THE CHILDREN OF THE GODS SERIES BOOKS 56-58

DARK HUNTER TRILOGY

I. T. LUCAS

Also by I. T. Lucas

THE CHILDREN OF THE GODS ORIGINS

THE CHILDREN OF THE GODS

PERFECT MATCH

PERFECT MATCH 1: VAMPIRE'S CONSORT
PERFECT MATCH 2: KING'S CHOSEN
PERFECT MATCH 3: CAPTAIN'S CONQUEST

THE CHILDREN OF THE GODS SERIES SETS

BOOKS 1-3: DARK STRANGER TRILOGY—INCLUDES A BONUS SHORT STORY: THE FATES TAKE A VACATION

BOOKS 4-6: DARK ENEMY TRILOGY —INCLUDES A BONUS SHORT STORY—THE FATES' POST-WEDDING CELEBRATION

BOOKS 7-10: DARK WARRIOR TETRALOGY
BOOKS 11-13: DARK GUARDIAN TRILOGY
BOOKS 14-16: DARK ANGEL TRILOGY
BOOKS 17-19: DARK OPERATIVE TRILOGY
BOOKS 20-22: DARK SURVIVOR TRILOGY
BOOKS 23-25: DARK WIDOW TRILOGY
BOOKS 26-28: DARK DREAM TRILOGY
BOOKS 29-31: DARK PRINCE TRILOGY
BOOKS 32-34: DARK QUEEN TRILOGY
BOOKS 35-37: DARK SPY TRILOGY
BOOKS 38-40: DARK OVERLORD TRILOGY
BOOKS 41-43: DARK CHOICES TRILOGY
BOOKS 44-46: DARK SECRETS TRILOGY
BOOKS 47-49: DARK HAVEN TRILOGY
BOOKS 50-52: DARK POWER TRILOGY
BOOKS 53-55: DARK MEMORIES TRILOGY
BOOKS 56-58: DARK HUNTER TRILOGY
BOOKS 59-61: DARK GOD'S TRILOGY

MEGA SETS

INCLUDE CHARACTER LISTS

THE CHILDREN OF THE GODS: BOOKS 1-6
THE CHILDREN OF THE GODS: BOOKS 6.5-10

TRY THE CHILDREN OF THE GODS SERIES ON AUDIBLE

2 FREE audiobooks with your new Audible subscription!

Published by Evening Star Press

EveningStarPress.com

ISBN: 978-1-957139-32-6

DARK HUNTER'S QUERY

1

ALENA

*A*lena, eldest daughter of the goddess Annani, a mother of thirteen, a grandmother of seventeen, a great-grandmother of twenty-three, and a great many times over grandmother of nearly every member of her clan, gazed at her phone's screen and sighed like a besotted schoolgirl.

In her over two millennia of existence, Alena had never reacted so strongly to a male, let alone to a mere depiction of one. The portrait had been created by a talented illustrator, but it hadn't been embellished in any way. The forensic artist had merely given life to a verbal description taken from a human's memory, and Annani had attested to its accuracy.

Annani had hung the framed original in her receiving room, a fond reminder of the male's father—the god Toven, whom she'd greatly admired in her youth. According to her mother, father and son looked so much alike that they were nearly indistinguishable.

Taken by the immortal's striking looks, Alena had captured Orion's image with her phone so she could gaze at it whenever she pleased, which was often. By now, she had every detail of the drawing committed to memory—the intelligent eyes, the chiseled cheekbones, the full sensuous lips, the aristocratic nose, the shoulder-length dark hair, the strong column of his neck—and yet she still felt compelled to pull out her phone and gaze at it.

Despite being an artistic construct, the drawing looked so lifelike, Orion's face so expressive, that it made her feel as if he were looking straight into her soul.

But it was all an illusion, and getting excited over a pretty face was as shallow as it got. She was too old to be blindsided by skin-deep beauty and wise enough to know that the only beauty that mattered was the kind found on the inside.

The male was gorgeous, perfect in the way all gods and the first generation of their offspring with humans were. It didn't mean that he was a good man, or that he could carry on an intelligent conversation, or that he was the truelove mate she'd been secretly hoping for.

Alena was the eldest, and yet the Fates had bestowed the blessing of a truelove mate on her younger siblings first. She wasn't jealous of their happiness and wished them the best their eternal lives had to offer, but she wanted her own happily ever after, and she was tired of waiting.

Except, Orion couldn't be the one for her, and if he was, the Fates had a really sick sense of humor. He was a compeller, and Alena could never be with a male who could take away her will at his whim. Just imagining being so helpless and at the mercy of another made her shiver. So even though his beautiful face evoked a powerful longing and caused a stirring—the kind Alena had never experienced before—and even though she pulled up his damn picture and stared at it numerous times a day, he could never be her truelove mate.

Her one and only probably had not been born yet, or he was making his way toward her while she was letting herself get enchanted by the pretty face of another.

Alena sighed.

Hopefully, the one the Fates chose for her would have longish black hair, piercing blue eyes, and a face that looked like it was lovingly carved from granite by a talented sculptor—precisely like Orion, just not Orion himself.

Could her fated one be Orion's father? Except, Orion hadn't inherited his compulsion ability from his human mother, and Toven was probably a compeller as well.

Maybe Orion had a brother? One who hadn't inherited the ability?

After all, Geraldine was also Toven's daughter, and she wasn't a compeller.

Hope surging in her heart, Alena closed her phone and put it back in her skirt pocket.

She was running out of patience.

Supposedly the Fates rewarded those who selflessly sacrificed for others or suffered greatly with the gift of a truelove mate. Had she sacrificed or suffered less than her siblings? Was that why she was the last one left even though she was the eldest?

Kian had dedicated his life to the clan, so she could understand why he'd been granted a mate first. Amanda had lost a child, which was the worst suffering Alena could imagine, so it was only fair that she'd been the next one in line to find her fated mate. Sari had worked almost as hard as Kian to better the lives of those clan members who'd chosen to remain in Scotland, so it was also fair that she'd gotten her happily ever after.

Alena deserved hers as well.

She wasn't a natural leader like Kian or Sari, and she hadn't suffered a terrible loss like Amanda, but she was the de facto mother of the clan, and she also sacrificed a lot to keep her own mother out of trouble.

Not that any of it had been a great sacrifice or had caused her any suffering.

Motherhood was the best possible reward in itself, and traveling the world with Annani wasn't exactly a hardship either.

As Annani's companion, Alena had been an unwilling participant in her mother's crazy shenanigans, but she had to admit that most of them had been fun and not overly dangerous. She also enjoyed the babies and toddlers who arrived at the sanctuary to be kept safe until it was time for them to transition.

Life had been good to her, but she'd been doing the same thing for two thousand years, and it was time for a change.

Her only solo adventure had been impersonating a Slovenian supermodel in the hopes of luring Kalugal out of hiding.

After the fun time she'd spent with the team who'd accompanied her to New York, it had been difficult to go back to the routine. For a few precious days, she'd enjoyed being different, being her own person and not her mother's shadow.

It seemed like such a distant memory, like it had taken place in another lifetime.

The face she saw in the mirror was the same one she'd been looking at for two millennia.

Gone was the sophisticated hairstyle she'd adopted for the New York trip, replaced by her habitual loose braid, her face was free of makeup, and she wore one of her long, comfortable dresses instead of the fashionable clothes Amanda had gotten her for that trip.

Those had been given away to charity soon after she'd returned from New York.

There was no reason to dress up in the sanctuary, where everyone expected her to look the part of Annani's devoted daughter—the goddess's companion and advisor—a part she'd been playing for so long that no one could envision her doing anything else, including herself.

Not that there was anything wrong with it.

Her position at Annani's side was a duty and an honor that Alena had proudly and lovingly performed for centuries—a position that could not be filled by anyone but her.

ORION

*O*rion regarded the leader of his captors, noting the hard lines of Kian's face, the stiffness of his shoulders, and the sheer size of him. The guy was big, he was gruff, but he wasn't cold, and that gave Orion hope.

So far, other than the damn tranquilizer they'd knocked him out with, these immortals hadn't treated him too badly. Nevertheless, they were holding him against his will, and even though the apartment he'd woken up in was as fancy as any high-end hotel suite, it was still a prison cell.

Other than having been born immortal, he hadn't done anything to them, and they had no reason to hold him, but he was at their mercy, his compulsion ability nullified by the earpieces they were all wearing.

Without it, he was as helpless as any human, and the only way out of the situation was to cooperate with his captors and give them what they wanted, which was information about his jerk of a father.

No skin off his nose.

If they could find the god, Orion didn't care what they did with him.

Kian put his paper cup down on the table and crossed his arms over his chest. "Now that you've eaten breakfast and gotten caffeinated, I want to hear the story of how you found your father and got him to admit that he was a god."

It was clear that the guy's patience was wearing thin, but Orion needed a little more time to think. The coffee break he'd practically begged Kian for had helped ease the pounding headache he'd woken up with, but his mind was still foggy.

He didn't mind telling them about his father, but there were other things he'd learned from the god that he wasn't sure he should share with them.

Did it matter if they knew that he was hunting for the god's other potential children?

They already knew about his sister and niece and had accepted Geraldine and Cassandra into their clan, but had their motives been pure?

They needed new blood for their community—more genetic diversity. They might try to get to his other siblings first and draft them into their clan.

Was that so bad, though?

Perhaps they could help him with his quest.

Orion had exhausted all of the information he had, but they might have access to resources that he didn't.

Damn, if only his head would clear so he could follow one thought to its logical conclusion instead of all his thoughts jumping around in his head like bunnies on speed.

Were these people trustworthy?

Were they a force for good or the opposite of that?

Was he lucky that they had found his sister and him?

The effects of the tranquilizer were beginning to wane, but he was still having a hard time reconciling what he'd learned from his captors with what he'd been told by his father. Some of it confirmed the god's story, but there was so much more that his father hadn't shared with him.

For nearly five centuries, Orion had been convinced that he was the only immortal, an anomaly, and then he'd met his father who'd claimed to be a god—not a deity, but a lone survivor of a superior race of people who'd been annihilated by one of their own.

Herman, aka Toven, had claimed that the gods from various mythologies had been real people. At the time, Orion had doubted his father's story, had suspected that the guy was either delusional or being deliberately deceitful, but his captors had confirmed everything Herman had told him. The gods hadn't been the constructs of human imagination, and what's more, his father wasn't the only survivor.

Had his father known about the two goddesses who'd escaped the attack and chosen not to tell him?

Had he known that some humans carried the dormant godly gene and withheld the information on purpose?

"Whenever you're ready," Kian prompted.

"Can I bother you for another cup?" Orion cast the guy a pleading look. "My head feels like it's stuffed with cotton. Usually, I don't suffer from such maladies, but the tranquilizer your guy injected me with must have been incredibly potent."

Kian grimaced. "It had to be to knock out an immortal."

"I'll brew a fresh pot," Onegus said. The male mated to his niece was the head of the clan's security forces, and yet he got up to reload the coffeemaker. "It will take a couple of minutes."

Apparently, these people didn't follow strict hierarchy. The guy could have asked one of the guards to brew the coffee but had chosen to do so himself. They acted more like a family or a group of friends than a military organization, which Orion took to be a good sign as to the kind of people he was dealing with.

Next to him, his sister winced. "I'm so sorry."

He patted her knee. "My head already feels much better."

"I didn't mean the headache." Geraldine smiled apologetically. "Well, that too, but what I'm really sorry about is entrapping you. You wouldn't be in this situation if I hadn't dug into my murky past."

"Why did you?"

7

"Do you mean why did I want to find out about my past or why did I help the clan trap you?"

"The first one."

"As long as I was oblivious about having had another life, I was content with the one I had. But after I discovered that I had a daughter who I couldn't remember, I had to find out how it happened. But I should have just moved on." She sighed. "In part, it's your fault that I didn't. You compelled me not to leave the house for more than a day, so I couldn't start my new life with Shai in his village."

Orion nodded. "Indeed, and that means that my capture is on me, and you have nothing to apologize for." He cast a sidelong glance at Kian. "I've been careful not to get noticed by humans, but I never anticipated other immortals. Although with the advent of the modern era and the proliferation of imaging devices, avoiding discovery by humans is getting more difficult. I can rely on my compulsion ability to get out of tight spots, but I can't compel inanimate objects, and nowadays, there are surveillance cameras everywhere and everyone has smartphones they can use to snap photos with. I had to develop new tactics to avoid getting my image recorded on electronic devices."

Ironically, though, his capture hadn't been the result of technology or even his negligence. Orion had followed the best protocols he could devise. What had gotten him in trouble was precisely the thing his father had warned him against—family, people he cared about, people who could lead others to him.

His sister and her daughters were his Achilles heel.

Next to him, Geraldine shifted her knees sideways and put her hands in her lap. "I have to admit, though, that your compulsion wasn't the only reason I didn't leave the house. As much as I hated the idea of trapping you, I wanted to talk to you and not forget the conversation as soon as you left. We pieced together most of what had happened to me, but there were still so many holes in the puzzle, and I wanted answers. I needed closure."

He put a hand on her knee. "I understand. You don't need to keep apologizing."

Geraldine lifted her big blue eyes to him, so much like his own that it was like looking in the mirror. "You're my brother, but I didn't know that, and I thought that you were my inducer. Do you know how awkward it feels now that I know the truth?" She shook her head. "It gets worse. When I finally recalled our interactions over the years, I was offended that you didn't find me attractive." She chuckled. "Although, I should have known something was up because I wasn't attracted to you either." She waved a hand over his face. "If you were ugly, that would have been understandable, but you are so gorgeous that I can't take my eyes off you."

Orion had never felt comfortable with the looks he'd gotten throughout his life, either covetous from those interested in him sexually or envious and outright hostile from others, but Geraldine was his sister, and her complimenting him on his good looks didn't feel as awkward. It reminded him of his mother and the way she used to regard him with love and adoration in her eyes.

"Thank you." Absentmindedly, he reached for Geraldine's hand and gave it a gentle squeeze. "I'm curious. How did you suddenly recover your memories of me? Did your mate have anything to do with that?"

"The goddess released them." Geraldine shifted her eyes to Kian. "Is it okay for me to reveal that?"

"It's fine."

So that was how she remembered him. Orion had wondered about that, thinking that maybe her boyfriend or one of the other immortals was powerful enough to unlock her submerged memories. But it had taken a goddess to release them, which meant that the others were not as powerful as he was.

He tucked away that bit of information for later use. "Is the goddess here?" He looked at Kian. "Can I meet her?"

Kian chuckled. "The Clan Mother is very curious about you, and I have no doubt that she will want to meet you as soon as possible. She's very fond of your father and speaks highly of him."

Orion grimaced. "He must've changed a lot since she last interacted with him."

"Here you go." Onegus handed him a mug of freshly brewed coffee.

"Thank you." Taking the mug with him, Orion leaned back against the couch cushions and crossed his legs at the ankles. "Perhaps I should start my story at the beginning, many years before I met my father." He took several sips from his coffee before putting the cup on the table.

"Please do," Geraldine said. "I want to know everything about you, or at least the highlights of your life."

Now that Orion's head was clearer and his thought process faster, deciding which information to share and which to withhold became easier.

The coffee break had been a test, and it had allowed him to observe his captors interacting with each other, and more importantly, with his sister and niece.

There was no faking the loving glances between Onegus and Cassandra and between Geraldine and Shai. His sister and niece were indeed happily mated to these clansmen, which made the men his family as well.

Besides, the clan had little to gain from what he could tell them, and he didn't have much to lose.

So far, Orion's query had yielded only one result—Geraldine—and he'd been unsuccessful in locating any of Toven's other children. Perhaps he and Geraldine were the only ones, or maybe he needed help locating the others.

3

KIAN

"*As* I mentioned before," Orion began, "I was fourteen when I discovered that I was immortal."

"Hold on." Geraldine lifted her hand. "That's not the beginning. I want to know where you were born, who your mother was, and how you ended up on the battle-field at such a young age."

Kian stifled a groan. At this rate, it would be nighttime before Orion reached the part about his father, and Kian had no intentions of staying in the keep for so long.

He called his mother when Orion had been captured, but because the guy had been knocked out cold, he'd had nothing else to report. His mother was no doubt anxiously awaiting an update and getting more aggravated with every passing moment.

Besides, as fascinating as hearing about Orion's life was, he was more interested in Toven's, and even that was not as important or as fun as spending time with his daughter.

Just thinking about Allegra's cute smiles and the adorable sounds she made eased the tension in his shoulders and lightened his heart.

Orion sighed and leaned forward to pick up his coffee mug. "The man who I thought was my father was a merchant in a small town near Milan. I was born nine months after he was killed in what is known as the Great Wars of Italy or the Habs-burg-Valois wars. Because of the opportune timing, no one ever suspected that the grieving widow gave birth to a child that wasn't her deceased husband's, and neither did I." He chuckled. "Although even as a small boy, I knew that I looked nothing like that fat, ruddy-cheeked man in the portrait hanging in our home's entryway. What little hair he had was light brown, and my mother was a blond." He lifted his hand and smoothed it over his chin-length raven hair. "As you can see, my hair color is nearly black."

"You have beautiful hair," Cassandra said. "Did no one wonder about the little boy who looked nothing like his deceased father?"

10

He shrugged. "My mother was smart. She told everyone that I was the spitting image of her cousin, and she repeated it enough times for the fib to become truth. I think that after a while, she started believing it herself."

"Did you believe the lie?" Cassandra asked.

"Why wouldn't I? I adored my mother, and I had no reason to doubt her."

Kian huffed out a breath. "You must have realized the truth after surviving the injury that should have killed you."

Hopefully, jumping ahead to that would shorten the story time.

"Not right away." Orion's lips lifted in a crooked smile. "I came up with several possible explanations, starting with a guardian angel and ending with a good witch."

"What about being bitten by a vampire?" Geraldine asked.

"That came later, after my fangs started growing. I panicked, afraid that I would become crazed with blood lust, so I packed up my things and was about to leave in the middle of the night. My mother intercepted me, and when I admitted my fears, she said that vampires didn't exist but that I might have inherited strange things from my father, who wasn't the man she'd been married to. She told me that I was old enough to learn the truth, and that if I wanted to live, I needed to keep it a secret."

"How did she manage an affair?" Cassandra asked. "I mean, war was raging, and her husband was gone. And how did Toven find her? Did he just stroll into town and seduce her?"

"I don't know. She didn't divulge any details, only that he'd been a stunningly good-looking man and very smart. I'm not sure that she remembered much more than that. When I started discovering my own powers, I realized that he must have tampered with her memories."

Geraldine tilted her head. "Do you think that Toven compelled her to be with him?"

Orion shook his head. "My father is a jaded bastard, but he's not a rapist. My mother accepted him with open arms. I know that it makes her look bad, but she'd been practically sold to her husband by her family, and the arranged marriage was a disaster. He was a terrible man, or at least that was what she claimed, and when he died, she rejoiced at finally being free and celebrated with a very handsome stranger."

"How did she remember her affair with Toven?" Onegus asked. "Did he leave at least some of her memories of him intact?"

"My mother was an artist." Orion looked at Geraldine. "Our father had a thing for creative women. Your mother was an artist as well."

Her eyes widened. "Did you meet my real mother?"

He nodded. "I did, but I'll tell you about that later. I don't want to jump all over the timeline."

Kian was still trying to understand Orion's answer to Onegus's question. "What does your mother being an artist have to do with remembering Toven?"

"Indeed." Orion smiled. "She told me that she'd drunk a lot of wine after her husband's death, and she didn't remember much about the man she'd celebrated her freedom with, but her artist's eye remembered enough of him to draw a portrait." Orion waved a hand over his face. "When I reached adulthood, I realized that I looked just like him, but that's getting ahead of the story as well. You wanted to know how I found myself on the battlefield at the age of fourteen."

Geraldine nodded.

"Quite simply, I was the only male in the household, and they demanded one from each family. My mother wasn't very wealthy, but she wasn't destitute either, and she tried to bribe the recruiters. They took her gold and drafted me anyway. Back then, a woman alone was powerless. There was nothing she could've done to prevent them from taking me."

Geraldine put her hand on his arm. "I can't imagine how terrified you were."

"I was. I just knew that I was going to die. I'd never trained with any kinds of weapons. Heck, I didn't know how to hold a pike or a crossbow."

As Geraldine's chin started to wobble and tears slid down her cheeks, Kian cast her an amused glance. "But he didn't die. That's not a ghost sitting next to you."

The redheaded guard snorted. "I disagree. We have with us the ghost of Orion's past."

4

ORION

*A*s everyone laughed, Orion closed his eyes. The horror of that day nearly five centuries ago was still fresh in his mind as if it had happened a week ago.

He didn't remember much of the battle or how he had been gutted. It had all been a blur of terror, and dying hadn't been the worst part of it. He'd been glad that it was over.

Except, he hadn't died.

Sometime later, he woke up with dirt filling his nostrils, his mouth, his throat. He'd been buried with the rest of the fallen. Choking, starved for breath, he'd clawed at the loosely compacted earth, had dug up against the flesh of the dead he'd been buried with, and had blindly inched toward the surface.

When he'd finally broken free, Orion had coughed and spat and vomited, and then lost consciousness again. The next time he opened his eyes, he had patted his stomach, searching for the injury, but other than caked-on blood, no trace of it had remained.

That had terrified him almost as much as regaining consciousness in the mass grave had. He'd thought that he was in hell, and in a way he was. Living was purgatory, and unlike the rest of humanity, his would last forever. He was stuck on this horrid plane of existence with no chance for parole.

"Orion?" Geraldine's soft voice pierced the darkness of his memories. "Are you okay?"

Fighting against the phantom choking sensation, he forced himself to suck in a breath. "Yeah, I'm fine. Nearly five centuries to the day, and I can still taste the dirt in my mouth."

"They buried you alive," Kian guessed. "They thought that you were dead."

Orion nodded. "I think that I was actually dead and was resurrected somehow."

The redhead leaned forward. "Was there water in the mass grave? Did it rain?"

"I don't think so." Orion wiped a hand over his mouth. "I remember that the dirt was dry. Why do you ask?"

"You might have entered stasis, but you could have appeared dead to humans even without going into that deep state."

"What year was that?" Shai asked.

"1525."

"So you were born in 1511," Kian calculated. "Was Orion your given name?"

He shook his head. "My mother named me Orlando. I've used many different names over the centuries, but I chose Orion after meeting my real father."

"When did you find him and how?" Kian asked for the fifth or sixth time.

But unlike before, this time he'd get an answer. It was a relief to jump ahead in the timeline, bypassing hundreds of terrible experiences, large and small, that had each left a scar on Orion's soul.

His body was a perfect machine that healed all injuries without leaving a single mark, but his soul was a different story. It was wounded, scarred, and aching, with no hope of ever recovering.

"Thirty-eight years ago, on Rue de la Jussienne in Paris, a chance encounter brought me face to face with my father. I was heading toward my favorite café when I saw him walking toward me. We both stopped at the same time and stared at each other. It was like looking in the mirror. And yet, it didn't occur to me that he might be my father. Everyone is supposed to have a doppelgänger, right?"

Cassandra snorted. "Not someone who looks like you." She turned to Kian. "Or you. Your godly heritage is unmistakable. No human is that perfect."

Kian arched a brow. "Did Toven also think that you were his doppelgänger?"

"No, he knew who I was, but he pretended that he didn't. He gave me a tight-lipped smile and kept walking. I hesitated for a split second before rushing after him. *Excuse me,* I said as I fell in step with him. *I wonder if we are related. Looking at you is like looking at the mirror.*

"We are not, he said. *You don't know me, and you've never seen me. Go away."*

"That's when I knew he was either the one who sired me or a half-brother of mine. He tried to use compulsion, but it didn't work because I had the same power. I told him the same thing Onegus said to me when I tried to use it on him. *Your tricks don't work on me. I'm just like you.*"

Cassandra grinned. "I would have paid good money to see the bastard's face when you told him that."

"He wasn't happy, and he was even less so when he realized that he couldn't get rid of me. I followed him to the townhouse he was renting at the time, and he had no choice but to let me in."

Kian leaned forward, bracing his elbows on his knees. "How long did it take you to force him to admit that he was your father?"

"Not long. I told him that I wasn't going anywhere until he told me everything I wanted to know."

"Did he?" Geraldine asked.

"He told me a lot, but apparently, not nearly enough."

5

VROG

Still baffled by the sudden early morning evacuation from his cell and transport to the village, Vrog sat on a barstool in Stella's kitchen and sipped on a cup of herbal tea that tasted like dishwater.

"I'm sorry that we don't have coffee," Stella said. "I was supposed to go grocery shopping this morning, but then Kian called with the good news—"

"And you got stuck with me," Vrog finished for her.

Vlad and Wendy were both at work, so Stella had kindly agreed to welcome him to the village and entertain him until Vlad returned from his shift at the bakery.

To say that it was awkward to be alone with her at her home was to put it mildly. Vrog sat on the stool stiff as a plank of wood, and Stella wasn't doing much better.

Like him, she probably expected Richard to walk in at any moment and kick him out. The guy hadn't been happy about the uninvited guest when she'd called him earlier.

"Would you like a tour of the village?" She pushed to her feet. "I can show you the construction site Richard works on."

"A tour would be lovely, but I don't think it's wise to antagonize your mate further. Hopefully, I'll be gone before he goes on break."

"Don't mind him." She rolled her eyes. "Richard is all bark and no bite. He just needs to get used to you being here. And as soon as you find a lady, he'll relax." She smiled conspiratorially. "Perhaps our tour of the village should start at the café. You'll get to say hi to Wendy and enjoy a decent cup of coffee."

He was on his feet in an instant. "Lead on."

"I knew you'd like the idea." Stella lifted a shawl off the couch, wrapped it around her shoulders, and threaded her arm through his.

He stopped and gently removed her arm. "We shouldn't act too familiar with each other. Richard still thinks like a territorial human, and if he smells me on you, he might jump to conclusions."

"He won't," she said but didn't touch him again. "Richard and I have bonded, which means that cheating is impossible. He knows that." She walked to the front door and pulled it open.

As Vrog followed her out, he made sure that there were at least three feet between them. "How come?"

"It's an immortal thing. It doesn't happen to everyone, but those who bond are physically incapable of feeling attraction towards anyone other than their mate."

"What happens if a mate dies?"

She winced. "It's bad. To lose a truelove mate is devastating, and it takes a long time for the addiction to wear off. Luckily for us, deaths are rare."

"I don't understand. Before, you referred to it as a bond, and now you're talking about addiction. Are the two one and the same?"

"Yes and no." Stella tightened the shawl against the morning chill. "The venom is addictive, but only if an immortal couple is sexually exclusive for a significant length of time. Historically, those who wanted to avoid the addiction played around, but that was during the gods' era, and since it wasn't relevant to the clan's situation, it was forgotten."

"Why wasn't it relevant?"

"Because none of us had long-term relationships, and we only hooked up with humans. Up until a few years ago, all clan members were Annani's descendants, too closely related to mate with each other, and there were no known immortals outside of our clan, other than the Doomers that is, but they didn't count."

"Your enemies. I remember you asking me if I was a Doomer. I didn't know what you were talking about."

She cast him a sidelong glance. "You still remember that?"

He nodded. "Over the years, I thought of you quite often."

She chuckled. "No doubt contemplating how to choke the life out of me to avenge your people, since you were convinced that I was responsible for their demise."

"Not always. Sometimes, I wondered about our son and what kind of man he turned out to be." He smiled. "Vlad has exceeded all my expectations. You've done a great job with him."

"Thank you." She let out a breath. "I'm very proud of Vlad."

Vrog had a feeling that he was making her uncomfortable. It was safer to talk about the clan and the problems it faced than about their shared history.

"So, back to the bond and addiction issues. How did the clan become aware of the venom's addictive properties?"

She seemed relieved. "No one remembered that until Kian and Syssi became a couple and bonded within days. When the addiction followed within less than a week, Kian was reminded of what Annani had told him about it many years ago."

"So, Kian's mate was the first Dormant your clan found?"

Stella nodded. "There have been more since, but the vast majority of clan members are still waiting for the Fates to bless them with a truelove mate."

"What about these newcomers you've told me about? Your former enemies. Can't they mate with clan females?"

She chuckled. "There is plenty of partying going on and hookups galore, but so far, only one couple has bonded." She sidled up to him. "There are many available females for you to choose from."

Vrog took a step sideways to put more distance between them. "I don't know how to act with an immortal female. Are there dos and don'ts that I need to know about?"

"You did fine with me."

"That's because I thought you were human."

"You were charming and sexy back then. Just act the same now, and you'll be fine."

That had been a long time ago before his entire family had been slaughtered and his world had fallen apart. He'd been carefree back then, or as carefree as a Kra-ell male living among humans could be. He'd been young and hopeful, but he was no longer that guy. In fact, Vrog could barely remember him.

6

ORION

Paris, France, thirty-eight years ago.

*A*s he followed the immortal through the door, Orlando half expected the male to slam it shut in his face, but he didn't. Instead, he took off his coat and scarf, hung both on a coat rack, and walked over to a bar cart.

Orlando remained standing at the doorway even though he had no intentions of leaving. If the guy didn't invite him in, he would stay anyway, but he wanted to see what he would do.

Lifting a bottle of Glen Grant 1953, the man poured the golden liquid into two glasses and then turned to look at Orlando. "Are you going to just stand there?" he asked in perfect Italian. "Come in, take off your coat, and close the door behind you. You're letting the draft in."

"How did you know that I was Italian?" Orlando hung his coat on the rack, walked over to the man, and took the glass from his hand.

"You have an accent."

"I do not." Orlando had an uncanny talent for languages. He could speak all of the Western European languages fluently with no trace of a foreign accent. He could also converse in twenty-some others.

"It's very slight, but I have a good ear." The guy sat down in one of the two over-stuffed armchairs facing the fireplace. "Take a seat."

"Thank you." Orlando looked around the living room, taking in the stacks of books and newspapers.

The place was clean but cluttered, and it was quite obvious that no woman lived in the townhouse. It was a bachelor's pad—an old bachelor who was more interested in the company of books than females.

The immortal took a sip from his whiskey. "How did you find me?"

"I wasn't looking for you if that's what you're asking. Our encounter was fated." Orlando lifted his glass. "Should we toast it?"

The guy shrugged. "I guess I should be intrigued, perhaps even happy to see you, but regrettably, I have lost the ability to get excited over anything." He took another sip from his drink. "When you've lived as long as I have, you'll understand." He grimaced. "It's all quite pointless."

Orlando knew precisely what the immortal was talking about. Life was worthless without people to love, and as a lone immortal, he was condemned to walking the earth alone.

"I've lived for nearly five centuries," he said. "I've lost people I loved, so I get it."

It seemed that this had been the right thing to say because the guy's expression softened a fraction. "What's your name?"

"Orlando Farnese."

A genuine smile brightened the male's face, a stark transformation from the deadened expression he wore like a dark cloak. "Oh, yes. I remember your mother." He pushed to his feet and walked over to a table that was laden with leather-bound books. "I have her portrait somewhere."

Well, that answered the question of how they were related. "You are my father." A statement, not a question.

The guy shifted his gaze from the books and leveled it at Orlando. "I thought that was obvious. You are the spitting image of me." He picked up one of the books, looked at the spine, put it down and picked another, and then another, until he found the one that he was looking for.

Clearly, the man hadn't lied about being emotionally dead. If Orlando had discovered that he had a son, he would have been over the moon. Perhaps the guy had spread his seed far and wide and had sired thousands of children over his long life. One more was of no consequence to him.

"You could have been my brother or my grandfather or an uncle."

"Not likely." The guy grimaced. "All of my relatives were long dead before you were born, and I'd given up on siring a child even before that, which was many thousands of years ago. You're most likely the only one." He brought the journal with him to the armchair, sat down, and flipped through the pages. "Here she is." He handed it to Orlando, opened on a sketch. "That's how I remember Gilia."

It was a portrait of his mother the way she looked in her youth—radiant, happy, sensual. It was a lover's sketch.

Even if the guy hadn't fathered a horde of children, he still must have dallied with thousands of women. To remember his mother's name, she must have left quite an impression on him.

It was a small consolation, but it was better than nothing.

Orlando scanned the writing underneath the sketch, but it wasn't in any language he knew. He kept flipping through several written pages until he reached the next portrait of a lovely young woman.

It seemed that his father kept track of his lovers, either as sentimental mementos or for some other reason.

"My mother must have left an impression on you."

"Gilia was a remarkable artist."

"She was. She drew a portrait of you and hung it in her bedroom. Even if I didn't grow up looking just like you, I would have recognized you from that painting."

Orlando handed the journal back. "By the way, what should I call you? Other than Father, that is."

The guy cradled the journal in his lap. "I go by many different names, but these days, I call myself Herman." He looked at Orlando from under lowered lashes. "I hope that you are careful and hide your immortality. You should also change your name every couple of decades or so."

"I do." Orlando's lips contorted in a grimace. "I wish you had been around when I was figuring out all of this on my own. Your advice would have been helpful."

Not a shred of guilt passed through Herman's cold eyes. "Do you ever check on your past lovers to find out if any of them has conceived?"

"I did at first, but I stopped when it became evident that I was infertile."

Herman smiled, but the smile didn't reach his eyes. "I thought the same thing, and yet here you are." He turned to the journal in his lap and started flipping through the pages. "Who knows? Maybe I have sired more than one offspring over the years."

Orlando glanced at the leather-bound book and then shifted his gaze to the many others stacked on top of the table and on the floor. "Do all of these contain portraits of your past lovers and their descriptions?"

Herman's eyes followed his to the stack on the table. "Many of them do. I can't share my life with a woman or even stay around for longer than a few days. There have been so many that my memories of them started to blur and became interchangeable. It upset me, so I decided to prolong my relationship with those who were special to me by immortalizing them in these journals and making them the heroines of the stories I write. Naturally, I'm the hero of each of my novels, albeit in disguise." He waved his hand at the stacks piled on the floor. "The other journals contain my stories."

"Is that how you support yourself? You write books?"

Herman laughed, but his laugh was mirthless. "I have more gold than I could ever spend. Writing just helps pass the time."

Given that Herman could live forever, he must have stockpiles of gold hidden somewhere. Hell, he probably had an entire goldmine that no one knew about.

The question was why he'd told him about it. Didn't he fear his treasure's discovery?

Orlando tucked the information away, and instead of commenting on the gold, he asked, "Do you publish your books?"

"Some, not all. Naturally, I use a different pseudonym for each book, and I vary the style. I don't want anyone tracking me by my stories."

Pushing to his feet, Orlando walked over to the bar cart. "May I?" He lifted the whiskey bottle.

Herman waved a hand. "Help yourself."

"Someone might recognize the style and figure out that these books were written by the same person." Orlando filled his glass to the brim and returned to the armchair.

"I'm not worried." Herman put his still half-full glass on the side table between the armchairs. "Back in the day, I was known as the god of knowledge and writing. I can write in many different styles."

For a moment, Orlando just gaped. "You are a god?"

Given Herman's pinched expression, he hadn't meant to disclose that. "A very minor one. Nothing to get excited about. It's not like I'm a deity and can perform miracles. Humans regarded my people as gods because we could manipulate their minds to think that we were divine. But we were just a more advanced species."

"Am I a god?"

Herman shook his head.

"Your mother was human, so you are only an immortal."

"I can also manipulate human minds. Doesn't that make me a god? What's the difference between a god and an immortal?"

Letting out a long-suffering sigh, Herman rose to his feet and walked over to the bar cart. "It's a long story, and what you can learn from it is not going to help you in any way." He refilled his glass even though it hadn't been empty. "It's getting late. You should leave."

Orlando had no intention of leaving without learning all that he could from his father. He had a feeling that tomorrow Herman would no longer be in the townhouse, and he would never find him again.

"Nevertheless, I would like to know what kind of blood flows in my veins."

7

ORION

"*W*hat do you know about mythology?" Herman put the glass of whiskey on the side table and walked over to the fireplace.

"Which one?" Orlando asked.

"Any of them." The god added a new log to the fire.

"I know the Greek and the Roman and some of the Norse."

"Good enough." Herman sat back on the armchair, stretched his legs in front of him, and crossed them at the ankles—a pose nearly identical to Orlando's. "They are all based on the more ancient myths of the Sumerian. The pantheon of twelve major gods remained pretty much the same, just with different names, but the Sumerian pantheon was the first, and it was based on real people."

"Are you an alien?"

"My parents and my older half-brother were born on a different planet, but I was born on Earth. Does that make me an alien?"

"If both of your parents were gods, then I guess it does."

"I guess." Herman took a small sip from his whiskey. "For a long time, I thought of myself as an honorary human. My father was what nowadays would be called a humanist. He championed human causes, and I followed in his footsteps. But I got disillusioned. No matter what I did, even pretending to be a real deity to make them fear me, they remained bloodthirsty savages. Whatever I tried to teach them, they managed to distort into something horrific—killing and maiming and torturing in my name." He emptied the rest of the whiskey down his throat and got up to refill his glass. "I decided that humanity was a lost cause, stopped playing God, and disappeared."

Orlando felt compelled to defend humanity. "Humans have made big strides. It's not as bad as it used to be."

"In some ways, they have." Herman sat back down. "It only took them five thousand years to become as civilized as they were back then. Without the powerful gods to guide and control them, they were no better than chimps."

"What happened to the gods?"

"Gone. My brother killed them all and died along with them." He shifted his deadened gaze to look at Orlando. "We can die, you know. Even I can't survive a decapitation or injuries that are too massive for my body to repair. Don't take your immortality for granted, and don't do stupid things. If you fall out of a plane, you'll die."

Was Herman trying to impart fatherly advice?

It was too little too late, but at least he was making an effort.

"I figured as much. I'm resilient, and I can compel and put humans under my thrall, but I don't have magic."

"Smart boy."

Orlando chuckled. "I'm nearly five centuries old. I had a long time to test my limits, and I'm not stupid. I'm also not a boy."

"I know. I just wanted to test how it felt to give fatherly advice."

So he'd been right. Couldn't fault the guy for trying, though, and what Herman was telling him about the history of the gods was not something Orlando could have found in books.

"Why did your brother kill the other gods?"

Herman shrugged. "He murdered another god, which was punishable by entombment. When the council found him guilty and passed sentence, he decided to get rid of them all, including our father and me. I knew that he was power-hungry and unstable, but I never thought that he would go so far. He must have lost his mind completely."

"How did you survive?"

"I got tired of listening to the endless and pointless discussions and snuck out. I was never interested in politics and voting to entomb my own brother depressed me. I flew to a faraway land I was researching at the time, and when I returned many months later, I found the entire region devastated. I flew to the north and searched for my brother in his stronghold. After I learned from his servants that he'd never returned, I compelled them to forget that they'd ever seen me, flew back to where I came from, and stayed there for a very long time."

"Until you got tired of humanity."

Herman nodded, emptied his third glass of whiskey, and got to his feet. "I'm tired, and I've told you enough. Please see yourself out."

"Wait." Orlando followed him. "Can I come back tomorrow, and we can talk some more?"

The guy's lips lifted in a mockery of a smile. "I won't be here tomorrow, and we are never going to see each other again. I wish you the best, but I don't wish to have a relationship with you."

Orlando had suspected as much, but he still asked, "Why not?"

"Because we look too much alike and it's dangerous for both of us."

"We can talk on the phone, and we can send each other letters. I don't expect you to be a father to me, but I could use a friend."

Herman shook his head. "I'm glad that we ran into each other and that I know that you exist. If I want to see you again, I will find you. Please, see yourself out." And with that, he turned around and climbed the stairs to the second floor, leaving Orlando standing in the middle of the living room alone with the coat rack by the door.

It seemed surreal that the guy didn't want to have anything to do with him, and Orlando wasn't going to beg the bastard to change his mind. Besides, even that wouldn't have touched the guy's dead heart.

Other than asking for his name, Herman hadn't asked him a single question. He was completely uninterested in learning anything about his only son, or rather, the only one he knew of.

His eyes darting to the journals, Orlando walked over to the table and lifted one. There were dates on the spines, and as he took each and examined a date, a plan started forming in his head.

Herman was a lost cause, but if he had sired more children, Orlando could locate them and do for them what he wished someone had done for him—befriend them and show them how to hide who they were while living among humans.

His best chance was to find the women his father had immortalized in his journals who were still alive. If he could track them down, he could find out whether they had children and then find them as well.

It was a long shot, but Orlando was eager to hunt for the brothers or sisters he might have. If he found even one, it would be worth the effort.

Without feeling an iota of remorse, he took the most recent journal—the one that was marked with a starting date of 1929 and no end date—and tucked it under his arm.

At the door he took his coat, shrugged it on, and zipped it over the journal.

Casting one last look up the stairs, he shook his head and saw himself out.

8

WENDY

*A*s Wendy prepared cappuccinos for Vrog and Stella, she watched the two talking at their table, and it was quite obvious that they weren't comfortable with each other, more so on Vrog's part than Stella's. He was leaning away from her as if her breath was stinky or her perfume overpowering, but Wendy was sure that neither was the cause.

Did he still think that Stella had been somehow responsible for his people's demise?

Except, even from where she was standing, Wendy could see that there was no hostility in Vrog's eyes, only wariness.

What was he afraid of?

She still remembered being in his situation. After a lifetime of bad experiences, it had been difficult to believe that Vlad and his clan were good people. Wendy hadn't had faith in anyone, and she'd treated Vlad deplorably.

And yet, he'd not only forgiven her but had fought his way into her heart, barreling through all of her prickly defenses and convincing her that she wasn't the evil bitch she'd believed herself to be.

Vrog needed almost as much help as she had back then, but unlike her, he didn't have anyone willing to fight for him.

She needed to find him a good female, someone aggressive who would appeal to his Kra-ell side, or maybe someone soft and loving who would appeal to his human half.

Working at the café, Wendy was uniquely positioned to do so, and as soon as she figured out which kind of female was best suited for him, she could start sending out feelers to see who was interested.

It shouldn't be too difficult to find him a suitable match. Vrog was a handsome fellow, and he seemed like a nice guy.

Hopefully, not many knew about his attack on Stella.

When the cappuccinos were ready, she loaded them on a tray, added a few pastries and sandwiches, and carried everything over to Vrog and Stella's table. "So, what do you think about the village so far?" She set the tray down.

"It's beautiful and so peaceful." Vrog reached for one of the paper cups and removed the lid. "A true paradise." He took a sip from the cappuccino and let out a sigh. "Divine."

"We ran out of coffee," Stella said. "Poor Vrog couldn't stomach the herbal tea, but it was the only thing I had."

Wendy frowned. "Do you have dietary restrictions like Emmett? Do you need blood?"

He shook his head. "I can exist on a human diet as long as it's mostly lightly cooked meat. I don't eat bread or pasta or rice, but I can tolerate some vegetables and fruits. And I love coffee." He took another sip, the froth painting him a milk mustache.

Wendy's eyes widened. "What about cows' milk? Can you tolerate it?"

"Cappuccinos are a weakness of mine, but I don't tolerate the milk well," Vrog admitted. "It upsets my stomach."

Wendy stifled a chuckle.

Contrary to what she'd thought before turning immortal, farting wasn't exclusive to humans and other mammals. She could just imagine how bad those produced by a lactose intolerant half Kra-ell male would be.

"I can make you a cappuccino from alternative milk. We have soy, almond, and coconut."

"Perhaps I'll try some next time." He took another grateful sip. "When is your shift over?"

"We close the café at six, but Vlad will be back much sooner. In any case, Stella can walk you over to our house, and you can make yourself comfortable there. Your room is ready."

"Thank you." He smiled. "It's so kind of you to invite me to stay with you and Vlad. It will give me an opportunity to get to know my son. I just wish there was something for me to do in the village. I don't like being idle."

"You can help out in the café if you want. Wonder and I can always use another pair of hands in here."

It would also put him on display for the ladies, which would make it much easier to find him a match.

"I would love to," Vrog said. "I can also assist in the construction project. The Guardian who transported me here said that Kian employs Chinese crews. I can translate if needed."

Wendy chuckled. "Do you really want to work so closely with Richard?"

He grimaced. "Good point."

Stella cast Wendy a reproachful look. "Don't make Richard into a monster. If he needs help translating from English to Chinese or vice versa, I'm sure that he would appreciate Vrog's offer."

9

GERALDINE

"That's one hell of a story." Kian pushed to his feet, walked over to the suite's bar that doubled as a kitchenette, and refilled his coffee cup. "So you got the journal, but you couldn't read it. If it was written in the gods' language, no one in the human world could have translated it for you."

"Fortunately, it was written in Aramaic," Orion said. "The first linguist I took the journal to recognized the language and referred me to another who was proficient in Aramaic. I had him translate the journal for me, and then I erased his memories of the work he had done."

"Was that how you found my mother?" Geraldine asked.

Orion nodded. "By the time I tracked her down, she was a grandmother of eight. Fortunately for me, she still lived in the same town and even used her maiden name in addition to her married one. I had to thrall her to admit that she'd had a daughter out of wedlock who she'd given up for adoption."

"Did she tell you why?"

As Orion took her hand in a show of support, Geraldine braced for the worst, but his tone was soft when he explained, "You have to understand that things were different back then. It wasn't easy to be a single mother, and very few ladies dared. They had special places for unwed pregnant women where they waited until their babies were delivered and then they were immediately taken to their adoptive parents. Your mother said it was difficult to give you up, but she never regretted her decision. She'd gotten married, had three kids, and lived a good life. She assumed that you did as well because she'd been told that the couple who adopted you were nice people."

"Maybe they were, but not to me. I was told that my adoptive parents sent me to work on a farm, and my aunt and uncle treated me like a slave." She rubbed her temple, trying to remember who she'd learned from. Had it been Darlene or Rudolf who'd told her about that?

His eyes were full of compassion as he gave her hand a gentle squeeze. "You were born an immortal, Geraldine. You could hear conversations that you shouldn't have been able to, you were too strong, too fast, and you never got sick. When you fell down and scraped your knees, they couldn't understand why you were crying because your knees looked perfectly fine. Your adoptive parents were terrified of you."

She snorted. "What did they think, that I was possessed by a demon?"

Orion nodded. "What else could they think? By the time they shipped you off to their relatives in Oklahoma, you'd already learned to stifle your abilities, but they were still scared of you. When you married Rudolf, and he didn't seem to notice anything strange about you, they were overjoyed. They thought that you were cured."

"I see." She pulled her hand out of his and folded her arms over her chest. "How did you find them, though? Did my birth mother know who adopted me?"

"She didn't, but she remembered the name of the lady who arranged the adoption, and I tracked her down. She remembered your case well."

"Why?"

He cringed. "They tried to give you back."

"How awful." Cassandra turned to Geraldine. "I'm so glad that you don't remember any of it."

"Right." Orion frowned. "It just occurred to me that you knew about Rudolf and Darlene, but the goddess couldn't have retrieved your memories from before the accident because they were lost forever. How did you find out about them?"

"It's a long story." Geraldine turned to Kian. "Is it okay if I tell Orion?"

"Go ahead." Kian waved a hand. "In the meantime, I'm going to step outside to make a few phone calls." He motioned for Onegus and Andrew to follow him out.

"Thank you." She shifted her eyes to Kian's guards, but neither one made a move to follow their boss.

Evidently, they deemed him safe with just Onegus and Andrew by his side.

She waited until the door closed behind them before turning back to Orion. "It all started with Cassandra meeting Onegus at a charity gala. Her boss needed a stand-in for his wife, who had a concert that night, so he invited Cassy. She and Onegus took one look at each other and immediately felt the connection."

"Oh, Mother." Cassandra rolled her eyes. "You don't need to embellish the story." She smiled. "I thought that Onegus was a stuck-up billionaire, but oh so handsome." She batted her eyelashes.

"Anyway," Geraldine continued. "They started dating, and when things kept blowing up around Cassy, Onegus figured out that she was the cause. Paranormal abilities are a strong indicator that a person might be carrying the godly genes, and that made him suspect that Cassy was a Dormant. Since the godly genes pass through the mother, he suspected that I was as well. But then, as he got to know me a little, he picked up on clues that led him to suspect that I was already an immortal. To test the hypothesis, he took my picture and gave it to Roni to run through clan-developed facial recognition software."

"Hold on a moment." Orion lifted a hand. "Our Roni? Your grandson?"

"The same." Geraldine smiled. "That's a story for another time, but I'll let Roni tell it to you when you meet him. He's an immortal now."

"What about Darlene? Did she turn immortal as well?"

Geraldine's smile wilted. "Not yet, and I hope she will attempt transition as well, but it's more complicated with her. Leo is one problem, and her age is another..."

"What about Leo?" Orion asked. "What does he have to do with it?"

"That's another long story. We have so many that it will take days to fill you in on everything. Let's get back to how I found out about my past. Roni recognized me right away from the pictures his mother had shown him. As it turns out, he already knew that I was immortal and had been searching for me for several years." She smirked. "You taught me to hide so well that even my genius hacker grandson couldn't find me. Anyway, Onegus and Cassandra decided to test how fast I healed to make sure, and Onegus's mother scratched me. When I healed almost instantly, they got the confirmation they needed that I was indeed immortal."

"Not just any immortal," Cassandra said. "Her healing was so rapid that we knew she must be close to the source, but no one could have imagined that she was the daughter of a freaking god."

"What does it mean, being close to the source?"

"Just what it sounds like," Shai said. "It means first- or second-generation immortal."

ORION

"*I* see." Orion ran his hand over his hair. "I still have so much to learn about immortals and gods and the history of our people. My father was very stingy with what he told me."

His prick of a father had told him just enough to get rid of him, but the joke was on him. Thanks to the journal Orion had swiped, he'd found his sister, and thanks to her, he'd found the descendants of a goddess who'd actually shared with them what she knew.

Geraldine patted his knee. "That's okay. Cassandra and I are learning new things every day. You don't have to figure out everything in one go. It's a lot to take in." She chuckled. "Isn't it ironic that I'm the one who knows more than you now?"

"It is. So, I guess Roni heard from Darlene about your relationship with your parents?"

"Not quite. He didn't know much. Cassandra and I devised a plan to meet Darlene. We pretended to be the daughters of her mother's twin sister."

"You don't have a twin."

"I know that." She scrunched her nose. "Though to be honest, I wanted to believe it, and I even convinced myself that having a twin was the only explanation that made sense. I couldn't fathom not remembering my own child, so having had a twin sister who was Darlene's mother and drowned was tragic but convenient."

"I'm sorry." He took her hand again. "I really thought that it was for the best. You didn't remember anything from before the accident, and I figured it was better to spare you from what you would anyway be forced to do in the near future. Imagine how difficult it would have been for you to fake your own death when you could no longer hide the fact that you were not aging."

"She could have dragged it on for a few more years," Shai said. "She could have waited until Darlene went to college instead of orphaning her at twelve."

"I know." Orion winced. "And if not for the accident, I would have helped her do just that." He turned to Geraldine. "Given the memory issues you had after recovering from the accident, it was too risky to send you back to them. I did what I believed was best for everyone, and I looked out for Darlene. I arranged for her to get a full-ride scholarship at an excellent university, and later, I got her worthless husband a well-paying job, which he lost when Roni was caught hacking. I had to wait for things to calm down before getting him a new one."

"We suspected that you were behind Leo's cushy new job," Cassandra said. "Thank you for that. I just wish that you had helped Roni to get out when he was caught."

Orion sighed. "I'm an antiques dealer, not an undercover operative. He was being watched twenty-four-seven by agents and by electronic devices. I could have handled the humans, but even that was too dangerous. I was afraid to tangle with the government."

"You were smart to stay out of it," the redheaded guard said. "It was one hell of an operation to get Roni out of there, and it took months of planning. There is no way you could've pulled it off on your own."

"I can't wait to hear that story, but let's finish this one first." He turned to Geraldine. "How did you approach Darlene?"

"Do you know about those genetic tests that you can mail order nowadays?"

"I've heard of them."

"Roni knew that his mother had done one, so he planted fake results for Cassandra and me at the same place. Cassy called Darlene and told her that we were such a close match that we must be cousins. We set up a meeting and got her to tell us about her father. Cassy suspected that Rudolf had something to do with my accident. That perhaps he wanted to kill me for the insurance money."

Orion shook his head. "Rudolf wasn't a bad man, and he loved you."

"I know that now." Geraldine heaved a sigh. "Anyway, long story short, we went to visit Rudolf, pretending to be Sabina's twin sister's daughters. We found out that you were not as careful as you thought you'd been. He'd seen you with me, and you'd left quite an impression on him. He was convinced that we were having an affair."

"Impossible."

"What? That he saw you or that he thought we were having an affair?"

"That he saw me without me seeing him. He was such a simple guy."

"Never underestimate the resourcefulness of a jealous husband," Cassandra said. "We got an incredibly talented forensic artist to draw your portrait from Rudolf's memory." She pulled out her phone, scrolled for a moment, and handed it to him. "See for yourself."

Orion glanced at the sketch, which was so incredibly accurate it could have been his photograph. "I'll be damned. That's incredible." He handed her the phone back. "The artist must have a paranormal ability to do that from Rudolf's forty-year-old recollection of me."

Geraldine snorted. "Tim is something else, and he charges accordingly. Poor Shai had to part with a big chunk of money for the service."

"I'll pay you back," Orion immediately offered.

"No need." Shai lifted his hand to stop Orion from pressing the point. "I did it for Geraldine."

He decided to let it go for now and repay the guy in some other way in the future. A priceless antique or a rare painting would do great as a wedding present.

When Orion nodded, Geraldine continued, "We told Rudolf that you were mine and Sabina's third sibling who had also been given up for adoption." She put a hand over her heart. "You should have seen the relief on his face. It was like a huge weight had been lifted off his shoulders." She lifted a finger to wipe a tear away. "Up until then, I didn't feel anything toward him, but that touched my heart."

"So you'd already known that I was your brother?"

She laughed. "I didn't. It was just a story we made up to ease Rudolf's tortured soul. He agonized about my supposed infidelity for four decades."

"Damn." Orion shook his head. "Talk about good intentions paving a road straight to hell. If I had known that he had seen me and was tormenting himself over an imagined affair, I would have thralled him to forget me."

"Didn't I tell you about it? Because Rudolf said that he'd confronted me about my alleged affair several times. According to him, I told him that I didn't know what he was talking about, and I don't think that I lied. You probably erased yourself from my memory after each visit."

"I did, and you never mentioned Rudolf's suspicions. Perhaps I made a mess in your head with thralling you to forget me and then releasing the memories when I returned for another visit."

"Did you thrall Rudolf not to notice my peculiarities?"

"I didn't need to. You'd been suppressing your abilities for so long that it was like you didn't have them, and he had no reason to suspect anything. Naturally, you didn't know why you had those abilities, but just to be safe, I compelled you not to show your hand."

She narrowed her eyes at him. "Why did you make me forget you? Did you even tell me who you were?"

"You asked me to do that, so you wouldn't miss me and also so you wouldn't accidentally blurt out anything about me. The way we set it up was for you to remember me as soon as you saw me and forget me once we parted, but after your injury, I had to be more careful. You really didn't remember who I was, and I decided not to tell you that you were immortal. I wasn't sure how long my compulsion would hold, and I figured that the less you knew, the better." He turned to look at Cassandra. "Even your own daughter didn't notice anything unusual other than your memory issues, right?"

Cassandra nodded. "She couldn't use her immortal strength even after we both knew that she was immortal." She grimaced. "You did a good job on her."

"I truly couldn't lift that planter," Geraldine said. "I gave it all I had, and it wouldn't budge."

"That's the power of suggestion," the redhead said. "I once saw a show where a hypnotist told a subject to forget the number four, and then he told him to count from one to ten. The guy counted three times, and each time, he skipped over the number four. He didn't even know that he was doing it."

11

KIAN

"So, what do you think?" Kian asked Onegus and Andrew as the door closed behind them.

"I didn't detect any lies," Andrew said. "He seems like a decent guy."

Onegus nodded. "I didn't smell deceit on him, only anxiety and then excitement when Geraldine and Cassandra arrived."

That had been Kian's impression as well, but he wanted a second and third opinion before allowing the guy into the village. Hell, he still wasn't convinced and planned to ask Edna to probe him.

Kian had to remind himself, though, that Orion's case was very different than Lokan's or even Kalugal's.

Orion was an unaffiliated immortal, who was pretty clueless about his heritage but still dangerously powerful. On the other hand, he cared deeply about Geraldine and Cassandra, and he wasn't the clan's enemy. Besides, Annani was probably already packing and getting ready to head over to the village.

She would demand that Kian invite Orion right away.

Andrew pulled out his phone and checked the time. "If you no longer need me, I should go."

"I'm sorry for keeping you for so long. I didn't expect Orion and Geraldine to go down memory lane." Kian chuckled. "But I should have." He clapped Andrew on the back. "Thank you for coming."

"Any time." Andrew returned Kian's clap.

When his brother-in-law headed toward the elevators, Kian pulled out his phone and called Edna.

She was in her city office today, which was only a few minutes' drive away from the keep. Hopefully, she wouldn't mind swinging by and probing their guest on such short notice.

"Hello, Kian," she answered.

"Good morning. Are you busy?"

"What do you need, Kian?"

"I need you to probe our latest guest at your earliest convenience. I have him in the keep. How soon can you get here?"

"Who's your guest?"

"Orion, son of Toven."

For a long moment, a loaded silence stretched over their connection. "So you've finally caught him."

"We did. The guy slipped by our surveillance and watched Geraldine and Shai from her neighbor's house. His mistake was to follow Shai, who lured him into a trap that we set up for him on Red Canyon Road."

"Why did he follow Shai?"

Kian chuckled. "I asked Orion many questions, but it didn't occur to me to ask that. I arranged for Andrew to be there when Geraldine, Cassandra, Shai, and Onegus came. He listened to Orion's story and then to Geraldine and Orion reminiscing about the past and comparing notes, and he didn't detect any lies. But I want to be absolutely sure about Orion's motives before I bring him to the village, which is why I need you to probe him."

He heard Edna getting up and walking. "What's your impression of him?"

"Andrew, Onegus, and I agree that he seems like a decent guy who was looking after his sister. The way he found her is a fascinating story, but even more so is how he met his father. That encounter had the Fates' fingerprints all over it."

"Interesting." He heard Edna unlock her car and open the door. "Where and when did he meet Toven?" She turned the engine on.

"It was a chance encounter thirty-some years ago on a street in Paris. Toven tried to get rid of Orion by using either thralling or compulsion, but neither would work on Orion because he's immune. He's a compeller himself, and apparently a powerful one. He followed Toven to his place of residence and demanded answers, but Toven brushed him off with the bare minimum of details and sent him away."

"Why? From what Annani told me about Toven, he sounded like a good guy. He didn't sound like the kind of male who discovers that he has a son and wants nothing to do with him."

"Quoting Orion, 'Toven is a jaded bastard who cares about nothing.'"

"Toven lost his wife in the bombing. Perhaps losing his mate broke him."

Using his fingers, Kian brushed his hair back. "I think my mother said that they weren't truelove mates, but that doesn't mean that he didn't love her. He'd been loyal to her." Kian chuckled. "In that respect, Toven was nothing like his father and brother."

"As I said, Annani's descriptions of Toven were favorable. Then again, given who his brother was and who his nephew is, it's possible that he flipped. Insanity runs in families."

Kian snorted. "And yet we allied with Lokan and Kalugal, who carry the same genes."

Edna let out a breath. "I really like Kalugal, and I like Lokan too, but I'm keeping my eyes on Kalugal, and so is Rufsur. If he starts acting insane and making plans to annihilate half the world, Rufsur is ready to stop him."

"Good to know that I'm not the only one who is wary of Kalugal's heritage." Kian glanced at Onegus, who was nodding his agreement. "When you get to the keep, head straight to the dungeon level. I'll probably still be outside in the hallway making phone calls."

"Very well. By the way, why are you not in there with Orion and the others?" Edna asked.

"I thought it would be a better utilization of my time while Orion and Geraldine are reminiscing."

"I would have found that conversation interesting," Edna said with amusement in her voice, "but I understand your need to wrap things up quickly and go home. Send my regards to Syssi when you call her."

"I will." Kian terminated the call.

Onegus arched a brow. "How did she know that you were going to call your wife?"

"If you're worried that Edna can probe us over the phone, she can't. She's just smart enough to deduce it."

"Yeah, but how did she know that you didn't call her already?" Onegus leaned against the wall and crossed his arms over his chest.

"I have no clue. Perhaps Edna had spoken with Syssi earlier, and Syssi told her that I haven't called her yet with updates about Orion." He sighed. "I need to call Annani, but I want Edna to probe Orion first. If he's hiding malevolent intentions, I'd rather know that beforehand."

"How come you didn't have her probe Vrog?" Onegus pushed off the wall.

"Because there was no point. Vrog is pretty transparent, and the only thing we have to worry about is his loyalty to Jade and what he might do if she orders him to go against us. But then we know the answer to that. Having Edna confirm that he's loyal to his former mistress would have served no purpose."

ORION

*W*hen Orion's cell door opened again, Kian returned with Onegus and a stern-looking woman. Andrew, the not-so-subtle lie detector, wasn't with them.

"This is Edna," Kian introduced the female. "She's the clan's judge and a member of the council."

Orion rose to his feet and offered her his hand. "Am I on trial?"

She gifted him with a smile that was just a tiny upturn of her lips. "In a way, but you are not on trial for past transgressions." She took his offered hand. "I'm here to assess your intentions, your aspirations, and the makeup of your soul."

She wasn't joking.

From the corner of his eye, Orion saw the redhead wince, and even the stoic blond let a shadow of emotion cross his eyes, but whether it was out of respect or fear, Orion wasn't sure. The guy was hard to read.

"That sounds ominous." He smiled down at her.

Despite her modest stature, she seemed like a force to be reckoned with, and given the respect on everyone's faces, it wasn't just his impression.

"If you have nothing to hide, this should go easy." She cast a quick glance around the room and nodded her hellos. "It's too crowded in here for what I need to do. Is there anywhere else you could all wait until I'm done?"

When Geraldine darted a panicked glance at Kian, the judge added, "I'll call you back in when I'm ready to share what I've learned."

"Of course." Kian turned to Geraldine and Cassandra. "You can wait in my old office. Onegus will show you where it is." He turned to Geraldine's mate. "I'll stay here with Anandur and Brundar. You can go with them." He turned to Edna. "If that's okay with you."

When the judge didn't object, Geraldine rose to her feet and put her hand on Orion's arm. "Good luck." She stretched up on her toes and kissed his cheek.

Cassandra cast him an encouraging smile before following her mother and the chief of security out.

As the door closed behind them, Edna sat on the couch and motioned for him to sit beside her. "Give me your hands, look into my eyes, and don't say a thing. If you do, Kian will suspect that you compelled me, and we don't want that."

Orion wanted to ask her what he should expect, but heeding her warning, he just nodded.

"What I do is similar to thralling, but I go much deeper. On my way down into the depths of your soul, I might see scenes from events that shaped who you are today, but I'm not going to reveal any of it. I'll only give my opinion about the kind of male you are."

Stifling a witty remark, he nodded again.

"I mean you no harm," Edna said. "If you resist my intrusion, I will have to push harder past your barriers, which will make the experience more difficult for both of us. If you relax and let me in, this will be over much faster."

He nodded again.

As he looked into her ancient eyes, the room faded away, and as her ghostly fingers gently sifted through his memories, he let her dive as deep as she wished.

Orion had nothing to hide, no crimes he felt guilty about or injustices he might have committed. There had been many sorrows in his life, but only a few regrets. He thought of himself as a good man. He was no saint, that was for sure, but he always tried to be the best version of himself.

When one lived forever, accumulating even small regrets could become a crushing weight over time. He was better off avoiding them as best he could.

Just as Edna had promised, her probe didn't take long, and once she was done, she gave him a genuine smile and let go of his hands. "Congratulations, you passed the test."

"Thank you." He inclined his head.

"What's your opinion, Edna?" Kian asked. "I need more than a pass or fail grade."

She turned to look at her leader. "Orion harbors no malevolent plans, not for the clan and not for anyone else. Family is important to him, and he is very protective of the one sister he has found so far and her family."

"Are you still searching for other siblings?" Kian asked.

Orion grimaced. "I've exhausted all the information contained in Toven's journal, and I've only found Geraldine. I was unable to track some of the women described in the journal, though, so perhaps there is still hope. Maybe with your clan's resources, you might succeed where I've failed."

"If there are any out there, it's imperative that we find them," Kian said. "I'll provide you with all the help I can." He shook his head. "I cringe thinking about unaffiliated immortals who have no idea who they are, why they are not aging, and where their special abilities come from. Some might use those abilities in unsavory ways, risking exposure and causing harm." He smiled at Orion. "I'm impressed that you didn't use your powers to take unfair advantage, especially since you had no mentor to teach you the proper rules of conduct for an immortal and instill in you the right values."

Orion cast a sidelong glance at Edna, who shrugged. "As I said, I'm not here to judge you on past misdemeanors. If you want to confess, it's up to you."

The way she phrased it made it evident that Edna didn't judge him harshly for what he had done. Hopefully, Kian wouldn't either.

"I used my powers when I needed to. I thralled women to forget my fangs, I compelled business associates to tell me the truth, and I forced those who tried to cheat me to give me a much better deal than I would have accepted if they were dealing fairly with me."

"I see no problem with any of that. I would have done the same thing."

Edna cleared her throat. "Strictly speaking, thralling and compulsion are only allowed to hide who we are and protect clan members from danger or discovery. That's why thralling the memory of a venom bite is sanctioned, while thralling a reluctant partner into your bed is definitely not."

Orion put a hand on his chest. "I would never do that. It's no different than rape, probably worse."

13

KIAN

*A*fter thanking Edna, Kian called Shai to let him know that it was okay to return and asked him to order lunch for everyone.

Several hours had passed since they'd had breakfast, and he didn't want to bring Orion to the village hungry and then worry about feeding him. He also needed to call Ingrid and have her prepare a house for the guy.

Thankfully, Kalugal's men had moved into their part of the village, so there was no shortage of available houses.

Perhaps he could fob off Orion on his cousin?

Kalugal had a cook, so the problem of feeding Orion would be solved.

Nah, he was overcomplicating things. Geraldine and Cassandra could take care of Orion's needs.

When the two couples returned, Kian rose to his feet. "I need to make a few more phone calls." He turned to Anandur. "Let me know when lunch is here."

"No problem, boss."

Stepping outside, Kian left the door open and headed to his old office to call his mother.

"Hello, my son. What news do you have for me of Orion? Is he okay?"

"We treat him as an honored guest, and I intend to invite him to the village, with proper security, that is."

"No cuffs," Annani commanded.

"None. I just don't want him to know where the village is, but that's not treating him any differently than the majority of clan members. Everyone knows the area, but only a select few know where the entrance to the tunnel is."

"Where is Orion going to stay?"

"There is no shortage of available houses, and when the new section of the village is completed and the furniture delivered, there will be an abundance of vacant houses even in the center of the village. I'm moving all the Guardians to the new homes."

"Exciting times. But what are you going to do with him in the meantime? Perhaps one of the homes in phase two would do. Is he used to luxury?"

"I don't know. But even if he is, it doesn't mean that I need to pamper him. What's good enough for my clan members should be good enough for him."

"What is he like?" Annani asked.

"He's okay. I had Edna probe him, and she didn't find anything that is cause for concern. Frankly, I'm starting to like the guy."

Orion was no Boy Scout, but he was a good male. He didn't use his powers to gain an unfair advantage, which was truly admirable since he answered to no one, and he cared deeply for his sister and her family, assisting them in any way he could.

"You have no idea how happy I am to hear that," Annani said. "I was afraid that you would regard him with suspicion like you did Kalugal."

"I'm still suspicious of that conceited know-it-all, but I also like him."

Annani laughed. "You like him because he smokes cigars and drinks whiskey with you. You found a partner in crime."

"Kalugal smokes *my* cigars and drinks *my* whiskey, but I don't mind. He's good company."

The guy was intelligent, well-read, easygoing, and he was good to his mate and to his men. That was good enough for Kian.

"Indeed. I am glad that you are getting along with your cousin, and now you have another one."

"Orion is not my cousin any more than Navuh is. Both are Ekin's grandsons, and Ekin was your father's half-brother, so that's a very distant relationship. And even though Kalugal and Lokan are the sons of Areana, calling them cousins is a stretch because you share a father and not a mother."

She sighed. "I like thinking of Lokan and Kalugal as close family. Fates know that these boys have no one else. Areana is locked up on the island, and Navuh regards them as potential enemies. We are the only ones who treat them like real family."

"True. I never thought of it from that angle."

"Well, now you do. Did Orion tell you anything about Toven?"

"Yeah." Annani wasn't going to like what Kian had to tell her about the god she used to be so fond of. "Orion met him only once, and at the time, Toven called himself Herman."

"Herman? Why on earth would he call himself that? Had he been hiding among the Germanic tribes?"

"It's possible, but he didn't tell Orion much." Kian repeated everything that Orion had told them about that fateful meeting with Toven.

"That does not sound like the Toven I knew. He must have been devastated when he learned the fate of our people. I, at least, had the Odus to keep me company. He had no one."

"He also lost his mate. I remember you telling me that he loved his wife and was faithful to her, but that they weren't truelove mates. Is that correct? Or am I confusing Khiann's parents' story with Toven's?"

"Both couples had good marriages despite not being truelove mates. That was why they could be separated for long periods of time without suffering terribly. Khiann's father was often gone for months, taking caravans to trade in faraway lands, and Toven was an explorer and a researcher. He was also gone for months at a time."

"Then Toven should have gotten over her death a long time ago."

"Perhaps he could not," Annani said softly. "He had been married for much longer than I had."

"Perhaps." Kian needed to change the subject before his mother started crying. As strong and as resilient as she was, it still pained her to talk about Khiann.

"I want to see Orion," Annani said.

"Of course you do. When should I expect you?"

"It will take Alena and me about an hour to pack and for the Odus to prepare the jet. The flight time is about five hours, so plan for Okidu to pick us up from the airstrip accordingly. Also, since there are so many houses available, have one prepared for us. We will be staying for a while this time, at least until Amanda delivers her daughter and probably a couple of weeks after that if not longer."

Ingrid would have a panic attack if he asked her to prepare two houses on such short notice.

"I'll see what I can do. If Ingrid can't manage a house for you right away, you can spend a couple of days with Syssi and me until the house is ready."

"I understand. But do the best you can. I would rather unpack once."

His mother had never packed or unpacked a suitcase, the Odus took care of that for her, but he wasn't going to point that out. "Naturally. I'd better let Syssi know that you will be joining us for dinner."

"Invite Orion to dinner as well."

He should have expected that. In fact, he should have thought of it himself. The problem was that the guy wasn't just any immortal. He was a compeller.

"We need to consider security, Mother. Orion is a compeller, and he's immune to compulsion by others. Even Toven couldn't compel him."

"Are you suggesting that I wear those earpieces?" Her tone was incredulous.

"I don't think we need to go that far. But instruct your Odus not to obey orders from you if they originate from Orion. I will also have the brothers attend dinner while wearing earpieces. They will know not to obey questionable orders from either of us."

"Sounds reasonable."

"We can discuss what to do about Toven when you get here."

"I want to find him, of course. Do you not?"

"I do, but even more important than that is finding his other children if he fathered any in addition to Orion and Geraldine. Those immortals could cause a lot of trouble, or worse, get caught."

"We can search for both," Annani said. "But we will talk about it over dinner tonight. I need to tell my Odus what to pack for me."

"Call me when you are within an hour of landing, and I'll send Okidu to pick you up. Syssi will need every spare moment of his help to prepare dinner for so many people."

"Who are you inviting other than the family and Orion?"

Kian loosed a breath. "If I invite Orion, I have to invite Geraldine and Shai, Cassandra and Onegus, and Roni and Sylvia. And since it's too early for me to trust Orion, I need Anandur and Brundar to be there with earpieces, but since I don't want him to think that I consider him a threat, I'll have them bring their mates along. The rest are the usual suspects—Amanda and Dalhu, Andrew, Nathalie, and Phoenix, and Jacki and Kalugal. Together with you and Alena, that's twenty-two people."

"Is your dining room large enough?"

The one in their new house was, but the crews were still putting final touches on it, and the furniture wouldn't arrive for another two weeks.

They might be able to squeeze twenty people into their current dining room, but perhaps it was better to move dinner to the backyard and bring in heaters. He needed to check the forecast to see if it was going to rain tonight.

"I need to talk it over with Syssi, and I should do that as soon as possible. Is there anything else you need to discuss with me before I go?"

"We can talk more when I get there. Goodbye, Kian."

"Goodbye, Mother. I'll see you tonight." He ended the call and then called Syssi.

She patiently listened as he gave her a quick summary of the day's events, the number of people they would be hosting tonight, and his suggestion to have the dinner in the backyard.

"Did you look at the forecast?" Syssi asked.

"Not yet."

"It might rain tonight. Maybe we should have it at Kalugal's place," she suggested. "I'm sure he wouldn't mind. Atzil can whip up a dinner for twenty with ease. He's used to cooking for a crowd."

"I'd rather cancel the whole thing than give Kalugal the satisfaction. Okidu can move the dining table into the living room and stick the living room furniture somewhere else."

"That could work."

"Thank you for doing this. I'll try to get home early and assist with whatever you need me to do."

She chuckled. "You have enough on your plate, and you shouldn't worry about me. I'll draft the queen of party organizing to help me prepare this lovely event."

"The queen is heavily pregnant. I doubt she can do much."

"She can conduct the orchestra from the couch. Amanda never does anything with her own two hands, but she's great at planning, organizing, and delegating."

14

ALENA

*A*nnani opened the door to Alena's suite and rushed in, in a flurry of nightgown and robe. "Pack your things, Alena. We are leaving within the hour."

Alena's heartbeat accelerated. "What happened?"

Her mother smiled. "Kian is moving Orion to the village, and we are going to see him tonight at dinner at Syssi and Kian's house. I am so excited to meet Toven's son. Are you?"

With how fast her heart was racing, to say that she was merely excited would be missing it by a mile. Terrified would be more accurate.

Alena hadn't expected to have to face Orion so soon, or ever if she could help it. He was a compeller, a possessor of a rare paranormal ability that gave her the creeps, but he was also the most attractive male she'd ever seen a picture of, and she yearned to meet him in person. Those two opposing forces were sure to mess with her head, and it would have been best to avoid walking into that landmine.

Except, her mother wanted to see Orion today, so that was happening whether Alena was ready and willing or not.

"What is Kian doing as far as precautions?" she asked. "Orion is a compeller."

Annani waved a dismissive hand. "So is Kalugal, and no one wears those special earpieces around him anymore." She turned toward the door she'd left open. "And if we don't need them around Kalugal, who is the son of our arch-enemy, we definitely don't need to wear them around Orion, who is not."

They didn't know what Toven was up to, but Alena didn't point it out. There were other considerations that her mother had conveniently forgotten. "You compelled Kalugal not to use his powers on clan members. Are you going to do the same with Orion?"

"I might not be able to. He told Kian that Toven had tried to compel him to go away but was unsuccessful. I do not know how strong of a compeller Toven is, and whether I am stronger than him or not. I will need to test it."

Great, so that one kernel of hope was gone. If Annani could have compelled Orion not to use his compulsion on her clan members, Alena might have given him a chance, but now it was out of the question.

"I don't like it. I know that there is no way I can convince you to wear earpieces when you meet Orion, but I'm definitely going to do so. I'll text Kian and ask him to send a pair for me with Okidu."

Annani regarded her with her ancient eyes. "I am a compeller as well. Are you living in constant fear of me using my power on you?"

"Of course not. You're my mother, and I trust you."

"Why do you trust me?"

Alena rolled her eyes. "Because you love me, and you know how much I hate the very idea of compulsion. I know you will never use it on me or any of your children without their permission."

"I compelled you once. Did you forget?"

"That doesn't count. It was for an excellent cause, and it was a blanket compulsion that covered everyone in the clan. There was so much mistrust between Kian and Kalugal and between Kalugal's men and our clan that the only way they could coexist alongside us was if you compelled everyone to get along and not harm each other."

"Nevertheless, you felt the power of my compulsion. Was it so terrible?"

"It wasn't," Alena admitted. "From you, it felt like love. But it wouldn't feel like that from anyone else, and especially not from a male." She shivered. "It's vile. It's a violation of the worst kind."

Annani shook her head. "I do not know why you have such aversion to people who possess the ability. Like with everything else, it depends on how they use it. A male is typically stronger than a female, and he can force himself on her. Does the ability to do so make him vile? Of course not. If he uses his superior strength to rape and plunder, then he is evil. But if he uses it to protect those who cannot protect themselves, then he is a hero."

It was hard to argue with that logic, but Alena was well aware that her aversion to compellers wasn't entirely rational, and she didn't even know why. It wasn't like she'd ever been a victim of compulsion or even of hypnotism.

"You are right, Mother, but I still prefer to wear the earpieces, at least until I'm convinced that Orion is a good guy."

"Fair enough." Annani looked down at her robe. "Oh my. In all the excitement, I forgot to get dressed before leaving my suite."

As usual, she looked magnificent even when wearing a nightgown. Not that it looked any different than her dresses. It was silk—because she didn't like any other fabric touching her skin, purple—because it complemented her fiery red hair, and floor-length—because she didn't like her feet showing.

Evidently, everyone had their quirks. Alena's was an allergic reaction to compellers, and Annani's was embarrassment over her tiny, child-like feet.

"That's okay, Mother. No one noticed because your dresses look like nightgowns anyway."

"They do." Annani chuckled. "I like to be comfortable but still stylish." She cast Alena a motherly smile before opening the door. "Tell Ovidu to start packing. I want to leave as soon as possible."

15

ORION

*A*fter Geraldine, Cassandra, and their mates had returned, and Kian had left again, no one bothered to close the massive door to Orion's comfy prison.

Evidently Edna's favorable opinion of him had put the suspicious Kian at ease, and he had slackened security.

"I can smell food." The redhead pushed to his feet. "That must be Edwin with the delivery." He walked out of the room and a moment later returned with a bunch of paper bags in hand and Kian in tow.

Orion liked the casual way these immortals interacted. They called each other by their first names, and although the guards regarded Kian with respect, they also treated him as a friend or a family member rather than their boss.

Well, the redhead did. The blond was doing an excellent impersonation of a statue and was impossible to read, except for that one glimpse of emotion he'd shown when Edna explained what she'd been about to do.

The experience had been intrusive and a little uncomfortable, but it hadn't been as bad as Orion had expected. She'd handled him with care.

"After we are done with lunch—" Kian accepted a box from the redhead "—we will head to the village." He leveled his intense eyes on Orion's. "I'm having a house prepared for you, so you can continue your reunion with your sister and niece from the comfort of your own home."

That didn't sound good.

Did Kian intend to keep him under house arrest?

"A whole house just for me? Can't I stay for a couple of days with Geraldine or Cassandra?"

"Perhaps during your next visit. Right now, the housing situation in the village is in flux, and the best solution is to give you your own place for as long as you want to stay with us. It's nothing fancy, but it's nearly brand new, and it's as nicely decorated as this place by the same talented interior designer."

That was a relief and a pleasant surprise, but he needed to make sure that he understood Kian's intentions correctly. "Thank you. That's very generous of you, but I can't stay for more than a few days. I have a business to run."

"I understand," Kian said. "As I told you, you're welcome to stay as long as you want." He opened the box and lifted a piece of eggplant with a pair of chopsticks. "Naturally, I count on you to keep our existence a secret just as you keep yours. The safety of your sister and niece depends on that." He put the piece of eggplant in his mouth.

"I would never do anything to jeopardize their safety, as well as yours and the rest of your people. I vow it on my life."

It was a shame that the lie detector guy was gone and couldn't vouch for the veracity of his statement, but it seemed that Edna's probe was enough to convince Kian of his good intentions.

"I count on it." Kian lifted another piece of eggplant and ate it.

Was he a vegetarian?

Orion had always been a carnivore and assumed that it was part of his unique physiology. His fangs, venom, and ability to thrall people and beasts alike were the traits of a predator, and by definition predators were meat-eaters.

Opening the box the redhead handed him, Orion was glad to find beef and broccoli. He looked at the tall guard. "How did you know what to order for me?"

The guy shrugged. "I didn't order it, Shai did, and the box had your name written on it."

"I told Shai what to order," Geraldine said. "More and more of my memories of you are slowly resurfacing, including the many lunches we had together. I even remember which dishes you used to order."

It was a nice feeling to have at least one person know and care about his preferences. Before, he hadn't dared to let her remember those things because her mind had been too fragile.

Casting a sidelong glance at her mate, Orion wondered if the guy was aware of the risk he and his people were taking by releasing Geraldine's memories. As long as she stayed in the village, that was okay, but if she ventured into the human world, she might forget not to say anything about immortals and their beautiful hideout.

"By the way," Kian said. "The Clan Mother is on her way, and you are all invited to dinner at my house." He smiled at Orion. "You are going to meet her much sooner than you hoped for."

He dropped his chopsticks into the box. "Tonight?"

"I told you that she's eager to meet you."

Geraldine put a hand on his arm. "You have nothing to fear from Annani. She is kind and friendly and much nicer than your father."

"That's not difficult to do." He gripped the chopsticks and lifted a piece of broccoli.

"Shai and I need to get a house of our own as well." Geraldine put her box on the coffee table. "And I need to start driving again so I can visit my friends. Shai is arranging a new fake driver's license and passport for me." She smiled at her mate. "I can finally leave the country and travel. I've seen nothing of the world yet."

Orion didn't know whether he should issue a warning or keep his mouth shut. Perhaps later, he would take Shai aside and tell him to proceed with caution.

Shai groaned. "I don't know if I can take a vacation that's longer than a couple of days." He cast a sidelong glance at Kian. "How are you going to manage without me?"

"I told you that you need an assistant, and I also asked that you put an ad on the clan's virtual bulletin board. I don't know why you're dragging your feet about that."

"What is it that you do, Shai?" Orion asked.

In all the commotion, he'd forgotten his original reason for following Shai. He still hadn't determined whether the guy was worthy of Geraldine.

Shai hadn't said much during the long hours that they had spent together, which was an admirable trait, provided that he did it out of respect and consideration and not because he had nothing to add to the conversation.

"I'm Kian's assistant." Shai avoided his eyes as if he was ashamed of his job.

"That's a very respectable position," Orion said and meant it.

"Shai is much more than that," Kian said. "I would have been lost without his eidetic memory."

Orion's appreciation for the guy ratcheted up by a few notches. "Do you remember everything?"

Shai nodded. "Word for word."

"What a great asset to have." Orion thought of all the ways a talent like that could be useful.

"Not as great as the power to compel," Shai said. "I would trade with you in a heartbeat, not because I'm power-hungry, but because it's a great defensive weapon."

"I'm glad that you think of my compulsion as a defense mechanism, but most people don't." Orion put the empty box on the coffee table. "They assume it's an offensive tool, which I admit it can be. But I would rather have your amazing memory and not be considered a threat." He pinned Kian with a hard stare. "As a compeller, I'm assumed guilty until proven innocent."

16

KIAN

*A*s the SUV's windows turned opaque, Kian felt Orion tense.

"What's going on?" he asked.

"Nothing to be alarmed about. It's a little trick we use to make sure even our own people can't find the village."

Letting go of the wheel, Anandur turned around and grinned at Orion. "From this point on, the autonomous driving engages. It will relinquish control to me when we reach the parking structure."

"You can't be serious." Orion cast a glance at Brundar, who sat beside him in the back seat, but when the Guardian didn't respond, he turned to look at Kian. "Unless you keep your people underground in that village of yours, I'm sure everyone has already figured out where they live. All it takes is to look at the landmarks."

"True, but they can't find the entrance to the tunnel, which is the only way in," Kian explained with no small amount of smugness. "When we get there, you will feel the car enter an elevator, which will take it up to the parking level. From there, another elevator will take us to the surface. The only other way into the village is by parachuting from above, but thanks to clever camouflage and signal disruptors, no aircraft fly overhead. You would have to use a very large bird to get over the village, but since dragons are extinct, you're out of luck."

"I was under the impression that Dragons were a myth."

"It was a joke," Kian clarified. "The bottom line is that our village is very well-hidden."

"I have to admit that I'm impressed." Orion folded his arms over his chest. "Not by the technology but by the resources your clan has to command to afford a project like that. How rich are you people?"

"We're doing well, but our humanitarian efforts are a big drain on our resources. We've organized a charity to help with the costs and the donations help, but we still fund about half of the operations."

"What's your gig?"

Kian didn't like that word in reference to a serious problem like trafficking. Hadn't Geraldine or Cassandra told Orion about the charity gala where Onegus and Cassandra had met? The donations had gone to the rehabilitation center for the victims.

"We fight trafficking," Brundar said.

Orion was so startled by the Guardian speaking that Kian doubted he'd noticed that they'd entered the tunnel.

"Human trafficking?"

Brundar cast him an incredulous look and didn't bother to answer.

"Is there any other kind?" Anandur asked.

Uncrossing his arms, Orion leaned closer to the redhead. "What exactly do you do to stop it?"

"We raid the brothels, rough up the scum, free the victims, and leave enough evidence for the police to lock the scum up." Anandur smiled evilly. "Sometimes we get too rough and the scum expires, but oh well, shit happens."

"We also rehabilitate the victims," Kian added.

Orion was about to comment when the car rolled onto the elevator platform, and the thing lurched up. "It's like science fiction. I feel like I'm entering Batman's cave."

"Not quite." Kian chuckled.

When the elevator door opened, Anandur drove the SUV out and pulled into Kian's parking spot. "We are home."

Brundar opened the door, got out, and opened the trunk to get Orion's suitcase and carry-on.

After they'd collect his things from the Airbnb he had been renting, Orion told them about the pizza delivery guy he'd hosted for an evening against the guy's will. What Kian liked about the story was that Orion had compensated the Uber driver for his time and for the use of his car. Provided that it was true, and Kian had no reason to doubt it, Orion had done precisely as he would have, which made him like the guy even more.

"I can take these." Orion took the luggage from Brundar's hands.

The Guardian didn't argue and headed for the elevators.

As they stepped out of the elevator and entered the pavilion, Orion's eyes widened. "What's all this?" He motioned at the artifacts housed behind the glass displays.

"Our shared cousin, Kalugal, is into archeology. He's been searching for clues about the gods' civilization and collecting artifacts that pertain to them. I'm afraid most of these were smuggled illegally from the countries they were discovered in, but I can definitely turn a blind eye to that. Technically, they belong to us."

"What do you mean, shared cousin? Are we cousins?"

Kian led the way out the doors. "In a manner of speaking. Mortdh was Kalugal's grandfather, and Toven was Mortdh's brother. That's how you and Kalugal are related. Kalugal's mother is my mother's half-sister from the same father but different mothers, and that's how we are related. So, you and I might not be cousins, but we share Kalugal as a second or third cousin." Kian chuckled. "In the clan, we make it easy. Everyone is a cousin unless they are directly your sibling or an uncle or an aunt, and of course your mother."

Orion arched a brow. "What about fathers?"

"Up until recently, there were no fathers in the clan. But things are changing." Kian smiled proudly. "I'm a father, and so is Andrew, and also one of the Guardians. Another Guardian mated a widow with two children and officially adopted them. Kalugal's wife is expecting, and so is my sister Amanda. Hopefully, the clan will have many more fathers in the not-too-distant future."

17

ORION

"$\mathcal{G}$et some rest," were Kian's parting words as he left the house that would be Orion's home for as long as he wished to stay.

The immortals' village was serene and beautiful, the only noises disturbing the quiet coming from the building project that Kian had promised to take him on a tour of.

"So, what do you think?" Cassandra sat down on the couch. "It's nice here, isn't it." She and Geraldine had come along to see the house. Their mates had bid him goodbye outside the glass pavilion, and Orion assumed that they had gone to work.

"It's a slice of paradise." He walked over to the sliding doors and opened them. "I've never owned a house."

"Why not?" Geraldine followed him out into the backyard. "It's surely not due to lack of funds."

He shrugged. "I have apartments in different cities around the world, but I keep them more as an investment than personal residences. I'm always traveling and staying either in hotels or Airbnbs."

She glanced back at the living room where his suitcase and carry-on had been left next to the front door. "For someone who lives out of a suitcase, you travel light."

"I don't need much."

He wondered whether the male he'd seen sitting on a bench across from the house was there to keep an eye on him.

Kian had done his best to make it seem as if he didn't consider him a threat, but Orion saw right through the act. The guy was right to be cautious, though. Orion meant none of them harm, but despite Edna's stamp of approval, Kian still didn't know him well enough to be sure of that.

The fact remained that he was a compeller, and apparently, it was a rare power that even immortals feared. That was why they'd been wearing specialty earpieces when they'd apprehended him. Kian hadn't, but his guards had, and Orion was willing to bet that the one sitting on the bench had them too.

"Do you want to shower and take a nap before dinner?" Geraldine asked. "If you need your clothes ironed, I can do that for you."

He wrapped an arm around her shoulders and kissed the top of her head. "I know how to use an iron. I've been a bachelor for most of my life."

She lifted a pair of sad eyes to him. "I remember what you told me about the woman you loved. Are you still mourning her?"

"I will never stop mourning her. Miriam was the love of my life."

"How long ago did she die?"

"Four hundred fifty-six years, two months, and three days ago." He walked back into the house through the sliding doors.

"That's a long time to mourn," Cassandra said. "This village is full of lovely immortal females who will be all over you once they hear that there is a new immortal bachelor in the village who is not Annani's descendant. Perhaps you should give them a chance."

Orion snorted. "Don't mind if I do. Vowing never to love again doesn't mean that I've abstained for all these years."

"Good. For a moment there, I thought that you had, and wouldn't that have been a great loss to females everywhere."

"I doubt that." He sat on the couch, taking Geraldine with him. "I'm not much of a catch."

He was old, and most people tried his patience. His encounters with women were purely physical, and he never spent the night with them.

The only one he'd ever woken up next to had been Miriam, the woman he'd been married to for thirty-three years, the woman who had known his secret but had taken it to her grave. She'd loved him with everything she had, and he'd loved her back just as much.

A love like that came once in a lifetime if one was lucky. There was no chance he could ever find someone to love like that again.

"Come on, Mom. Orion had a very tiring day. We should let him rest."

Geraldine rose to her feet. "We need to go grocery shopping. I opened the fridge, and there was nothing but beer and sodas in there."

That piqued Orion's interest. "There is beer?"

Cassandra grimaced. "It's probably Snake Venom. It's potent, which is why the clan males love it, but it tastes vile. I wonder who put it there."

"I bet it was Anandur," Geraldine said. "That's a sign that he likes you."

"I've heard of Snake Venom." Orion opened the fridge and pulled a bottle out. "Since you say that it tastes terrible, I won't offer you a beer, but would you like some sparkling water?"

"I'm good." Cassandra walked into the pantry. "There are two boxes of crackers and two kinds of cereal in here. Do you want some crackers with your beer?"

"Why not." He popped the cap off and took a careful sip. "That certainly packs a punch."

"Men." Cassandra opened the box of crackers. "Don't tell me that you actually like it."

"It's not bad." He took another sip.

After the day he'd had, whiskey would have been better, but beggars can't be choosers, and this high-alcohol-content beer hit the spot.

Geraldine put a hand on his bicep. "Are you going to be okay here by yourself until Cassandra and I return with the groceries?" She fiddled with her necklace. "I also need to stop by the house and get a change of clothes. I can't go dressed like this to dinner with Annani."

He looked her over and saw nothing wrong with the outfit she had on. Geraldine had always been a smart dresser, even when finances had been tight and she'd made her own clothes. He would have gladly covered all of her expenses, but he couldn't have done that without leaving clues. The only safe way to help her had been anonymously buying her quilts.

"You look beautiful as always, but if you want to go home and change, don't hesitate because of me. I'm used to being alone." He turned toward the living room window and looked at the walkway, where the man still sat on the bench and pretended to watch something on his phone. "Besides, I have this guy to keep me company. If I get bored while waiting for your return, I'll join him on the bench and strike up a conversation." He smiled at Cassandra. "Maybe I'll ask him about the village's single ladies."

18

ALENA

*A*s Okidu pulled the limo into its parking spot, Kian opened the back door for Annani and offered her a hand up.

"Good evening, Mother. How was your flight?"

"I took a nice nap." She kissed his cheek. "I was hoping for a vision of Toven, but evidently, I only get visions of my children."

Alena stifled an eye roll and took Kian's offered hand. "Good to see you, Kian." She kissed his other cheek. "How is our newest guest doing?"

Despite the butterflies flapping around in her stomach, she'd somehow managed a bored tone. If she didn't get a hold of herself and that schoolgirl crush she'd developed over a sketched portrait, she was going to embarrass herself.

It was difficult to hide attraction from immortals, but Alena was old and experienced, and she knew how to handle herself. She would do just fine, and no one would be any the wiser.

"After I brought him to the village, Geraldine and Cassandra stayed with him for most of the time, only taking a couple of hours off to get groceries. After they left, he took a long nap, showered, shaved, and got ready for dinner."

"How do you know all that?" Annani asked.

"I posted a Guardian in front of his house."

Annani leveled Kian with a hard look. "How would a Guardian who is outside the house know that Orion shaved? Did you put surveillance cameras inside to spy on him?"

"I did, but not in the bathroom. He must have heard the electric shaver. There is one in the living room, and the feed from it goes into the server for safekeeping. Unless he gives us a reason to suspect something, no one is going to watch it."

As Okidu, Ovidu, and her mother's three butlers each pulled a suitcase out of the trunk, Kian arched a brow. "Did you bring your entire wardrobe along?"

"We are going to stay for at least a month." Alena fell in step with him. "And you know Mother—she needs a different gown for every day."

Annani huffed. "My silk gowns do not take much space, and they do not weigh much either. Alena and I visited a baby store in Anchorage, and there were so many beautiful outfits for babies and toddlers and such marvelous toys that we ended up buying half the store. We have a lot of presents for all the little ones."

"Not just for the little ones," Alena said. "We got something for everyone. After all, we will be staying for the holidays."

Kian held the elevator door open for them. "Don't tell me that you got gifts for every clan member."

"I wish I could." Annani glanced at the Odus, who were staying outside to wait for the next elevator to arrive. "Alena and I would have needed many more suitcases."

The clan didn't celebrate during the various human holidays, but since the newly transitioned immortals missed the end-of-year festivities they had been so fond of as humans, Annani had decided to start a new gift-giving tradition during the holiday season. Alena was still trying to figure out how to add more celebratory flair to it, a symbol like the Christmas tree or the menorah could have been helpful—something people could gather around.

So far, the new custom hadn't taken root, and only a few clan members exchanged gifts during the holidays, but if she came up with a party theme, perhaps more would join. It was a nice tradition.

As the elevator door opened and they entered the pavilion, looking at Kalugal's display of artifacts gave her an idea. Perhaps she should research Sumerian mythology and find a symbol her people would be comfortable with. Nothing came to mind readily, but it had been many years since she'd read the Sumerian legends.

The clan's large golf cart that was parked outside the pavilion doors was the size of a limo and could seat eight, or in their case, the three of them, the four Odus, and all of the luggage.

As Kian helped Annani up, Alena walked around to the other side and climbed in. They waited for the Odus to load the luggage and get in as well, and then they were off with Okidu driving the thing.

"Which home are we getting this time?" Alena asked.

"Shai's. I convinced him to get a new house for him and Geraldine in the newer part of the village, right next to the house Onegus and Cassandra are getting. Shai's roommate is moving in with Onegus's."

"Is it going to be ready on time?" Annani asked. "You did not know that we were coming until this morning, and then you were busy interrogating Orion."

"I owe Ingrid a big bonus for what I put her through. I gave her four hours to get Shai and his roommate's things moved to their new homes, and the house scrubbed clean and prepared for you and Alena. She mobilized several Guardians to help her with the task and was done in three."

"The woman is a miracle worker," Alena said. "She deserves a promotion."

"She's already got it. I let her use one of the houses in phase two as her headquarters, and I authorized her to hire five full-time employees to tackle the new homes in the last building phase. She's strutting like a peacock through the village, telling everyone about her new design center."

"I want to see it," Annani said. "Put it on my calendar, Alena."

She pulled out her phone. "You have Wednesday early afternoon open. Is two o'clock okay?"

Annani nodded. "Coordinate it with Ingrid."

"Of course." Alena added a reminder to call the designer later and put her phone away. "Before I forget, did you bring me the earpieces I asked for?"

"Yes." Kian reached into his pocket and handed her a clear box. "These are William's newest edition, and they are much better than the previous versions. They are smaller, so they are less obvious, and the AI filters the voices and slightly alters their frequencies in real time instead of translating them into machine voices. Before, everyone sounded the same, and it was disorienting and uncomfortable. With these, you will still recognize the voices and who they belong to, but they will sound a little different."

"Wonderful." She put them in her skirt pocket. "Will you be wearing a pair?"

Kian shook his head. "Anandur and Brundar will, and Okidu and Onidu will be there as well. That should be enough. Even if Orion had nefarious intentions, which Edna assured me that he doesn't, he wouldn't dare to use compulsion on you or anyone else during dinner. You really don't need the earpieces, but it's up to you."

She patted her pocket. "I'll use them. At least until we know for sure that he can be trusted."

"Fair enough."

Their mother didn't look happy about it, but she refrained from saying anything. They'd had that discussion before.

When Kian's phone pinged with a message, he pulled it out and read it. "Syssi says that Kalugal and Jacki are already there. And the brothers arrived with their mates even before I left to greet you."

Alena checked the time on her phone. "It's not eight yet." They still had eighteen minutes, and her family was not known to be punctual.

"Kalugal probably thought that he could share a cigar with me before dinner." Kian smiled. "I wonder if Orion likes cigars."

"You should ask him," Annani said. "Perhaps you could bond with him over whiskey and cigars as you did with Kalugal and Dalhu."

His lips twisted in a grimace. "I wouldn't call it bonding. Kalugal is just pleasant company, and so is Dalhu when he actually speaks. Orion seems to be a decent fellow, and he certainly knows how to tell a story. He's quite likable."

As soon as Kian had brought up Orion again, Alena's heart rate accelerated.

In mere minutes, she was about to come face to face with her silly crush, and it would take all of her self-control to hide her infatuation.

Kian frowned. "Are you cold, Alena? Your cheeks are red."

Mortified, she lifted her hands to her heated face. "I must be. My coat is in the suitcase. It's usually so warm here, even during the winter, that I thought I wouldn't need it, but it's colder than usual."

Annani cast her a curious glance. "The cold has never bothered you before."

Reminded of the theme song from *Frozen*, Alena was overcome by an urge to sing it. When the movie had first come out, she'd sung it over and over again, but never in public.

At first, she just hummed the melody, but as the song seemed to rise from inside her, demanding to be heard, Alena ignored her mother and brother's amused expressions and started singing loud enough for the entire village to hear. "Let it go, let it go, can't hold it back anymore—"

19

ORION

*W*hen a knock sounded on the door and Orion opened up, he wasn't surprised to see the guy who'd been sitting all day on the bench in front of the house.

"Good evening. I'm Mason, and I'm here to escort you to Kian's house." The guy extended his hand and smiled.

"Orion." He shook what was offered.

Mason had chin-length hair, which would never have been allowed in the human army or police force, but apparently these immortals were not sticklers for the rules. Besides, Mason had probably been chosen for the job because of his long hair. It served to obscure the special earpieces that nullified Orion's compulsion ability.

Evidently, Kian didn't want him to feel like he wasn't trusted but still considered him a threat.

What about thralling, though? It didn't require speech to be effective. It worked telepathically, so earpieces were useless against it. If he could thrall Geraldine, which he had done in the past, he most likely could thrall Mason as well.

Did Kian know that?

Since the Clan Mother had seen Geraldine's memories, they should have known that Orion could thrall immortals.

It was an inexcusable oversight, which made him wonder about the quality of the rest of the clan's security measures. Perhaps they weren't as thorough as Kian liked to think they were.

"Are you assigned to guard me?" he asked the guy.

Mason nodded. "I'm assigned to assist you in any way you require."

It was a nice way to put it. "But you're a guard, right?"

"Guardian."

"Like a Guardian angel?"

Mason chuckled. "I would like to think that I am, and sometimes the trafficking victims we rescue call us that." His eyes clouded with sadness. "When they are not too traumatized and don't think that every male is a monster." He loosed a breath. "Anyway, members of the clan's security force are called Guardians."

"I would like to hear more about those rescues. Would you like to come in?"

The Guardian lifted his phone and glanced at the screen. "Perhaps some other time. It's twenty minutes to eight, which gives us just enough time to get you to Kian's house in time for dinner without rushing."

"Then let's go." Orion stepped out and closed the door behind him. "Is it okay to leave it unlocked? I don't have a key."

"No one locks their doors in the village. There is no need."

Orion arched a brow. "Is everyone perfectly behaved?"

"I wouldn't say that, but no one enters someone else's house without permission or takes something that doesn't belong to them."

"So what's considered misbehavior?"

"Gossip is a big issue in a small community like ours, and since most of us are related, everyone thinks that they have the right to butt into everyone else's business."

The guy didn't realize how lucky he was to have a big family that gave a shit about him.

"That's not so bad." Orion cast the Guardian a sidelong glance. "Other than dealing with pesky relatives, do you like living here?"

The guy turned puzzled eyes on him. "What's not to like? Other than the damn gossip, the place is perfect."

"It looks new. Where did the clan live before?"

"The Guardians and some of the civilians lived in the keep, and the rest were scattered throughout. When the Doomers murdered one of ours who lived alone in San Francisco, Kian ordered everyone to move into the keep, but people weren't happy living in a concrete and glass tower, so he started the village project."

"Who and what are the Doomers?"

"That's a long story."

Orion lifted his hand and looked at his watch. "We have fifteen minutes."

"I guess that's enough. You are Toven's son, right?"

"Yes."

"The Doomers are the followers of his brother's son Navuh, who in some ways is worse than his father. He's not as powerful, but he's smarter and not as impulsive. He's the master of long-term planning."

"I thought that no one other than Toven and the two goddesses survived."

"Some of the immortals survived as well. Those who were in Mortdh's stronghold in the north escaped the nuclear wind, or so we think, about the wind, I mean. No one knows for sure what actually destroyed the southern region. It might have been a hydrogen bomb or something else completely."

Orion was about to ask about the bombing when he heard soft singing that quickly grew louder. The woman's voice was beautiful, powerful, defiant, sexy. It wasn't what most men would consider a siren's song, but it was to him.

He needed to find out who the woman behind the voice was.

"Who's the singer?" he asked Mason.

The guy chuckled. "I know only one female who can sing like that, but I haven't heard her sing in a very long time."

"Who is she?"

"Alena, Kian's elder sister. Most of the time, she's such a quiet, soft-spoken female —motherly, sweet, and gentle as can be. Until she starts singing." He cast Orion an amused glance. "We used to tease her that she could topple the walls of Jericho if they were still standing. Maybe that's why she stopped."

"That's a shame. She has an amazing voice." Orion stopped talking and listened.

The melody sounded familiar. He'd heard it before, but he'd never paid attention to the lyrics. This time he did because it was impossible not to when sung with so much emotion and with so much conviction.

It was about fear and isolation, about being tired of acting good while a storm was raging inside her, about refusing to bow to expectations, about letting go.

"She sounds frustrated," he murmured.

"Nah." Mason waved a hand in dismissal. "It's just a catchy song. The funny thing is that Alena kind of looks like Elsa. She's also blond and wears her hair in a thick braid." He chuckled. "And Alena also lives where it always snows."

"Who's Elsa?"

The Guardian stopped and turned to look at him with amused disbelief dancing in his eyes. "Have you been living under a rock? Who doesn't know who Princess Elsa is?"

"A princess?"

"Yeah, not just any princess, a Disney princess or rather queen." Mason frowned as if it was an important distinction. "I think Elsa was a queen, not a princess."

"Oh." Orion finally got the reference. "She's a character from a Disney movie. I don't have children, so I don't watch those kinds of movies."

"They are not just for children." Mason resumed walking. "They are fun to watch at any age."

"I'll take your word for it."

20

ALENA

*T*he song ended just as Okidu parked the cart in front of the house.

Kian clapped. "That was one hell of a performance. I haven't heard you sing in ages."

Alena shrugged. "My voice is not very good. It's just loud." Compared to her mother's voice, hers was like a trombone to a harp—loud and limited in range. "I use singing to relieve tension, and I usually do that in the shower in the sanctuary, where no one can hear me. I don't know what possessed me to bellow it over the entire village."

"You have an amazing voice." Kian helped Annani down. "You're just as good if not better than the original singer of that song."

She got down and followed them up the front steps. "That's nice of you to say, but it's not true."

Syssi threw open the door. "Alena, was that you singing?"

"Guilty. Mother said something about the cold never bothering me before, and that triggered the damn song. When the movie first came out, I couldn't stop singing it. It's an earworm."

Syssi grinned. "I didn't realize it before, but that song could be about you. The snow princess who craves freedom and adventure."

That was why she'd been singing it so obsessively until she'd forced herself to stop. "It's just a song."

Annani embraced Syssi. "Alena doesn't think that her voice is good, and when I say that it is lovely, she tells me that I am hearing it with mother's ears. Perhaps if more people complimented her on it, she would sing more."

When they entered the living room, which had been transformed into a big dining room, Amanda, Jacki, and Kalugal gushed over her singing as well, and Alena wanted to hide somewhere until everyone forgot about it.

Thankfully, Dalhu didn't say a thing, but he smiled at her and nodded as if to say that he agreed with the others.

"Where did the living room furniture go?" she asked to change the subject.

"It's out on the back patio." Syssi walked over to the sliding doors and flicked the backyard lights on. "I just hope it doesn't rain. The patio is covered, but it's windy, and the wind will blow the rain inside."

"Let's cross our fingers that it doesn't." Alena pulled out a chair next to Dalhu, the only one who seemed safe not to start talking about her singing again.

"Anything new and exciting happen during the month we were gone?"

Amanda patted her very pregnant belly. "I grew to mammoth proportions. I have six weeks to go, but I think this girl is not going to wait. She's ready to come out."

"All in good time." Their mother put a hand on Amanda's belly.

"I'm finally showing." Jacki patted her small bump. "But I'm still good to go."

"Go where?" Syssi asked.

"To visit the Mosuo. Kalugal was busy and kept postponing it, but I convinced him that it had to be done now or not at all. I'm not traveling when I'm Amanda's size or after the baby is born."

Alena leaned over the table. "Do you know whether you're having a boy or a girl?"

Jacki nodded. "We are having a boy."

Next to her, Kalugal puffed out his chest and grinned. "Allegra and Amanda's daughters need a couple of boys to chase after them."

Kian growled, probably because he didn't want any boys chasing after his precious Allegra, but Syssi smiled. "Hopefully, another couple will conceive soon, and we will have another boy."

Annani lifted a brow. "Did you forget about Ethan?"

"Of course I didn't. We need one more boy for Phoenix."

When the doorbell chimed, Alena tensed. Was it Orion? Would she finally get to see him in person?

Holding her breath as Okidu rushed to open the door, she remained seated at the table and listened to him welcome the latest arrivals.

"Good evening, Mistress Geraldine, Master Shai. Good evening, Mistress Cassandra, Master Onegus. Good to see you, Mistress Sylvia, Master Roni."

One after the other, the couples entered the living room, and Alena rose to her feet to greet them. She was embracing Cassandra when the doorbell chimed again, and Okidu opened the door once more.

This time she knew it was Orion, felt it in her bones.

Alena shook her head. She wasn't superstitious, and her senses weren't that good. It was simply statistically probable that it was him.

"Good evening, Master Orion," Okidu said.

Rooted in place and holding her breath, Alena waited for him to emerge from the foyer, and when he did, the impact of his presence was even more powerful than what she'd been prepared for.

He was nearly as tall as Kian, perhaps a half an inch shorter, broad-shouldered but not overly muscled, and his face was just as perfect as Tim's drawing. But the portrait couldn't convey the power in the eyes that scanned the room and landed on her with the intensity of a heat-seeking missile.

21

ORION

She was beautiful, and Orion knew without having to be told that she was the singer he'd heard on the way.

The song might as well have been written about her.

A pale blue dress adorned her tall but very feminine body, and a thick blond braid was draped over an ample breast. Her shoulders were squared, her chin was up, and her stormy blue eyes gazed at him with an intensity that looked more like animosity than the admiration he was used to from females.

As Kian walked up to him, blocking his view of the snow princess, Orion couldn't help the urge to lean sideways so he could keep looking at her. Perhaps if he smiled, she would smile back, instead of looking as if she wanted to trample him under her feet.

"Good evening, Orion." Kian offered him his hand. "Let me introduce you to my mother, the goddess Annani." Following Orion's gaze, he turned to look at the blond beauty and smiled. "This is not Annani. This is my sister Alena."

It took a moment for the meaning of Kian's words to sink in, and another split second for Orion to tear his eyes from the ice queen and look at her brother.

"I know." He plastered a smile on his face. "The singer with the lovely voice whom I heard on the way."

Behind Kian, Alena uttered a frustrated groan that didn't fit her royal demeanor.

Ignoring his sister, Kian led Orion to the head of the table, where a stunning beauty with a mane of red hair and a knowing smirk on her angelic face regarded him with amusement in her ancient eyes.

He bowed deeply. "It's an honor and a pleasure to make your acquaintance, Clan Mother." That was the title Mason had told him to use, and given her nod of approval, his greeting had been well executed.

"The pleasure is all mine, Orion." With a wave of her hand, she indicated her wish that he sit next to her.

A butler rushed over and pulled out a chair for him.

"Thank you," he told the guy before lowering himself to the seat.

Again, there was approval in her eyes. "Do you prefer Orion, or should I call you Orlando?"

"I go by Orion these days."

She nodded. "It suits you better than Orlando. You can call me Annani." She flashed him a bright smile. "After all, we are family. And speaking of family, let me introduce you to those you have not met yet."

When Orion turned to look at his dinner companions, he realized that Geraldine and Cassandra were there as well, and so was Roni, who he hadn't seen in years. Having been blindsided by the goddess's magnificent daughter, he hadn't noticed them before.

"You already know Kian," the goddess said. "And I do not need to introduce you to Geraldine and Cassandra and their mates, or to Roni, but the lovely lady sitting next to him is his mate, Sylvia."

"Hi." Sylvia smiled. "I'm so excited to meet you."

"So am I," Roni said. "You might know me, but I don't know you. Did we meet before I turned immortal? Have you thralled or compelled me to forget you?"

Orion shook his head. "I've watched over your family from afar."

"So you never thralled or compelled my mother?"

"I did not."

"Let us continue with the introductions," Annani said. "You can discuss family matters with Roni later."

Orion bowed his head. "My apologies, Clan Mother. Please, continue."

She smiled, her eyes sparkling with amusement and mischief that belied her age. "The lovely blond beauty you could not take your eyes off of when you walked in is my eldest daughter Alena."

"Enchanted." He turned to look at her and dipped his head.

She'd chosen the farthest seat from him on the other side of the long table, and he had to crane his neck to look at her above everyone's heads.

"Nice to meet you," she murmured so quietly that he wouldn't have heard her if he were human.

Where was that powerful voice that had carried over the entire village?

The goddess frowned, but then shifted her gaze to a stunning, very pregnant brunette. "This is my youngest daughter, Amanda, and her mate Dalhu."

The guy nodded his hello but didn't smile. Amanda grinned and waved. "We'll talk later. I have so many questions."

It seemed that Amanda was the opposite of Alena—a confident extrovert who didn't take no for an answer.

"And this is Syssi." The goddess took the hand of the smiling woman sitting next to her son. "My favorite daughter-in-law."

"I'm your only daughter-in-law," Syssi said before turning to him. "Welcome to the clan, Orion."

"Thank you, but I'm not going to stay long. I have a business to run and more siblings to look for." He turned to Kian. "I appreciate your offer to help me search for them."

"The one who can help you the most is Andrew, my brother-in-law. You met him this morning."

"The truth detector."

"That's me." Andrew turned to the brunette sitting next to him. "This is my wife Nathalie, and that's our daughter Phoenix."

The little girl, who apparently had been hiding from him behind her mother's side, peeked her dark-haired head out. "Are you my uncle?"

As he glanced at Andrew for directions, the guy nodded and mouthed, "Just go with it."

"Yes, I am."

"Can you play horsey with me after dinner? Uncle Kian gets tired too fast, and Uncle Anandur says that I'm too big for playing baby games. Uncle Brundar doesn't like to play kids' games at all, and Uncles Shai and Onegus never come to family dinners." She eyed Onegus as if assessing whether he would be a willing victim.

Andrew stroked his daughter's silky dark hair. "Don't pester Orion, Phoenix. He just got here."

She pouted. "Okay. He can be my horsey next time."

"It will be my pleasure." Orion winked at the child.

22

ANNANI

*A*nnani observed Orion's interaction with her family and could not find fault with a single thing.

Toven's son was behaving perfectly. He was polite, well-spoken, charming, and utterly unintimidated by her or Kian.

It rankled a little that he did not regard her with the same awe and reverence as others who had met her for the first time, but then she was not the first god he had met, and according to Kian, Orion's single encounter with Toven had left him unimpressed.

What a shame.

Toven used to be such an upstanding god. He was as brilliant as Ekin and as dedicated as his father to the improvement of human society. What had happened to him?

Perhaps loneliness had driven him mad.

Fates only knew what would have happened to her if not for her seven Odus and the kernel of hope that the soothsayer had planted in her heart.

The Odus had ensured her survival in more ways than just keeping her safe and nourished. They had kept her company when she had not wanted to engage with the primitive northern tribe that had accepted her as their goddess, had helped her build a proper shelter and had kept it warm and clean. But none of that would have sufficed if not for the hope that one day Khiann would return to her in one form or another. Without that hope, her will to live would have winked out.

After five millennia, that hope was nothing more than a dim flicker, but in the past, it had gotten her over the hardest times. Then her children had been born, and then her grandchildren, and their children and grandchildren and so on, filling the empty spaces in her heart with love and joy. Not fully, there would always be a large hole that only Khiann could fill, but enough for her to enjoy living even without her beloved.

Could Orion be Khiann's reincarnation?

Annani cast him another glance. He was very handsome and charming and intelligent, but he did not spark anything in her. She had met human males who had excited her more.

Alena, on the other hand, was completely smitten with Orion and fighting it with everything she had, unable to get over her aversion to compellers long enough to judge the male for everything he was aside from that.

Perhaps he could win her over. It would require patience and understanding that not many males were blessed with, but if Orion was as taken with Alena as she was with him, he would put in the effort.

If not, he probably was not worthy of her.

Closing her eyes momentarily, Annani prayed to the Fates, wishing that Orion and Alena were truelove mates. With all her siblings happily mated, Alena felt left out and wondered whether the Fates did not deem her worthy. It was absurd for her to think that, and it pained Annani that her daughter believed it.

With her thoughts wandering Annani had forgotten that she had not finished introducing her family to Orion, and Kalugal seemed upset, probably thinking that she had overlooked him, or worse, not considered him part of the family.

"My apologies, Kalugal. I should have introduced you first. After all, you and Orion are cousins."

"No need to apologize, Clan Mother." He put on one of his winning smiles. "I can introduce myself." He shifted his eyes to Orion. "I am Kalugal, grandson of Mortdh, your father's brother, and sitting beside me is my better half—my wife, Jacki."

Orion's smile was wide and genuine as he answered, "Well met, cousin Kalugal and the fair Jacki. I feel blessed that my sister and I, as well as my niece and my nephew, have become part of such a big and wonderful family of immortals."

Looking at Annani, he put his hand over his heart. "It has been a difficult and stressful day for me. But now that I know who your people are and understand that they had no choice but to approach me with caution, I'm just grateful to be here. Knowing that my sister and I are not alone in the world has eased something inside of me. So even when I go on my travels, collecting antiques and finding buyers for them, it will no longer feel as if I'm flying solo. I have a people I belong to."

Annani was not the only one who wiped tears from her eyes. Nearly every female at the table did the same thing, with Alena being the most notable exception. She did her best to pretend that Orion was not there.

It was such strange behavior for her. Alena was usually easygoing, mellow, and accommodating.

"Fates willing," Kian said. "We will find more of your siblings." He reached for a bottle of wine and uncorked it. "Let's make a toast."

On the other side of the table, Anandur uncorked another bottle of wine, and together he and Kian poured wine into everyone's glasses.

"To family." Kian lifted his goblet.

"To family." Orion clinked his glass with Kian's.

23

ALENA

*T*hankfully, once dinner was over Orion had gone outside with Kian and the other guys to smoke, and Alena could finally take a full breath and remove the annoying earpieces. They distorted everyone's voices and had gotten uncomfortable after a while. How did Anandur and Brundar tolerate wearing those things?

"What's gotten into you?" Amanda asked quietly. "You've been on edge the entire evening."

"I don't know what you're talking about." She smiled at her sister. "How is my niece doing in there?" She put her hand on Amanda's belly.

"She's kicking up a storm, but don't change the subject. There is definitely something going on for you to sing your heart out like that." She lowered her voice further. "Is Mother getting on your nerves?"

Alena's eyes darted to Annani, who was busy cooing to Allegra and oblivious to everyone else.

"Not at all," she whispered. "In fact, I'm a little worried about her. She hasn't come up with any risky shenanigans lately."

"Maybe that's the problem." Amanda rubbed slow circles over her belly. "Without Mother providing excitement, you're bored, and the tedium is getting to you."

There was some truth to Amanda's observation.

Alena winced. "Way to make me sound pathetic. I need my mother to stir things up to make my dull life exciting."

Involuntarily, her gaze shifted to the glass doors and to the men outside, or rather to one man. Perhaps that was why she was fascinated with Orion. He was dangerous, and that made him thrilling—sexy.

It was the bad-boy allure that she hadn't understood before.

Damn, she needed to stop right away. During dinner, she'd masked the scent of her attraction to him by keeping herself angry. Anger was a potent emotion, even stronger than arousal, and the scent it emitted was dominant.

Amanda chuckled. "Oh, I get it now. You've been cruising on neutral for so long that you don't know what to do when someone shakes up that equilibrium. A certain someone who's about six foot three inches tall with lips that are just begging to be kissed, not by me of course, because I'm taken, but they could be all yours."

"Stop it," Alena hissed.

The men were all outside except for Roni, whose ears had perked up the moment Amanda started her teasing about Orion. Syssi was pretending that she didn't hear a thing, and perhaps she didn't since the cappuccino machine was making all those grinding and thumping noises, and Callie and Wonder were busy discussing Callie's plans for opening a gourmet restaurant in the latest section of the village.

Cassandra and Geraldine, however, had heard every word and were eyeing her with curiosity.

"Oh, come on." Amanda tried to cross her arms over her belly, which put them right under her chin, so she gave up and put her hands on the table. "Since when are you so prissy? What's wrong with Orion?"

"He's a compeller."

"He's a good man." Geraldine came to his defense. "And he's been so lonely for so long." She sighed. "He lost the woman he loved and has never recovered from the loss."

"That's so sad," Amanda said.

It shouldn't have pained Alena to hear that Orion had loved someone so dearly and had lost her, but it did. Not because she was jealous or begrudged him the love, but because she wished he hadn't gone through the heartache.

He'd had no one to guide him, no one to tell him to keep his relationships with human women purely physical. She could imagine him as a young man, yearning for the love and connection with another and thinking that he could somehow make it work.

Kian had fallen into the same trap despite their mother's warning, and it had scarred him for life. Perhaps if he hadn't married Lavena at nineteen and then had to leave her a year later pregnant with their daughter, he wouldn't have become so grumpy and cynical.

"Poor guy," Alena murmured.

Roni groaned. "If it's going to be one of those talks, I'd better join the guys outside." He rose to his feet.

"Coward," Sylvia chided him playfully.

Leaning down, he kissed the top of her head. "You can come along."

"I want to hear the story about Orion's great love. You can go."

"I don't remember the details," Geraldine said after Roni closed the sliding door behind him. "Or perhaps Orion didn't tell me more than what I remember." She lifted her hand to her temple and rubbed it. "It was a long time ago. I asked him if he had someone special in his life, and he said that he had once, but after he lost her, he vowed never to love again because it was just too painful. When I asked if she had left him, he said that she had died, and he looked so sad that I didn't want to pry and ask him how it happened. Now that I know he's immortal, I assume that she died from old age."

"That's not likely," Cassandra said. "He couldn't have stayed with her for so long without her discovering who and what he was."

"Don't forget that Orion is a compeller," Alena said. "He could've compelled her to keep quiet about his fangs and everything else that was different about him."

"That's true," Cassandra agreed. "But even if they kept moving, people would have wondered about a young man married to a much older woman."

Alena shrugged. "He could have compelled their neighbors to ignore that as well. A powerful compeller can get away with almost anything."

24

ORION

*I*n Kian's backyard the air was fresh, and the cool night breeze crisp and soothing on Orion's frayed nerves.

He'd done okay, his mask of composure never once faltering under the goddess's intense gaze.

She'd asked him many questions, for which his answers had hopefully been truthful. Orion couldn't remember half the things he'd said because his attention had been split between Annani and Alena, most of it commanded by the goddess's intriguing eldest daughter, who hadn't spared him a single look all throughout dinner.

His eyes had darted to her numerous times, but she hadn't even turned her head in his direction. It had been more than indifference—it had been hostility.

For some reason, Alena did not like him.

Was she a contrary person? Was that why she was the only one of Annani's children who was still single?

Was it by choice?

He'd garnered that she was the goddess's companion, so maybe she didn't wish to settle down with a male. Or perhaps she just hadn't found the right one yet?

He shouldn't be having these thoughts about her. A magnificent female like her deserved much more than he could offer, which was passion and perhaps occasional companionship, but not love. His heart had been buried with Miriam, and he'd vowed never to love again.

Except, a small voice at the back of his head whispered that Miriam wouldn't have wanted him to be alone. She'd actually said it on her deathbed, beseeching him to move on and live his life. He'd promised that he would, and he had. He'd built a profitable business, he traveled all over the world and met interesting people, and he shared his body and his passion with numerous females. Miriam hadn't been specific, so technically he hadn't defied her deathbed wish by avoiding relationships and therefore love.

He had a life, but he hadn't moved on.

Perhaps it was time to fulfill that part of Miriam's wish.

He'd been devastated by pain and grief when he'd made that vow, and he never wanted to experience such devastation again. But Alena wasn't human, and if he allowed himself to love her and she loved him back, they could have eternity together.

Yeah, no.

It hadn't escaped his notice that in addition to the two Guardians, Alena was the only one at the dinner table who was wearing earpieces.

No one else deemed him a threat, not even the goddess, who'd said she was going to test her own power of compulsion on him at some point. Although, after he'd warned her that it wouldn't work because he would obey her every wish regardless of whether it was imbued with compulsion or not, she might choose to forgo the test.

"Orion." Kian motioned to the humidor on the coffee table. "Pick a cigar."

The living room furniture had been moved to the back patio to make room for the large dining table. The men had spread out, with Kian and Kalugal sharing the couch, Andrew and Dalhu each commandeering an armchair, and Shai, Onegus, and the Guardians making do with outdoor chairs.

Roni had stayed inside, saying that he wasn't a fan of cigars.

"Which one do you recommend?" Orion sat between his cousins.

It wasn't the most comfortable seat, but his other option was a chair next to the Guardians, and that would have sent the wrong message.

"They are all superb," Kian said. "You can't go wrong with any of them."

Orion picked a short one that was aptly named Short Story by Arturo Fuente. "I'm not much of an expert. The last cigar I smoked must have been twenty years ago."

"Then you should take it easy," Kalugal advised. "You might get lightheaded."

As the patio doors opened and his grand-nephew stepped out, Orion took a quick glance inside, his eyes searching for a long blond braid. He saw her sitting between her sister and Geraldine, her pale cheeks slightly flushed as if she was embarrassed about something. The faint splash of color made Alena look young and innocent, but he knew both to be untrue. As the goddess's eldest daughter, she might be twice as old as he was, and he doubted she'd retained any innocence after living that long.

"Did they kick you out?" Anandur asked Roni.

"Nah. They started talking about mushy stuff that made me uncomfortable." He sat next to the Guardian. "Sylvia says that I'm on the spectrum because I can't handle emotions, but that's not true. I love her. Isn't that enough?"

Anandur clapped him on the back. "Your brain is mostly made of code and numbers. There isn't much left to process anything else."

"True," Roni admitted. "If all people have about the same number of neurons and synapses, then when most of them are taken by something a person is passionate about, other areas suffer."

"You should ask Amanda." Andrew crossed his arms over his chest. "Maybe each person has a different number of brain cells and connections between them. After all, some people are smarter than others, right?"

Orion wondered if the same was true for various paranormal talents. Did his ability to compel rob him of intelligence or some other ability he might have possessed? And why should Roni ask Amanda? Was she an expert on the subject?

"Amanda is a neuroscientist," Kalugal said. "She researches paranormal abilities."

"Did I ask that out loud?"

"No, but you were frowning, so I assumed you were wondering about that." Kalugal smiled condescendingly. "How old are you, Orion?"

"Over five hundred years old. Why?"

"If Andrew told Roni to ask William about neurons and synapses, what would you have thought?"

Orion guessed where Kalugal was going with that question, and he didn't like that the guy was making assumptions about him. "Who is William?" He pretended not to catch Kalugal's drift.

"It doesn't matter. He's a male."

"So what?"

"You would have assumed that William knew something about the brain that others didn't, but you wouldn't have assumed that about a beautiful woman like Amanda."

"Is that so?" Orion arched a brow. "Are you a mind reader?"

"No, I'm a compeller like you." Kalugal grinned. "I wonder, though, which of us is more powerful."

25

KIAN

*K*alugal and Orion were about to engage in a pissing contest, and Kian wasn't going to do anything to stop it because he wanted to find out who was more powerful as well.

"I didn't know that you were a compeller." Orion turned to look at Kalugal. "Kian only told me that you're an archeologist."

"That's just a hobby of mine. My business endeavors are varied, and I was born with the ability to compel, which has proved very useful over the years."

"Yeah," Kian grumbled. "To get insider information and make a fortune on the stock market."

"It also saved my life," Kalugal countered. "It allowed me to escape my father."

His father was Mortdh's son, and therefore Orion's first cousin. Or was it second because Mortdh and Toven shared only a father and had different mothers?

"Excuse me." Orion pushed to his feet. "The smoke from your cigars and my own is too much for me."

The guy had probably been uncomfortable sitting between them and turning his back to one in order to look at the other.

Lifting one of the outdoor chairs, Orion brought it over and set it down next to Dalhu's armchair.

"I'm getting bits and pieces of information, and it's all becoming a soup in my head. I need someone to explain things to me in order. Who are the main players of the immortal world? Who were the gods? What did they do before Mortdh killed them?"

"That's a lot of information to cover in a short time." Kian took a puff of his cigar. "What do you want to know first?"

"Let's start with compulsion. Can't all immortals do that to some extent? Can they compel humans? I know that Geraldine didn't have the ability even before the accident, but I assumed it didn't manifest because she'd never needed it."

"All immortal males can thrall," Onegus said. "The females can as well, but since they have less need for it, not many bother to learn how. Compulsion is a rarer ability, and even more so the ability to compel other immortals. That's why Brundar and Anandur are still wearing earpieces. We would like to think of you as family, but trust takes time to build."

"What about Kalugal? Do you wear earpieces around him too?"

Kalugal chuckled. "They were much more careful with me when we first met, and they didn't trust me until the Clan Mother compelled me to do no harm to her clan members. For some reason, you've gotten the red-carpet welcome."

Kian arched a brow. "Some reason? You are Navuh's son. He's not. That's why."

Kalugal hitched his brow even higher. "You've just met him this morning, and you don't know a thing about him. He could be an ax murderer."

Andrew's shoulders started shaking, and then a laugh bubbled out of him. "I don't know why everyone is afraid of ax murderers as if any others are less deadly. Dead is dead."

"The conversation has just turned too morbid for my taste." Roni rose to his feet and walked over to the bottle of whiskey Kian had left on the dining table. "If you don't mind, I'll pour myself a glass."

"You can go back inside," Shai suggested. "I'm sure the ladies are not talking about anything gruesome or morbid."

"No, thank you. I want to find out who is the stronger compeller."

"So do I," Kian said. "Let's test it." He leveled his eyes at Orion. "After that, I'll tell you everything you want to know." He lifted his cigar. "Or at least as much as I can squeeze in as long as my cigar lasts."

"Then let's make it quick." Orion turned to Kalugal. "Give me your wallet."

The order had been directed at Kalugal, but Kian found himself reaching into his pocket, and he saw Roni do the same.

"No." Kalugal grinned at Orion. "I'm immune to your compulsion. Let's reverse the roles, shall we?"

"Do your worst," Orion challenged.

Kalugal took a puff of his cigar, pretending to consider that. "Since you are not a clan member yet, I'm not bound by Annani's compulsion to do you no harm. Are you sure that you want me to do my worst?"

"It was a figure of speech." Orion took a look around the backyard. "Thankfully, you can't tell me to jump off a cliff because there are none."

"Actually, there is one, just not in Kian's backyard. But I would never do that." Kalugal smiled evilly. "What I want you to do, Orion aka Orlando, is to stand on one foot and quack like a chicken."

Orion grinned. "It's quack like a duck, but I'll do neither. I'm immune to your compulsion as well."

Kalugal didn't look happy. "That only proves that we are immune to each other's compulsion. It doesn't prove who is stronger."

"Does it matter?" Orion asked. "I hardly ever use my ability, and only when it's either necessary or deserved."

"Same here." Kalugal tapped on his cigar to dislodge the ash. "My interest is more general, and it has to do with my father's legions of warriors. He has them all under his compulsion, and I admit that I'm not nearly as powerful as he is, so I can't wrestle control over them from him. I wondered whether you could."

Kalugal had never shown any interest in the island or taking down Navuh. Had it all been a lie?

"What sparked this sudden interest?" Kian asked. "You said over and over again that the island is of no interest to you."

"My only interest in the island has to do with my mother, but she does not wish to be freed. At this point, it's a purely hypothetical end-of-days kind of scenario. If anything happens to Navuh, for whatever reason, the outcome would be disastrous. Without his control, his warriors would spread out like a plague over humanity. I'm not powerful enough to contain them all, but perhaps Orion is."

26

ORION

"How many warriors are we talking about?"

"Twenty-some thousand," Kalugal said. "My father has them recite devotions several times a day, which is how he reinforces the compulsion."

"I don't think I can compel so many at once, nor do I want to. Politics was never something I wished to get involved in."

"It's more than politics," Kian said. "But I doubt you are powerful enough. Power grows with age, and Navuh is even older than Annani. Not by much, but he obviously inherited his father's ability, which was formidable."

"He's also smart," commented Amanda's mate. "And careful. Anyone who thinks that they can take that island from him is fooling himself."

Given Kian's somber expression, he shared Dalhu's opinion.

"What about the goddess?" Orion asked. "If she's powerful enough to compel Kalugal to behave, then she should be able to control those warriors."

"I will never risk it," Kian said. "I don't want her anywhere near that vile island or Navuh. He has her sister. That's bad enough."

Orion cast a sidelong glance at Kalugal. "Is your mother under your father's compulsion? Is that why she doesn't want to be freed?"

"It's complicated." Kalugal puffed on his cigar. "She claims that he doesn't compel her. She's convinced that they are truelove mates, and that without her, he would become an even worse monster than he is now. It might be true, or it might be all in her head."

"Perhaps things have changed since you escaped."

"We found a way to keep in touch with her," Kian said. "My mother talks with her twice a week, and Areana hasn't changed her mind about Navuh. From what the other compellers we have report, you can't compel someone to love you or feel any other emotion toward you. You can only compel her to stay with you. Is that your experience as well?"

So, they had other compellers in addition to Kalugal, just not as powerful.

"I've never tried to compel anyone to love me. The only woman I've ever loved didn't need to be compelled, and after she died, I did my best to prevent anyone from falling in love with me again."

"I'm sorry." There was genuine compassion in Kian's eyes.

Orion nodded. "So am I. But it is what it is. My love couldn't prolong her human life."

Even after over four centuries it still hurt to think of her, but now was not the time to show weakness, and Kian's cigar was one-third shorter than it had been when he'd made the bargain with him. "I fulfilled my part, and now it's your turn. I need a comprehensive overview of the immortal landscape—history, politics, ongoing conflicts, and future prospects. I need to familiarize myself with this new world I find myself in." He leaned down and reached for Kian's lighter. "Do you think you can fit all that in before your cigar is done?"

Kian examined his Fuentes whatever-the-name-was and smiled. "It has an hour left in it, and I will be done long before that."

Andrew pushed to his feet. "I'll leave you to it. Phoenix is making faces at me through the sliding door."

They all turned to look, Orion included, and everyone smiled at the little girl standing on the other side of the glass with her tiny hands pressed to the door and making funny faces at her daddy.

Lucky guy.

Orion kept watching as Andrew opened the door, flung his daughter into his arms, and started kissing her cheeks. Giggling, she cupped his face and kissed him back. The happiness on her face was heartwarming.

"Adorable child." Orion turned back to Kian. "I still remember Cassandra at that age. She was always such a serious girl. I guess having a mother who needed constant help wasn't easy. I wish I could have hired a nanny for her."

"Why didn't you?" Shai asked. "You could have taken them both with you and compelled them not to say anything about your special abilities. In fact, they didn't even have to know that you were immortal. Don't get me wrong, I'm glad that you didn't, but I'm just curious."

"Cassandra was human, and I didn't know that she could one day turn immortal. I wanted her to have a normal life, which she wouldn't have had with me. I traveled a lot, for my business and in search of my other possible siblings." He took a tentative puff on his cigar. "I still don't understand how the bite can induce a Dormant into immortality and where and how to find Dormants."

27

KIAN

"*Y*ou wanted a comprehensive overview, so I'll start at the beginning, but I'll try to squeeze as much as I can into the time we have." Kian tapped his cigar over the ashtray.

"The gods were a small group of either refugees or exiles from a different place in the universe. We don't know where they came from or why. For a while, I entertained the idea that they might have been a divergent species of humans, survivors of a different epoch, perhaps pre-diluvial. But Kalugal and his brother Lokan gleaned some more information from Navuh, who'd learned it from his father, which made that theory obsolete. Now, the leading theory is that the gods were genetically enhanced humanoids, and that humanity was actually created by them as a race of servants."

"That explains why humans are so easily led by the nose," Roni said. "They were engineered to follow and not ask too many questions."

Kian grimaced. "You sound like Navuh."

"Did he say that?"

Kalugal nodded. "Same exact words."

Roni shrugged. "We know that he's not stupid."

Orion frowned. "Doesn't Annani know where her people came from?"

"Her parents didn't tell her," Kian said. "The younger generation of gods were kept in the dark, so to speak, because the original settlers didn't want their children to know about their bloody history. They tried to create a utopia for the gods and for the humans they were in charge of, establishing just laws and practicing an assembly-style democratic rule combined with a kind of monarchy. The position of head god was hereditary, but the ruler couldn't make any major decisions without getting approval from the gods' council. Some decisions could be passed by a simple majority, while others required a unanimous vote."

Orion nodded. "Toven told me that his brother was sentenced to entombment by the council of gods for murdering another god. To avoid the sentencing, he attacked the assembly and killed them all, perishing alongside them."

"That's correct. A decision that grave required a unanimous vote, which was why all the gods attended the assembly and could be destroyed in one fell swoop. It also meant that Toven voted to entomb his brother for the crime of murdering my mother's truelove mate—her husband, Khiann."

Orion's eyes widened. "Toven didn't tell me that." He frowned. "But you are not a god, so Khiann wasn't your father."

"He was murdered mere months after they were mated. There wasn't enough time for my mother to conceive." Kian took another puff of his cigar. "But I'm getting ahead of the story. Mortdh was a powerful god, and he didn't want to answer to Ahn, the ruling god and my mother's father. He built a stronghold in the northern part of the region and amassed power. Hoping to keep Mortdh from starting a war, Ahn promised him Annani's hand in marriage. Once Ahn stepped down, his daughter would have become the next leader, and as her mate, so would Mortdh. Ahn believed that would assuage Mortdh's aspirations for rulership in the interim."

"Was he wrong?" Orion asked.

"Annani believed so. She was convinced that once they became the ruling couple, Mortdh would get rid of her. He wouldn't have been satisfied to rule at her side. He wanted to rule supreme. My mother is a very smart lady, so I believe that her assessment of Mortdh was correct. She's also cunning. She could have invoked her right to choose a mate and break off the engagement that way, but she knew that would offend Mortdh's honor and would result in a war. If she found a truelove mate, though, war could be averted. Or so she hoped."

When Orion frowned again, Kian lifted his hand. "To refuse the gift of a truelove mate was to offend the Fates, and no one, including Mortdh, could officially go against the Fates' decree. He would have lost popular support, and since he was a savvy politician, she hoped that would stay his hand."

"Good plan," Orion said. "But isn't finding a truelove mate a difficult thing to do?"

"It is," Kian agreed. "Khiann was a childhood crush of Annani's, and she decided that he was the one. She pursued him and convinced him to ask for her hand."

"Your mother is beautiful. She probably didn't have to work hard to convince him."

Kian smiled. "Her beauty aside, when my mother decides on something, no one and nothing can stand in her way."

Orion shook his head. "Let me guess. Mortdh was offended anyway and murdered Khiann."

"Mortdh felt humiliated, but more than that, he was furious about losing his shot at the throne. He tried to murder Khiann covertly, but the men who accompanied him on his murderous mission betrayed him and testified before the gods' council, sealing his fate. My mother sat in the assembly until the sentencing was passed. But while the gods debated how to bring Mortdh to justice, news arrived of him preparing forces to march against them, and Annani realized that she was in grave danger. If he attacked and won, he would make her life a living hell to punish her for humiliating him. So, she snuck out, loaded her servants and a few belongings on her flying machine, and escaped."

"My father said that he'd gotten bored with the endless discussions, and he snuck out as well. I wonder if he noticed that Annani had done that first."

"He might have thought that she was too upset to attend. She told me that she'd cried a river during the proceedings."

"What about her sister?" Orion asked. "Kalugal's mother?"

"When Annani broke off the engagement, Ahn offered Mortdh his other daughter, Areana. Reluctantly, Mortdh accepted the offer, but Areana wasn't the one he wanted. She was Ahn's daughter with a concubine, not his official wife, so she was not in line to rule even though she was older than Annani, and she was a widow."

"Did Annani have any other siblings?"

"No. Which meant that if anything happened to Annani, Areana could become the next ruler of the gods. That was the consolation prize that Ahn dangled in front of Mortdh."

"If Annani had the right to choose her mate, I assume that Areana had that right as well. Why did she agree to marry Mortdh?"

"Because she wanted to please her father," Kalugal said. "He never thought much of her, and when he summoned her and asked her to take Annani's place, she agreed, hoping he would finally appreciate her." He grimaced. "Mortdh was insane, but Ahn was an asshole. He treated my mother badly, barely deigning to acknowledge her as his daughter because she was a weak goddess."

"How did Areana end up mating Mortdh's son, though?" Orion asked.

"Turns out that Navuh had a crush on my mother, which she hadn't been aware of," Kalugal said. "My father wasn't a god, so she never considered him as a contender even though he was Mortdh's official heir and the most powerful immortal in existence. Besides, she mourned her first husband many decades after his passing and turned down full-blooded gods, so he never dared to approach her. She agreed to wed Mortdh out of duty and considered it a sacrifice for her people. Mortdh left Navuh to escort Areana to his stronghold in the north, but when she asked to stay a little longer to attend Annani's wedding, Navuh agreed. After the wedding, she left with an escort of Ahn's men, but Navuh intercepted her on the way, one thing led to another, and they became involved. When news of Mortdh's demise along with the other gods reached the north, Navuh took Areana as his mate and hid her from the world, claiming that he was protecting her from his immortal warriors. He told her that they were overcome with grief and rage and would want to take it out on the last remaining goddess. Most of them had families in the south."

"Why would they be angry at her?" Orion asked. "None of it was her fault."

Kalugal shrugged. "Navuh probably made it up. As Mortdh's only son, he inherited his father's stronghold, which already had several thousands of immortal warriors, and as the most powerful immortal, his rule was uncontested. But Areana was a full-blooded goddess, and even though she was less powerful than him, she outranked him. He didn't want anyone to know that he had a goddess in his harem. Navuh kept his father's immortal concubines in there for show, but he never graced their beds. He has remained loyal to my mother, which is proof that they are indeed truelove mates."

"Annani wasn't even sure that her sister had survived," Kian said. "She lived with terrible guilt for thousands of years, thinking that if Areana made it to the north, she was suffering endlessly at Navuh's hands. We've discovered only recently that Areana has been living like a pampered queen in the lap of luxury, but that's a story for another time."

"It's a good story, though." Kalugal smiled. "Remind me to tell it to you some time."

28

ORION

"What are you doing tomorrow?" Orion asked.

"In the morning, I'm in the office." Kalugal stubbed out his cigar. "But I would love for you to come visit Jacki and me in our home in the evening." He turned to Kian. "How about the entire family comes over to dinner at my place? You haven't seen it yet."

"You keep saying that it's not ready. I was waiting for an invitation to a house-warming party."

"Where do you live?" Orion asked. "I'm not sure I'm free to come and go as I please yet."

"I live right here in the village. My men and I have our own section, which we just recently moved into. I'm still waiting for some artwork and furniture to arrive, but Jacki is pestering me to invite everyone over even though some pieces are still missing."

Orion shook his head. "Your story and how you ended up with Annani's clan is another missing puzzle piece, but you can tell me all about it tomorrow. I think Kian skipped over the part of how the immortals came to be. If the stories of the Bible reflect reality, then I assume that at some point the gods decided to slum it with humans."

Kian nodded. "In the beginning, unions with humans were indeed prohibited. But there weren't enough gods to provide genetic diversity, and combined with their extremely low fertility rate, they feared eventual extinction, so unions with humans were sanctioned, provided that they were consensual. I guess that the creatures they'd created to serve them turned out to be much smarter than the gods had originally planned, and to the gods' credit, they acknowledged that and treated humans with kindness and respect."

"I'm glad to hear that, although I have my doubts. Perhaps that's how they wanted to go down in history."

"It's possible," Kian agreed. "My mother's version of the gods' era might be somewhat embellished to make them look better than they actually were. But let's continue with how the immortals came to be. Compared to the gods, human fertility was robust, and many immortal children were born, but when those immortals took human lovers, their children were born human, or so it initially seemed." Kian took a small puff of his cigar.

The thing was down to less than one-third of its original length, and Orion was running out of time, but it wasn't a big deal. Kian could continue the story at Kalugal's tomorrow.

"I assume that those children had the godly genes, but they were inactive," Orion said.

"Precisely. They discovered, probably by chance, that a venom bite could activate those genes and induce transition into immortality, but only for the children born to female immortals. The children born to immortal males and their human mates didn't possess the godly gene."

Orion rubbed a hand over his jaw. "Maybe the children of the males have the genes as well but require a different mode of activation?"

For a long moment, Kian just looked at him with a deep frown. "You know what? You might be onto something. We've always taken it for granted that the children of the males didn't have the genes because that was what the gods believed. But what if they were wrong?"

Anandur shifted in his chair. "I hope they were right because it would really piss me off if they weren't."

From the corner of his eye, Orion saw Shai close his eyes and wondered why Anandur's words had upset him.

"Why wouldn't you want the gods to be proven wrong?" Orion asked Anandur.

"Because that would mean that hundreds of clan males were deprived of the joys of fatherhood based on a false premise."

Kian lifted his hand. "Even if the children of the males have the gene and there is another method of activating them, we couldn't have discovered it up until very recently. Genetic sequencing wasn't developed enough, and the equipment needed was too pricey even for the clan's deep pockets. We might have the ability to test it now, though. William is searching for bioinformaticians to recruit for another project we are working on, and once he gets a team together, he and Bridget might be able to finally identify what makes us different. Once they do, we could possibly find out whether children born to male immortals with humans have the gene."

"We have no children to test," Onegus said. "Nowadays, everyone uses birth control, and the chances of immortal males causing unintended pregnancies is practically nonexistent."

The topic was fascinating, and Orion was surprised that no one had thought of testing children of the males before, but given the state of Kian's cigar, he didn't have much time. Some of his questions could wait for tomorrow, but there were several he didn't want to wait to hear the answer for.

"How does the venom bite activate a Dormant?"

"We don't know," Kian said. "What we found out was done through trial and error rather than a scientific study. We know that for an adult female Dormant to transition the venom bite is not enough, and insemination is needed to boost the effect. For a male, the venom bite suffices, probably because it's done during a match and the composition of the venom is more potent when its production is triggered by aggression as opposed to sexual arousal."

"What about younger Dormants?"

Kian winced. "Boys and girls can be activated once they reach puberty, which is about the age of thirteen, and at that age, the venom is enough, and sex is not required. For very young girls, being around my mother is enough. Phoenix is already immortal."

"What about very young boys?" Orion asked. "How come being around the goddess doesn't activate them? Was it even tried?"

"Of course it was, but for some reason, it didn't work."

29

SHAI

*H*ope surged in Shai's heart.

Kian hadn't dismissed Orion's idea out of hand. He'd actually planned on having William and the new team of bioinformaticians identify the immortal gene and then search for it in children born to immortal males and human females.

What if Rhett could turn immortal?

What if he had the godly genes and William's team found a way to activate them? That seemed like a much easier problem to solve than not having the genes in the first place.

It would probably take a long time for the research to be done, but Rhett was still young. He still had time.

It was ironic that Orion, who didn't know anything about immortals aside from his own experience, would ask the question no one else had thought to ask.

But it also made sense.

Only someone without preconceived notions could challenge a belief that had been held for thousands of years.

The problem was finding children of immortal males to test. When the time came, and they searched for test subjects, Shai would have to reveal the secret he'd kept for nearly twenty years and accept whatever punishment Edna or Kian decided on.

If there was even a sliver of a chance of Rhett becoming immortal, Shai would do whatever it took to make it happen.

"That's so odd," Orion murmured. "Why would being in the goddess's presence activate the little girls but not the boys?"

Kian leaned forward and stubbed out his cigar. "As I said. I don't know." He rose to his feet. "We should go back inside."

Orion followed him up. "I still have so many questions, but I guess I can save some for tomorrow." He smiled at Kalugal.

"Or I can stay out here with you. Would you mind entertaining me until you're done with your cigar?"

"By all means." Kalugal motioned to the seat Kian had vacated.

Uttering a groan, Kian walked over to the table and refilled his glass of whiskey. "I'd better stay and make sure he's not feeding you embellished stories."

Kalugal arched a brow. "Why would you think that? Have I ever told you untruths?"

"You're prone to exaggerations. I want Orion to get the facts as best as we know them."

Kalugal regarded him with thinly veiled amusement. "What's gotten you riled, cousin? It couldn't have been me because I hardly said a word."

"It wasn't you." Kian downed the whiskey in one go and didn't offer an explanation for what was bothering him.

The air between the two seemed to crackle with tension, and it seemed to affect Orion.

"My apologies for bringing up a painful subject," Orion said. "It must be difficult for the immortal males who were not blessed with immortal mates to be denied the joys of fatherhood. That brings me to the next question, which is why so few males are fathers. Is there a prohibition on mating within the clan for genetic reasons?"

The guy was smart to figure that one out, or perhaps Cassandra and Geraldine had told him that during the long hours they'd spent with him.

"Annani's descendants are considered closely related and therefore forbidden to each other," Kian said. "And until recently, we didn't know of any immortals aside from the Doomers, who are all male and are our sworn enemies."

"I assume that you're referring to Navuh's followers," Orion said.

"DOOM is the acronym for The Devout Order Of Mortdh Brotherhood," Kalugal clarified. "The clan nicknamed them Doomers."

"Why are they all male?" Orion asked.

"Because my father doesn't allow the females born to Dormants to be induced and transition into immortality. He doesn't want them to lose their human fertility. He needs them to keep producing children for his army and his breeding program. The boys are induced and join the warrior ranks, and the girls join their mothers as breeding mares."

Orion's eyes blazed with inner fire, and when he opened his mouth, Shai saw that his fangs had elongated. "That's despicable."

"I agree." Kalugal puffed on his cigar. "That's why I was curious about your powers. If you happen to be as powerful as my father, perhaps you could do something about it."

Just like Kian, Shai wondered about Kalugal's sudden interest in the welfare of the island's population. He hadn't shown concern for them before.

"You mentioned that they live on an island. Where is that?" Orion asked.

"A small rock somewhere in the Indian Ocean. They manage to hide their existence well, but we found out where they are. Nevertheless, we can do nothing to liberate the Dormants and other humans they hold captive. We don't have the military power, and we can't just blow the place up because not everyone on that damn rock deserves to die, and least of all my mother."

"Of course." Orion pushed a dark strand of hair behind his ear. "Perhaps if we combined our powers we could overthrow your father."

"I wish it were that simple." Kalugal sighed. "It's not enough to eliminate him. Someone has to take control over those hordes of warriors and keep them contained. That means staying on that godforsaken island and ruling over scores of hoodlums and emotionally handicapped Dormants and humans. Who wants to do that?"

"Your brother," Kian said. "Lokan, Kalugal's brother, is also a compeller, but not as strong. He can only compel humans, and he has aspirations for the island and dreams of turning it into a utopia."

"He's a dreamer, all right," Kalugal said. "I'm not a pessimist, but I consider myself a realist, and I don't see a solution to the island's problem that will not result in thousands of lives lost."

"What does Navuh do with all those warriors?" Orion asked.

"He used to instigate wars and send them to fight on the side of his protégés," Dalhu said. "Now he uses them to sell drugs and run prostitution."

Orion's fangs descended even lower. "Is he involved in trafficking?"

"Of course," Kalugal said. "The island serves two purposes. One side is home to the Brotherhood, and the other is known as Pleasure Island. It's the most exclusive brothel in the world, serving the super-rich, powerful, and depraved. Lately, though, my father has started inviting brains to the island. He finally realized that brute strength was no longer the best qualifier for his soldiers, so he's working on improving the stock, breeding brainiacs. I think that's why it has been so quiet lately. Navuh is not in a rush, and he can afford waiting a couple of decades to build a smart army and amass weapons. In the past, even the thousands of immortal soldiers were not enough to take over the world, but with today's technology, it can be achieved with a much smaller force of smart cyber warriors."

So that was why Kalugal was suddenly interested in taking over the island.

"I don't get it." Orion looked between Kian and Kalugal. "If it's a known brothel, the island's location can't be secret."

"Windowless private transport planes." Kian looked like he'd lost the last of his patience and was on the verge of exploding. "I'm going inside," he proclaimed and strode toward the sliding doors.

This time, they all rose to their feet and followed him.

30

KIAN

*K*ian was bristling with anger, mostly at himself. Kalugal's comment about Navuh's future plans was nothing that hadn't occurred to him before, but the issue that Orion had raised had not.

Why hadn't he thought to ask his mother to run a test on a child of an immortal male?

Her blood could potentially be the other method of activation, and if it wasn't, it would not harm the child either. They should have given it a try a long time ago, as soon as Annani and Alena had found out that it activated the girls.

He felt like punching a wall, and he probably would have if he didn't have a house full of guests. His mother and sister had been sitting on this secret for two thousand fucking years.

Kian hadn't known. His mother had shared the secret only with Alena because the first child they'd tried it on was hers. He'd found out when Annani had given Syssi a small amount of her blood to help her pull through her transition.

And what about Bridget and William? The two big brains on his council? Why hadn't it occurred to them that the children of immortal males could have the genes but needed a different method of activation?

They shouldn't have blindly accepted that the method the gods had discovered over five thousand years ago was the only one.

Except, those two didn't know about Annani using her blood to activate the little girls, so they could be forgiven, but not his mother and sister, and not he.

Most likely it wouldn't work, but until they tried and failed, the guilt was going to eat him alive. Not that it wouldn't if it worked. He would live with the guilt for not trying it sooner for the rest of his immortal life.

Syssi walked up to him and wrapped her arm around his middle. "What's wrong?"

He couldn't tell her the secret of Annani's blood, but he could tell her about Orion's theory.

"Orion offered a fresh perspective on Dormants. We accepted the gods' conclu-

88

sion that only the children of immortal females carried the dormant godly genes, and therefore could be activated. We didn't consider that the children of the males might carry the genes as well but require a different method of activation. If that's true, I will never forgive myself for not investigating it sooner."

His mother turned to look at him. "I assure you that the gods tried everything they could think of to activate the children of the male immortals. My aunt and uncle were relentless in their research, and they found no way to do it."

Alena, knowing what he knew, looked just as disturbed as he was. "What possible other method that we haven't tried yet could there be?"

Was that her way of telling him that she didn't think Annani's blood could activate the children of the males? Had they tried?

He couldn't ask her in front of everyone, but the first chance he got, he was going to have a private talk with her and Annani.

"We didn't have a way to do that before," Amanda said. "But with how fast the field of gene editing is growing, we might be able to turn anyone immortal in the not-so-distant future."

Kian arched a brow. "Are you serious?"

"We are not there yet, and it might take a couple more decades, but I'm hopeful." She turned to Shai. "You said that you read some articles on the subject. And since you remember everything you read verbatim, you can probably explain it better than I can."

Shai shook his head. "Remembering is not the same as understanding, and I'm not a scientist. Perhaps it would be better if you do that."

"Not really." She leaned back as much as her belly allowed. "Because you are not a scientist, you will explain it in laymen's terms, and everyone will get it."

"Very well." Shai walked over to the other side of the table so everyone could see him. "New genome editing technologies allow scientists to change DNA, by adding, removing, or altering genetic material at specific locations in the genome. The newest technology was adapted from a naturally occurring genome editing system in bacteria. The bacteria capture snippets of DNA from invading viruses and use them to create DNA segments called CRISPR arrays. Those arrays are like an instruction manual to defend the organism when the same virus invades it again. When it does, the bacteria produce RNA segments from the CRISPR arrays to target the virus's DNA and cut it apart, disabling it."

Annani tilted her head. "I understand how it can be used to fight viruses, but how can it turn a human into an immortal?"

"Currently, scientists use that mechanism to fight diseases," Amanda said. "But it can also be used to modify genes. They use the cell's own DNA repair mechanism to add, delete, or replace genetic material with a customized DNA sequence. At this time, the editing changes are limited to somatic cells, which means that the changes only affect certain tissues and are not passed from one generation to the next. Because of ethical concerns, changes to genes in egg and sperm cells and to embryos are illegal in many countries, but that's where the juice is, that's where the answers to what makes us immortal are hidden, and that's how we will be able to transfer our enhanced genes to the next generation."

Cassandra nodded. "I've read that soon genes could be not only altered but built from scratch by artificial intelligence. That whole field of research seems like science fiction to me."

Kian hadn't understood half of what Shai and Amanda had said, but he'd gotten the gist of it. Since he suspected that the gods themselves had been genetically engineered, he believed that when the genes responsible for their longevity and various other enhancements were identified, regular humans might one day be turned immortal.

The potential was exciting for the clan but terrifying on a global level. What if everyone lived forever? Immortals didn't multiply as fast as humans, but their numbers still grew.

If all of humanity became immortal, even given the same low fertility rate as the clan immortals, there would be a population explosion. Kian didn't want to imagine the terrors that would bring about.

31

VROG

*V*rog pulled on the T-shirt Vlad had loaned him. He'd been given clothes by the Guardians in the keep, but most were too loose on his slim frame. His son's shirt was a little tight, and it reminded him of the way he used to look when he was Vlad's age.

He hadn't been much older than his son when he'd fathered him, and in retrospect, he was less mature.

Vlad was a pensive young man, a good son to his mother, and a good mate to Wendy. He was also hard-working, kind, and intelligent.

Vrog was so undeservedly proud of him. Other than contributing his genes, he hadn't done anything. Worse, he'd demanded that Stella abort the pregnancy. He was so ashamed of it now but was too much of a coward to apologize to both mother and son.

Perhaps he would do that over dinner.

Wendy had invited Richard and Stella, the sweet girl intending to bring their ragtag family closer, but Vrog doubted Richard would be on board with that. The guy would celebrate the day he left the village and returned to his school.

The truth was that he missed the place, missed the students and even the chatty Doctor Wang. Vrog was respected there, even admired, and for a good reason. He was the founder, the one who kept the thing running like a well-oiled machine. Without him, the school would not collapse right away, but it would deteriorate over time. An organization was only as good as the people running it.

It always started at the top.

In the village he was a nobody, and that wasn't going to change. They didn't need him, and he had nothing to contribute.

Stella and several of the others had talked about him founding a school in the village, but it would take a long time and many more children before the clan would need one.

With a sigh, he pulled the T-shirt down to smooth out the wrinkles, opened the door, and headed toward the living room.

"You look awesome," Wendy said. "I knew Vlad's shirt would fit you. You guys are almost the same height, and you are both slim."

He smiled and took the dish she handed him. "Where should I put it?"

"On the table."

Vlad was in the kitchen, an apron tied around his waist, flipping steaks over the griddle. "I left yours almost rare." He lifted an overflowing platter to show Vrog. "This is all for you."

"Thank you." He had to find a way to pay for the extra food he was consuming, but he knew that they wouldn't hear of it, and he didn't want to offend them.

As the doorbell rang and Wendy rushed to open the door for Stella and Richard, Vrog took in a deep breath.

"I brought a casserole." Stella handed Wendy a glass dish.

"And I brought wine." Richard walked in with a bottle in each hand and cast Vrog a semi-friendly look. "You drink wine, I hope."

"I do." Vrog took the plate of steaks and put it on the table. "Vlad was kind enough to prepare nearly rare steaks for me. I don't know how to repay his and Wendy's kindness."

"Oh, stop it." Wendy slapped his arm. "We are a family. When Vlad and I come to visit you in China, you will return the favor."

"I will. That's a promise."

"And when is that?" Richard pulled out a chair for Stella. "I mean, when do you plan to go home?"

"Soon." Vrog took a seat across from the guy. "I just want to spend a few more days with Vlad and Wendy."

"You can stay as long as you like." Wendy put a salad bowl on the table and sat down. "I need more time to find you a good match."

That got Richard smiling. "I know just the lady for you."

"Who?" Wendy asked.

"Ingrid."

Stella winced. "Really? Is that your idea of a joke, Richard?"

"What's wrong with Ingrid?" Vlad asked. "She's a very talented lady."

"She was Richard's first immortal lover, which is why he's suggesting her."

"Well, yeah." Richard's expression was the picture of innocence. "I know her, and I know what she likes. I think she'll like Vrog." He smiled evilly. "She's not very picky."

"Richard!" Stella admonished.

"What?"

"That was offensive."

He snorted. "Ingrid was with me, so when I say that she's not very picky, I'm also insulting myself, and therefore it shouldn't be taken as an insult."

"I'm not offended," Vrog said. "And if Richard thinks that the lady will find me agreeable, then I'm more than willing to make her acquaintance."

Vrog didn't care if the woman was a bombshell or a hag. He just wanted Stella and Richard to stop fighting because of him. He'd done enough damage already, and he was there to make amends, not to cause more strife.

3 2

RICHARD

*R*ichard was starting to warm up to Vrog. The guy was polite, deferential, and did his best not to step on anyone's toes.

Perhaps he wasn't so bad.

After all, Vlad was one of the best people Richard knew, and half of his genes had come from his father, so there was that.

The guy could eat, though. Vlad took after Vrog in that regard too. They both were skinny and yet consumed huge quantities, however in Vrog's case, it had been almost exclusively meat. Vlad enjoyed carbs like any normal human.

When the pile of steaks on Vrog's plate was demolished, the guy put his fork and knife on top of it, reached for the napkin, and dabbed at his mouth like some damn aristocrat. "I remember Stella mentioning that you guessed Vlad's origins during a virtual adventure you both participated in. Could you tell me more about it?"

Richard lifted a brow. "You told him about that?"

"It's not a secret." Stella shrugged. "Many people know about our virtual adventure, and most everyone knows about Emmett confirming Syssi's amazingly accurate depiction of the Kra-ell."

Vrog gaped at her. "Is Kian's mate a seer?"

"She has visions," Stella said. "But the odd part is that she originally came up with the Kra-ell story for the virtual adventure company, and she was convinced that it was a product of her imagination. But she described a female-dominated society that was nearly identical to the Kra-ell, and she even named her imaginary people Krall. Coincidence? I think not. Anyway, William, who is the clan's tech genius, wanted us to test the program because Richard was still human back then, and he needed a human test subject. I chose the Krall adventure, but it turned out very differently than what I expected."

As Stella dove into the story, Richard was reminded of details he'd forgotten. It had been one hell of an adventure, and even though it had been terrifying and heart-wrenching at times, he liked the role he played and what it had shown him about himself.

He was damn proud of the hero act he'd pulled off.

The only thing that he didn't remember fondly was the damn fish stink during their escape from the Krall territory. They had been smuggled out in a fishing boat, hidden under a tarp, and he could still smell it.

"Why are you grimacing?" Wendy asked.

He waved a dismissive hand. "The experience was amazing, but it was too damn realistic. We escaped in a fishing boat through the Arctic Sea, freezing our asses off, and dying from the smell of rotten fish."

Vlad chuckled. "But you had your happy ending—a small house with a white picket fence and a vampiric, blood-sucking baby boy."

"That was how Richard guessed my secret," Stella said. "Subconsciously, I must have included clues about Vlad's heritage when I filled out the questionnaire."

Richard leaned back and puffed out his chest. "Yeah, a blood-sucking little Vlad was a big fat clue. Everything about the adventure was fun, though. I got to play the hero, rescue the woman I love, and come out in one piece."

"That sounds amazing," Vrog said. "Do you think Kian will allow me to experience a virtual adventure like that?"

"I don't see why not." Vlad uncorked one of the wine bottles.

"You'll need a partner," Richard said. "The Krall adventure is not a solo experience. But don't worry, the software will find your perfect match." He winked. "Who knows, maybe it will be Ingrid. I wonder if she's filled out the questionnaire."

Stella elbowed him in the ribs. "You've been with so many of the clan females. Can't you think of anyone but her?"

"She deserves a break. But it's not up to me, is it? Let the computer match up Vrog with the best female for him."

Vrog was watching their argument with a puzzled expression on his face. "You told me that bonded mates can't feel attraction to anyone other than their partner. How come Richard sampled so many different females?"

Richard winced. It was better to get it over with and tell the guy about his first job in the village before he heard it from someone else.

"I wasn't as lucky as you. When I arrived in the village, I was a human who was potentially a Dormant, but after several failed inductions, I lost hope of transitioning, and I knew that my days in the village were numbered. Then Amanda came up with the idea to sell my stud services in daily auctions to speed up the process of finding my one and only. And that's how I became the clan's gigolo."

"Is that how you found Stella?"

She snorted. "No. I would never buy a male's sexual favors in an auction. The Fates steered us toward each other, but I was too hardheaded and judgmental, and I didn't snatch up Richard when I first met him." She smiled at him apologetically. "I'm sorry. If I hadn't run off the first time we met, you would have been spared all that hard work."

"Did any of the ladies conceive?" Vrog asked.

Richard shook his head. "I know it's sacrilege to say this in the clan, but I'm glad none did. I only want children with Stella."

33

ALENA

*K*ian's accusations hurt.

After implying that Annani's *presence* might have activated the children of immortal males, he'd started on the boys born to immortal females, saying that he didn't understand why what worked for the girls didn't work for them.

What did he think? That they hadn't tried to use Annani's blood to activate the boys?

Alena couldn't believe that her brother could be so dense.

Neither she nor Annani would have been able to look Amanda in the eyes if they could have prevented Aiden's death and hadn't.

Even after all these years, Alena still teared up whenever she thought of her sister's grief. There was nothing worse for a mother than losing her child, and she prayed to the Fates she would never have to experience it herself.

"It is getting late." Annani rose to her feet and put her hand on Alena's shoulder. "We should head home." She shifted her gaze to Shai and smiled. "Thank you for letting us have your house on such short notice. It must have been a hassle to move your things so quickly."

"My pleasure, Clan Mother." He inclined his head. "I was glad for the excuse. Without it, Ingrid would have dragged her feet about getting Geraldine and me a new house. She has her hands full these days."

"Congratulations." Annani turned to Geraldine. "Are you staying in the village tonight?"

She nodded. "I waited for Orion to show up, and now that he is here, I can finally move in with Shai. For now, I just brought one suitcase, but later we will get the rest of my things and put the house up for rent."

Alena snuck a quick sidelong glance at Orion to see if Geraldine's words had angered him, but he had a small smile on his face, just a curve of one side of his lips that made him look even more roguish.

From the fond way he regarded his sister, niece, and nephew, it was obvious that he cared deeply for them. That was one point in his favor.

He was also so damn handsome, which she shouldn't give him points for because his looks had more to do with who his parents were and not with anything he had done. He seemed to be a good guy, though, and he wasn't intimidated by her big, overbearing family, which earned him two more favorable points.

Perhaps he was worth taking a risk on.

Except, his compulsion ability was worth at least five unfavorable points, which brought his balance down to a negative two.

Alena lifted a hand to her ear, realizing that she'd removed the earpieces when he'd gone outside and forgotten to put them back in when he returned. As a surge of fear speared through her, she had to stifle the urge to stick her fingers in her ears.

"May you enjoy many happy years in your new home," Annani said. "It amuses me to think that our bodies outlast the houses we build. Even our castle in Scotland, which is only a few centuries old, is crumbling and needs constant repairs, while our bodies still operate at optimal levels." She smoothed a hand down her hip. "We owe our thanks to those genetic engineers who perfected our genome. Perhaps the next step should have been to engineer self-repairing houses."

As a quick look at Kian revealed that his mood hadn't improved, Alena wondered if he was still thinking about the possibility of the children born to male immortals having the godly genes.

His frown was so deep that his brows were nearly touching.

Syssi leaned her head on his arm. "I thank God, the Fates, and the universe every day for the gift I was given. I get to spend eternity with the man I love and with our daughter. I hope we will have more children, but even if Allegra is the only one, I will still consider myself blessed beyond measure."

Kian's expression softened, and his forehead smoothed out. "So do I." He kissed the top of her head before pulling out of her hold. "I need to escort Annani and Alena to their new home, but I won't be long."

As if they needed him to escort them. He probably wanted to talk to them in private

"Thank you." Annani reached for Syssi's hand and pulled her into her arms. "It was a lovely evening."

"Tomorrow at our place," Kalugal said. "Everyone is invited, including Andrew and Nathalie and their adorable little girl who needed to go to sleep." He waved a hand around the room and everyone gathered. "It's not an official housewarming party, so don't bring gifts. I'll remind Andrew and Nathalie to bring Eva and Bhathian along." He turned to Orion. "You'll get to see all the little ones we currently have in the village. Eva and Bhathian have a little boy." He put his hand on Jacki's small belly. "Soon, there will be two more. Our son and Amanda's daughter."

Alena snuck another glance at Orion, curious to see his reaction to the pitiful number of children the clan had.

His face was surprisingly unguarded for someone who had walked the planet for over half a millennium, and his expression was more contemplative than sad or puzzled.

"When are you planning on having the official party?" Onegus asked Kalugal.

"Are you asking in your capacity as the chief? Or do you just want to know?"

"Both. But I was wondering what's taking you so long. You moved into the house over two weeks ago."

"Jacki and I are waiting for the last of the furnishings and decorative pieces we ordered. Hopefully, everything will arrive by the time we return from our trip."

"What trip?" Kian asked.

"I told you that I arranged to do some digging in the Mosuo territory. Jacki wants to see an archeological dig, but I don't want to take her to Egypt, where it's hot and humid. The Mosuo live around Lugu Lake, which is located in a high plateau amidst the Xiaoliangshan hills of Western Yunnan and enjoys temperate weather."

"I'm excited," Jacki said. "I just wish we had some company. I enjoyed our trip to Scotland so much. Does anyone want to join us?"

"When are you leaving?" Kian asked.

"Wednesday." Kalugal wrapped an arm around his wife's shoulders. "If any of you want to come, let me know, and I'll get Phinas to reserve rooms in the hotel."

Alena would have loved to go, but as usual she could only go where her mother wished to visit. And even if Annani was as intrigued by the Mosuo as Alena was, there was no chance Kian would allow them to join Kalugal without him being there and at least fifty Guardians to watch over them.

"How long are you going to spend there?" Shai asked.

"A couple of weeks," Jacki said. "But we might shorten or lengthen the visit depending on what we find."

"I hope that you are taking some of your men with you," Kian said. "I don't know how safe it is, especially since you are looking for clues about the Kra-ell."

"I'm taking Phinas and two more men. That still leaves plenty of space on my jet." He looked around the assembled company until his eyes fell on Alena. "How about it? Are you in?"

"I wish I could, but I'll have to take a raincheck."

34

ORION

*W*hile everyone was saying their goodnights and thanking their hosts for dinner, Orion wondered whether Mason would be outside waiting to escort him back to the house.

The guy had acted as if he'd been there to help Orion, but as evidenced by the earpieces the guy wore, it was obvious that his job was to guard the *dangerous* compeller.

Evidently, Alena viewed him as a threat as well.

Why, though?

Kalugal was probably just as powerful a compeller as he was. Did she wear protective earpieces around him also?

If compulsion was such a rare ability, it wasn't likely that Alena had encountered a nasty compeller and had a bad experience. Perhaps it was just a subconscious fear, like some humans feared snakes even if they'd never seen one.

Orion grimaced. That wasn't a good comparison.

"We can walk you back to your house," Geraldine offered as they stepped out onto Kian's front porch. "That's where our new house is, right next to Onegus and Cassandra's."

"Sylvia and I are in the second phase as well." Roni led the way, going down the steps.

As Orion had expected, Mason was waiting for him outside.

"I see that you have a full escort." The guy pushed his hands into his jeans pockets. "I guess you don't need me." He nodded to Onegus and the others. "I'll see you tomorrow morning."

"Good night, Mason." Orion had hoped to grill the Guardian about Alena and get as much background information on her as he could, but it would have to wait until tomorrow.

As the seven of them started toward their section of the village, Orion fell in step with Onegus. "So you are the chief of security here."

"I am."

"And you are also Cassandra's mate."

"I am that as well."

Orion smiled. "We are family. Do you really need to waste a Guardian on me? I'm not a threat to anyone here."

"I don't think that you are, but I'm a cautious fellow, and I just met you earlier today. Besides, you can use Mason or any other Guardian I post in front of your house as your personal tour guide. Their instructions are to be friendly and helpful."

"Mason followed your instructions perfectly." He cut a glance at the chief. "Can I ask you a question about Alena?"

Onegus narrowed his eyes at him. "What do you want to know?"

"What does she have against compellers? Did she have a bad experience with one?"

"Not that I'm aware of. We are all wary of compellers, especially powerful ones that can compel immortals."

"Your Clan Mother is a compeller."

"Annani never uses her power on us. The only exception was when Kalugal and his men joined the clan. There was a lot of mistrust going both ways, and everyone agreed that the only way to solve that was to have Annani compel everyone to do no harm to one another. We knew she was going to do it, we knew why, and everyone agreed that it was necessary. No one's will was taken away from them."

"Could the goddess compel me to do no harm as well? It bothers me that Alena regards me as a threat."

"You like her," Cassandra said. "And she likes you."

That was news to him. "She does?"

Grinning, Geraldine nodded. "We overheard her talking with Amanda. She didn't admit anything, but Amanda thought that she liked you."

Roni groaned. "You sound like a bunch of middle schoolers. She likes me, she likes me not," he taunted.

"I have no problem admitting that I'm intrigued by the lovely Alena. I just want to figure out why she was the only one other than Kian's bodyguards who was wearing earpieces."

"Alena is Annani's eldest daughter," Shai said. "And she deserves only the best."

"Are you implying that I'm lacking in any way? I hate to use the term, but I'm a demigod just like her."

"You vowed never to love a woman again. Alena deserves a male who will give himself to her fully, while you can only give her your body."

Cassandra snorted. "Alena might look all prim and proper, but she didn't produce those thirteen children by immaculate conception. She must have hooked up with many human males to do that. So why not Orion?"

Orion was still stuck on the number. "Thirteen children? How is that possible? Aren't immortals supposed to be nearly infertile?"

"Alena is a miracle," Onegus said. "If not for her fertility, the clan wouldn't exist. Sari has no children, Amanda lost her first son and is only now pregnant with her second child, and Kian's children would have been born human if he didn't find Syssi who was a Dormant and turned immortal. Alena is the de facto mother of the clan."

"Does it bother you?" Geraldine asked softly. "That she has so many children, and grandchildren and so on? Nearly every member of the clan is her descendant."

"Why would that bother me? I'm just awed." He shook his head. "Thirteen children. That's a lot even for a human."

"And yet, she's never been in love," Shai said. "Her entire life is about duty to her mother and to the clan. Ponder that when you lust after her."

"Shai!" Geraldine slapped his arm. "Why are you being so mean to Orion?"

He chuckled. "I'm not being mean, I'm giving him advice. If he breaks Alena's heart, what do you think Kian would do to him?"

35

ALENA

*A*s they entered Shai's former house, Alena was impressed with the cleaning job the Guardians and the Odus had done.

The place was sparkling clean, and everything looked brand new. They must have polished the wood, vacuumed the couches, and sprayed fresh scent all over the place.

There were only two bedrooms, which didn't leave room for the Odus, but since they didn't need to sleep or rest, they also didn't need beds. Still, she would have felt better if they had a place of their own and didn't have to spend the night sitting quietly in the living room.

She looked at Kian. "Do you have anything you can give our Odus to do during the night? They can clean up the office building or do some gardening."

He shook his head. "I prefer for them to stay with you and guard you. But if you want to send a couple of them to our house, they are welcome to stay with Okidu in his room."

"That would be lovely." Annani walked over to the couch and sat down.

Immediately, Oridu rushed to her. "Does the Clan Mother require refreshments?"

"I could use a cup of tea, thank you." Annani looked at Kian. "Can I offer you some?"

"Yes, please." He sat on one of the armchairs facing the couch.

"Please make tea for the three of us, Oridu."

He bowed. "Right away, Clan Mother."

As Alena joined Annani on the couch, Kian cast a quick look at the four Odus gathered in the kitchen. "I assume that all of them are safe to talk around?"

"Of course," Annani said. "They will never repeat a word."

"What Orion said about activating the children of the males got me thinking. Did you try the same method you use to activate the daughters of our females on the sons?"

"Naturally," Annani said. "After the experiment worked with the first baby girl, Alena and I tested it on every new child born to her, boy or girl. Unfortunately, my

101

blood did not induce the boys' transition, but fortunately, we had you to activate them."

He let out a breath. "That's a relief but also a disappointment. I wish that what Orion said was true, even if it worked only on the males' daughters. I would hate myself if we didn't try." He smiled. "It's not like there would have been many who needed your special blessing."

Annani nodded gravely. "If you find a child sired by an immortal male with a human, I am willing to give it a try. The worst that could happen would be a boost of health for the child."

Kian leaned back and crossed his legs at the ankles. "Sometimes it takes an outsider to ask a question that those on the inside never thought to ask. We took for granted that the gods had determined that the children of immortal males didn't carry the immortal gene, and we never thought to question that assertion. Now that we are on the cusp of developing tools that would allow us to play with the genome as the gods did, I wonder if we should."

Alena chuckled. "This gives the phrase 'playing God' a whole new meaning."

"Thank you." Annani took the cup of tea Oridu handed her and took a sip. "The gods tampered with the human genome, enhancing it just enough to create servants who were intelligent and obedient. But humans did not turn out exactly as they had intended. In a way, they were like today's artificial intelligence. They learned fast, and every generation was smarter than the one before it. Soon, they became just as intelligent as the gods, and since they multiplied rapidly as they had been designed to do, they became a threat."

"The law of unintended consequences," Kian said as he put his teacup on the coffee table.

Annani nodded. "Even though most humans were obedient and easy to control, some of them were ambitious and had minds of their own. Those outliers made the gods realize that they could not regard humans as mindless servants, and they enacted laws to govern them that mimicked their own. In the end, the gods were not destroyed by humans as they had originally feared, but by one of their own. Nevertheless, Mortdh would not have been able to amass power if not for the immortals and humans he commanded. So in a way, my father was right about humans posing an existential threat to the gods."

"What are you trying to say, Mother? That we need to be careful about tampering with genes?" Kian crossed his arms over his chest.

She shrugged. "I was just thinking out loud. This is not an easy issue that can be resolved over a cup of tea. There are pros and cons to be weighed, both moral and ethical, and the real danger is that you can never be sure of what that tampering will produce."

36

VROG

*V*rog had spent half the night thinking about the Kra-ell virtual adventure, and the other half dreaming about it. It had been a damn sexy dream, and when he woke up, he was determined to try it out.

He found Vlad in the kitchen, kneading dough.

"What are you making?"

"Wendy's favorite breakfast, lunch, and dinner. Beignets."

"I don't know what that is." Vrog pulled a mug out of the drying rack and filled it with coffee from the coffeemaker. "I've spent a lot of time thinking about that virtual adventure that Stella and Richard talked about. How difficult do you think it would be to arrange one for me?"

"Not difficult at all. I can take you to William after breakfast."

"It's Saturday. Does he work on weekends?"

"To William, the lab is not his workplace. It's his home. He's always there. Anyway, he'll give you a questionnaire to fill in, run it through the program, and hopefully, your perfect match will be somewhere in the village and interested in the same adventure."

"So it's an inside program. I can't be matched with a human female."

"You can." Vlad rolled out the dough. "You can go online and buy an adventure package in the Perfect Match studios. I think they have one in Beverly Hills, which is not too far from here. They can match you with a compatible human, but they are pricey. The one in the village is free."

"Price is not an issue, but I prefer to be matched with an immortal female. How does it work? Would I know who she is?"

Vlad shook his head. "Couples can choose to go together and have a joined virtual adventure. But if you want to find your perfect partner, it's anonymous. If you like her very much, you can put in a request to meet her, but she's not obligated to agree." He smiled shyly. "In fact, there is no guarantee that she is indeed a she. Unless you specify that she must be female in real life, you might get matched with a male who

103

wants to play the part of a female. But if he's your perfect match, then hey, why not, right?"

Vrog stared at his son, not sure whether Vlad was serious or pulling his leg. "The computer will not match a straight male with a gay one because that wouldn't be a perfect match. It would be a mismatch."

Vlad laughed. "Yeah, you are probably right. Unless the straight guy is secretly gay, that is. Not everyone is brave enough to admit their desires."

"True." Vrog took a sip from his coffee. "But I don't have these kinds of secret desires. I have others."

"Oh yeah? Like what?"

"Like the kind a father doesn't discuss with his son."

Vlad's amusement faded. "I don't want to hurt your feelings, but it's easier for me to think of you as a friend or a distant relative. Perhaps that will change in the future, but for now, that's the best I can do."

It hurt, but Vrog appreciated Vlad's honesty. "That's better than thinking of me as your enemy."

"I'm glad you're not taking it to heart. I like you, just not as a paternal figure." Vlad smiled again. "And since we are friends, you can tell me about your secret desires, if it's not too kinky, that is. I'm a simple guy with simple tastes."

Vrog was relieved to hear that. "So am I." He shifted on the stool that was too short for his long legs. "I always wondered how it would feel to be with a Kra-ell female. I would like to experience that at least once in my life."

Vrog's heart ached at the thought that they might be gone. He hadn't loved Jade or any of the others, but he'd admired and desired them. He'd hoped that his loyal service would earn him an invitation to one of their beds, but they had either been killed or abducted before it could have happened. Now, his only option was to experience a Kra-ell female in a fantasy that would probably not reflect reality.

Then again, if the creator of that fantasy was a seeress, she might have pierced the veil and seen a real Kra-ell coupling.

"I heard that they are vicious," Vlad said. "Why would you want that?"

"I'm just curious."

37

ALENA

*I*n the morning, Alena emerged from her bedroom, dreading breakfast with her mother.

Last night, she'd ducked into her room as soon as Kian had left, thus avoiding Annani's interrogation about her reaction to Orion. There was no doubt in her mind that Annani had known precisely what was going on.

They'd spent over two thousand years together, but although her mother could read her like an open book, the reverse was not true. The only thing predictable about Annani was her unpredictability, and that she was sure to surprise Alena with yet another one of her schemes that walked the razor-thin line between daring and reckless.

Perhaps that was the secret juice that kept Alena from going crazy.

Her childbearing years were long behind her, and the sanctuary, although beautiful, was stifling. If not for their frequent trips and her mother's shenanigans, the tedium would have been unbearable.

"Good morning, Alena." Annani put the newspaper down. "Did you sleep well?"

"Not really." Alena pulled out a chair and sat down.

Ovidu rushed over and poured her a cup of coffee. "Would you like an omelet, mistress?"

"Yes, thank you." Alena stirred cream and sugar into her coffee and took a sip.

Annani observed her for a moment before saying, "I want to discuss with you our plans for celebrating the holidays."

That was good. As long as her mother didn't bring up Orion and Alena's attitude toward him, she was willing to talk about any topic under the sun.

"What do you have in mind?"

"You said that we needed to choose a symbol for our holiday celebrations, and I found the perfect solution not just for one annual celebration but for two." Annani smiled triumphantly. "The summer and winter solstices. They are not directly related to any religion but rather symbolize the changing of seasons and celebrate nature. What do you think?"

"I think that you are brilliant, Mother, and I love the idea. Except, what actually symbolizes the solstices?"

Annani waved a dismissive hand. "I am sure that you will come up with something by Monday evening. I want to host the close family for the winter solstice celebration. You will handle the decorations, the Odus will prepare the feast, and we will hand out presents."

"A wonderful idea, Mother."

For a few moments they sat in silent companionship, with Alena thinking about winter theme decorations and where she could get them before Monday evening, but then Annani smirked, and Alena braced for what she knew was coming.

"Orion is very handsome," her mother said.

Here it comes. Alena stifled a groan and nodded. "Mm-hmm," she agreed noncommittally.

Annani smiled knowingly. "It is obvious that you find him attractive. Why do you try to hide it? You are not a bashful girl."

Alena snorted. "You are the only one who still calls me a girl. I'm ancient, Mother. And bashfulness has nothing to do with it."

"Then what does?"

"I've already told you why he can't be a contender for me." She braced her elbows on the table, which she knew annoyed her mother, but she didn't care.

"His compulsion ability should not be a deterrent." Annani cast her a stern look. "You cannot condemn Orion for something he was born with, and you offended him by wearing those ear contraptions throughout dinner. I saw him casting quick glances at you, and whenever he did, he had a hurt look in his eyes."

Alena hadn't noticed, but she didn't doubt her mother's observation.

"Maybe he was constipated."

"Alena!" Annani admonished. "Immortals do not suffer from that malady, and furthermore, this is not a topic that should be mentioned while eating." She waved a hand. "You should go over to his place and make amends."

"We didn't quarrel, so there is nothing to make amends for."

"You could be more friendly. Invite him for a walk, show him the village, or take him to the café."

Alena narrowed her eyes at her mother. "Why are you pushing me at him?"

Annani sighed. "No matter how old you are, I am still your mother, and I want what is best for you. The Fates sent Orion to us for a reason, and I do not think that they intended him for another female. He might be your one and only."

"If he's the one the Fates chose for me, then they have a really sick sense of humor. Compellers make my skin crawl, and that's who they send me? What did I do to deserve that punishment?"

"You are being childish, Alena, and it does not suit you. I want you to go to Orion's house and invite him for a walk. It is not a mother's suggestion. It is the Clan Mother's directive."

Her mother had never pulled rank on her or any of her other children. Well, she had done so once when Kian had wanted to marry Lavena and Annani forbade it. He'd done it anyway and suffered mightily for it.

Her mother had been right then, so maybe she was also right now.

106

"Here is your omelet, mistress." Oridu placed the plate in front of her.

"Thank you." Alena unfurled the napkin and placed it over her lap. "I'll do as you ask, Mother. I'll invite Orion on a walk around the village." She would do so while wearing earpieces, but Annani didn't need to know that.

The question was what to wear to control her raging attraction to him.

A chastity belt?

Perhaps Merlin could brew her a potion that suppressed desire.

Her mother smiled benevolently. "Thank you for being so agreeable, Alena. I assure you that you will not regret it."

"I know." Alena smiled sweetly. "But don't expect some grand romance to come out of it. I'm just going to take him on a walk so he doesn't think I hate him."

38

KIAN

*A*nnani's front door swung open just as Kian was ascending the stairs, and Alena walked out with Ovidu in tow.

The Odu bowed and kept the door open for him. "Good morning, Master Kian."

"Good morning." Halting on the mid stair, Kian waited for Alena to reach him. When she leaned to kiss his cheek, he noticed that she was still wearing the earpieces he'd given her the day before. "Going to see Orion?"

She leaned away to look at him. "How did you know?"

He pointed to her ear. "Unless these are a new fashion accessory or you forgot to take them out and slept with them in, Orion is the only reason for you to wear them."

Last night, when he'd escorted Alena and Annani home, Kian had been too consumed with his seething anger over their presumed oversight to notice, but he doubted she'd left them in.

Wincing, Alena lifted a hand to her ear. "These are too uncomfortable to forget about. Mother thinks that I was rude to Orion, and she wants me to make amends by inviting him for a walk around the village. I'm to give him a tour."

"Amends, eh?" He shook his head. "She's playing matchmaker."

"I know. But it's easier to do what she wants than argue."

Kian snorted. "I know what you mean. You are an angel to put up with her for all these years."

"Not so loud." Looking over her shoulder, Alena cast a furtive glance toward the open door. "She might hear you," she whispered.

He hadn't said anything that their mother wasn't aware of, but it was offensive nonetheless, and he didn't wish to hurt her feelings.

"You're right." Kian climbed the last stair. "Enjoy your walk with Orion."

"I'll do my best."

When he walked inside, he found Annani sitting on the living room couch with a newspaper spread out in front of her.

"Good morning, Mother." He leaned to kiss her cheek.

She beamed at him. "I am so glad you came." Folding the newspaper, she put it on the coffee table.

"You texted me and asked that I come over." He sat next to her. "I am not in the habit of refusing your summonses."

"Those are not summonses." She looked at him down her delicate nose. "Those are invitations."

"You told me to come alone."

"I did not want to bore Syssi with what I needed to discuss with you. I know that she likes to stay in bed on Saturday mornings."

"That she does. Only now, she brings Allegra to our bed in the mornings so we can cuddle with her. Not that our daughter is far from us during the night. Syssi still keeps her in a bassinet next to our bed."

Annani tilted her head. "Does it not interfere with certain activities?"

Kian stifled a chuckle. "From time to time, we roll the bassinet to Allegra's room and turn the baby monitor on."

His mother frowned. "Only from time to time?"

"A couple of times a day."

She smiled. "That is much better."

"Now that we are done discussing my sex life, what did you want to talk to me about? And does it have anything to do with you sending Alena to invite Orion on a walk?"

"I have no secrets from Alena, so no, there is no connection. She has a strange aversion to compellers, and I figured that the best way for her to get over it was by exposure. That is what they recommend for children who are afraid of dogs—get them accustomed to a cute little puppy, then to a medium-sized friendly dog, and eventually a big one."

This time Kian couldn't stifle the laugh bubbling out of him. "So if Orion is the puppy, who is the big dog?"

"Well, that would be Navuh, but I do not wish Alena anywhere near him. I will be satisfied if she is comfortable with the puppy."

"Orion is no puppy. He's cultured and polite, but don't mistake it for weakness."

Annani smiled. "I certainly hope that he is no weakling. Alena would trample all over him if he were."

That was a surprising thing for his mother to say about his sweet, even-keeled older sister. "She would never do that. Alena is pure heart."

"She is also an immortal female who is a demigoddess." Annani flipped a strand of her hip-length hair over her shoulder. "We are predatory by nature, and we want our males to be strong, so we test them, push them, and if they yield too easily, we lose interest." She smiled. "Perhaps we have more in common with the Kra-ell than we would like to believe."

Kian nodded. "It occurred to me that we might share a common ancestry, with the Kra-ell being a more primitive version of us."

"Or they might be us before the enhancements. They have shorter lifespans, do not heal as fast as we do, and they cannot activate their Dormants. All that talk about the scientific advancements in genetics got me thinking about them and their plight. Genome editing might provide a solution for them as well as for the children of immortal males."

"Is that what you wanted to talk to me about?"

"It was one of the topics. Is there anything we can do to hasten the progress?"

"We don't have any special knowledge to contribute. We helped along with technology, but that was thanks to Ekin's tablet and William's ability to figure out the information contained in it. Regrettably, the tablet didn't contain any information or instructions on genetics."

"But Okidu's journals do. When I heard the talk last night about genome editing, that was the first thing that came to my mind."

"William is searching for bioinformaticians to assemble a team that will help him tackle the journals. We don't know how much of the information contained in them will be helpful in that regard. Those are instructions on how to build Odus, not how to turn humans into immortals."

"Are we talking months or years?" Annani asked.

"I can't even answer that. We will know more once William and his team make some initial progress."

"I understand." She shifted her legs and adjusted the skirt of her dark-green gown. "The other thing I wanted to talk to you about is searching for Toven. Orion must have some clues that can point us in his direction."

"He mentioned a journal that he'd pilfered from Toven. Monday, I'll ask him if he will allow us to make a copy. I hope he has it with him."

"Why wait until Monday? Why not do that today or tomorrow? I have plans for Monday that I also need to discuss with you."

"Patience, Mother." He leaned closer to her and kissed her cheek. "Orion needs to get to know us better before he trusts us with that journal."

Her eyes blazing mischief, Annani smirked. "Why do you think I sent Alena to invite him on a walk?"

He arched a brow. "Because you wanted her to get over her aversion to compellers?"

"Well, that too," Annani agreed. "And I also think that they would make a nice couple. Orion is so ruggedly handsome, even more so than Toven. His mother must have been a very beautiful human."

"I suppose so." Kian leaned back and crossed his legs at the ankles. "So, what plans did you have for Monday, Mother?"

"Oh, yes." Her eyes sparkled. "Alena and I decided that the clan needs more celebrations, but since we have no official holidays, we would adopt a human one that is not tied to any particular religion. Starting with this Monday, we shall celebrate every winter and summer solstice."

"That's a great idea, but we can't arrange a clan-wide celebration in one day. Is it important to have the party this Monday?"

"That is the date of the winter solstice, so we cannot celebrate it a week later, but what Alena and I have in mind for this year is just a small family gathering. We will host a family dinner and distribute the gifts we brought with us. However, for the next solstice celebration, we will plan ahead and make it a grand event."

39

ALENA

*W*hen Alena neared Orion's house and didn't see a Guardian in front of it, two warring emotions ran through her, one right on the heels of the other.

The lack of a Guardian meant that Orion had gone out, and the Guardian had followed as he'd been instructed to do.

It was a relief not having to face him, but it was also a disappointment.

All that prep and pep talk on the way had been wasted, and she would just have to do it all over when Annani sent her again later.

"Shall I knock on the door, mistress?" Ovidu asked.

"I don't think Orion is home."

The Odu tilted his head. "I can hear two males conversing inside."

Perhaps Shai or Onegus were visiting him, and Onegus had dismissed the Guardian or had sent him to get something. In either case, she could turn around and tell Annani that Orion was busy.

Except, that was not going to fly with her mother. Annani would demand to know what Orion was busy with, and unless Alena knocked on that door and heard from him why he couldn't join her on a walk, her mission would not be deemed completed.

"I'll do it." Alena ascended the stairs. "You can wait for me on the porch." It was weird enough that she was showing up on Orion's doorstep uninvited. Having her butler with her would make it even more awkward.

She could have left Ovidu home, but he was an added layer of protection that she wasn't willing to forgo. Orion could physically overpower her and pull the earpieces out, the Guardian assigned to him might not reach them in time to help her, and Ovidu might be the only one who could save her mind from being overwhelmed by Orion.

She had to admit that it was an absurd scenario, but she wasn't taking any chances with a compeller.

Damn, she was overthinking this. It was only a walk through the village. He wasn't going to kidnap her even if he wanted to.

It wasn't a big deal, and she should relax.

"As you wish, mistress." Ovidu dipped his head and sat down on one of the two wicker outdoor chairs.

They were a deviation from Ingrid's usual decorating style. Most other homes in the village had either a wooden bench or loveseat swing on their front porches. Ingrid's idea had been to promote neighborly feelings, but most people didn't use them, preferring their private backyards.

Aware that she was letting her mind wander to buy herself another moment before knocking, Alena took a deep breath, plastered a pleasant smile on her face, and knocked.

When the door opened, though, revealing Orion in a pair of sweatpants and an unbuttoned shirt, Alena reconsidered her previous assessment.

Orion was a big deal and then some.

His bare chest was a work of art, hairless and tan and ripped with lean muscles, which hadn't been as noticeable under the dress shirt he'd worn the day before.

"Alena." Even with the damn earpieces distorting his voice, the way he said her name was like a soft caress over the most intimate places on her body.

But that was all he said and then he just stared at her as if he was as lost for words as she was.

"Hi," she finally managed to say. "May I come in?"

"Forgive me." With the spell broken, he shook his head and opened the door all the way. "I was just stunned to see you on my doorstep. What a pleasant surprise."

Mason, who was apparently the Guardian assigned to him, rose to his feet and smiled. "Good morning, Alena."

What was he doing inside the house? Wasn't he supposed to sit on the bench outside and do his best to be unobtrusive?

"Good morning." She forced a smile back.

"I invited Mason for a cup of coffee." Orion hurriedly buttoned up his shirt. "I hope that's okay, and he's not going to get in trouble for coming in."

"Not at all. It was nice of you to invite him."

"Can I offer you a cup as well? It has just finished brewing."

"Thank you. That would be lovely." The fake smile remained on her lips as her mind processed the scene she'd walked in on.

Mason was a handsome guy, and Orion had invited him in while wearing a pair of sweatpants that hung low on his hips, an unbuttoned shirt that left his magnificent chest bare, and no shoes on his sexy feet.

Had she been pining after a guy who was not interested in females?

"Please, take a seat." Orion motioned to the couch.

"Perhaps I should leave," Mason said.

"Don't leave on my account." Alena sat down. "The three of us can have coffee together, and then we can all go on a tour of the village, which is why I'm here this lovely morning. Ovidu is waiting outside." She'd felt compelled to add the last sentence, so neither Orion nor Mason would think she was there for the same reason Mason was.

The Guardian's expression turned rightfully doubtful, but he didn't say a thing.

Alena didn't live in the village, so although she knew the place well, she wasn't the best choice of a tour guide.

"Who's Ovidu?" Orion asked.

"My butler. The Clan Mother asked me to show you around." That should suffice as an explanation, and it was also the truth.

Alena wasn't there because she wanted to seduce Orion. Mason could have him.

Was she disappointed?

A little.

A lot.

"Why is he waiting outside?" Orion asked. "Invite him in."

"He's perfectly fine on your front porch."

Evidently, no one had told Orion about the Odus, and he assumed Ovidu was a clan member.

Well, in a way, he was, especially after Okidu and Onidu had rebooted and had become sentient. She still had a hard time wrapping her mind around that and even a harder time deciding whether she wanted Ovidu to reboot as well.

For a moment, Orion didn't move, looking at her as if he was waiting for her to change her mind about inviting Ovidu in, but when she didn't, he shrugged. "I'll get the coffee."

As he ducked into the kitchen, Mason and Alena sat in awkward silence, and when he returned a few moments later with a tray, they were both relieved.

Orion set down the mugs, cream, and sugar on the coffee table, but he didn't join her on the couch. "I would love to go on a walk, but I need to get dressed first. I was told that there is a café in the village, so perhaps we can stop for breakfast there." He smiled apologetically. "When I woke up this morning and saw Mason sitting outside on the bench, his breath misting because it was so cold, I took pity on him and invited him to share breakfast with me, but you came before I had a chance to make it."

Why had he felt the need to explain? Was he embarrassed about getting caught with Mason in the house?

A sidelong glance at the Guardian confirmed that he still looked like he would rather be anywhere but there.

Alena didn't know Mason well, but she'd never heard anything about him being into males, and Orion's invitation might have put him in an uncomfortable spot. In fact, he was probably grateful to her for showing up and saving him from having to reject unwanted advances.

As Orion sat down on the armchair next to Mason's, Alena cast another quick look at the Guardian, but he didn't seem bothered by Orion's proximity.

Perhaps she was reading the situation wrong?

She turned to Orion and smiled. "You are used to being around humans who are bothered by cold temperatures. We are immortals. The cold doesn't bother us as much. Nevertheless, it was nice of you to invite Mason in."

A smile bloomed on Orion's gorgeous face. "Right, you sang to that effect." He rubbed a hand over his stubbled chin. "The cold never bothered me anyway," he sang the line in a lovely baritone.

"You have a good voice."

"Not as good as yours."

Mason downed his coffee in one go and pushed to his feet. "I'll be outside keeping Ovidu company." He rushed out before either of them had a chance to stop him.

"Was it my singing?" Orion asked.

She laughed a little too merrily to cover her embarrassment. "I think it was me." She took a sip of the coffee and then rose to her feet. "Why don't you get dressed, and I'll see what I can make you for breakfast."

The horrified look on his face was hilarious. "I can't have the Clan Mother's eldest daughter making me breakfast."

"Why not?"

"It's just not right."

"What's not right is me taking you out on a walk on an empty stomach." She waved him off. "Go already. I don't have all day."

"Yes, ma'am."

40

ORION

rion felt like pinching himself to make sure that he wasn't dreaming.

Alena, the goddess's eldest daughter, was in his kitchen making him breakfast.

Did she even know how to cook?

She had a butler, who she'd left outside to wait for her.

It must be a dream.

Last night, after he'd returned to his temporary abode, he searched the village streaming service for that song she'd sung and found the animated movie. He'd watched it from start to finish and had listened to that song two more times.

The fairytale ice princess looked a lot like Alena, with the same big blue eyes and the same blond braid that she wore draped over her ample chest. Well, Alena's chest was ample, while the Disney princess's was less so. The other difference was that Alena was not icy.

In fact, he had a feeling that under her amiable expression and the quaint dress, there was a wild, passionate female just itching to get out.

Smiling, he looked at the suitcase that he'd left open on the floor and debated what to wear.

Alena's style was simple, old-fashioned. She hadn't bothered with anything fancy for dinner at her brother's house either, and this morning, she wore a long-sleeved cream-colored dress with small pearl buttons down the front and a flowing calf-length skirt. No makeup, no heels, and no jewelry except for a thin gold chain draped around her neck, the pendant dipping between those ample breasts.

She was a breath of fresh air—beautiful without putting any effort into it, direct and assertive despite her soft appearance, and she had an amazing singing voice to boot.

A true princess.

Pulling on a pair of slacks, Orion zipped them up, added a belt, a button-down that was his least formal, and pushed his feet into a pair of loafers.

A quick pass with the shaver got rid of his morning stubble, and a splash of cologne completed his primping. He tucked his useless phone in one pocket and his wallet in the other, more out of habit than expecting to have any use for either.

His phone had no reception in the village, and he didn't know whether the café accepted cash or credit cards. Perhaps it was free to clan members.

When he walked out of the bedroom, he was greeted with a pleasant smell of toast and eggs. It evoked a bitter-sweet feeling, the homey smells reminding him of Miriam—the only woman who'd ever cooked for him.

"Just in time." Alena waved a spatula in the direction of the kitchen counter.

Orion pulled out a stool and sat down. "Given that you have your own butler, I'm surprised that you know your way around a kitchen. Is he a new addition to your staff?"

"I've had Ovidu since I was born. He was my nanny." Alena transferred the omelet she'd made onto a plate and added toast, a container of butter, and another of jam.

Orion frowned. "How is that possible? You were Annani's firstborn. The clan didn't exist yet, and there were no other immortals."

"The Odus were Annani's servants, and she took them with her when she fled to the north." She pointed to his plate. "Eat. It's getting cold."

"I'm waiting for you."

"I've already had breakfast." She poured coffee into two fresh cups, set them down on the counter, and sat down on the stool he'd pulled out for her.

"I remember now Kian mentioning something about your mother loading her servants onto her flying machine. For some reason, I assumed that they were human females, ladies-in-waiting sort of servants. I should have known that they were immortal. She wouldn't have taken humans with her."

Had those servants fathered her children? Was that the reason she'd taken them along?

"They were neither." Alena cradled the coffee cup between her palms. "I hope Kian doesn't consider this classified information, but the Odus are a very advanced sort of cyborg."

"The Odus?"

She nodded. "That's what their kind is called, but Annani didn't like to refer to them as things, so she gave each one a distinct name. Her servants are Oridu, Ogidu, and Oshidu. Mine is Ovidu, Kian's Okidu, Amanda's Onidu, and Sari's is called Ojidu."

"I can't wait to meet your Ovidu. Does he look humanoid?"

She laughed. "Did Annani command all of your attention last night, so you didn't notice the servers? Those were Okidu and Onidu. They made all the food, set the table, served the meal, and cleaned up afterward."

"Impossible." He shook his head. "I remember thinking that they looked old for immortals, so I assumed that they were humans."

"We don't have humans in the village. Well, except for a couple of Dormants that is. And the construction workers…" she chuckled. "I guess we have plenty of humans in the village, just not as household staff."

"Who made the Odus?"

"We don't know. We assume that they were created on the gods' home planet and that their owner sent them to Earth to save them. Annani's father-in-law found them in the desert, and his son Khiann offered them to her as an engagement gift."

"Save them from what?"

Alena rolled her eyes. "Finish your breakfast, and I'll tell you on the way. We are supposed to be going for a walk."

Right. It was probably considered improper for her to be alone with him in his house. Nowadays, no one followed those outdated propriety rules, but Alena had been born in a different era, and so had her brother, whom Orion really did not wish to piss off.

41

ALENA

*A*s Alena and Orion walked out the front door, Mason and Ovidu rose to their feet.

"You can take a break, Mason." Alena smiled at the Guardian to put him at ease. "Ovidu will suffice as my chaperone." She winked at him.

The guy hesitated, his hand closing around the phone in his pocket.

"You don't need to call Onegus to ask his permission. Tell him that I authorized your break." She made her tone just a smidgen stricter than usual to let him know it wasn't up for discussion.

"Yes, ma'am." Mason planted his butt back on the chair.

"Go home, Mason. I'll call you when I return Orion safely to the house."

Reluctantly, the Guardian obeyed.

"Shall we?" She descended the stairs.

Following her down, Orion offered her his arm as if they were a couple in the Victorian times about to stroll through a city park.

Heck, why not.

She threaded her arm through his. "This will give people the wrong idea, you know."

"In what way?"

"They will assume that we are a couple."

"And that's bad?"

"No. It's just not true."

He cast her a roguish smile. "It could be true."

"Is that an offer?"

"I would very much like to get to know you better, Alena. I will consider it an honor if you accept my suit."

That was ridiculously old-fashioned but kind of sweet. The question was whether he'd meant it.

What about Mason?

Had she seen what hadn't been there?

Probably.

Orion seemed very focused on her, and his offer indicated that he was interested in more than just friendship. Then again, she'd started the flirtatious conversation, so he might have felt obligated to continue.

"Well?" Orion said. "I'm still waiting for an answer."

Alena flashed him a smile. "I'm old, but I like to think of myself as a modern female. You don't need to announce your intentions and get my permission."

That was a very noncommittal answer, and she was proud of herself for coming up with it.

Orion sighed dramatically. "There are advantages and disadvantages to the old customs, and to the new. In the old times, the guesswork was taken out of courtship. A lady either rejected a gentleman's suit or accepted it and things progressed from there. Nowadays, there are so many variations of possible relationships, or rather encounters. I had one lasting relationship a long time ago, and too many brief encounters. It's a novelty for me to court a lady."

"That's more than I had." Alena was curious about that one lasting relationship Orion had, but she didn't want to pry. If he wished to tell her about it, he would. "I only ever experienced encounters."

"And yet somehow you produced thirteen children. I'm told that for an immortal female, that is considered miraculous."

He'd sounded sincere, but just to be sure she snuck a sidelong glance at him to examine his expression and was relieved that he looked impressed rather than put off.

Alena had never told any of the human males she'd hooked up with about her children or any other personal details, keeping the encounters purely physical. To shield her heart and avoid false expectations, it was better to share with them as little as possible.

It felt uncomfortable to speak to a stranger who knew things about her because someone had told him. If she found out who that was, she would give them a piece of her mind. But it could have been anyone. Even Geraldine and Cassandra, who were new to the clan, knew about her children.

"My mother was also super fertile for a goddess. She had five children, while most of the goddesses she'd known had been lucky to have one. I probably inherited my super fertility from her, and my human side made me even more so."

"Your sisters were not so blessed." Orion halted. "Hold on. It just dawned on me that you said five. Annani talked about four children."

"Lilen was killed in battle. He was born between Kian and Sari."

Even though it happened centuries ago, it still hurt to talk about him.

"I'm so sorry." Orion put a hand over the one she put on his arm, the weight and warmth of it surprisingly comforting.

"It was a long time ago, and it plunged our mother into the depths of depression. She only managed to climb out of that black hole of despair when Sari was born. She was such an adorable baby. Kian and I doted on her. I guess we also needed help to get over our grief."

Orion nodded. "I know what you mean. I carried my grief around for a long time. I still do, but it's not as heavy as it used to be before I found Geraldine. For a while, life seemed a little better, a little brighter, but then she had a terrible accident, and I was terrified of losing her as well. Thankfully, she made it, and then Cassandra was born, and life got better once more." He flashed her his sexy roguish smile. "It's getting so much brighter now that I will soon need to wear shades."

Alena laughed. "It's winter, so we can get away with not wearing them. But summers in Southern California are brutal on our eyes. The sun is blinding."

He tilted his head. "So sensitivity to the sun is a common trait among immortals?"

"Only first-generation immortals like us. Although Amanda is less sensitive than Kian and I are, and Sari lives in Scotland, where the sunlight is manageable even in the summer."

Orion stopped and looked at the house they'd passed. "Did you notice that we are walking in circles? Isn't that the house I'm staying in? They all look alike, but I think that I would know the difference."

"You are right." Alena chuckled. "I wasn't paying attention, and I let you lead the way. What a lousy tour guide I am."

The roguish smirk was back. "On the contrary, you are the best guide I've ever had."

As she pondered what he meant by that, Orion lifted his head and sniffed the air. "I can find the way to the café if that's where you wish to go."

"You can smell it from here?"

He tapped his nose. "I adopted the name Orion for a reason. I'm a hunter."

Oh, boy, she was in trouble.

The predatory gleam in his eyes awakened the attraction she'd managed to suppress by convincing herself that he wasn't interested in her. But there was no way he'd missed the flare of desire that had shot through her a moment ago.

She needed to cloak herself in anger once more, but as hard as she tried, she just couldn't summon it.

Letting out a breath, she tugged on his arm. "Lead the way, oh mighty hunter."

42

ORION

$\mathcal{T}$he village café was teeming with people who said hello, nodded, smiled, and waved, and none of it was fake or forced. Alena was well liked, and because he was with her, everyone was friendly toward him as well.

After waiting in line with everyone else to get their cappuccinos and pastries—no special treatment for the goddess's daughter—they'd had to wait for a table to become available.

When a couple got up and waved Alena and him over, Orion had a feeling that they had done so out of respect for her.

"Thank you." She smiled as the male held the chair out for her.

"Have a lovely day," his partner said.

"I'm amazed at this place." Orion set down their tray. "The vibe is so positive." He took another look around. "Is it always this pleasant?"

"I don't know about always, but it is when I'm here. Not because of me, but because of my mother. Annani's presence in the village is a mood booster for everyone." Alena lifted her cappuccino cup and took a sip. "Being around her is like being plugged in. Didn't you feel that yesterday at dinner?"

The truth was that he'd been so preoccupied with thoughts of the demigoddess sitting across from him that his attention had been divided between her and Annani, which had probably diminished the impact of the goddess's electrifying personality.

"The Clan Mother is awe-inspiring." He said what he thought she'd expected him to say.

Alena smiled behind her paper cup. "For some reason, you didn't seem as impressed or awed as others upon first meeting her. Is it because you've already met a god?"

Orion thought back to his one meeting with his father. "Frankly, I was so angry at him that I didn't feel awed at all. He acted like a bastard and tried to get rid of me. I had to follow him and force my way into his house for him even to deign to talk to me."

"He didn't exude power?"

"Not like your mother. Even in my distracted state, I felt that Annani was a powerhouse."

"Why were you distracted?"

He smiled. "Why do you think?"

A lovely blush colored her pale cheeks pink. "You tell me." She still tried to hide behind that paper cup, holding it between her palms right in front of her face.

"I heard an enchanting siren's song on my way to Kian's house, and then I met a beautiful demigoddess, whom I recognized right away as the singer of that song. However, unlike most of the people at dinner, who were comfortable with me and didn't fear my evil compulsion power, she wore earpieces and did her best to ignore me. While her mother introduced me to my dinner companions, I kept thinking about the lovely demigoddess and stealing covert glances at her, hardly paying attention to the most powerful being in the world."

Alena's blush deepened. "I have an irrational fear of having my will taken away from me and my mind not being my own. I'm sorry if the earpieces offend you, but building trust takes time."

"What if I vow never to compel you for any reason?"

She looked into his eyes, assessing him, but even though he assumed the most innocent expression he could muster, Alena shook her head. "How can I be sure that you will keep your vow? You are very charming, and I like you, but I don't know you."

She was right. He'd vowed never to love again, and here he was, courting the goddess's daughter as if he could offer her everything she deserved, including his heart on a platter. Evidently, he wasn't very good at keeping his vows.

Except, that vow had been different. He had known then as he knew now that Miriam would have never wanted him to take it.

The vow not to use compulsion on Alena was simple and easy to keep.

"I can swear on my sister's life. You know how much Geraldine means to me."

Alena looked at him, her eyes stripping him bare. "I believe that you mean it, but you can't really make that vow. What if I hold a knife to Geraldine's neck, and the only way you can stop me is to compel me?"

"That's the silliest argument I've ever heard. You would never do that."

Putting her cup down, she leaned closer and assumed what she must have thought was an evil expression. "How do you know? You've just met me. I could be a psychotic killer."

Orion laughed. "I'm willing to risk it."

Alena threw her hands in the air. "I'm not the sweetheart that everyone thinks I am." She let out a breath. "I'm so tired of this role. I'm over two thousand years old, and I need a change of pace. Heck, I need a major makeover."

Leaning toward her, he reached for her hand. "You're perfect the way you are, but if you are not happy, make whatever changes that will make you so."

She loosed another breath. "I don't know where to start."

"Go out with me."

Alena waved a hand at their surroundings. "I am out with you."

"I mean on a proper date that is not in the village—a restaurant, a show, a movie, dancing—whatever is your fancy, I'm your man. Provided that your brother doesn't object, that is."

"Kian? He has no authority over me. I can do as I please."

"I know that you can, but I'm not sure that I'm allowed to leave the village. Kian has a Guardian watching me twenty-four-seven. I don't know if he'll allow me to go out with you."

"Let's check." She pulled out her phone from a pocket in her dress. "When do you want to go?"

"Tomorrow, if that works for you. Tonight, we are invited to Kalugal's."

"Thanks for reminding me." She cast him a small smile. "I forgot about that."

43

KIAN

*K*ian had spent over an hour with his mother, listening to her stories about how smart Toven was, and how she couldn't understand how he'd changed so much. With Alena gone on a walk with Orion, he hadn't wanted to leave Annani alone until her second guest of the day arrived, but the moment Ella and Julian had shown up, he'd bid everyone goodbye and rushed home.

What the hell was Annani going to do if Alena mated Orion?

Their mother needed a companion, someone to take with her on her travels, someone to talk to. She didn't do well on her own.

Did she expect Alena and Orion to live with her in the sanctuary?

Did she delude herself that Orion would happily give up his freedom and his business endeavors to travel with her and Alena all over the world?

Kian wouldn't put it past her. She'd coerced Wonder to move in with her and bring Anandur along, but the two had been so miserable there that she had to let them go.

Perhaps the best solution was for her to move into the village.

The sanctuary had been built a long time ago, before the village existed, and Annani loved it, but maybe it was time for a change.

They could convert the sanctuary into a vacation destination for the clan, or have people live there in rotations throughout the year, just to keep it from falling apart. A lot of resources had gone into building it, and it could prove essential in case of an emergency—a fallout shelter of sorts.

His phone rang as Kian was ascending the steps to his front porch, and as he pulled it out of his pocket, he was surprised to see Alena's contact on the screen.

Kian frowned. She almost never called him, and she was out on a walk with Orion. That could only mean trouble.

"Are you all right?" he barked into the receiver.

"I'm very well, thank you. Orion wants to take me out on a date, and he asks if he's allowed to leave the village."

Letting out a breath, Kian opened the door and walked inside.

His knee-jerk instinct was to decline the request, but he had no real reason to do so. Orion was not a prisoner, he was a guest, and he was not a bad choice for Alena, provided he wasn't hiding some dirty secrets or dastardly plans. But since Edna had cleared him, Kian had no excuse to veto the date other than his overprotective instincts. When it came to his mother and sisters, and even more so his wife and daughter, he was extremely risk averse.

If he said no, Alena would go over his head to Annani, and their mother was going to overrule him. His best course of action was to allow it but to insist on precautions.

Kian walked over to the couch and sat next to Syssi. "Orion is not a prisoner, and if he wants to leave, he can. But since you are going with him, you'll have to take at least one Guardian along."

Smiling, Syssi put down her tablet and leaned her head on his shoulder.

"Really?" Alena's tone was incredulous. "I don't need a chaperone, Kian."

Syssi chuckled and mouthed, "She doesn't."

"Not my rules, Alena. Mother's. I'm not allowed to go anywhere without two Guardians either."

"Amanda doesn't have to, and neither does Sari. Mother is worried about you because you are a potential target, but no one outside the clan even knows that I exist."

He sighed. "Humor me, Alena. We've known Orion for all of twenty-four hours. I'd rather err on the side of caution."

"Fine. We will need a car, though. Neither of us has one."

"Okidu can take you with the limo."

"I don't want to be driven around in a limo. Can we borrow your SUV instead?"

"When and for how long?"

"One moment." Alena muted the phone and came back a moment later. "We will leave the village Sunday at around noon and come back late in the evening."

"That's a long date."

"If that's a problem, I can ask Amanda if I can borrow her or Dalhu's car."

"She can have mine," Syssi offered.

He kissed the top of her head. "You can have the SUV. My only plans for tomorrow are to spend time with my wife and daughter, so I don't need the car. But Okidu will drive it, and you're taking Mason or one of the other Guardians with you."

"It's not going to be a very romantic date with a butler and a Guardian tagging along, but I'm willing to compromise." She chuckled. "I know that you regard this as a big concession on your part, so thank you. I want you to know that I appreciate it."

"You're welcome. I hope you'll enjoy your date." He ended the call and put the phone in his pocket.

"Alena and Orion," Syssi murmured. "They make a good couple."

"Annani thinks so as well."

"And you don't?"

"I think it's too early for matchmaking. Orion seems like a decent fellow, and Edna approved of him, but we know very little about him. If he proves to be as good as he seems, then he is probably the best match for Alena. A mating between them could also benefit the clan. If we ever find Toven, a union between Orion and Alena will ensure cooperation between him and Annani. An alliance with a powerful god like him could prove invaluable to us."

Syssi lifted her head off his arm. "From what Orion told us, his father doesn't care much about him or anyone and anything else. He might not give a damn about Orion and Alena's mating. He just wants to be left alone."

"Tough luck. Annani wants me to find him. I need to schedule a meeting with Orion and Onegus and talk strategy. Annani also wants us to find Toven's other children."

"If he had any," Syssi said. "Most gods didn't have more than one or two children. Your mother was very fertile for a goddess."

"You're probably right, but she wants us to help Orion search for them, and what Annani wants, Annani gets."

44

ALENA

*A*lena put the phone away and smiled apologetically. "I'm sorry about the escort. But just so you know, Kian is usually much more suspicious and careful about newcomers. That he agreed to let you take me out at all is a big deal. In fact, I'm sure he wouldn't have if not for my mother being here and pushing for us to get together."

She shouldn't have said that.

Orion looked like he'd just won the lottery. "Is she now?"

Alena shrugged, affecting nonchalance even though she knew that he could see through it. "She's interested in an alliance with your father. This is purely political maneuvering."

That was partially true, but not entirely. Annani thought that they were a good match, and she wanted to see all her children happily mated. But had she thought it through? Did she realize that she might lose her companion?

Orion put his large hand on top of hers. "I don't care what your mother's or brother's reasons are. I only care about yours. Do you want to go out with me because you like me and want to get to know me better, or are you doing it to please your mother?"

It would have been easy to tell him that she was doing it for Annani or for the clan, but that would be a lie, and it would hurt his feelings.

Letting out a breath, she pulled her hand from under his. "I like you, or at least the version you've shown me so far. But I've lived a long time, and I know better than to base my opinion upon first impressions. In my experience, there is almost always something rotten just underneath the surface, and often it's enough to just lightly scratch the decorative veneer to reveal it."

He gave her a roguish smile, his lips curving on one side of his mouth and creating a dimple in his cheek. "I might not have lived as long as you have, but I have spent most of it interacting with humans, so I assume that the sum of my experiences is greater than yours. And yet, I don't second guess my first impression of you. I know that nothing ugly is hiding under the surface."

Her gut instinct said the same about him, but Alena wasn't her mother, and she didn't act on impulses or feelings. She weighed each decision logically. That was why she was such a perfect companion for Annani.

Alena was the counterbalance, the voice of logic, and her mother relied on her to push back against schemes that were too dangerous.

Still, she didn't want Orion to feel guilty until proven innocent. The earpieces that she was still wearing were offensive enough.

She gave him an encouraging smile. "My gut tells me that you are a good male, but I'm a cautious female. Given my position, I have to be."

He seemed confused, but a moment later, his eyes started glowing as if what she'd said either angered or excited him. "Do you mean your position as the goddess's eldest daughter? Are you targeted by your enemies, the Doomers?"

Understanding dawning, her heart warmed. He'd thought that she was in danger, and his protective instincts had flared.

How sweet.

"Didn't you hear my conversation with Kian? The Doomers don't even know that my sisters and I exist. They are only aware of Kian, and not even by name."

The glow in his eyes dimmed. "So what did you mean by position?"

Should she tell him? What would he think of her spending her life as a mere companion? She wasn't a leader like Kian and Sari, or a scientist like Amanda. She was just a mother, and her mothering days were long gone.

"I'm Annani's companion," she said quietly.

"You are her right-hand daughter, then, her second-in-command. That makes you a target for your enemies whether you realize it or not."

Alena chuckled. "I'm nothing as important as that. Our mother leaves the management of the clan to Kian and Sari, who act as regents on her behalf. She seldom interferes in day-to-day matters, but she stays informed. My job is to keep Annani company so she won't be alone and also to keep her out of trouble. She's quite impulsive and adventurous, and she often disregards safety. My siblings count on me to rein her in."

"Do you enjoy it?"

She flipped her braid back. "It's never dull with Annani around. She keeps me on my toes and generates excitement the equivalent of a rollercoaster ride or a NASCAR race. I'm the opposite of her, and we balance each other well. Without Annani, my life would probably have been very boring."

45

ORION

Orion had a feeling that Alena didn't think much of her position as Annani's companion.

"You're very fortunate to have such a wonderful relationship with your mother. My father doesn't want me in his life at all."

She lifted her eyes to him. "If he had offered you a position as his companion, would you have taken it?"

He took a couple of seconds to think it over. "If what he did was interesting, involved a lot of travel, and wasn't evil, then yes. I would have loved to have the opportunity to spend time with him, learn from him. Alas, that wasn't meant to be."

"I'm sorry he was such a jerk to you. But it's his loss." She lifted her paper cup and drank the last few drops. "We've been hogging this table for too long. People are waiting for us to leave."

Orion doubted that was the reason they were being gawked at, but since he preferred to have this talk with her in a more private setting, he rose to his feet and collected their cups and plates. "Are you up for another walk?"

She followed him up. "Your house is twenty minutes from here, and I promised Mason to escort you back, so we are walking."

"If you're tired, I can find my way back on my own." He tossed the paper things into the recycling bin and the leftovers into the trash.

"I'm not tired." She waited for him to put the tray away. "I enjoy talking to you."

His heart soared like a schoolboy's. "I'm glad." He offered her his arm.

Her butler appeared out of nowhere and started trailing them.

"Where has he been all this time?"

"Helping Wonder and Wendy clean up," Alena said. "The Odus don't get tired, and they like being useful."

Since the Odus were machines, and therefore had no likes or dislikes, he assumed that she'd meant that they'd been programmed to be helpful. Or maybe they did have preferences?

"You still didn't tell me what the Odus' previous owner saved them from."

When she hesitated for a moment, he suspected that she didn't want the butler to hear, and when she looked over her shoulder, his suspicion was confirmed. "No one knows for sure," Alena said quietly. "We have a theory that is based on a vision, so it's not entirely reliable, but on the other hand, so far Syssi's visions have never been proven wrong, so what she saw might be a true account. It's also substantiated by some other bits and pieces of information that my mother learned' from her husband. I will tell you about it later, though. It might be upsetting to you-know-who."

"You said that he's a cyborg. Does he have feelings?"

"That's also a complicated story that I would rather tell you some other time."

"On our date?"

She leaned on his arm and whispered, "Only if he and the Guardian Kian assigns to us are far enough not to overhear." She lifted her head and smiled conspiratorially. "Tonight at Kalugal's might be a better idea. We are invited, but the Odus are not."

"Excellent. But as curious as I am about your butler, I'm much more curious about you."

"I think we've already covered my entire life. Would you like me to take you on a tour of the village's gym and training center?"

"Certainly, and on the way you can tell me more about your children. Do any of them live in the village?"

"Just one at the moment. The rest are either in Scotland or in the sanctuary."

"Where is the sanctuary?"

She tensed. "That's a well-guarded secret. So much so that neither I nor Kian nor my two other sisters can find the place. The only ones who know are Annani and the Odus, who fly us back and forth. But since no one can torture the information out of them, the secret of the sanctuary's location is safe."

"What about hacking into their brains? I'm told that there is no computer in existence that can't be hacked."

Alena snorted. "Perhaps if the gods landed on Earth and captured the Odus, they could hack into their stored data. But no human or immortal can penetrate a computer brain created by alien technology from alien materials."

"Fascinating, but we are back to talking about the Odus when I want to talk about you."

"I'm not nearly as interesting as they are."

"I disagree." He slowed his steps. "Did you have feelings for any of your children's fathers?"

Did she even know who they had been?

"Yes." She smiled. "Feelings of gratitude for the gift of motherhood—to the Fates for blessing me with an incredible fertility for an immortal female, and to the men for contributing their genetic material. Each of my children is a unique individual, and they are all good people thanks in part to the upstanding human males I chose to father them."

He tilted his head. "How did you know that the men you chose were good people if you only met them once?"

A soft blush bloomed on her cheeks. "I've never taken a male to my bed without vetting him first. For me, choosing the right males with the right traits was more important than physical gratification. Besides, the Fates made me fertile for a reason, and I like to believe that they had a hand in each one of the conceptions, allowing only the best to take root."

"So it was all about duty? About creating the clan?"

"Oh, no." She laughed. "I love children, and during the years they were growing up, I was the happiest and the most fulfilled."

"How far apart were your children born?"

She sighed. "It's strange, but I delivered all thirteen during the first five centuries of my life. After that, my fertility apparently ran out, which shouldn't have happened to an immortal whose body doesn't age." She looked at him from under lowered lashes. "And it wasn't for lack of trying. I wouldn't have minded having a hundred children if I could."

46

GERALDINE

*G*eraldine huffed out a breath and sank onto the couch. "I forgot how tiring it is to move."

Cassandra sat down next to her. "That was actually easy. We only brought over clothing. We still need to pack the artwork and all your knickknacks."

"The exhausting part is not hanging my things in the closet. It's the emotional drain." Geraldine sighed. "I'm going to miss our old house, which isn't old at all. It was brand new when you bought it, and it symbolizes so much." Tears gathered in the corners of her eyes. "You bought it after your big promotion. It was your way to show that you'd made it, that you'd succeeded, that you'd proven yourself."

"It's just a house, Mom." Cassandra draped her arm over Geraldine's shoulders. "You've always told me that a home is where your loved ones are, and since we are here, this lovely new house is our home. It's next door to Onegus and me on one side and Orion on the other. It doesn't get any better than that."

"Yeah, it does. If Darlene transitions and moves here as well, it will be even better. Since Orion is not staying, she can move into his house."

"Maybe he will stay," Onegus said. "He's just gotten here, and he seems very interested in Alena. They went on a long walk this morning, then spent over an hour in the café, and they are going on a date tomorrow."

"Awesome." Cassandra pumped her fist in the air. "Nothing like a good woman to help a guy make up his mind about staying."

"Alena doesn't live in the village," Shai pointed out. "If they bond, he will have to move with her to the sanctuary."

Cassandra shrugged. "Then we need to convince Alena to move into the village. I'll start the campaign tonight at Kalugal's."

Shai's expression remained doubtful. "Alena is the Clan Mother's companion. She can't leave."

"The Clan Mother will have to find a new companion," Geraldine said. "As a mother, she needs to think about her daughter's happiness first." She lifted her eyes to Cassandra. "It was difficult for me when you moved out, but I dealt with it because I wanted you to have a life with Onegus."

"Oh, Mom." Cassandra leaned and kissed her cheek. "I love you."

"I love you too, sweetheart." Geraldine scrunched her nose. "Are you busy tomorrow?"

"I don't have any plans other than playing house with Onegus. Why?"

"If I want to be able to visit my friends, I need to start driving again, but I haven't driven in so long that I've lost my confidence. Can you take me out for a spin tomorrow?"

"Sure thing. We can drive to the mall and pick up stuff for our new houses. I want to replace Ingrid's artwork with something more exciting."

Geraldine winced. "I'm not ready for such a long drive. I need to start on a deserted road where I can't hurt anyone."

"I'll take you," Shai said. "I've put in an order for a clan car for you. It should get here in about three weeks."

"Thank you." Geraldine rose to her feet, walked over to him, and kissed him lightly on the lips. "Why didn't you tell me sooner?"

"The order went out only yesterday, and I thought to surprise you when the car got here, but since it's such a long wait, you would've asked about it eventually, and I would've told you anyway."

"That's so sweet of you." She kissed him again. "I need to come up with a good story to explain to my friends why they can't visit me in my new place."

"You can use the same story—" He stopped himself. "You know, the one about your fiancé working for a reclusive billionaire who demands that his employees and their families live on his estate, but doesn't allow visitors."

That was the story Shai had told Rhett, but Cassandra and Onegus didn't know about the son he'd kept a secret for nearly twenty years. It was so sad that Shai had to be a lawbreaker to be part of his son's life. The stupid law that prohibited immortal males from sharing the lives of their children had to go.

Perhaps she could mention it tonight to Kian or even the goddess herself. But if she did, they might wonder why. She could make it sound like a random thought, and with her fragile mind, no one should think much of it. They would just assume that she'd gotten confused.

Except, it would stress Shai out, so maybe she shouldn't.

"When is Orion taking Alena on a date?" Cassandra asked. "I mean, what time?"

Onegus arched a brow. "Why?"

"I just thought that if Orion is busy with Alena, we can call Darlene and invite her to have lunch with us. I spoke with her yesterday, and she said that Leo wasn't back yet. His business trip got prolonged."

"What does that have to do with Orion?" Onegus asked. "Do you want her to meet him?"

"No, not yet." She turned to Geraldine. "I didn't make any plans with Darlene because I knew that you wanted to spend as much time with your brother as possible before he left, but since he's going out on a date with Alena and won't be here anyway, we can move our plans regarding Darlene a step forward."

47

KIAN

"Kalugal's mansion is so impressive," Syssi said as Okidu drove the large golf cart over the bridge into Kalugal's section of the village.

"What you see is just what's above ground," Kian said. "Most of the structure is underground, and it's much grander on the inside."

"I know." She smiled at him. "I have seen the blueprints. But I didn't see the façade Gavin designed. He did a magnificent job of making the visible section impressive despite its modest size and security limitations. Hiding the structure from passing aircraft is one heck of an architectural challenge."

Syssi's comment on security had Kian seeking out the hidden cameras aimed at the bridge, but he couldn't detect them even though he knew they were working just fine. William's crew had done a good job of making them invisible.

If Kalugal had discovered them, he hadn't done or said anything about them. They were still transmitting images twenty-four-seven to the clan's security center. But that was the extent of what Kian had done to keep an eye on his cousin and his men. There were no Guardians posted on or near the bridge, and there was no gate either.

Only a small fraction of the security measures he'd originally planned for the place had ended up being implemented.

During the months it had taken to complete the building project, Kian's mistrust of Kalugal had significantly lessened. He no longer worried about his cousin making a move against the clan, but that didn't mean that he knew what Kalugal was up to. He and his men spent long hours in their city office building, including Saturdays and some of them even on Sundays.

That was a significant departure from the days of Kalugal not having enough work to keep his men busy.

It occurred to Kian that he had a new tool in his arsenal to use to find out what Kalugal was working on.

Orion was not bound by Annani's compulsion, and he was a powerful compeller

134

who could ask one of Kalugal's top men a few questions on Kian's behalf. He wouldn't dare to refuse the request, especially now that he was interested in Alena and needed the clan's help to search for his father and siblings. The guy had a lot to gain by helping out.

Furthermore, as long as Kian didn't use the information against his cousin or his men, getting some questions answered was not a violation of the accord.

Kalugal, however, might be of a different opinion.

When Okidu parked the golf cart behind the smaller one that Anandur had driven over, Kalugal and Jacki came out to greet them. The couple waved hello at the brothers and their mates and then walked over to the larger cart.

"Good evening, my dear family." Kalugal rounded the vehicle to where Annani was seated and offered her a hand to help her down. "Welcome to our home, Clan Mother."

"Thank you." She took his hand and let him assist her. "It is very impressive."

Kalugal offered his hand to Alena next.

"Give me both hands," Amanda told Dalhu. "I'm a whale. I need a crane."

"You're not a whale, but you have a crane." He put his hands under her armpits and lifted her down.

"Where are the little ones?" Jacki asked as Andrew and Nathalie got out of the long limo-style golf cart.

"Ella, Wendy, and Lisa are watching Allegra, Ethan, and Phoenix. We decided to get babysitters and have us a grownup evening." She winked at Syssi.

When everyone disembarked, Okidu got back behind the wheel and drove to pick up the second group of guests.

"Aren't they too young to take care of babies?" Kalugal asked.

Syssi winced. "Phoenix and Ethan are not a problem, but I'm worried about Allegra. She's still so tiny."

"Don't worry," Amanda said. "Ella has plenty of experience babysitting. She helped Vivian raise Parker, and he grew up to be a fine young man. Besides, you're five minutes away. If Allegra gets fussy, Ella can call you, and you can rush over."

"Yeah, you're right." Syssi forced a smile. "I should trust her."

Syssi had wanted to leave Allegra with Okidu, but Kian still didn't feel comfortable doing so. He trusted Okidu, but not a hundred percent. Not enough to leave his vulnerable little daughter with him.

Jacki and Kalugal led them up the steps, and as Kalugal opened the massive front door, he turned to his wife. "Should we wait with the grand tour until everyone arrives?" .

"We can do two tours." Jacki put a hand on his chest. "I'll lead the first one while you wait out here for the others and give them a tour when they arrive."

Kalugal didn't look happy, and Kian knew why. He wanted to show off, and he wanted to see Kian's reaction to the extravagant opulence.

Heck, why not.

He didn't mind letting the guy enjoy his moment.

"How about we take a tour of the grounds while we wait for the others," Kian offered. "And then both of you can share the joy of giving everyone a tour of the interior."

Kalugal looked to his wife for approval of Kian's plan.

She nodded. "Good thinking. We will do it your way."

48

ALENA

*A*s Orion and the other guests arrived, Alena's heart did a happy flip and started beating like a frantic butterfly.

After they were done saying their helloes, and Kalugal led them inside his mansion, Orion fell in step with her.

"Did you get any rest?" he asked.

"My mother had visitors, and my presence was required."

"You must be tired."

"Not at all."

She'd spent the afternoon smiling and nodding and pretending to listen, while replaying her morning with Orion in her head and going over their conversation so she wouldn't forget any of it.

"How about you? How did you spend your afternoon?"

"I watched *Frozen* again."

She chuckled. "You didn't."

"I did, and I enjoyed every moment of it." He leaned closer to whisper in her ear. "I want to hear you sing it again, preferably just for me."

Was he actually interested in hearing her sing, or was it a sexual innuendo?

"Aboveground, we have the entry, the family room, the secondary kitchen, and the staff bedrooms." Kalugal headed toward a wide staircase that led to the lower level. "The main living quarters are underground. But don't worry, it's not stuffy or dark. We have motorized skylights that can be opened to allow fresh air in, and there is plenty of natural light."

Kalugal's house was amazing, and it reminded Alena of the sanctuary, just without the indoor tropical paradise built under a dome of ice.

If someone flew a drone high over his house, they would only see treetops. Just as in the rest of the village, clever mirror placement multiplied the visual greenery and hid the rooftops. If the drone flew lower, under the tree canopies, it would see an average-sized home with expensive finishes, manicured grounds, and what looked like reflective tiles embedded in the ground in between shrubs and bushes and flower beds. Those tiles were actually the skylights, coated with reflective material and angled so they reflected the greenery.

It was just as luxurious as the sanctuary, but not nearly as large. Then again, the only people living in the house were Kalugal and Jacki and a staff of two, while the sanctuary was home to over seventy people.

"Here is our home gym." Kalugal pushed the double doors open. "It includes a lap pool a hundred feet long—that's two-thirds of a regulation Olympic pool."

"I'm impressed," Orion said. "But what do you need a private pool for? The one in the clan's training center is true Olympic size, and it's available to everyone."

"I like my privacy." Kalugal put an arm around Jacki's rounded middle. "And I don't like anyone gaping at my wife while she's in a bikini."

"Kalugal is a snob," Kian murmured next to Orion. "And he's a competitive bastard. Since I have a lap pool in my backyard, he needs to have a bigger one."

Alena stifled a chuckle.

"Are we done?" Amanda asked. "It's not easy walking around with this belly."

"Yes, of course." Kalugal led them out into the wide hallway. "Just one more room to see." He pushed another set of doors open. "Our twenty-four-seat home theater. After dinner, we can come here and watch a movie."

"You must be doing very well for yourself," Kian said. "This must have cost a fortune, and you also doubled your donations to our cause, for which I haven't thanked you yet. Your contribution is much needed and appreciated."

"You're very welcome." Kalugal cut a sidelong glance at Annani. "But that was Jacki's doing. She convinced me that if I expect my good fortune to continue, I need to contribute some of it to a good cause. The two causes I chose were the clan's fight against traffickers and another organization that fights world hunger." He puffed out his chest. "Frankly, I didn't think that donating would make me feel so good. I started the donations as a bribe, and I didn't expect to keep making them for long, but Jacki was right when she said that it was the right thing to do. I feel like I'm making the world a little better and paying forward the good fortune I've been given." He smiled lovingly at his wife.

Annani put her hand on his arm. "Areana will be proud of you when she hears this. I assume that you did not tell her yet because she did not mention your increased contributions when we talked last week."

"What I want to know," Kian grumbled, "Is how you make all that money. Is it all stock market gains?"

"In a way, but not exactly. I'll tell you about it over cigars and whiskey after dinner."

49

ORION

*K*alugal put his fork down and wiped his mouth with a napkin. "I would like your honest opinion, Orion. Now that you can compare Atzil's cooking to the Odus's, whose is better?"

The dinner served by Kalugal's cook hadn't been as fancy as the one served by Kian and Amanda's butlers, but the food was tasty in a hearty way that he preferred.

"It's a matter of taste." Lifting his wine goblet, Orion took a sip while catching a glimpse of the cook's white apron peeking from behind the opening to the kitchen. "I enjoyed Atzil's cooking more because I prefer simpler, heartier dishes. The Odus prepared a sophisticated meal, which probably appealed more to others."

Kian chuckled. "You're a politician, Orion."

"I told the truth and nothing but the truth. But if we are already talking about the Odus, I would like to know what their previous owner saved them from by sending them to Earth." He shifted his eyes to Syssi. "Alena told me that you had a vision about that."

As all eyes turned to Alena, the silence around the table was deafening.

"Was that supposed to be a secret?" she asked. "Because no one told me that it was."

Kian was shooting daggers at his sister, but he didn't say a word.

"It is not a secret," Annani said, defusing the tension. "My father-in-law found the Odus in the desert, and they immediately recognized him as their master." She looked at Orion. "They had been programmed to find a god and become his or hers, but other than that, all their other previous programming had been wiped. They only retained basic functioning and learning capabilities. My father-in-law told Khiann that the Odus had been created to be servants. He hinted that they had been misused in warfare and that the winning side decided to decommission them, and the technology of how to make them was erased. We speculate that the owner of the seven did not wish to see them destroyed and sent them to a distant colony of the gods where he believed they would be appreciated."

Syssi put her napkin over her plate. "In my vision, I saw scores of Odus being loaded into shuttles. Nothing was said in that vision, so I don't know for sure that they were being loaded to be ejected into space, but the feeling was somber, depressing."

"Perhaps they were loaded on the shuttle to be sent into battle," Orion suggested.

"Perhaps." Syssi lifted her wine goblet. "That would be a somber event as well."

Kian still looked as if someone had pissed in his soup, and Orion had a strong feeling that it was in his best interest to steer the conversation away from the subject of the marvelous Odus. For some reason, Kian either didn't like talking about them, or he didn't want Orion to learn too much about them.

Not that he could blame the guy. A greedy person might decide to steal one of those amazing creations and sell it to the highest bidder. Human AI was nowhere near as sophisticated, and companies working on developing it would pay many millions to put their hands on a perfectly functioning cyborg so they could reverse engineer it.

Assuming an amiable expression, he turned to their host. "Something you said during the tour intrigued me. You said that you started donating to the clan's humanitarian cause as a bribe. Was that in exchange for Kian allowing you and your men to live in the village?"

Kalugal looked at his wife, who smiled and nodded, and then at Kian, who shrugged. He took Jacki's hand, lifted it to his lips, and kissed it. "I did that to win Jacki's love."

"He kept me as a hostage," Jacki said. "He scared the hell out of me just to verify that what Kian had told him was true, and to make amends and convince me to give him another chance, Kalugal made me a deal. For every day that I agreed to stay with him, he would donate twenty-five thousand dollars to the clan's charity."

Orion arched a brow. "That's a lot of money. He must have done something really bad."

"Oh, he did." Jacki cast a mock stern look at her husband. "But he apologized profusely and paid for it dearly, so I forgave him."

50

KIAN

*A*fter coffee had been served, Atzil's chocolate soufflé had been devoured, and Annani had invited everyone present to celebrate the winter solstice at her place, Kalugal rose to his feet. "Whoever wants to join Kian and me for whiskey and cigars out in the gazebo, please follow."

As usual, the ladies were happy to see them go. Kian could only imagine what they talked about when the men were not around, but he didn't care as long as Syssi enjoyed herself. She loved being a mother, but he'd noticed that she'd become restless lately, and this outing without Allegra was good for her.

For a change, she could spend time with her friends, not as the hostess but as a guest and without having to keep an ear on the baby monitor and rush out the moment Allegra uttered a sound.

Kalugal led them up the stairs and into his garden, which was walled off by greenery rather than a fence. A gazebo on a raised platform was already set up with a couple of bottles of superb whiskey and a box of cigars, the fire pit in its middle warming up the night's chilly air.

"I hope you approve." Kalugal opened the lid. "I got us genuine Cohibas from a reliable source. Those are not fake, my friends. Enjoy."

Seated around the fire pit, each holding a cigar in one hand and a glass of whiskey in the other, they took a few moments to savor the tastes, the smells, and to compliment their host.

It was decadent.

Kian had never felt like a privileged rich male when he smoked in his modest backyard. It felt like a well-earned reward after a long day at work, or when he had guests over, a way to be a good host and connect with his male friends.

At Kalugal's though, everything was grand, over the top, and screamed money.

Taking one more puff, Kian turned to his cousin. "So, what's your money-making secret?"

"I've always been good at spotting opportunities." Kalugal puffed on his cigar.

"But I have to admit that I was a little slow to jump on this one." He smiled at Kian. "But not too late to make a fortune."

He had their attention.

"You do like drama, cousin. Enough with the intro and give us the juicy details."

Looking even smugger than usual, he lifted three fingers. "Blockchain technology, cryptocurrency, and Web 3.0—the new true global democracy."

Kian shook his head. "Cryptocurrency is unreliable. It has nothing to back it up. It's just an imaginary construct and it can disappear into the thin air it has been created from."

Kalugal smiled indulgently. "I was of the same opinion when I first read about it, but I've since changed my mind, and I'm a much richer man for it. Especially since I minted one of the most popular coins, and it's selling like crazy."

The guy was a gambler, and minting his own coin was a genius move, but he could lose all that money just as fast as he'd made it. Besides, Kian was sure that cryptocurrency wasn't the only thing keeping Kalugal busy these days.

"Good for you." Kian took a sip from his whiskey. "But I'm not a gambler. I'm not investing in cryptocurrency."

"You'll regret it." Kalugal smirked. "The dollar is just as imaginary a construct as crypto, but unlike crypto, the government does whatever it wants with it. When they print money, they devalue the worth of what's in your bank, and there is no way to bounce back from that. That money will never regain its worth. Crypto is volatile now, but it will eventually stabilize, and the government can't put its greedy paws on it."

"I'm glad that it's working for you, and I appreciate the doubling of your contributions, but for now, I'm not ready to jump in."

"You don't have to invest in cryptocurrency. There is a lot of money to be made by investing in companies that develop blockchain technology and the new internet. That's more up your alley as an investor. Although, I know that you prefer a more hands-on approach. You don't like just putting in money, you like developing the technology."

Kian nodded. "You got me pegged, cousin. I find it much more satisfying to be part of the creative process."

"What is Web 3.0?" Orion asked. "I didn't even know that there was a Web 1.0 or Web 2.0." He smiled apologetically. "I was never tech-savvy."

"Web 1.0 was the beginning of the internet," Shai said. "Users passively surfed for information but didn't generate content. In Web 2.0, users generate content and interact with sites and other users through social media. I don't know much about Web 3.0, though. Is it run by artificial intelligence?"

"Web 3.0 is the new democracy," Kalugal said. "Currently, the internet is dominated by tech giants who censor users and exploit their data for profit, selling it to advertisers and to other more nefarious parties. There is hope that Web 3.0 will have a decentralized infrastructure. A lot of it will run on blockchain, which means that the data will belong to the users, and they will be compensated for it, not the tech behemoths."

"A brave new world," Anandur teased. "I want to learn more about it."

"That's a smart man." Kalugal waved his cigar in Anandur's direction. "Crypto currently represents seven percent of all global currency." He cast Kian a sidelong glance. "Do you really think that it's going to disappear? Just think how much more you'll be able to do for the clan and for the humanitarian causes the clan supports with the fortunes you can make if you jump on this spaceship before it breaks orbit and shoots for the stars."

"Nice analogy," Shai said.

Kian leveled his eyes on Kalugal. "What I want to know is what you're going to do with all that money."

"Conquer the world, of course." Kalugal laughed. "Money makes the world go round, right? So those who have the most of it determine which way it spins and at what speed."

51

ALENA

"Thank you for a fantastic evening." Alena kissed Jacki's cheek.

"I'm glad everyone enjoyed themselves." Kalugal walked them out the door.

Up front, Okidu and Onidu were waiting with the golf carts, but Alena wasn't ready to call it a night. She and Orion had barely exchanged a few words throughout the evening, and the morning they'd spent together seemed like it had happened days ago.

"Alena?" Kian turned to her after helping Annani into the cart. "Are you coming?"

"I'd rather walk some of this off." She patted her belly and smiled at Orion in a blatant invitation. "Anyone want to join me?"

He dipped his head and offered her his arm. "It will be my pleasure to walk you home."

Kian's grimace was enough to scare off the most ardent suitor, but Orion wasn't easily deterred and kept his expression neutral under her brother's hard stare.

Alena had known that Kian wouldn't approve. Other than Anandur and Brundar, they had no other Guardians with them, and Ovidu had stayed in the house, so there was no one to chaperone her. But she didn't need to be guarded from Orion, and she wasn't asking Kian's permission.

"Anandur will go with you," Kian said.

The Guardian didn't look happy, and she couldn't blame him. He wanted to go home to his mate instead of performing a needless task because Kian was an over-protective brother.

"Orion will suffice as Alena's escort, Kian." Their mother's tone brooked no argument. "I am sure he can handle any night prowler that might slither into our very safe village." She winked at Alena.

As a blush warmed her cheeks, she didn't know whether to be angry at her mother or grateful. Annani's wink and smile sent a clear message that she didn't expect Alena to arrive at their house anytime soon.

Orion bowed his head. "I'll guard Alena with my life. Goodnight, everyone." He didn't wait for a response before leading Alena out of Kalugal's front courtyard.

"I'm sorry about that," she said quietly. "It's nothing personal against you. He would have done the same with any male other than a clan member." She let out a breath. "Kian is trying to adapt to the times, but he is still such a damn chauvinist. If the roles were reversed, and I was a clan male and you a newfound immortal female, he wouldn't have been worried one bit."

"I don't think that's true. Kian is more worried about me than others because of my compulsion ability." He cast her a bright smile. "Thank you for not wearing the earpieces tonight. I take it as a vote of confidence and trust in me."

She reached into her pocket and closed her hand around the two small devices. Coming here tonight, she hadn't planned on being alone with Orion, and she'd been sure he wouldn't use compulsion with Annani around, but now that they were alone, a sliver of fear crept into her heart.

"I have them in my pocket," she admitted. "But I'm not going to put them in. I trust you."

He stopped and turned to face her. "You can't imagine how much that means to me. You can be absolutely sure that I will never compel you to do anything."

"What if I ask you to do it?"

"Why would you?"

Smiling, she threaded her arm through his and resumed walking. "Amanda once asked Kalugal to compel her not to crave cheese. She's a vegetarian, but she wanted to go full vegan like Kian."

"Did he do it?"

"He wasn't happy about it, but after some convincing, he did, and it worked. Amanda couldn't touch cheese for days. But then she got tired of it and asked our mother to remove the compulsion."

Alena had told Orion the story as a subtle hint that she wasn't completely helpless against his compulsion. If need be, Annani could free her from it.

"Your mother must be more powerful than Toven, both in ability and in strength of character. After the demise of the gods, he allowed ennui to overtake his soul, while Annani found a worthy goal to keep her going. I kept watching her tonight and admiring how lively and passionate she is. The contrast was so stark."

"Don't judge your father too harshly. We don't know what his story is. He might have started out like she did but failed and got discouraged and disillusioned. Fates know we had so many setbacks over the years that it's a miracle my mother never gave up. Not even after Lilen's death."

"That's what I meant by strength of character. Your mother kept fighting no matter what obstacles she faced. To me, that is even more admirable and awe-inspiring than her innate godly powers."

When they reached the house Alena shared with her mother, Alena regretted not being able to see whether the lights were on inside. For security reasons, all windows in the village had been equipped with motorized shutters that were timed to close at nightfall to prevent lights from betraying their location.

Orion climbed up the steps with her and stopped by the front door. "I don't wish us to part."

Was that a question in his eyes? Was he waiting for her to invite him in?

Her mother wouldn't mind, but Alena hesitated.

She didn't want to treat Orion like one of her casual hookups. It was nice to be courted for a change and get to know a guy before getting intimate with him. On the other hand, she hadn't been with a man for a long while, and Orion was sexy as sin.

"We can sit on the bench for a little bit," she suggested.

"Okay." He took her hand and led her to the wooden bench under the living-room shuttered window.

When they sat down, he hesitantly wrapped his arm around her shoulders, and when she leaned her head on him, he let out a relieved breath.

The guy was over five centuries old, and she'd managed to reduce him to a schoolboy.

Why was she acting so prim and proper with him? Especially given that her primal instincts urged her to throw him on the porch floor and rip his clothes off?

Because she was Annani's eldest daughter, and he knew who she was.

With human partners, she didn't need to act like a lady, she didn't need to act at all unless she wanted to play. She could assume any role—wanton or shy, assertive or submissive, passionate or reserved. It didn't matter what they thought of her because she never saw them again. She was never interested in getting to know them, developing a relationship.

It was easy to just bed a guy and leave. There was no emotional attachment.

With Orion, she didn't know how to act or what to do.

Because with him, she wanted more.

52

ORION

Orion was keenly aware of the goddess's presence on the other side of the wall. The power Annani radiated couldn't be contained by wood, plasterboard, and the best insulation money could buy.

He'd recognized its signature as soon as they neared the house, and now, sitting so close, he could no longer convince himself that it was all in his imagination.

Did the goddess's power dim when she slept?

She was awake now, he was sure of that, waiting for her daughter to return.

What was the protocol for courting a demigoddess?

Should he even be doing this?

He craved Alena as he had never craved a woman, not even the love of his life.

Miriam had been beautiful, soft and gentle, and he had loved her deeply. But even though he'd been a young man back then, the passion he'd felt for her had been a pale echo of the inferno Alena ignited in him.

The desire was primal, demanding, as if his body recognized its equal and was desperate for her—a strong immortal female who he wouldn't have to hold back with, who could keep up with his stamina, who could possibly exhaust him instead of leaving him only partially satisfied.

Damn, he felt so guilty for having those thoughts.

He wasn't in love with Alena like he had been with Miriam. The novelty of an immortal female was probably to blame for his raging desire, and once he bedded Alena and his hunger was satiated, he would be able to think clearly and examine how he really felt about her.

Except, this could not be a one-time thing for either of them, and if they crossed that line, the consequences would be significant. Especially for him.

Kian would murder him if he misled Alena or hurt her feelings.

Unless he was certain that he could offer her his heart, he should stop right now and find an excuse to cancel their date tomorrow.

The thought made his gut clench so painfully that he had to suppress a wince.

146

For a guy who prided himself on his cool head and decisiveness, the wavering between extremes was unsettling. For the first time in centuries, Orion wasn't sure about anything.

Logically, he was willing to let go of the vow he'd made centuries ago to never love a woman again, but his heart and gut were not in agreement.

Not consistently.

One moment he was convinced that Miriam would have wanted him to love again and that she would be angry at him if he squandered the only opportunity to mate his equal in every way—a demigoddess who would live as long as he did and not die on him within a few miserly decades. But the next moment he saw his long-dead wife looking at him with accusation in her tear-filled eyes, asking him if he'd ever truly loved her and calling him an oath breaker.

"What's wrong?" Alena asked. "You made a sound as if you were in pain."

"It's nothing. I remembered something upsetting."

"Do you want to talk about it?"

"Not really."

Alena looked offended. "I should get inside," she said quietly, but didn't make a move to get up.

"I didn't want to tell you about the thing that upset me because I didn't want to spoil the mood. I had a wonderful time with you today."

"It's okay." She smiled at him. "We barely know each other. You don't need to tell me anything that you're uncomfortable with."

He swallowed. "I'm not used to talking about myself. I've spent my life among humans, hiding who I was."

Her eyes softened. "That must have been so difficult, being all alone."

"I didn't realize how much until I got here, until I met you."

She smiled, and he wanted to kiss her so badly, but would he be able to stop at just a kiss?

And what about the goddess?

Would she rage at him for taking liberties with her daughter?

Rising to his feet, Orion offered Alena a hand up. When she took it, he slowly pulled her against his chest, giving her every opportunity to back away.

She didn't.

Closing the last inch of distance between them, she tilted her face up with a coquettish smile lifting her lush lips. "Am I getting a kiss goodnight?"

He wanted to tell her that she could get much more than that, but instead, he stifled the impulse and took her lips.

53

ALENA

*O*rion's lips were soft, smooth, his mouth warm, gentle, and as Alena twined her hands around his neck and kissed him back, the world and all of her earthly concerns receded, leaving only the here and now, only Orion.

Letting go of her lips, he leaned away and gazed at her with wonder in his eyes. "Your eyes are glowing," he murmured.

"So are yours."

One side of his lips lifted in a satisfied smirk, forming a dimple in his cheek. "Are they now?"

Immortal, she was with an immortal male, and everything about this kiss was different from any she'd received or given before.

"Your fangs have elongated as well." It was the first time she'd seen a male's fangs up close and imagining what he could do with them shot a blast of desire through her.

Damn, that was hot.

Orion smiled, baring those beauties for her to admire. "I've never smiled while aroused before. It feels like an unleashing."

And then he showed her what he'd meant by that.

His hands, which had been roaming over her sides before, slipped away, not to let go, but to secure a better hold on her. One gripping her waist, the other her hair, he tipped her head back and plunged his tongue into her welcoming mouth.

A soft moan leaving her throat, Alena gave herself over to the kiss, to Orion, and when a moment later he twisted them around and pushed her against the front door, she dropped her hands from his neck and cupped his glorious behind.

She'd been eyeing it hungrily all evening, and it felt just as hard and muscular as she'd imagined.

Encouraged by the move, Orion slid a hand down to her thigh and hoisted it up around his waist. Thankfully, her long loose skirt did not hinder the maneuver, the thin fabric allowing her to feel every delicious grind of his hard length against her core.

They were making a ruckus, and Alena had no doubt that her mother could hear everything, but she didn't care. She'd witnessed Annani seduce men often enough, and her mother had seen her do the same. They'd been careful to never take things beyond casual flirting in front of one another, but with their enhanced hearing, complete privacy had not always been possible.

When he left her mouth, she was about to protest, but then he began exploring her neck, his fangs scraping delicately over the soft skin, and her protests died on her lips.

She dug her fingers into his bottom, which earned her a stinging ear nip, and when she retaliated by digging her fingers deeper into the hard muscle, he seized her mouth again to plunder it.

Fates, how she wanted him to reach under her skirt, tear her panties off, and plunge that long, hard length into her. But they were out in the open, necking like a couple of horny teenagers, not by the front door, but actually leaning against it, and she couldn't allow a random passerby to catch her acting like that in public.

Uttering a frustrated groan, she pushed on his chest. "We have to stop, Orion."

He let go of her immediately. "I'm sorry." He backed away.

"Don't." She put a hand over her racing heart. "I loved every moment of it, but we can't be doing this out here."

His fully elongated fangs protruding over his lower lip, and his eyes glowing blue light, Orion was a gorgeous predator, and Alena wanted him so much that she had to bite her lips to stop herself from inviting him inside.

Annani wouldn't say a word, but it would be highly inappropriate.

"Come to my place." He reached for her hand.

"Not tonight," she heard herself saying. "We shouldn't rush into this."

Nodding, he wiped a hand over his mouth. "You're right. We shouldn't."

He didn't sound convinced at all, but she appreciated that he wasn't trying to pressure her.

"Good night, Orion." She leaned over and kissed him one last time, intending it to be a soft parting kiss, but Orion had other ideas.

His arms locking around her, he took over the kiss, and soon they were exactly where they had been a few moments ago, their lips and tongues and hands roaming, touching.

This time it was Orion who let go first. "I'd better go before I do something stupid and take you right here on this porch." He walked backward down the steps.

She managed a chuckle. "The clan's rumor mill would keep turning for months." She lifted a hand and waved. "Good night, Orion."

"Good night, Alena. Don't forget, tomorrow at noon."

"I'll be ready."

She opened the door and ducked inside.

Thankfully, it was dark, and there was no one in the living room. Down the hallway though, the door to her mother's room was open, and a movie was playing on the television—a comedy, given her mother's laughter.

Alena stopped at Annani's door. "I'm back, Mother. I'm going to sleep. I just wanted to say good night."

Annani tore her gaze away from the screen and gave Alena a bright smile. "Good night, my dear daughter. I wish you sweet dreams."

54

ALENA

*A*lena stood in front of her closet and looked at her collection of dresses. Why on earth had she donated the clothes Amanda had gotten her for the New York gig?

She knew perfectly well why she'd done it.

It had been too upsetting to see all those fashionable outfits hanging in her closet, remembering the fun she had while pretending to be a supermodel, and knowing that she had nowhere to wear them.

While traveling with her mother, they both tried to look as ordinary as possible so as not to call attention to themselves. Annani shrouded herself, but while it was effortless for her mother, keeping a shroud for a prolonged period of time was tiring for Alena. Besides, dressing plainly did the trick for her. She was pretty, but she wasn't a stunning beauty like her mother or like Amanda.

Except, now she had nothing to wear for her date with Orion.

Perhaps she should call Amanda and go over to her place. They were almost the same height, with Amanda being about an inch taller but slimmer, or she had been before the pregnancy. Before, Amanda had also been less endowed, but the difference had shrunk to about half a cup size, if that.

Hopefully, she hadn't donated all her pre-pregnancy clothes, which knowing her sister was very likely.

Amanda was a fashionista, and she seldom wore the same article of clothing more than a few times before donating it. She probably planned on getting a whole new wardrobe as soon as she regained her pre-pregnancy figure.

"Here you are." Her mother glided in through the open closet door, the glow from her luminescent skin casting light on the row of dresses. "Are you hoping new outfits will materialize if you stare at your closet for long enough?"

"I don't have anything nice to wear for my date with Orion. I love my comfortable, soft dresses, but no one else does. He will not be impressed if I show up in one of these."

Annani chuckled. "Orion will not care what you are wearing, my dear. You can show up wearing a potato sack, and he will still look at you as if you are the most beautiful woman he has ever seen because you are."

"Thanks for the pep talk." Alena leaned down and kissed her mother's cheek. "But for this date, I want to look like a young woman from this generation. I'll call Amanda and ask her if she can lend me one of her outfits."

"That is a very good idea. Your sister loves giving makeovers, and you will make her day by requesting one." Annani took a quick glance at the mirror and flipped the mass of her red hair back. "I will be out most of the day and evening, visiting clan members, so enjoy your time with Orion and do not hurry to come back." She smiled. "In fact, you do not have to come back tonight at all." She winked at Alena and then motioned for her to dip her head so she could kiss her cheek. "Have fun, sweetheart."

"Thank you, Mother. I will."

"Oh, before I forget." Annani turned around. "We need to get decorations for our solstice celebration and put them up, so do not make plans with Orion for tomorrow, unless he wants to come over and help, that is."

"I'll ask him."

"Are you inviting Eva and Bhathian?"

"Would they be offended if I did not?"

Alena shrugged. "You have to draw the line somewhere, or you will have to invite the entire clan."

"Indeed."

When Annani glided out of the closet, Alena pulled out her phone and called Amanda.

"Good morning, Alena." Amanda sounded breathless. "To what do I owe the pleasure of you actually picking up the phone and calling me at eight in the morning on a Sunday?"

"Did I wake you up?"

"No, but I was lounging in bed with a book, and my phone was in the kitchen. Do you know how hard it is to get up and then run with a belly this size?"

Alena cleared her throat.

"Oh, right. You do. My bad. I'm not thinking straight this early."

"So I guess coming over to borrow an outfit for my date with Orion is out of the question?"

"Are you kidding me? I would not miss such a rare opportunity. Be here in ten minutes. I'm getting dressed and having Onidu brew us coffee."

Alena chuckled. "I'm on my way."

5 5

ORION

*O*rion walked into the living room wearing a white button-down shirt, gray slacks, and black dress shoes. He thought that he looked quite dashing, but the grimace on Geraldine's face said otherwise.

"Why are you making that face?"

"Is that what you are going to wear?"

He looked down at his slacks, searching for a stain or a crease, but they were clean, and he'd just ironed them. "What's wrong with it?"

"You look like an insurance salesman. A very handsome one, but still. Don't you have a nice pair of jeans and a polo shirt?"

"I don't wear jeans. I detest them. The most casual pair of pants I have is light gray linen, and those are summer pants."

"Let me see." She rose to her feet.

He shook his head. "You're not going into my bedroom. Wait here, and I'll get them."

Her eyes sparkled with interest. "What are you hiding in there?"

"A big mess," he cast over his shoulder.

It wasn't that bad, but he hadn't made the bed, and his clothes were still in the suitcase, which was indeed quite messy.

The pair of linen pants were badly wrinkled, and he debated whether he should show them to his sister.

He enjoyed her being there, advising him on what to wear on his date with Alena even though he didn't need advice.

It just felt nice.

Geraldine had always been a good listener, and he'd shared many things with her before, but the difference was that this time he wouldn't have to make her forget what he'd told her.

It was such a relief to see her happy and healthy and dealing well with her memory issues. He wondered whether having a mate with an eidetic memory was beneficial to her, or did Shai just make her happy.

What a strange and lovely pair they made.

Perhaps those Fates the clan believed in knew what they were doing, and maybe pairing him with a female who had a strong aversion to compellers wasn't their idea of a joke but a way to heal old wounds.

Alena didn't remember anyone compelling her to do something she hadn't wished to do, but if part of the compulsion was to forget the encounter with the compeller, she wouldn't remember it, and there was nothing that could be done to retrieve that memory.

The goddess had been able to override Kalugal's compulsion of Amanda because she'd known precisely what he had compelled Amanda to do. In Alena's case, that couldn't be done. Annani couldn't compel her daughter to remember something she'd forgotten without knowing what it was.

The only thing the goddess could do was to thrall Alena and have a look at her memories, but if the compulsion to forget had been strong, even that probably wouldn't work.

Holding the pair of linen pants in his hand, Orion returned to the living room and sat on the couch next to Geraldine. "How did the goddess retrieve your memories of me? Did she just tell you to remember, and you did?"

Geraldine shook her head. "The Clan Mother asked me to relax, and then she spent a long time sifting through my memories. Why do you ask?"

"Alena is irrationally afraid of compellers. I suspect that she encountered a compeller before, and the experience was traumatic. Perhaps she can't remember it because she was compelled to forget it."

Geraldine's eyes widened. "Do you think Kalugal did that to her? Other than you and the goddess, he's the only one who could have done it. Oh, wait. I was told of one more person who can compel immortals, but I don't think Alena ever met him."

"Who is that?"

"His name is Emmett Haderech, and he used to be a cult leader, but then the clan caught him."

He was about to ask her more about that when a knock sounded on the door.

"That's probably Mason." Orion opened the door to let the Guardian in.

"Hi." Geraldine pushed to her feet. "I should be going."

Geraldine, Cassandra, and their mates were also going out for lunch to meet with Darlene, and the plan was to tell her about her dormancy and offer her immortality.

Orion thought that it was premature, and to do so in a public place was a mistake, but Geraldine had insisted that it was a rare opportunity to talk to her daughter while Leo was not around.

"If I didn't have a date, I would come with you."

"Why?"

"I don't think your plan for Darlene is a good one."

"Oh. We are not meeting her today after all. She called Cassandra and told her that Leo was coming back today."

"Good. It will give us time to come up with a better plan."

Geraldine eyed him from under lowered lashes. "You can't compel Darlene to agree. The decision has to be hers."

Did she really think that he would do that even if Darlene wasn't his niece? The only times he bent people's will to his was when it was either a life and death situation or they were trying to cheat him.

"I would never even try to convince her to consider transition, but I could compel her to keep it a secret, which would allow her more time to think it through. Thralling her to forget what you tell her only a few minutes later is not going to give her enough time. How can you expect her to make a decision like that on the spot?"

She let out a breath. "Yeah, that occurred to me as well. We will talk about this after your date." She lifted on her toes and kissed his cheek. "Have fun with Alena, but don't do anything to upset her."

"Why would I do that?"

Geraldine shrugged. "You're a nice guy, but sometimes people say things that they don't mean or that just come out wrong, and feelings get hurt. Alena is Annani's eldest daughter, and she's loved by her clan. If you do or say something stupid, you will wind up with a lot of enemies."

Smiling, he took her hand and clasped it between his. "I appreciate the sisterly advice, but I'm over five hundred years old, and think I know how to handle myself around a lady."

5 6

ALENA

*A*lena brushed nervous fingers through her hair. Amanda had trimmed and styled it the way she'd done for the New York trip, and she had also done Alena's makeup. It was subtle, and the change wasn't huge, but the eye shadow and mascara made her eyes pop.

Her sister hadn't been happy when Alena refused to have foundation on her skin, or blush, or lipstick.

She didn't like the caked-on feeling of cosmetics, and even the eye makeup bothered her. She'd put up with it during the New York mission because she'd been playing a part, but it was not needed for her date with Orion. For that, she wanted to be herself.

What a lie.

Glancing at the mirror by the entry door, Alena grimaced. The slim black pants and loose white blouse were not her usual style, and neither were the three-inch heels, but she craved change, and updating her appearance seemed like a good place to start.

It was easy.

The rest was not.

Leaving the sanctuary, no longer accompanying her mother on her trips, coming up with adventures of her own...

Was she ready for that?

Was it even happening?

Alena shook her head at her reflection in the mirror. It was only a date. She and Orion had shared one passionate kiss. It wasn't as if they were truelove mates ready to ride off into the sunset.

The moment she felt his presence on the other side of the door, her heart rate accelerated, and when the knock came, she took a long, steadying breath, forced her lips to curve in a smile, and opened up.

Orion looked splendid in a white button-down and a pair of gray slacks, the white accentuating his tanned skin and nearly black hair. He was a magnificent male, and she couldn't wait to peel these nice clothes off him.

As his eyes widened and then blazed with inner light, Alena's smile relaxed.

"Hello," she managed to chirp as she lifted her small purse off the entry table.

"You look different." He offered her his arm.

On the path behind him, Mason grinned like a fiend and gave her the thumbs up.

She threaded her arm through Orion's. "Good different or bad different?"

"Do you need to ask?" He led her down the steps.

"In fact, I do. This is Amanda's work." She waved a hand over herself. "The hair, the clothes, the makeup. I don't feel like me."

"It's still you no matter what costume you don, but I know what you mean." He smiled. "Geraldine said that I looked like an insurance salesman and asked if I had a pair of jeans. She was surprised that I didn't, but I never saw the appeal, and if I had worn a pair, I would have felt like an imposter. I guess it's because I'm old."

Compared to her he was a youngling, but even though he knew that she was over two thousand years old, Orion had never commented on her age, and Alena appreciated it.

"I can't stand jeans either. They are so uncomfortable."

He leaned closer. "I bet they would look good on you, though. You have amazing legs."

A blush creeping up her cheeks, she cast a quick glance over her shoulder at Mason, but the Guardian must have been listening to music on his earpieces because his expression remained neutral.

"You've never seen my legs," she whispered into Orion's ear. "So how do you know that they are amazing?"

A predatory gleam sparkled in his eyes. "I felt one around my waist, and it was perfect, and since it is safe to assume that the other one is its precise twin, they both are." He released her arm only to drape his over her waist. "I hope to see them in their full glory soon."

Alena didn't know whether to applaud his boldness or to be offended by it.

He'd been polite and reserved until their kiss last night. Had it emboldened him?

Pretending innocence, she arched a brow. "Is that an invitation to the beach? It's a little cold this time of year, but we can go to the pool in the training center. It's kept warm."

He chuckled. "Actually, the beach is where we are heading, but not for a swim. To do that, I'd rather take you to Hawaii or the Caribbean, where the water is warm year-round."

That sounded so lovely that Alena stifled a wistful sigh. "I would love that, but it is not in the cards unless you don't mind traveling with my mother and four Odus. Not that I know for sure that Annani would agree for you to come along, but since she likes you, she might."

"Can't you go anywhere without her?"

"I can, but unless it's necessary, I don't like leaving her alone."

"Was it ever necessary?"

"Once." Alena smiled. "I went on a mission to New York with a team of Guardians. It was so much fun."

"Are you allowed to tell me about it? I'm sure it's a fascinating story."

"Frankly, I'm not sure. I'll have to check with Kian."

He arched a brow. "You said that you don't answer to him."

"I don't, but when it's a question of security, and lives are at stake, I'd rather make certain."

Areana's communication with her sister and son was better kept confidential. Although most of the clan was aware of them, so it wasn't such a well-guarded secret.

"Lives at stake sounds ominous."

"It might be a slight exaggeration. By the way, where are we going? Did you choose a restaurant?"

He nodded. "Onegus recommended a place, and I have a feeling you will see some familiar faces when we get there." He turned to smile at Mason. "He didn't say anything, but I doubt one Guardian and one Odu are deemed sufficient protection for Annani's heir apparent."

57

ORION

*A*lena shook her head. "Annani is going to live forever, so the title is meaningless."

There had to be a reason the goddess was keeping her eldest daughter close, and Orion doubted that it was only because she needed a companion. She must be grooming Alena to become the next Clan Mother.

"What if she decides to step down?"

"She already has. Kian and Sari are running the clan, and our mother gives them almost complete autonomy. She's like the queen of England—a figurehead."

"I think she's much more." Orion smiled as he saw Kian's butler inside the pavilion, waiting for them with his chauffeur hat clutched in his hands. "Our other escort awaits."

"Hello, Okidu," Alena said. "Thank you for driving us today."

The cyborg's smile looked too human, too genuine for a machine. "It is my pleasure, mistress." He bowed his head. "But I do wish you would reconsider the limousine. It is so much more comfortable than Master Kian's SUV."

"I don't wish to draw too much attention, Okidu. The SUV is perfect."

Clearly disappointed, the butler bowed again. "As you wish, mistress."

The cyborg was quite opinionated for a machine. How intelligent was this AI? Or was that just mimicry and the Odu had repeated Kian's opinion?

Orion wished he knew more about technology. With his endless lifespan, he had the time to learn whatever he pleased, but he'd never been drawn to the sciences. He loved art in all its various expressions—drawings, paintings, sculptures, furniture, architecture, literature, poetry—but since he had no talent to create things, he collected them and sold them for profit.

When they reached Kian's SUV, Orion was surprised to see that it was an older model from more than five years ago. Surely Annani's regent could afford a new car every couple of years or so? Was he keeping the older model to avoid attracting attention? Or was the vehicle equipped with specialized technology that was deemed too costly to switch over to a new one often?

As images of the Batmobile flitted through his mind, Orion stifled a chuckle. Perhaps not being technologically savvy had its advantages. He could suspend disbelief more easily and let his imagination soar.

"What are you smiling about?" Alena asked as they settled in the SUV's back seat.

"I was wondering if this automobile could turn into an aircraft or a submarine like in the comics."

Mason, who sat next to Okidu, turned to look at him. "Are you a fan of comics?"

"I'm a collector, and furniture is not the only thing I deal in. A few years back, I found a box of original comics in an estate sale that was worth a fortune. I had some fun with them before selling them. I also watched the Marvel and DC Universe movies." He cast an apologetic glance at Alena. "I hope you don't think less of me for enjoying such trifling entertainment."

She laughed. "You watched *Frozen* three times. I think Marvel and DC are a step up."

He narrowed his eyes at her. "To have an opinion, you must have watched them as well."

"Guilty." She leaned her head against his shoulder. "They are fun to watch and don't leave me sad. There is enough sadness in the real world. When I need an escape, I prefer it to be a fun place."

"I couldn't agree more." He reached for her hand, enveloping it in his.

With Okidu and Mason listening to every word, they talked about many more trivial things on their way to the restaurant. It was located on a hotel rooftop and overlooked the ocean. Onegus had recommended it, and he'd even reserved two tables for them and asked that they would be within sight of each other but not too close.

The table the waiter escorted them to was the best the place had to offer, right against the railing, with the Venice boardwalk below and the ocean no more than fifty feet away.

People usually gawked at Orion, but with Alena at his side, most of the gawking rightfully went to her. She was a rare beauty, soft and feminine, but with an inner core of strength and determination that shone through her eyes.

Orion hadn't met Sari, but out of the three siblings that he had met, Alena was the best choice for Annani's heir. Kian was too focused on security and making money to support the clan and its various humanitarian endeavors. Amanda didn't seem interested in a leadership position. Alena was wise, coolheaded, and empathic, and he guessed that her mother had chosen and groomed her to step into her physically tiny but metaphysically enormous shoes.

Once the goddess decided it was time for her daughter to lead the clan, as a figurehead or more if she chose to, Alena could not only slide into that role with no difficulty, but she would also be accepted by the clan as its Clan Mother with no reservations.

58

ALENA

*A*fter their lunch had been served and consumed, Alena excused herself to the bathroom, not just because nature called, but because she wanted to text Kian and ask him if she could share with Orion the story of her New York adventure.

It wasn't that she needed to impress him. For some reason, he seemed overly impressed with her already, but she wanted him to know that she could be more than just the responsible and dedicated daughter everyone saw her as. She could be fun as well.

Kian's return text was short. *Just make sure no one other than Orion can hear you.*

Frankly, she'd expected more opposition and was surprised that he'd agreed so readily. He either trusted Orion or wanted to win him over.

With her mother pressuring Kian to find Toven, he needed Orion's cooperation, and that was probably the reason why he was being so uncharacteristically accommodating.

Her lips quirking in amusement, she texted back. *Aren't you afraid that Orion is Navuh's spy and that revealing Areana's secret rebellion might endanger her?*

His reply was *Very funny. I'm not that paranoid.*

As she put the phone back in her purse, Alena was suddenly worried that her teasing might have planted the idea of Orion being a spy in Kian's head. Despite his protests, her brother was paranoid enough as it was.

The next item on her agenda was figuring out where and when she could tell Orion her story. The safest place would be back in the village, but she wasn't ready to end their date yet.

She could cast a silence shroud around them, but with so many people on the rooftop terrace of the hotel, that wasn't practical, and a walk on the beach while wearing Amanda's pumps wasn't either. They were slightly too small and pinched her toes.

Perhaps Gerard could squeeze them in for dinner. His place was built to provide privacy for his clients, and he wouldn't dare refuse a request from his grandmother. She knew that he always kept one booth on standby for his star clients, and hopefully it was available.

Leaning against the sink in the ladies' room, she typed up a text and sent it, but she didn't stay to wait for his reply. *By Invitation Only* wasn't open yet, so he probably wasn't busy in the kitchen at the moment, but knowing her grandson, he didn't carry his phone with him. Not that she blamed him. If he wanted a moment's peace, he needed to turn the thing off.

Her phone buzzed as she returned to the table, and as she sat down and pulled it out of her purse, she had to smile at Gerard's answer.

How can I say no? Of course, I'll have a table for you and your date. I heard of Orion's capture, but I was too busy to come to the village and get a look at him. Thank you for bringing Toven's son to see me. Your reservation is for six.

Apparently, Gerard's curiosity was a stronger motivator than his love for his grandmother.

"Good news?" Orion asked.

"Yes." She put the phone away and leaned forward. "Have you heard of an exclusive restaurant called *By Invitation Only?*"

"I think so. Very rich people buy memberships for the privilege to make reservations, and then they have to pay extravagant amounts for the meal itself."

"You've heard right. My grandson is the chef, and he owns it together with Kian. I texted him to ask if he could squeeze us in tonight, and he said of course." She chuckled. "Not out of respect for his grandmother, but out of curiosity. He heard about you and can't wait to meet you."

Orion frowned. "I thought that all local clan members lived in the village."

"The vast majority do. I think Gerard and Brandon are the only exceptions."

"Which one is the chef?"

"Gerard is the owner of the restaurant. Even though he's much younger than Brandon, he's my daughter's son, and we are quite close. Brandon is my many times great-grandson, so to him, I'm more like a distant aunt."

Leaning forward, he said quietly, "Tell me about your children. Who are they, and what do they do?"

"Why do you want to know?"

"Because I want to know everything about you, and your children are no doubt a big part of your life."

"They are." She leaned back. "First came three girls—Sorcha, Morag, and Alisa. After that, two boys—Tavish and Malcolm. Then five girls—Blair, Una, Alison, Innis, and Lyell. Next, two more boys—Caelan and Arran. And last but not least, my youngest, Gavina."

"Nine girls and four boys," Orion said.

She nodded. "How about you? Did you ever have children?"

59

ORION

The question hit Orion hard.

He'd given up on having children centuries ago, and when he'd learned that he wasn't infertile, he hadn't internalized that until Alena had voiced her question.

He could one day be a father.

Could he, though?

What if he turned out to be a jerk like the god who'd sired him?

And who would he have his children with? Alena?

It had been on the tip of his tongue to ask her whether she wanted to have more children, but he swallowed the words. If she could have more, he had no doubt that she would.

For the clan.

"I never had children," he said instead. "I thought that I was infertile."

Her eyes turning sad, Alena nodded. "Perhaps you were lucky not to have fathered children. I can't imagine how terrible it is to outlive your offspring." She pushed a strand of hair behind her ear. "After Lilen was killed, I cried myself to sleep for years. During the days, I had to be strong for my mother, who just fell apart and was like a walking ghost, but at night I allowed the tears to flow." She let out a shuddering sigh. "Some nights, I wished not to wake up the next morning and face the gaping hole in my heart again, but I knew it was selfish of me to wish for death as a way out of my misery. My mother needed me, my people needed me, and quitting was not an option."

He reached for her hand and brought it to his lips for a soft kiss. "I wish I could have been there for you."

She smiled. "It happened before you were born. I'm ancient, Orion."

"You're like a superb wine, aged to perfection."

She chuckled. "That was smooth." Then the merriment faded from her lovely face, and she lifted their conjoined hands to her cheek. "Neither of us is a stranger to loss."

Someone must have told Alena about his wife, probably Geraldine, but it wasn't a secret, and eventually he would have told her about Miriam, but their first official date was not the right time for it. Then again, Alena had told him about her own devastating loss, so maybe he should share his as well.

"Did Geraldine tell you about Miriam? The woman I was married to a long time ago?"

Alena nodded. "Geraldine didn't mention her name, but she told me that you loved her very much and never truly recovered from her loss."

"Never is a strong word," he admitted. "It no longer feels like a gaping hole in my soul, but I still think about her often."

"Tell me about her."

He arched a brow. "Are you sure? Former loves are not what a couple on their first date should be talking about."

"Miriam helped shape the kind of man you are today. To know you, I need to know the kind of woman she was. But if it still hurts too much to talk about her, and you don't want to, I'll understand."

"It doesn't hurt." He let go of her hand, leaned back, and lifted the wine glass that the waiter had refilled for them while Alena had been in the ladies' room. "In fact, I need to talk about her so I won't forget. After nearly five centuries, my memories of her are starting to fade."

"You were very young when you married her."

"I was twenty-one."

Alena smiled. "The young love the most fiercely."

"We did, very much so."

"How did you hide your fangs from her?"

"I didn't. Miriam knew I was different and loved me anyway." He ran his fingers through his hair. "At first, I hid it from her, thralled her after each time we made love, but she was smart, and she figured it out. I was afraid she would think I was a monster, which was what I thought I was, but she said that I was pure goodness, and that having fangs might make me strange, but it didn't change who I was on the inside."

"She was a remarkable woman." Alena reached for her wine glass. "Especially given the time she lived in, with all the superstitious nonsense humans used to believe in."

"She was, and she was taken from me too soon. Miriam was twenty when I married her. She died at fifty-three."

"That was a good lifespan for that time. Back then, most humans didn't live past forty. Your venom probably kept Miriam healthier than most."

"I suspected that. She didn't age as fast as other women, and I hoped that was because she was with me. But I couldn't save her in the end." He lifted his eyes to her. "If I had known of your clan's existence, do you think your doctors could have helped her?"

Alena shook her head. "The knowledge my mother took with her out of Sumer was all about technology. Her uncle, from whom she pilfered the tablet, was an engineer and inventor, not a doctor. Back then, our healers knew no more than the human ones, and the same goes for today. We have no advanced medical knowledge. If we had, we would have shared it with humanity."

In a way, that was a relief. As it was, he'd lived with enough guilt for not being able to save Miriam, always thinking that there was something he could have done, some expert he could have found who would have known what to do. But if even the clan, with all their godly knowledge, wouldn't have been able to save her, then there had been no cure, and perhaps it was time to let go of the guilt.

60

ALENA

*A*lena had known that the walk down the Venice boardwalk was a stupid idea, and now her poor toes were paying for it dearly.

When Orion had suggested it, she hadn't wanted to admit the pinching shoe situation. Besides, a walk on the beach had sounded romantic, and she hadn't wanted to miss out on it just because of her footwear.

"What's the matter?" he asked when she winced.

"I'm not used to wearing heels," she said, admitting to a partial truth that was not as embarrassing as telling him about the half-size-too-small shoes she'd borrowed from her sister just because she'd wanted to look pretty and sophisticated for their date. "I don't know what possessed me to wear them."

"You thought that we would be sitting most of the time." He looked down at her feet. "Let's head back, and you can take the shoes off. After all, we are on the beach, so it's not a big deal to walk barefoot."

Knowing what went on in Venice at night, she'd rather not.

"That's okay. I'll survive a few more minutes until we get back to the car."

He glanced at his watch. "Can we arrive at that restaurant earlier than six?"

She laughed. "Gerard wouldn't let us in. He only opens the place at six. But we can go for a drive, and I can show you the sights. How familiar are you with the greater Los Angeles area?"

"I've never lived here if that's what you're asking. I have several wealthy clients who I occasionally visit in Beverly Hills and Bel Air, owners of high-end galleries who are interested in particular period pieces I specialize in, and there is Geraldine."

"Let me guess. You are unimpressed with the city."

He smiled apologetically. "Frankly, it's not very interesting. The architecture is blah, most of the stores are inside malls, and there is no real center. I like New York, Manhattan especially, and I like Boston. Other than that, most of my favorite cities are in Europe."

"You said that you travel a lot. Where is your home?"

166

He shrugged. "I don't think about any of the flats I own as home because I never stay long in one place. I treat them as an investment more than anything else. I have an apartment in Manhattan, a townhome in Paris, a flat in London, and a flat in Milan."

"You are a true international man."

He nodded. "You said that you travel a lot as well."

"I do, but other than that one New York adventure, it's always with my mother. We have our own jet, and our trips are usually short. We only stay a couple of days and then return home to the sanctuary."

"Why do you call it a sanctuary? Are the trafficking victims you rescue brought over there?"

"That would have been impractical. We have a local sanctuary for them. I think my mother started calling it that because it's a place of rest and relaxation. Using some of the gods' technology, the clan built an oasis in the snow for Annani."

"Alaska or some other eternally snowy place?"

Behind them, Mason cleared his throat, reminding her that she should be careful with what she said to Orion.

She ignored him. "It's in Alaska, but as you know, Alaska is vast, and the sanctuary is small. No one other than the Odus knows how to find it. They fly the jets in and out, shuttling clan members back and forth."

"On windowless planes?"

"Our jets use the same technology as the clan cars. The windows turn opaque." Not on Annani's jet, but he didn't need to know that.

Besides, even though she'd looked out the windows plenty of times, Alena still couldn't have found the sanctuary if her life depended on it. It was located in the mountains where there was always snow, and to her, one snowy mountain looked like another. Perhaps if she'd paid better attention, she could have memorized some distinguishing features, but navigation was never her strong suit.

"Is your home called sanctuary because it's the goddess's secret shelter?" Orion asked.

"That's one reason. Beside being my mother's happy place, it also serves as a safe place for expectant mothers. They come to the sanctuary to deliver their babies, where they are safe until they are ready to transition. Not all do, and we didn't have any for the longest time, but it's there for anyone who needs it."

"Is it a happy place for you as well?"

She took a moment to think about it, and then nodded. "When we have babies and children in the sanctuary, it is, but when many years pass without any young ones, it gets boring despite the waterfalls and the tropical greenery under a dome of ice."

"I would love to see the place. Do you think that I would be allowed?"

If he was her truelove mate, then yes, he would.

But was he?

The guy was still mourning the woman he'd loved even though centuries had passed. Had Miriam been his one true love?

He might think so, but a bond was only possible between immortals, or between a Dormant and an immortal, and Miriam couldn't have been a Dormant. She would have transitioned if she were.

When Kian had fallen in love with Lavena, he'd believed that she was his one and only, but falling in love so deeply was often a young heart's folly. Kian had been with Lavena for a little over a year, and if he'd been with her as long as Orion had been with his wife, he might have realized that she wasn't the be-all-end-all he'd believed her to be.

Orion had been married for thirty-three years, and his love for Miriam had time to mature and deepen. It hadn't been just a young man's infatuation—it had been the real thing.

When he'd lost Miriam, Orion had been so devastated that he'd vowed never to love again.

But then, he'd never expected to encounter an immortal female who would live as long as he did. That was a game-changer that Orion was well aware of.

Otherwise, he wouldn't be here with her.

Alena knew that he desired her, and he also seemed to admire her, so perhaps love was possible, but if they were truelove mates who'd been fated for each other, shouldn't they have fallen in love at first sight?

But what she felt for him was not love. It was a strong like with a hefty helping of lust.

As they reached the car, Okidu rushed to open the door for her, and as soon as she was seated, Alena kicked the damn shoes off and sighed in relief.

"I have an idea." Orion slid next to her. "How about we stop at a shoe store and get you comfortable shoes? I don't want you to suffer, and I also don't want to cut our date short."

She gave him a grateful smile. "That's so sweet and considerate of you." Not to mention sexy.

Imagining Orion kneeling at her feet and putting shoes on them was so damn erotic that she had to bite on her lower lip to stifle a moan.

He grinned. "So I guess it's a yes?"

"It's a yes, please."

Damn, she'd sounded like she was pleading for something that had nothing to do with shoes but everything to do with him kneeling between her legs.

61

ORION

For some reason, Alena seemed disappointed as they left the shoe store, but Orion didn't have the foggiest idea why.

She'd spent over two hours trying on nearly every pair of shoes they had in her size and had ended up buying four pairs. He'd tried to pay for them, but she wouldn't hear of it, had paid for them herself, and walked out in a pair of black pumps that looked as comfortable as they were stylish.

What had she expected from him that he'd failed to deliver?

A silly thought of another princess story flashed through his head, the one with the glass slipper. Had she wanted him to put the shoes on her feet?

He would have done so gladly, but only in the privacy of his bedroom. He would have kissed each toe separately, driving her crazy before dipping between those long legs of hers and kissing a much softer place. But to do so in a shoe store would have been scandalous.

Besides, Mason had been with them, so even the most innocent flirting had been out of the question. The most Orion was comfortable with in public was having his arm around Alena's shoulders or her waist and a chaste kiss on the cheek.

As Okidu pulled up in front of the valet station, Alena tapped Mason's shoulder. "You can't come in with us. Gerard won't have a table for you."

"I know. I'll stay in the car with Okidu. I've already cleared it with Onegus."

A guy in a blue blazer who didn't look like he was a valet waited until they got out of the car. "Good evening, Ms. Alena, Mr. Orion. I'm Caleb, your host for tonight."

"Good evening, Caleb," Alena said.

As they followed the guy through a lush garden, Orion leaned closer and whispered in her ear. "Are any of Gerard's people like us?"

She shook her head.

Good, so Caleb couldn't hear him. "Did I do something to upset you in the shoe store?"

"No, why do you ask?"

"You seemed disappointed when we left, but you liked the shoes, so I figured it must have been something I did or didn't do."

"It wasn't because of you." She took his hand and gave it a squeeze. "I got tired of us having no privacy and Mason trailing us everywhere." She looked at him and smirked. "That's why I came up with the idea to come here in the first place. I knew he couldn't follow us into the restaurant, so we could finally enjoy each other's company without an audience."

"Beautiful and clever." Orion lifted their conjoined hands and kissed her knuckles. "Am I lucky or what?"

"It depends," she murmured.

"On what?"

She shook her head. "Never mind."

It had been a long time ago, but Orion hadn't forgotten the lessons he'd learned from his marriage to Miriam. When a woman said never mind, it was a very bad sign, and the worst thing a male could do was to pester her to explain what she meant by it. The best thing to do was to wait until her mood improved and then prod gently, showing her that he hadn't forgotten and that he cared.

Lifting Alena's hand, he kissed her knuckles again. "You'll tell me when you're ready."

The doubtful look she cast him wasn't encouraging, but he was a patient man, and he would eventually get her to tell him what had bothered her.

Inside the restaurant, the host transferred them into the care of a pretty young woman who led them to a secluded corner booth. "Can I get you something to drink while you look over tonight's offerings?"

"Just water for me," Alena said.

"Sparkling?"

"Yes, please."

"Same for me." Orion picked up the wine menu. "I'll let you know our wine choice later."

"Very well." The waitress dipped her head and walked away.

"Gerard has a different menu for every night," Alena said. "He also keeps adding new dishes, which keeps the members coming back."

Orion cast a look around the opulent dining establishment, noting that all the tables were occupied. "He's definitely doing well for himself."

"Gerard will probably show up for a couple of seconds to satisfy his curiosity, and then we will not see him again. He's way too busy in the kitchen lording over his staff."

"I heard that." A smiling man in a chef's outfit sauntered toward them. "Alena, you look as lovely as ever, my dear cousin." He winked at her before embracing her briefly.

"Thank you." She smiled. "Gerard, meet Orion. Orion, this is Gerard."

The chef offered Orion his hand. "When I heard the news, I couldn't believe it. What an incredible coincidence that your sister and niece both found their way into the family and brought you to us as well."

"Indeed. The Fates must have been involved." Orion hadn't believed in fate or the Fates before he'd been captured by the clan, but he was becoming a convert.

Gerard cast him a knowing look. "My cousin is a very special lady. I hope you know that."

There was a threat implied in that statement.

"I do."

"She is loved and admired by the entire family. If anything were to happen to her, many people would be upset."

"I know that, and I can assure you that she's perfectly safe with me. I'll protect her with my life." He meant every word.

"You'd better." In a flash, Gerard's expression turned from threatening to haughty and condescending. "I must return to the kitchen. Thank you for choosing *By Invitation Only* for your outing tonight, and I hope you enjoy your dinner."

"I'm sure we will," Alena said.

62

ALENA

It was silly to feel disappointed over a fantasy that couldn't have been realized even if Orion could have read her mind. And yet here she was, sitting in a booth in the fanciest restaurant in town, feeling frustrated and antsy.

Perhaps her long hiatus from sexual activity was to blame, or maybe her valiant effort to hide her attraction from Orion had finally collapsed under the onslaught of his male pheromones.

She would have gladly skipped dinner and dragged him to the nearest private place where she could have her way with him.

Except, with Orion it wouldn't be enough, with him she wanted more, but his heart still belonged to a woman who'd died four and a half centuries ago.

Could she win his heart?

Her mother would not have shied away from the challenge. On the contrary, it would have made Orion even more appealing to her because he wouldn't have been blinded by her beauty and might have actually resisted her for a little bit.

Annani would have told her to fight for what she wanted, even if it meant going against a ghost, and not to give up until she won.

Her mother would have been right.

Hiding behind the two-foot-tall menu, Alena pretended to ponder the selection while contemplating her next move.

Tonight, she was going to seduce Orion, and the night after that, and the one after that, until he couldn't imagine himself going to bed without her, until he couldn't be apart from her for more than a few hours without missing her terribly.

The question was how to get rid of Mason.

After driving them back to the village, Okidu wouldn't follow them to Orion's house. He would go back to Kian and Syssi's. Mason would follow his orders, though, and at the end of his shift, he would be replaced by another Guardian.

Did she care that they would know that she spent the night with Orion?

If there were no Guardians assigned to watch him, she might be able to sneak out in the early hours of the morning and get back to her and Annani's place unnoticed.

The problem was that Orion's house was in phase two of the village, while their place was in phase one and right next to the office building. Someone would notice her slinking around for sure.

Except, why hide their relationship?

Kian had brought Syssi over to his place and had seduced her within days of meeting her, if that. Amanda had closely followed their story and had reported the highlights to her and their mother, but several years had passed since then, and Alena didn't remember all the details.

In any case, Kian hadn't courted Syssi for days on end, and no one had batted an eyelid over it. Why should it be different for her?

Just because she was a female and however many times great-grandmother of most of the clan didn't mean that different rules applied to her. If she wished to do so, she could spend the night with Orion and then bring him over to have breakfast with Annani for all to see that he was hers.

Stake her claim, so to speak, in which case the Guardians had to go for sure.

If she was making it official that she considered Orion a potential mate, Kian needed to stop treating him as a suspect.

Putting the menu down, Alena gave Orion a tight smile. "I need to powder my nose." She pushed to her feet. "I'll be back in a minute."

The perfect gentleman that he was, Orion got to his feet as well. "Have you decided on your selection?"

She hadn't read even one line on the menu. "Everything Gerard makes is delicious, so it's hard to decide. I'll ask the waitress to recommend a course." She gave him another come hither smile. "Or you can choose for me. We can share."

"As you wish." Orion remained standing until she turned the corner, staring at her with his blazing eyes.

Given that glow, he was just as hungry for her as she was for him.

In the ladies' room, Alena pulled out her phone and texted Kian. *I intend to spend the night with Orion, and I don't want Guardians snooping around. I also want you to stop the surveillance feed from the house. I don't want to feel self-conscious.*

The three dots indicating that he was typing kept blinking for a long time, but his answer was short. *Your safety is paramount. The Guardians stay.*

He must have typed several different answers and then erased them, but if he expected her to accept his final version, he didn't know her very well.

Alena typed back, *Did you have Guardians watching you when you and Syssi first got together?*

This time the reply came back quickly. *Syssi was human and harmless. Orion is neither.*

Alena ground her teeth. Kian had no authority over her. In fact, as the eldest, she could pull rank over him.

Theoretically.

She'd never done that before, had never felt the need, but as the saying went, there was a first time for everything. Alena typed, *Get rid of the Guardian, or I will. This is not a request, and the same goes for the feed—kill it.*

His reply was short and to the point. *As you command, sister mine. Just be aware that you're assuming responsibility for the consequences, whatever they might be.*

She answered, *I'm well aware of that. Thank you for not fighting me harder on this.*

Alena didn't expect an answer, but a moment later, another text came in. *Who am I to stand in the way of true love? It would seem that the Fates have spoken, and if not, and you are wrong about him, you can't blame me for not warning you.*

63

ORION

*L*eft alone in the booth, Orion tried to figure out what was bugging Alena. The answer she'd given him might have been true, but he doubted that.

Mason had been trailing them the entire day, but she hadn't been bothered by it until the shoe store.

His only clue was the scent of her arousal that had flared as soon as he'd mentioned buying a new pair of shoes, but he'd dismissed it as a female's footwear obsession.

Not that he'd encountered a woman who'd gotten sexually aroused by shoes before, but he'd read and seen films about men with shoe or feet fetishes. If males had a thing for shoes, why not females?

After all, Alena had ended up buying four pairs, so there was that. But although they were elegant and fashionable, he wouldn't call them sexy.

Practical was a more fitting description of the footwear Alena had selected.

But even if she had gotten stilettos, which Orion had to admit evoked erotic imagery, he wouldn't get excited by seeing them in a store or a box. On her feet, though, especially with nothing else on, that was a different story.

The waitress hovered nearby, waiting for Alena to return from the ladies' room, and as soon as she did the woman pounced with her pitcher of chilled sparkling water and a ready smile.

"Have you made your selections?"

"We did." Orion turned to Alena. "Do you still want me to order for you?"

She waved a hand. "Go ahead. Everything Gerard creates is superb."

"Thank you." The waitress inclined her head. "I'll convey your compliments to the chef."

"No need," Alena said. "He's heard it from me many times. We are cousins."

"Oh." The waitress's eyes widened. "That's nice," she stammered, probably not knowing what else to say.

Feeling sorry for her, Orion saved her from having to comment by placing their order. "I would also like a bottle of the Ovid Napa Valley 2016 red wine." He handed her the menus.

"That's a very good choice, sir." She smiled and scuttled away.

"You know that it will cost you a fortune. Gerard does not give family discounts. In fact, he wouldn't have made a table available for anyone else other than Kian and my mother on such short notice."

"Do I look worried?"

She smiled. "I just don't want you to think that you need to impress me. I'm already impressed."

He arched a brow. "I'm glad to hear that, but I don't know what I have done to earn that. I haven't done anything of note since I got here."

Her hands steepled in front of her mouth, Alena hid a small smile. "You survived on your own, and when you discovered your sister, you took care of her the best way you knew how."

"You must be easily impressed."

She shrugged. "Not really. I'm the daughter and companion of a goddess. It's not easy to impress me at all."

Alarmed, he glanced at the other tables. "You should lower your voice when you talk about her."

"There is no need to whisper in here." She waved a hand at the booth. "I cast a silencing shroud around us the moment the waitress left."

He hadn't known that was even possible. "Can you teach me how to do that?"

"Just imagine us encased in a bubble and then will it into existence. My shroud only works on humans, but yours might work on immortals as well. You have the power of a god."

"I'm glad that you are no longer afraid of my compulsion ability."

Alena leaned forward and leveled her eyes at him. "I trust you, Orion." She left it at that, but her eyes told him the rest. *Don't make me regret it.*

"I trust you too." He reached for her hand and gave it a gentle squeeze.

She looked confused. "What can I ever do to you?"

"You have enormous power over me, but I know that you won't use it. I trust you."

"Give me an example."

"You can get upset with me and tell your mother and brother that I'm a horrible person and that I shouldn't be allowed anywhere near the clan. You can also capture my heart and then break it."

She arched a brow. "Can I capture it, though? Is it even available?"

That was a poignant question, one he would have answered very differently only a couple of days ago. "It's not available to just anyone, but it could be yours if you want it."

64

ALENA

For a long moment, Alena was speechless. What could she say to that? What could be said?

Orion hadn't told her that he loved her, he only said that he could, but even that was a huge deal for a guy who'd believed that he would never love again.

That he was opening himself up to her was precious.

"It means a lot to me to hear you say that." She reached for her glass of water. "I know it must have been difficult for you to open your heart to me."

He let out a breath. "Miriam wouldn't have wanted me to be alone. The vow I made all those years ago was not to her. In fact, she asked me to live my life, and I did not honor her by vowing not to love again. It was an expression of my grief and despair, the absolute certainty that I never wanted to experience that kind of suffering again."

Reeling from his confession, Alena hadn't noticed the waitress approach their booth until the woman was standing right over her, a bottle of wine in her hand. Quickly dropping the silencing shroud, Alena forced a pleasant smile onto her face.

The woman expertly uncorked the wine, poured it into their glasses, and then waited for them to taste it and make a comment.

"Excellent," Orion said. "Thank you."

She nodded her head, promised that their first course would be arriving shortly, and pivoted on her heel.

As soon as the woman was a few feet away, Alena recast the silencing shroud around them.

"Are we in a bubble again?" Orion asked.

"Yes."

"That's a very useful trick. What else can you do?"

It seemed that Orion had reached his limit of emotional revelations and needed a change of subject.

"I can thrall, but I don't have much use for the skill. Frankly, I don't have much use for shrouding either because my mother takes care of that when we travel together. It's as effortless for her as breathing, while it's work for me."

"What are the rules regarding thralling and compulsion? I'm still not clear on when it's allowed and when not. Clearly, shrouding is permitted, and I wonder what the difference is."

Wow, he was really crawling back into his shell after his confession. Clan law was the last thing Alena wanted to talk about while she had seduction on her mind, but it seemed like Orion needed a palate cleanse, so to speak.

"Both thralling and shrouding affect human minds. Shrouding changes what they see, hear, smell, and even touch, while thralling is more invasive and changes what they remember and what they believe. Thralling can also be used to look into people's recent memories or those that have left a lasting impact on them. Because it is intrusive and has the potential to cause permanent damage, it is only allowed to conceal immortals' existence and when lives are in danger. Shrouding is allowed unless it is used to gain an unfair advantage. Compulsion, curiously, is less dangerous to human minds than thralling. I assume that they work on different areas of the brain and use different brain wavelengths."

"Are there any immortals who can thrall others of their kind?"

She shook her head. "So far, we've only encountered immortals who can compel other immortals, but not thrall. I don't know about shrouding, though. Once you learn to use it, it would be interesting to see whether it works on us the same way as your compulsion. I know that Kalugal's shrouding does, but I don't know to what extent."

"If Kalugal's shrouding can do that, then mine should as well. What about the goddess? What can she do?"

Alena hesitated. "Why do you want to know?"

"I'm just curious."

"The gods can do to immortals everything that immortals can do to humans, but even among the gods, their abilities and power vary. Areana, my mother's half-sister and Kalugal's mother, is a very weak goddess who can't even do what any strong immortal can. Kalugal's father, who is a first-generation immortal like you and me, is much more powerful than her. In fact, he's the most powerful immortal to ever exist."

"So I've been told." Orion crossed his arms over his chest. "How does his power manifest?"

"He has an entire army of immortal warriors under constant compulsion. I can't imagine the energy he needs to pump into that. I wouldn't be surprised if that was one of the reasons he lost his mind."

"And still, his mate loves him."

"She does." Alena leaned back. "Mentioning Areana reminded me of the New York mission that I promised to tell you about. Kian said that it was okay as long as no one overheard me."

Orion grinned. "That calls for another glass of wine." He refilled their glasses.

65

ORION

The arrival of the first course had put a halt to Alena's story, but given how tiny the dish was, the delay had been short.

Putting his fork down, Orion smiled. "This little thing was as pretty as it was delicious, but if the main course is proportionally small, we will have to stop for a hamburger on the way back."

Alena laughed. "Don't worry. By the time all five courses are done, you won't be hungry. You won't be overstuffed either, and your wallet will be much lighter." She leaned closer. "Besides, when we get back, I can whip something up for you. Geraldine and Cassandra did a good job filling up your fridge and pantry. There is plenty for me to work with."

The hinted message wasn't lost on him, not with the way her eyes blazed, and her intoxicating feminine scent flared. She had plans for tonight that he was a thousand percent on board for.

"Can we skip the rest of the meal?" His words came out a little slurred, not because of the two glasses of wine he'd had but because his fangs had elongated.

His eyes were probably glowing like a pair of torches.

"No, we can't." Her smile was full of promise. "I'm a decent cook, but nothing I make could ever equal Gerard's creations."

Pretending that they were talking about food, Alena was teasing him and enjoying every moment of it. She knew perfectly well what had been on his mind when he'd suggested skipping dinner.

"Are your clan members aware of your evil streak?"

She assumed an innocent expression. "I'm only looking out for your culinary delight. I wouldn't want to deprive you of one of the best gourmet offerings in the world."

He could play along. "I prefer a home-cooked meal."

"So do I, but sometimes, I need something to whet my appetite first."

He let out a breath. "At least distract me with the story of your New York mission."

"With pleasure." She lifted her wine goblet and took a sip.

"It all started with Lokan, whom you haven't met yet, wanting to find his mother and not being scrupulous about the means." Alena went on to tell him about the two Dormants with telepathic powers whom Lokan had tried to kidnap and use to infiltrate the harem and the trap they'd set up for him. The plan had nearly failed, but all had ended well.

It was a fascinating story that provided him with a lot of information about Navuh, the clan's archenemy, and Pleasure Island—his secret base in the Indian Ocean.

No wonder Kalugal had wanted to find out how powerful Orion's compulsion ability was. The people living on that island, humans and immortals alike, were deprived of the most basic rights, and they needed to be liberated. The problem Kalugal and his brother faced, though, was that unless they could take control of the immortal army, removing Navuh from power would do more harm than good, and neither of them was powerful enough to do that. Besides, whoever took the reins would be chained to that island, and it seemed that Kalugal had much loftier goals.

Alena paused her story when the second course arrived—a small salad that was as artfully presented as the appetizer.

Once they were done with that, Alena continued, "When we found Areana, she revealed that she and Navuh had another son who was nearly as powerful a compeller as his father, and who escaped his father's stronghold during World War II. He was presumed dead, but both Areana and Navuh knew the truth because Kalugal shouldn't have been anywhere near the nuclear bombing site. Secretly, Navuh hired human detective firms to look for Kalugal, but they couldn't find him."

Alena lifted the wine glass, and Orion refilled it for her. "But then the clan found Kalugal with your help."

"Nope. I did my part to the best of my ability, but the mission failed nonetheless." Alena took a couple of sips and put the glass down. "After Areana told us about Kalugal, we didn't have the slightest idea where to even start looking for him until Syssi had a vision of him walking into the New York Stock Exchange. We knew from Areana's story that Kalugal loved his mother very much, and that's how the idea of me impersonating her was born. We are about the same height, and we are both blonde, but it took a lot of makeup to make me look like her." Alena smiled wistfully. "It was so much fun pretending to be a supermodel. It was such a different persona from my regular one that I wasn't sure I could pull it off, but I did. My face was plastered over the sides of buses and billboards, it was in fashion magazines and even on the subway. I had a blast, but Kalugal was no longer in New York and saw none of what I'd done. So, it didn't work."

Alena affected a sad face, but her eyes still shone with excitement.

"It must have been hard to return to the quiet life of the sanctuary," Orion prodded gently.

She sighed. "You have no idea. It took me forever to stop feeling restless and confined even though my mother has taken me on many other adventures since."

"But they were not your own. You didn't star in them."

She nodded. "Does it make me selfish not to want to walk in my mother's shadow for a change?"

"Not at all. I think you've been doing that for too long." He leaned forward and took her hand. "How would you like to go on an adventure with me?"

"What kind of adventure?"

"Hunting for Toven and any other children he might have sired." He needed to qualify that. "But I also need to make a living, so some of it will involve hunting for antiques as well."

For a long moment, she looked into his eyes, a hundred different emotions floating through hers. "If you're waiting for me to say that I would love to, the answer is yes, but that doesn't mean that I will. I can fantasize about a new life all I want, but I have responsibilities no one else can assume."

He gave her hand a light squeeze. "We shall see about that. The Fates might surprise you with a new twist you didn't see coming."

She smiled. "I didn't see you coming, so that's an unexpected twist."

"A good one, I hope."

"The best." She squeezed his hand in return.

66

ALENA

$\mathcal{A}$s the four of them left the pavilion, Okidu bowed. "Good night, Mistress Alena, Master Orion. I shall see you again tomorrow at the party." He pivoted on his heel and walked into the night.

"What party?" Orion asked.

"The winter solstice party my mother and I are hosting." Alena threaded her arm through his. "Did you forget?"

"I must not have paid attention. I didn't realize it was tomorrow."

He must have been really distracted by her not to have heard Annani invite everyone who was at Kalugal's on Sunday to the celebration.

"If you want, you can come over tomorrow afternoon and help me decorate."

His eyes widened. "I didn't get anyone presents." He looked at the two bags of shoes he was holding. "We should have gone shopping."

"No need." She patted his hand. "We didn't get you any gifts either. We've got presents mainly for the little ones, and just a few for the grownups. Our plan was to arrive in a few weeks, and the presents weren't about the winter solstice either. My mother and I were searching for something the clan can celebrate that isn't tied to any particular religion, and we just came up with the idea of celebrating the solstices when we got here." She smiled. "When Annani heard about your capture, she couldn't wait another minute to meet you. We rushed over as soon as our things were packed, and the jet was ready for takeoff."

"I hope she wasn't disappointed."

"You're kidding, right? You are the spitting image of Toven, and she adored your father. Besides, you are charming, intelligent, and caring. What's there not to like?"

He grinned, that adorable dimple making an appearance. "I'm glad you think so."

Mason cleared his throat. "I will part ways with you here. Good night."

"Good night, Mason." Alena cast him a smile. "Thank you for the escort."

"It was my pleasure." The Guardian bowed his head and then walked away as briskly as he could without actually jogging.

Evidently Kian had been true to his word and had instructed Onegus to remove the Guardians. Hopefully, he had done the same for the surveillance feed.

It was a relief to be spared the unpleasant task of telling Mason that he had to leave, and probably also having to argue the issue with Onegus. She'd been serious when she'd told Kian she would do it herself, but it was good that she didn't have to. Her energy would be much better spent on more pleasant activities.

"How did that happen?" Orion watched Mason disappear behind the curve. "Am I not considered a threat anymore?"

"You're not a threat to me, and I told Kian to get rid of the Guardians." She didn't mention the surveillance since Orion didn't know about it.

He arched a brow. "And he actually agreed?"

"I put my foot down."

"Good for you." He transferred the bags to one hand and wrapped his arm around her waist. "I knew that there was a steel core under that soft appearance."

Not many people realized that, but it was true. She'd been with Annani nearly every step of the way, building up the clan and shoring up her mother when the goddess's resolve had faltered.

Orion saw her, the real her, which made him even more dear to her and strengthened her resolve to pursue this thing between them to wherever it might lead.

Strolling along the village's central path, they arrived at Shai's former house in minutes, but when Orion stopped, Alena tugged on his arm and kept on walking.

Hadn't she made her intentions clear?

When she'd said she would come to his place to cook for him, Orion had seemed to get it, but perhaps he was the kind of guy who didn't like to assume anything and needed things to be spelled out rather than just hinted at.

Her walking past her house must have made it crystal clear that she hadn't been talking about actually whipping up a meal for him, and as the scent of his arousal flared, his hand tightened on her waist.

When she leaned into him, he relaxed his grip and smoothed his hand down her hip and then up again, igniting the banked flames of her passion. It shouldn't have been enough to make her breathless, but it was, turning her knees to jelly.

They walked the rest of the way to his house in silence, the sexual tension sizzling between them so strongly it was a wonder that her hair didn't turn into a frizzy halo.

The door wasn't locked, and as Orion closed it behind them and dropped the bags on the floor, Alena didn't care whether Kian had disconnected the surveillance feed or not.

"Kiss me," she breathed.

She expected him to grab for her, was hoping for it, but when Orion reached for her, his hand was gentle. Pulling her against his chest, he lowered his mouth to hers and kissed her ever so softly.

As Alena slid her arms around his neck, pressing herself against him as she deepened the kiss, Orion's hands roamed along her sides, but he didn't get swept away in her passion.

He was holding back, treating her as if she was made from porcelain and might break if he unleashed even a fraction of himself on her.

She knew the ferocity was there, the wildness hidden, suppressed. No matter how charming and civilized he was on the outside, Orion was a first-generation male immortal, the most dangerous predator on earth. She craved the wild ferocity he was stifling with an intensity that bordered on insanity.

Perhaps he needed a little prodding.

"I'm immortal." She nipped his lower lip. "I'm not a breakable human." When he hissed, she nipped his lip harder. "You don't have to hold back with me."

Panting, he lowered his forehead to hers. "I don't know if I can. I've been holding back my entire life."

"So have I." She took his hand and led him to the bedroom.

67

ORION

$\mathcal{W}$ith a growl, Orion swept Alena into his arms and crushed his mouth over hers. There was nothing remotely gentle in the way he handled her now, but given the way her scent had intensified, it was precisely what she wanted.

Their mouths still fused, he carried her to the bed, set her down, and kneeled at her feet.

Alena sucked in a breath. "What are you doing?"

He smiled up at her. "I'm going to ravish every part of you, starting with your feet and going up from there." He took off one shoe, tossing it behind him.

Lifting her foot to his lips he kissed one toe at a time, and when she giggled, he tickled her arch with a quick sweep of his tongue.

"Stop it." She tried to pull her foot out of his grasp.

"Why?" He lifted her other foot, took the shoe off, and tossed it aside.

"My feet are not fresh." She tried to pull her foot out of his grip.

"They are perfect." He held on and kissed each toe.

When she leaned back on her forearms, he pulled down her pants, getting dizzy when the scent of her hit him full force.

"I have to taste you." He moved the gusset of her sensible cotton panties aside and without much preamble, licked into her.

"Fates," she hissed. "Don't stop."

He had no intentions of doing so, but he wanted better access, and her panties had to go, as well as her blouse and her bra. He wanted her fully bared to him, wanted access to every part of her—a full possession with no inch of her untouched by his hands, his lips, his tongue.

Moving with immortal speed, he had her just as he wanted in a matter of seconds, and as he knelt between her legs again, his shoulders spreading her thighs wide, a sense of rightness swept over him.

"You're mine," he growled as he licked between her wet folds, finding her entrance and spearing his tongue into her.

He didn't know what had possessed him to say that to Annani's heir. What right had he to call her his?

Thankfully, Alena seemed too lost in her pleasure to have heard the words that had tumbled out of his mouth. And yet, he couldn't help the disappointment of her not claiming him as hers in return.

"Orion—" she moaned his name as her body convulsed in a violent climax.

He sucked and licked, helping her ride the wave for as long as it lasted, and when she finally stopped shuddering, he kissed her folds one last time and leaned away to look at the goddess sprawled on the bed before him.

"Magnificent," he whispered as he shucked his clothing and rose over her.

As his shaft nudged at her entrance, his mouth found her nipple, but when she lifted her hips to draw more of him inside her, the last of his control snapped, and he had to let go.

He surged all the way home, joining them, and the world around them receded into nothingness. There was only her and him and the bed they were on, and as he began moving, going faster and stronger than he'd ever dared before, she was right up there with him, taking everything he had to give her and demanding more.

Her hips lifting to meet him stroke for stroke, her nails scoring his back, and the heels of her feet digging into his buttocks, she was just as wild as he was, if not more.

It took mere minutes for them both to reach the point of no return, and when she turned her head and exposed her neck to him, it took all the restraint he could muster to lick the spot first to anesthetize it before sinking his fangs into her flesh.

Alena groaned, and as her release barreled through her once more, his own shattered through him in an explosive rush.

He must have passed out, waking up from his stupor long minutes later and realizing that he was crushing Alena under his weight.

Not that she was complaining. A blissed-out expression on her beautiful face, she was out like a light. He hadn't expected her to black out like a human woman, but apparently the venom worked on immortal females the same way.

Rolling to his side, he took her with him and held her close. She was so warm, so soft. He kissed her flushed cheeks, her eyelids, her nose, nuzzled her neck, and yet she didn't open her eyes. He knew she was floating on the cloud of post-venom euphoria, and he wanted her to enjoy every moment of it, but he already missed her, wanted her eyes to open and gaze at him and tell him that he had pleased her.

6 8

ALENA

*A*lena was soaring over marvelous landscapes, only dimly aware that they weren't real. She'd never felt so relaxed, so happy, so fulfilled, and she didn't want it to end.

And yet, through the haze, she felt Orion's soft lips peppering her face with kisses, and it was the sweetest thing any male had ever done for her after they'd satisfied their needs.

It was as if he loved her, as if he couldn't wait for her to return to him from her trip over the clouds, and the tugging on her heart was stronger than the blissful pleasure. As lovely as soaring was, the emotion conveyed in those kisses meant more to her. It was real. The surreal landscapes were not.

As she forced her eyelids to lift, her eyes beheld the most handsome face she'd ever seen, and a smile lifted her lips. "Hello," she murmured.

"Hello to you too." He softly kissed her lips. "I'm glad to have you back with me."

"I never left." She cuddled up closer and pressed her nose into the crook of his neck. "I felt your kisses." She kissed that warm spot that smelled heavenly. "But it took me time to decide if I wanted to cut my trip short and come back to you. It was my first venom bite, and it exceeded my wildest expectations."

The smug satisfaction on his beautiful face was precious. "There are plenty more where that one came from."

"There are? From what I hear, immortal males can have multiple orgasms but can only generate enough venom for one bite a night."

"Is that a challenge?"

Alena yawned. "I'm too tired for issuing challenges."

He seemed disappointed. "How many times can immortal females climax in one night?"

"I don't know, but I assume at least as many times as the males." She ran her fingers over his hairless chest. "Or more." She followed her fingers with her lips.

"You smell so good." She licked his skin. "And you taste good as well." She slid down his body, kissing his chest and belly on the way to the prize.

He swallowed hard but didn't stop her.

Why would he?

She was about to pleasure him with her mouth. What male wouldn't love that?

His manhood was proudly erect as if he hadn't just climaxed, and as her lips brushed over the tip, it twitched in welcome, and as she rubbed her cheek against the velvety skin, his fingers threaded in her hair.

They both sighed when she took the tip into her mouth, her tongue pillowing him as she gently sucked.

His fingers tightening on her scalp, he tried to keep still, but he was fighting a losing battle with his hips, a fight that she wanted him to lose. One hand holding onto his shaft, the other clasping his muscular buttocks, she took him deeper, circling her tongue around the hard length pressing into her mouth.

Every twitch of his went straight to her sex, and as he watched her pleasuring him, his rugged breaths spurred her to take him even deeper. She wanted him to lose control and thrust into her throat, but he never gave her more than what he thought she could handle.

Forcing her throat to open as wide as it would go, she simply sucked him in deeper and kept him there until he swelled to the point that she was choking around him and had to release him to take a breath.

"Come here." He pulled her up his chest and rolled on top of her. "That was amazing, but I'd rather not finish inside your mouth."

"Why not?" She pouted.

"Because—" He thrust into her and her eyes rolled back. "We both enjoy this more." He retreated and surged back in.

"Yes." She locked her ankles on the small of his back.

This time their lovemaking was less frenzied, and as he dipped his head and kissed her, the kiss was slow and lazy, his tongue thrusting inside her mouth to the rhythm of his manhood doing the same between her lower lips.

The slow and tender didn't last long though, and soon he was thrusting between her legs with the same ferocity as before, and as she sank her tiny fangs into his neck, he roared his climax and shot his seed into her, pulling another orgasm out of her.

69

ORION

$\mathcal{F}$or long moments they lay on their sides, chest to chest, tangled in each other's arms, panting from the powerful climaxes that had torn through them, satisfied, but only partially.

Orion could go for rounds three and four if Alena was up to it.

As if she'd read his mind, a ripple from the muscles in her sheath coaxed a twitch from his shaft.

"You're incredible." He kissed a spot on her neck right below her ear.

"So are you." Her hands circled to the back of his neck, massaging for a moment before continuing down to his shoulder blades and then further down his back to cup his buttocks.

He trailed his fingers up the soft underside of her arm, circling the crease at her elbow, and as she shivered, he dipped his head and took her lips in a soft kiss.

As she kissed him back, her hands went back up to caress his side, his ribs, his pectorals. And as their passion flared, he rolled over her and braced his weight on his forearms, still kissing her, still buried deep inside her, but not moving.

He wanted to savor the closeness while his brain was still functioning and not consumed by lust.

She lifted her long, powerful legs and wrapped them around his hips, caging him between them.

The message was clear, and as he retracted and surged back in, her sheath tightened and rippled along his shaft. When she nibbled on his lower lip and then pulled it between her teeth and sucked, he became undone.

Drawing his hips back, he slammed back in, and his thrusting became faster and harder, she met him blow for blow, and then with a strength that he'd never encountered in a female before, she flipped them around and rode him even harder than he had ridden her.

With her long blond hair flying, her heavy breasts bouncing with each lift and descent, her lips red and swollen from their kisses, Alena was a dream vision, a fantasy he never wanted to end.

The force with which she slammed down on his shaft was incredible, and although his hand gripped her hips, she didn't need him to lift her.

Orion had never expected to be taken like that but being possessed by this amazing female didn't diminish his masculinity one bit.

On the contrary, he'd never felt as desired, as wanted as he did lying nearly passively under Alena and letting her take him for the ride of his life.

Her body gripping him wet and tight, her hands gripping his shoulders, she brought him to the cusp of a climax, but he held back, waiting for her to reach her peak and milk his seed out of him.

Going faster and faster, she threw her head back and commanded, "Now, Orion!"

The orgasm exploded out of him with a force he'd never experienced before, his muscles locking, and her sheath milking him just as he'd imagined, exquisite relief pouring out of him.

Despite the powerful climax though, his hunger wasn't satiated.

Rolling them over, he started thrusting again, and in mere moments, another orgasm ripped out of him with a roar that must have been heard across the village.

He had just enough presence of mind to roll to his side instead of collapsing on top of her.

"Wow," Alena whispered into his chest. "That was one hell of a ride." She chuckled. "You won."

"I didn't realize that it was a competition."

"You are still hard inside of me, which means that you can go for another round, but I am exhausted, so you won."

He brushed a strand of damp hair away from her flushed cheek. "My manhood might entertain the idea, but I don't think the rest of my body is up to the task. It's a draw."

"I'll take it," she murmured sleepily. "I don't even have the energy to get cleaned up."

"I'll take care of you." He feathered a tender kiss on her cheek.

He wasn't sure how he would muster the energy to get up and do that, but not taking care of her wasn't an option.

Alena's answer was a smile and a soft sigh, and then her breathing evened out, becoming deep and slow.

Orion gave himself a few more moments to watch her beautiful face as she slept. After catching his breath, he gently extracted himself from her arms and padded to the bathroom.

KIAN

"*I* apologize for the early hour," Kian addressed the team gathered around his office conference table. "But given the winter solstice celebrations later this evening, I thought you'd rather be done early."

Many were not celebrating the new holiday Annani had decided on. It would take time for the tradition to take root, but he was accommodating those who wished to gather with their closest friends and family tonight and needed time to decorate and prepare a festive meal.

"Thank you," Vrog said. "I promised Wendy and Stella to help them decorate. Richard is busy at the construction site."

"How are you getting along with him?" Mey asked.

"He's not as hostile as he was at the beginning."

"I'm glad." Mey cast him a reassuring smile.

"How do you like the village?" Yamanu asked.

"It's beautiful and peaceful, and everyone is very friendly. I like the feeling of community." He turned to Kian. "I'm impressed with your leadership and what you've achieved here, and I'm not saying that to get on your good side. This place is as close to utopia as it gets."

Kian knew full well that not everything was as perfect as it appeared, and Kalugal was not the only one who schemed and planned in secret. Then there was the gossip, which often grated on Kian's nerves, the lack of privacy, and the right everyone felt to butt into others' business and offer their advice. Their community was a strange hybrid creature of a large family, a society with its own laws, customs, and beliefs, a business organization, and a self-ruled democratic monarchy.

Vrog wasn't going to stay long enough to experience all that, though. Kian needed him back in China to assist Mey in her continued investigation of echoes left over by the Kra-ell.

"Thank you, Vrog. I'm glad to hear that you're enjoying your stay, but it will have to be cut short. You're leaving on Wednesday along with Mey, Yamanu, and a couple of Guardians. I need the investigation to continue as soon as possible."

Vrog was visibly taken aback. "I thought I would have more time. Can you postpone it for another week? I'm just starting to get acquainted with my son and his fiancée." He ran a hand over his dark hair. "I am also looking forward to the Kra-ell virtual adventure William is setting up for me. I filled out the questionnaire on Saturday, and I'm just waiting for William to find me a match."

"If you want, you can come back to the village after Mey is done with her echoes investigation. Your help deciphering the files you promised me would be invaluable."

"You can go on the virtual adventure when we return," Mey said. "Besides, William might find you a match today and schedule it for tomorrow."

Vrog let out a breath. "Why the rush, though?" He looked at Kian. "Last we spoke, I was under the impression that you were not in a big hurry."

"I wasn't, but I am now. Kalugal is leaving for the Mosuo territory on Wednesday. He suspects that an earlier group of Kra-ell influenced the Mosuo society, and he wants to search for artifacts or any other clues that would confirm his suspicions. I want the two teams to work in tandem and, if needed, assist each other. If Mey finds more clues in the echoes, she can communicate her findings to Kalugal and potentially point him in the right direction and vice versa. What you need to decide is whether you want to return here after the assignment or remain in your school."

Vrog looked conflicted. "Can I come back here for a few weeks? I can't abandon the school completely because it will fall apart without me. I'm the one bringing new students in and keeping the administration accountable to the so-called board of directors." He smiled. "That has only one member. I originally founded the school as a cover, but it has become my life project. I'm proud of what I've created." He sighed. "The clan will not need a school for many years to come, and I'm not the kind of male who could be happy idling. I would be delighted to visit, though, if you allow me."

"How much longer do you think you can pull it off?" Yamanu asked. "You're not aging, and eventually people will start noticing."

Vrog shrugged. "I can pretend for at least another twenty years, and by then, the clan might have enough high school-aged students for me to build a school for them. I'll bring a lot of valuable experience to the table."

"A lot can happen in twenty years," Kian said. "So there is no point in making such long-term plans. After you fulfill your obligation to me by assisting Mey and providing the documents you found, you can come here for a longer visit."

"And after that?" Vrog asked.

"You have my permission to visit the village whenever you want, but precautions will have to be taken. You will have to coordinate your visits with Onegus, the security chief. He will provide you with itineraries that will bring you here in a roundabout way that is difficult to follow. You will also need formal invitations from Vlad and Wendy because they will be responsible for you during your stays."

Vrog inclined his head. "That's very kind and generous of you. Thank you."

"You're welcome."

"So." Yamanu leaned back and crossed his arms over his chest. "Who is coming with us this time?"

"Jay, Alfie, and of course, Morris. You don't need Arwel and Jin this time, and you definitely don't need Stella and Richard. Vrog can translate for you."

ALENA

*A*s Alena's awareness re-emerged from under the hazy clouds of dreams, the strong arms holding her tight were a reminder of where she was and with whom.

The room wasn't dark, which meant…

With a start, her eyes darted to the window, and as she'd suspected, the motorized shutters were up, and the sky was the color of early dawn—the top a deep cerulean blue, the bottoms streaked with bronze, orange, and yellow colors.

"Good morning." Orion's hand started a slow track down her spine. "Did you sleep well?"

"What time is it?"

"A little after six in the morning. Is that a problem?"

"People will see me leaving your place, and the rumor will spread like wildfire through the village."

His hand on her back halted. "You can stay until the afternoon, and when you leave, they will assume that you came to visit me earlier today."

She let out a breath. "With the clothes I chose for our date, everyone would know that I didn't dress like that for a day in the village. You've seen my regular style."

He continued his up and down track over her back. "If you wish, I can accompany you and compel everyone we encounter on the way to forget that they saw you."

"That won't be necessary." Alena shifted to her back, and Orion followed, leaning on his elbow as he gazed down at her face.

"I've run out of ideas." He dipped his head and kissed her lips. "Well, I do have some, just not for getting you home unnoticed." He put a hand on her stomach. "As far as I'm concerned, we can stay here until the food runs out, but even after that, I'm sure Geraldine would be more than happy to replenish the supplies."

Alena smiled. "It's tempting." She could see herself spending an entire month with Orion, making love and getting to know each other. "I'm expected to be back to help my mother host the winter solstice celebration tonight."

He kissed her again and then lifted his head with a smirk tilting up one corner of his sensuous mouth. "That gives us at least twelve hours. I'll barricade the doors, you'll turn your phone off, and we will spend the entire time in bed."

Alena laughed. "Kian would jump to conclusions and come by with a bulldozer to knock the walls down. He's done that before."

"To you?"

"Not to me. He did that to Amanda." Her bladder sending an urgent message to her brain, Alena winced and pushed on Orion's chest. "I need to use the bathroom."

He scooted a few inches to the side. "Go ahead."

For a brief moment, she considered pulling the sheet off the bed and wrapping it around her nude body, but then discarded it and proudly padded to the bathroom with all her femininity on display.

After all, Orion had already seen, touched, licked, and kissed nearly every inch of her, so what was the point in pretending modesty she didn't feel?

Alena had no issues with her body.

Nevertheless, she closed the bathroom door behind her. If this thing between them lasted, she might one day be comfortable enough with him to leave the door open while she used the toilet, but not just yet. It was too familiar, too intimate.

Then again, he'd cleaned her after their lovemaking, and there was nothing more intimate than that.

No one had ever done that for her, not because her casual lovers had all been selfish men, but because she'd always left while they had still been asleep. It was easier to sneak out after her needs had been met and not face the awkward morning after.

She hadn't felt awkward with Orion, though. It was as if they'd known each other for years, and waking up next to him in bed was the most natural thing in the world.

Damn, if he didn't feel the same about her, she was in deep trouble.

Searching through the vanity drawers, she found a new toothbrush still in its original box. After brushing her teeth and combing her hair with her fingers, she opened the door and sauntered back into bed.

The fresh minty smell coming from Orion revealed that he'd used the other bathroom in the house. "You could have come in." She lay next to him and draped an arm around his middle.

"I assumed you wanted privacy." He pulled her closer to him. "So, what's the plan for the rest of the day?" His hand trailed down her hip and then around to cup her bottom.

She smiled. "You are on the right track."

ORION

"I wish I at least had a change of underwear." Alena pulled on her pants.

"You can use one of mine."

She stopped. "I'll take you up on your offer." Pulling her pants back down, she put them on the bed and then walked over to his suitcase that still lay open on the floor.

"Bachelors." She shook her head as she crouched next to it. Pulling out a pair of boxer briefs, she tugged them on over her long, magnificent legs.

The rest of her was still deliciously bare.

Orion found it curious that the order in which Alena dressed was like a male would. Women tended to get dressed from top to bottom while men usually dressed bottoms first.

Not that there was anything unfeminine about her. Alena was femininity personified and gloriously so. She was soft and curvy in all the right places, but she was statuesque and strong. She was also soft-spoken, gentle, and kind, but she didn't shy away from confrontations, and put her foot down on what mattered to her.

Not many would have dared to order Kian around, but Alena had done it and gotten her way. She was the older sister, that was true, but Orion doubted Kian had obeyed her wishes out of respect for her seniority. He'd probably been so stunned by her demand that he'd capitulated out of shock.

Fishing her blouse out from under the bed, she winced and brushed the dust off with her hand.

"You can use one of my shirts as well," Orion offered.

She glanced at the suitcase, shook her head again, and turned to him. "Why aren't you getting dressed?"

He was in bed, lying on top of the messy sheets and wearing the towel he'd wrapped around his hips after their joint shower. "I enjoy watching you getting dressed in my bedroom too much to miss out on a single moment."

A smile bloomed on her face, accompanied by a slight reddening of her cheeks.

"If you want to have breakfast with my mother while wearing a towel, that's fine with me, and I'm sure that she wouldn't mind either."

He was out of bed in one second flat. "You didn't say anything about breakfast. Did she invite me, and I forgot that too?"

Had he been so consumed by Alena that he might have missed the goddess's invitation?

"Annani didn't invite you." She buttoned up the blouse. "I am inviting you. Otherwise, I will spend what's left of the morning getting interrogated about last night." She smiled at him sweetly. "Since you were an active participant, you can answer half of her questions."

Orion swallowed. "If you need me to shield you from your mother, I will, but are you sure it is wise for me to show up for breakfast the morning after?"

"It's very wise." Alena leaned down to fish her shoes from under the bed. "You haven't grown up among immortals, but our attitudes about sex are very different from those of humans. My mother will be overjoyed that we spent the night together and that I found pleasure in your arms." She pushed her feet into her shoes and cast him a seductive smile. "Many times over."

As the towel rose, lifted by the pole that had sprung up between his legs, Alena licked her lips. "Save it for later, lover boy. I've already texted my mother that we are coming over." She waved a hand at him. "Get dressed."

Letting the towel drop, he sauntered toward her and enveloped her in his arms. "Is later a promise?"

Her expression softened. "What do you think?"

"I hope that you will spend tonight with me as well, but I don't want to presume."

She chuckled. "You're allowed to presume."

"I'm a simple male, and I need to be told things in black and white. Is it a yes or a no?"

She lifted her arms and folded them around his neck. "It's a yes. I will spend tonight with you, but this time, I'll bring a change of clothes." She kissed him for a long moment before pushing on his chest. "If you need to take a cold shower before getting dressed, hurry up and do it. Keeping my mother waiting will not endear you to her. She doesn't appreciate tardiness."

He definitely didn't want to upset the goddess today or any other day for that matter.

There was no willing his erection to deflate, which forced him to dress top to bottom to Alena's great amusement.

"If you keep watching me, it will take longer for me to get ready."

"Fine." She tore her eyes away from his erection and turned on her heel. "I'll wait for you in the living room. You have two minutes."

ALENA

"Good morning, Mother." Alena walked over to Annani's chair at the dining table, leaned down, and kissed her cheek.

"Good morning, Clan Mother." Orion sketched a deep bow.

"It is almost good afternoon." Annani grinned from ear to ear, "So good afternoon to both of you." She waved a hand. "Please, take a seat and let us dine." She turned to Orion. "My Oridu made Okidu's famous waffles. You are in for a treat, and you do not want to eat them cold."

"Thank you, Clan Mother." He bowed again and then rushed to pull a chair out for Alena.

The poor guy didn't know what to do with himself, but he'd bravely accompanied her without complaint, ready to incur Annani's wrath if the goddess didn't approve of their night of passion. Alena had told him that he had nothing to worry about, but he hadn't been convinced.

Obviously, she'd been right because Annani was beaming with barely contained joy.

As Oridu served them waffles topped with strawberries and whipped cream, Annani lifted the dainty porcelain cup to her lips and sipped on her tea.

"I cannot wait for us to find your father, Orion. I cannot believe that our children are about to be mated, and I am sure the news will gladden him no matter how jaded he has become."

As usual, her mother went overboard.

Alena put her fork down and cast Annani a suffering glance. "Please, Mother. Don't read too much into us spending the night together. Orion and I are just enjoying each other's company for now, and it is too early to talk about matehood or marriage."

They hadn't bonded overnight, and Alena hadn't expected them to. Well, there had been that small kernel of illogical hope that it would happen to them as fast as it had for Lokan and Carol. But even Kian and Syssi hadn't bonded after their first night together, and they were still deeply in love after over four years of marriage.

She and Orion had just met, and they weren't in love, not yet. They were good together, though, in bed and outside of it, so the prospects of them bonding were also good.

With a sigh, Annani put her teacup down. "The Fates have brought Orion to us for a reason, Alena." She smiled fondly at him. "You are each other's perfect match."

He cast Alena a pleading look. "I hope you are correct, Clan Mother."

"I am never wrong about matters of the heart." As she lifted her empty cup, Oridu rushed over to refill it. "When the Fates brought Amanda and Dalhu together in the most unconventional way, my son was overcome with worry for his sister, but I knew she was safe with Dalhu even though he was still a member of the Brotherhood back then. I knew he would never harm her."

"That was different," Alena said.

"Of course." Annani smiled at her indulgently. "A relationship between Orion and you is easy. There are no obstacles standing in your way. Amanda had a much more difficult time convincing Kian and the rest of the clan to accept a former enemy."

If only that was true.

"Orion and I face different difficulties. Perhaps they are not as extreme as what Amanda and Dalhu had to overcome, but Amanda had no duties to the clan. She could've basically done whatever she pleased."

Her mother arched one perfect red brow. "What challenges stand in your way?"

Alena really did not want to answer that. Why was her mother pushing her to say that she viewed her as an obstacle to her happiness?

Annani took another sip of tea and put the cup down. "I want you to do what is right for you, Alena. Do not concern yourself with me or your duties to the clan. Those are minor considerations compared to finding your truelove mate." She shifted her gaze to Orion. "I hope that mate is you."

74

VROG

*A*fter the meeting in Kian's office, Vrog had spent the rest of the day helping Wendy, Stella, and Wendy's mother decorate the house while anxiously awaiting a call from William. Not directly to him since he didn't have a phone, but to Vlad, who would in turn call Wendy, who would let him know whether a match had been found for him.

As the hours ticked off though, he'd started losing hope. Computers were fast, and if there was a match for him, it would have been found in seconds. If William hadn't called, it was because none was found or the female declined to participate for whatever reason.

The match was supposed to be anonymous, so hopefully it wasn't because he was Kra-ell, but then the clan females knew precisely which males could be their potential matches, and there weren't that many unrelated and available males in the village. Another possibility was that a rumor had spread out about him looking for a match, and none of them wanted him.

"Don't look so sad," Wendy said from up on the ladder. "You'll be back here before you know it. Two weeks max, and then you can stay for as long as you want." She cut off a piece of tape and attached a section of the paper garland to the door frame.

"That's not why he's moping around," Stella said. "He was looking forward to the virtual adventure, but it doesn't seem like it's happening today."

Wendy rolled her eyes. "Of course not. Everyone is busy with this new holiday Annani came up with. No one can commit to three hours in the lab today."

"If a match was found, William could have scheduled it for tomorrow," Vrog said. "I leave on Wednesday."

"True." Wendy came down the ladder. "I bet William is busy with something else and didn't even run your questionnaire through the software yet. He didn't know that you were leaving so soon." She walked over to the kitchen counter and lifted her phone off its charger. "I'll text him that he needs to hurry up."

The polite thing to do would be to stop her from bothering the tech genius while he was no doubt busy decorating and making other preparations for the festivities, but Vrog's curiosity was burning hot for the Kra-ell virtual adventure, or rather the Krall, as Kian's wife had named it.

When Wendy's phone pinged with an incoming text, Vrog held his breath.

"I knew it," Wendy said. "He didn't run it yet. He's super busy. His crew is installing holiday lights all over the village, and he's writing a program to make them twinkle in sync with the music he's going to run through the loudspeakers." She put the phone back on its charger. "I'm so excited. We will have a festive spirit throughout the village."

Vrog sighed in relief, but his disquiet had lessened only a fraction. As he'd told Kian, the village was as close to utopia as he'd ever imagined a community could be, but it was not a good fit for a half Kra-ell male like him.

He was very good at hiding his inner nature, at putting on a civilized façade, but he was an aggressive male who needed an outlet for his baser needs, and he hadn't had one since they'd caught him in China.

"What's wrong?" Stella asked. "You still look upset."

"I'm not upset. I'm just restless. I need to go on a run or lift heavy weights to release stress." Or engage in sexual activity, but he wasn't going to add that.

"Tomorrow, Vlad can take you to the gym," Wendy said. "You can run on a treadmill and lift weights and even spar with the Guardians who train there."

"Sounds good." Vrog wiped his sweaty palms on his borrowed jeans. "I think I'll go for a short run if you don't mind."

"Of course not." Wendy put a hand on his arm. "Just come back in time to shower before dinner."

"Thank you." He looked into her soft brown eyes. "You're very kind."

She smiled. "I'm just paying forward the kindness that was extended to me, and I wish with all my heart for you to find as much happiness as I did."

75

ANNANI

*A*nnani surveyed the hearth Alena and Orion had decorated with candles and pinecones and cloves. The mantel had evergreen garlands draped over it, and beautifully wrapped gift boxes were piled on the floor in front of it.

It was almost time, and she was happy with how everything had turned out.

Orion had left to change into festive clothes, Alena was in her room getting ready, and the four Odus were putting finishing touches on the tables and chairs that had replaced the living room furniture, to accommodate her guests.

It was going to be a joyous celebration, but Annani wished she could have invited more people over.

When Kian's new home was ready, she could host a much larger party there, but that would be next winter solstice. For the summer solstice celebration, the village square would be perfect.

Sari could come with her people, and so could everyone from the sanctuary. There was no reason to leave anyone to guard a place that no one outside the clan knew existed.

She could lock it up for a few days.

Her eyes darting to Alena's room, tears welled in their corners as she thought about a future without her sweet daughter to keep her company, to keep her grounded, to keep the loneliness at bay. But Annani was a mother, and her children's happiness would always come before her own.

She had often wondered who could possibly be worthy of a treasure like Alena. The Fates must have heard her plea and answered by sending the most perfect male for her eldest daughter.

Orion was powerful, honorable, charming, handsome, intelligent, kind, and dedicated to his tiny family. Annani had no doubt that he would extend the same kind of dedication to his new one.

All that remained to be seen was whether they would bond, but Annani's gut told her that they would, and it also told her that she would probably return home alone.

Alena was going to remain in the village with Orion or join him on his search for Toven and possibly more of his siblings.

With a sigh, Annani walked up to the window and looked at the beautiful sanctuary her son had built for their people in the Malibu mountains. Perhaps she should come live at the village as well and bring whoever wanted to leave her northern paradise to Kian's southern one. Alaska could serve as a vacation spot for the clan and a potential escape shelter if the unthinkable happened and Navuh discovered the village.

Could she do it, though?

The three separate clan locations were strategically important. It would be nice to move everyone into the village, but it would not be prudent.

Besides, Annani liked her independence, and she did not like having Kian hovering over her and demanding to know where she was going and why. But those were minor things that could be discussed and agreed upon before any final decisions were made, and no decisions were required at the moment. She could take her time and give living without Alena a try.

As her heart squeezed and another tear found its way down her cheek, Annani put one hand over the aching spot and wiped the tear with the other.

Perhaps it would not be so bad. Perhaps she would ask one of the other sanctuary occupants to be her companion or she could rotate between several.

For now, though, she needed to put on a happy face and celebrate the winter solstice with her family.

"Everything is ready, Clan Mother." Ogidu bowed. "Would you like to inspect the tables?"

She gave them a cursory glance and nodded her approval. "You have done a splendid job. Thank you."

The tables were covered with white tablecloths and decorated with small pinecones. Sage and cloves were scattered among lit candles, and crystal goblets stood in front of every plate.

As the door to Alena's room opened, Annani affected the expression her daughter was used to seeing on her and smiled. "You look lovely."

"Thank you." Alena smoothed a hand over her long skirt. "I need to update my wardrobe, but this will do for tonight."

The makeup was gone, her hair was back in its usual thick braid, and a thin band adorned her head. Alena was effortlessly beautiful, and Annani did not want her to change.

"You need to stay true to yourself, my daughter. Do not change to please anyone other than yourself, not Orion, not Amanda, and not me." Annani waved a hand over her long silk gown. "None of my children approve of my style, but it is mine, and it pleases me."

"You are stunning no matter what you have on, Mother." Alena leaned down and kissed her cheek. "But wearing a bra, at least for today, would have been appreciated."

Annani huffed. "That would have made me terribly uncomfortable the entire evening. Why would my children want me to suffer so?"

"Oh, Mother." Alena rolled her eyes. "We would never want that. But doesn't it bother you that you make your male guests uncomfortable?"

Annani smiled. "Not at all. It is good training for them to focus on a female's eyes and not her chest."

76

KIAN

*I*t didn't escape Kian's notice that things had progressed between Orion and Alena. At the dinner table the two were seated together to Annani's left, while he and Syssi were right across from them to Annani's right, giving him a perfect vantage point to observe his sister and her new love interest smiling at each other and holding hands under the tablecloth, as well as Annani and the expression of smug satisfaction on her face.

Hadn't she realized what a union between Alena and Orion would mean for her?

Could it be that their mother had tired of Alena's company and wished to make a change?

Kian doubted that. More likely, Annani was putting her daughter's needs and happiness before her own, as any mother should.

Leaning toward Syssi, he kissed her cheek and whispered in her ear, "I love you."

Grinning, she kissed him back and lifted her glass. "Happy solstice, my love. I'm looking forward to thousands more."

As he clinked his glass with hers, other couples followed suit, and then Kalugal rose to his feet and turned to Annani. "I would like to propose a toast."

Annani nodded. "Of course."

He smiled. "First of all, many thanks to the Clan Mother and Alena for coming up with this wonderful new tradition for the family to celebrate and for hosting this dinner."

As everyone clapped and then lifted their glasses, Kalugal continued. "To many more joyful family celebrations."

Annani's face beamed with happiness as she lifted her glass higher. "To our ever-growing family." She cast a quick smile at Orion.

The guy didn't look comfortable. In fact, he looked like the cat who'd snuck into the kitchen, had been caught with his nose in the cream bowl, and was still waiting for his punishment to be announced.

Despite being a powerful immortal, Orion was behaving like a human from a different time period, when seducing a lady without asking for her hand was a grave crime that could cost a guy his head.

"I would like to propose another toast," Annani said. "To Alena and Orion, may they find love and joy with each other."

Apparently, their mother had noticed the same thing he had and wanted to put poor Orion at ease, but by doing so, she'd embarrassed Alena.

His sister's cheeks reddening, she cast Annani a withering look. "Thank you, Mother."

Annani ignored the sarcastic tone and smiled sweetly at Orion. "Is there something that you would like to toast?"

The guy cleared his throat, glanced at Alena, and then at Kian. "Yes." He rose to his feet and lifted his glass. "To my newfound family and friends, thank you for welcoming me into your clan. In my wildest dreams, I could have never imagined that such a large and virtuous community of immortals existed, and that it was led by an incredible goddess—a goddess who is just, kind, wise, and cares deeply for her people as well as humanity at large." He turned to Annani and bowed deeply. "Thank you for never losing your spirit and your drive to better everyone's lives, immortals and humans alike." He lifted his glass higher. "To Annani!"

As everyone oohed and aahed and clunked their glasses, the cynic in Kian wondered whether Orion was a superb actor or a great manipulator. With one toast the guy had cemented his place in the clan without having been offered membership.

Naturally, Annani wouldn't have it any other way, especially now that Alena had claimed Orion for herself, but things hadn't been official, not until Orion had gotten up and declared himself a member of the family.

Presumptuous? For sure. Gutsy? Somewhat. Manipulative? You bet.

Except, the non-cynical part of Kian had heard the sincerity in Orion's voice and believed that the guy had meant every word he'd said.

"Oh, Orion." Annani sighed. "Thank you for your lovely toast. I am overjoyed to welcome Toven's son into my clan, and I hope to one day welcome your father and your other siblings as well."

ALENA

*A*lena was glad for the loose dress she'd donned for dinner. She'd eaten too much, not because everything the Odus had prepared had been delicious, although it was, but because she was nervous, and stuffing her face had been a good way to avoid conversation.

Annani had put both her and Orion on the spot with her comment about their relationship, and even though Orion seemed unfazed by it, Alena was still seething.

Her mother's intentions were good, but as usual, her methods could use some refinement. As someone who had lived for five millennia, Annani should have developed more subtlety, but Alena suspected that her mother was just too impatient to bother. The goddess was used to getting what she wanted when she wanted it and how she wanted it, and this time, she wanted a union between her daughter and Toven's son.

Preoccupied with her thoughts, Alena hadn't been paying attention to the conversations going on around the table until Kalugal said, "I haven't heard yet whether any of you have decided to join Jacki and me on the trip to the Mosuo territory."

"Where is that?" Orion asked.

"In China." Kalugal took a sip of his coffee and looked at Kian. "Have you told the newest member of our family about the Kra-ell?"

"I've heard the name mentioned before," Orion said. "But not who they are and their connection to the Mosuo people in China."

"The Kra-ell are a different kind of immortals that we've recently discovered," Kian said.

Wide-eyed, Orion kept looking at Kian, but that was all her brother had to say.

Kalugal picked it up from there. "We know very little about the Kra-ell. So far, we've found only two members of their original community, and we have three of their descendants. The rest of their tribe is presumed dead—ambushed and murdered either by their own rebelling half-breeds or another tribe. We don't know whether there are more of them, but we suspect that small communities like the one those two males belonged to are scattered throughout the globe. The reason we are interested in the Mosuo is that their unique and peculiar social structure closely resembles that of the Kra-ell. Both societies are female dominated, with children belonging to the female's household and raised by her family. The fathers have visitation rights." He shifted toward Jacki and put his arm around her shoulders. "But where the Kra-ell had a good reason for structuring their society that way, the Mosuo didn't, which leads me to believe that they were influenced by contact with the Kra-ell. I have organized an archeological dig in their territory, and since my wife wanted to visit an archeological site, I figured that she would enjoy a lakeshore vacation in Yunnan, China much more than a dusty dig in Egypt."

"What was the reason you were referring to?" Orion asked. "I mean for the structuring of the Kra-ell society."

"Four to five Kra-ell males are born for each female. To prevent endless fighting over females, they organized themselves in family structures that were not couple based. Two or more Kra-ell females share a harem of males, and the children belong to the tribe. One female is the ultimate leader, and the others are her lieutenants. The males are not allowed to even initiate sex. They have to get invited, and then they have to fight the female to prove their worth."

"Their females are nasty," Amanda said. "They enjoy inflicting pain."

As an argument started about the Kra-ell females and whether their nastiness was biologically necessary for the process of natural selection or cultural in nature, Alena tuned it out and imagined a lake-shore vacation—a real lake, not the glorified pond of the Scottish arm of the clan.

When no one won the argument, Orion asked Kalugal, "What are you hoping to find?"

"Clues to a Kra-ell presence that predates the arrival of these latest newcomers." Kalugal shifted his gaze to Kian. "We are also sending a crew to investigate the Kra-ell tribe's former location. Hopefully, we will collect enough information to give us a better picture of who they are, where they came from, and what they are after." He smiled at Kian. "My cousin is worried that they might pose a threat to the clan."

It hadn't escaped Alena's notice that Kalugal had started to talk in terms of 'we.' It seemed that Orion's arrival had solidified the ties between their two groups because Kian had not corrected him even once. Furthermore, her brother hadn't appeared to be even annoyed by that.

"And you're not worried?" Orion asked Kalugal.

"I think that if they haven't bothered us so far, they are not going to, but I'm a curious fellow, and I'm a passionate part-time archeologist. I'm assisting Kian's investigation for purely selfish motives."

"What else is new?" Kian muttered under his breath.

ORION

*A*fter another round of coffee and tea had been served, Kalugal's wife said, "Lokan and Carol are joining us."

Kian's sharp inhale made everyone's eyes turn to him. "Isn't that incredibly dangerous?" he asked.

Kalugal shrugged. "Lokan and Carol are isolated, and they miss hanging out with people they don't need to pretend around. Naturally, they will take precautions." He leaned back and took his wife's hand. "We all use Turner's evasive protocol. I'm not saying that it's infallible, but I believe it's good enough. Besides, they will have me there, and I can compel immortals, so I think my brother and his mate will be safe."

"We will have a wonderful vacation on a lakeshore," Kalugal's wife said. "I've seen pictures and YouTube videos of the area, and it's breathtaking."

Alena sighed. "I would love to join you, but I can't."

"Why not?" the goddess asked.

"Because it's not safe for you to go, and I can't go without you."

"Nonsense." Annani waved a dismissive hand. "I am not a child who needs to be looked after. I am in the village, with plenty of things to do, people to visit, and you, my dear, need a vacation. I can survive a couple of weeks without you." The goddess turned to Orion. "Do you have anything important that you need to do over the upcoming weeks, or can you accompany Alena to China?"

Next to him, Orion felt Alena tense.

This was precisely what she craved—an adventure that didn't involve her mother —and he'd be dammed if he didn't help her get what she wanted.

"I can combine business with pleasure." He squeezed Alena's hand under the tablecloth. "I deal in antiques, and since Kalugal is running an archeological dig there, he might find artifacts that he's willing to part with. I have several clients who I can interest in artifacts from China."

"Then it is settled," Annani said. "Alena and Orion will join Jacki and Kalugal."

Kian lifted his hand. "Not so fast. I'm not going to allow Alena to head into danger without a heavy Guardian escort, and Kalugal's jet has limited seats."

Kalugal snorted. "I'm taking three men with me. Besides, if I thought that the Mosuo territory was dangerous, do you think I would take my pregnant wife there?"

Kian pinned his cousin with a hard stare. "When I sent the team to investigate the Kra-ell former compound, no one expected to encounter any trouble. Nevertheless, I had an uneasy feeling despite sending two head Guardians and two additional ones to safeguard the ladies. You know how that story ended. Need I say more?"

"What happened?" Orion asked.

"One of the teammates was attacked."

Kalugal shook his head. "By her former lover who would have never hurt her."

"First of all, we don't know that." Kian crossed his arms over his chest. "And secondly, that's beside the point. The point is that the team was taken by surprise, and that they weren't prepared. I don't want to repeat the same mistake with anyone, and especially my sister."

Kalugal cast a quick glance at Orion before going back to his verbal ping-pong with Kian. "Alena will have three strong compellers with her. Orion, me, and Lokan. Do you really think that anyone would be able to get to her?"

Kian's hard expression didn't soften. "You'll be busy with other things, and you need to sleep sometimes. I want Alena to have Guardians whose only job is keeping her safe."

"We are short on Guardians," Alena said. "Besides, Mother and I travel with just our Odus, who don't need to sleep, and who can handle any threat to us. I can take Ovidu with me. Together with Kalugal's men, that should suffice."

This time some of the hardness left Kian's face. "Ovidu is a good idea, but I want one more warrior in addition to Kalugal's men watching your back."

Like everyone else at the table, Orion read between the lines. Kian wanted his sister to be protected by someone he trusted, and he apparently didn't trust Kalugal or his men, and he didn't trust Orion either.

Orion put a hand over his heart. "I vow to protect Alena with my life."

Kian didn't look impressed. "When was the last time you fought anyone, Orion?"

"It has been several centuries," he admitted.

"The only weapon that you know how to use is your compulsion ability, which I don't discount, but you have no training to speak of. You are a civilian."

Meaning, not good enough to protect his sister.

"That might be true, but I have a vested interest in keeping Alena safe." He draped his arm over her shoulders. "She's precious to me. Wouldn't you tear out the throat of anyone threatening your mate?"

Kian's eyes blazed, and as he opened his mouth to speak, his fangs were elongated. "I certainly would, but I'm trained. You're not."

His brother-in-law cleared his throat. "When was the last time you visited the training center?"

"It's been a while," Kian admitted. "But I can still kick your ass."

"I have no doubt." Andrew chuckled. "But what I'm trying to say is that Alena will be safe with three compellers, three warriors, and one Odu. And let's not forget Carol. She is a force to be reckoned with as well."

ALENA

*E*xcitement rushed through Alena, electrifying her like a live wire. She was going on another adventure, only this time it would be even better than New York because she wouldn't be sleeping alone at night. Orion was coming with her.

She knew that he'd agreed to accompany her only because she'd told him that she craved adventure, and he wanted her to have it.

Alena could fall in love with him just for that.

Wow, she needed to put the brakes on that.

They'd met just three days ago, for Fates' sake, and Orion had vowed never to love again. But that was focusing on the half-empty portion of the glass instead of the half-full, and that had never been Alena's style. She shouldn't fear the hope surging in her heart. She should allow it to take flight and electrify her like it was doing now. She should focus on the positives.

Kian and Syssi had fallen for each other in a matter of days, and Orion had admitted that his wife hadn't wanted him to be alone. He was ready to open his heart to her.

"What about finding Toven?" Cassandra asked. "Doesn't he take priority over the Kra-ell? If Orion is going to China, who is going to lead the investigation?"

And just like that, the hope winked out.

Kian had no say in what Alena did, but he could prevent Orion from going to China with her, and there was no point in her going without him.

Their mother waved a hand in dismissal. "Orion can do that once he returns."

Orion shook his head. "There isn't much I can do. I've exhausted everything from the journal I took from Toven. I was hoping that the clan has resources I did not and can access more information."

"Where is that journal?" Kian asked.

Orion hesitated for a split second before replying, "I have it with me."

Kian eyed him with renewed appreciation. "Thank you for trusting us with that. Will you allow us to make a copy?"

"Of course. But it's written in Aramaic. Can you read it? It's not one of the languages Google can translate."

Kian chuckled. "I would be very surprised if it could, but maybe someone should come up with artificial intelligence translations for dead languages." He shifted his gaze to Kalugal. "It could prove very useful to you. Imagine how much time it would save you deciphering those tablets."

"Not likely," Kalugal said. "The problem with the tablets is that they are missing pieces, and I doubt AI can tackle that. Not yet."

Kian shrugged. "It was just an idea." He turned back to Orion. "I can't read Aramaic, but Edna can. I'll ask her to translate the journal, and we will take it from there. It will probably take her the entire two weeks you are gone, if you're planning to stay that long, that is. Perhaps you and Alena will choose to return earlier."

Orion seemed conflicted. "After the trip to China, I will have to make a few stops in Europe for auctions I've already committed to. I won't be able to return here until a month from now."

Alena's heart sank. He was going to leave her for two whole weeks. How was she going to survive without him?

Damn, she shouldn't let herself fall down the rabbit hole like that. They hadn't bonded yet, thank the merciful Fates. She'd survived alone for over two millennia, she could survive two weeks.

But what if they bonded while vacationing at Lake Lugu?

Orion's hand tightened around hers. "I hope that you will accompany me on those trips. I know that we've only met, but I can't imagine being without you."

Across the table, Syssi sighed.

Alena's heart did a happy flip, but then she looked at her mother. "I would love to if it's okay with you."

"What about me?" Amanda asked before Annani had a chance to respond. "My baby will arrive in less than a month. I want you here with me. You promised."

It was so much like the spoiled princess to think only of herself, but given how terrified she was of losing another child, Alena forgave her. "We will be back before your due date. If Orion's obligations prevent it, I'll come alone."

Kian cleared his throat. "Aren't you going to ask if I approve of your travel plans?"

Alena's knee-jerk response was to say no, but Kian had been more accommodating than usual with her and Orion, and she didn't want to repay him with rude dismissiveness.

"If you want to suggest safety precautions, I'm willing to take them under consideration. Just please, don't overdo it."

He gave her a smile. "I wouldn't dream of it. If the Chinese part of the trip goes without incident, a couple of Odus will suffice for the European part." He turned to Annani. "I'm sure you will have no problem with contributing one of your Odus to Alena's entourage and programming him accordingly."

Annani pretended to consider it for a moment and then laughed, the sound so beautiful it lightened the mood in the room. "It would be my pleasure." She pushed to her feet. "Who wants to help me give out the gifts?"

"Me!" Phoenix rushed to her many times great-great-grandmother.

Reluctantly, Alena pulled her hand out of Orion's. "I should help."

"I'll come with you." He followed her up.

Kian leaned back and folded his arms over his chest. "Bring the journal to my office tomorrow morning. Shai will copy it with the utmost care and return it to you before your trip."

Orion swallowed. "Will it be okay if I copied it for you?" He glanced at Shai. "No offense, it's just that this journal is priceless to me for many reasons."

"No offense taken," Shai said. "I understand."

Alena understood as well, and her heart swelled in appreciation. Orion was doing it for her, bargaining his most treasured possession to Kian for the privilege of spending time with her.

She wanted to tell him that he didn't need to do it, that her time belonged to her and that she decided how she wanted to pass it, but that would have taken away from what he considered a sacrifice, and she didn't want to diminish it in any way.

Besides, letting Kian have a copy of the journal would help find Toven and possibly Orion and Geraldine's other siblings.

Alena hoped that they would find many. If they were good people like the two they had found so far, then all of their lives would benefit from Toven's children joining their clan.

What about Toven himself, though?

Could Annani find happiness with him despite her vow to never love again?

Perhaps Annani could learn from Orion's story of love lost and then found again centuries later. If Khiann had loved her as much as Orion's human wife had loved him, then he wouldn't have wanted her to spend her eternal life alone either.

It wasn't Alena's place to suggest that to her mother, though. All she could do was to tell Annani Orion's story and let her decide whether it applied to her or not.

Alena had taken care of others her entire life, never thinking of her own needs and desires. She'd earned the right to her own happily ever after, and for now, she should focus just on that.

DARK HUNTER'S PREY

1

ORION

"Don't worry." Alena put her hand on Orion's cheek. "Kian is not going to pull the big brother routine on you." She smiled. "He can't because I'm older, but he's no doubt going to warn you again to keep me safe, or else."

"Your brother doesn't intimidate me." He planted a chaste kiss on her cheek. "Enjoy your shopping spree with Amanda, and don't worry about me. I'll be fine."

Alena needed new clothes for their trip to Lugu Lake, and Amanda had insisted on accompanying her and providing stylistic expertise.

"I'd rather spend more time with you." Alena wound her arms around his neck and pulled him down for a proper kiss.

They were standing in front of the office building in full view of everyone who cared to look their way, especially Kian, whose office windows faced the village square, but if Alena wanted a kiss, Orion wasn't going to deny her.

They'd spent another incredible night of passion together, and parting ways was doing unexpected things to his gut, but maybe his unease had more to do with the journal tucked inside his pocket than being separated from Alena for a few hours.

When her phone rang, she reluctantly let go of him. "I'd better go. Amanda is waiting for me in the parking garage."

"Have fun."

"You too." She smiled before pivoting on her heel and heading toward the glass pavilion.

As he watched her walk away from him, he tried to focus on the gentle sway of her hips, the casual confidence of her gait, the thick blond braid swinging from side to side with each step, and not on the tightening sensation in his chest that grew worse along with the distance between them.

Alena was spectacular, and for some reason, she found him worthy as a potential mate. Hopefully, their trip to China would solidify her decision and not weaken it. They'd known each other for all of four days, and thinking about forever was premature, but he couldn't help it. He was consumed by her, utterly enamored and helpless to resist.

Orion patted the pocket containing his father's journal, unease churning in his gut. He hadn't expected it to be so difficult to hand it over, and he had to remind himself that he was doing it for Alena.

The journal was a bribe, a show of goodwill that had convinced Kian to let him accompany his sister to China.

Besides, Orion wasn't giving up the original up, only a copy of it. The journal traveled with him wherever he went, safely tucked away in his carry-on luggage, but the truth was that he should have made a copy years ago and kept the original in a safe.

Perhaps it hadn't occurred to him before because theft hadn't been a consideration. After all, the journal wasn't valuable to anyone but him. Still, he should have considered that accidents happen, and it could get damaged or lost.

Since stealing it from the god nearly four decades ago, Orion had only parted with it once when he'd given it to a linguist to translate.

Back then though, separation anxiety hadn't been an issue because he hadn't formed an attachment to the manuscript yet. In the beginning, it had only been a means to an end, providing him with clues about Toven's lovers, which in turn could potentially lead him to discover more of Toven's children.

In time, however, the journal had become so much more to him.

Looking at his father's sketches and neat handwriting, he felt grounded, connected to the god—the father whom he'd only gotten to know through those handwritten pages—a father who didn't want anything to do with him.

Orion wished things could have been different between them, but all he had of his father was the damn journal, and despite the resentment he felt for having been so rudely and unequivocally dismissed, it was important to him.

It had provided solace when things spiraled out of control, the way they had after Geraldine's near-fatal accident, and it kept the ennui at bay when life felt pointless and everything seemed meaningless.

Flipping through the pages, looking at the lovingly sketched portraits of his father's beautiful lovers, Orion would imagine the kind of children those women might have brought into the world—half-brothers and sisters to him and Geraldine with whom he could connect. And sometimes, he would pick up the journal to remind himself not to become like his father—an emotionally-bankrupt empty shell.

Although given how meticulously Toven had been recording details about his former lovers, or at least those who'd left an impression on him, immortalizing them in his journals, the guy wasn't as dead on the inside as he'd wanted Orion to believe he was.

The jerk had claimed to have lost the ability to care about anyone and anything, but those lovely drawings and poetic descriptions belied the stony cold manner in which the god had treated Orion.

It made the rejection worse.

A lifeless sociopath couldn't have filled pages upon pages of numerous journals with portraits of beautiful young women, capturing with his pencil their unique characters as well as their outer beauty.

Perhaps Toven had a preference for the company of females?

Orion could understand if the god had grown disillusioned with the males of all species—human, immortal, and god alike—but still retained some fondness for the females. If Toven's gripe with the various sentient inhabitants of the earth was their bloodthirstiness and cruelty, then females were far less prone to these afflictions than males.

Would his father have reacted differently if he'd encountered Geraldine on a Parisian street instead of him?

Perhaps the god wouldn't have dismissed a daughter. Perhaps he wouldn't have told her to get lost and that he never wanted to see her again.

But Toven hadn't known about Geraldine. The god had been convinced that he was infertile, and coming face to face with his doppelgänger had been a shocker.

Maybe later, he'd regretted throwing Orion out? Or maybe Toven was so consumed with self-loathing that he couldn't stand the sight of a son who looked exactly like him?

What if his father had come to regret not knowing whether he had any other offspring?

According to Alena, most gods were lucky to produce one or two children, so it was possible that throughout Toven's very long life, he had fathered only two.

Alena, his lovely, beautiful Alena, was over two thousand years old, and unlike other immortal females, she'd been miraculously fertile. Curiously though, all of her thirteen children had been born during the first five centuries of her life. And it wasn't as if she'd been abstaining since.

What if Toven had experienced the same spikes and dips in his fertility? What if he had fathered many children thousands of years ago and then none until Orion and Geraldine?

Perhaps Alena would be the same? What if she was capable of having more children?

Orion certainly hoped so, provided that they were his.

Before being captured by the clan and learning the particulars of immortal fertility, he'd given up hope of ever becoming a father, but now that he knew that fatherhood was still a possibility, he was once again allowing himself to yearn for a child of his own, provided that Alena was the mother.

Ugly jealousy clouding his reasoning, he resented those thirteen human males who'd fathered her children, and he felt guilty for it. He should regard them as sperm donors, but that wouldn't be true. Alena had told him that she felt grateful to those males for the gift of motherhood and for contributing their genetic material to make each of her children a unique individual. She attributed her children's good qualities to the upstanding human males she'd chosen to father them.

He should be glad that her experiences had been positive, and he was, but he was also insanely jealous, not only of those who had fathered her children, but of every male who had ever laid hands on her, and there had been many.

Damn, he shouldn't feel so possessive of her—he had no right. Hell, he'd known her for all of four days, but in that short time she'd become indispensable to him.

Too indispensable.

What if things didn't work out between them?

How could he go on without her?

He couldn't, and getting aggravated thinking of all the males she'd been with as he was heading into her brother's office was the last thing he should be doing.

Kian was super protective of his sisters, and if Orion let the less than perfect side of him show, the guy might decide to retract his approval and forbid him from accompanying Alena to China.

Hell, getting Kian's permission to go with her on that trip was why Orion was standing in front of the office building with the journal in his pocket, and he should get on with it.

He'd wasted enough time on what ifs. Sharing the journal with the clan was the right thing to do regardless of creating goodwill between him and the brother of the woman he wanted. The clan would put it to good use, possibly helping him locate Toven and perhaps additional siblings who would enrich his and Geraldine's lives.

2

ALENA

*A*s Onidu helped the heavily pregnant Amanda step out of the limousine, Alena was reminded of the less than fabulous moments of her pregnancies. She'd loved the feeling of a life growing inside of her, and she'd cherished every moment of the journey, but some moments had been better than others, and feeling like a bipedal whale had not been among her fondest memories. Neither had been the frequent visits to the bathroom, especially since toilets back then had not been the porcelain thrones of today.

"It's so nice of your friend to open her boutique for us an hour early." She followed Amanda to the front door.

Her sister chuckled. "For me, Joann would open it in the middle of the night and on her birthday, and not because I thralled her to do so. She knows that I'll make it worth her while." She rang the doorbell.

"Don't count on me filling Joann's coffers. I'm not going to buy that many outfits. You'll need to get some as well."

"No way." Amanda patted her big belly. "I'm not getting anything new until I can fit into size six again."

Alena patted her arm. "Don't be silly. You never wear anything more than a couple of times anyway, and by the time you get your pre-pregnancy figure back, you'll have grown tired of those 'enormous' size eight outfits and will buy new ones."

"Good point." Amanda rang the doorbell. "That's odd. I've never had to ring twice before."

The door banged open, and a tall, leggy blonde with an apologetic expression on her perfectly made-up face walked out. "I'm so sorry for keeping you waiting. I was upstairs unpacking a new delivery, and my hair got tangled in one of the plastic ties." She gently embraced Amanda and then turned to Alena. "You must be Amanda's sister, but you two look nothing alike. You're both gorgeous, of course, just in different ways." She paused her rushed monologue to take a breath. "You must forgive my blabbering. After hearing so much about you, I'm just so excited to finally meet you. I'm Joann." She offered Alena her hand.

"I hope you heard good things." Alena cast Amanda a sidelong glance. "What stories have you spun about me?"

Her sister waved a dismissive hand and pushed past Joann into the boutique. "I told my dear friend that you need an entire new wardrobe for a romantic vacation to a lake located high up in the mountains of China. I checked, and it gets really cold there at night. In fact, the temperature drops to near freezing this time of year, so regular Southern California attire won't do."

"Don't worry." Joann put three of her expertly manicured fingers on Alena's arm. "I've made a few emergency phone calls to colleagues of mine who offer exclusive designer attire for colder climates, and I had everything you need delivered. One of those shipments was what I was busy unpacking when you rang the doorbell."

Alena could just imagine the price tag that came with such a bespoke service. She had plenty of money, but she didn't like frivolous spending. A donation to a worthy cause would make her much happier than wasting a small fortune on a fancy new wardrobe.

Her sister, however, didn't have such qualms. Donating her designer outfits after she'd gotten tired of them was what Amanda considered to be a worthy charitable contribution.

"What about Amanda?" Alena asked. "Did you prepare a selection for her as well?"

"Of course." Joann smirked. "I wouldn't neglect my best customer." She glanced at Amanda, who was pressing the heels of her palms into the small of her back. "Let's get you ladies comfortable." The boutique owner motioned for them to sit down on the two white chaises. "Coffee? Tea?"

"Coffee," Amanda said.

"Tea for me, thank you." Alena forced a polite smile.

When the woman strutted away on her four-inch heels, she pinned her sister with a hard look. "Yesterday, you said that I needed a few key items. From what Joann said, it sounded like I will leave with truckloads of new outfits."

Amanda chuckled. "Only a couple of truckloads, darling. No need to be so dramatic."

"I'm not the dramatic one in the family," Alena murmured under her breath.

"I heard that." Amanda leaned back and lifted her legs onto the chaise. "Don't be such a mood spoiler, Alena. Not everything in your life needs to be about service to the clan. You deserve some pampering, and you can afford to be frivolous for a change."

There was some truth in her sister's words.

Alena would probably end up buying too many outfits that she would never get to wear after the vacation was over, but if it made her sister happy, she could live with that.

Amanda was putting up her usual façade of a spoiled rich princess and pretending that everything was okay, but Alena didn't buy the act. She knew that her sister was terrified of becoming a mother again.

Talking about her fears with Vanessa would have benefitted Amanda, but since she was refusing to admit them even to herself, shopping therapy would have to suffice.

"After we are done here, do you think you'll have enough energy left for a little more store hopping?"

Amanda's eyes sparkled. "What else do you need to get?"

"I need to buy clothes for Orion. I've seen what he has in his suitcase, and there is nothing in there warm enough for Lugu Lake's cold nights. He also doesn't have anything that's suitable for a visit to an archeological dig. At the very least, he needs hiking shoes and a warm coat."

"Do you know his size?"

Alena arched a brow. "Intimately."

Her sister laughed. "I meant shoe size. How intimate did you get with his feet?"

Leaning forward, Alena whispered conspiratorially, "He has the sexiest feet ever. Am I weird to find a male's feet so attractive?"

"Not at all, darling." Amanda pushed up against the chaise arm and tried to cross her arms over her belly. "I think Dalhu's feet are very sexy, and I also buy him clothes and shoes, but that's because he hates shopping. Orion seems like a stylish guy, though, who doesn't need help in that department. Besides, you've known him for four days. Isn't that too soon to start dressing him up? If you ask me, that's more intimate than sex."

Well, for immortals, it might be.

Alena shrugged. "I don't feel as if only a few days have passed since we met. I feel like we belong together, and since we do, I need to take care of my man." She smiled apologetically. "Still, I don't want to appear too pushy or presumptuous, and I don't want him to think that I'm mothering him, but he needs clothing for the trip, and he doesn't have time to get it himself. He's meeting with Kian to talk about Toven's journal and to devise a strategy to find him. It might take all day, and we are leaving early tomorrow."

Amanda's expression turned serious. "I hope that Orion feels the same, and if he wants a life with you, he needs to accept you for who you are, and you are a mother at heart. You need to take care of others. If he can't deal with that, then he's not the one for you."

3

ELEANOR

"*I*'m worried." Emmett got to his feet and walked over to the suite's balcony. "We've left Leon and Anastasia to run Safe Haven without giving them proper training." He turned around and looked at Peter. "Can you call your former partner and check how they are doing?"

"I can do better than that." Peter pulled out his phone. "We can have a video chat with Leon and Anastasia, and you can ask them anything you want."

"I'd appreciate that."

So far, Eleanor's fears about Peter and Emmett being at each other's throats hadn't been realized. On the flight over, the two had been civil to each other, but that was probably because they'd each gotten their own little pod in the business class section of the cabin and had slept on the red eye from Oregon to West Virginia.

Sharing a two-bedroom suite didn't seem to be a problem either.

"It's nine o'clock in the morning in Safe Haven," she said. "Leon and Ana are having breakfast right now. Are you sure it's a good time to call them?"

"It's the perfect time," Emmett said. "If they are in the dining room with Riley and her cohorts, it's even better. I want Riley to know that I'm checking up on her."

"Leon can handle Riley," Peter said.

"He doesn't know her," Emmett countered. "She seems agreeable and effusive, but she is cunning and manipulative. She'll have him wrapped around her little finger without him being any the wiser."

Peter shook his head. "Anastasia knows her well, and she's a smart girl. Riley won't be able to manipulate her."

"Anastasia didn't spend all that long in Safe Haven, and she wasn't in management." Emmett let out a long-suffering breath. "She was a maid, for heaven's sake. She barely interacted with Riley."

"We need to get ready." Eleanor rose to her feet. "The funeral is at three o'clock, and it's half an hour's drive."

"What about the call?" Emmett asked.

"Safe Haven survived without you for months, and it will survive a couple more weeks."

She didn't add that if he was that worried, he should have stayed behind instead of twisting Kian's arm to let him join the mission. Not that she minded. It was good to have him with her.

"We have plenty of time." Peter ignored her and placed the call.

"Good morning," Leon answered. "How was your flight?"

"Great. We flew business, and we had those seats that turn into beds, so we slept like the dead. Listen, Emmett is worried that he left you without proper instructions. Can you tell him to relax?" Peter switched the phone to a video call and positioned it so Leon and Ana could see Emmett.

"Don't worry, Emmett," Anastasia said. "Safe Haven runs like a well-oiled machine. As long as nothing unexpected happens, everyone knows how to do their jobs. All that Leon and I have to do until you come back is supervise and handle the unexpected. What could possibly happen over the next week or two?"

"A lot," Emmett said. "But you are right about everyone knowing their jobs." He puffed out his chest. "The standard operating procedures I put down are so clear that a trained monkey could follow them and do a great job."

"Then you shouldn't worry." Eleanor clapped him on the back. "I'm going to get dressed."

"Good luck," Anastasia said. "Leon and I are keeping our fingers crossed for you."

"Thank you."

A lot was riding on her today, and Eleanor would be lying if she claimed that she wasn't nervous.

Roberts's widow was hosting a late luncheon after the funeral, which would provide the perfect setup for what Eleanor needed to do. All the trainees were attending, as well as the higher-ups who would decide the paranormal program's future.

Convincing the bosses to let her take over the program shouldn't be too difficult, even without the use of compulsion. With the fake doctorate the clan had arranged for her, she had the right credentials, and as someone who had been instrumental in finding talent for the program, she was also the best candidate to run it after its two founders had died.

Her second task was to check which of the trainees were unhappy and wanted to leave the program, so she could recruit them for a different kind of job and offer them a new life. The third was to find someone who worked in the Echelon system and compel them to supply the clan with the information they needed.

Kian wanted access to what the spying system was collecting about mentions of paranormal abilities. He also wanted her to give the person a list of Kra-ell words. If spoken or written over communications lines that weren't as secure as the clan's system, they would get flagged, and the clan would be able to find the source.

All three tasks were super important, and it made her feel good that she'd been entrusted with them. Did it mean that Kian no longer regarded her as an outsider?

Eleanor wasn't sure about that.

Perhaps Kian trusted her, which in itself was a huge achievement, but he still didn't think of her as a clan member. He'd accepted her proposal to run Safe Haven alongside Emmett too easily. Was it because he was glad of the opportunity to get rid of her?

4

KIAN

"*G*ood morning." Kian motioned for Orion to take a seat at the conference table next to Onegus.

"Good morning." The guy smiled tightly.

The journal he was holding with a white-knuckled grip was bound in brown leather, with the date of January 1929 embossed on its spine and no end date. If that thing contained all of Toven's lovers for over half a century, then the god either wasn't very active sexually or recorded just a small fraction of the women he'd been with.

"Do you mind if I take a look?" Kian extended his hand. "Or do you prefer for me to wait until the copy is ready?"

With an effort, Orion released his death grip on the thing and handed it to Kian. "Be careful with it. Some of the pages are loose."

"Of course."

Following Syssi's advice, Kian tried to put himself in the guy's shoes. It was a hack she'd suggested to help him develop empathy, but so far it had been only marginally useful. Often, Kian found himself feeling ambivalent about things that meant a lot to others and vice versa.

When he tried to imagine how he would have felt if that leather-bound five-by-eight journal was all he had from his father, Kian realized that it would have held no sentimental value for him.

He'd never been overly curious about the human who'd fathered him. His mother had told him fantastic stories about the Scottish warrior who'd sired him, but Kian regarded them more as fanciful tales than an accurate description of the man.

Besides, he wasn't a sentimental guy, especially with regard to mementos.

Still, out of respect for Orion he handled the journal with care, gently flipping the pages and admiring the beautifully crafted sketches. He didn't know much about art, but the portraits were pleasing to the eye and seemed to have been drawn with a fondness for the subjects.

"Toven is talented." He handed the journal back. "But then he had thousands of years to hone his skill." Kian chuckled. "That being said, I doubt I would have graduated from drawing stick figures even after a thousand years of daily effort. I just don't have the eye or the inclination for artistic expression."

As the door opened and Shai entered with a cardboard tray of coffees, Orion snatched the journal off the table and put it in his lap.

"Good morning, Shai." He gave the guy a smile. "Is one of those for me?"

"Naturally." Shai handed each one of them a paper cup filled to the brim with the aromatic dark-roast brew from the café. "Tell me when you're ready, and I'll show you how to operate the scanner."

"Where is it?" Orion glanced at Kian's desk, his eyes passing over the device without recognizing it for what it was.

Shai pointed to the scanner. "It's the thing that looks like a desk lamp. You put the book open on the tray, and it scans both pages. It's just as time-consuming as with a traditional scanner, but the way it's designed makes the copying gentler on the original. You don't have to flatten it because the software compensates for the curvature and flattens the image. It's not perfect, but it's good enough for what we need."

"I'll start on it right away." Orion pushed to his feet. "Can you show me how to operate it?"

"Drink your coffee first," Kian said. "Copying the manuscript will take you several hours, so you'd better get caffeinated before you start."

Orion nodded. "I'll just put the journal next to the device, so it's safe. I don't want it anywhere near food or liquids."

When he returned to the conference table, Kian put his coffee cup down and leaned back. "By the way, do you have the original translation with you? It could save Edna a lot of time."

"I don't." Orion removed the lid from the paper cup and took a sip. "By now, I know everything written in it by heart, so I no longer need it. Besides, I like the idea of a fresh set of eyes tackling the translation. I don't know how good the original was, and Edna might do a better job. Perhaps she will uncover new hints that had been lost in the original translation."

"Good point," Kian agreed.

"I have a question," Shai said. "Do you happen to remember some of the titles of Toven's novels?"

Orion shook his head. "I don't. Why?"

"You were correct in your assumption that an author's anonymous work can be identified by his writing style. If we can find even one book written by Toven, we might be able to find others, and if he used traditional publishers to sell his novels, we could get them to reveal information about him. Even if they never met him in person, they must have paid him, and money leaves a trail."

5

ORION

*O*rion shook his head. "Toven said that he changed his writing style from book to book so no one could recognize that they were written by the same author."

"He might think he's clever," Shai said. "But with today's artificial intelligence technology, it is possible to detect style even if the author makes a deliberate attempt to hide behind a pseudonym. Last night, I did some research on the subject and found out interesting stuff about the famous J. K. Rowling, author of the global phenomenon called Harry Potter. She wanted to prove that Harry Potter was not a fluke and that she could succeed as an unknown author writing in a very different genre. When some stylistic similarities were noticed between the new detective story she wrote and the Harry Potter books, they were run through stylometry software, and it was proven that they were written by the same person. Usually, software like that is used to detect plagiarism, but it could also help us find books written by Toven."

"Provided that they are available in digital form," Kian said. "Not all books are."

"True," Shai agreed. "But perhaps some are. It's the only lead we have."

"We have the journal," Orion said. "But it's written in Aramaic. The translation will eliminate any stylistic identifiers, provided that there are any. Toven is a very old and very smart god. I'm sure he did a superb job varying styles."

"We should consult William," Kian said. "He's an expert on anything that has to do with software." He pulled out his phone. "I'll cast the call on the screen so it will be as if he's here with us instead of dragging him away from his lab." He glanced at Orion. "I love modern technology. Don't you?"

Orion chuckled. "I like everything about it save for learning to use it and the potential dangers it poses for us. Every day, something new comes up that the young people of this generation adapt to in an instant. An old immortal like me has trouble catching up."

Kian nodded, but Orion had a feeling that the guy didn't share the same sentiments. He was probably one of those who understood technology on an innate level and quickly adapted to innovation.

As if to prove him right, Kian pressed a button on a remote, and a large screen descended from the ceiling, covering the entire wall of windows behind Kian's desk and darkening the office. A moment later, a bespectacled guy popped up on the screen, occupying most of its area.

"Good morning, Kian. To what do I owe the pleasure of this call?"

"I'm here with Orion, Onegus, and Shai, and we have some AI-related questions for you." Kian pressed another button on the remote, and a camera descended from the ceiling, its lens rotating until it was trained on the conference table. "Can you see us?"

"Yes." William smiled. "It's my pleasure to finally meet you, Orion. After the meeting, come over to my lab. I have a clan phone ready for you."

"Right," Kian said. "I forgot to mention that. Our phones work all over the world and are secure. All communications with clan members are to be made from that phone."

"Thank you." Orion inclined his head. "A smartphone was one of the innovations I adapted to very quickly and now can't live without. I didn't expect its lack to make me so uncomfortable."

"It's easy to get used to good things," Kian said. "And it's always difficult to go back to the way things were before."

"How true," William said. "So, what did you want to ask me?"

After Kian explained the problem in a few words, William turned to someone else who was not in the camera's view. "What do you think, Roni?"

As his nephew rolled his chair over so they could see him, Orion smiled and waved. "I didn't know that you and William shared an office."

"I have my own," Roni said. "But I like working with William. Two brilliant minds are better than one. As for your question, I think that with some tweaking by our very talented William, the software will detect style even in a translated text, provided that the sample is big enough. How long is Toven's journal?"

"Not that long," Orion said. "No more than twenty thousand words, if that."

"It might be enough, but I would have preferred a larger sample."

Kian frowned. "No offense, Roni, but you're a hacker. What do you know about literature and style?"

Roni grinned. "I don't need to know anything about literature. The same software that can analyze the writing style of novels can analyze computer code. Not many people realize that, but coding is a form of expression and it's not anonymous. How do you think hackers are exposed? Plagiarism is not exclusive to creation in human languages. Code gets plagiarized as well. To prove that plagiarism has occurred, researchers create abstract syntax trees that show the code's structure, the same way it would have been done with any human language." He chuckled. "Or immortal, for that matter. But in order for the algorithm to learn Toven's style, it needs a large sample—at least one full-length book."

That explanation had flown over Orion's head, but he understood enough to figure out how Roni's hacking related to Toven's writing. The other thing he realized was that it was imperative for him to remember at least one of the many titles he'd seen scattered around Toven's townhouse nearly four decades ago.

"Can immortals undergo hypnosis?" he asked. "What I saw in Toven's place should be in my head, recorded in my subconscious, but I need someone to help me retrieve it. I heard that hypnotists can do that."

"Maybe the Clan Mother could thrall you," Onegus suggested. "Thralling shares many attributes with hypnotizing."

Kian nodded. "It's worth a try. I'll give her a call to see when she's available."

6

ANNANI

"Master Kian and Master Orion." Oridu bowed. "The Clan Mother is expecting you."

As they entered the living room, Orion inclined his head. "Good morning, Clan Mother. Thank you for agreeing to see us."

Sitting on the couch, Annani gave her son and her adopted nephew a welcoming smile. "Good morning to you too. You were lucky to catch me between appointments. Unfortunately, I cannot spare more than half an hour, so we need to do this quickly."

"This is important, Mother." Kian leaned to kiss her cheek.

It was indeed important, but not for the reason they were there. Orion had just handed Annani the perfect excuse to test her powers on him, and she was sure Kian was not only aware of that but had planned for it.

If she could retrieve Orion's submerged memories, she could also do much more.

Orion nodded. "Half an hour should suffice. I only need to remember the title of one book, and I'm sure that I have it stored in my subconscious mind."

"Come." She patted the seat next to her. "Sit with me."

As Orion sat beside her on the couch, Kian walked to the other side of the room and sat on a barstool, probably so his presence would not affect her concentration.

"Give me your hands," she commanded Orion. When he tensed, she gave him a reassuring smile. "My thralling is not like Edna's probing. In fact, you will probably not feel it at all."

"I didn't mind Edna's probe." He shifted a little closer. "I don't have anything to hide from you or the rest of your clan. I'm just a little nervous."

Of course, he was.

It was not easy to submit one's mind to another's scrutiny, even if one had nothing to hide. Additionally, Orion might feel reluctant to show her his memories because the freshest ones included intimate moments with Alena.

Annani would have to be careful to avoid those, not just out of respect for her daughter's and her mate's privacy but because they were irrelevant to what she was after. The best way to prevent an accidental peek was to divert Orion's focus to the subject at hand.

"If you follow my guidance, this should not take long. Relax, close your eyes, and visualize Toven's townhouse. Start from the moment you entered."

Loosing a long breath, Orion relaxed his shoulders and closed his eyes. "I'm ready."

When she entered his mind with surprising ease, Annani wondered whether it would have been more difficult if he had resisted her.

She was ready to scan the room for book titles, but she had not prepared herself for the shock of seeing Toven through Orion's eyes.

He was not the same male she had known five millennia ago. His eyes were still his most striking feature, the intelligence palpable even through someone else's eyes, but the spark of interest that had shone so brightly before was gone.

Orion had been right about his father appearing emotionally numb.

As Annani's heart squeezed with sorrow, she refocused on the physical resemblance between father and son. They looked a lot alike, but as someone who had known Toven well, Annani could easily discern the differences.

Who was the more striking one, though?

Orion was more animated, bright eyed, but even though he was by no means simpleminded, he lacked his father's sharp intelligence, which had always been what had attracted Annani to Toven. However, looking at him through his son's eyes and with the perspective of age, she wondered whether Toven had always been somewhat cold, and she just had not been aware of that. The male was ruled by logic, not heart, and he had probably been that way even when she was a young girl.

"I see a title," she murmured. "It is written in Russian."

Orion's eyes popped open. "It says *An Angel in Moscow.*"

"You can read Russian?" Kian asked.

"I do." Orion turned back to Annani. "Did you see any other titles?"

She shook her head. "That was the only one you noticed."

"Let me see if I can find it online." Kian pulled out his phone. "That's the precise translation? *An Angel in Moscow?*"

When Orion nodded, Kian typed on his screen. "Interesting." He frowned.

"What did you find?" Annani asked.

"Nothing that's related to Toven, but there is a book called *Angels over Moscow—Life, Death and Human Trafficking in Russia – A Memoir* that's written by an American doctor. I find it quite serendipitous."

"What makes you so sure that it wasn't written by Toven?" Orion asked.

"First of all, the writer is a female, and her name and photo are included in the article about the book. Secondly, it's a memoir, not a novel." He kept reading for a couple of moments. "Although the way it's written, it could be a novel. After skimming through the excerpt, I'm actually intrigued, and I never read memoirs."

"What about the title I saw?" Orion asked.

"The search didn't reveal anything. Perhaps it was published only in Russia." He walked over to the couch and sat next to Orion. "Here." He handed him the phone. "Type the title in Russian."

"That's not going to be easy." Orion sighed. "I can speak and read it but not write in it."

"Take your time. We are not in a rush."

It took Orion a long time to type the three words in Russian, and when the search did not bring up any results, he looked disappointed. "What now?"

"Not everything is online." Kian took the phone from him and put it in his pocket. "We will have to search in Russian libraries." He chuckled. "I bet Turner has someone who can do that for us."

"Turner," Orion said. "I've heard that name mentioned before. Am I ever going to meet the guy?"

"I'm sure you will soon." Kian rose to his feet. "Turner is a great strategist, and I wouldn't be surprised if he comes up with a new angle that we haven't considered. But it will probably have to wait for after your vacation."

7

KIAN

*N*ow that Kian had proof that Annani could thrall Orion, he felt much better about Alena going with the guy to China. If he tried to compel Alena to do anything she didn't want to, Annani could override his compulsion. It didn't seem likely, and Kian wasn't really worried about Orion stepping out of line, but he wanted added protection for Alena nonetheless.

Since Lokan was joining their group at Lugu Lake, it was possible that he would be followed. It was highly unlikely, but Kian had no tolerance for risk where the Brotherhood was concerned. Then there were the Kra-ell, who had probably lived in the area thousands of years ago but were long gone by now. Still, on the remote chance that they were still there, he wasn't taking any chances where his sister was concerned.

If he could, he would send an entire contingent of Guardians with her, but she would never agree to that, so one Head Guardian and three compellers would have to do.

As Annani took another peek into Orion's memories of his encounter with Toven, Kian pulled out his phone and texted Arwel. *I need you to go to China after all, but not with Mey and Yamanu. I want you to accompany Alena and keep an eye on her. You can bring Jin along.*

Having his mate with him hadn't hindered Arwel's performance before, but Kian would have preferred that the Head Guardian's attention was fully on Alena and not split between her and his mate. On the other hand, having him join the expedition along with Jin would be a much easier sell than sending Arwel alone.

Alena and Jacki would be glad of the additional female company, so Alena wouldn't object.

Arwel's return text arrived a few moments later. *I spoke with Jin, and she's excited to go.*

Kian typed back. *I'm glad. Come over to Annani's place. I want her to transfer command of Oridu to you.*

When Annani let go of Orion's hands, her disappointed expression told Kian that she hadn't found any more titles hiding in the guy's subconscious.

"I'm sorry." Orion raked his fingers through his hair. "I wish I'd paid more attention and read the titles on the spines."

"It is what it is," Kian said. "Don't beat yourself up over it."

Orion nodded. "I keep thinking about other ways to find Toven. He said that he had a lot of gold, and that means that he had to store it somewhere and sell it from time to time to cover his expenses. Perhaps Roni can hack into the gold depositories."

"It's worth a try." Kian put his phone back in his pocket. "Arwel is coming over in a few minutes."

"What for?" Annani asked.

"I assigned him to the Mosuo trip, and I want you to transfer command of Oridu to him."

Annani arched a brow. "I planned on transferring command to Alena. Is there a specific reason you want Arwel to command the Odu?"

"Arwel is a Guardian. If the group is attacked, he would know how to defend them better than Alena would. Naturally, she will retain command of Ovidu, but I want Oridu at Arwel's disposal."

"Alena is not going to be happy about that." Annani cast a sidelong glance at Orion, who pretended as if the discussion had nothing to do with him. "You agreed that two Odus would suffice as her guard."

Kian shrugged. "I changed my mind. Besides, Arwel is bringing Jin along, and I'm sure Alena and Jacki will be glad to have her with them."

Annani smiled. "Clever, Kian."

"Is Kalugal's jet big enough for two more passengers?" Orion asked.

"It is. And before you ask, Kalugal knows better than to refuse my request to add additional security for my sister."

When a knock sounded at the door, Oridu rushed to open it for the Guardian. "Good morning, Master Arwel." He bowed. "Please, come in."

"Thank you." Arwel strode in. "Good morning, Clan Mother." He bowed to Annani. "Hello, Kian, Orion."

"Have we met?" The guy pushed to his feet and offered his hand to the Guardian.

"We haven't." The two shook hands. "But we are about to get very well acquainted over the next two weeks."

"I'm looking forward to it."

As Orion smiled, Kian wondered what Arwel's opinion of him was. The Guardian's empathic ability lent itself to character evaluation, but it wasn't always accurate.

Arwel had thought that Eleanor was evil when he'd first encountered her. She'd been filled with hate and resentment, but it hadn't corrupted her to the core. After having been shown kindness and acceptance, the woman had changed a lot. Her character was still abrasive, and she was extremely ambitious, but now she used those qualities for the clan and strived to prove herself.

Kian still didn't trust her a hundred percent, but if she managed to achieve all the objectives he'd tasked her with in West Virginia, he might have to get over the remaining vestiges of doubt and officially acknowledge her contribution to the clan with some kind of title or position.

He would need to give it some further thought or perhaps ask Syssi to come up with something appropriate.

"Oridu," Annani called him to her. "As we have discussed earlier, tomorrow you will join Alena and Orion on their trip to China, but there was a slight change of plans. Instead of obeying Alena's commands, you will obey Arwel's."

"As you wish, Clan Mother." Oridu bowed. "Should I obey both their commands or just Master Arwel's?"

Annani shifted her gaze to Kian. "I suggest both. Do you object?"

"What happens when their commands contradict each other? One has to be the primary and the other the secondary. I want Arwel to be the primary."

Annani didn't look happy, but she nodded nonetheless. "Very well." She turned to Oridu. "You are to obey both Mistress Alena and Master Arwel. But if their commands are contradicting, you should obey Master Arwel over Mistress Alena."

8

EMMETT

*E*mmett sat on the bed in his and Eleanor's hotel bedroom and watched her pull on a pair of silky black nylons, shimmy into a tight black dress, and then push her feet into a pair of black pumps.

"You look good." He reached for her hand and pulled her into his lap. "Too good. Let me come with you, or I'll go crazy thinking about all those humans ogling what's mine."

"We've talked about that." She put her hand on his cheek and gave him a little peck on the lips. "Peter is coming as my date."

"He can come as your brother. I want to be your date for the funeral."

She rolled her eyes. "I can't show up with two guys. I'm not a family member, and I can't justify bringing additional guests who didn't know Elijah to the funeral."

"You can do whatever you want. You're a compeller, and so am I. Who is going to tell us that we can't be there?"

She furrowed her eyebrows. "You have a point. But there is no need for you to come. Actually, it's better that you don't. I'm going to lay on the charm and pretend to flirt with the big honchos that will decide the program's future, and I don't need you growling at every male I talk to."

"I'm not going to growl. Didn't I behave admirably so far? I'm playing nice with Peter despite the coveting looks he sends your way."

"You're imagining things. Peter has absolutely no romantic interest in me. In fact, I hope he will find a connection with one of the trainees. Naomi is pretty, but she's only twenty-one, so she might be too young for him. Abigail is not as good-looking, but she's thirty-two, and she's a healer—gentle, soft-spoken, and curvy—the opposite of me. I think she and Peter would be perfect for each other."

That eased some of the pressure in Emmett's chest, but he still didn't want her going without him. It wasn't about jealousy but about his need to protect her. Eleanor was a confident, strong female, and Peter was a good Guardian, but neither of them could match Emmett's compulsion ability or physical strength.

No one could protect Eleanor better than he.

"I'm glad that you're thinking about hooking Peter up with someone else, but he's not the reason I want to come with you. You're my mate, and I need to protect you. I can't do that from the hotel."

Her eyes softened. "I'm not walking into the lion's den. It's just a funeral with mostly old people attending. And as you said yourself, I'm a compeller. What could they possibly do to me?"

"Just let him come," Peter said from the other side of the door. "He's not going to stop begging, and he might crawl after you to the car, holding on to your ankles. I really don't want to see that."

"Fine." She let out a breath. "Do you have anything appropriate to wear?"

Emmett smiled triumphantly. "I came prepared."

"Of course, you did. You knew that you were going to win."

"I don't give up easily, and you love me because I'm tenacious." He tightened his arms around her and lifted his lips to hers.

Eleanor gave him another small peck. "I love you for many reasons, but we don't have time. If you want to come, you need to get dressed." She pushed on his chest. "Let me go."

"One more kiss, a proper one, and I will."

A loud groan sounded from the other side of the door. "You know that I can hear every word. This is not the village, and the soundproofing here sucks."

Emmett smirked. "I know."

9

VROG

*I*t was lunchtime at the café, Wendy's busiest time of the day, but instead of letting Vrog help, she'd told him to sit on a barstool, learn to use his new phone, and do what Kian had asked of him.

The device looked like an iPhone, or one of its Chinese-made clones, but it was much more sophisticated.

"Does William have my number?" he asked Wendy when she had a moment between taking orders from customers.

"He's the one who programmed your phone, so naturally, he has your number. Did you send the emails Kian asked you to?"

"Not yet. I'm still figuring out how to use this thing."

She rolled her eyes. "The same way as any other cellphone."

"Not exactly, but similar enough." He tapped on the icon that looked like an envelope, hoping it was an email service. "I got the email. I'm good."

She gave him a quick smile before turning to her next customer.

Kian wanted the team to stay at the school instead of a hotel, which made sense, since it would be more convenient and save them on travel time, but it would be difficult to explain to Doctor Wang and the rest of the school's faculty.

Vrog had never hosted guests at the school's staff quarters before.

Could he claim that they were all prospective teachers? He could make the principal forget that he'd ever seen Mey and Yamanu before, but that was never foolproof. Doctor Wang was a smart fellow, and his mind was not as easily manipulated as those of others. For it to hold it would have to get reinforced daily, and that was too much of a hassle. Vrog needed an excuse that retained the fake identities they'd provided to the principal before.

He could tell Doctor Wang that Mey and Yamanu were interested in purchasing the school, and that they wanted to experience it firsthand before making their decision. The poor guy might get distressed by the prospect of foreigners buying Vrog

I. T. LUCAS

out, but he could reassure the principal that no staff members would be replaced following the change of ownership, so Wang should not worry about losing his job.

Not that he would ever sell the school, but it was a good story. Later, he would tell Wang that the deal fell through.

As before, Alfie, Jay, and Morris would pose as Yamanu and Mey's personal staff members, and naturally, they would need to stay close to their bosses, so accommodations had to be prepared for them as well.

"Vrog," Wendy whispered close to his ear. "Don't look now, but Dorothea is eyeing you, and I think she's about to come over and talk to you."

"Who is Dorothea?" he whispered back.

"To your left. The tall brunette with the waist-long hair."

That sounded promising. Tall brunettes were his preferred type.

Pretending to move the phone's screen out of the direct sun, he took a peek.

The female was indeed looking at him, but he wasn't sure if there was interest in her eyes or suspicion. So far, most of the looks he'd gotten were of the second kind, and she was too far away for him to detect her scent.

"I don't think she likes me very much," he whispered to Wendy. "She's just curious."

"That's a good start," she whispered back.

As he typed an email to Wang, Vrog kept checking on Dorothea out of the corner of his eye, but she never made it to the counter and eventually left with a friend.

Could she be his match? Had she come to the café to take a look at him?

He was still awaiting William's call, hoping that a match had been found for him. But if Dorothea was the one the software had matched him with, he knew she would decline to participate.

When his phone rang Vrog was so startled that he almost dropped it, and when he saw William's name as the caller, he almost dropped it again.

"Hello, William. Do you have good news for me?"

Wendy abandoned her customer and came over to listen.

"I do," William said. "The software found you a match, but the lady can't do it tonight."

"Did you tell her that I'm leaving tomorrow?"

"She was very sad to hear that, but she couldn't change her plans for today. She said she'd wait for you to return. I didn't tell her that you're probably not coming back. Should I?"

"No. I'll be back."

Vrog hadn't been sure before, but now that he had a confirmed match with a female who was willing to wait for him to return, he wasn't going to disappoint her.

"Does she know who I am?"

"It wasn't too difficult to guess. It's a small village. But I didn't confirm her suspicion. Fortunately, you are not the only one who's leaving tomorrow, so she can't know for sure. Kalugal is taking three of his men to China as well."

"Kian told me about the Mosuo trip. That's the reason my visit is ending too soon."

"I'm sorry about that," William said. "What should I tell the lady? Are you sure that you're coming back?"

"I am, but I don't know when that will be. It depends on Mey and how successful she is with finding echoes left by my people."

238

10

ELEANOR

*E*leanor surveyed the crowd gathered at the chapel in the funeral home. Up front, Roberts' widow was seated between her adult children, their spouses, and her grandchildren. Other family members filled the three rows behind her, and the rest were colleagues—past and present—everyone from the paranormal program, including the new doctor, the nurse, the other instructors, and the bosses, two of whom were in uniform and the other two in civilian attire.

So far, no one had asked why she'd brought two men with her, but then they'd arrived when nearly everyone was seated, so other than a few curious looks, no one had had a chance to ask her anything.

She'd approached Dora to offer her condolences, and the tears in her eyes had been genuine—not for Roberts, who'd been a prick, but for his widow, who'd lost a life-long partner. Perhaps Elijah had been a good husband in his old age, but even if he hadn't, he and Dora had been together for decades, and his widow would miss him.

After wiping her tears and regaining her composure, Eleanor had located the members of the paranormal program and given them a genuine smile, but it hadn't been reciprocated.

They hadn't changed much since the last time she'd seen them. James had lost more hair, Mollie had gained a few pounds, Sofia had changed her hair color from mousy brown to fiery red, and Spencer had lost his baby face to a scruffy beard. The others hadn't changed at all. Naomi, Abigail, Jeremy, Andy, and Dylan looked the same as they had before, except for the hostile looks they were sending her way.

Without periodic reinforcements, her compulsion over them had worn off, and their true feelings for her had re-emerged.

Oh well, she could always compel them again, but she had no doubt that it would be more difficult this time. They were no longer the naive recruits she'd lured into the program with promises of earning big money by serving their country. Now they were jaded, suspicious, and not as easily impressed.

Once the service was over and everyone moved into the luncheon reception area, Eleanor found the one higher-up she knew. The colonel might not be the one making hiring decisions, but he could refer her to someone who was.

Leaving Peter and Emmett at the buffet, she walked over to the man. "Good afternoon, Colonel Crowley." She offered him her hand. "Do you remember me? I'm Eleanor Takala." She affected a charming smile. "I worked closely with Elijah and Edgar to create the paranormal program from its very inception."

"Of course, I remember you." He shook her hand. "Although I have to say that your sabbatical has done wonders for you. You look incredible, Eleanor."

"Thank you. I also used the time off to finish my doctorate." She leaned closer. "With that degree in my pocket, I'm the most qualified candidate to replace Roberts as the head of the paranormal program. I know the objectives, I know each one of its current members, and I'm available immediately. With me, the program will continue without a hitch. Not only that, but I'm also the only one who was able to recruit real talent. After I left, Elijah didn't add a single new paranormal. Without me, this program will die. You need me."

That speech should have been good enough even without the element of compulsion she'd added to it, but since she'd been as subtle as a bull in a china shop, Crowley might have been put off by her aggressiveness. The compulsion served to overcome any such personal misgivings, making it impossible for him to reject her offer out of hand.

Crowley regarded her for a long moment, his dark brown eyes boring into hers as if he was trying to see into her soul. "You've convinced me that you're the best candidate for the job, but I need to convince others. I know that you didn't leave the program voluntarily, and I need to know why Roberts kicked you out."

Grimacing, she cast a sidelong glance at the widow and then leaned even closer to the colonel. "It doesn't feel right to talk about it here. Can you walk outside with me for a moment?"

"No problem."

As he offered her his arm, she threaded hers through it and cast a quick look at Emmett, telling him with her eyes not to follow.

He didn't look happy but nodded and turned to Peter.

When the door closed behind them, Crowley pulled out a cigarette box. "This is a nasty habit, but it provides the excuse for much-needed breaks." He flipped the top open and offered it to her.

"No, thank you. I don't smoke."

"Will it bother you if I do?"

"Not at all." She smiled. "I didn't want to say anything next to Dora and her family, but Roberts and Edwards were a couple of philandering bastards. They both hit on me at one time or another, and they hit on the young recruits as well."

"Interesting. No complaints were filed."

First of all, that was a lie. None might have been filed recently, but there had been several in the distant past, and given that Crowley didn't seem shocked in the least meant that he was aware of that.

Bastard.

He was probably guilty of the same thing and didn't think it was a big deal. The good-old-boys covered up for each other.

Eleanor struck a pose and pinned him with a hard stare. "I know of several complaints that were filed a couple of decades ago when both Roberts and Edwards were a little younger and still using their station and influence to coerce subordinates into sexual situations they would have never agreed to otherwise. They also threatened anyone who might have dared to come forward, explicitly and implicitly. I was fired and denied access to the facility precisely for that reason, and frankly, I stayed silent out of fear for my life."

"Really?" He arched a brow and puffed on his cigarette. 'What made you come forward now?"

She smiled coldly. "They are both dead, and I doubt anyone else is motivated to go to such extremes to prevent this from getting out. I would rather not cause their widows additional grief, but I can easily collect a number of testimonials from their other victims. That's neither here nor there, though. You wanted to know why I was kicked out despite the exemplary service I provided, and now you know."

The colonel wasn't a stupid man, and she didn't need to spell out the threat for him to understand what would keep her quiet.

"I can't give you an answer on the spot. I will need to schedule an interview for you to present your qualifications. Also, we will need to run a new security check on you."

"Naturally." Roni had already taken care of that, and since her doctorate was from an online university, there was no one for the Feds to interview. The records would show her as attending online courses for the past six years and earning her doctorate a little over a month ago.

11

ANNANI

"*R*onja." Annani opened her arms. "You look absolutely amazing." She hugged her friend and then smoothed her hands over the woman's defined biceps. "What a transformation."

Ronja looked at least ten years younger since the last time Annani had seen her, and if she did not know better, she would have thought that Ronja had transitioned.

"Thank you." Her friend smiled. "Merlin's health regimen works, and not just on me."

"I want to hear all about it." Annani took her hand and led her to the couch. "You look so much thinner and more toned. How long ago did you start exercising?"

"About six weeks ago. I didn't actually lose that much weight. Only seven pounds, but Merlin says that I lost much more than that, but the fat was replaced by muscles." She sighed. "I love the way I look, but I don't like how sore I am most days."

Annani frowned. "Is Merlin being too rough with you?"

Ronja tilted her head. "He has to be, or I wouldn't get out of bed in the morning. I hate running, and I hate lifting weights, and I hate swimming more than both. The only activity I kind of enjoy is bike riding."

Annani laughed. "I do not think we are talking about the same thing. I was referring to Merlin being sexually rough, not his training routine."

Ronja's cheeks reddened. "We haven't done that yet."

"Why not?"

"You know why." Ronja pushed a stray strand of hair behind her ear. "But I have to admit that I'm fighting a losing battle with my hormones." She smiled shyly. "Merlin is exercising alongside me, and his transformation is even more dramatic than mine." She laughed. "He was always handsome, but he has turned into an irresistible hunk, and the sly man knows it. He flexes his new muscles whenever I look at him and gives me those sexy looks that make my heart flutter."

"Only your heart?" Annani waggled her brows.

Ronja's blush deepened. "Among other things."

Annani was overjoyed to see her friend not only looking healthier and more beautiful but also happier. Merlin was good for her.

She patted Ronja's knee. "Well, you know what I think about your abstinence, so I am not going to repeat it. Tell me how Lisa is doing."

"She's wonderful. Out of solidarity with me, she joins us on our morning jogs and sometimes also the afternoon swims."

That was admirable, but it was also hindering romantic progress. Merlin could not put the moves on Ronja with Lisa around.

"You two should go on a vacation," Annani suggested. "Just you and Merlin."

"I can't." Ronja crossed her legs. "I can't leave Lisa alone."

"You could take her to Scotland, leave her with David and Sari, and tour the country with Merlin, but winter is not a good time to visit Scotland. The Highlands are cold even in the summer."

"I went to Scotland with my first husband. It's beautiful, even more so than Norway." She uncrossed her legs and leaned forward. "Speaking of vacations, though, I heard that Alena is joining Kalugal and Jacki on a trip to China. Are you going to be okay without her?"

"Of course," Annani said with more conviction than she felt. "I have you to keep me company while she is gone."

Ronja seemed taken aback. "I can't possibly take Alena's place. She's your heir, your second-in-command, so to speak. I'm just a simple woman."

Obviously, Ronja was not thinking about the next two weeks but more long-term. Was she afraid Annani would take her away from Merlin and Lisa?

Even if she was free to go, Ronja was no substitute for Alena.

"First of all, you are not simple, and secondly, no one can take Alena's place, and I am not looking to replace her. I just need a friend."

"I can do that. I hope." Ronja averted her eyes. "You are a goddess, Annani. And I'm just a simple mortal who has just a smidgen of your spark in me. I try not to think about your glowing skin and ignore the power you emit, but the truth is that next to you, I feel insignificant. I don't think that makes me a very good friend."

"Nonsense." Annani took Ronja's hand. "I know that I am a lot to take in, and we have not spent enough time together for you to get comfortable with me. But in our souls and hearts we are the same. We are both mothers, and we are both widows. We have experienced the same kinds of sorrows and the same kinds of joys, and since people are shaped by the sum of their experiences just as much as they are shaped by their genetics, you and I are more alike than you think."

1 2

ELEANOR

"*L*et's make a toast." Eleanor raised her wine glass. "To Elijah Roberts, may he rest in peace."

As the paranormal program's members lifted their glasses, some repeated her words while others nodded in agreement.

Surprisingly, none had refused her invitation to a local bar after the service was over. She hadn't even had to resort to compulsion to get them to agree.

Unlike Jin and her cohorts, those who had stayed were not aware of Eleanor's real role in the program and had only remembered her as their recruiter—the one who supposedly had negotiated the extravagant pay for them. They might not like her as a person, but they were smart enough to realize that befriending her could benefit them.

"What now?" Mollie asked. "Are they going to end the program? My annual contract is about to end, and I have no idea what to do on the outside."

"You could start a psychic lost and found," Jeremy suggested. "Or help the police solve crimes."

Mollie's talent was post cognition, so Jeremy's ideas for her future employment weren't wrong, except for the fact that no one was hiring.

She snorted. "What would that pay? Not a quarter of a million a year, that's for sure."

"The program is not going anywhere," Eleanor said. "Not if I can help it. In fact, I'm working on a plan to move it out of the crypt you've been complaining about to a beautiful beachfront property in Oregon. I also plan to recruit new talent."

Jeremy eyed her from below his dark lashes. "How are you going to achieve all that?"

"First of all, I'm going to take over as the program's director, and then I'll offer the higher-ups a deal they can't refuse on the new location I've scouted for them."

"They have no use for us," Abigail said. "We are not worth the expense, and they are going to get rid of us soon."

Eleanor frowned. "Did someone tell you that?"

Abigail shrugged. "It's easy to deduce. Only James, Mollie, and Spencer were ever sent out on an assignment. The rest of us are treated like lab rats. They just keep testing us."

"We are still learning," Sofia said. "My telekinesis has gotten better since I've started training."

"You can affect a dice or coin in motion," Dylan said. "Your talent is only useful in Vegas, but if you get caught, well, you know what happens to cheaters in casinos."

Abigail's comments gave Eleanor the opening she needed. "If I can get any of you out of your contracts, who would want to leave? Raise your hands if you do."

No one did.

"What if I can get you the same pay on the outside?"

This time everyone lifted their hands.

There was no way Kian would approve paying the nine remaining members of the program a quarter of a million each for doing basically nothing. He had no use for their talents, and he was only interested in them as potential Dormants. She had no doubt, though, that those who had the godly genes would trade the pay for immortality.

"I see. So you love the pay and hate your jobs."

"I hate living underground," Naomi said. "And I hate being treated like an experiment, which is what we are really here for. But my family and I need the money. I'm treating this as a necessary evil to secure a better future."

Spencer, who so far hadn't said anything, kept glancing between Eleanor, Emmett, and Peter. "You, your boyfriend, and your cousin all have spectacular auras. Are you on something?"

Eleanor tensed. "What do you mean? Like drugs?"

Spencer shrugged. "That's what it looks like to me."

"What you see," Emmett said. "Is the aura of enlightenment. All three of us have reached deep within and brought forth the best version of ourselves. With proper training, all of you can have auras that glow as brightly."

"How is enlightenment achieved?" Andy asked. "Through meditation?"

"Among many other techniques."

As Emmett launched into one of his sermons, Eleanor let out a relieved breath. Her mate was a masterful bullshitter, and right now, she was grateful for that talent. If not for him, she would have had to compel Spencer to keep his mouth shut about their glowing auras.

The troubling thing about that was that the kid could apparently identify immortals. If he turned into one himself, he would keep it to himself, and perhaps his ability could be used to the clan's benefit in some way.

It was a shame, though, that he couldn't detect Dormants by their auras. That would have been super useful.

Perhaps he could train himself to do that?

Obviously he couldn't do it now, or he would have noticed that the four trainees who'd escaped the program had auras different than regular humans. But perhaps he'd attributed it to their paranormal abilities?

Nah, then all of the program's members should have glowing auras, including Simmons, who had been a Dormant.

"I have a question for you, Spencer," she said when there was a momentary lull in

Emmett's lecture. "Are the auras of people with paranormal talents different than of those without?"

"Every person's aura is different," he hedged.

"I know, but you noticed that my aura, as well as Peter's and Emmett's, shone brighter, and I wondered whether it was because of our enlightened state or because of our paranormal abilities."

Spencer's eyes widened. "You have a paranormal ability? You never told us about it." He looked at James, who was sitting to his right. "Did you know?"

The telepath shook his head. "She can be very persuasive. Maybe that's her talent."

He had no idea how close to the truth he was.

"That's right," Eleanor confirmed. "Emmett and Peter are both telepaths," she added before anyone had the chance to ask. "But not very strong ones."

That earned her a brow lift from Emmett. "I can be very persuasive as well."

"Yes, you can, dear." She patted his shoulder. "But back to the auras." She looked around the bar. "Are the auras of those seated around this table noticeably different than those of other people in the bar?"

Spencer looked around. "I really can't tell because they are all different. Only the three of you have brighter ones."

Eleanor wasn't ready to give up yet, but she couldn't keep leading the kid on without revealing too much. Perhaps she would get him alone some other time, tell him precisely what she was after, and then compel him to forget it.

13

VLAD

$\mathcal{V}$lad carried a tray of freshly baked cupcakes to the living room and put it down on the table.

"They smell divine," Wendy's mother said. "Thank you."

"You're welcome." He sat down next to Vrog, who seemed to be uncomfortable with Margaret and Bowen for some reason.

Naturally Wendy had noticed and was trying to cover up for him by chatting up a storm. "Anyway, as I was telling Vrog, the Fates must have planned our journey all along. Otherwise, there is no way my mother and I would have ended up being rescued by the clan."

Margaret smiled at her mate. "I was rescued by Bowen, but only because I fell and broke my knee, and that happened only because the clan faked a fire in Safe Haven to rescue Eleanor and Peter. I didn't need rescuing."

"That's arguable," Bowen said. "Emmett compelled you to fear outsiders. You needed to be rescued from that."

Next to Vlad, Vrog groaned. "I must apologize for my tribesman's misuse of power. He shouldn't have held you against your will and prevented you from contacting Wendy."

So that was Vrog's problem. He felt guilty by association.

"I don't blame Emmett for that," Margaret said. "He thought that he was protecting me, and he was probably right. Roger, my ex-husband, was an abusive man, and Fates only know what he would have done to me if I showed up on his doorstep."

Bowen growled. "I should've killed the maggot a long time ago. The only reason he's still alive is that you don't allow it."

Margaret patted his knee. "He's not worth it. Besides, Vlad thralled him to never harm anyone again. Right, Vlad?"

He nodded. "Can we change the subject, please? This talk is upsetting Wendy."

It was upsetting him too.

"Yes, it is." Wendy backed him up. "Let's talk about cheerier things, like Vrog's match for the virtual adventure. William called earlier to tell him that he found a match, but the lady was unavailable to do it today, so it will have to wait for Vrog to return." She smiled triumphantly. "And that means that he's coming back after the team completes the assignment at his school."

"That's wonderful," Stella said. "I'm glad that you decided to return to us."

"It wasn't just because of that." Vrog leaned forward and snatched a cupcake off the tray, probably just to have something in his hands because he wasn't going to eat it. Grains and baked goods didn't agree with his digestion. "I haven't had enough time with my family." He looked at Wendy. "I hope it's okay with you if I come back here and stay a little longer?"

"You're always welcome here," Wendy said. "Our home is your home."

From the corner of his eye, Vlad saw Richard grimace, but he didn't say a thing, which was smart. Stella had been upset with him for the way he mercilessly teased Vrog, and he'd promised to curb his jabs at the guy.

Bowen grinned as he wrapped his arm around Margaret's shoulders. "You've changed so much since I first met you, Wendy. You're like a different person."

She blew him an air kiss. "Thanks in part to you. Your fatherly advice helped both Vlad and me. If not for you, we might have not ended up together."

"Love has a way of overcoming obstacles." He took Margaret's hand. "It might have taken you longer without my sage advice, but you would still have ended up together. The Fates wouldn't have allowed things to unfold any other way."

After casting Bowen a fond look, Margaret turned to Vrog. "Emmett told us that the Kra-ell revere the Mother of All Life, but he didn't elaborate. What does that entail? Do they have a shrine for her? Are there any special holidays to celebrate her?"

"There was no shrine, but there was an altar in Jade's house for the Mother. I don't know what the purebloods do with it other than consecrate vows and celebrate children's transition into adulthood. Those were the only two I took part in. On my thirteenth birthday, I got my first weapon. It was a hunting knife, which I used to cut off my hair for the first time ever and put the braid on the Mother's altar. Then I used it to make a cut in the palm of my hand and drip blood over the braid. After that, Jade ignited my tribute and chanted some ancient Kra-ell prayer that I didn't understand."

"We also have a rite of passage celebration for our boys at thirteen years of age," Bowen said. "But instead of making sacrifices, our boys challenge an older immortal to a fight, get bitten, and transition."

"Do you have another celebration upon completion of training?" Vrog asked.

"We don't. Did you?"

"The second time I was brought before the altar was upon the completion of my training to vow my eternal loyalty and servitude to Jade. I had to cut my palm again and drip blood into a chalice. This time, Jade cut her palm as well and combined her blood with mine. She again chanted something incomprehensible and set our combined blood offering on fire."

"Very voodoo-like," Stella said. "I wonder whether those were legitimate Kra-ell rituals, or did Jade invent them to scare the hybrid young men into serving her for as long as they lived."

14

ORION

"*I* don't like it that you're leaving so soon." Geraldine wiped tears from her eyes. "I've just found you, and we've gotten to spend so little time together."

Orion put a hand on her arm and smiled. "You've never lost me. You just didn't remember me."

When Geraldine had organized the goodbye dinner for their small family, Orion had expected her to be a little sad, but not the tears. Before, he'd had to thrall her every time they'd parted, and he saved himself the sorrow of seeing her cry. This time around no thralling was needed, and he was thankful that Geraldine had Shai and Cassandra to console her so he could feel less guilty about leaving.

"You know what I mean." Geraldine waved a hand. "Don't mind me. I'm really glad that you are going on a romantic getaway together with Alena and the other couples. I hope you have a wonderful time."

Orion wondered whether Kian might have agreed for Geraldine and Shai to join the expedition. Perhaps even Cassandra and Onegus. Could Kalugal's jet even accommodate so many passengers?

In either case it was too late to suggest that, and besides, Orion was a guest himself. For him to invite others to join would have been inappropriate.

"Thank you," Alena said. "We'll be back before you know it. Two weeks is nothing when you have eternity to look forward to."

"True." Geraldine forced a small smile. "Besides, Cassandra and I are going to be so busy that the time will fly. We have two houses to decorate, and we also need to convince Darlene to attempt transition."

"We are not going to try to convince her," Cassandra said. "We are only going to give her the option and explain the risks. I don't want to pressure Darlene to take a potentially deadly risk. I don't need that on my conscience."

Orion shook his head. "Wait until I come back. You need me to compel Darlene to keep what you tell her a secret. We agreed that thralling her to forget about her godly genes right after you tell her about them is a bad idea."

"I agree," Onegus said. "With Orion, Kalugal, and Eleanor gone, we have no compellers left to take care of that. We need to wait until at least one of them returns."

"What about Parker?" Shai said. "He's a decent enough compeller."

Onegus gave him an incredulous look. "You are kidding, right? Parker is a kid."

"So what? He's a tested and proven compeller. We can bring him along to lunch or dinner with Darlene, test his ability to compel her, and if it works, we can tell her about her chance at immortality. She needs a strong motive to leave Leo."

Cassandra sighed. "That's another thing I don't want to pressure her to do. We might think that Leo is a bastard, but that's our opinion of him. Darlene might love the guy despite him being an asshole. Maybe he has redeeming qualities we don't know about."

"Like what?" Geraldine asked.

"He might be great in bed, or he might be good at telling jokes, or whatever. There is no accounting for taste."

Onegus's lips twisted in a grimace. "I'm sure she will change her mind about her hubby after she finds out that he sold out their son for reward money."

That was news to Orion. "What did Leo do?"

"When we arranged for Roni to meet his parents, we took extensive precautions that should have kept him safe. We couldn't understand how the meeting place was compromised until Andrew discovered that Leo told the agents in charge of Roni's investigation where the meeting would be."

"Bastard." Orion's fangs punched out. "Why would he do that to his own son?"

"There was a big reward offered to whomever provided information that led to Roni's capture," Shai said. "Apparently, Leo loves money more than he loves his son."

"Roni might not be his," Geraldine said. "When we talked about the genetic testing, Leo made some snide remarks about wanting to see Roni's results. We think that he suspects Roni might not be his son."

Orion rubbed a hand over the back of his neck. "Darlene was married to Leo for many years before they had Roni. Perhaps they couldn't conceive, and she used a sperm donor without telling Leo?"

Cassandra crossed her arms over her chest. "I hope the sperm donor was the total package and that Darlene got the donation the natural way. That would serve Leo right. Even if Roni is not his biological son, he still raised him as his, and he should act as a father, protecting his son, not selling him out. The guy must be a total douchebag to do that."

15

ALENA

*A*s Alena and Orion arrived at the village's parking garage, a small crowd was already gathered, ready to board the bus. The two teams leaving for two separate destinations in China were heading to the clan's airstrip, where one team would board Kalugal's executive jet and the other the clan's.

Alena watched Mey and Jin hug and shed tears as if they were parting for months, which was kind of silly since they were sharing a ride to the airstrip and were not parting yet. After that, they would be separated for only a week or two, so that wasn't a big deal either, and it was certainly nothing to shed tears over. But then she and Annani hadn't done any better.

They had said their goodbyes in the house, and both of them had fought tears, not because of the upcoming trip and the short separation, but because they were keenly aware that it might be the first of many goodbyes if Alena and Orion bonded and she had to leave the sanctuary.

After spending twenty centuries together, she and her mother didn't know how to live without each other and adjusting would be difficult. Annani had done a much better job of putting on a brave face than Alena had managed, but then she was doing the right thing by encouraging her daughter to live her life to the fullest, and she wasn't the one leaving.

Alena, on the other hand, was overcome with guilt.

"I don't like traveling by bus," Kalugal grumbled as Okidu opened the vehicle's door. "The ride to the airstrip would have been a perfect opportunity to show off my new limousine."

Chuckling, Kian clapped him on the back. "Stop being such a snob. The seats on the bus are just as comfortable as the ones in the limousine."

"Perhaps in yours, but mine is newer and more luxurious."

"You'll have plenty of opportunities to show it off when we return," Jacki said.

Next to Kian, Syssi sighed. "I wish I was going with you."

Amanda nodded. "Me too, sister, me too." She wrapped her arm around Syssi's waist. "Perhaps in a year or two, when our daughters are a little older, we will travel somewhere exotic together. I've never been to Tibet, and I would love to see it."

As if to remind them that she was there, Allegra kicked her little pink blanket off and made a sound that was a clear demand to be picked up. It wasn't a whine or a cry, but a mixture of a huff and a gurgling growl.

Alena laughed. "She's becoming more like her daddy by the day." She reached into the stroller and picked her niece up. "Aren't you, sweetie?" She kissed both warm cheeks, inhaling the baby's scent and getting drunk on it.

Science called it an oxytocin rush, a hormone that was responsible for the bond between mothers and their babies, and Alena was definitely addicted to it. Some people got high on drugs or drunk on alcohol; she got high on babies.

Catching Orion looking on with a smile on his face and softness in his eyes, Alena walked over to him. "Would you like to hold her?"

He shook his head. "I've never held a baby. I don't know how."

"Did you ever hold a puppy?"

He nodded.

"Then you'll do fine." She handed him Allegra.

Immediately, Syssi and Kian both stepped up to Orion, hovering within catching distance in case he dropped their precious bundle.

But they shouldn't have worried. Orion's instincts worked perfectly, and as he held Allegra against his chest and smiled down at her, she smiled back and reached with her tiny hand to grab his hair.

"Ouch." He laughed. "Her grip is surprisingly strong for such a small hand."

"That's my daughter," Kian said proudly but didn't offer to help poor Orion, who didn't know what to do.

Syssi took the little fist between two fingers. "Let go of Uncle Orion's hair, Allegra."

The baby gave her a defiant look and held on.

"Let go." Syssi pried the tiny fingers apart and then took the unhappy Allegra from Orion. "She's also stubborn like her father and doesn't like to be told what to do."

"She's a leader," Kian said.

"Master." Okidu bowed. "All the luggage is safely stowed. Should I ask everyone to board the bus?"

"Yes." Kian tore his eyes from his daughter. "I wish you all a safe, successful, and enjoyable trip."

Alena embraced Syssi and then Amanda. "Don't you dare go into labor while I'm gone."

"Don't you dare not be here when I do," Amanda countered.

Next, Alena hugged Kian. "Do me a favor and try to visit Mother more often. She's going to be lonely without me."

"We will," Syssi said. "I'm going to make sure that she never dines alone. Unless she's meeting other clan members over dinner or lunch, she will dine with Kian and me, or just me when Kian is at work."

"Hey," Amanda pouted. "What about me? I'm her daughter too."

"We'll share," Syssi offered. "Or we can all dine together every day."

"That would make Mother very happy." Alena gave her sister one last kiss on the cheek before taking Orion's hand. Together, they boarded the bus and sat down behind Mey and Yamanu.

"Have a safe voyage, everyone," Kian called out as Okidu closed the door.

16

ORION

$\mathcal{A}$s the bus cleared the tunnel, Orion expected the windows to clear, but they stayed opaque. Was it because they weren't as sophisticated as the ones in the private cars? Or did they function just as well, but he and the others weren't supposed to know where the clan's airstrip was?

His bet was on the second one.

Despite Kian's claims of tight budgets due to the expenditure on humanitarian efforts, the clan seemed very well off, and what Orion found admirable was that the wealth seemed to be more than fairly distributed among the members. Everyone got a share, whether they contributed to the community or not, but those who worked for the clan got compensated according to their contribution. The beauty of the system was that everyone was free to pursue their dreams and interests whether they were profitable or not, but work was still incentivized, and so was education.

According to Shai, young clan members had to be twenty-five to be eligible to share in the clan profits, but if they were full-time students in good academic standing, they got their share as soon as their first semester was successfully completed.

He wondered what happened when someone dropped out. Did they lose their share and have to wait until they reached the age of twenty-five?

Orion had a feeling that Kian wouldn't have left such a loophole for youngsters to take advantage of. The guy was pragmatic, and he wouldn't allow anyone a free ride, but he was also generous.

According to Cassandra, Guardians were very well paid, and Shai, who was just an assistant, had quite a nest egg saved up. Kalugal and his men probably didn't get a share in the clan's profits, but did they become eligible when they mated a clan female?

Orion still had so many questions, and hopefully some would be answered during the trip. He also needed to learn the names and positions of most of his fellow travelers.

Leaning closer to Alena, he whispered in her ear, "I don't know half of the people on this bus."

She chuckled. "I'm such a bad host. It's just that it feels so natural to have you with me that I keep forgetting you are new to all this. Let me introduce you." She motioned for him to get up.

First, she stopped next to the couple sitting in front of them. "I'll start with Mey and Yamanu. Yamanu is a very special Guardian. He has the power to thrall thousands at one time, and the same goes for shrouding. His ability equals or maybe even surpasses that of the most powerful gods."

The guy grinned. "You're making me blush, Alena. Orion and I have met before." He winked at him. "But you might not remember me. That tranquilizer shot knocked you out before we had a chance to get introduced." The guy offered him his hand. "No hard feelings, eh?"

"None." Orion shook the guy's hand.

He remembered the Guardian, but he hadn't known what Yamanu was capable of.

"I'm impressed by your ability. I'm a first-generation immortal, and I can't do even a fraction of that. How did you become so powerful?"

"It's a long story," Yamanu said. "The gist of it is that I channel all of my energy and focus it into the thrall or the shroud, and I need others to shield me when I'm in that state. One day, I'll tell you how I discovered my ability."

"I'm looking forward to it."

"I'm Mey," his mate said as she offered her hand. "It's a pleasure to meet you, Orion."

"You are the one who can hear echoes in the walls." He gently shook her elegant, long-fingered hand.

She smiled. "That's me."

As an idea popped into Orion's head, his hold on her hand tightened. "How do you feel about a trip to Paris?"

Looking confused, she cast a questioning glance at Alena. Her mate's reaction was more extreme. The friendly smile was gone, and Yamanu looked as if he was about to tear Orion's throat out.

"I'd better explain," he said as he quickly let go of her hand.

"Yes, you'd better," Yamanu hissed from between elongated fangs.

Were all immortals that fang-trigger happy? Or was it territorial posturing when another male was perceived as showing interest in their mate?

Orion's control over his fangs was much better than that, and he doubted that they would elongate even if someone flirted with Alena.

Right. He was such a hypocrite. Only yesterday, he'd been battling feelings of anger and resentment when thoughts of her former lovers flitted through his head.

Casting an apologetic smile at Yamanu, Orion took a step back. "The reason I suggested Paris was that I would like Mey to listen to echoes at a townhouse my father stayed in many years ago. I'm sure you're aware who he is."

Mey nodded. "The god Toven. By now, I doubt there is anyone left in the village who hasn't heard about him."

"I met him nearly four decades ago in Paris. It was a chance encounter that he wasn't happy about, and he got rid of me as soon as he could. The Clan Mother wants to find him, and it has just occurred to me that you might find out more about him from listening to the echoes in that house."

"That depends," she said. "I only hear echoes of highly charged emotional moments. Do you know how long he lived there?"

The surge of hope in Orion's chest took a nosedive and got crushed on the rocks suddenly filling his gut. "Not long, and I doubt he could get emotional over anything anymore. There are probably no echoes of him left."

"I'm sorry." She offered him a consolatory smile. "In any case, I'm willing to give it a try." She looked at her mate. "I would love to visit Paris again. Especially since this time, it will be with you."

His friendly expression back on, Yamanu took his mate's hand and kissed the back of it. "As soon as this assignment is over, I'll request time off so we can go to Paris."

Leaning over, she kissed his cheek. "Let's wait for spring, my love. Paris in the winter is not as pleasant."

17

ALENA

"This is Jin, Mey's sister," Alena introduced Arwel's mate next. "The clan sprung her from the government's paranormal program, but that's also a story for another time."

"Hi." Jin offered Orion her hand. "Welcome to the clan."

"Thank you. What is your special talent, if I may ask?"

"I can tether people. I tie a string of my consciousness to theirs, and I can see and hear everything they see and hear. That's how I captured Kalugal."

"That's how you tried to capture me," Kalugal corrected. "Instead, I ended up capturing your mate and your best friend." He wrapped his arm around Jacki's shoulders. "The best catch I've ever made."

By the time Kalugal had finished telling Orion the story of how Jin had tethered him in a club, how the clan's plan had gotten spoiled by a crazed human with a gun, and everything that had followed until he'd moved his base into the village, Okidu had parked the bus at the clan's airstrip.

After they'd disembarked and waited for the Odus to unload the luggage and then load it into the jets, Yamanu put his enormous hand on Orion's shoulder. "Before we go our separate ways, let me introduce Vrog."

The Guardian seemed to have forgotten all about the misunderstanding regarding the Paris offer and was back to his usual friendly self.

"Vrog, this is Orion. Orion, this is Vrog." Yamanu grinned. "Vrog should be thankful to you. When we caught you, Kian authorized Vrog's move to the village because he needed the dungeon apartment for you."

"Thank you." Vrog shook Orion's hand. "You and I have a lot in common. We are both newcomers to the clan, and we are both leaving before we've had a chance to acclimate." He smiled at Alena. "The notable difference is that you are leaving with your true-love mate, while I'm leaving alone."

Orion didn't correct Vrog's misconception. Instead, he clapped him on the back.

"Your one and only is somewhere out there, waiting for you. The good news is that as an immortal, you will never run out of time to find her."

"I wish that were true, but I'm not immortal, only long-lived compared to humans. Hopefully, though, it won't take me that long to find the one I belong to."

"I hope that you don't mean Jade," Arwel said.

"No, of course not. I meant the female who will own my heart, not just my vow of loyalty."

"You are Kra-ell," Orion said. "It took me a while to connect the dots."

"I'm half Kra-ell and half-human."

"Yeah, that's what I meant." Orion regarded the guy with curiosity in his sapphire blue eyes. "Are you hoping to find a Kra-ell female? Or are you hoping to catch the eye of someone in the village?"

Vrog lowered his eyes. "I don't think I'll ever find a Kra-ell female, and even if I did, she wouldn't want me. The pureblooded females don't take half-breeds into their beds, and neither do the hybrid females. The only way a half-breed can have long-lived children is if she invites a pureblooded male to breed with her."

"I see." Orion seemed lost for words.

"Don't look so glum." Yamanu squeezed Vrog's shoulder. "You're much better off with a clan female. They don't bite." He laughed. "Much."

As Yamanu's group separated from theirs and headed to the clan's jet, Kalugal led the rest to his. "Ladies first," he said as he motioned for Alena to follow Jacki up the stairs and then Jin.

"Wow." Alena looked at the plush armchairs. "This is even fancier than my mother's jet, and it's bigger than the clan's largest plane." She turned around to look at Kalugal. "What do you need such a large jet for?"

He chuckled. "If your brother were here, he would have said that I'm a competitive bastard and that I need to have everything bigger than his."

She arched a brow. "Is that really why you got it?"

"Among other things." He motioned for her to take a seat. "I enjoy luxury, and I love showing off, but I also love a good bargain. This beauty was for sale at a bargain price because the guy who'd commissioned it needed the money for something else. It's a little too big for what I need, and it barely fits in the clan's hangar, but I couldn't refuse such a sweet deal. I quickly grabbed it before someone else had a chance to."

As the others got on board, Kalugal finished the introductions. "This is my second-in-command, Phinas."

"I'm his third." Phinas shook Orion's hand.

"Not true," Kalugal said. "You and Rufsur are both my seconds." He turned to Orion. "Rufsur is mated to the lovely Edna, whom you had the pleasure of meeting."

Again, Orion didn't contradict him. "Indeed. But I didn't meet Rufsur. He must be an impressive fellow to snag such an important member of the clan."

Kalugal chuckled. "Rufsur is not nearly as smart as Edna, but he has other qualities she appreciates." He motioned for his other two men to step forward. "This is Shamash, who holds a position similar to Shai's, and this is Welgost, who's my equivalent of Anandur, sans the red hair and about six inches in height and breadth, but no less deadly."

"Well met." Orion shook both men's hands. "I'm looking forward to spending the next couple of weeks with you all."

18

ANNANI

*A*nnani could have walked to Ingrid's new design center, but without Alena by her side, it felt awkward to amble through the village. It was a silly sentiment. She had visited the village without Alena, and before that the keep, and she had never felt strange about taking a walk by herself.

Well, usually Kian had a guardian or two trailing her, but she had paid them no attention. Curiously, he had not assigned any to her during this visit. Or maybe he had, but they were keeping their distance?

She hoped none had to chase the golf cart on foot.

As Oshidu parked the cart in front of the house that Ingrid had converted into her workplace, the woman trotted out on her high heels with a big smile on her face.

"Clan Mother." She bowed. "It's such an unexpected honor to have you come visit my new design center."

Annani accepted Oshidu's hand to step out of the vehicle. "Congratulations." She pulled Ingrid into her arms. "With how hard you have been working for years now, you should have gotten some staff to help you out a long time ago."

"Most of the time I didn't need help," Ingrid admitted as she led Annani up the steps to the front porch. "And whenever I did, I asked for the Guardians' assistance, and they never refused me. But with the newest section of the village nearing completion and Kian wanting everything done yesterday, I need a dedicated crew. I just hope I will have work for them after the project is completed."

"I'm sure you will." Annani looked around the living room that had been converted into a design showroom.

Framed photographs of Ingrid's various projects hung on the walls; a few were of houses in the village, but most were of the clan's hotels. Furniture catalogs and fabric samples were strewn over two presentation tables, but from the artful way they were arranged, they had not been just randomly tossed there.

"Knock, knock," a male's cheerful voice sounded from the other side of the door. "May I come in?"

Ingrid arched a brow. "I have no idea who that might be." She sniffed the air and frowned. "I smell chocolate cake, do you?"

Annani nodded. "Open the door, dear. I think someone came with some sweet offerings for you."

Ingrid hesitated. "I didn't invite anyone. I have the next two hours blocked off for your visit."

Another knock sounded on the door. "Is anybody in there?"

Annani smiled. "Your secret admirer is persistent. I do not mind meeting him, especially since he came bearing sweet gifts."

Reluctantly, Ingrid walked over to the door and yanked it open. "Atzil, what are you doing here?"

"I brought you a cake." He thrust a baking dish into her hands. "To celebrate the new design center."

Annani had a feeling that the man was not aware of her being inside, which was a testament to how enamored he was with Ingrid.

Usually, Annani's power radiated so strongly that everyone in her vicinity was aware of her presence unless she deliberately tamped it down.

"Thank you," Ingrid said. "That's very kind of you, but I have a visitor right now. Can you come later?"

"Nonsense," Annani called out. "I want a taste of that chocolate cake."

As Ingrid opened the door all the way, the stunned expression on the man's face made Annani smile.

"Do not look so shocked, Atzil. Please, come in."

"Clan Mother," he whispered and then bowed nearly all the way down to the floor, but did not move an inch. "I should leave."

"Come in." Annani imbued her voice with command, not to compel the poor man, but to release him from his paralysis.

"Yes, Clan Mother." He bowed again and then took a few steps in before halting in the middle of the room.

Ingrid seemed as lost as he was, standing next to him with the cake in her hands. "Would you like some tea with the cake, Clan Mother?" she asked.

"That would be lovely." Annani walked over to the couch and sat down. "Atzil, come sit with me." She motioned to one of the armchairs facing the couch.

"Yes, Clan Mother." He sat on the edge of the chair with his hands clasped in his lap and his eyes downcast.

"You can look upon my face, Atzil. I promise that you will not go up in flames."

That got a little smile out of him. "I am so sorry for coming here unannounced. I thought that since it was a place of business, that was okay. I wanted to thank Ingrid for the beautiful job she has done on my house."

Annani tilted her head. "I thought that you lived with Kalugal and Jacki?"

"I do, but I also have my own place if I wish to sleep there." He cast a quick glance toward the kitchen, where Ingrid was preparing tea. "Kalugal doesn't need me all day long. If I want, I can prepare the meals and leave. Others can take care of the cleanup, but I like to supervise. A kitchen needs to be kept clean at all times. I never compromise on that."

"That is admirable." Annani smiled. "But then it goes well with your name."

When he looked confused, she realized that he might not know the meaning of it. "Your name means noble, which implies high moral and ethical standards."

"In which language?"

She waved a hand. "Several of the ancient ones." She looked up at Ingrid, who came into the converted living room carrying a tray with three teacups, a teapot, and artfully arranged chocolate cake squares. "These cake pieces look almost as good as they smell." Annani cast Atzil a sidelong glance. "Between your baking skills and Ingrid's design flair, you could produce masterpieces together." She clapped her hands. "Like wedding cakes."

19

RONJA

"*Y*ou're doing great, Ronja." Kri loaded weights to one side of the barbell and then to the other.

Ronja doubted she could even lift one of those plates or whatever they were called. She chuckled. "I'm using just the bar with no weights on it, and I can do no more than twelve repetitions. How much weight did you just put on yours?"

"I'm not going too heavy because I don't want to bulk up too much. It's a total of one hundred pounds. Fifty on each side."

Did Kri realize how ridiculous that statement sounded? Ronja hadn't visited the gym while still living in the human world, but she was quite sure that male body-builders didn't put much more weight on their barbells. Or maybe they did?

She wouldn't know.

"I find it funny that to you, a hundred pounds is a light weight. I can't imagine being able to lift that much even after years of training."

"Human females can lift that and more, but you are a beginner, and for a fifty-something human who has been training for only six weeks, your progress is impressive. Watching how well you're doing makes me less anxious about you attempting transition."

Ronja felt her cheeks reddening. Did everyone know her plans?

"I'm just trying to get healthier. I haven't decided yet if I'm going to attempt it."

"Yes, you did." Kri lifted the barbell effortlessly.

"I did what?"

"You've already decided that you're going for it. Otherwise, you wouldn't be here every day at seven in the morning, doing something you really don't like doing." She gave her a sly smile. "Don't try to deny it. I see you walk into the gym every morning, looking like you'd rather be anywhere but here."

Ronja wondered whether she'd been so obvious or Kri was very good at reading people. She'd only spoken with the Guardian a few times, and their conversations had been brief and not personal.

At first and second glance, the female was intimidating, but if she cared enough to fear for Ronja's safety then perhaps there was a soft heart beating under all that muscle.

"You're partially correct," Ronja admitted. "I'm about fifty percent sure that I want to attempt it." She shook her head. "No, that's a lie. I'm a hundred percent sure that I want to transition, but I'm also a hundred percent terrified of attempting it."

"That's perfectly understandable, but you should not wait too long. Do it while the Clan Mother is here."

It was a little ridiculous for an advanced society of people to believe in the power of blessings. Ronja had trained as a nurse and had been married to a doctor. She knew first-hand that spirituality only helped to relieve anxiety but didn't deliver miraculous healings.

"With all due respect, I don't put much faith in blessings, even those given by a goddess."

"Don't belittle it." Kri put the barbell down. "It's not superstition, and it's not anything mystical. Think about it this way. If Annani's mere presence induces transition in young Dormant girls, then it makes sense that the power she radiates has something to do with it. It might not be enough to induce transition in an adult, but it must be the boost that helps them through when difficulties arise. It worked for Syssi, Andrew, and Turner. All I'm saying is that you shouldn't dismiss anything that might help you, and don't attempt transition without Annani being nearby to offer you her blessing. Unlike compulsion, her blessings don't work over phone lines."

"Your theory is the first one that actually sounds logical." Ronja set the bar back on the rack. "Thank you."

"You're welcome." Kri turned to look at the gym's double doors a split second before they were pushed open, and Merlin walked in. "Thanks to you, our doctor looks terrific too." The Guardian winked at Ronja before sauntering over to the next station in her morning circuit.

"Hello, gorgeous." A grin splitting his handsome face, Merlin walked over to Ronja and kissed her cheek.

"Hello to you too. What took you so long?"

After their morning run, Merlin had gone back to his house to check on a potion he'd left brewing over a very low flame. It shouldn't have taken him more than a few minutes, but more than half an hour had passed, which meant that he'd either gotten distracted by something or someone needed his help or advice.

"During the run, I had an idea that I wanted to check on. It took me a while to find the right book."

She arched a brow. "What's the idea?"

He picked a dumbbell from the rack and started working his left bicep. "I remembered reading about an Indian recipe that combined several herbs and spices and was supposed to help longevity. Originally, I dismissed it as just another folk remedy, but yesterday I stumbled upon a scientific study that was done on that combination of herbs." He smiled sheepishly. "I wanted to take another look at the ingredients, but then I got distracted and forgot all about it, until this morning when you mentioned the curry dish you were planning to cook later today. Curry is one of the ingredients in that remedy."

That was Merlin to a tee, and she was willing to bet that he'd forgotten about the potion. "Did you remember to check on the potion brewing in your kitchen?"

His eyes widened. "Damn. I forgot all about it." He put the dumbbell back on the rack. "I need to go."

He was such a classic smart guy, with so many thoughts and ideas crowding his head that he couldn't keep them all straight.

"I'll come with you."

"I don't want you to miss out on your workout because of me."

"We can jog to your house. That counts as a workout, right?"

His lips quirked up in a smile. "It sure does."

2 0

MERLIN

$\mathcal{M}$erlin was a good actor who had honed his skills over many decades of working with human patients, but he didn't know how much longer he could pull this off.

It was getting harder and harder to treat Ronja as a friend and not make any sexual advances.

For a male, it was impossible to hide his desire even from a human with a weak sense of smell, so there was no way she'd missed the evidence of his arousal every morning when she showed up on his doorstep wearing those tight exercise pants and figure-hugging small shirts.

Even Lisa had noticed.

Several times, he'd caught the minx smiling knowingly and averting her eyes.

Ronja, however, was either clueless or pretended not to notice. In either case she chose not to react, and he had to respect her wishes, but he was running out of patience.

Even now, as they jogged to his house, he found it impossible to keep his eyes from being drawn to her bouncing breasts and his mouth from watering as he imagined his lips on her nipples after he'd gotten rid of what was covering them.

Fates. He shouldn't think such thoughts. It was only making him more miserable.

"You're awfully quiet," Ronja said as they neared the house. "Still thinking about that Indian recipe?"

"Not quite."

"What's on your mind?"

"You," he admitted.

"What about me?"

Did she really have to ask?

"You look very beautiful this morning. Is this a new exercise outfit?"

She smiled shyly. "I'm surprised that you noticed. You're usually oblivious to things like that."

He was, but not when the décolletage dipped so low. Her other exercise outfits were more modest.

Was that a hint?

Should he ask?

Ronja jogged up the stairs ahead of him and opened the door. "Nothing's burning, so that's a good sign."

Except for him, nothing was on fire.

In the kitchen the potion was bubbling on top of the low flame, but that was what it was supposed to do. Once most of the liquid evaporated and all that remained was the paste, it would be ready for the next step in his experiment.

"I was wondering." Ronja leaned against the kitchen counter. "Who are you going to test the poultice on? Immortals don't need it."

He shrugged. "I'll find a volunteer or two in the city."

Her eyes widened. "Are you going to just walk into a hospital, find injured people, and use the poultice on them?"

He shrugged. "I've done that many times before. This is an improvement on a tried and tested formula, so there is no chance of me doing them any harm. I'm only going to help them heal faster."

"Test it on me."

"You're not injured."

"I'll make a cut on my arm, and you can treat it with your poultice."

"Never." As he walked over to her, the urge to kiss her was so strong that he doubted he would be able to refrain from taking her lips. Cupping her cheek, he looked down into her pale blue eyes. "I will never allow harm to come to you."

Staring into his eyes, she swallowed. "Yes, you will. If you induce my transition, you might be the one to harm me."

Merlin recoiled, his erection deflating in an instant. "Are you trying to push me away?"

She shook her head. "I'm only stating the obvious. We have been tiptoeing around the subject for weeks, and I appreciate it that you gave me space and didn't push me to decide one way or the other, but I can't keep going on like this, pretending as if there is nothing between us and we are just friends." She reached for his hand and pulled him to her. "I want you too much."

Thank the merciful Fates.

His arousal kicking back up, he pressed himself against her and took her lips in the gentlest of kisses.

Moaning into his mouth, she cupped the back of his neck and kissed him back. He'd expected Ronja to be shy or hesitant, but she proved him wrong, thrusting her tongue past his lips and exploring the way he wanted to explore her.

With a groan, he wrapped his arm around her waist and brought her flush against his chest. Rubbing himself against her softness, he deepened the kiss, devouring her with his lips and his tongue until she pushed on his chest, and he realized that she needed to come up for air.

Letting go, he leaned his forehead against hers. "We can use protection. Sex does not have to equal induction."

Still panting, Ronja lifted her eyes to him. "I don't know what to do. Kri said that I shouldn't wait. She said that I need to do it while the Clan Mother was in the village so she could give me her blessing and help me pull through if needed. Before, I thought that it was just a spiritual thing, and that Annani couldn't really help me, but Kri made a valid point. If the little girls transition just from being around the goddess, then she must radiate some kind of power that induces transition. It's not strong enough to induce an adult Dormant, but it can help me pull through."

Merlin had his own suspicions about the Clan Mother's so-called blessings, but right now, he was focused on only one thing—getting Ronja naked and exploring her lush body like he'd dreamt of doing for months.

Except, he was a doctor first and a male second, and Ronja's immortal life was his first priority. His raging erection would have to take a back seat to that.

Leaning away from her so he could collect his thoughts, he ran a hand over the back of his neck. "Kri made a very astute observation. Naturally, it has occurred to me before, but the Clan Mother has avoided discussing it with Bridget or with me, saying that not everything in the universe has a scientific explanation, and that we should have faith as well. She seems to care very much about you, so perhaps if I request an audience with her and ask her more questions about the way she induces the girls' transition, she might actually give me some answers this time."

21

VROG

"Welcome home, Mr. Wu." Doctor Wang inclined his head. "Mr. and Mrs. Williams, it's a pleasure to see you again, and I'm delighted that you loved our school so much that you decided to invest in it."

Mey smiled and shook the guy's offered hand. "We were indeed impressed, and when we met with Mr. Wu in the States and heard more about his future plans, we decided to come back and give the place another look."

The principal cast Vrog a worried glance, but he didn't inquire about those plans or his place in them. That would probably come later when they were alone.

Vrog and Yamanu discussed thralling Wang to forget that he'd ever seen them before, but they'd decided to wait until the end of their visit to erase his memories. Frequent thralling was harmful to humans, so it was better to do it only once. In fact, the entire faculty would need to be thralled after interacting with the Americans for several days, but Yamanu said that he could handle that in one go.

The guy was incredibly powerful in that regard, probably as much as Jade. Vrog was curious which one of them would have emerged triumphant if they were to compete. From what he'd surmised, the Kra-ell ability worked a little differently than what the clan used. It had an element of compulsion in it that thralling didn't have.

Thralling could change people's memories and make them think that they made the decisions the thraller wanted them to make, but they still retained their free will, and if they realized that the thoughts in their head weren't their own, they could theoretically resist.

"Let me show you to your rooms." Dr. Wang motioned for them to follow him.

Since classes were still in session, they didn't encounter any of the teachers on their way to the staff quarters, saving Vrog the need to introduce them twice. He planned to do that tonight over dinner in the staff dining hall.

Wang opened the door to the first room. "This one is for the three gentlemen." He motioned for Alfie, Jay, and Morris to enter. "It is right next door to the Williams' room."

Three narrow beds had been squeezed into the small space, with two chairs serving as nightstands. There was no other furniture or decorations.

Looking at the room through their eyes, Vrog felt embarrassed about how spartan it was compared to the lavish accommodations in the village, or even in the clan's dungeon. "I apologize for the modest size and decor. It has its own bathroom, though."

"It's perfectly fine." Jay walked in and sat on the narrow bed.

Alfie opened the door to the bathroom, took a look at the shower curtain, and closed the door.

Wang looked at Vrog with worry in his eyes. "These are the best rooms we have."

"That's okay. The Williamses knew not to expect luxury."

"I'm sure we will be comfortable." Mey smiled at him. "I wasn't always wealthy. I grew up in a very modest home."

Reassured, Wang opened the door to the other room. "I hope that meets with your approval."

At least the room had a double bed, but even though it was a standard length, it was not long enough for Yamanu. Vrog was not as tall, and he had a special bed commissioned for himself. Yamanu wasn't going to be comfortable, but he didn't seem concerned.

"Perfect." He rolled his and Mey's luggage inside the room.

Wang looked relieved. "I took the liberty of arranging a welcome dinner for our guests. All the teachers are eager to meet the American investors."

"Thank you." Vrog was impatient to end the tour. "Our guests are tired from their trip and would like to rest."

"Yes, of course." The principal bowed. "Dinner is at six."

That was in less than an hour, which didn't leave them much time for what Mey wanted to do.

"We will see you at dinner, Doctor Wang," Vrog said. "Thank you for taking care of all the arrangements."

When the principal finally left, Vrog let out a breath. "Would you like to freshen up before I take you up to my suite? I suggest we make that our headquarters."

"Lead the way." Yamanu motioned.

His place was not much fancier than the rooms they'd been given, but it was more spacious and had its own sitting room. It was also more private. Vrog had made sure that no one could eavesdrop without him knowing.

When they entered his apartment, he walked over to his bar cabinet and opened the doors. "Can I offer anyone a drink before dinner?"

"What do you have?" Yamanu sidled up to him.

"Rum, whiskey, wine, but no beer. I don't have a refrigerator up here. I should get one."

"No worries." Yamanu pulled out a bottle of wine and turned to his mate. "Would you like some?"

"I'd rather have some water if you have any."

"It's not chilled." Vrog opened a drawer and pulled out a bottle.

"That's fine." She took it and sat on the couch. "Where do you suggest I start listening to echoes tomorrow?"

"Where did you listen to them before?"

"Two of the school dorm buildings. I got the best results from the kitchen and from a storage room."

"There are two storage buildings that survived the fire. You can try your luck there."

22

ALENA

*I*t was a little after six in the evening when the limousine pulled up in front of the lakeshore hotel. Kalugal had hired two of the most luxurious vehicles available, along with drivers that would stay with them for the entire duration of their trip. As expected, the hotel he'd booked for them was the fanciest the lake had to offer. It was comprised of several buildings that monopolized the entire peninsula. The hotel was surrounded by water on three sides, offering a panoramic view of the lake.

As Alena stepped out of the limousine, the hotel's front door flew open, and a small figure with a mop of blond curls rushed out, squealing all the way it took her to reach them.

Alena braced for impact, but at the last moment Carol beelined for Kalugal, nearly tackling the guy to the ground as she leaped into his arms.

"I missed you all so much." She let go of Kalugal to embrace Jacki with a little more care and then leaned away. "Let me see that belly." She put her hands on Jacki's slightly rounded abdomen. "How is my nephew doing? Do you feel him moving around already?"

"All I've felt so far are little bubbles, but Amanda and Syssi tell me that this is how it feels in the beginning, and that soon I will start feeling him move."

"How far along are you?"

"Twenty-one weeks, give or take a couple of days."

"Time flies."

"When you're having fun, right?" Jacki waved at Lokan, who was leisurely strolling over, a big grin spread over his handsome face.

"Working with Lokan on a new fashion line is fun, but I miss you all terribly."

As Lokan and Kalugal embraced, clapping each other on the back, Carol walked over to Alena and Orion. Hugging Alena with much less enthusiasm than she'd hugged Jacki and Kalugal, she gave Orion a thorough once-over.

On the one hand, Alena was glad that her cousins had become such an integral part of the clan, which was nothing short of a miracle. The sons of their archenemy had become close family, and that was wonderful. But on the other hand, she felt slightly offended by Carol's preference for her mate's brother and his wife. After all, Alena had been Carol's several times great-grandmother for much longer than Kalugal had been her brother-in-law.

In a way, it was Alena's own fault. She'd never emphasized her role as the clan's foremother, had never wanted any titles or special treatment just because the Fates had gifted her with incredible fertility. But perhaps she should remind her family of their lineage from time to time.

She turned to Orion. "Let me introduce my five-times great-granddaughter, Carol." She smiled sweetly. "Carol, this is Orion, Toven's son."

The slight jab seemed to fly over Carol's head.

"Hello." She offered Orion her hand. "I've heard a lot about you and your sister." She sighed dramatically. "I miss home and being part of everything that's happening in the village. Hearing about it secondhand is not the same."

Sidling up to Carol, Lokan wrapped his arm around her shoulders. "You hurt my feelings, love. Am I not keeping you happy?"

Carol kissed his cheek. "You are." She pulled out from under his arm to greet Jin, Arwel, and Kalugal's men.

Alena waited for Lokan and Orion to shake hands and introduce themselves before asking what was probably on everyone's mind. "Aren't you taking a huge risk coming to the lake?" She glanced around. "We are out in the open where anyone can see us."

"Don't worry about it, cousin." Lokan tilted his head back and breathed in. "The road you took to get here is the only one leading to the lake. If anyone was following us, we would have seen them coming from miles away."

Carol came over and leaned against her mate's side. "As far as everyone is concerned, Lokan and I are meeting potential investors." She glanced around and then leaned closer. "Chinese intelligence is no doubt aware of where we are, but Navuh has no access to it, so we are good."

"Let's move the party inside." Lokan started toward the front door. "I have a couple of tables reserved for us in the restaurant."

As the Odus and Kalugal's men hefted the luggage, their group headed to the hotel's lobby.

"You can leave everything here," Carol said. "Or have the Odus carry it to the rooms. Do they know what goes where?"

"Of course, mistress." Ovidu bowed.

"I'd rather finish checking in first," Kalugal said. "Dinner can wait a few more minutes." He leaned closer to his brother. "This place looks even better than the pictures on its website. I love the vaulted glass ceiling. It reminds me of my new house in the village. The difference is that the vaulted skylight is the only source of natural light to the great room that's belowground."

"I can't wait to see it," Carol said. "I need to come home for a visit." She threaded her arm through Lokan's. "But not without my mate. We need to find a way to smuggle him out safely."

As the discussion about a possible visit continued, Alena tuned it out and looked at the lobby's architectural details and design touches.

Syssi would have approved of the architecture, and Ingrid would have approved of the decor.

The soaring vaulted ceiling was supported by massive stone columns and had murals painted on it. The marble floor was polished to perfection, and the Chinese-style furniture seemed of the finest quality.

The hotel's main building looked like a Chinese palace.

"This is the most luxurious hotel in the entire area," Carol said. "And since we are talking Chinese scale, that means hundreds of miles in each direction. The rooms are spacious, the beds are luxurious, and the water pressure in the shower is great."

"How is the food?" Orion asked. "Did you have a chance to sample it?"

"I've had better," Carol admitted, "but the service is incomparable. They are really doing their best to impress their guests."

As an army of bellboys descended on the Odus and Kalugal's men, taking the luggage off their hands, the Odus looked to Alena for instructions.

"You can go up and start unpacking," Alena said. "After you are done, you can retire to your room."

"Yes, mistress," they said in unison before pivoting on their heels and following the bellboys.

When their group headed to the hotel's restaurant, Orion leaned closer to her. "This was the first time that I've observed them acting like robots. I wonder if I would have suspected something was off about them if I didn't know that they were cyborgs."

"You would have excused that as their familiarity, being twins, or training. The mind likes to organize things in familiar patterns, and when something doesn't make sense, it just reshapes it until it fits the preconceived mold."

23

ORION

Once dinner was served, Kalugal cast a shroud around their table so they could talk freely, but Orion couldn't understand how Kalugal had solved the problem of the staff seeing them talking soundlessly. Since none of his dinner companions seemed to be concerned, it was either a different kind of shroud than the one he'd experienced Alena casting, or Kalugal planned to thrall the waiters later.

"How does your shrouding work?" Orion asked. "The waiters can't hear us, but they can see our lips moving. I assume that you have a solution for that."

"Naturally," Kalugal said. "What we say sounds like gibberish to them, and they assume that we are talking in a foreign language they've never heard before."

"What happens if they ask us something? Do you have to drop the shroud?"

Smiling, Kalugal shook his head. "My shrouds are very sophisticated. If you look directly at them when you speak, they will understand you."

"Once again, I'm impressed with your ability. I'm not even going to ask how that's possible because I still don't know how shrouding works. Is it similar to compulsion?"

Kalugal smoothed a hand over his neatly trimmed goatee. "The best description I can come up with is that it's thralling with an element of compulsion. I imagine what I want the humans to hear, and then I will that into their minds." He smirked. "But that's not the impressive part. As you know, my shrouding works on immortals as well as it does on humans. What's truly marvelous is that I can pick and choose who I'm shrouding. While everyone around this table can hear and see each other, the humans cannot. It's a very delicate and complicated operation. In addition, once I cast the shroud, I can maintain it effortlessly while enjoying my dinner and conversing with you."

Kalugal loved to show off, but he was entitled to his bragging rights. "Is there a chance you can teach me how to do that?"

"I don't know that I can, but I'm willing to give it a try."

Lokan put his chopsticks down and dabbed at his mouth with a napkin. "Kalugal told me that you inherited the compulsion ability from your father, and that you can also compel immortals."

"I can."

"How many people can you compel at once?"

"I don't really know. I think twelve was the most I've ever attempted, but those were humans. I have no idea how many immortals I can compel at the same time. Are you asking because of your father's island?"

Lokan nodded. "The only way to wrestle control from him without causing a much bigger problem is for someone to step in and take his place. Over time, after a long re-education effort, the need to keep all the warriors on a tight leash might diminish, and hopefully, one day it won't be necessary at all."

"My brother is an optimist," Kalugal said. "A dreamer."

Lokan didn't dispute Kalugal's claim. "I want a better life for everyone on that accursed island." He looked his brother in the eyes. "You know how bad it is. What they do to the Dormants and the other women they bring over to serve in the brothel. And the thing is that they are not even aware of how bad they have it because they are all either thralled or compelled into thinking that they have it good." Lokan smoothed his hand over his straight dark hair before shifting his eyes to Orion. "Can you blame me for wanting to make it better?"

"No, I can't. And if I could do something about it, I would. But I don't think that I can control a hundred immortals, let alone several thousand. I'm not your solution."

Orion wondered whether Toven could take over for his nephew.

How powerful was the god?

He probably wasn't as powerful as Navuh, or he wouldn't have failed so miserably at all his attempts to bring civilization to the savages.

If he was, Toven could have just compelled them to abandon their bloodthirsty ways until the behaviors he wanted to instill in them became so ingrained that no further compulsion was needed.

That was what Lokan envisioned for the island's hoodlums, and he was right about the method, just not about the means to achieve it.

Orion was not his solution.

"How about your father?" Lokan asked.

Orion smiled. "I was just contemplating the same thing. Toven is a compeller, but I don't know how strong. He told me that he'd failed in all of his attempts to improve the lives of humans, and that they always managed to twist his teachings into horrific acts of cruelty. If he was as powerful as your father, he could have forced the savages to be peaceful."

"Perhaps it didn't occur to him to try," Carol suggested. "Lokan has had a long time to think about the best way to rehabilitate these warriors and turn them into decent males."

"Toven has had even longer," Alena said. "But it's not fair to compare his situation to Navuh's. Controlling the island's population with compulsion is possible only because Navuh also controls who can get in and who can leave. There is practically no outside influence. Toven didn't have that luxury."

"The Brotherhood's home wasn't always on the island," Lokan said. "Its first home was Mortdh's stronghold in Baalbek, and there were at least five others before

Navuh bought the island and moved the Brotherhood there. That being said, even before the island, the warriors had not been exposed to much outside information, firstly because it wasn't freely available, and secondly because they were kept too busy training and fighting to ponder or question anything."

24

ALENA

*A*fter everyone was done with their meal, and the waitress came over to offer them a dessert menu, Alena was curious to test Kalugal's claim about his shroud.

"What do you suggest for dessert?" she asked while looking directly at the woman.

"Here is the dessert menu." The waitress pulled a stack of red cardboard cards from her apron pocket and distributed them around the table.

The card was printed in Chinese on one side and English on the other, and as Alena went over the selection, she felt Kalugal drop the shroud. She had to admit that his was subtler than hers. The difference between having the bubble he'd created around them and its absence was barely discernible, while her silence shroud felt like being in a fish tank.

Leaning back, Kalugal regarded the young woman with the usual one-sided tilt of his lips that made him look as if he was smirking. "Min," he read her name tag. "My friends and I would like to take a tour of the lake. Can you recommend a guide?"

The hotel had a concierge service, so Kalugal didn't need the waitress's recommendation, and Alena suspected it was just a conversation starter intended to make her feel at ease so he could ask her more questions.

"The boat rental place is a good place to start. They offer a great rowing tour. There are also walking tours around the lake, which is a good way to see the scenic beauty of the surrounding area. There are several old temples along the lake's shores, and beautiful vista points to take pictures of the lake from."

"Is it a difficult trek? My wife is expecting, and I don't want her to exert herself."

"There are two guided treks. One takes a day, and the other is more leisurely and takes three days, but if you prefer something less tiring for your wife, perhaps a horseback tour would be better."

"What is there to see other than the spectacular nature?" Carol asked.

"Oh, many things." Min smiled. "The trek passes through the Lusoshui village of the Mosuo, several temples, pyramidal stupas, and altars. The hotel concierge can make the reservation for you, and a guide will come to pick you up from the lobby. They can also book the rowing tour for you." She turned back to Kalugal. "What would you like to order for dessert?"

As Kalugal looked at the menu and made his selection, Jacki put down the brochure she'd picked up in the lobby and looked at Min. "It says here that Lugu means falling into water. Do you know who fell into the water? Is there a legend about it?"

"There are many legends about the lake, but not about anyone falling into the water. The most well-known one is about the spirit Goddess Gemu who had many lovers among the male spirits of the area. When one of them came to visit and found her with another, he felt humiliated and turned his horse around. She ran after him, but all she found was a hoofprint at the foot of the mountain. Gemu was sad that he'd left and started crying. She cried so hard and for so long that the hoofprint filled with her tears and turned into a lake. When the male spirit saw that, his heart softened, and he threw a few pearls and flowers into the water." Min smiled. "The tear-filled hoofprint is Lugu Lake, and the pearls and flowers are the small islands scattered throughout it."

Jin chuckled. "The legend reflects the sexual practices of the Mosuo."

The waitress kept her expression neutral. "There are several variations of the same legend, but in all of them, Gemu had many lovers."

When Min had left with their orders, Kalugal cast the shroud again. "Aside from their female-dominated society, the Mosuo have several other beliefs and customs that echo those of the Kra-ell. They have taboos on needless killing of animals and felling of trees. From what Emmett told us about the Kra-ell, they drink the blood of animals but don't kill them. Killing an animal and eating its flesh is not forbidden, but it's considered wasteful, and when it's done, a portion of the meat needs to be offered as tribute to their goddess, the Mother of All Life."

"What about the falling into the lake?" Arwel asked. "That got me more intrigued than the other silly legends about the goddess's tears filling up a hoofprint. What if a group of Kra-ell landed in the lake?"

"How deep is it?" Jin asked.

Lokan pulled out his clan-issued phone. "Its maximum depth is 307 ft. It's about six miles long and three miles wide. I don't know how large their pods were, and whether it's deep enough for a massive craft to splash into it from space. But let's check." He typed the inquiry into the search engine. "Ha, that's interesting. Apparently, most of the space capsules that have splashed into the ocean only went six to eight feet down before floating to the surface. The Freedom 7 Mercury capsule went all the way to the bottom, but it doesn't say how deep that was."

Leaning back, Kalugal supported his elbow with one hand and smoothed the fingers of the other over his beard. "Alien landing pods would be much more sophisticated than the primitive capsules human early space exploration employed. I bet they were amphibian and possessed navigation abilities. Probably flying capabilities as well. They were most likely modestly sized and not very long-ranged, but they had to have some mobility."

"Where are you going with this?" his brother asked.

"Oh, I'm just letting my imagination soar. What if the Kra-ell created an underwater base in the lake? What if they did that in many places around the world? There are numerous accounts given by credible witnesses of unidentified submerged objects. I always dismissed them as hallucinations, the same way I did sightings of unidentified flying objects, but perhaps it's worth looking into. My dismissal was mainly due to the familiar terms the witnesses used to describe what they'd seen, which often matched the technology of the time or the science fiction they'd been exposed to. But what if they'd been thralled or compelled to see things not as they appeared? We know that the Kra-ell possess those abilities, and according to Emmett, some of them could compel entire herds of animals." He smiled. "Since humans exhibit many traits of a herd-like mentality, that applies to them as well."

25

ORION

"Not too shabby." Orion walked over to the chaise and sat down. "I've been in plenty of hotel rooms during my travels, and this is nicer than most." He beckoned her to join him.

Her hands on her hips and her head tilted to the side, Alena remained standing in the middle of the room. "It's fancy alright, but the soundproofing is bad. I can hear Jin and Arwel talking in the next room over. Kalugal got the presidential suite on the third floor for him and Jacki, so at least they have some privacy."

Apparently, his mate had been preoccupied with the same thoughts that had kept him busy throughout dinner. After the long journey during which they hadn't done more than hold hands, he couldn't wait to get to their hotel room and make love to Alena.

His lady wasn't a meek lover, and she could get quite loud when in the throes of passion. He wouldn't have it any other way, but given the circumstances, they would have to get creative.

"Do they have another suite? I'll gladly pay for an upgrade."

"I don't think they do." She walked over to the balcony and opened the French doors. "It's freezing." She closed them and looked out through the glass. "The lake is so dark at night."

Pushing to his feet, Orion walked up to Alena and wrapped his arms around her. "We will just have to be very quiet." He put his lips on her neck and inhaled. "I love your scent," he whispered in her ear before taking the soft earlobe between his lips.

As his hands roamed over her sides and his lips trailed the column of her neck, a soft moan escaped Alena's lips, and her head dropped back on his shoulder. "Let's get into the shower. The water will mask the sounds of our lovemaking."

"I can be silent as a mouse." He cupped her breasts and trailed kisses up her neck. "Can you?"

She shook her head. "Not for long."

"Then I'll have to do this." He turned her around and fused their mouths.

Kissing her, he reached for the curtain and pulled it closed, and then made quick work of getting her naked. When he was done, all that was left were her shoes.

Taking a step back, he admired the beauty before him. "The best of sculptors could not have created such perfection."

Alena wasn't shy, and the pose she struck was more about looking sexy than trying to shield her ample breasts. Smiling confidently, the fingers of her right hand lightly touching her left arm and her head slightly tilted downwards, she gazed at him from under lowered lashes.

His eyes caressed every inch of her, starting with her beautiful face, down her long neck to her substantial breasts, her narrow waist, the flare of her generous hips, her long legs.

"Did you have your fill?" she murmured.

"I will never get enough of this." He put his hands on her waist and lifted her, intending to take her to bed.

"Shower," she insisted. "We've had a long day of travel."

"It's small."

Most of the bathroom area was taken up by a big tub, but Orion wasn't keen on submerging himself in one that had served many guests before him, and the shower was not built for two.

"We will make it work." Alena kicked her shoes off and nipped his ear.

Orion knew better than to argue.

"Yes, mistress," he mimicked Ovidu's subservient tone.

Alena gave the impression of being a soft, accommodating female, and most of the time she was precisely that. But in the short time he'd been with her, he'd discovered the steel core underneath. Alena didn't compromise on what was important to her, and right now, it was showering before making love.

Changing directions, he crashed his lips over hers and carried her into the bathroom.

As he set her down, Alena stepped into the enclosure, cranked the faucets all the way, and reached for the soap. Slowly lathering her skin, she taunted him with a seductive smile as her hands ran all over her lush body.

In seconds, he shucked his clothes and joined her inside. They were both statuesque, substantial people, so even with their chests flush against each other, their bottoms hit the shower's glass enclosure on both sides.

He had a feeling that the whole thing would fall apart as soon as things got heated.

"There are only two ways this can work." He cupped her bottom. "Either like this." He lifted her and let his shaft tease her entrance. "Or like this." He turned her around, her back to his front. "What's your preference, princess?"

She chuckled. "Why do I have to choose when I can have both?"

"True." He slid down her body until his face was flush with her round bottom.

With his hand on her inner thigh, he lifted her leg to the side and dove in. His fingers digging into her glorious ass, he kept her in place as he lapped, kissed, and nibbled. She tried to move, her hips undulating in response to the onslaught, but he held her firmly in place. Releasing one side, he wrapped his arm around her and touched his finger to that most sensitive bundle of nerves at the apex of her thighs.

As he speared his tongue into her wet sheath and applied gentle pressure to her clit, the tiny inner muscles rippled around his invading tongue, and then she bucked against him, the orgasm exploding out of her with a muffled groan.

After helping her ride out the aftershocks, he kissed her soft petals and pushed to his feet, sliding up her silky skin. "Wait in bed for me," he commanded in her ear. "I'll wash up and join you in under a minute."

Panting, her hands pressed against the glass enclosure, she turned her head around and kissed the underside of his jaw. "Yes, sir."

26

ALENA

The climax Orion had wrangled out of her notwithstanding, Alena felt disappointed as she padded to the bed with a towel wrapped around her. In her fantasy Orion would take her from behind in the shower, but practicality prevented her fantasy from materializing.

The shower was too cramped, and the enclosure too flimsy for a couple of immortals in the throes of passion. They would have demolished the thing, which she wouldn't have minded paying the hotel for, but broken glass would have not been conducive to lovemaking.

Looking at the four-poster bed though, she had an idea for how she could still have some of her fantasy, just without the water and the glass.

In addition to the four posts, the bed had a tall headboard and a matching footboard. If she waited for Orion leaning against either one, he would guess what she was after. He might be in a bossy mood, but she knew he would follow her cues nonetheless.

Her male was eager to please, which was a very good quality for a mate to have. Alena was a generous lover, and she expected the same in return.

Dropping the towel, she climbed on the bed and knee-walked to the headboard. The top provided a good grip for her hands, but given how powerful immortal lovemaking got, that position would make the bed bang against the wall while she was trying to minimize noise.

Leaning against the footboard might produce similar results, though.

The chaise would have to do.

In fact, the way it was built was perfect for a very naughty pose. One side was higher than the other and curved, providing a perfect perch for her belly, and the other side didn't have an armrest at all.

Smiling, she quickly got off the bed and assumed the pose she'd envisioned on the chaise lounge.

As the door opened and Orion stepped out, naked and magnificently erect, her core clenched in anticipation.

The hiss he emitted had her shiver in the most delicious way.

"I wish I had my father's talent." He walked over and smoothed a hand over her arched back all the way to her behind. "But I would never show the drawing of my Venus to anyone."

The god had no place in their hotel room, but she felt like commenting nonetheless. "He never intended anyone to see the drawings he made of his lovers."

"True. And yet, he drew them partially covered." Orion's hand traveled down the swell of her buttocks, his fingers lightly brushing against her lower lips. "I would draw you completely nude." He dipped his head and kissed one cheek and then the other before delving into her with his tongue.

That wasn't what she wanted. As talented as he was with his tongue, she needed that magnificent shaft of his inside of her.

As if reading her mind, or maybe tasting her need, Orion climbed up behind her. "Gods, I need this." He teased her entrance with his erection, coating it with her juices before surging into her in one powerful thrust.

Despite herself Alena cried out, not because the penetration was painful, but the opposite of that. It felt perfect, and as he started pumping into her, she gripped the curved armrest and readied for the ride.

Holding her hips with both hands, he pistoned in and out of her with the power of a freight train. The lewd sounds their bodies were making as they slapped against each other only added to the experience, and as she clamped her teeth on the armrest to muffle her moans, his lips closed on her shoulder to stifle his groans.

At some point, he pulled her upright, her back flush against his chest, and kept riding her hard. When his tongue swiped over the spot his lips had claimed moments ago, the anticipation of what was coming next ripped an orgasm out of her, and as his fangs pierced her skin, she cried out, not caring about who heard her.

27

CASSANDRA

*G*eraldine tapped Onegus's shoulder. "Where is that restaurant you are taking us to?"

Why was she asking him, the one behind the wheel, and not Shai who was sitting next to her in the backseat?

Besides, Cassandra had told her twice where they were meeting Darlene, once before she'd called her sister to invite her to lunch, and a second time after they'd set the time.

Geraldine was getting better, there was no doubt about it, but whenever she was stressed, her memory issues resurfaced.

"It's a private lounge in one of the clan's hotels," Onegus said.

"Isn't that dangerous?" Her mother's tone was bordering on panicked. "What if Darlene is followed? We don't want to bring the government to a property that belongs to the clan."

Cassandra had explained that too, but Geraldine either didn't remember it or was too stressed to recall their conversation from yesterday.

"I have a Guardian trailing Darlene. If he notices that she's being followed, we will cancel the lunch."

"What if she has her phone on, and they follow the signal?"

"Cassandra made the arrangements with Darlene over the phone, so they already know where Darlene is going, who she's meeting, and why." Onegus had the patience of a saint. "The only reason they might have to follow her is if they suspect that Roni will be there. But they have no reason to think that."

By now, the agents keeping an eye on Darlene in the hopes of finding Roni knew about her two recently discovered cousins. Thanks to Leo, though, they also were aware that Cassandra knew how to reach Roni. But when she'd called, Cassandra hadn't mentioned him, or even told Darlene that Onegus and Shai were joining them, and the reason she'd given her sister for the meeting was that she and Geraldine missed her and wanted to see her.

The lunch meeting necessitated her taking half a day off work, but there was no avoiding that if they wanted to see Darlene without her hubby present. During the day, Leo was busy at the gallery and couldn't join them, so lunch was the best time to talk to her privately.

Clutching her purse, Geraldine looked tense. "Forgive me for asking so many questions, but I still think it looks suspicious. Why would three cousins who live in the same city meet in a hotel for lunch?"

"The hotel is a public place," Onegus said. "No one knows that it belongs to the clan because it's held by a subsidiary of another larger company, which belongs to yet another one abroad, and the connection to the clan is very well-hidden. The hotel restaurant is open to the public, and in addition to the hotel's guests, business-people from nearby office buildings dine there. The private lounge is just a room inside the restaurant that is frequently used for business meetings. Even if Darlene's phone is being tracked, and her location is known, all they will see is her going into the hotel restaurant."

Cassandra turned around to look at her mother. "You're overthinking it, Mom. By now, they are keeping a minimal lookout for Roni. He's eluded them for so long that they should have given up already."

"And yet they offer a reward for information that would lead to his capture." Geraldine sighed. "I don't know how we are going to tell Darlene that Leo sold out his own son for that reward money."

Shai took her hand. "That he didn't get because we were careful and changed plans as soon as we noticed agents snooping around Nathalie's café. We are just as careful now, so you have nothing to worry about."

"That's not true," Geraldine said. "Of course, I have reason to worry. Darlene is going to be devastated when she hears that. I don't want her to be in pain."

Cassandra huffed. "I think this plays beautifully into our plans. Hearing what scum Leo is will make it easier for her to leave him. We can bring her to the village, and she can find a nice immortal male to console her. If Roni is right, the only reason she hasn't left Leo yet is that she's afraid of having no options and being alone. If we convince her that she'll be a most desirable catch for the immortal males in the village, it will give her the courage to leave the jerk."

"We're making too many assumptions," Shai said. "What if Darlene is happy with Leo? What if Roni is wrong and his own opinion of his father is coloring his opinion of their relationship? What if Darlene knew about Leo selling Roni out? Today's meeting is about getting answers to these questions. We will decide how to proceed only after we know what Darlene wants and where she stands in regard to Leo's betrayal of Roni."

"My daughter would never betray her son," Geraldine said. "I might not remember her and the kind of person she is, but she is my and Rudolf's daughter. I would have never done such a thing, and after meeting Rudolf, I know he wouldn't either."

"It's the classic nature versus nurture argument." Cassandra sighed. "You and Rudolf were not the only influences in her life, and genetics don't determine every-thing. I want you to mentally prepare for the possibility that Darlene knew about Leo's betrayal of Roni."

28

GERALDINE

For the rest of the drive, Geraldine didn't ask any more questions. Cassandra seemed annoyed with her, probably because she'd forgotten what she'd already told her, but that was what usually happened when she got anxious. Her mind just stopped working right, and Geraldine wasn't even sure that it was a memory problem. She just couldn't handle stress well, or at least not as well as others.

If only she was more emotionally resilient, life would have been easier. She worried about telling Darlene about Leo's treachery and how it would affect her. And she worried about Darlene attempting transition at forty-nine. She worried about Shai's son, and whether he carried the immortal gene after all, and whether the clan would find a way to activate his Dormant genes with the help of that new gene-editing technology that was named crisper, or was it crispr? It was probably an acronym, but she didn't know of what.

Perhaps with Shai at her side, she shouldn't be as worried, but despite his eidetic memory, he didn't have the answers to everything. He just knew a collection of facts that was sometimes useful.

Too much had happened too fast for her to adjust, even if it was all good. She'd found a true-love mate, she'd found a new home where she belonged, and she'd found her brother. But what if her good fortune ran out?

What if pushing Darlene to leave Leo and attempt transition was the wrong thing to do?

"What's wrong?" Shai squeezed her hand. "You're very quiet."

"I'm not sure that we should tell Darlene about Leo. What if it makes her so upset that she keels over? I don't know anything about her medical history. She might have a heart condition, or diabetes, or whatever else humans her age suffer from. She's forty-nine."

Shai chuckled. "She'll be fine. If you're worried about shocking her, we can tell her about it in a roundabout way. Besides, she's not going to remember it after we are done with her, so if she gets overly upset, at least it's not going to last long."

Geraldine nodded. "I try to tell myself all those things, but I can't stop worrying anyway. She's my daughter, and I want what's best for her. The problem is that I don't know what that best is."

"That's simple," Cassandra said. "You can't beat immortality. If she has even a slim chance of achieving that, it's worth the risk."

As Onegus pulled up into the valet station, Geraldine's heart started racing, and her palms got sweaty. "I'm scared."

"I know, love." Shai kissed the top of her head. "Let's just take it slowly, okay? We are not going to drop it on Darlene right off the bat. Let's enjoy lunch first."

"Okay." She took his offered hand and stepped out of the car.

"The restaurant is on the seventy-second floor." Onegus led them to the elevators. "This building is a new concept that combines hotel rooms with offices. The guest rooms are on the top ten floors, and the rest are office suites."

The elevator to the top floor was so fast that Geraldine felt her ears pop, and as the doors opened and they walked out, the view that greeted them was spectacular. The entire metropolis was spread out before them, or at least most of it.

Onegus stopped by the hostess's station. "MacBain. I reserved the private lounge."

The woman made a show of checking her ledger and then lifted her head with a smile. "Welcome to the Seventy-Second, Mr. MacBain." She pulled out five menus and then looked over their party of four. "Are we waiting for another guest?"

"She should be here at any moment," Cassandra said. "We can either wait for her here, or you can show her to the private lounge when she gets here."

The hostess was about to answer as the elevator door opened, and Darlene stepped out. "That was quite a ride." She patted her ears. "I can't hear anything."

"Hi." Cassandra gave her a one-armed hug. "Blow your nose. That will clear your ears."

"Yeah, that's what I do on flights." Darlene turned to look at Shai and Onegus. "I didn't know that you two were coming as well. I'm glad that you are joining us, but I'm surprised."

"It was a last-minute decision." Shai leaned toward her and kissed her cheek. "Onegus and I had a meeting nearby, so we thought why not combine business with pleasure. I hope that you don't mind."

"No, of course not."

"Let me show you to the private lounge," the hostess said.

That got Darlene's attention. "Are we dining in a private lounge?"

"Working for a very rich guy has its perks." Onegus winked.

29

CASSANDRA

*N*ormally Cassandra was a straight shooter who didn't mince words, but the situation with Darlene needed a more nuanced approach. She could let Onegus handle it, which he would no doubt do better than she could ever hope to, but Darlene wasn't his sister, and it wasn't his responsibility to tell her about her scum of a husband or offer her immortality.

She should hear it from her family.

Another complication that had somehow escaped Geraldine's list of worries was that when they told Darlene about her chance at attempting immortality, they would also have to reveal that Geraldine and Cassandra were not her cousins.

Cassandra had no doubt that the shock of learning that Geraldine was Darlene's long-presumed-dead mother would be much worse than her sister learning about her husband's treachery. She hadn't pointed it out to Geraldine because her mother was already stressed enough.

"Let's make a toast." Cassandra lifted her wine glass. "To family."

Looking a little confused, Darlene lifted her glass and clinked it with Cassandra's. "To family, old and new."

"I bet you're wondering why the four of us cornered you into this private dining room." That wasn't the soft delivery Cassandra had hoped for, but they didn't have all day to dance around the issue.

Darlene put her glass down. "I had a feeling that the story about the business meeting wasn't true. What's going on?"

"We've learned something very upsetting about Leo."

Darlene swallowed. "Does he have a mistress? Is that why he goes on all those business trips?"

"He might, but that's not it. Did you know that there was a substantial reward offered to whoever provided information that led to Roni's capture?"

She shook her head. "How substantial?"

"Half a million dollars."

Darlene smiled proudly. "My Roni is worth a lot more than that, but I'm sure he's tickled silly by that amount. What does it have to do with Leo, though?"

Unless Darlene was an excellent actress, she really didn't know about the reward money or about Leo selling his son out.

Cassandra leaned forward and reached for her sister's hand. "Do you remember that we changed the meeting place with Roni because agents were snooping around the original place?"

She nodded.

"We couldn't figure out how they'd found out about it. Later, we learned that Leo had sold Roni out. He was the one who told the agents where the meeting was about to take place."

For a long moment, Darlene just gaped at her, and then the waterworks started. "Oh, my God. I can't believe that he did that. What a colossal jerk." She fisted her hand. "If he were here, I would punch him right in the teeth. How could he?"

Next to Cassandra, Geraldine sniffled. "I didn't want to tell you. I knew how upset you would be."

"How did you find out?" Darlene asked Cassandra and then turned to Onegus. "Was it through your security connections?"

He nodded. "After Leo's comment about wanting to see Roni's DNA test results, I suspected that he had something to do with compromising our meeting location. I have agent friends who work for a different department than the one Roni worked for but have access to the same files. I asked one of them to check, and he provided the information."

"When did you find out?"

"A while ago," Onegus admitted. "We debated whether to tell you or not. Geraldine was afraid it would upset you."

"Of course, it upsets me." Darlene sighed and picked up a napkin to dab at her eyes. "But it shouldn't have surprised me. Leo has always suspected that Roni wasn't his, but he never had the guts to demand a DNA test."

"Was he right?" Cassandra asked.

Darlene nodded. "We've always had relationship problems. Well, not in the beginning, but after years passed and I couldn't get pregnant, he blamed me, assuming that I was the infertile one because nothing could be wrong with him. I went to the doctor, and when she couldn't find anything wrong with me, she suggested that Leo might be the infertile one. He refused to get checked, saying that the doctor was incompetent and that I should go see a specialist. I was angry that he wasn't willing to even consider that it might be his fault. We fought over this and many other things, and finally, I got fed up and left. He didn't even try to stop me." Darlene dabbed her eyes again. "I think that he was happy to be rid of me."

"You met someone," Cassandra guessed.

Darlene nodded. "I wasn't ready to file for a divorce yet, but I was hurt and angry, and my confidence was shot. I needed to prove to myself that I was still desirable. I wasn't picky, and I said yes to the first guy who offered." She chuckled. "He was a geeky software engineer who couldn't believe that I said yes. I didn't know that he was a genius, but I guess I got lucky. Roni wouldn't be nearly as smart if Leo was his father."

30

GERALDINE

*G*eraldine had so many questions she wanted to ask her daughter, and more than that, she wanted to take her into her arms and console her, but she could do neither since the waitress had returned with their order.

When the woman left and closed the door behind her, Onegus asked, "How long were you and Leo separated?"

"Not long." Darlene unfurled the napkin and spread it over her knees. "A couple of months, maybe even less than that. I still worked back then, and Roni's father was the IT person for the firm. I didn't know that he'd been mooning after me for the entire year and a half he'd known me. We went out a few times, but it wasn't serious. Not on my part anyway. I still loved Leo and hoped that he would come to his senses and apologize for being such a dick. But it didn't happen."

"What did you do when you found out that you were pregnant?" Geraldine asked.

"I freaked out. I didn't want to divorce Leo, so I called him and suggested that we go to couples therapy. Surprisingly, he agreed. I took it as a sign that he missed me and wanted me back but had been too proud to initiate the reconciliation. Naturally, I did everything to be the perfect wife he wanted, and we got back together. When I told him that I was pregnant a month later, he was overjoyed. Frankly, I don't think he started suspecting anything until Roni's superior intelligence started manifesting. They have similar coloring and the same slim build, but neither Leo nor I are that smart. When Roni got a little older, and his contrary character started to become more apparent, he and Leo fought nonstop. I think that was when Leo started suspecting that Roni wasn't his."

"Did he confront you about it?" Shai asked.

Darlene sighed. "Many times. I denied it, of course. When I called him paranoid and pretended to encourage him to take a paternity test, he backed off, only to bring it up again when we had yet another fight. But I never thought he would go as far as selling Roni out. He raised him as his son. How could he have done that?"

Cassandra crossed her arms over her chest. "A better question is why did you put up with him for so long? Leo is obviously a prick."

"Guilt. Fear." Darlene wiped tears from her eyes. "What am I going to do now? How can I stay with him after he did a thing like that?"

"Do you love him?" Geraldine asked gently.

"I don't know. I'm used to him, and I don't want to be alone."

"What if I could promise you a better future?" Cassandra said. "What if you could live next to Roni and his mate, have handsome men vying for your attention, and all of your needs met? Would you leave Leo then?"

"Sure, but you can't promise me all that."

Cassandra smiled. "Yes, I can, and much more than that. I can offer you immortality."

Darlene's tears dried in an instant. "You're either crazy, or you think that I am, in which case, I really resent you for making fun of me."

"I wouldn't dream of it." Cassandra uncrossed her arms. "But I see that you are not ready for the red pill yet. Let's eat first, and when you feel up to it, I'll tell you precisely how you can have all the wonderful things I've offered you."

"What red pill?"

"Didn't you see *The Matrix*? The red pill represented the willingness to learn a potentially life-altering truth, and the blue pill represented staying ignorant. Which one would you choose?"

"I remember now." Darlene reached for a glass of water with a shaking hand. "The truth was much worse than the fantasy, and one character betrayed the rebels in exchange for erasing that knowledge from his mind. So maybe choosing the blue pill is the smarter option."

"Not in this case." Cassandra grinned. "The red pill we offer you will reveal a truth that is better than your wildest fantasies."

Geraldine wasn't sure Cassandra had it right. The truth in the so-called red pill could tempt Darlene with a promise of eternal life but also deliver premature death.

31

KIAN

"Come in," Kian said as a knock sounded on his office door.

He was expecting Edna sometime that afternoon, but not this early. Perhaps she'd cut her workday short. After all, it was Friday, and people were getting ready for the weekend.

"Hello, Kian." The judge walked in and sat down on one of the chairs in front of his desk. "I didn't see Shai on my way in. Did he take a day off?"

"He's in a lunch meeting with Geraldine's daughter." He looked at his watch again. "I wonder how it's going. They are supposed to tell her about her possible shot at immortality, get her reaction, and then thrall the memory away."

Edna lifted one sculpted brow. "That's an odd way to go about it. Now that we have several compellers in our midst, it would have been better to compel her silence instead of thralling her."

"I agree. The problem is that except for Parker, all of our compellers are away at the moment, and Cassandra didn't want to wait. I think she hopes that Darlene will just decide on the spot and come back with them to the village, but that's unrealistic."

"I don't know the woman, but without a very compelling reason to jump ship, most reasonable people would need some time to mull over a decision like that."

Kian nodded. "How is translating Toven's journal going?"

Edna sighed. "I haven't read anything in Aramaic in a very long time, and my initial progress was painfully slow. It's going faster now, and I have about half of it translated. He recorded detailed descriptions of his lovers, including their full names, the month, year, and location of the encounter. I bet that Orion looked into that and checked whether these women produced children nine months later, but what I found more interesting was the pattern I discerned."

"That the women were all artistically inclined? Orion said that Toven had a thing for artistic females."

"That too. Toven wasn't moved by physical beauty alone. He preferred ladies who piqued his interest, who were creative and were independent, or as independent as the times allowed women to be back then. He also preferred big cities, and during the time period that particular journal covered, he visited the US many times. So far, the cities mentioned in the journal were New York, Boston, Chicago, Philadelphia, San Francisco, Houston, Miami, and Honolulu. In Europe, the only cities mentioned were Paris and London, and there were none in East Asia or Africa or South America. That doesn't mean that he didn't visit there, though. He might have just not taken lovers while there. It makes perfect sense. Women were more progressive in the West, and large cities provided him with the anonymity he needed."

Leaning back in his chair, Kian crossed his arms over his chest. "How does that help us find him, though?"

"I think he's in the US, probably on the East Coast. We know what he looks like, but not precisely enough to use facial recognition software to find him by his driver's license or passport. I wonder if William can tweak the program to broaden the match. It might produce thousands of results, but it shouldn't take too long to sift through them. If he can include British and French databases in his search that would be even better."

"That's a very smart idea. I'll ask him if that's possible. Anything else that you found and took note of?"

"For now, that's it. I'll work on the rest over the weekend and make a list of all the cities his affairs took place in and the corresponding dates. Perhaps I can narrow it further."

Kian nodded. "The problem is that the last entry was made nearly four decades ago. Toven might have moved to a new territory."

"It's possible," Edna said. "But for now, that's all we have to work with. What about the other idea of locating his novels by his writing style?"

"Turner's guy is searching through Russian libraries and used books stores for the title Orion remembered seeing at Toven's place. Their cataloging system is not nearly as thorough as the one we have here. We will also use your translation of the journal. I hope that Aramaic translates well into English."

Edna grimaced. "It does not, but Toven has a very distinctive writing style that I doubt he was able to change enough for the novels he published. Once I'm done with the translation, it's worth a try to run it through a style-detecting software."

"Of course." Kian uncrossed his arms and leaned forward. "I wonder if Eva and Geraldine have more in common than they realize. What if Eva wasn't induced by Kalugal but was born immortal?"

Edna shook her head. "Eva said that she'd thought it was the flu. She wouldn't have gotten sick if she were immortal. She also remembers her parents, and she wasn't adopted."

"Perhaps she just felt down emotionally and thought that it was the flu?"

Kian knew that he was grasping at straws, but that nagging suspicion that there was more to Eva's story refused to abate. "Also, record keeping back then wasn't as efficient, and her parents might have opted for a private adoption without any intermediaries. That was also done back then."

"What about her senses? Did she always have super strength and super hearing, or did she start noticing that after her so-called flu?"

"That's actually a very interesting question. Eva thought that her powers were the result of tampering with her DNA that was done during her training with the DEA."

"As far as I remember her story, she was oblivious until she cut her finger one day, and it healed almost instantly. She was probably blocking her super senses like Geraldine did, or thought that it was normal to hear and see as well as she did. Personally, I don't think the Fates would have sent Kalugal Eva's way if she didn't need activation. But if you still have doubts, you can call her and ask."

Despite his nagging suspicion, Kian had to accept that all the evidence confirmed Eva's induction by Kalugal.

Perhaps Eva's grandmother was Toven's daughter?

"No, you're right. The simplest explanation is usually the right one. We know for certain that she and Kalugal hooked up, and there was no way he wouldn't have noticed her strength and stamina when he had sex with her. She must have been still human back then."

32

ANNANI

*T*he house felt empty with Alena and Oridu gone. Annani still had Ogidu and Oshidu, so she wasn't alone, and she had been trying to distract herself by making back-to-back appointments with various clan members, but she could not fill every moment of every day.

Besides, she needed time to rest and gather her thoughts, or so she had been telling herself, but the truth was that she was very happy about Merlin's request for an audience. Not only did it fit in nicely between two appointments, but she also enjoyed the quirky doctor's company.

Merlin was a positive male with a good sense of humor and a seemingly bottomless trove of knowledge. He was always a pleasure to be around, and he was entertaining.

Except, she had a good idea why he had requested an audience with her, and there was nothing amusing or entertaining about that. She could not tell him the truth about her blessing, but she wanted to reassure him that it was helpful and had proven to be highly effective in aiding Dormants' transition.

Merlin was smart, and he might figure it out, but as long as she did not admit the truth, he had no proof and did not know it for a fact. If he was ever captured by their enemies or by humans who sought the secret of immortality, he had a better chance of withholding information he was unsure of.

When the knock sounded at the door, Oshidu walked over to open up for Merlin, and Ogidu rushed out of the kitchen with the tea and canapés she had requested him to prepare for the meeting with the doctor.

"Good afternoon, Clan Mother." Merlin bowed his head. "Thank you for agreeing to see me on such short notice."

"It is always a pleasure to talk to you, Merlin. I was very glad to grant your request." She motioned to the armchair. "Please sit down and help yourself to some canapés."

Ogidu lifted the teapot and poured tea into Annani's cup.

"Would you like some tea, master?"

"I would love some." Merlin lifted the cup for the Odu to fill. After taking a few polite sips, he put the cup down and smiled. "I promised to update you on Ronja's progress."

"Indeed." She put her cup down as well. "I saw her on Wednesday, and I was amazed at the transformation. If I did not know better, I would have thought that she had already transitioned. You look amazing as well, Merlin."

He inclined his head. "Thank you, Clan Mother. Ronja and I have been working very hard, exercising, eating healthily, drinking plenty of water, and of course, my health-boosting potions had something to do with it as well."

"Do they work on immortals?"

"We don't need them because our bodies are programmed to operate optimally, but I believe that there is always room for improvement." He flexed his muscles. "I'm proof of that. I was perfectly healthy, but my posture wasn't great, and I was a bit on the scrawny side. After training alongside Ronja, I look much better, and I feel better as well. But as far as health-boosting potions go, I don't think they have much effect on immortals. Unless we abuse our bodies on a daily basis, they repair whatever needs fixing on autopilot. Humans, on the other hand, need all the help they can get." Leaning forward, he looked into her eyes. "Speaking of help, I would like to find out more about your blessings and how they help Dormants transition."

She arched a brow. "Is Ronja ready to attempt it?"

A sly smile lifting his lips, Merlin nodded. "My new and improved physique has proven to be a very effective aphrodisiac. Ronja admitted that she could no longer resist me. But joking aside, the reason she finally capitulated was a conversation she had with Kri."

"Good for Kri." Annani lifted her teacup. "That girl does not mince words. What did she tell Ronja to convince her?"

"Kri advised Ronja to attempt transition while you are in the village."

"I told her the same thing." Annani crossed her feet under her long skirt. "I would think that my word would carry more weight than Kri's, but apparently, it is not so."

"Ronja thought that the blessing was a spiritual thing and that the effect it had on transitioning Dormants was a psychological rather than physical one. Kri had an interesting observation that convinced Ronja the blessing was much more than a mood booster for the transitioning Dormant and his or her mate. She said that if your presence alone is enough to activate the dormant little girls, then you must be emitting something that activates their dormant genes. It might not be enough to induce transition in an adult, but it can provide the extra boost to get them over the most difficult part of it."

"Kri is a smart girl." Annani took a sip from her tea and waited for Merlin's question. When it did not come, she leveled her eyes at him. "Was there a question in that story which I missed?"

He nodded. "Are you aware of emitting something that activates the Dormants?"

"Of course." She put her cup down. "Well, I do not feel it, if that is what you are asking, but I have been told by many that being in my presence is like being next to a small nuclear power source." She laughed. "Thankfully, I am not radioactive despite having glowing skin. But I am radiating something. Blessedly, it has only positive effects and no negatives."

She had not lied. Everything she had told Merlin was the truth, just not the whole truth.

"Is that all?" Merlin asked. "What do you do when you bless a Dormant? Do you concentrate that power somehow? Do you put your hands on them to imbue them with your power? Forgive me, Clan Mother, but as a scientist, I like to know how things work."

"I forgive you." She gave him an indulgent smile. "But I keep what I do to channel my power a secret for a reason, and I have no intention of letting anyone witness the ritual. What I can tell you, though, is that spirituality is only one component of the blessing, and it is more for my benefit than the transitioning Dormant. It helps me concentrate and channel my power. What I can also tell you is that without my blessing, those Dormants I helped might not have made it. If I were a totalitarian ruler, I would have forbidden you from inducing Ronja without me being nearby to help if needed. But since I do not like to assert my will on others, and I prefer people to listen to my advice because that is the prudent thing to do, I leave it up to you and Ronja to make the final decision."

Merlin dipped his head. "Thank you, Clan Mother. You are as wise as you are gracious."

33

DARLENE

*L*eo had warned Darlene that there was something wrong with her newfound cousins. He'd said that their stories didn't add up, but she'd been so happy to have found them, or rather at having been found by them, that she'd ignored the seeds of doubts he'd planted in her head.

She'd done a little online research and found plenty of information about Cassandra, but none about Geraldine. She didn't know Shai's last name, so she couldn't check up on him, but she found Onegus's while reading an article about the gala where he and Cassandra had met.

What was written about him didn't match what he had told her and Leo at all. According to the article, he was a reclusive billionaire, the founder of the charity that helped rehabilitate rescued victims of trafficking.

He was not the head of security.

Still, their story had been plausible enough until Cassandra had started pushing her to leave Leo and talking about that immortality nonsense. If it was only Cassandra, Darlene would have dismissed it as the blabbering of a crazy person, but the others hadn't denied her claims.

They were all in on it, and they had ganged up on her while Leo was away, spinning lies about him.

Telling them about Roni's real father had been so stupid. Now they could use it against her, forcing her to do things that she wouldn't otherwise agree to.

She was such a stupid cow.

She'd just proven Leo right and justified all the times he'd called her that.

How was she going to get out of the mess she'd created?

"Stop stressing," Cassandra said. "Your nervous energy is killing my appetite."

"I can't help it." Darlene shoved another piece of chicken into her mouth.

When she was nervous or unhappy, she ate more, not less. No wonder Cassandra looked like a supermodel while she looked like a pumpkin. And just to prove that she wasn't only a stupid cow but also a fat one, when there was nothing left on her plate, she reached for the last piece of bread in the basket and shoved it into her mouth as well.

Cassandra pushed her half-eaten entree away from her and picked up her wine glass. "So here is how it's going to happen. I will tell you a lot of things that you are probably not going to believe, and then I'll ask you to make a decision. After that, Shai is going to erase your memory of this entire conversation, and we will take it from there." She glanced at her watch. "I'm just waiting for Roni to get here."

Darlene frowned. "What do you want from him?"

"I thought that you would be more inclined to believe your own son than a cousin you've just met." As Cassandra turned to Geraldine, her eyes softened. "You know what's coming, right?"

Tears glistening in her eyes, Geraldine nodded.

"Are you ready?" Shai asked. "We don't need to do this today. If you need more time, that's fine."

Why were they all coddling Geraldine?

If anyone needed reassurance it was Darlene, the woman who they were trying to deceive, the one who was outnumbered and alone.

Roni was coming, but would he stand by his mother's side? Or was he going to stick with these strangers that claimed to be related to him?

"I need to visit the ladies' room." Darlene pushed to her feet.

Perhaps she could duck into the elevator before they could notice.

Could they really erase her memories?

"I'll go with you." Cassandra got up.

Darlene sized her cousin up and realized that she didn't stand a chance against that Amazon woman. With heels on, she was well over six feet tall, and she looked toned. Darlene hadn't visited the gym in years, and her idea of exercise was pacing around the kitchen island, which was sizable, but given that she usually snacked while doing it, it really didn't count.

God, if she got out of this bizarre situation without losing her husband or worse, she was hitting the gym, and to make sure that she actually followed through, she was going to hire a personal trainer.

As dreams of a better, stronger body and a brighter future eased some of her anxiety, Darlene gave Cassandra a forced smile. "I can find the way to the bathroom on my own."

"I know you can." Cassandra put her hand on Darlene's arm in a gesture that might have been intended as reassuring but came across as threatening. "I need to visit the ladies' room as well."

Darlene doubted that, but it wasn't as if she could get rid of her imposing cousin. "Let's go. I want to be back before Roni gets here."

"Same here." Cassandra took hold of her arm and led her out of the private lounge. "It was difficult enough to drag him out here. I promised him that it wouldn't take long and that we wouldn't waste his valuable time."

"Does he know what this is about?"

"I only told him that you would need someone you trust to tell you the story. I wish I had thought of that ahead of time, but I didn't expect you to panic. It will also make it easier on Geraldine." Cassandra pushed the door to the ladies' room open.

"Why is everyone so concerned with her?" Darlene asked. "She is not the one that is getting slammed with nonsense from *The Matrix*."

"Let's wait for Roni." Cassandra opened one of the stalls and motioned for Darlene to go in. "I'll be right here if you need me." She winked.

34

CASSANDRA

*A*s the door to Darlene's stall closed, Cassandra leaned against it to make sure the little mouse didn't get any ideas of escape into her head.

Pulling out her phone, she texted Roni. *When are you getting here?*

His reply text came in a minute later. *At the valet. Will be there in two.*

Cassandra let out a breath. She should have thought of bringing Roni along, but it hadn't occurred to her until Darlene revealed her big secret. That was the reason she'd stalled and told Darlene that they would continue talking after the meal. She'd needed to give Roni enough time to get there. He would be so glad that Leo wasn't his biological father. He didn't like the guy, and the feeling was mutual.

Even if Roni wasn't Leo's biological son, the guy had still raised him from infancy into adulthood. He should have loved Roni even though he suspected that he wasn't his. But Leo was a jerk who hadn't been a good husband or father, and yet Darlene clung to her marriage despite everything.

Did she love him, though?

When the toilet was flushed in the stall behind her, Cassandra pushed away from the door and waited for Darlene to step out.

"Roni should be here in a minute."

Darlene nodded and walked over to the row of sinks to wash her hands. "I thought that you needed to use the bathroom yourself." She looked at Cassandra through the mirror.

"I thought I did, but when I got here, the sensation passed."

Raising a brow, Darlene turned the faucet off and dried her hands with a towel. "Just admit that you accompanied me to make sure that I didn't escape."

Cassandra shrugged. "What can I say. You caught me."

"Why is this so important to you? Why do you care if I stay with Leo or not? It's none of your business."

"I just want what's best for you." Cassandra took Darlene's arm and led her back into the lounge.

Roni came in a moment after they'd sat down. "Hi, everyone." He walked over to Darlene and leaned to kiss her cheek. "How are you holding up, Mom?"

"I'm confused and worried. Cassandra told me that you have all the answers."

Roni gave Cassandra an accusing look. "Thanks, auntie."

"She will be more accepting of what we need to tell her if it comes from you."

"Right." Roni motioned for Cassandra to get up and let him sit in her chair. "So here is the thing, Mom." He took her hand between his two. "You and I carry godly genes. Mine were activated, and I am now immortal. Yours can be activated as well, but not without risk. The transition into immortality is dangerous for older Dormants, and you are pushing the limit of what's safe, but I still think that it's worth the risk."

Darlene gaped at him. "Are you on drugs?"

He grinned. "I knew that you would think that. Just look at my teeth." He closed his eyes, and soon his fangs started elongating. He'd probably imagined making love to his mate, or maybe attacking another immortal male.

"What the hell?" Darlene's eyes widened. "Are those prosthetics?"

Roni sighed, and his fangs retracted. "I hoped that I wouldn't have to do this, but you leave me no choice." He pulled out a small switchblade from his pocket, flipped it open, and plunged it into the palm of his hand.

"What are you doing?" Darlene shrieked.

"Just watch my hand," he commanded.

As the skin started knitting together, Darlene sucked in a breath, and when the cut disappeared, she gripped Roni's hand and wiped the few drops of blood away with her finger. "It was a trick. You used one of those prop knives and dripped a few droplets of blood on your hand."

"You've seen the skin knitting together, but here," he handed her the switchblade. "Check it out for yourself."

Darlene turned the miniature weapon this way and that, opened it, closed it, opened it again, and then handed it back to Roni. "I can't believe it."

"I know you can't." Roni took her hand again. "But it's real, and it could be yours, but you can't stay with Leo. He doesn't have the godly genes, and when you transition into immortality, it will be really difficult for you to hide it. You'll be stronger, faster, your hearing and eyesight will improve, and your wrinkles will disappear. You will look much younger."

"You should have started with that," she murmured. "How, though? Where did we get it from? My mother wasn't immortal, and my father's aging process is just as predictable as any other human's."

"Actually," Geraldine said. "Your mother is an immortal. I am not your mother's twin sister's daughter, Darlene. I am your mother."

35

DARLENE

*D*arlene felt as if someone had kicked her in the gut. The young woman who she'd believed was her cousin, the one who looked years younger than her, was her mother?

"Prove it. What was my favorite dessert?"

Tears slid down the imposter's face. "I don't remember. The day you thought I died, I almost did. I must have collided with a boat and suffered a severe brain injury. If I hadn't been immortal already, I would have died. In fact, a normal immortal would have died from an injury like that, but I wasn't just any immortal. I'm the daughter of a god, and the amazing healing abilities I inherited from my father saved my life. But since I regrew a large chunk of my brain, all my memories from before the accident were gone. I had to learn everything from scratch, even how to speak. Fortunately, my brother found me and took care of me. He chose not to tell me about the family I had before to save me from having to go through the anguish of leaving you later on. I wasn't aging, and eventually, I would have been forced to really fake my own death and disappear. Orion thought that he was doing the right thing, but I wish he hadn't kept me in the dark. I wish I had spent a few more years with you, at least until you were old enough to go to college. But what was done is done, and I only discovered recently that I had another daughter. You can't imagine how upset and heartbroken I was about it. So much so that I was convinced it couldn't be true and that I really had a twin sister who was your mother." Geraldine reached across the table for Darlene's hand.

Darlene leaned back, pretending not to notice the gesture. Even if everything Geraldine had said was true, she still wasn't ready to forgive her for the charade she'd pulled, pretending to be her cousin. She'd had plenty of opportunities to come out and admit who she really was.

"Who is your other daughter?" Darlene suspected who she was, but she wanted her suspicion confirmed.

"Cassandra is my younger daughter," Geraldine, or rather Sabina said. "You and I lost so many years, but we can have eternity to make up for it. All you have to do is decide whether you are willing to take the risk, and whether you are willing to leave your old life behind. From what I've heard so far, leaving Leo shouldn't be a great heartache for you."

"Why do I need to leave him?" Darlene narrowed her eyes at the woman claiming to be her mother. "Why is it so important to all of you?" She turned to Roni. "Do you hate your father so much?"

As the words left her mouth, she wondered whether anyone present had already shared her confession with Roni.

"He sold me out for money," Roni hissed, the fangs he'd shown her before elongating once again. "Leo doesn't think that he's my father, and even though I look like him, I don't think he is either. I can't remember him ever hugging me, or giving me a ride on his shoulders, or coming to any of my school events, or congratulating me when my science project won first prize in the entire county. I thought that he was just a cold bastard, but to sell me out was a new low that I'm not willing to ever forgive him for. He doesn't deserve the title of father."

Every word was true, and each one was like a punch to her stomach. Leo had always been cold, but she'd blamed his upbringing for it. His parents were two dry sticks who looked down their noses at everyone because they were rich, and their grandparents had been the founders of whatever.

"You are the smart one in our dysfunctional family, Roni. What do you want me to do?"

"I don't want you to do anything that you don't want to, but I want you to know that you have options, and I want you to choose what's best for you."

"I don't know what's best for me. What do I need to do to start the transformation to immortality? And what are the risks?"

Roni grimaced. "That's not something I'm comfortable explaining to my mother. Cassandra should do that."

Darlene turned to her sister. "Well? Do I need to get bitten by a werewolf or something?"

"That was actually a very good guess. You need to get bitten by an immortal male while having sex with him, and if you really like him and bond with him, that makes your chances of transitioning even better."

"You can't be serious." Darlene looked at Roni. "Don't tell me that you had to have sex with a male to transition into immortality."

Roni chuckled. "Thankfully, male Dormants only need to fight an immortal male to activate their genes. The venom needed for the induction gets produced in response to aggression as well as to arousal."

If it were anyone but Roni, Darlene would have suspected that they were pulling a joke on her and that at any moment, someone would shout, you've been pranked! But she'd known Roni all of his life, and he wasn't a good actor, nor was he a jokester.

"What are the risks?" She looked her son in the eyes.

He was the only one she trusted.

"The clan's doctor says that the older Dormants have a difficult time, and that the transition could be potentially deadly for them, but so far, everyone who has attempted it made it through. For some, it was easy, while for others it was more difficult, but no one has died."

"How old was the oldest person who transitioned?"

"I think Turner was forty-seven." Roni looked at Onegus. "Or was it forty-eight?"

"He was forty-six at the time," Onegus said. "But Turner was also sick. He had cancer."

Cassandra waved a dismissive hand. "Everyone knows that women are more resilient. You're forty-nine and in good health. You'll be fine. Besides, you are the granddaughter of a god, which means that your genetics are superior. Your transition should be easy."

"A god? What do you mean by that?"

"Do you remember what you learned in school about Greek and Roman mythology? Both are based on a more ancient pantheon of gods that originated in Sumer. Those so-called gods were genetically enhanced humanoids who came from somewhere else in the universe, and like it says in the Bible, they took human lovers and produced us—immortals who possess a diluted version of their powers. Long story short, our grandfather is the god Toven. He and two other goddesses were the only ones who survived the cataclysm that destroyed all the other gods."

Darlene's head was spinning enough as it was, and adding an alien grandfather to the mess was too much for her to absorb all at once.

It was easier to focus on the details than on the big picture.

She shifted her gaze to Cassandra. "Did you transition?"

Her sister nodded. "It was an easy process for me, which is why I'm confident that it will be easy be for you as well."

36

RONI

*R*oni struggled to keep his expression neutral and not let his mother see the storm brewing inside of him. She needed to choose between him and his father, between living a second-rate life or grabbing the opportunity given to her with both hands and joining him on the other side.

What would it be?

So far, she'd chosen Leo at every juncture. She'd never come to Roni's defense when his father had been mean to him, and when he'd confronted her about it in the past, her defense had been that parents needed to show a united front. That might be true if both parents were doing what they were supposed to, but not when one was being an asshole and the other a doormat who'd never stood up for herself or for her child.

Would his mother finally grow a pair and show some backbone?

"So, what's next?" Darlene asked.

"It depends on what you decide," Onegus said. "If you don't want to leave your husband and would rather spend the rest of your human life with him, we will respect your wishes and thrall you to forget this entire exchange. Cassandra and Geraldine will go back to being your cousins, and you'll continue believing that Roni works for some secret organization. However, if you decide that you want to jump on the opportunity right away, you can leave your old life behind today and come with us to live in our secret community. You'll have plenty of immortal males to choose from, and once you find one you like, you can start the process. But if you need more time to think it through, that's totally understandable. We will thrall you to forget what you've learned today, but the next time we meet we will bring a compeller along. When we release your submerged memories of today and answer more of your questions, the knowledge will be secured by a compulsion to never utter a word about it to anyone outside of this group. That will give you time to think it through."

Darlene cast Roni a sidelong glance. "Why didn't you bring that person along today?"

He'd wondered the same thing. "You should ask Cassandra. She's the mastermind behind this."

Cassandra pinned him with an incredulous stare. "Did you forget that we have a shortage of compellers at the moment? The only one available is Parker, and he's just a kid. I didn't want to drag him into this unless it was absolutely necessary."

"Right. I did forget." Roni turned to his mother. "If you want my opinion, just come with us now. Leo can rot in hell for all I care. Don't even pack a suitcase, so the agents watching the house won't know that you're going anywhere. I can replace everything that you leave behind. The clan pays me very well for my services."

Looking into his eyes, Darlene shook her head. "I guess Cassandra told you about Leo not being your father. Otherwise, you wouldn't be talking like that."

"She told me no such thing." He turned to Cassandra. "What is my mother talking about? And why didn't you say something before?"

Cassandra lifted her hands in the air. "Don't blame me. I had my suspicions, but until your mother confirmed them today, I didn't know that Leo wasn't your real father."

Roni shifted his eyes to his mother. "Does he know?"

She shook her head. "He suspects, but he's never had the nerve to test it."

"Who is my real father?"

She smiled. "He's just a guy I dated for a couple of weeks while I was separated from Leo. He doesn't know, and I'd like to keep it that way. By now, he's probably married with two and a half kids. He was the IT person in the firm I worked for at the time, and he was very smart and very sweet." His mother chuckled. "You inherited your smarts from him, but not his personality. In that, you were more like Leo— sarcastic, judgmental, and you have a superiority complex."

A growl started low in Roni's throat. "I'm nothing like that jerk. I was thrown into the adult world much too early, and I had to survive. My crusty attitude was my shield, my armor."

Onegus cleared his throat. "If that were true, you would have turned into a sweetheart after joining the clan. But we both know that didn't happen."

Roni shrugged. "It was too late for me to change." He turned to his mother. "How do you want to do this?"

"I don't want my memories erased." She turned to Geraldine. "So, the memory issues you and Cassandra said plagued your mother were actually yours?"

Geraldine nodded. "My brain healed, but not completely. When I get stressed, I still forget the most basic things. It's not a good feeling."

"I believe you." Darlene sighed. "But how can I just leave everything behind? And what about Leo? It's true that he hasn't been the best of husbands or fathers, but he wasn't a monster. He deserves an explanation."

"Call him or write him a letter," Cassandra said. "Admit that Roni is not his and file for a divorce."

For a long moment, Darlene chewed on her lower lip, and then she shook her head. "I can't do it like that. I'm sorry. Can you let me walk away with my memories intact if I promise not to breathe a word of it to anyone?"

"We can't," Onegus said. "After Leo sold Roni out, we are even more wary than usual."

"I understand." She lowered her eyes. "Then do what you must and let's all meet at a later time. You will have to explain everything to me again when you bring along that compeller of yours to ensure my silence."

The boulder in Roni's gut dropped to the bottom. His mother was once again choosing damn Leo over him.

"As you wish," Onegus said.

Darlene lifted her eyes to Roni. "I just need a little more time to think things through. Can you understand that?"

"Yeah. I guess." He pushed to his feet. "I need to get back to work." He forced a small smile. "Do you need me for anything else? Or can you handle the rest without me?"

Roni still couldn't thrall, so he would be no help to them in taking care of his mother's memories. In a way, it was a relief that she wouldn't remember any of that.

He wished he could forget it all as well.

37

ALENA

*A*s the canoe gently glided through the lake's placid water, Alena leaned her head on Orion's arm. "This is one of the most beautiful places I've ever visited, and I've been all over the world."

"I agree," Kalugal said. "Lugu Lake is a hidden gem."

After breakfast, they'd taken the waitress's suggestion to book a boat trip on the lake. The simple dugout was larger than the traditional pig troughs, as the canoes were called by the Mosuo. Each of the four benches was just wide enough for a couple to sit snuggled together, and it glided over the water nearly soundlessly, not disturbing the serenity of the lake.

Kalugal's men followed in another boat that Phinas had insisted on renting without a guide. Originally the proprietress had refused, but when he'd offered her double the price, she'd relented. In the unlikely event of an attack, Phinas didn't want to have to worry about the human tour guide.

The two Odus had been left behind in the hotel, which Arwel hadn't been happy about, not because he thought he needed them for Alena's protection, but because Kian would have a fit when he found out.

There were two problems with taking the Odus along. The first was practical. The Odus might be too heavy for the flimsy canoes. The other one had to do with what might happen if they accidentally fell into the water. They wouldn't float and hauling them out would require a motorboat and a cable, which would betray that they weren't human. A lot of mind scrubbing would ensue, and that was not something Alena wanted to deal with on her vacation.

But those were minor considerations compared to a possible reboot. Okidu and Onidu had both rebooted after prolonged submergence in water, and until it was proven that their following emergent sentience didn't pose a risk to the clan, Alena didn't dare risk Ovidu rebooting. If she was ever forced to decommission him because he was dangerous, it would break her heart.

"Why is the boat called a pig trough?" Carol asked Lamai, the pretty Mosuo girl who captained their boat. She was young, no more than eighteen or nineteen, and dressed in her people's colorful traditional outfit, including flowers in her hair and strings of beads around her neck.

"It's because of the legend," the girl said in heavily accented English. "A long time ago, there was no lake here. One day the water came from the Gamu mountain and flooded the valley. When that happened, a mother was feeding the family's pigs with her children playing next to her. When she saw the water coming, she put her children in the pig trough and saved them. She died in the flood, but the children who survived became the ancestors of the Mosuo people. That's why we call Lugu Lake the Mother Lake." She smiled proudly. "The mother's courage and sacrifice was the foundation of our matriarchal society."

Orion leaned and whispered in Alena's ear. "I wonder if some ancient Kra-ell visitors caused the flooding or it was a natural phenomenon."

Smiling, Alena lifted her head off his shoulder and turned to look up at his handsome face. "It's just another legend that explains how the lake was formed. It's a little more believable than the mountain spirit's tears filling a giant hoofprint, but it's probably just as untrue."

"You never know." Amusement danced in his eyes. "People think that the Sumerian legends are made-up stories as well."

With his lips hovering so close and that dimple in his cheek making him look so roguishly attractive, Alena wanted to kiss him long and hard for all to see, not just because she craved him nearly nonstop, but because the tour guide was eyeing Orion with hunger in her eyes.

Why had the girl set her sights on him when the other males in the boat were nearly as handsome?

Kalugal had the vibe of a rich man about him, and he had the bad boy charm most women found irresistible, Lokan looked elegant and sophisticated, and Arwel had the most unique colored eyes and misleadingly vulnerable expression that made women want to take care of him. And yet, out of all these magnificent males, Lamai coveted Orion.

Well, he was the most handsome of the four and the kindest, but he was just as taken as the others, and Lamai was out of luck.

"I don't think that the Kra-ell are that technologically advanced," Kalugal said quietly enough for the girl not to hear but loud enough for the immortals.

"It's not complicated to do," Arwel said. "If they had explosives, which given that they were space travelers, I'm sure they had, they could have caused an avalanche that formed a natural dam. The water wouldn't come in a torrent, but it would gradually rise until it filled the valley."

"Lugu Lake is one of the deepest natural lakes in China," Lamai continued her tour guide speech. "The average depth is forty-three meters, and the deepest is ninety-three meters. If you look over the side of the boat, you'll see that the water is very clean. You can see for many meters down."

"But not all the way down," Lokan murmured. "If I was part of an ancient expedition to earth and feared the local savages, I would have built a subterranean base and then flooded the basin to hide it."

"The Kra-ell are different from us," Arwel said. "They don't like living underground. Emmett was miserable in the keep."

"One male's preferences are not indicative of the entire species," Kalugal countered. "Don't forget that he's half-human, and the human side of him might not have liked living underground while the Kra-ell might have loved it. Besides, safety comes before comfort, and we know that a subterranean base is not a bad idea. I would love to explore the possibility."

Alena let out a breath. "We decided to wait with the investigation until Monday and enjoy the weekend sightseeing. Can we give the conspiracy theories a rest for a while?"

"Why?" Kalugal sounded amused. "They are so much fun."

"I want to hear more about the lake and the Mosuo culture," Jacki said, loud enough for the girl to hear.

"I'll be delighted to tell you more about my people. Our main industries are tourism and fishing. The lake is rich with fish, and its beauty attracts many visitors. It is said to be like a quiet, beautiful girl. The lake changes colors like a girl changes dresses. In the morning, the sun paints it gold, during the day it is a beautiful blue and green, and when the sun goes down, it is dark green. The lake has five islands and three semi-islands, which are compared to a girl's jewels."

As their boat reached the middle of the lake, one of the guides on a nearby boat started singing in their native language. Even though it sounded like Chinese, it wasn't. Soon after the first girl began singing, all the other guides, including Lamai, joined her, their song rippling over the surface of the lake.

"One thing is for sure," Jin said. "The Mosuo women are not like the Kra-ell females. They seem so nice and gentle."

"Seem is the operative word," Kalugal murmured. "You need to ask their men how they are in bed."

Jin chuckled. "Are you curious?"

"Of course, I am."

Was Orion curious as well? He must have noticed the looks the girl had been sending his way.

"The Mosuo are human," Alena said. "We don't even know if their customs were influenced by the Kra-ell, but even if they were, the Kra-ell sexual practices just don't fit human nature and would have served no purpose. The Mosuo didn't suffer from a shortage of females that needed to be compensated for, and their survival didn't depend on producing the strongest, most aggressive offspring. Besides, if the men weren't happy, they would have rebelled. I think that they had a sweet deal in the Mosuo culture, and that's why it survived for so long. The women take care of pretty much everything."

Jacki snorted. "That's no different from most human cultures. Women work, take care of the children, pay the bills, clean the house, and the men think that they are saints for helping out when they feel like it."

"Excuse me?" Kalugal protested. "Is that your experience with this male?" He pointed at himself.

"I'm pampered silly. But I wonder what would have happened if we weren't rich and we didn't have Shamash and Atzil to take care of all the housework. Do you even know how to operate a washing machine?"

"I don't have to know. With my brains, there is no way we could have ever been poor enough not to afford domestic help."

Alena stifled a laugh. Kalugal was such a snob. She'd had a butler from the day she was born, and yet she knew how to cook and how to operate modern household appliances. The difference between them was that she didn't consider housework beneath her, while Kalugal obviously did.

38

ORION

*A*s their boats neared the second of the seven islands on their tour, an older guy wearing a Hawaiian shirt and a rumpled tweed jacket waved at them.

"I wonder what he's doing there all alone." Carol waved back. "There are no boats moored at the dock." She turned to Lokan. "Can you sense if there are any more people on the island?"

Lokan shook his head. "I only sense him. Besides, I wouldn't call this rock an island."

Orion didn't sense the presence of anyone else either. "Perhaps there is a dock on the other side as well."

"There isn't," their guide said.

As their boats docked, the guy grinned. "Hello, fellow travelers."

"Hello," Alena answered. "Are you stranded here? Where is the rest of your group?"

"Oh, I'm not stranded. I asked the young lady who brought me here this morning to leave me so I could explore at my leisure. She'll pick me up when she returns with another group of tourists. I thought that it was her, but your guide is a different young lady."

"We can offer you a ride back." Alena glanced at Phinas, who was shaking his head.

If the man wanted to hitch a ride with them, they would have to twist Phinas's arm to allow him on his boat.

"That's very kind of you." The guy smiled. "But I still have some exploring to do, and Milu will be worried if she comes back for me and I'm not here." He leaned closer to Alena. "I promised her a generous tip for picking me up. I don't want to disappoint her." He straightened and offered Alena his hand. "Doctor Herbert Neisman at your service." He smiled. "But call me Herb, and don't expect me to know anything about medicine. The only service I can offer is to put you to sleep with talk about ancient languages. I'm a doctor of philology, not a medical doctor."

"I happen to find old languages fascinating." Kalugal offered Herb his hand. "Which ones do you specialize in?"

"The Kra-Dai languages. The Kra family of languages in particular."

The small hairs on Orion's neck prickled. "Kra-Dai? What languages are those?"

"It's a family of tonal languages found in mainland South Asia, South China, and Northeast India. It's spoken by roughly ninety-three million people and includes ninety-five languages, the majority of which belong to the Tai branch. The modern Kra language family, however, is only spoken in southern China and northern Vietnam. There are about twelve Kra languages, with about eight thousand speakers, and they include at least four mutually unintelligible varieties."

That didn't sound like a lot of people and given how much they drifted apart as to be unintelligible, the original language was probably very old.

"Fascinating." Kalugal smoothed a hand over his goatee. "What does Kra mean? Is that a name of the people speaking it?"

"The word Kra in Porto-Austronesian means human, and as you know, Austronesian is one of the world's major language families."

Orion had never even heard the term, and he thought of himself as a well-informed man with well-rounded general knowledge.

Had Kalugal heard about it? As an amateur archeologist, he might have.

The guy was nodding sagely as if he knew precisely what Doctor Herbert Neisman was talking about, but that didn't mean much. Kalugal could be completely clueless and still pretend as if he was knowledgeable in the subject.

"What's particularly interesting about the Kra languages," Herb continued, "is that they contain words for metalworking, handicrafts, and agriculture that do not correspond to any of the other languages in the broader category of the Kra-Dai languages family. That suggests that the Kra people developed technological innovations independently from their contemporaries, or perhaps preceded them."

Orion hadn't been emotionally invested in the Kra-ell investigation, but as more pieces were added to the Kra-ell puzzle, he was starting to get excited.

"I have to admit that I've never heard of the Kra languages." Kalugal didn't show even the slightest reaction to the doctor's explanation. "I'm more familiar with other ancient languages—Sumerian, Hattie, Minoan."

When Herb's eyes widened with delight, Kalugal lifted his hand. "I'm just an amateur archeologist, and my knowledge of these languages is rudimentary."

"He's being modest." Jacki wrapped her arm around Kalugal's middle. "He can translate ancient texts written on crumbling tablets with half of the symbols missing. That requires much more than just a rudimentary familiarity with those languages."

"What tablets?" Herb asked.

"Fragments of tablets is more like it," Kalugal said dismissively.

Orion remembered Kian saying that the artifacts on display in the village's entry pavilion had been illegally smuggled out of the countries they'd been excavated in. No wonder Kalugal was being evasive.

"Which hotel are you staying in, Herb?" Carol asked, probably to change the subject for Kalugal's sake.

"The Lake Lodge."

"It's only a few minutes' walk from our hotel," Kalugal said. "You should join us for dinner tonight. I would love to hear more about the Kra people and their languages."

"I would be delighted. What time?"

"We are late diners," Jacki said. "Is seven too late for you?"

"No, it's perfect. I'm a night owl myself."

"Tell me, Herb." Kalugal started walking down the path toward the island's interior. "What are you researching on this little jewel?"

"The temple, of course. Unlike the others in the area that are Buddhist, this one is dedicated to the goddess, and it's much older." He smiled at Kalugal. "As an archeologist, I'm sure you will find it fascinating, and since I'm one of the few who can translate the inscriptions, you're very lucky to have bumped into me. I can translate them for you."

"Indeed. Are you up to showing my friends and me the temple today?"

Herb beamed. "It would be my pleasure. Follow me."

Orion leaned closer to Alena and whispered in her ear, "Can this be a coincidence? An ancient language named Kra?"

"I don't think so," she whispered back. "I got goosebumps when Herb said that Kra means human in that language. Ell means god in a lot of the languages spoken around the Mediterranean. Maybe Kra-ell means people who are half-human and half-gods."

"But that describes us better than the Kra-ell."

"I know. The pieces of the puzzle don't fit yet, but as we collect more of them, we might be able to discern a pattern."

39

ALENA

*A*s the philologist led them to the ruins of the goddess's temple, Alena held on tight to Orion's hand. Not all of the lake's islands and peninsulas were covered in such dense greenery, but this one was uninhabited and overgrown with bushes. Fates only knew what crawled under the thicket, and Alena wasn't fond of snakes and spiders and other creepy-crawlies.

The climb to the top of the hill took a good twenty minutes, not because it was so steep or the distance long but because there was no path.

"It seems that the goddess doesn't have many followers," Kalugal said. "Given how everything is overgrown, no one comes to see her temple, not even the tourists."

"It's not in any of the tour guides," Herb said. "The locals are all Buddhists with a twist. Some of their old traditions and legends are intertwined with their particular brand of Buddhism."

As they climbed the last several feet, the ruined remains of the temple looked more like a heap of rocks than a structure, but it was obvious that it had never been more than a small shrine.

"I know that it doesn't look like much," Herb said. "But I discovered something that you might find interesting." He pushed aside several branches to reveal an engraving in the stone. "If you look closely, you can see that it's a woman's face, and she looks fierce. The symbols are in better condition, and I wonder if they were added at a later time. 'Oh, Mother of Life, death and destruction, be pleased with me, oh dreaded one, be pleased with me, you who shapes the world, be pleased with me, you who are beyond comprehension and time.'"

Pulling out his phone, Kalugal snapped a picture of the engraved rock face and then moved aside to let the others get closer.

Not much of the original face engraving remained, but the mouth with a pair of fangs protruding over it was unmistakable.

As goosebumps rose over Alena's arms, Orion rubbed his hands over them. "Is it common for goddesses to be depicted with fangs?" he asked Herb.

"I'm a philologist, not a historian, but I'm a fan of mythology, so I know a thing or two about the various gods and goddesses. Several Indian goddesses are described as skinny, small-breasted, and bearing fangs and fierce expressions. Their depiction represents their ever-present primordial hunger and their power of destruction and death. There is also Wadjet, the fanged cobra goddess of ancient Egypt, or Nehkbet, the vulture-goddess of Upper Egypt. But unlike the Hindu goddesses, they were not bent on destruction and death. Wadjet and Nehkbet were the protective goddesses of the king, and Wadjet was nurse to the god Horus, helping his mother, the goddess Isis, to protect him from his uncle Seth."

Herb scratched his balding head. "I'm sure I'm forgetting someone. I think that some of the Native American goddesses had fangs as well."

"I wonder if I could get a permit for a dig here," Kalugal said.

Herb shook his head. "The locals don't even allow motorboats on the lake. They don't want to disturb its tranquility or pollute the water. The Chinese government pushed hard for it, and motorboats were delivered to the lake, but there was so much opposition that their use was quickly discontinued. The lake isn't big, and the canoe rides provide income for the Mosuo people who live around it. They can't live on fishing alone."

"My partner secured permits for a dig a little farther up the Lugu river," Kalugal said. "There used to be an ancient outpost built on a river island, but that one is much bigger than this one."

Herb looked impressed. "Your friend must be well connected. I wanted to visit the site but was refused entry. Is there a way you could arrange for me to see the excavation?"

"I haven't been there yet." Kalugal wrapped his arm around Jacki's shoulders. "My wife wanted to explore the lake first. I'm probably going to head out there tomorrow, but I need to check with my partner whether it is safe before I allow visitors on site." He smiled. "I don't know how litigation works in China, but even if that's not an issue, I don't want any accidents on my conscience."

"I understand." Herb nodded. "Will you let me know?"

"Of course."

"We should head back," Jacki said. "Our guide is probably getting impatient."

The girl hadn't accompanied them to the top of the hill, preferring to remain with her boat.

"I'll stay here for a little longer." Herb pulled out a handkerchief from his back pocket and wiped his forehead. "Does the invitation to join you for dinner still stand?"

"Of course." Kalugal gave him one of his charming smiles. "It was a pleasure to make your acquaintance, Doctor Herbert Neisman, and I'm looking forward to continuing our conversation over dinner."

After everyone had said their goodbyes, and their group started their descent down the hill, Alena asked, "Is it just me, or did that engraving look a lot like what I imagine a Kra-ell female would?"

"I had the same thought," Kalugal said. "That's why I took the picture. I want to send it to Vrog and to Emmett and ask them if she looks anything like the Mother of All Life that the Kra-ell worship. I'm also curious whether the symbols resemble the Kra-ell language."

"Are we coming back here tonight?" Arwel asked. "We can bring some tools and dig around for clues. If the Kra-ell worshiped their goddess on this hill, they might have left some tributes that we can date. It will give us an idea when they'd arrived here."

"If they ever did," Kalugal said. "As Herb said, a depiction of a fanged goddess is not such a rare occurrence. Kali, one of the Hindu main deities, is always drawn with fangs and with a long, protruding tongue."

"Why the tongue?" Carol asked. "What does it symbolize?"

"Hunger, most likely," Jacki said. "The warrior goddess who devours her enemies and licks their blood."

Carol shivered. "All this talk about blood freaks me out." She leaned closer to Jacki. "That's why I'm not fond of the newest additions to our clan. Did you meet Vlad's father?"

Jacki shook her head. "I didn't."

"I did," Arwel said. "He's a decent fellow. Don't hold his heritage against him. After all, he contributed half of Vlad's genes, and Vlad is one of the best people I know."

"True." Carol nodded. "Will I get to meet him during this trip?"

"It remains to be seen," Arwel said. "If we find something that we think he should take a look at or vice versa, and pictures are not enough, then I might suggest that he and the team investigating the school join us."

When they were back on the boat, Kalugal pulled out his clan phone again. "Let's see what we can find about the goddess Kali."

Jacki leaned closer to him to look at the screen. "Aren't you going to send the photo from the shrine to Vrog first?"

"It can wait." Kalugal peered over his phone for a long while, uttering all kinds of surprised sounds and nodding as if what he was reading confirmed his suspicions. "The goddess Kali is considered to be the master of death, time, and change. She is said to be the supreme of all powers, and the ultimate reality. She is also the mother of all living beings." Kalugal lifted his head and looked behind him. "Sounds familiar?"

Arwel shook his head. "You are all getting carried away. I can accept that the Kra-ell influenced the lifestyle choices of the Mosuo, but I'm not buying that they also influenced the entire Indian culture. That's taking it too far."

"Why?" Alena said. "A small group of gods influenced the entire Western civilization from a small settlement in Sumer. A small group of Kra-ell who settled in a different corner of the globe might have influenced the cultures of the people of that part of the world."

They no longer bothered to speak quietly, and their guide was following the conversation with curious eyes. "Who are these gods you talk about?" the girl asked.

Kalugal cast her an indulgent smile. "We are talking about legends and mythology. Those are all just fantasies that people came up with to explain the world to themselves. It's like your legend of how the lake was formed. No one truly believes that it's made from a goddess's tears, right?"

The girl smiled. "It's a nice story."

"Indeed." Kalugal went back to reading on his phone. "There are even more similarities between Kali and Jade. Kali is often depicted as standing on top of her husband, Shiva, who lies prone on the ground. It says here that it's never Kali who calms Shiva when he's misbehaving, but Shiva who must calm Kali. Her eyes are often described as deep red with rage and maybe intoxication, her small fangs some-times protrude out of her mouth, and that lolling tongue." He chuckled. "The Indian patriarchal society had trouble reconciling Kali's dominant pose with her husband lying literally under her foot, so they came up with an explanation. Kali was called to destroy a demon army, which she did, but with her blood lust out of control, she couldn't stop rampaging. Shiva was called to stop her, and as he lay under her feet, Kali realized that she had stepped over her husband's chest and was so embarrassed that she extended her tongue in modesty and shame."

Jin snorted. "Right. To me, the foot over Shiva's chest and the lolling tongue look like signs of triumph and dominance."

"I think so too." Kalugal returned the phone to his pocket. "It would be fascinating to discover the origins of that story—the Sumer of the East."

4 0

VROG

*T*he files Vrog had recovered from the safes were locked in a fire-proof cabinet in his office. If he'd learned anything from the fire that had destroyed the compound, it was that Jade had been smart to lock all important possessions and documents in the two safes. She probably hadn't expected fire or flood, only theft, but Vrog had taken the lesson to heart.

Anticipating the worst and preparing for it was smart. Hoping for the best was not.

Vrog's hand trembled as he opened the cabinet and pulled out one of the ledgers. Taking it with him to the desk, he sat down and opened it at the first page. It was handwritten in the Kra-ell language, and he wondered whether Jade had preferred to record their tribe's accounting the old-fashioned way, handwritten with pen on paper, as a security measure or because there was no way to program the Kra-ell language into accounting software.

The fact that she'd kept the ledgers locked in a safe suggested that she'd been worried about privacy, and no one could hack into handwritten books. The question was who she'd been protecting the information from, humans or another Kra-ell.

As he flipped through page upon page of neatly written columns, he also wondered whether it was Jade's handwriting or did it belong to one of the other females. He doubted she would have entrusted any of the males with so much information. The Jade he remembered kept things close to the chest, so to speak.

It felt strange to allow Kian to have a look at the ledgers, and probably Shai and the clan's hacker as well. Kian wouldn't do the investigative work himself. He would assign it to his assistant and others who knew how to follow a money trail.

Vrog should have done it himself a long time ago.

He'd excused his reticence as lack of resources, but the truth was that he'd been afraid to attract attention to himself by following the money and looking into the tribe's various holdings.

As long as no one tried to recover the tribe's riches, whoever had sacked the compound wouldn't suspect that anyone had survived the attack and wouldn't come back to finish the job. But twenty years was a long time, and perhaps it was safe to do so now.

Or not.

Was he signing his own death sentence by giving the journals to Kian?

As soon as the clan started investigating what happened to all that money, the killers might come back. Vrog could potentially hide in the clan's village, but what if they harmed the students or the staff?

Could he risk that?

It was too late to change his mind. He'd promised Kian to deliver the files, and Vrog wasn't the kind of male who went back on his word. Not intentionally anyway.

When his clan phone buzzed with an incoming message, he picked it up expecting it to be Mey. Earlier, he'd left her in one of the storage buildings, with Yamanu and the two Guardians watching over her as she listened to the echoes. Perhaps she'd found out something new.

But the message wasn't from Mey. It was from Kalugal.

At first, all he saw in the picture the guy had sent him was a brown-grey rock covered in moss, but when he read Kalugal's explanation, he enlarged the picture with his fingers and took a closer look.

Kalugal asked whether the carving looked anything like the Mother of All Life that the Kra-ell worshiped, but it was hard to tell. The full lips and the small protruding fangs could have belonged to a Kra-ell female, and they could have been a rudimentary drawing of the Indian goddess of time, doomsday, and death. Since there was no body, and just a few lines of the face had survived the elements, it was impossible to tell. If it was the goddess Kali, she would have four or ten arms and some sort of a headdress.

Lugu Lake, where Kalugal and his team were visiting, was close to Tibet, so discovering a shrine dedicated to Kali wouldn't be overly surprising.

He texted back, explaining why he couldn't say for sure that it was or wasn't the Kra-ell deity, and that it was most likely the Hindu goddess Kali.

His phone rang a moment later.

"Can you talk?" Kalugal asked.

"I'm alone if that's your concern."

"Could Kali be based on a Kra-ell female or on legends of the Mother of All Life?"

"I will have to look into the stories about Kali, but what I can tell you for sure is that the Mother of All Life had only two arms. She had fangs, she was thin and tall, and she was dark-haired, but that's where the similarities end."

"What about her dominant pose with her foot over the prone body of her husband Shiva?"

Vrog chuckled. "Unlike the Mother of All Life, Kali didn't have a harem of husbands to serve her needs."

"Those variations are to be expected," Kalugal said. "Just as Western cultures adapted the stories about the gods to fit their religion and their world view, Eastern cultures might have done the same to a Kra-ell influence. The Indian culture was and still is patriarchal. They made Kali as fearsome and as dominant as their world view allowed. I'm not saying that Kali is for sure based on a Kra-ell deity or living female, but it's worth pondering."

41

RONJA

*R*onja had spent the afternoon planning, or rather attempting to plan, how she was going to seduce Merlin. Not that she would have to work hard for it, but she wanted to make it special, elegant, refined—a night to remember for eternity, and not because she was embarrassed by it.

Without a plan, she was bound to attack him.

Not that Merlin would mind.

He wanted her, he'd made it quite obvious, and since he hadn't left the village without her, she also knew that he hadn't been with anyone else. For an immortal male that showed extraordinary restraint, and she loved him all the more for it.

Except, she hadn't told him that she loved him yet, not in so many words, but he shouldn't have trouble guessing her feelings. Over the past two months they'd spent many hours together, and they had all been enjoyable despite the undercurrent of sexual tension, or perhaps because of it.

It might have not been love at first sight, but then that was reserved for the young and naive, not a middle-aged woman who'd been married twice, cheated on by her first husband, and widowed by her second.

Merlin had grown on her gradually, but Ronja had known she was in love with him for weeks.

What was there not to love?

He was brilliant, handsome, funny, and he needed her, not just as a friend and a sex partner, but for organizing his messy life. She wasn't nearly as smart as he was, but she had a methodical mind while Merlin's was all over the place, which made them perfect for each other. With her monitoring everything he worked on and keeping his house from falling into disarray again, she freed him up to think. His mind could wander in whichever direction he pleased without worrying about all the things he might have forgotten.

Merlin had told her many times about how invaluable she'd become to him, and that since she'd taken over organizing his work and everything else in his life he'd become so much more productive.

It was a good feeling to know that, in her own way, she was contributing to the creation of great things. With her, Merlin might come up with new cures that would help countless people. After all, most of his research wasn't on how to heal immortals but on how to cure humans.

Fates, she felt so absurdly happy and fulfilled that she was afraid to rock the boat and introduce a new variable that might ruin the good thing they had going. Then again, the clock was ticking both on her window of opportunity to transition and on Merlin's patience, and frankly, hers as well.

Ronja had always been a passionate woman who'd enjoyed sex, and going without for so long was frustrating, especially when it was offered to her on a silver platter with a cherry on top.

As much as she wanted to honor Frank's memory and mourn his death for a full year, she was reaching a breaking point and could no longer wait.

"Bye, Mom." Lisa kissed her cheek and then pranced toward the door.

"Where are you going?"

"To Parker's house." Lisa paused with her hand on the door handle. "Magnus bought a movie projector, and we are going to watch all the Harry Potter movies."

"That will take all night."

"I know." Lisa smiled. "Don't wait up for me. I'm going to try to stay awake for as long as I can, but as the only human among five immortals, I stand no chance. I'll probably fall asleep on their couch."

"Five? Who else is joining the Harry Potter marathon?"

"Ella and Julian."

"That sounds like fun. Say hello to Parker's family for me."

"I will." Lisa opened the door. "Hey, why don't you call Merlin and invite him over? That way, I won't feel too guilty about leaving you alone on a Friday night."

Ronja felt her cheeks heating up. "That's a good idea. Perhaps we can watch something as well."

As the door closed behind Lisa, Ronja released a breath.

The stars seemed to be aligning in formation tonight, all pointing in one direction—her bedroom.

As Merlin had said, sex didn't have to mean induction. They could use protection. Perhaps they should start with that. It definitely made the decision to go for it much easier.

Well, easier did not mean easy.

Ronja had only been with two men in her life, and she'd been married to both for a very long time. She'd been just a young girl when Michael had seduced her, beautiful, desirable, and as perfect as a human girl got to be. She'd still been beautiful and desirable when she divorced Michael and started dating Frank, so getting naked with him had not been a problem.

But she was much older now, and despite all the progress she made over the past several weeks, all the excess weight she'd lost and the muscle she'd gained, she was still a middle-aged woman who'd had three kids, and her body was far from perfect.

Heck, she didn't remove her bra until it was time for bed, even if she was alone in the house, and not just because her large drooping breasts didn't look good. They were uncomfortable.

How was she going to bare herself to Merlin, who looked like a male model in his mid-twenties or early thirties?

He'd only ever seen her dressed in flattering outfits, push-up bras, and tummy control panties that streamlined her silhouette and concealed the flabbiness. Without those props, she wasn't as good-looking as he thought she was.

What if he got turned off when he saw her naked?

Closing her eyes, Ronja sighed. One way or another, it was going to happen, and since Annani was in the village, the sooner the better.

Hopefully, Merlin was starved for sex enough to overlook all of her imperfections.

42

MEY

*M*ey walked out of the storage building and shook her head. "There was nothing of interest in there."

That wasn't entirely true, but what she'd heard in the echoes had nothing to do with the Kra-ell, and a lot to do with the current inhabitants of the school. As it turned out, the storage building had been frequently used for amorous encounters between teachers, administrators, groundskeepers, delivery people, and Fates knew who else.

Mey was still trying to shake off what she'd heard, and the sounds of passion hadn't even been the worst. There had been screaming arguments about broken promises, crying fits about real and perceived betrayals, mean-spirited gossip, and evil plotting against this one or that.

It was good that the faculty had no idea what she could do, or some members would have been very worried.

Yamanu pushed away from the wall he'd been leaning against and put his arm around her shoulders. "If you didn't find anything, why are you shaking your head?"

"People are nasty when they think no one can see or hear them, and I was never into pornography. This storage building was used more as a shag-pad than to store stuff."

Both his brows shot up. "Is that so? Who shagged whom?"

"It wasn't the Kra-ell, and thankfully, not the students. I only saw and heard adults, and given their clothing and vernacular, they were all contemporary. I wonder if Vrog knows what's going on under his nose. It seems that everyone is shagging everyone else, people are plotting and scheming to get promoted and to get others demoted, and don't even start me on the drama."

Yamanu sighed. "It's a shame that you can't share what you see and hear with me. I could have used the entertainment. I'm so bored that I'm reduced to watching reruns of old episodes of *South Park*."

"My poor baby." She leaned closer and kissed his strong jaw. "You don't need to trail after me. I'm perfectly safe on my own here."

She felt awkward with Yamanu and the two Guardians following her around. It was a school, not an enemy camp.

"Stella and Richard thought that they were perfectly safe in that sleepy little town, and they got a nasty surprise. I'm not gambling with your safety. Especially not here."

"Why? Do you sense anything?"

Yamanu wasn't empathic, but he was very intuitive, and it would be a mistake to ignore his intuition's warnings.

He shook his head. "It's a general feeling of things not being right about this place, but it might be because of what happened here two decades ago. I think the impact it left on the compound is overshadowing any current or impending threats." He rubbed a hand over his jaw. "I wonder if that's why my intuition didn't warn me when Vrog planned his attack on Stella."

"Maybe you didn't feel anything because he wasn't going to harm her. The Fates had no reason to sound the alarm."

"I didn't consider it from that angle, but you might be right."

Smiling, she looped her arm around his waist. "Of course, I'm right. I always am."

"Naturally." He grinned. "You're as wise as you are beautiful, my mate, and I'm always awed by you."

He stopped next to the second storage building. "Do you want me to come in with you?"

"What for? All you'll see is me sitting on the floor with my eyes closed. I look like I'm meditating."

"Can't you narrate what you're seeing and hearing? That would be very entertaining."

"I wish I could, but I can't. It would break my concentration." Looking over her shoulder at Alfie and Jay, she had an idea. "Why don't the three of you play cards or something while I'm inside. You could entertain each other."

"As I said, my mate is brilliant. We don't have cards, but we could play the stone game, provided that we can find a fourth player." Yamanu turned his head to look over his shoulder. "And here he comes." He smiled at Vrog, who was heading their way. "What's up, buddy?"

"I came to ask the same of you. Did you hear any interesting echoes?"

Mey grimaced. "Yes, but not the ones I was hoping for. Do you know what the faculty has been using that storage building for?"

Vrog frowned. "Other than storing classroom or janitorial supplies?"

Mey had a feeling that the guy had no clue. Dalliances between the staff members were prohibited, and given how straitlaced Vrog himself was, he probably expected everyone to uphold the same standards.

"Let me put it this way. You should really relax the rules and allow the faculty and other staff to have intimate relationships. That way, they wouldn't have to sneak into the storage building to have fun."

His eyes widened. "Are you sure it was the current staff?"

"Positive. And the drama, oh, my. You have no idea."

"No, I don't, and I prefer it that way."

"Why don't you allow it?" Yamanu asked. "These people live and work here, and they didn't sign up for a monastery."

I. T. LUCAS

"I can't allow it." Vrog sighed. "It would be like opening Pandora's box. My major concern is sexual coercion, with senior faculty members taking advantage of junior members. Then there are the squabbles, the lovers' spats, the jealousies, you name it. If they are not supposed to be doing any of it, they can't complain to me about it."

"Forcing them to live like monks is not the solution, though." Mey pointed to the door of the other building. "I hope this one will have less of what I saw in the other storage building, and at least a scrap of what I'm looking for."

"Perhaps the Kra-ell didn't leave echoes because nothing emotionally charged happened in there." Vrog started toward the other building. "Which makes sense. I don't think the purebloods bothered with fetching supplies. That's what the human servants were for."

"You mean slaves," Yamanu said. "If they weren't allowed to leave and weren't paid for their labor and for their blood donations, then the right term is slaves."

"True." Vrog sighed. "But things are not much better for many people in this part of the world. I'm not saying that to excuse what the Kra-ell did, and they would have probably done the same if they settled in the West, it's just that most of the humans living on the compound didn't think that their lot in life was so unfair or terrible. Some even appreciated the health benefits of occasionally donating their blood to the Kra-ell."

Mey didn't know much about the local population's attitudes, but people were the same everywhere, and no one enjoyed having their freedom taken away from them or serving as breeders for aliens.

"What kind of things were stored in there back then?" Mey asked. "I assume that there was no need for school supplies, not in these quantities." She waved at the building they'd come from.

"Dry goods, extra clothing for the humans, bedding, bathroom supplies, etc. When I got here, there was almost nothing in these buildings, and whatever was left was saturated with smoke. I disposed of it."

"That's odd. If the compound was taken in a surprise attack, then the storage building should have been full. Your leader sounds like the type who would not allow supplies to dwindle. She would have been on top of that."

Vrog nodded. "Jade was like a general, and she ran the place efficiently. She probably put one of the purebmooded males in charge of inventory to make sure that no one was taking more than they were supposed to. But don't forget that the compound stood in ruins for months before I got back here. The locals probably took everything that was salvageable."

"Makes sense," Mey agreed. It wouldn't even have counted as looting because there had been no one left to claim the goods.

"Why would Jade be concerned with people taking more than they were supposed to?" Yamanu asked. "What would the humans have done with extra supplies? It's not like they could have smuggled stuff out of the compound."

Vrog smiled. "Never underestimate the ingenuity of people."

Yamanu looked doubtful. "If they couldn't smuggle themselves out, how could they smuggle supplies and what for?"

"They were thralled to fear leaving. The fear instilled in them was so powerful that their hearts would give out if they tried."

"A simple solution to prevent theft would have been to thrall them not to steal."

328

Mey sniffed the air as they got closer to the other building. "It smells nice. Was it converted to serve as the school's laundry?"

Vrog nodded. "I turned the back part of this building into a laundry and kept the front for storage of maintenance supplies."

"Can I go in there?" Mey asked. "Or are people working there?"

"For now, you can listen to echoes in the storage part. You can check out the laundry during the weekend." He typed in the code and opened the door.

Mey stepped over the threshold. "Wish me luck."

Vrog didn't let go of the door. "Before you go, I wanted to give you a quick update about the other group's progress at Lugu Lake."

"Did they find anything?" Yamanu asked.

After giving them a summary of his conversation with Kalugal, Vrog pulled out his phone to show them the photo Kalugal had taken. "What do you think?"

Mey lifted her eyes to him. "You're asking me? I've never seen a picture of the Kra-ell goddess."

"Have you seen pictures of Kali?" Vrog asked. "She's the Hindu goddess of time, doomsday, and death."

"Of course," Mey said. "Who hasn't? She is the blue goddess with a long red tongue and four arms."

"She also has fangs." Vrog took his phone from her and typed Kali in the search field. "Like in this picture."

Mey took the device. "I've never noticed the fangs before. The necklace of severed heads must have distracted me."

"What I don't understand," Yamanu said, "is why would anyone worship such a terrible goddess."

"Kali is both terrible and wonderful," Vrog said. "According to legend, she became terrible only when she was called to defend her people. She used her power to defeat demons and assist the gods, and she's revered for it. She's also the goddess of life, and some refer to her as the Mother and the essence of all existence."

43

MERLIN

A bouquet of flowers in one hand, a bottle of wine in the other, and six packets of condoms in his pockets, Merlin left his house and headed to Ronja's.

After she'd called him, he'd made a mad rush to the city to purchase the necessary items for a night of seduction.

Hopefully, he hadn't forgotten anything—

Damn, he should have gotten her chocolates. He had a stash of Godiva boxes at home, which he kept on hand for his fertility patients. Should he turn back and get them?

Nah, it was bad luck to re-enter the house, and even though Merlin wasn't superstitious, tonight he wasn't taking any chances.

Because tonight was *the* night.

Annani had confirmed that what she did for the transitioning Dormants wasn't a morale boost that had a placebo effect but was a real exchange of energy. She had refused to give him specifics, but what she'd told him was enough to reassure him that she could save Ronja if her transition became life-threatening.

Then Ronja called to invite him for dinner at her house, emphasizing that Lisa would be gone all night and that they would have the house to themselves. He couldn't have hoped for a clearer message than that.

Well, if she told him to bring condoms that would have been clearer, but Ronja was old-fashioned, and unlike the young women of today, she still believed that subtlety was classier.

He wondered whether Lisa's absence was what had prompted Ronja to take the plunge tonight. Privacy hadn't been the reason behind her reluctance to take their relationship to its natural next step because his house was always available to them. Since Ronja had taken command of it, his bedsheets were clean, smelled fresh, and his bed was always made, so that shouldn't have been an obstacle. But perhaps Ronja felt more comfortable seducing him in her own place?

Damn, if his erection became any harder, he would require hospitalization.

He needed to deflate that bad boy, or it would ruin the evening.

Perhaps going over the list of symptoms and various forms of nephrotic syndrome would do the trick, and if that didn't work, he had plenty of other lists he could go through, and the more troubling the disease, the better.

High blood pressure, swelling in the feet, hands, and around the eyes, weight gain with fluid retention and swelling— Merlin went through the list of symptoms twice, and by the time he reached Ronja's house, he had everything under control.

Ringing her doorbell, he was sure that he wasn't going to embarrass himself, but as soon as Ronja opened the door, that conviction evaporated into thin air.

"You look stunning." He gaped at her lush body that was encased in a sexy, form-fitting black dress, and those black stiletto shoes—damn—they made her legs look so good—

All he could think about was Ronja with nothing on except for those shoes, her legs wrapped around his waist, and him buried deep inside of her.

Forcing his eyes to shift to her face, he focused on her pale blond hair, which was gathered in an elaborate updo, with soft curling strands left loose to frame the long diamond earrings that shimmered with every move of her head.

With the outfit and the hair and the makeup, she looked like a pinup, and she had done it all for him.

Ronja definitely had seduction on her mind.

Should he go over the list of epidermal parasitic skin diseases? That was a sure erection deflator. *Scabies, pediculosis, tungiasis...*

"Thank you." She took the flowers and the bottle of wine from him. "You look very handsome yourself." She walked over to the kitchen and pulled a vase out of the cabinet. "When did you have time to get these? I called you less than two hours ago."

"I made a quick run to the city."

She smiled. "Just to get me flowers?"

"And wine. Don't forget the wine." He'd spent a small fortune on that bottle. "I hope it goes with whatever you made that smells so good."

Ronja smiled. "Today's meal is not perfectly aligned with your health guidelines, but it's not terrible either. I made almond-crusted trout with mashed potatoes and grilled vegetables."

"That sounds healthy and delicious."

She chuckled. "Not really. There is a whole stick of butter in the dish, but that's what makes it so tasty."

"Butter is the secret of life," he quoted. "What movie?"

"*Last Holiday.*"

"That's my girl." He leaned and kissed her cheek.

44

RONJA

"This is delicious." Merlin cut another piece of the fish and arranged the almond slices, so they covered the morsel evenly. "I love everything you cook, but this is your best one yet."

"I'm glad you like it."

Ronja pressed her fork into the mashed potatoes, making a lattice design. She was too nervous to eat, or maybe she just wasn't hungry because she'd been snacking while she cooked, or maybe her control-top panties were too tight.

It had been a mistake to put them on. They made the dress look ten times better on her, smoothing out her muffin top and creating the hourglass figure she'd once taken for granted. But she should have considered her plans for later tonight and worn something looser that didn't leave red compression marks on her skin.

Perhaps she should excuse herself and go change into a robe? It would take at least an hour for the marks to fade.

"Ronja," Merlin said quietly. "Why aren't you eating?"

She forced a smile. "I'm not hungry. I snacked while I cooked."

"You haven't touched your fish." He pulled her plate toward him and cut a nice little piece. "Just one bite. Once you taste it, your appetite will awaken."

Reluctantly, she opened her mouth and let him feed her the small piece of fish. It was good, even better than she'd imagined, but her stomach was still tight like a drum, and not just because of the damn compression panties.

"Good, right?"

She nodded.

"Have another one." He quickly cut another piece and put it in front of her mouth. "Open wide." When she took it, he nodded his approval and cut another piece for her.

Ronja shook her head. "Stop feeding me. I cooked for you, and you're not eating."

"I like feeding you." He made small circles with the fork in front of her face.

"Please, for me." His eyes were bright like twin flashlights as they focused on her lips. "I love seeing you eat."

Was he imagining her lips closing around his erection? Was that why his eyes were glowing?

Was this a kind of foreplay?

Neither of her husbands had ever fed her, and she had to admit that she liked Merlin being so focused on her, watching her so intently, taking care of her.

As something loosened deep within Ronja, she smiled and opened her mouth. Merlin growled his approval and kept feeding her until there was nothing left on her plate, and she felt like her belly was going to win the war with her panties and burst them at the seams.

"No more." She lifted her hands. "Now, you finish yours."

His eyes still trained on her lips, he put the fork down and leaned closer. "You are mine." He put his lips on hers, his tongue penetrating her mouth and stroking leisurely.

She was breathless when he leaned back and looked at her. His glowing eyes were full of sexual promise, and then he was kissing her again, his tongue invading, probing, caressing, elaborating on that carnal promise.

Ronja was on fire, her breasts and her core tingling, aching with need. It had been so long, and she was so damn hungry. She gasped when his fangs scraped her lower lip, not expecting them to elongate that quickly. It was a little scary, but the small fear only added fuel to the inferno raging inside of her. He was careful though, and as his lips left hers to trail down her neck, he somehow managed to keep his fangs away from her skin.

Was she crazy for wanting him to scrape her again? To bite her?

Leaning away, he looked at her with hooded eyes. "Can I take you to bed now? Please say yes."

She wanted to, boy, how she wanted him to do precisely that, but her damn inhibitions were raising their head again. There was no way in hell she was letting him undress her and see those granny compression panties. "Can I ask you for a favor?"

"Anything."

"Can you give me fifteen minutes to slip into something more comfortable?"

He seemed understandably confused by her request, but then he nodded and smiled. "Take all the time you need and call me when you're ready."

"Thank you."

When she rose to her feet, he caught her hand and pulled her down onto his lap. "I need one more kiss to tide me over."

As his hand started a slow track from her hip and up her side, she jumped off his lap before he could feel what was under her dress, leaned down, and pecked him on the lips. "This will have to do for now."

45

MEY

*T*he remaining storage area of the second building was indeed much smaller than the first, no bigger than a four-car garage, maybe even smaller than that. The windows were closed and barred, but because of the laundry on its other side, it lacked the slightly musty smell she'd suffered through in the other building.

The organization style was the same, though. Neat rows of fully stocked industrial metal shelving took up most of the space, holding big boxes of toilet paper, cleaning supplies, bedding, towels, and other bathroom necessities.

The only open area was in the front of the room right by the door, and that was where Mey chose to sit down. Crossing her legs in the lotus position, she closed her eyes and started the meditative process.

She still felt overstimulated from the echoes she'd heard and seen in the other building, as well as from the conversation with Vrog and all the new bits and pieces of information she'd just learned. It took her a long time to quiet her mind enough to reach the state necessary to open herself to the echoes.

When the scenes started playing, she braced for a long and protracted drama-fest similar to what she'd been subjected to in the other building. If she were lucky, the old echoes would have been more emotionally charged than those that had been created after the compound had been turned into a school.

At first, the two ghostly spindly forms that appeared in her mind's eye were not substantial enough to make sense of other than their humanoid form, and unlike most of the echoes that started with a built-in soundtrack playing the moment they popped into her mind, the two forms were utterly silent as they entered the storage building and locked the door behind them.

When the forms became more substantial, Mey realized that they were females, and they weren't human. The two were very clearly Kra-ell and not hybrids but purebloods. Even in their semi-ghostly echo form, they looked so alien that Mey wondered how they'd ever managed to pass for humans.

It was difficult to assess their height, but if the entry door was the same size as the

334

current one, the taller female was at least six foot four inches tall, and the other maybe an inch or an inch and a half shorter. They were so slim that they looked almost skeletal, but not gaunt like some of the runway models, just narrowly built. They were both nearly flat-chested, had no hips to speak of, and their waists were so tiny that she could probably close her hands around them and her fingers would touch. Nevertheless, there was power in those seemingly insubstantial bodies, and they moved with the sinuous fluidity and gracefulness of immortals.

Even if Mey hadn't known anything about them, she would have recognized them as predators—dangerous, lethal, even cruel.

Still, despite the lack of feminine curves and the twin hard expressions they wore, they were both beautiful. Long black hair cascaded like a gleaming curtain down their backs, their dark eyes large in their thin faces, too large, and the corners were slightly elongated but not in the same way Asians' eyes were. In fact, the eyes were the females' most alien feature. Well, that was true until they started talking, or rather arguing, and Mey saw their fangs and their tongues, which were definitely more alien than their eyes.

Except for a word here and there, she was unable to follow the rapid exchange in Kra-ell. Giving up, she paid closer attention to those fangs which, unlike hers and Jin's or even those of the male immortals, were quite long in their retracted state. Then again, given the explosive animosity between the two Kra-ell females, their fangs might have been in their elongated state in response to aggression.

Even more interesting than the fangs were their tongues, which had a pattern of dark coloring down the middle that made them look as if they were forked.

Was that a natural feature or were the patterns tattooed?

Mey had seen humans with tongue tattoos, so alien ink wasn't such a far-fetched idea, and since the Kra-ell didn't heal as fast as immortals, perhaps they'd found a way to mark their bodies permanently, which the immortals couldn't do.

None of the hybrid Kra-ell she knew had a pattern of different coloring on their tongues, but maybe because they were mixed the different coloring was less evident. She and Jin had none, but then they were only one-quarter Kra-ell.

In either case, if the tongue marking was natural, it was a recessive trait that didn't get transferred to hybrid offspring.

As the arguing became more heated, the taller female backhanded the other one, the force of the blow sending the shorter female flying across the room and crashing into a shelving unit.

The shelving and everything on it went down, but not the female. It was as if she was made of rubber, bouncing up, and with a roar, launching herself up at the aggressor, flying at her with fully extended fangs and toppling her to the ground.

As the females clawed and bit each other, the savagery was too much for Mey, and she averted her eyes.

At least her suspicion about their fangs being elongated in aggression had gotten confirmed.

Mey managed to keep her concentration and stay in place as long as the ghostly figures kept wrestling and crushing into shelving that wasn't near her, but as the brawling got closer and closer to where she was seated, Mey fought the urge to get out of their way, even though she knew they weren't real and couldn't hurt her.

When they crashed right through her, she lost the battle with her concentration and was thrown out of the echo.

No, no, no. She closed her eyes and tried to calm herself down enough to regain access to the echo, but it was no use.

Mey knew that she had to rest and give it a try another time.

After all, the echoes weren't going anywhere, and they would still be there tomorrow and the day after that, years and decades from now. Even if she hadn't lost her concentration, she would have to watch the replay of the scene many more times before she could decipher the rapid Kra-ell exchange.

She was curious about the impetus for the fight, but even if she never found out what the females had been fighting about, it was a rare glimpse into an alien society of which she was a distant member.

With a sigh, Mey pushed up to her feet and walked to the door.

Outside, Yamanu, Vrog, Alfie, and Jay were seated on the ground, a pile of small rocks between them, looking like a bunch of boys on a school playground.

What would Vrog's students think if they saw him like that?

He would have to thrall their memories away.

Yamanu took one look at her and knew that something had gone wrong. "No luck, eh?"

She crouched next to him. "I wouldn't say that. I struck gold in there. I saw two pureblooded females go at each other's throats, but then they started brawling, their ghostly forms crashed into me, and I lost concentration. I will have to come back another time and watch that echo again."

"What did they look like?" Vrog asked.

"Very tall, very skinny, with long black hair, long white fangs, and black tattoos on their tongues. One was a little taller than the other."

"Those were not tattoos," Vrog said. "The purebloods are born with them. None of the hybrids had the markings, so I assumed it was a trait that manifested only when both parents were pure Kra-ell. Did you notice any other distinguishing features?"

Mey shrugged. "They were both very beautiful but had no feminine curves whatsoever. They both had the same dark hair and the same alien-looking eyes." She chuckled. "Like those little gray aliens with enormous black eyes, except the eyes of the Kra-ell females weren't all black, just too big for their faces and oddly shaped. Other than that, they looked like human eyes, with a pupil and an iris, just very dark." She looked at Vrog. "Was that common for the females to go at each other so viciously? I thought that only the males fought each other for the females, not the other way around."

"I've never seen them fight," Vrog said. "They presented a unified front, but maybe they fought for dominance in private, or maybe they just needed to release some steam. Did you catch any of what they said to each other?"

Mey shook her head. "Is there a chance you could coach me on some more Kra-ell? They were talking so fast, screaming and hissing at each other that I couldn't understand what they were saying."

"It would be my pleasure," Vrog said. "We can work on your Kra-ell through the weekend, and then you can try the echoes again on Monday. I'm very curious about that fight and what it was about."

46

RONJA

*I*n her bathroom, behind a locked door, Ronja peeled off her dress, unhooked her bra, and then hesitated before shrugging it off.

Should she leave it on?

It was a sexy bra, a black lace and satin pushup balconette that kept her breasts where she wanted them. She had the matching panties somewhere in her lingerie drawer, still with the price tag attached. She could swap them for the control top and that would solve her biggest problem. Merlin would assume that she'd had them on all along.

She hadn't laundered them, though, and she didn't like putting on anything that hadn't gone through the wash yet, but she would make an exception this time. After all, it wasn't as if anyone tried on panties in a lingerie store. They were clean.

With the bra back in place, she peeled off the tight panties and put on a robe before ducking into the bedroom. She found the sexy panties that matched the bra, ducked back into the bathroom, tore the tag off, and put them on. Red marks marred her skin where the other pair had dug into her flesh, but other than that, she looked okay. Not great, but pretty good for a middle-aged mother of three. She'd lost weight, and at her age that meant loose skin, and that wasn't attractive at all, but there wasn't much she could do about it.

Ronja didn't know what was worse, the loose skin muffin top or the padded one she'd had before.

Whatever. Merlin knew that she wasn't a spring chicken, and he wanted her anyway.

After rubbing some lotion over the marks, she spritzed a little perfume on her hair and the panties that still smelled like the store she'd gotten them from and took off the robe.

Ronja planned on waiting for Merlin in bed, so the robe wasn't needed.

Turning the lights off, she quietly opened the door, leaving it slightly ajar before dashing to the bed and slipping under the cover.

"I'm ready," she said barely louder than a whisper, not sure at all that the words were true, but it was time, and she wasn't a coward, so ready or not, she was having sex with Merlin tonight.

Naturally, Merlin heard her. As he pushed the door open, light spilled in from the hallway, and as he sauntered into the bedroom, she saw that he was holding a glass of wine in each hand.

"Are you comfortable, my beautiful Ronja?" He prowled over to the bed, sat next to her on top of the covers, and offered her a glass of wine. "You seem tense and unsure of yourself, and it's not like you. Did I do anything to make you nervous? Do you want to wait a little longer?" He smiled. "It will kill me, but if you are not ready, tell me, and I will go home, or we can go back to the living room and watch a movie."

"I'm ready." She took a sip from the wine and then another one. "I'm just nervous because I'm a vain woman who is no longer in her prime and feels insecure about baring herself to a man who looks half her age."

Merlin frowned. "You are hot, Ronja. Every morning when you show up on my doorstep with those sexy exercise clothes of yours, I get so hard I can barely walk, let alone run. Do you know what I have to do to be able to jog with you?"

"What?"

"I go over lists of conditions and symptoms like I did in medical school. That's the only way I can stop thinking about those bouncing breasts of yours and that magnificent ass that I can't wait to sink my teeth into."

Ronja laughed. "Don't you dare put your fangs anywhere near my ass."

His eyes blazed blue green in the dark. "What about other parts of your body? Can I bite your neck?"

As she imagined that, her new panties dampened. "Yes."

"Where else can I bite you?" He took the wine glass from her hand and put it on the nightstand. "Can I bite your inner thigh?" His hand tugged on the blanket, and as she let go of it, he pulled it down her breasts. "Or here?" He ran a finger over the swell of her breast.

"Just the neck for now," she breathed.

"That's a shame." He dipped his head and kissed each swell before tugging the bra cups down and exposing her nipples. "One day, I'll bite you here." He lightly pinched her right nipple and then licked the small hurt away. "And here." He repeated the same on the other side. "And maybe, when you learn to trust me, I'll bite you down here." He tossed the blanket aside, exposing her fully. "Gorgeous."

MERLIN

"So soft." Merlin trailed his finger over the top of Ronja's sexy black panties. Her skin was so pale in contrast. "Will you allow me to kiss you here?" He lowered his head and pressed a kiss to her mound over the satin and lace.

"Yes," she breathed. "Don't you want to undress too?"

"Not yet." He smoothed his finger down the side, eliciting a shiver from her. "I want to take my time with you." He kissed her a little lower, finding her panties soaked through.

"I thought that I would be scared." She reached with her hand and cupped his cheek. "Of your fangs, I mean. Not you."

"And you're not?" He lifted his head and let her see his fully elongated fangs.

The room was dark, but the light coming from his eyes should be enough for her to see what she would later feel.

"I'm not scared. It's you, the same kind male I fell in love with, just with fangs."

His throat dried out in an instant. "You love me?"

She reached for him, winding her arms around his neck. "Wasn't that obvious?"

"I was hoping that you feel about me the same way I feel about you, but I wasn't sure. I didn't want to pressure you, so I held back, but I wanted to tell you for weeks that I love you."

Her smile was radiant as she leaned up and kissed him softly, her tongue darting out and licking around his fangs.

With a groan, he pulled away. "If you keep doing that, I'm going to come in my pants, and I'm way too old for that."

She gazed at him from under her long lashes. "There is no reason to hold back. I'm ready, and I'm aching." She trailed her hand down her belly and pushed past the elastic into her panties. "Right here." Her eyes rolled back as she lightly rubbed her clitoris.

It was the most erotic thing he'd ever seen, and as he snaked his finger under the gusset, her hips bucked up in a blatant invitation.

She was drenched, and as he dipped his finger in her wetness and dragged it up to where her fingers were pressed, she let her hand fall to the side to give him access. "Get undressed, Merlin. I want to see you. All of you."

"Not yet, love. I'm trying to pace myself so I can give you the attention you deserve, and I'm afraid that if I take off my clothes, I will lose control. I can't let it happen. You are still human, and you're fragile."

She chuckled nervously. "You will have to take them off at some point."

"Yes, but I need to prepare you first. It has been a while for you."

"For you as well." She said it as a statement, but there was a slight questioning note in her tone.

"Yes, it has. I've been waiting for you." He kicked off his shoes and stretched out on the bed next to her. "You were worth the wait." Lowering his head, he kissed her deep and long while gently massaging that most sensitive spot on her body.

When he slipped a finger inside of her, she bucked up against his hand, and he swallowed the moan she emitted. As he kept devouring her mouth and pumping his finger in and out of her, the faster he finger-fucked her, the lewder the wet sounds became, and combined with the overpowering scent of her desire, he was on the brink of spilling in his pants or ripping his zipper open and plunging into her with one brutal thrust.

Gathering the last of his self-control, he did neither, but he wasn't going to last much longer, which meant that he had to wrest a climax out of her lightning fast.

Given the churning of her hips and the sounds she was making, that shouldn't be hard to do.

Adding another finger, he let go of her mouth and lowered his head to her nipple, lapping at it once, twice, and sucking it into his mouth. Ronja was almost there, he could feel the small muscles in her sheath rippling against his fingers, and as he added his thumb to the play and gently rubbed her clitoris, she exploded with a scream.

48

RONJA

*T*he orgasm exploded out of Ronja with the force of a hurricane, and for long moments, she couldn't move, couldn't open her eyes, couldn't even thank the male who'd given it to her.

She hadn't been with anyone since Frank had died, but lately, she'd gone back to pleasuring herself. Heck, she'd done that last night thinking about Merlin and coming hard as she imagined him between her legs and at her neck.

Ronja had hoped that last night's powerful orgasm had taken the edge off, so once she let loose, she wouldn't attack Merlin like a crazed succubus. It had done the job in that regard, but she'd still climaxed like a firecracker after two minutes of foreplay.

A gentle hand on her cheek and a kiss on her lips forced her to open her eyes, and the sight that greeted her was precious. Even though Merlin's eyes were aglow, and his fangs were at the longest she'd ever seen them, he didn't look alien, or scary, he just looked like a man in love.

A very naked and very hard and very thick male in love.

During the scant moments of her post-orgasmic bliss, he'd managed to get his clothes off and mount her, but he made no move to penetrate her.

"Hello, beautiful." He dipped his head and kissed her softly. "I need to ask you a question."

If he wanted to propose, that was wonderful, but it could wait. She needed that thick, pulsating length inside of her.

Ronja lifted her arms and looped them around his back. "Does it have to be now?" She ground herself on his erection. "I might have orgasmed harder than I ever did before, but that only whetted my appetite for more."

His smile was all about male pride and satisfaction as he slipped his hand under her butt and tucked her closer, the head of his erection probing her entrance. "Glad to oblige, my love, but I need to know whether you want us to use protection or not."

That was a tough call.

Ronja had planned for their first few times to be just about making love and not about her transition, and that necessitated the use of condoms. But now that she felt the velvety skin of him, she didn't want to sheath it in rubber.

Damn, she was such an airhead.

The same kind of frivolous behavior had gotten her pregnant with twins at nineteen and forced Michael to marry her. Then again, the twins were a blessing, and she'd been in love with Michael and had wanted him to marry her, so that hadn't been a mistake.

Perhaps this time it wasn't either.

It was the voice of her intuition, and it was telling her that it was time and that her gamble would pay off.

"No condoms." She tightened her arms around him. "I'm a hundred percent in. I want eternal life with you, Merlin, and that life begins tonight."

As the tenderness and love in his eyes became tinged with fear, he lowered his head and rested his forehead against hers. "I love you, Ronja, and I will continue loving you even if you choose not to transition. Are you absolutely sure?"

"I am." She caressed his back. "But I don't want anything to diminish the pleasure of our first time. If wearing a condom would make you less anxious, it's fine with me."

Her only warning was a growl that started deep within Merlin's chest, and then his manhood speared into her with one glorious thrust, filling her so completely, so perfectly, that it brought tears to her eyes.

As Merlin froze above her, his expression of lust replaced by alarm, she shook her head. "You're not hurting me. It just feels so perfect that I was moved to tears."

He smiled, flashing her those dangerous fangs, and thrust deeply. She arched up, meeting him stroke for stroke. As he started a steady rhythm, penetrating and retreating, she gripped him tightly, her fingers digging into his back muscles, her mouth finding a spot on his chest that she just had to lick.

He tasted as good as he smelled.

"You feel so perfect, Ronja."

She didn't answer, not with words, but she did with her body.

As another climax tore through her, she turned her head to the side, exposing her neck, and as she heard him hiss, she shut her eyes tightly, expecting the pain, welcoming it but also fearing it.

When his fangs penetrated her skin, the burn was worse than she'd expected, but it didn't last more than a couple of seconds, and then it was gone, and she orgasmed again, and again, and just when exhaustion began to wash over her, she was hit with a boost of energy and whisked away onto a cloud.

She was soaring high above magnificent landscapes that were totally alien, and yet felt more like home than everything she was familiar with. They were about love and tranquility, about a sense of rightness, of being one with the universe. She was no longer Ronja. She was a goddess, an angel, a free spirit not bound by any laws of men or nature, but she felt safe. She wasn't going to get lost because she was tethered by love, and all she had to do to find her way back home was to follow that golden line of light.

49

MERLIN

*M*erlin held Ronja in his arms for nearly three hours, her head tucked into the crook of his neck, her hair tickling his nose, the scent of their lovemaking permeating his nostrils.

As she soared on the clouds of venom-induced euphoria, or maybe just slept and dreamt, he hadn't dared close his eyes for longer than it took to blink, not because he was worried about her being out for so long, but because of who she was to him and what was at stake.

He'd been with enough human females before to have absolute certainty that the venom bite was not harmful.

On the contrary, once the women woke up, some as soon as an hour later while others took up to six, they felt wonderful. Rejuvenated, satisfied, and relaxed.

He'd always stayed to make sure that they were fine and to thrall the memory of his bite from their minds. They'd remembered spending several hours of passion with the quirky doctor, but they hadn't remembered that the doctor was not human.

If they wondered about the venom-induced trip, they dismissed it as a strange dream, or maybe even suspected him of slipping them a hallucinogenic, but none had ever complained.

Dipping his head, he pressed a soft kiss to the top of Ronja's head. He'd done that many times over the three hours or so since she'd checked out, but so far she hadn't even stirred. This time, though, her lips lifted in a little smile, and yet she didn't wake up. It wouldn't be long now. The smile meant that her consciousness was surfacing, and that her trip was almost over.

He hoped she'd enjoyed the ride, and he had no intention of letting her see how worried he was once she opened her eyes.

Up until now, her transition had been hypothetical, something that needed to be decided on in the future. As such, he could think about it rationally and refer to the excellent statistics the clan had with transitioning Dormants so far—a hundred percent success rate. But statistics didn't mean shit even if they had a one in a million chance of death when that death was of the one you loved.

In his case, it was even worse because if Ronja didn't make it, he would be the one responsible. It couldn't be blamed on some random act of fate or nature, a disease that there was no cure for, or an accident. It would be entirely on him.

If he hadn't pressured her into it, if he hadn't bitten her, her life wouldn't be in peril.

If she died, it would destroy him. He wouldn't be able to go on, and he would have to find a way to end his own life. Jumping off a plane with no parachute should do the trick, but he wouldn't need to resort to such extremes.

After all, he was a doctor, and there were poisons that in the right dosage could kill even an immortal.

With a sigh, he looked down at Ronja's peaceful sleeping face, leaned down and kissed her warm cheek. He shouldn't entertain such morbid thoughts on what should be the happiest day of his life.

Ronja had told him that she was in love with him, and he had known that he loved her for weeks now. There was no doubt in his mind that they were true-love mates, and if so, the Fates were responsible for their mating and wouldn't let anything happen to her.

Right.

Since when did he believe in all that spiritual crap?

He was a scientist, and it was against his religion to invoke the Fates or any other supernatural power. But as the saying went, there were no atheists in the foxhole, or in the hospital, or wherever else people fought for their lives and stared death in the face.

Merlin had cared about many people over the long centuries of his life, immortals and humans, but he'd never been in love before, and it was terrifying.

5 0

ORION

*W*hen their group arrived at the hotel restaurant, Orion expected the philologist to already be there, and a frown creased his brow when he didn't see him. "I hope Herb was picked up by his tour guide. I don't think it's safe for a middle-aged human to stay the night on that tiny island. His Hawaiian shirt and tweed jacket do not offer much protection from the elements, and it gets freezing on the lake at night."

Kalugal didn't seem to share his worry as he walked past, following the hostess. "If he doesn't show up in the next half an hour, I'll call the Lake Lodge and ask to speak with him. If he's not there, I'll send one of my men to that island."

"Thank you." Orion pulled out a chair for Alena. "I don't mind rowing over there myself. I could use the exercise."

"I'll join you." Alena sat down. "It sounds romantic."

"It's dangerous," Arwel said. "You can send one of your Odus."

"I don't want them anywhere near water. They are so heavy that I don't know if it's safe for them to be on one of those narrow canoes. Besides, I don't think that they like the idea of being on a boat." Alena pushed a strand of hair behind her ear. "Ovidu seemed very glad to be left behind this morning."

"Did you reboot him?" Carol asked.

"Not yet. Annani and I discussed it, and we decided to wait a little longer and see how Okidu and Onidu are doing and that the reboot doesn't have an adverse effect on them."

Orion followed the conversation with interest. "Do the cyborgs require rebooting?"

"One second." Kalugal lifted his hand. "Okay, you can talk now. I cast a shroud to muffle our conversation."

Jacki kissed his cheek. "You are so talented, my love."

Alena smiled at the couple before turning to Orion. "They don't. In fact, my mother refused to let anyone probe them or test them, fearing that it might cause

345

damage that would be impossible to fix. The first reboot happened by accident when Okidu fell into the ocean, and it took a long time to pull him out. The Odus are very heavy, so he sank all the way to the bottom, and they needed to hook a cable to him and drag him back to the boat, where they used a crane to haul him out of the water. When he woke up, so to speak, Okidu started acting differently. He appeared more sentient, and then one day, he decided to reboot Amanda's butler because he needed help with a surprise he was preparing for Kian's birthday. Now we have two sentient Odus and five who are not."

"What was the present?" Orion asked.

Alena averted her eyes. "It's a very closely guarded secret. I'm sorry, but Kian would have my head if I tell you."

As an uncomfortable silence stretched across the table, Orion tried not to feel hurt. For a newcomer, he'd been entrusted with many of the clan's secrets and even with the goddess's heir. That was much more than he could have expected, and he shouldn't feel offended that they were still withholding information from him. It would have been irresponsible of them to do otherwise.

"That's okay." He lifted Alena's hand to his lips and kissed the back of it. "I don't need to know everything there is to know about the clan. I'm not a member yet."

"Most members don't know about it either," Arwel said. "It's a security issue, and we cannot afford any slackening in that."

"I understand perfectly." He kissed Alena's hand again to reassure her that he wasn't holding it against her.

Even if they had been already mated for many years, he wouldn't have expected her to share everything with him. She was an unofficial leader of her clan, privy to classified information, and there were things she couldn't share even with her mate.

"By the way." Arwel turned to Kalugal. "Did you mean what you told Herb about visiting the dig tomorrow? Weren't we supposed to wait until Monday?"

"I changed my mind," Kalugal said. "I'd rather tour the place and explore it freely without the workers snooping around us and watching what we do. My partner sent me a video of what they've found so far, and I can't wait to see it, but I was serious about going alone. I want to check the safety measures before I bring my pregnant wife there."

"You're not going alone," Jacki said. "Besides, I thought that the Chinese worked seven days a week."

Carol chuckled. "It's a myth. The Chinese are hard-working people, but they are not machines, and they get weekends off just like everyone in the West. If they work in a factory, they have shifts, and in case of an emergency, they stay overtime to solve the problem, but that's no different from how it's handled in the West."

"What about bribes?" Phinas asked. "I read that businesses in China have to pay hefty bribes to operate."

"Speaking of business," Kalugal said. "How are your double endeavors progressing? The fashion line and recruiting high-ranking Chinese officials to work for the Brotherhood?"

Lokan cast a quick sidelong glance at Phinas and Kalugal's two other men who were sitting on the other side of the long table, but then shook his head. "It's going slow, and the bribes are indeed a big problem."

51

ALENA

*A*lena could understand Lokan's instincts kicking in and making him wary about talking in front of Kalugal's men, but he had nothing to worry about. Or so Alena hoped.

Annani had compelled all clan members and all of Kalugal's men to not cause harm to one another. But did that include Lokan?

As Carol's mate, he was a clan member, but since he was still serving Navuh and the Brotherhood, it was a loophole someone could use to circumvent the compulsion.

Not that it was likely. Kalugal's men were loyal to him, and they had proven that loyalty countless times. They would never do anything to endanger his brother. Besides, they had as much to fear from Navuh and the Brotherhood as any clan member, probably more. If any of them was ever caught, Navuh would make an example out of them to scare the others into obedience.

"You can get away with not paying the bribes," Jacki said. "Why not compel them to do whatever you want them to do?"

"It's not that simple," Lokan said. "The bribe-takers are well organized, and it's part of doing business in China. I can compel those who come to collect the bribe money, but I have no access to their bosses. If the money doesn't get to them, I can kiss any progress goodbye, or worse." He leaned back in his chair. "Don't forget that I'm a foreigner, and they can kick me out very easily.

"Who do you need to bribe?" Alena said. "Is it like organized crime and you have to pay protection money?"

"That too," Carol said. "The bribe-takers are mostly local officials. We even have to pay to get access to materials, equipment, and other supplies needed to run the business. Perhaps it's not as bad in other provinces, but Beijing is the worst."

"Are Chinese entrepreneurs in the same boat as you are?" Arwel asked.

"Slightly less," Lokan said. "The statistics I read say that Hong-Kong-owned firms pay the most, followed by other foreign-owned firms, and the Chinese firms pay the

I. T. LUCAS

least. The spread is about twelve percent. The highest bribes are paid by real estate and manufacturing firms. Corruption is a plague, and the government is trying to crack down on it, but it's like fighting trafficking. As long as big money can be made with relatively little effort, the cockroaches will find a way around the strongest of pesticides."

"Ugh." Carol shivered. "Why did you have to talk about cockroaches at the dinner table? It's gross."

"My apologies." He leaned toward her and kissed her cheek.

As the restaurant door opened and the philologist walked in, Kalugal snapped his fingers, letting everyone know that he'd dropped the shroud.

"Doctor Neisman." He rose to his feet. "My companions and I were worried that you were left stranded on that island." He pulled out the chair he'd reserved for Herb. "If you didn't show up just now, I would have called your hotel to check whether you had returned to your room."

"I'm so sorry." Herb sat down. "I started reading up on Kali and lost track of time." He chuckled nervously. "I'm the definition of an absentminded professor."

He hadn't mentioned being a professor before. As far as Alena knew, a person could have a doctorate, but unless they were employed by a university as teachers or heads of research, they weren't called professors.

"Where do you teach?" Alena asked.

"Brown University."

"Lovely place," Kalugal said. "I once dated a girl from Brown."

Jacki elbowed him in the ribs. "You said that you didn't date anyone before me."

He smiled indulgently. "Dated is a figure of speech. I just don't appreciate the modern lingo referencing amorous encounters. The romance is gone from it."

At the mention of romance, Orion's hand found Alena's under the table, and as he teased her palm, the way she knew he would later tease other places on her body, Alena felt her cheeks get warm.

Luckily, everyone's eyes were on Kalugal, and Herb gazed at him with renewed admiration. "It's so refreshing to see a young man like you who appreciates the finer nuances of language."

"Thank you." Kalugal dipped his head. "Language has power, and the words chosen to express feelings feed back into those feelings. We need to be careful in the way we communicate and even in the way we think."

"I couldn't agree more." Herb turned to look at the waitress who'd been waiting patiently to take their order. "If you don't mind, I would like to order and keep discussing the use of language over dinner. I'm famished."

348

5 2

ORION

*T*he sexual tension Kalugal's innocent comment had ignited refused to abate despite the food Orion shoved in his mouth. As his mind got stuck running in circles and replaying all the marvelous moments of him and Alena making love, his appetite for her nullified his interest in the meal he was consuming on autopilot.

The same couldn't be said about Herb, who kept refilling his plate from the communal platters as long as there was anything left on them. He was very polite about it, though, always asking if anyone else wanted the last few bites. Naturally, they had all indulged him by telling him to go ahead.

When the professor finally pushed his plate away and leaned back, the buttons of his Hawaiian shirt strained to hold his bloated belly inside, and a few gray hairs poked through the gaps.

"Thank you for dinner." He rubbed a hand over his belly. "The Mrs. always tells me that it's not healthy to wait until dinner to eat and that I should consume smaller portions throughout the day, but I get so absorbed in my work that I forget to eat until hunger is gnawing at my belly, and then I overindulge."

"Where is Mrs. Neisman?" Carol asked.

"Back in the States. Our youngest daughter is about to have her first baby, and Matilda flew to Seattle to be with her." He smiled sadly. "We have three daughters, and each one of them lives in a different state. It's so difficult for Matilda. I have my work to keep me busy, but she retired a couple of years ago, and she gets lonely."

The guy didn't know how lucky he was. Orion couldn't imagine having one daughter, let alone three. He and Alena hadn't talked about the future yet, but she'd told him that she loved children and would have loved to have a hundred if she could, but it seemed that her fertility had run out, and his hadn't manifested yet and maybe never would.

What were the chances of them having a child together?

Geraldine had told him about a clan doctor who was working on improving immortals' fertility. If things went well and they bonded, perhaps the doctor might be able to help them conceive.

Casting a sidelong glance at Alena, Orion imagined her pregnant with their child, her delicate hands resting on her rounded belly, and happiness illuminating her beautiful face.

"So, Herb." Carol turned to the professor. "What did you find out about the monster?"

He frowned. "What monster are you referring to?"

"Kali, of course."

He seemed offended on the goddess's behalf. "Kali is not a monster. She's vicious but also nurturing. She is complicated, feared, and adored at the same time. She represents all of existence and encompasses the two forces governing it—death and destruction on one side, creation and salvation on the other. She symbolizes death's inevitability, but at the same time, she makes the passage easier by encouraging acceptance and dispelling fear."

The professor's speech was interrupted by the waitress. "Can I take away some of these?" She motioned at the mostly empty platters.

"You can take all of it," Kalugal said. "I would like to see the dessert menu for tonight, and another serving of tea would be great."

"Right away, sir." The young woman inclined her head, and a moment later, several busboys rushed over to clear the table.

"How old is Kali's worship?" Lokan asked.

Orion had wondered the same thing and even planned to search for answers on the internet, but it had been a busy day, and he hadn't had the opportunity. If the myths about Kali originated with the Kra-ell's Mother of All Life, the start of Kali's worship could provide them a rough time estimate for when the first Kra-ell had arrived.

"Kali's name first appears in a holy Hindu text. The oldest estimated age of that text is seventeenth-century BCE, and the most recent eleventh-century BCE. Kali is also described in the Devi-Mahatmya portion of the Markandeya Purana historical texts. What's somewhat confusing about the Hindu pantheon is that one god or goddess can have many manifestations. Kali is also the great goddess Devi, who is also known as Durga. Her other names include, Sati, Rudrnai, Parvati, Kamakshi, and others that I can't recall at the moment."

"Interesting," Carol said. "I don't know much about the Hindu pantheon, but I remember hearing a story about the god Shiva, and a wife named Parvati, and another wife named Kali. I thought he had several wives, but from what you're saying, it's a different manifestation of the same one."

Herb grinned. "Isn't that just brilliant? Women are such complicated and multifaceted creatures, and the Hindu tradition captured the female essence so beautifully. Kali is the goddess of fertility and time. She is the protector and defender who is called upon in times of great calamity. She is the symbol of productivity, the cycles of nature, the creator who takes life to give new life. She's the destroyer of evil, ignorance, and selfishness, and the nurturer of all that is good in humanity."

"I like her," Jin said. "She's a kick-ass goddess."

"Like the Kra-ell's Mother of All Life?" Arwel said so quietly that only the immortals heard him.

"She's a warrior," Herb said. "When demons needed slaying, and Parvati was too gentle to deal with them, she called upon Kali—her fiercer manifestation to come forward. Kali decapitated the demons and swallowed some in her enormous mouth. That's why she is often depicted with blood-smeared lips, holding weapons in her four, eight, or ten arms, and wearing a skirt of severed hands and a garland of skulls."

"She sounds terrifying and horrifying," Alena said. "More of a destroyer than anything else."

"Don't forget that those she slew were demons, real or figurative." Herb pulled out his phone and scrolled through until finding what he was looking for. "This is Kali at a dinner party. As you can see, her plate is painted in reds and purples, reminding us that she drinks the blood of demons."

"Lovely." Alena grimaced and passed the phone to Orion. "I hope that I'm not going to dream about her tonight."

53

ALENA

*A*lena opened the balcony doors of their hotel room and stepped outside. The two rocking chairs with a small table between them reminded her of Kian. As she imagined her brother sitting outside and puffing on one of his cigars, she wondered what he would have made of their discoveries from earlier today.

Leaning her elbows on the railing, she looked at the lake. Most of it was dark, with the exception of an area that was bathed in moonlight, shimmering with a silver light.

Were they seeing real mythological patterns that aligned with what they knew of the Kra-ell? Or were they mistakenly assigning meaning where there was none?

Orion walked up behind Alena and wrapped his arms around her. "What are you thinking about?" He kissed the side of her neck.

Closing her eyes, she let her head drop back against his chest. "When you are kissing me, I think of nothing at all. I just feel."

He nuzzled her ear. "Is it just me, or does the goddess Kali perfectly fit the Kra-ell deity?"

"Kian always warned us against seeing patterns and giving them unwarranted interpretations. Just like humans, our brains are programmed to see patterns, but that doesn't mean that what we deduce from those patterns is true. Many of the ancient gods and goddesses were depicted as terrifying and destructive, and not all mythologies were based on our ancestors."

As he trailed kisses down her neck, his hands traveled up her sides and then closed over her breasts. "How about we give the scary gods and goddesses of other mythologies a rest for tonight and move to more enjoyable topics?"

Alena smiled. "What topics do you have in mind?"

His fingers teased her nipples. "The worship of one very beautiful goddess who is gentle and sweet and not terrifying in the least."

"I could be terrifying if I wanted to."

"Not a chance." He turned her around to face him. "I'm running the water in the tub. It's probably full by now." He dipped his head and kissed her lightly. "I plan on giving you a very thorough wash, starting with your dainty toes."

Said toes curled inside her ballet flats. "Sounds delightful."

"I'm glad you approve." He lifted her into his arms and carried her to the bathroom.

Alena laughed. "I've never understood what was so special about a male carrying a female, but I get it now. It's sexy as hell."

"Is it, now?" He lowered her onto a chair he'd positioned in front of the bathtub and went to turn the faucets off. "I don't know what's sexy about hell. Isn't hell supposed to be hot?"

"That's the idea." Alena kicked her shoes off. "Maybe it started with hot as hell, which would make sense, and then it morphed into sexy as hell. Or perhaps it started with sexy as sin and turned into sexy as hell."

"We could ask Herb." He knelt at her feet and reached for the waistband of her trousers. "Your new wardrobe is sexy and sophisticated, but I liked your long dresses better."

She arched a brow. "Really? Amanda said that I looked quaint in them."

"So?" He gently pulled her pants down. "You looked like the fairytale princess you are, and the dresses were easy to take off. What more can a male ask for?"

She leaned and kissed the top of his head. "You say the nicest things."

He still hadn't told her that he loved her, but then she hadn't said the words either. Were they in love, though? Or were they still in like and lust?

Orion lifted on his knees and started on her blouse buttons. "Wait until I get you naked. I will have even nicer things to say."

"Oh, yeah? Like what?" She helped him with the last two buttons and shrugged the blouse off.

He sucked in a breath. "Keep the new lingerie when you go back to wearing the soft dresses you like. Talk about hot as sin and sexy as hell. Or is it the other way around?"

It was just a white lace bra, but it was low cut, leaving most of the swells of her breasts exposed. But if it got Orion to look at her like that, she was going to buy it in every color.

"Should I leave it on?" she breathed as he leaned to kiss the top of her breasts.

"As beautiful as it is," he reached behind her and popped the clasp, "it can't compare to the beauty of you in nothing at all." He slid the straps down her arms and tossed the bra aside.

Lifting her off the chair, Orion kissed her long and hard before lowering her into the tub.

Alena scooted to the side. "Aren't you going to join me?"

"Not yet." Orion took a washcloth, squirted liquid soap on it, and knelt by the tub. "Lift your foot." When she did, he took hold of her heel and ran the washcloth over her foot. "You have the prettiest toes I've ever seen." He lifted her foot to his lips and started kissing one toe at a time.

With a moan, Alena let her head drop back on the lip of the tub and closed her eyes. "This feels so good."

His strong fingers pressed into the arch of her foot. "I've only just begun."

54

ORION

*A*s their limousine bumped and swayed over the unpaved road, their driver swore in Chinese and then quickly apologized for it. Orion couldn't converse freely in the language, but he picked up enough of it to get the gist. Besides, some things were universal, and cussing sounded the same no matter which language it was uttered in.

Kalugal said something about compensating him for damage to the vehicle, which seemed to mollify the guy, and he cussed no more even though the ride got even bumpier over the last section of the path.

When the vehicle finally stopped next to a dusty truck that was parked a hundred feet or so from the riverbank, they all sighed in relief.

"Whose truck is that?" Lokan asked.

"My partner's, Jianye," Kalugal said. "I asked him to meet me here and walk me through the security measures he's taken."

"I'm glad I had a light breakfast," Alena said as she took Orion's hand. "I didn't expect the road to be a goat trail." She cast Kalugal an accusing glance. "Did you know that it was unpaved?"

"Of course."

"So why did you bring us here in the limousines?"

He arched a brow. "Would you have preferred a yak ride?"

"You have a point," Alena conceded.

"I hope my baby is okay." Jacki caressed her small belly. "He got quite a roller-coaster experience today."

"He's fine," Kalugal reassured her. "Right now, he's the size of a banana and is surrounded by protective liquid."

Jacki's lips twisted in a grimace. "Please don't compare our baby to a banana."

"I didn't. All I said was that he was the size of one." For the first time since Orion had met Kalugal, the guy seemed impatient with his wife.

Perhaps it was worry that shortened his temper.

Kalugal had wanted to go to the dig alone, check the safety of the site, and come back to get them only after making sure that it was okay. But Jacki had insisted that it was a waste of time and that he could check the site while the rest of them waited on the riverbank. If it wasn't safe, they would at least get to see the scenic route leading to the islet in the middle of the wide river.

In Orion's opinion, it was worth the nearly one-hour-long bumpy ride to just get a look at the ruins from the riverbank. The ancient trade post had been carved into the rock, starting on top of the high platform and going down.

He wondered how the platform had been naturally formed in the middle of the river, and if the locals had a legend for that as well. The walls of the outpost were at least fifty feet tall, and a massive gate once guarded the only entrance. All that remained of it was the opening, which was about thirty feet tall and had carved pillars on both sides that were more decorative than functional.

As their group walked the last few feet to the bank, Kalugal's local partner waved and smiled from the rope bridge that had been erected between the riverbank and the excavation site. After a short round of partial introductions, the two made their way across the bridge, while the rest of them waited to hear Kalugal's verdict about the site's safety.

"I'm glad that we are immortal," Alena whispered in Orion's ear. "That bridge doesn't look too solid."

Wrapping his arm around her waist, he nuzzled her neck. "How good of a swimmer are you?"

"Not great, and I'm not looking forward to getting wet. The middle rungs of the bridge are submerged. I also don't like the idea of the outpost being carved going down. Kalugal said that this site has been excavated before, and that the previous archeologists dug through several strata of habitation. It made me wonder how deep down they went. If they dug below the river's surface level, the whole place could be flooded."

"Don't worry," Jacki said. "They've been digging here for over two weeks, and nothing's happened. Why would anything collapse just from us walking around and looking?"

"I don't know." Alena rubbed her hands over her arms. "I have a bad feeling."

Orion's shoulders stiffened. "Do you often get premonitions?"

She chuckled. "Very rarely, and I'm usually wrong, so don't mind me. I guess it has become a habit of mine to issue warnings about all possible mishaps. With my mother's complete disregard for safety, I had to be the voice of reason." She sighed. "I hope she's doing okay without me."

"Have you called her since we got here?" Carol asked.

Alena shook her head. "She told me not to call unless it was an emergency. She wants me to enjoy my vacation and not worry about her, but it feels so strange. I want to call her and tell her about how beautiful it is out here, and about all the interesting things we've learned from the philologist."

"So call her," Carol said. "I think your mother wants to prove that she can survive just fine without you, but there is no reason to go cold turkey about it. I think that both of you will feel much better if you talk at least once a day."

"What do you think?" Alena turned to Orion. "Should I call my mother?"

He glanced at the ruins, but Kalugal and his partner had disappeared beyond the gate and were nowhere to be seen.

"Kalugal's inspection of the site might take a while, so you have time to call your mother. The only thing I'm not sure about is whether it is smart to defy the goddess's command. Will she be okay with you disobeying her wishes?"

Alena shrugged. "The worst she will do is pretend to be upset with me, but I think she'll be glad I called." She pulled out her phone and frowned. "That's strange. I have no reception here." She looked up. "And it's not even cloudy. Clan phones are supposed to work everywhere."

"Let's see." Arwel pulled his out. "You're right. Something must be interfering with the satellite connection." He turned to Lokan. "Do you have the Brotherhood's phone on you?"

Lokan shook his head. "I left it in the hotel."

"Damn." Arwel put the phone in his pocket. "I'm going to jog back to the limo and check with the driver if his phone works."

"I'll come with you," Jin said. "I don't think he speaks any English, and you might need me to translate."

"I'll go with you as well," Lokan said. "I speak fluent Chinese."

55

ALENA

"I feel naked." Alena looked at her useless phone. "Does anyone have a theory about why our phones don't work here?"

The driver's phone didn't work either, but that was because the nearest tower was at the lake, and the area of the ruins didn't get coverage. He'd told Lokan that he'd lost reception twenty minutes into the drive. That had probably been another reason for the man's cussing bout.

The satellite phones should have been fine, though.

"Maybe the satellite is malfunctioning," Arwel said. "Although it has never happened before."

"Should we even go into the outpost without our phones?" Carol asked.

Arwel looked conflicted. "I don't think we should. We should buy walkie-talkies and leave someone on the outside with one."

"Where are you going to find them?" Lokan asked. "All you can get around the lake are touristy things."

"The boat operators might have them," Carol said. "I didn't see ours carry a walkie-talkie, but she probably had one. How else is she communicating with her dispatcher?"

"We had no problems using our phones on the lake." Alena lifted her phone again, hoping that by some miracle a signal would show. "The guides can use phones. They don't need walkie-talkies."

It would be a shame to come all the way out here and not visit the ruins just because they didn't have reception. If people worked on that site Monday through Friday without it, their group could manage an hour sightseeing with no connection. People had done just fine without instant global connectivity up until about a decade ago, and now they couldn't function without it?

It was ridiculous.

Alena dumped the device in her purse and crossed her arms over her chest. "We are already here, and we are going to see the damn site with or without reception. It's not like we always had cellular phones. We've spent the vast majority of our lives without them."

"Kalugal is coming back," Jacki said.

As Alena turned to look at the swaying rope bridge, her bravado of only moments ago evaporated. She had no idea how Kalugal was crossing it so calmly. One wrong step and he would plunge into the river's freezing water.

It was good that the Odus had stayed behind. The flimsy bridge would have come apart under their weight.

"It's safe," Kalugal announced. "As long as we don't go inside any of the dwellings, there shouldn't be a problem."

"Our phones don't work," Arwel said.

"I know. There is no reception here."

"That shouldn't affect our satellite phones," Lokan said.

"Jianye says that there's some sort of natural interference in the soil. Supposedly there are large deposits of copper in the river's sediment and in the rock platform." Kalugal smiled. "Although Jianye thinks that the culprit is a naughty spirit. The workers are complaining about their tools and lunches disappearing."

"I don't think it's safe to go in without the ability to communicate," Arwel said. "I don't even like being here, on the riverbank, without a line to the outside world."

"That's fine." Kalugal waved a dismissive hand. "There is no one for miles around, and we are only going to walk through the outpost's main boulevard and look at the artifacts that have been found so far. I don't expect it to take long, and I'll inform the drivers that they should come to look for us if we don't come out in an hour."

"I'll do that for you," Jianye said.

"Thank you." Kalugal offered him his hand. "Thanks for coming out here during the weekend. I appreciate that."

"No problem." The man smiled. "My compensation is more than adequate."

As the two said their goodbyes, Arwel walked over to the bridge and examined it. "The bridge looks well built, but I suggest that we cross it one at a time."

"The water is pretty shallow here," Kalugal said. "If we didn't mind getting wet, we could have walked across. In fact, when they installed the bridge, that's how they did it. Anyway, my long preamble was to explain why I feel it's safe for us to cross two at a time."

Alena wanted to kiss Kalugal on both cheeks. Walking across the rope bridge together with Orion would be much less scary than crossing alone.

"The current is strong," Arwel said. "If anyone falls and loses their balance, they might get carried away."

Jin rolled her eyes. "You probably mean us, the fragile females. I assure you that each one of us can swim against the current. We are immortal, in case you've forgotten."

Alena wasn't sure at all that she could battle the current. She wasn't a strong swimmer, and that was why she never ventured into water that was deeper than she could stand in. Nevertheless, she refused to be the only one who acted scared.

She was Annani's daughter, and she should be fearless, or at least pretend that she was.

Arwel nodded. "Two at a time it is."

"Shall we, my love?" Kalugal offered Jacki his arm.

Brave girl.

Then again, if Kalugal felt that it was safe for his pregnant wife, then Alena really shouldn't worry.

Except, phobias were not rational, and Alena seemed to be afflicted with several.

"Let's go." Jacki took Kalugal's offered arm without a moment's hesitation.

As the two of them made their way slowly across the swaying bridge, Alena held her breath, and when they stepped onto solid ground on the other side, she finally let it out.

"Who's next?" Arwel asked.

"Lokan and I." Carol took her mate's hand and led him toward the bridge.

The two made it across much faster than Kalugal and Jacki had, and since Arwel wasn't going to do it until Alena got safely to the other side, it was her and Orion's turn.

"Don't worry," Orion said. "I won't let you fall." He took her hand.

The next five minutes were the longest of her life. How had the others done it so fearlessly?

The gaps between the wooden slats were so wide that one wrong move could end up with her plunging into the water, and the whole thing swung like a pendulum. Holding Orion's hand on one side and the rope railing on the other, Alena concentrated on putting one foot in front of the other and not thinking about the water below.

By the time she made it safely to the other side, she was drenched in sweat and shaking.

"I don't know why I was so scared." She smiled apologetically. "Even if I fell, I would have just gotten wet and cold. The current doesn't look that strong, and even I could swim ashore."

"I blame your mother." Carol patted Alena's arm. "Just don't tell her that I said that."

"What does my mother have to do with my anxiety?"

"Because of her shenanigans and your constant exposure to stress, you have developed low-level anxiety. Two thousand years of trying to tame a mischievous goddess would do that to a person."

Alena was about to deny Carol's observation when she realized that there might be something to it. She was aware that most of her fears were irrational. She had no reason to fear compellers when her mother could free her of compulsion if needed, and she had no reason to fear the rickety bridge because a fall from it would be harmless. But knowing something intellectually was not the same as internalizing it and believing it on a visceral level.

Perhaps she should have a talk with Vanessa and see what the therapist thought of Carol's observation.

5 6

ORION

*A*s they crossed what used to be the outpost's gate, Orion was glad to see that Alena's anxiety had been replaced by curiosity.

"Please stay on the main boulevard and don't walk into any of the structures," Kalugal warned.

What he called a boulevard was actually a trench. From what Orion could see, the ancient builders had started digging down in the middle of the plateau to carve out the main throughway, and then continued carving on both sides to form the homes and shops and other structures. It was quite ingenious. First of all, they hadn't needed to bring any building materials to the site, and secondly, the steep sides of the plateau provided a natural barrier, so they hadn't needed to build protective walls either. What he found curious, though, was that the outpost had only one gate. For strategic reasons at least two gates were needed, one on each side of the islet, and preferably an escape tunnel that ran under the riverbed.

"All I see are piles of rocks," Jin grumbled.

"Let me explain what you are seeing," Kalugal said. "Most of the dwellings are underground, and they were excavated from the top down." He motioned for them to get closer. "These steps are hewn out of the rock, and they lead into a hidden entrance." He took the steps down and crouched. "This one is blocked, either on purpose or because of crumbling rock." He pushed up and took the steep steps out of the small tunnel.

"Did they find any homes that were easy to access and not walled off?" Jacki asked.

"Jianye said that they found some dwellings that survived nearly intact. The workers erected a tent at the end of the boulevard to house the artifacts they found, and that's where we are heading."

"How old are these ruins?" Orion asked.

"About twenty-one to twenty-three hundred years old."

Alena chuckled. "They are not much older than me and there isn't much left of them. It always amazes me that our bodies can keep regenerating as they do."

Over the many years of his life, Orion had often thought about how his body's regeneration worked, what was special about it. Except, everything that had to do with science usually went over his head, and when he tried to educate himself about human biology, he'd usually given up after a page or two of explanations that had his eyes glazing over.

Given that his father was the god of knowledge, he should have been better at the sciences, but evidently, he'd inherited his mother's brain and not his father's, just without her talent. He had a good eye for art and appreciated it, but he couldn't create it.

It occurred to him that he hadn't tried many forms of artistic expression yet. He might have a talent for sculpting, or glass-working, or pottery, or songwriting, or any of the other creative endeavors he planned to experiment with one day. As an immortal, Orion had endless time to explore his talents, but that was also why he hadn't yet. There was no rush to do anything.

His body was going to keep repairing itself and serve as housing for his soul for a very long time.

"Kian said something about the gods being genetically engineered. Is that fact or a hypothesis?" he asked Alena.

"It's a strong hypothesis," she said. "Another hypothesis is that the Kra-ell are an older version, perhaps even the original, and that we are a later development."

"Do you have anything to substantiate the belief that they came from the same place as the gods?"

She shook her head. "We don't, but it makes sense."

As they kept their leisurely stroll down the avenue, and Kalugal pointed out another set of stairs leading down to a residence, Jacki stopped.

"Check if the doorway is still intact. I want to see one of those dwellings."

"It's not safe." He carefully descended the stairs and crouched to look through the opening. "This one is not blocked, but it's a twenty-foot drop down. The people who lived here probably had a ladder that they could detach in case of an invasion. Anyone trying to go down this hole would have been immediately killed or injured, either by the defenders or by the fall."

Orion followed Kalugal down and took a look through the hole. "I wonder how they were eventually overwhelmed. Are there any signs of fire? Because that would have been one of the ways to do it. They could have shot flaming arrows into the homes and set them on fire."

"The stone wouldn't have been affected, but if they had wooden furniture, that would have been an effective method." Kalugal pulled out his phone and shone the flashlight into the hole. "I don't see any scorch marks, and my partner didn't mention it either."

"Would sooty marks have survived over the centuries?"

"Oh, definitely. This outpost was still active in the fourteenth century of the Common Era."

"Then I really can't see how it fell."

"Are you guys coming up?" Jacki said. "If I can't go down there, I want to at least see the artifacts."

Kalugal looked up and smiled at his mate. "You wanted me to take a look."

"Yeah, but since we can't go in, we should move on." She tapped the fingers of her hand over her other arm. "If we had a ladder, though, we could take a look inside. I'm sure we can find one that the excavators used."

When he started shaking his head, Jacki put her hands on her hips. "Stop with that overprotective act of yours. These ruins stood here for hundreds of years, and whatever was supposed to collapse already did. Those homes are like caves that are carved into the rock, so it's not like they have walls that rotted away."

"She has a point." Alena joined Jacki, looking down at them. "This is an archeological site. We should be able to find a ladder lying around somewhere."

ALENA

$\mathcal{A}$s their tour of the ruins progressed, Alena stopped worrying about the lack of phone reception.

It seemed perfectly safe, and the tent with the artifacts was about a hundred feet ahead. The place was completely devoid of vegetation, which was odd since the area received a good amount of precipitation, double what California got annually, but the upside of that was no hidden creepy-crawlies hiding where she couldn't see them but could still hear them.

Having enhanced senses was mostly advantageous, but sometimes she wished her hearing wasn't as good. If she didn't hear the damn bugs, she could pretend that there were none. After all, most were harmless, and even those that were poisonous couldn't kill an immortal. If she was stung by a scorpion, she would be uncomfortable, but she wouldn't die.

"Are you thinking the same thing I'm thinking?" Orion wrapped his arm around her waist.

"That depends. What were you thinking?"

"The area of the lake is covered in lush greenery, but this place is barren as if it was somewhere in the desert. Could the copper in the soil do that?"

"Excess copper is toxic to plants," Kalugal said. "But that's not the only reason."

Alena waited for him to continue his explanation, but he got distracted as Jacki lifted the tent's flap and motioned for them to walk in.

Long worktables were piled with dusty artifacts that Alena didn't find overly exciting. Shards of pottery, some tools, pieces of cloth—very little remained of the people who'd once lived in the outpost. It made her sad to look at those scraps and think that this was all that was left of them.

"What's fascinating about this site," Kalugal said as he walked over to one of the tables and lifted what looked like an arrowhead, "is that older artifacts are found near the surface while more recent ones are buried deep below. What my partner thinks happened was that subsequent inhabitants kept digging deeper to build their abodes, and that's why the deeper we dig, the newer the stuff gets."

"What's that?" Jacki lifted an artifact. It was a mask of a scary-looking face that had huge ears and big slanted holes for eyes. "Oh, wow." She swayed on her feet and leaned against the worktable.

Kalugal was at her side in a flash. "What's wrong?"

She waved him off, but he wouldn't let go. "Talk to me, Jacki. What's going on?"

When he tried to pry the mask from her hands, she held on, clutching it to her chest. "The poor child. She's so scared."

"What child?" Kalugal's tone turned urgent. "Are you having a vision?"

Jacki nodded. "A little girl. This thing scared her. She ran away and hid from it." She turned in a circle and walked over to the tent's eastern side. "It was right here." She backed away and walked toward the entrance. "There are stairs here that lead to a tunnel."

Still holding the scary statue clutched to her chest, Jacki walked out and squeezed herself between the tent's wall and the rock face.

"Wait." Kalugal took hold of her elbow. "You'll tear your skin on that rock."

"It's right here." Jacki crouched next to the boulder. "Can you move it?" Her voice wavered. "She's inside. I hope she's still alive. How did this boulder get here and block the entrance to the tunnel? Did someone trap her on purpose?"

"Who would do a thing like that?" Jin said. "And why?"

Thinking about a child trapped underground had Alena's heart hammering against her ribcage. "The who and why doesn't matter right now. We need to get her out, and once she's safe, then find the ones responsible and bring them to the authorities."

As the males got to work dismantling the tent's eastern wall to make room, Alena wrapped her arm around Jacki's shaking shoulders. "How often do you get visions?"

"Not often, but this was a strong one." She lifted a pair of worried eyes to Alena. "I don't know when this took place. It might have happened a long time ago, and all we will find are bones." She shivered. "But it could have also happened yesterday or a couple of days ago, and we might be able to save the girl."

As the seven males got behind the boulder and pushed, Alena regretted not having the Odus with her. As strong as immortal males were, the Odus were stronger.

"On the count of three!" Kalugal called out.

The males grunted, and slowly, the boulder started moving.

"Again! One, two, three!" The boulder moved another inch.

On Alena's right side, Jin bristled. "If there was any space to put my hands on this rock, I could have helped. I'm strong."

"I'm sure you are." Carol patted her back. "But let the boys do their thing."

"A child's life is at stake," Jin hissed.

"Perhaps." Carol caressed her back as if she was trying to tame a wild mare. "If Jacki's visions are anything like Syssi's, the girl could have run into that tunnel centuries ago, or she might run into it centuries into the future. Visions are tricky that way."

58

ORION

*T*he damn thing must have weighed a couple of tons if seven immortal males could barely move it. Orion was covered in sweat, and his palms were slick on the boulder's smooth face.

If not for Jacki's panicked insistence that there was a child trapped in the tunnel, he would have given up. But on the slight chance that her vision was true, he couldn't.

Still, he couldn't shake the feeling that the entire scenario didn't make sense. Who rolled the boulder over the entrance and why?

He doubted that anyone had trapped the child on purpose. It was more likely that the workers Kalugal's partner had hired had done that without knowing that the child was there, but even that didn't make sense. First of all, they were human, and there was no way they could have moved the thing without proper equipment. And secondly, why would they do that when it made erecting the tent more difficult?

Perhaps it had been a security issue, and they didn't want anyone falling in?

If not for that massive boulder, they wouldn't have had to put up the tent at an odd angle. Most likely, it had been there when the tent went up, which also meant that the child couldn't have gone into the tunnel recently.

Jacki's vision was probably about a past event.

Hopefully, the girl had made it out before someone had decided to block the entrance, or she'd found another way out. If not, they were going to find either a skeleton or a rotting corpse, which would devastate Jacki and probably the other females as well.

Hell, who was he kidding. It would crush him too. He'd never dealt well with death, not when it was of people he cared about, and not even of strangers, and especially not children.

When they managed to move the rock by a few inches, Kalugal called a halt to their efforts. "Let's see what we got here." He used his phone to shine light through the small opening they'd created.

"Here." Jin handed him a flashlight.

"Thank you." He tucked the phone in his pocket and turned on the strong beam. "Yup, just as I suspected."

"What?" Jacki peered over his shoulder. "What do you see?"

"A long drop and no ladder. There is no way a small child could have jumped down and not injured herself."

"She wasn't that small. She was eleven or twelve, with a dirty face and wild eyes. She went down a flight of stairs, though. I didn't see a drop."

"Could you have mistaken a ladder for stairs?" Carol asked.

"Maybe." Jacki pinched her forehead between her thumb and forefinger. "She was so terrified after seeing that mask, screamed so loudly, and ran so fast that I might not have paid attention to details."

"The mask is a depiction of Cancong," Kalugal said. "The legendary first king of Shu."

"I don't care whose head it is. Can you move the boulder enough for us to go down?"

"We can't go down because there is no ladder."

Jacki lifted a brow. "I could jump twenty feet down as a human, so don't tell me we can't do it."

Turning the flashlight off, he pushed to his feet. "First of all, you are pregnant, and there is no way you are jumping even five feet and risking our baby. And secondly, how do you propose that we get out once we find her or realize that she's not there? Jumping twenty feet up in the air is beyond my capabilities, so it's sure as hell beyond yours."

"We can tie a rope." Jacki turned to Phinas. "You can climb a rope, right? And you can pull us up one at a time."

The poor guy looked to his boss for help. "What do you want me to do?"

"Find a damn rope." Jacki stomped her foot. "Every minute we waste arguing out here, the girl might be dying down there."

Closing his eyes for a moment, Kalugal let out a long-suffering breath. "Find a rope, Phinas." He lifted a finger to shush Jacki. "But you are not coming down. Phinas and I will go, and the rest of the men will stay out here to guard you."

"Like hell." Her hands on her hips, she stared him down. "I'm the one who had the vision, and I saw the girl running through the tunnel. I'll recognize the twists and turns and show you where to go. You'll be lost without me."

"I found a ladder." Phinas dropped a large bundle of ropes and wooden slats at their feet. "That's what the workers use to go down the holes, and it should be sturdy."

Kalugal looked conflicted, but Orion knew how it would end. Jacki would have her way, and if she went, the other ladies wouldn't want to be left behind, and if they went down the tunnel, the other males would go as well to provide them protection.

"Did anyone see a canteen lying around?" Jacki asked. "We should bring water with us. The girl might be dehydrated."

"She might be dead, my love." Kalugal took his mate's hand. "Your vision might be from a long time ago."

"I know. But it's not centuries old. The girl wore pants and a puffer jacket. Those became popular only a few years ago."

Alena shook her head. "They've been popular since the forties, and especially in China."

5 9

ALENA

*A*lena felt quite useless as she watched the men push and grunt to get the opening wide enough for them to go down through. Jin and Carol went to look for more flashlights, Jacki was the one with the vision, and Alena was left with nothing better to do than watch Orion's muscles bunch and swell as he strained along with the others.

With a child's life possibly on the line, ogling her guy was just wrong, and so was feeling all warm and fuzzy about the teamwork she was witnessing. Orion was quickly becoming part of the family, cooperating with her cousins, their men and Arwel as if he'd known them for years instead of days.

Kalugal wiped his hands on his slacks and turned to Phinas, who was just as out of breath as the others. "I want that ladder secured to this damn boulder."

"I'm on it, boss." Phinas entered the tent and a moment later returned with a big hammer and a bunch of bolts.

"Stand back," he told everyone as he started hammering the bolts into the rock.

When he was done Kalugal pulled on the rope ladder to test the bolts, and when it didn't budge, he motioned for Phinas to grab the other side and pull along with him to test its strength.

Satisfied with the results, Kalugal dusted off his hands and turned to his wife. "Is there any chance I can convince you not to come down there with us?"

She shook her head. "You need me. If we had functioning phones, I might have been able to guide you from the surface, but we don't, and without me, you will not know where to go."

"I don't like it, but you are right."

"We've got lights for everyone." Jin and Carol came out of the tent holding hard-hats with attached lights and several flashlights.

"I'll take a flashlight," Jacki said. "I'm not wearing a hat some sweaty guy had on for days."

After that comment, Alena snatched a flashlight as well, and so did Jin and Carol.

The guys had no choice but to use the hardhats.

As Phinas dropped the ladder into the opening, Welgost went down first. "All clear," he called from the bottom. "Send Shamash down. We will hold the ladder for the ladies."

After Shamash joined Welgost, Jin tucked the flashlight in her waistband and approached the ladder. "Wish me luck."

Arwel went down right after her, then Carol volunteered to go next, and Lokan followed.

"Who's next?" Alena asked.

"You go." Jacki waved her on. "Kalugal and I will be the last."

Orion rubbed his hands, trying to get the dirt off them. "Shouldn't we leave someone on top to guard the opening?"

Kalugal looked conflicted. "No one can move that thing, so I'm not worried about that, but if someone wants to sabotage us, they can cut off the ladder. On the other hand, if Jacki is down there, I want all the men there to protect her. It's a tough call."

"Why would anyone want to sabotage us?" Jacki asked. "Besides, the two limo drivers know to come look for us if we are not out in an hour." She looked at her watch. "We've been here only twenty minutes or so. Do you want to send someone to tell them to wait longer before they come looking for us?"

"I don't know how reliable those drivers are, and I prefer them not knowing that we are going down."

"Why?" Alena asked. "I think someone should know in case we encounter trouble down there. If someone cuts the rope ladder, the drivers wouldn't know where to look for us."

Kalugal arched a brow. "Do we really need the help of two humans? If we can't handle whatever is down there, they for sure can't either, and neither can anyone else they might bring from the village to help."

Alena chuckled. "Since they are probably Chinese government agents in disguise, they might be better trained than you think."

Smiling, Jacki kissed her husband's cheek. "Alena is onto something. If these guys are government agents, they wouldn't allow anyone to come up here and cut the ropes."

"You're putting too much faith in your assumption that those two are indeed agents." Kalugal took her hand. "And as I said, we don't need them. Unless a battalion of Kra-ell purebloods is hiding down there, seven immortal males should be able to handle whatever we encounter."

"Then why are you so worried about me?" Jacki asked.

"What worries me is a cave-in, or some other accident that the so-called agents wouldn't be able to help us out of anyway."

Alena was losing her patience. Did they forget why they were going to all that trouble?

A child's life was at stake. "We don't have time for this." She gripped the ladder and started climbing down.

As someone who was anxious about most things, Alena surprised herself with how confident she felt descending into the semi-dark cavern.

The hardhats and flashlights provided enough light for her to see the interior of the hewn-out chamber, and it was big. This wasn't a family dwelling, or even a shop. It looked more like a chapel, especially given the altar on its far end.

ORION

"Where to, lady seer?" Kalugal asked.

The cavern was empty of any artifacts. It was just a roughhewn-out chamber, with a raised platform and a crumbling rock cuboid on top of it that had probably served as an altar.

Orion could see two exits, or rather holes that possibly led into tunnels or other chambers, but Jacki didn't point to either of them.

"It's over there." She walked up to the stone wall and started patting it. "I saw her going through here." She moved a foot to the side and patted the rock there. "Here. This one seems to move." She pulled out a few of the rocks that had been arranged to conceal the opening.

It had been done so well that Orion wouldn't have noticed it, and it confirmed further that Jacki had really seen the girl going in there, and the vision hadn't been a hallucination or something her brain had conjured up.

"Let me." Phinas motioned for her to step aside before gently knocking on the rock wall with the wooden side of his hammer. "It's hollow on the other side." He turned to Kalugal. "Should I break through?"

"Go for it," his boss told him.

Taking a step back, Phinas swung his hammer with all his might, and the rock crumbled under the onslaught, revealing a passage. Phinas swung it a few more times to clear the way, and when he was done, Welgost entered the tunnel first.

It was obvious that the girl hadn't gone through there recently and that Jacki's vision was of either a past or a future event, but by now they were committed, and Orion doubted he could convince anyone to just let it go.

"It reminds me of a video game Mey and I used to play." Jin held on to her flashlight as if it was a weapon. "It was a labyrinth, and there were traps at every turn. It took us weeks to get to the end without getting killed and having to restart the game from the beginning. I wonder if there are any traps in here."

"Indiana Jones," Carol whispered. "Did you see that movie? Talk about traps."

"I'm more worried about spiders and scorpions," Alena said. "Those were in *The Mummy*." She shivered. "I have a love-hate relationship with that movie. I loved Brendan Fraser, and I even thought that the actor playing the Mummy was sexy. But all those bugs gave me the creeps."

"Arnold Vosloo was a major hunk." Carol sighed. "I had a movie crush on him."

"Who is Arnold Vosloo?" Jin asked.

"The Mummy, of course." Carol rolled her eyes. "You were how old when it came out? Two?"

"The tunnel is clear," Welgost poked his head through the opening. "But it gets very narrow and shallow, and I had to crawl part of the way. It opens up to another chamber that has three different tunnels branching off of it."

"Damn it," Alena whispered in Orion's ear. "I hate tight spaces."

He wrapped his arm around her waist. "Would it help if I crawled right behind you and sang praises to your glorious bottom?"

Kalugal stifled a chuckle, and so did Arwel.

Jacki let out a relieved breath. "So far, so good. I was afraid Welgost would find a body." She took her husband's hand. "Let's go."

"Hold on." Jin walked up to her. "In your vision, how far into the tunnels did you follow the girl?"

"What do you mean?"

"Did you see her crawl through a narrow tunnel?"

Jacki shook her head.

"Then perhaps this is not the right one."

"She entered through here." Jacki rubbed her temples. "It's odd. I didn't see her break or move the rock either, and yet I knew that the opening was there. Visions are not movies, they are more like dreams. I get bits and pieces of information, and my brain arranges it into a comprehensive story. The girl might have crawled through the tunnel, but since I didn't see that part of her escape, my brain filled the gap with what I expected to see, which was the girl running through the tunnel system."

Jin groaned. "What is going to happen when we reach a juncture you didn't see in your vision? How will we know where to go?"

"Right." Jacki pinched her forehead between her thumb and forefinger. "I saw her running through the tunnel until she reached a chamber and sat down on the floor. She hugged her knees and cried. I kind of expected to find her in that chamber. But what if that wasn't her final destination?"

"We should mark our way going in," Orion suggested. "If the tunnel system is extensive, we might get lost." He turned to Jacki. "You didn't see the girl going out, so you wouldn't know how to guide us out of here."

"True." She gave him an apologetic smile. "It always looks so easy in the movies, doesn't it? What should we use to mark the juncture points? Should I tear off pieces of my shirt and tuck them into crevices on the way?"

"I have a better idea," Phinas said. "I'll hammer signs, marking each entrance and exit point. No one will be able to erase or remove them."

"Brilliant idea." Orion clapped him on the back. "And a great utilization of what we have on hand, which is plenty of hewn stone walls, a hammer, and brute strength."

ALENA

*A*lena was not dressed for crawling over dirt and rocks. The stretchy black pants would be ruined, and there was no way her elegant, form-fitting puffer jacket would survive either. It was meant to keep her warm, not withstand sharp stones.

She would gladly sacrifice both for a chance of finding the girl, but she didn't really believe they would. Still, on the very remote chance that the child was still there, they had to keep going.

Pulling out the flashlight from her purse, she shone it at the small opening that looked like a maw with jagged teeth.

"Are you going in?" Orion asked.

She wasn't sure. The others had already gone in, and only she and Orion remained in the cavern. It was tempting to stay behind and let the others handle the situation, but if there was indeed a scared young girl somewhere in those tunnels, Alena couldn't in good conscience leave the task of calming her to people who had no experience handling children.

"Yeah." She sighed. "For a moment, I contemplated staying here for all the wrong reasons. If there is a scared child in these damn tunnels, she needs a gentle hand and a patient voice, and I don't know how good the others are at that. None of them are parents."

"True, but one is an empath, and two are compellers. I'm sure that between them, they can handle one scared girl." He turned her to him and planted a soft kiss on her lips. "We could stay here and make out."

"Don't tempt me." She kissed him back before slinging the strap of her purse across her body. "I just need to figure out how to crawl while holding the flashlight."

"I can give you the hat." He took off the hardhat and handed it to her.

"What about you?"

He grinned. "I'll follow your scent."

"Naughty boy." She kissed him and put the hardhat on.

It smelled gross, but given the situation, it was just one more small concession that she had to make.

Crouching, she studied the narrow opening that couldn't be more than three feet in diameter. Orion was tall, and his shoulders were broad. He might have a hard time crawling through it, but since the others had made it to the other side, he should be fine.

Taking in a deep breath, she crawled in. The tunnel was even tighter than she'd imagined, but the hardhat provided plenty of illumination, so at least she could see where her hands were going and that she wasn't touching any creepy-crawlies. If she accidentally put her hand or knee on a scorpion and got stung, she would become more hindrance than help to the rescue mission.

She couldn't have crawled more than five feet when her sleeve snagged on the stone wall, and she heard the fabric tear.

"Damn, there goes a one-thousand-dollar jacket."

Behind her, Orion chuckled. "It's a very nice jacket, but why on earth would you pay that much for a puffer?"

"Amanda. Should I say more?"

"No need. Don't move!"

Suddenly, he was on top of her, and she was squashed beneath his weight.

"Orion! What has gotten into you?"

His arm shot up, and a moment later she heard something land with a squish behind her.

"Sorry about that." He kissed her neck before crawling off her. "There was a spider the size of my hand over your head."

Alena squeaked and redoubled her crawling speed. "Where is it now?"

"It's dead. I squashed it with my hand."

"Are you okay?"

"Except for having spider slime on my hand, yeah, I'm fine."

"Gross. But what if it were poisonous?"

"It wasn't, and normally I wouldn't have killed it, just tossed it aside, but I know how squeamish you are about creepy-crawlies."

Her knight in shining armor, or rather her knight with a slimy hand.

Alena smiled. "Thank you."

As she saw the light at the end of the tunnel, she breathed out. It was only light from the flashlights and hardhats of the others, but right now, it was just as welcome as sunlight.

"I was starting to worry." Arwel offered her a hand, helping her out of the narrow opening. "What took you so long?"

"We had an encounter with a spider." Orion emerged from the small opening.

He looked much worse for wear than she was, with his coat ripped in multiple places but mainly on the shoulders, which was the widest part of him.

"Come take a look." Kalugal beckoned them over. "We found something very interesting."

"What is it?"

"Look at the engraved writing. Jin says this looks like Kra-ell symbols."

"Can you read it?" Alena asked.

Jin shook her head. "Emmett tried to teach us, but it was too difficult, and we decided to focus on understanding spoken language."

"I snapped a photo." Kalugal lifted the device to show her. "When we are back where our phones work, I'll text it to Emmett."

"Check with Kian first," Arwel said. "Or better yet, text it to him, and let him decide if he wants to text it to Emmett or to Vrog."

Alena expected Kalugal to disregard Arwel's suggestion, but to her great surprise, he nodded. "You are right. I don't want to get in the middle of the clan and Kra-ell politics."

"You are part of the clan," Alena said.

"Thank you." He dipped his head. "Nevertheless, I'd rather stay out of its politics."

"People," Jacki said. "Let's find the girl first and investigate the Kra-ell later. We are wasting precious time."

They probably weren't because the girl was no longer there, either because she'd been trapped in the tunnels and died there or because she found a way out. Hopefully, it was the latter and not the former.

ARWEL

*A*rwel wanted it to be over. He wanted Jin and Alena out of the damn tunnels, preferably riding the limousines to the hotel. But it wasn't his show, and no one would listen to him if he suggested abandoning a child to her fate.

Never mind that they were chasing a ghost.

"Which way?" Kalugal asked Jacki.

As she looked between the three openings, Arwel wondered if she'd seen in her vision which one the girl had taken or if she was making things up on the spot.

She was desperate to find the girl, convinced that she was still alive and in need of rescuing, and she might be willing to lie to get them to continue the search.

"This one." Jacki pointed to the opening that was next to the carved words.

As Welgost went ahead once more, Orion examined the carving. "This is not very old." He ran his finger over the grooves. "If you are looking for ancient Kra-ell, that wasn't them."

"How can you be sure?" Kalugal asked. "This is hard rock, not the sandstone that the rest of the structure is carved out from. Sheltered from the elements, it could have been preserved in pristine condition for centuries. And that's a curiosity in itself. How did this stone find its way into these caverns?"

"Could it be a large meteorite?" Carol suggested. "That would explain why this rock is barren while everything in the surrounding area is lush with greenery."

"That's not a bad guess," Kalugal said. "That could also explain why we have no reception. Perhaps the copper has nothing to do with it."

"Haven't you checked?" Arwel asked.

"I didn't have a reason to doubt Jianye's explanation. But perhaps I should bring an expert to investigate the composition of this rock."

"Good idea." Jin turned to Orion. "So, why do you think this was not done by the Kra-ell?"

"I can't read it, but the symbols look familiar. Also, if these were ancient, the edges would have been more rounded. This still looks rough."

"It's not Chinese," Lokan said. "Perhaps it is Tibetan?"

"All clear," Welgost called out from the opening.

This time the tunnel allowed for walking upright, but Arwel and the other males had to bend their heads and hunch their shoulders, or they would have bumped into the tunnel's sides.

"I can't believe that I'm saying this." Alena tapped her hardhat. "But after Orion saved me from a spider in the other tunnel, I'm glad for this stinky headgear protecting my hair from overhead bugs."

"The hero," Jin murmured under her breath.

"He squashed it with his hand," Alena added.

"Ugh, that's gross," Carol said.

Jin shivered. "Yeah, I agree."

Walking behind her, Arwel put his hand on her shoulder in what he'd intended as a reassuring gesture but achieved the opposite.

Uttering a very girly squeak, Jin jumped and bumped her shoulder on the jagged stone wall. "Ouch." She rubbed the spot.

"I'm sorry." Arwel reached for her. "Let me kiss it and make it better."

Turning a pair of angry eyes at him, she batted his hand away. "Why did you do that? You scared the crap out of me. I thought it was a spider."

"I'm sorry," he repeated. "I thought that you weren't scared of them."

"I'm not." She huffed and kept on walking. "That doesn't mean that I like it when one crawls over my body."

The tunnel terminated at a small chamber that was barely big enough to contain all of them.

A pile of firewood in the corner indicated that someone had definitely used it as a shelter, and given the fresh smell, it had been quite recently.

Perhaps a family lived in those tunnels, and the child they were looking for had a father, brothers, and uncles who could pose a threat. Not that a few humans worried him, especially with two powerful compellers in their group, but they could be a nuisance.

"Someone was here recently," Arwel said to Kalugal.

"Evidently."

In addition to the opening they'd come through, there was another opening on the opposite wall, but even though it was dark, Arwel could see the narrow staircase that had been hewn out of the rock. It didn't go down in a straight line but curved a few feet in.

Kalugal took the flashlight from Jacki and aimed it at the shaft. "Did you see the girl going down there?"

Jacki shook her head. "This cavern is where I saw her sitting on the floor, and that's where the vision ended." She turned around and pointed at a niche carved into the stone. "She sat over there, next to the pile of wood. But since there are only two openings in this cavern and we came from that one, she must have used the one going down."

Arwel still thought that they were on a wild goose chase. The people using the tunnels now might have no connection to the girl, and Jacki's vision was about events that hadn't happened recently. The child might have hidden in the cavern, had a good cry, and then gone back the way she'd come.

Kalugal handed Jacki the flashlight back. "Since this is where the vision ended, there is no reason for you to continue. Phinas and I will go down to investigate, while the rest of you head back. You can wait for us in the comfort of the limousines."

His tone brooked no argument, and not because he'd used compulsion. As charming and as easygoing as Kalugal appeared most of the time, he had no problem letting the alpha in him emerge when needed.

Arwel agreed with Kalugal. He wanted Alena and Jin out of the underground, and although he would have preferred to be with them, he knew that Kalugal and Lokan could offer them better protection. Compulsion was a very effective, nonlethal weapon against humans.

Jacki didn't look happy, but she must have realized that arguing with her mate would be futile, or maybe she just feared discovering a body instead of a live girl. "Take Welgost with you as well. Shamash will keep me company, and so will Lokan, Orion, and Arwel. You're not the only one who is worried about your mate's safety." She took his hand and brought it to her cheek. "I worry about you too."

63

ORION

$\mathcal{O}$rion cast a sidelong glance at Alena. Should he go back with her? Or should he volunteer to go with Kalugal?

Perhaps he should replace the guy. After all, Kalugal's mate was pregnant, and he probably wanted to stay by her side. As the leader of their group, he'd felt that he needed to lead the search for the girl, but was he the best-suited male for the task?

From the little Orion had learned about the guy from Geraldine and Alena, he'd been a warrior earlier in his life, but many decades had passed since then, and during that time the only battleground Kalugal had seen was on Wall Street.

"I should go." Orion turned to Arwel. "You're a trained Guardian, and you have experience dealing with traumatized girls. I think you should come with me, and Kalugal should go back with Jacki."

When Alena put a hand on his bicep, he thought that she was going to object to his proposal, but she smiled and nodded, approving and encouraging.

He could fall in love with her just for that.

Hell, who was he kidding? He was already in love with her, and the twinge of guilt that rushed through him at the realization wasn't as bad as he'd expected.

Miriam would have approved of Alena.

Jin huffed. "If you macho guys are all done flexing your muscles and thumping your chests, I suggest that we start moving." She shone her flashlight at the opening and started down the stairs.

"Hold on." Arwel rushed after her. "Let's talk it over."

"There is nothing to discuss. Orion is right. Kalugal should go with Jacki, and you should search for the girl because you are the best-trained member of our group." She cast Welgost an apologetic smile. "I know that you were a soldier, but that was a long time ago. Arwel is an active Guardian."

"Orion, Phinas, and I will go." Arwel took hold of her arm. "You should go with Jacki, Carol, and Alena. I want you to watch their backs."

As they looked into each other's eyes, a silent exchange passed between them, and at the end of it, Jin nodded. "Fine." She looked at Kalugal. "Are you okay with this plan?"

Smiling, he wrapped his arm around Jacki's waist. "I'd rather stay by my mate's side, so yes, I find this plan acceptable."

Orion wondered what Arwel's comment and Jin's subsequent acquiescence was about. What had Arwel meant when he'd told Jin to watch the ladies' backs? Didn't he trust Kalugal and Lokan? They were Alena's cousins. Maybe he was worried about Welgost and Shamash?

Or perhaps it had just been an excuse to convince Jin to head back with the others, but Orion doubted she would have fallen for that if she didn't believe that she was needed. But for what? She looked like a fierce female, but she wasn't a Guardian.

"Let's move out, gentlemen." Arwel picked up a stick from the pile and cast one last glance at his mate before heading down the tunnel.

"Be safe." Alena took off the hardhat, put it on top of his head, and kissed his cheek before turning around and following Lokan and Carol into the tunnel they'd come through.

Orion watched her until she disappeared inside and then followed Phinas down the steps.

The stairwell was narrow and its ceiling low, forcing them to bend and hunch, but thanks to their hardhats, the shaft was well lit.

The going was slow, with Arwel carefully assessing the stairs and tapping with his stick before putting his foot on the next one. "I think we are below the waterline," he said. "I wonder if this is an escape route for the outpost."

"Could be." Orion looked behind him at Phinas. "It seemed odd to me that the place had just one gate. Typically, even a settlement as small as this one would have two or three exit points. Strategically, it's not wise to have just one entrance."

"I'm surprised that we didn't encounter any traps." Arwel kept his routine of tapping each stair before placing his foot on it.

"Why would there be traps on an escape route?" Phinas asked.

"To slow down anyone chasing those escaping." Arwel stopped. "Can you smell that?"

Orion sniffed the air. "Smell what?"

"Fresh water. There must be an underground reservoir nearby."

"Oh, that. Yeah, I smelled the water, but I thought it was the river above us. What makes you think that there is a subterranean source?"

"It smells different than the aboveground running water," Arwel said.

Orion sniffed the air again, noting the subtle difference. "Yeah, I can smell the difference. Now that you've brought it to my attention, I can smell both sources of water."

64

ALENA

*A*s their group emerged at the second cavern, Alena didn't relish the prospect of crawling back through the narrow tunnel into the first big chamber, especially without Orion watching her back.

This time it was Shamash behind her, and she was very conscious of him watching her butt as she slowly crawled ahead of him.

Welgost got to the other side first, and the vile curse she heard him utter didn't bode well. When a few seconds later his sentiment was repeated by Jacki, just in less flowery language, Alena knew that they were in trouble.

"We are trapped," Jin said. "How did they move that damned boulder back?"

As Lokan offered Alena a hand to help her out of the narrow opening, the darkness that greeted her confirmed what her friends had said. The opening they'd created by moving the boulder aside was closed, and the ladder was gone.

"What the hell?" Carol dusted her pants off. "Who could have done that?"

"And why?" Lokan asked.

"Maybe the Chinese government wants us dead." Carol sat on the ground and leaned against the stone wall. "What do we do now?"

Kalugal looked up at where the opening was. "I don't think that they moved the boulder back because that would have been impossible for humans to do without proper equipment. They probably covered the opening with something lighter. The problem is that it doesn't matter what's up there because none of us can jump that high, and even if someone could, he couldn't jump and push whatever is blocking the entrance at the same time."

"We need to build a ramp," Lokan said. "Phinas took the hammer, though. I can turn around and catch up to them, have them come here and help us. Between the seven of us, we could take turns hammering at the walls and chipping rocks to build the ramp from."

Kalugal shook his head. "That would take days."

"Do you have a better idea?" his brother asked.

"Yeah. We need to find another exit. Those stairs back there probably lead out of the outpost."

Kalugal tried to sound unconcerned, but Alena could hear the worry in his tone. Heck, she was worried too. Would her Odus come to look for her if she didn't return to the hotel by nightfall? Would they even know where to look for her?

"There is no need to panic," Kalugal said. "Even if we don't find another exit, our drivers will eventually come looking for us, and we can shout to them that we are trapped down here."

"What if the drivers were the ones who did it?" Carol asked. "They looked fishy."

"If not them, then my partner and his crew will come back on Monday and find us. It's not like we can die down here." He cast a worried look at Jacki. "As long as we find water, we should be fine until we are found."

With a sigh, Alena walked over to where Carol was sitting on the ground and joined her. "I should have listened to my intuition and stayed on the riverbank when we found out that our cellphones don't work here."

"Let's get back to where Arwel, Orion, and Phinas went," Jacki said. "I don't want to just sit here and wait."

Kalugal nodded. "I want Jacki to rest for a few minutes, and then we will turn around and join the others."

"Someone needs to stay here," Lokan said. "In case anyone comes looking for us."

"They wouldn't know to look down here." Kalugal rubbed a hand over the back of his neck. "If not for Jacki's vision, we wouldn't have known that there is anything down here."

Alena pulled out her phone, but it still had no reception. "What if we play music? I have some songs stored on my phone. If I put it on full volume, whoever is on top might hear it."

"I have music too." Carol pulled her phone out of her purse. "When yours dies, I will play mine."

"My phone is fully charged." Alena looked at Kalugal. "When we go back, I can leave it here playing as loud as it can go."

Jin, who'd been pacing the entire time, stopped and turned to Kalugal. "Whoever did that wants us dead. I'm afraid for Arwel and the others. What if there is another entrance and the enemy is waiting on the other side to finish us off?"

Alena jumped to her feet. "We need to warn them."

"I'll catch up to them," Lokan looked at Carol. "You can follow at a slower pace."

"We go together," Kalugal said. "It was a mistake to split up."

65

ARWEL

"*D*on't you think that we can go a little faster?" Orion said as Arwel prodded the next stair with the tip of his staff. "We've traversed at least a hundred stairs, and none of them were rigged. I think it's safe to assume that there are no hidden traps in here."

"I prefer to err on the side of caution." Arwel went down another step and prodded the next two.

The smell of water was getting stronger. By now, they were so deep in the ground that the river was probably flowing overhead, and he was smelling both the river and an underground reservoir that was massive.

Another two stairs down, another tap, and then a faint click that he'd almost missed. The split second it had taken the sound to register in Arwel's mind might have cost him his life if he were human. Only his fast reflexes saved him from getting skewered as he hurled himself back and slammed into Orion, who slammed into Phinas, and what saved them from tumbling down head over heels was the narrowness of the passage. They were wedged between the two walls.

Orion groaned. "Remind me never to doubt you again."

Arwel chuckled. "You can bet on it." He pushed himself off the guy and looked at the rusted bolt that was embedded in the stone wall right where his neck had been a moment ago.

As he examined the rigging mechanism, Arwel was impressed by its simplicity and effectiveness. A piece of rebar, a couple of strings, and a well-hidden plate on the stair that had been camouflaged with dirt.

"This is all done with modern materials." He showed the others. "Someone is using these tunnels, and he or she has enemies they fear."

"What makes you think that?" Orion asked. "Maybe there is a hidden treasure down here, and whoever is guarding it wants to eliminate anyone who gets close."

"Perhaps." Arwel looked down the stairs to where his staff had fallen. "We will need to be extra careful from here on out. If there was one trap, there will be others. We go slow."

"We haven't been going fast," Phinas grumbled. "Do you want to use my hammer?"

"Keep it. It's not long enough."

"That's what she said." Orion laughed. "I'm sorry, but I just couldn't help myself. You two were asking for it."

Arwel rolled his eyes but smiled nonetheless. The joke defused some of the tension.

Without his staff, Arwel had to resort to brushing over each step with the tip of his shoe, moving the dirt to check for hidden plates.

Thankfully, no more traps were sprung until he reached his stick. Clutching it, he'd never been more grateful for a piece of wood.

Five steps down, another click sounded, and this time, Arwel immediately jumped back, but instead of a bolt firing at him from the side of the stairwell, an avalanche of rocks fell, pelting the three of them, but mostly Arwel, who was closest.

"Damn it." He brushed the rocks off him. "I didn't expect that."

"Are you okay?" Orion asked. "I smell blood."

"It's nothing." Arwel wiped his bloody forehead with the sleeve of his jacket. "It will heal in a moment."

The next fifteen steps didn't trigger any new traps, and as Arwel had suspected, at the bottom of the staircase was an underground water basin, housed in an enormous natural cavern.

Shafts of pale light shone from holes high above, which meant that they'd cleared the river and were well on the other side of it.

"An entire village could hide here," Orion said. "If there are fish in the water, they could have survived here indefinitely."

"Indeed." Arwel looked around, checking for possible exits, traps, storage bins, fire pits, any signs of habitation, but the place looked like it had never been visited by humans. Except, given the hewn-out stairs leading down to it, people had made use of this hidden gem in the past, and with some digging, Kalugal's team would probably find evidence of that.

"Perhaps the girl is hiding somewhere down here," he said more to himself than his companions.

"She wouldn't have died of thirst here, that's for sure," Phinas said. "And if she knew how to fish, she could have survived on that. But I wonder how she avoided triggering the traps."

"Maybe she wasn't heavy enough," Orion said.

Arwel shook his head. "I doubt that those primitive traps were calibrated for weight. She must have known which steps to avoid."

ALIYA

*A*liya watched the intruders from her perch high above the cavern. They didn't know yet that they were trapped, but they would discover that soon when they made their way back.

With the other entrance blocked, the only way out was through the lake, then a climb up the rock face to where the opening to the staircase was, and then up the stairs to the surface.

It would never occur to them to swim across the nearly freezing water, and even if it did, they wouldn't find the entrance to the staircase.

She still couldn't understand how they'd known to push the boulder aside to get into the large chamber, or how they'd known to break through the barrier she'd so carefully camouflaged and find the other entrance to the tunnel system. It had taken her many days to block that entrance and make it look like the rest of the stone wall, so even if someone got into the large cavern, they wouldn't suspect that it served as an entrance to an extensive system of tunnels.

No one was supposed to know about it, and even the crew searching for artifacts in the ruins had no clue that it was there.

But these men weren't regular humans.

Humans wouldn't have been able to move that boulder without a bulldozer, and other than the rope ladder they'd used to go down into the large cavern, she hadn't found anything that would indicate the use of pulleys or anything else that could have helped them move it. The system of pulleys she'd constructed was still hidden in the same spot she'd left it, safely stowed away in one of the ancient, ruined dwellings.

When she'd discovered that her hiding place had been compromised, Aliya had been certain that the Kra-ell had somehow found her, but looking at these males now, she was no longer sure.

Two of them had dark hair and olive-toned skin, so perhaps they were hybrids, but the third was too fair to be a Kra-ell. As sunlight from one of the shafts hit his hair, it gleamed with golden hues, a color no Kra-ell or a hybrid she'd known ever had.

The question was what she was going to do with them. She couldn't just wait for them to die because it might take months until they starved to death, and what was she supposed to do in the meantime?

Besides, these three couldn't be the only ones who'd entered the tunnels. When she'd returned from her hunt, Aliya had found two limousines parked on the river-bank. The human drivers had been smoking and chatting as they'd waited for their customers to return, completely oblivious to the huntress who could take them down with two well-aimed arrows.

Not that she would.

Humans were not her friends, but they weren't her enemies either, and taking a life without proper cause was an affront to the Mother of All Life.

As Aliya examined the way the males were dressed, they didn't impress her as rich guys who would hire two limousines with drivers for just the three of them.

She'd seen some of the wealthy tourists visiting the Mosuo villages, and they'd been much better dressed.

The three must have split up from a larger group, and the others were probably somewhere else in the labyrinth of tunnels.

It had been a stupid move to block the other entrance.

If she'd thought it through instead of succumbing to the surge of rage and thirst for vengeance that had clouded her mind, she wouldn't have done it. But all she could think about was killing them all, and she hadn't stopped to consider that this was her home, and she didn't want anyone rotting away in it. Not even her enemies.

Now that the rage had subsided and reason returned, Aliya considered unblocking the other entrance. If these intruders didn't find what they were looking for, they would just leave and never come back.

What were they looking for, though?

Had they come for her?

How did they even know that she was here?

She'd been hiding for years, and no one in the Mosuo village should remember her because she'd compelled them to forget her.

Perhaps they'd come for the same reason she and her mother originally had.

Either way, they weren't going to find anything, she'd made sure of that, and if they could, they would eventually leave.

She needed to unlock the entrance now before it was too late and they discovered that the ladder was gone and the boulder was back in place. That would give her away as surely as if she'd walked up to them and flashed her fangs.

For them to remain oblivious to her presence, she had to put everything back the way it was, and hopefully they wouldn't notice that things were not precisely as they'd left them.

But to do that, she needed to wait for these three to get out of the cavern. If these were indeed Kra-ell hybrids, which was the most logical explanation for their ability to move the boulder, they would notice her the moment she moved.

But to get to her, they would have to swim through the lake, and by the time they made it to the other side she would be long gone. Except, that would defy the purpose of the entire operation.

They would know that she'd been hiding in these tunnels, and in order to escape them, she would have to run away and keep running because they would come after her.

Her only option to eliminate the threat was to kill them all, including the limousine drivers. But even though the Mother might forgive her for taking those lives in self-defense, Aliya didn't want the humans' deaths on her conscience.

67

ORION

"*W*ell, this looks like a dead end." Orion turned in a circle. "The visibility is pretty good thanks to the shafts drilled through the earth, and there are no other openings that I can see. Unless she had a boat here and rowed away, she must have found some other way to get out of here."

"She could have swum," Phinas said. "What I wonder is who made those shafts and why."

"The same people who dug out the tunnels and carved the stairs out of the rock." Crouching next to the small subterranean lake, Arwel put his hand in the water. "If she swam through, she would have suffered from hypothermia and drowned. The water is too cold for a human to survive."

That seemed like an awful way to die, but he reminded himself that the girl might have never existed, and if she had, it had been a long time ago and she'd got out before someone rolled the boulder over the opening to block it.

In fact, he was quite sure that if a child got lost in these tunnels and was later found by her parents, the villagers would have pooled their resources to block the entrance and prevent other children from playing dangerous games.

"Maybe she wasn't human," Phinas said. "Or maybe she was a spirit. Don't forget that we are chasing after a phantom seen in a vision. You all seem to give it a lot of credence and given that the vision was my boss's mate's and it was about a child, I didn't argue or question the wisdom of it. But we've reached the end of the line. We should go back."

"You can't." Lokan walked out of the tunnel opening. "Someone removed the ladder and pushed the boulder back over the hole. We need to find another exit."

"Where are the others?" Arwel asked.

"Making their way over. I convinced Kalugal to let me run ahead to warn you in case the perpetrators were planning an ambush." He looked around the cave. "Did you check the perimeter? There are plenty of hiding places in these rocks, and we are easy targets standing here in the light coming down these shafts. Someone might shoot us from there." He pointed at the stone wall across the water and the many ledges and niches that were visible from where they stood.

There were probably many further down that they couldn't see.

"We can handle ourselves," Arwel said. "You should have stayed behind to protect the ladies."

"With how narrow these passages are, it wouldn't have made a difference, and we feared for you." Lokan smiled at Arwel. "Your mate wanted to be the one to rush over, but I convinced her to stay with the group and let me go ahead." He looked at the hammer in Phinas's hand. "If we don't find another exit, our only option would be to build a ramp, and this hammer might be what saves us."

Arwel shook his head. "Who could have blocked the entrance and why?"

"Beats me." Lokan lifted his eyes to the shafts of light. "It looks like we are only forty feet or so from the surface. Maybe we can climb up and enlarge one of the openings."

As Orion shifted his gaze to where Lokan was pointing, he caught a movement from the corner of his eyes. Quickly turning his head in that direction, he saw a long black braid whipping around a protrusion that was high up on the stone wall across the small lake. It lasted no longer than a split second, and then it was gone.

"There!" He pointed. "I saw her. There must be an exit on the other side."

"Are you sure that it was the girl?"

"All I saw was a long dark braid. It could have been an adult male for all I know."

"We need to follow her." Arwel started removing his clothes.

"What are you doing?" Orion asked.

"Yeah." Jin entered, followed by the others. "Are you nuts?"

Arwel removed his shoes and socks. "I'm going to swim over to the other side, but I don't want my clothes to get wet, so I'm going to make a bundle and tie it to my head. That way I can put them back on when I get there."

"Smart thinking." Orion started undressing as well.

Phinas hesitated for a moment, but then turned to Lokan and handed him the hammer. "This is yours now, in case you'll need to build the ramp after all."

68

ALIYA

*A*liya ran, her long legs taking the narrow stairs four at a time, her arms pumping, her breath leaving her mouth in a mist as it met the cold air.

She'd been up and down these accursed stairs so many times, her leg muscles didn't have to strain as hard as theirs no doubt would, and she could outrun them. Not expecting anyone to get that far, she hadn't rigged them with traps, so there was nothing to slow them down.

How had they evaded the traps she'd set on the other staircase?

What to do now? Where would she go?

When the fourth male entered the cavern and started talking to the other three, Aliya had hoped that they would be distracted enough not to notice her moving around the ledge and ducking into the stairwell. But one of them must have heard her, confirming her suspicion that they were not human.

How many of them were there?

The fourth one said something about the others coming, and Aliya thought that she'd heard a woman's voice, but she wasn't sure. Was it a good or bad sign that they had females with them?

She didn't know and couldn't risk finding out. Her only option was to run as far away from this place as she could and start over somewhere else.

As bitter tears stung the corners of her eyes, she wiped them away with her sleeve and kept racing to the top.

Life had been hard enough for her as it was, and starting from scratch with nothing but the clothes on her back was terrifying.

But maybe it was time.

She'd lived in these ruins for far too long, only venturing into the village when she had no other choice. Maybe someplace else, people would be more accepting of a hybrid freak like her. Maybe she could blend in better and pretend to be human.

The Mother had gifted her with an uncanny ability to learn new languages fast, and Aliya had taught herself English, Japanese, and a little bit of Swedish, the languages spoken by most of the tourists who loved visiting the Mosuo.

There was no way she could blend in among the Japanese, but she might be able to do so among the Americans or the Europeans.

Except, she had no money, nothing she could trade, and she wasn't willing to steal anything that was not necessary for her survival. Food and small tools were okay, and they didn't cause real hardship to those she stole from, but stealing money was on a different level, one she'd hoped never to stoop to.

Today, though, was the day she'd been fearing for years. Her enemies had found her and were either going to kill her or drag her with them to their stronghold. So today was not a day to stick to her morals and principles. Today, she was going to ignore them all to survive.

If she made it out before they caught up to her, she would compel the two human drivers to leave their passengers behind, sending one driving all the way to Lijiang, and the other one to drive her to Shangri-La. She'd heard the tourists talking about it, and it was supposed to be a beautiful place. She didn't know whether it was big or small, but she knew it wasn't too far away.

Or maybe she should compel the driver to take her all the way to Beijing?

Her mother had told her that it was a marvelous city with many millions of people, and Aliya tried to imagine that many people in one place. Supposedly, that was where they came from. Not from the city itself, but somewhere in that area.

She had never left the compound before they'd been forced to leave, and she didn't remember the area or the names of the towns and villages they'd passed through. She had been just a young girl, traumatized, scared, and she remembered very little of their journey across the country.

Perhaps it wouldn't be wise to go to Beijing if it was so close to that place of blood and loss. Perhaps she should ask the driver about another big city where a strange-looking woman could disappear.

69

ALENA

*A*s Orion stripped to his undershorts, Alena shivered, but it wasn't because she was excited to see his magnificent body. It was a sympathetic response. It was so cold in the cavern, and the water was even colder. The subterranean lake wasn't big, it was more of a large pond, and it wouldn't take them long to get to the other side, but if they were human, they probably wouldn't have made it. Hypothermia would have disabled them in minutes.

"How did that person get to the other side?"

"Probably from the outside." Arwel gave Jin a quick hug before wading into the water with his bundle of clothes tied around his head like a strange-looking turban.

How did he expect to keep that from falling into the water?

"Be safe." Alena helped Orion tie his own bundle in a similar fashion.

"Don't worry." He gave her a quick kiss before following Arwel and Phinas, who were already swimming with steady, measured strokes and keeping their heads upright.

"It's all my fault." Jacki let out a breath. "That vision must have been of a past or future event, and I shouldn't have roped everyone into following. Now we are stuck here." She walked to where Lokan was guarding the entrance to the tunnel with Phinas's hammer and lowered herself to the ground. "At least we have water, right? We can survive here for a long time."

"We won't have to." Kalugal sat down next to her. "Arwel, Orion, and Phinas will find the exit, come around, and move the boulder. We will be out of here in time for lunch."

Jin grimaced. "Don't talk about food. I'm hungry."

They'd eaten a big breakfast, so Jin's hunger was probably the result of stress and not a need for food.

Kalugal glanced at his watch. "It's after two in the afternoon. I wonder if our drivers are starting to get worried."

"I just hope that they are still there." Carol joined them on the ground. "And I hope our guys are not rushing into a trap."

While Arwel had been tying up his bundle of clothes, he'd told them about the traps he'd sprung on the stairs coming down. The rest of them had been lucky that there hadn't been more.

As the three men walked out of the water on the other side, their bundles of clothing still on their heads, Alena let out a relieved breath. The three of them were shivering badly, but as they quickly got dressed, the shivering stopped.

Orion waved at her before starting the climb to where he'd seen that dark braid, the other two following him up.

"We found another staircase!" Arwel shouted. "We are going in."

"Be careful!" Lokan yelled back. "Watch out for traps!"

As an answer, Phinas gave him a two-fingered salute and ducked behind the ledge after the others.

Pushing to her feet, Alena started pacing along the pond's shore. "This whole thing doesn't make sense unless there are Kra-ell hiding in these tunnels. They would have been strong enough to push the boulder back. Jacki's vision might have accidentally sent us straight into their lair."

"Perhaps it wasn't accidental," Jacki murmured. "What if the Fates wanted us to find them?"

"There are no Kra-ell in here," Lokan said. "If there were, we would already be dead. I wouldn't be surprised if some local punks decided to play a trick on a bunch of tourists just to amuse themselves. From what I read about the Mosuo, the women do everything, and the men have very little to do, which is not healthy for young males. If they are not kept busy working or training, they are bound to get into trouble. Young bucks have excess energy they need to dispense one way or another."

Alena doubted that was the explanation, but Carol seemed to agree. "Boys can do some really stupid things when they are bored. Stupid, cruel, and sometimes even deadly."

"What about the girl?" Jacki said. "Do you think she might have used the other exit to get out of here?"

Alena nodded. "Maybe in the summer, the water is not as cold, and she could swim over."

"It wasn't summer in my vision." Jacki shifted her weight. "She wore a puffer, remember?"

"Maybe she had a raft or a boat hidden somewhere here," Carol said.

70

ALIYA

$\mathcal{A}$s Aliya pushed open the wooden grate at the top of the staircase and peeked out, she cursed. The damn limousines had vanished along with her escape plan.

Her other option was the canoe she'd left on the other side of the ruins, but that meant running across the rope bridge, entering through the gate, and climbing down the rope she'd anchored to the top of the wall.

Except, the canoe could only take her down the river to the lake, and that would not solve her problem of having no home and nowhere to hide. She would have to go into the village and use her hypnotic power to coerce one of the matrons to allow her into her household and give her a place to hide.

It was a shitty plan, but it was better than nothing. Right now, she had to evade the men chasing her and make sure that they didn't know where to find her or that she was even there.

They couldn't have seen much of her on that ledge, not enough to know that she was the one they were looking for, so she might be able to pull it off, but she needed to move fast.

She had a decent head start on them, but they would probably reach the surface before she could make it to her boat, and even if she made it, they would see her rowing down the river.

The good thing was that without a boat of their own, they couldn't follow her unless they swam after her. The bad thing was that they would see her and her canoe and would know where she was headed.

Glancing at the dense greenery behind her, Aliya considered for a moment running into the woods and hiding there until they left. The advantage of that plan was that it would give her time to formulate her next step. The problem with that was that if these men were Kra-ell, they were excellent hunters, and without a large body of water to mask her scent, they would be able to find her and hunt her down.

The river was her only option.

Heaving herself out of the hole, Aliya grabbed the grate and shoved it back in place before sprinting toward the bridge. She wasn't sure that it had been wise to waste that extra second putting it back. If they were strong enough to move the boulder, they would have no problem moving the heavy grate out of the way. Still, it might slow them for a moment.

As she cleared it on the other side, she heard a thud that sounded a lot like the grate hitting the ground and allowed herself one look over her shoulder, gasping when she saw one of the males emerge from the hole.

How in the name of the Mother had they caught up to her so fast? They would have had to swim through the lake and climb up the wall, which should have taken them between five and ten minutes. They shouldn't have been able to close the gap by climbing the stairs faster than she had.

If they were that fast, there was no way she was going to make it to the boat before they caught up to her.

Fear adding power to her tired muscles, she ran even faster, leaping over piles of rocks and dodging the larger ones. The good thing was that she was very familiar with the place and knew where all the obstacles were. The bad thing was that she could hear them gaining on her.

71

ORION

 rion pushed the grate up, tossed it aside, and heaved himself up the rest of the way to clear the hole. He didn't wait for Arwel and Phinas and sprinted after the woman.

The dark braid flying behind her identified her as the one he'd seen on the ledge in the cavern, but she was definitely not the girl from Jacki's vision.

Given her height and speed, she was not only a fully grown woman, but also immortal, either a descendant of the gods or the Kra-ell. The way she was sprinting and leaping over obstacles could have won her a gold medal in the human Olympics, and even though he was pushing himself to the limit, he was barely gaining on her.

Behind him he could hear his two companions running, and as he hit the bridge, he had to slow down once they jumped on and the whole thing swung and shook. He wasn't afraid of hurting himself in a fall, but he couldn't afford the lost time that would cost him the female.

The thing was, Orion wasn't even sure why he was chasing after her other than the need to get answers. Now that they had found a way out of the tunnel system, they would somehow manage to move the boulder and get the others out of there as well.

Except, the female couldn't have been operating alone. Even an immortal couldn't have moved the boulder and blocked the entrance to the tunnel by herself. She'd either had help or knew who had done that.

Were there more immortals hiding in the area?

Were the tunnels their home?

And why did they want to trap a group of people whom they must have assumed were innocent tourists?

Had they done it before?

Was that what happened to the young girl in Jacki's vision?

Anger over the needless cruelty adding fuel to his leg muscles, Orion ran faster, closing the distance between himself and the fleeing female.

She climbed the steps to the top of the wall with incredible speed, but he was even faster, and when he was almost within reach of her, she leaped over the side of the wall.

Without thinking, he leaped after her, grabbed the back of her jacket and twisted midair, hurling them both back into the hollowed-out ruins.

Their fall wasn't graceful, with him absorbing the brunt of it with his back, her landing on top of him, and the both of them rolling down the steps right into Arwel and Phinas and taking them along for the ride.

As soon as they stopped rolling down, she leaped and started running again.

This time, Arwel chased after her while Orion checked himself for broken bones.

His reprieve didn't last long, though.

Both Arwel and Phinas were getting their asses handed to them by that slim female, probably because they were trying not to hurt her, but she was not only incredibly strong and desperate, she was also terrifying.

If he didn't know about the Kra-ell, he would have thought her a demon.

Red blazing eyes, fangs as long as his, and a crazed expression on her face, she snarled, kicked, bit, and punched whatever part she could reach on the two males trying to apprehend her without hurting her.

Their fangs didn't even elongate.

Orion wondered whether it was physically impossible for an immortal male to respond with aggression to a female even if she was the one attacking, or were Arwel and Phinas just capable of great self-control?

That being said, if he didn't knock her out, she might manage to escape. Besides, she was hurting his friends, and that was unacceptable.

With a groan, Orion grabbed a rock, heaved himself up, and got into the fray. He didn't waste time trying to grab hold of the snarling beast. As soon as the opportunity presented itself, he hit the back of her head with just enough force to knock her out but not kill her.

Her red eyes rolling back in her head, she crumpled to the ground.

Breathing heavily, Arwel bent down, bracing his hands on his thighs. "Thank you." He lifted his head and smiled at Orion. "It has been a long time since someone handed me my ass like that, and never a female. Now I understand how Anandur and Brundar felt after Wonder took both of them down."

"That's a story I want to hear," Phinas said before turning his face sideways and spitting out blood. "We should tie her down before she comes round. I don't think I can last another round with her."

He'd said that with a straight face, but Orion was sure Phinas was exaggerating.

Arwel shook his head. "Do you think ropes would hold her?"

"Do you have a better idea?" Orion crouched next to the unconscious woman and checked her pulse, relieved to find it going nice and steady.

He still didn't know much about immortals and even less about the Kra-ell, who the woman obviously was. Orion had been careful with the force he'd applied, but a blow to the head could cause serious damage even to an immortal, as evidenced by what had happened to Geraldine.

"She's fine." Arwel rubbed a hand over his bruised neck. "I can hear her heartbeat. Did any of you notice that our rides are gone?"

Orion hadn't, and given Phinas's grimace, he hadn't either.

The limousines had been parked on the other side of the ruins, not visible from where they were standing.

"How will we get back to the hotel?" Phinas asked. "And what are we going to do with the hellion?"

72

ARWEL

"We need to get to the others." Arwel bent down, hefted the unconscious woman up, and slung her over his shoulder. "For such a skinny thing, she's surprisingly heavy."

"And strong like two males," Phinas said. "I'm still waiting to hear the story of how Wonder overpowered Anandur and Brundar."

"I'll tell you about it on the plane back home, but the gist of it is that Wonder is also incredibly strong, but unlike this one, she's not a fighter."

"Then how did she overpower two Head Guardians?" Phinas fell in step with him.

"She was pushed into using her strength by the circumstances."

"This lady might have felt the same about us," Orion said. "Are we taking her with us?"

"I don't know. We need to find out where the rest of her tribe is. I didn't hear or feel anyone in the tunnels, but then I didn't feel her either until we started chasing her up the stairs. She emitted very little emotion."

Orion dusted his clothes off as best he could, but he'd taken quite a fall, and even before that, his clothing wasn't in great shape. Arwel could only imagine the reaction of the hotel's concierge when he saw them coming in looking like that.

"Can the three of us move the boulder?" Orion asked.

"Let's check whether it is in fact the boulder that's blocking the entry." Arwel adjusted the woman draped over his shoulder like a sack of potatoes. "If she was working alone, she might have pushed over something lighter to close the opening."

"We need to tie her up," Orion said, "before she starts waking up." He looked at the ground and picked up a round rock. "I have a feeling that I will need this again."

"Aren't you a compeller?" Phinas asked. "Why don't you just compel her to obey you?"

Orion snorted. "In all the commotion, it didn't even occur to me. I could have yelled at her to stop instead of chasing after her." He tossed the stone aside. "Would compelling this woman be sanctioned by the clan, though? I don't want to break any rules."

What had Alena done to the guy to make him so afraid to use his talent?

Arwel hoped that she hadn't invoked some nonexistent clan rules about compulsion to keep him in check because there were none. What applied to thralling also applied to compulsion, restricting its use to concealment of immortals' existence and matters of clan security.

Both of those applied to the situation, and yet Orion seemed hesitant to use compulsion on the woman.

"In my capacity as Head Guardian," Arwel said. "I'm authorized to give you permission to compel this woman to cooperate with us. But even if I wasn't here, this is a very clear case of protecting clan members. The same circumstances that allow thralling also allow compulsion."

"Good to know. So, we don't need to tie her up?"

"It depends on how strong of a compeller you are, and how susceptible she is to compulsion. You might need that rock after all."

Arwel's empathic ability picked up on the woman's fear a moment before she bucked up and tried to escape his hold.

"Don't move!" Orion said.

The woman stopped her struggles, but Arwel was paralyzed as well, and so was Phinas.

Fates, how Arwel hated the feeling of having his will taken over by another. He still remembered how helpless and desperate he'd felt when Kalugal had captured him.

Unlike Kalugal though, Orion used his compulsion like a sledgehammer instead of a delicate scalpel. It was powerful but unrefined. Perhaps he needed to take lessons from the master.

It took Orion a moment to realize that what he'd done stretched further than he'd intended, and then he said, "Arwel and Phinas, you can move."

"Thank you," Arwel bit out. "Compulsion is a precise art. When you imbue your words with compulsion, you should be very careful with how you phrase things and who you direct them at."

The woman groaned, but the command not to move also prevented her from moving her lips, so she couldn't speak.

"I'll be damned," Arwel said as he saw the boulder covering the entrance. "I need to question the lady." He lowered her to the ground, arranging her body so she was leaning against the boulder.

Her eyes were wild with terror, and her fangs were fully elongated and protruding over her lips. Compulsion didn't work on involuntary body functions, to which the elongating of fangs and venom creation belonged.

"Ask her where the rest of her people are, and command her to tell the truth."

Orion crouched in front of the terrified woman. "We mean you no harm. You have nothing to fear from us. But we need to get our friends out of the tunnels, and one of the women is pregnant, so swimming in near-freezing water is out of the question. We need to move that boulder, and we can't move it alone. We need the help of your tribesmen."

73

ALIYA

*T*he male who'd commanded Aliya's body not to move had kind eyes, and he wasn't Kra-ell. He wasn't human either, though.

What was he?

And did he and his friends really mean her no harm? The way they chased her down had implied otherwise, but given that one of the members of their group was a pregnant female, it was no wonder that they'd been so desperate to find a way out that didn't involve her swimming through the subterranean lake's freezing water.

Still, even though Aliya could understand why they had chased her with such determination, she couldn't tell him that she was alone. The Mother only knew what they would do to her if they found out that no one would come to her rescue.

"Answer me truthfully. Where are the other members of your tribe?" When she didn't answer, he narrowed his eyes at her, and they no longer looked kind. "You are allowed to move your mouth, and you are allowed to speak, but you are not allowed to move your hands or legs, and you are not allowed to bite or head-butt any of us either."

The one with the shoulder-length tawny hair chuckled. "You're learning, Orion. That was a very precise compulsion. But what if she doesn't speak English?"

Orion didn't shift his eyes as he answered the male. "She understood when I commanded her not to move." Staring into her eyes, he asked, "Where is the rest of your tribe?"

"I don't know." Her spoken English was good, but her accent was terrible.

If she didn't make any effort to make it better, maybe they wouldn't be able to understand her. The one named Orion hadn't commanded her to speak clearly. She couldn't keep her mouth shut and refuse to answer him, but she could mumble her responses in her bad accent.

"What's your name?"

She wanted to resist the command, but it was impossible. "Aliya," she blurted.

He smiled. "That's a very nice name. How come you don't know where the rest of your tribe is?"

"Most are dead. Some might have been taken away."

She suspected that the bad Kra-ell hadn't attacked just for the fun of it. They had probably been after the pureblooded females, and maybe even after the hybrid girls. Females were most precious to the Kra-ell, and there weren't enough of them to go around. The males had to share them, and maybe some had thought to fix the situation by abducting the females of another tribe.

Orion frowned, but she didn't know whether it was because he hadn't understood her or because of her answer.

The tawny-haired guy crouched next to Orion. "Were you a member of Jade's tribe?"

Aliya's heart stopped, or at least that was what it felt like. How could he have known about that unless he was one of the attackers? But they had been Kra-ell. Or maybe not?

It wasn't like she'd seen them.

She'd escaped along with all the other humans that had been told to leave and forget that they'd ever lived in a Kra-ell compound. The command to forget had worked on the humans, but not on her, and yet the male in front of her was holding her imprisoned in her own body with hardly any effort.

Then again, neither he nor his companions looked like they had even a drop of Kra-ell blood in them. Orion's eyes were the kind of purple blue no Kra-ell or hybrid she'd ever seen had. The other one's were turquoise, a color that the Kra-ell eyes sometimes turned, but the rest of him didn't match. The third one had brown eyes, olive-toned skin and dark brown hair, so he could potentially be a hybrid, but he also looked too human to be one.

What if not all Kra-ell looked the same, though? What if there were others who looked like these men?

"Answer my question," he commanded.

"Yes." She spat on the ground between his legs. "Were you one of the murderers who killed my father?"

His eyes softened. "Neither my friends nor I had anything to do with that."

The tawny-headed male smiled, revealing two rows of teeth that looked very human. "As you can see, we are not Kra-ell. We are a different breed of immortals. Fate brought two members of your tribe to us, and they told us about Jade and about the attack. We came here because of the Mosuo. Their tradition and lifestyle so closely resemble that of the Kra-ell that we suspected it was influenced by them."

"If there are no others," the third male said, "how the hell did you move that boulder by yourself?"

Aliya could answer that without being compelled to. Baring her fangs, she smiled at him. "As you've experienced, I'm very strong."

"You're not that strong." He turned to the compeller. "Make her tell us how she did that. Jacki, Kalugal and the others are waiting to hear from us, and I want to get them out of those damn tunnels. We need to somehow move that rock."

Orion nodded. "Tell me how you moved the boulder, Aliya."

"With the help of pulleys and a lot of muscle."

"Where can we find these pulleys?"

"I hid them in the ruins. If you let me move, I'll take you to them. It's too difficult to explain where they are hidden."

Apparently, Orion's compulsion left her some maneuvering space. All she had to do was not disobey his commands completely but rather dance around them like she had just done.

Maybe she could get free after all?

Orion smiled, but it wasn't a friendly smile. "You must think me a fool, but I assure you that I'm not. I will let you move, but only on my command. You'll be like a marionette with me as your puppet master."

She didn't know what that French-sounding word meant, but it was easy enough to guess what Orion had in mind.

74

ORION

*O*rion was beyond impressed. If Aliya had made the traps and also constructed a pulley mechanism herself, then she was very smart, resourceful, and cunning.

He was curious to hear the rest of her story, which was no doubt going to be fascinating. She must have been a small girl during the attack and had somehow managed to escape, but how had she gotten from a small village near Beijing all the way to Lugu Lake, and why?

"I need to get down there." She pointed to a flight of stairs leading to one of the underground dwellings.

The carved-out staircase was barely wide enough for one person, and he didn't want her to go alone. It might lead to another tunnel through which she could escape.

But he was a compeller, and he should be able to direct her with precise phrasing to go down, get the pulleys, and come back up. But what if there were no pulleys down there?

If he told her to come back with the pulleys, she could use it as a loophole to disobey his command. The girl was damn smart.

"You can go, but you have to come back in less than ten minutes with or without the pulleys."

That should do it.

She was back in less than five.

"Give them to Phinas," Orion commanded. "When we get to the boulder, show us how to use them."

After she'd shown them how to tie the ropes and what to do, Arwel cast her an appreciative glance. "That's ingenious. Where did you learn how to do that?"

She shrugged. "I used the tools I could find, and I modified what I've seen others use to drag heavy rocks."

"Show me how to pull," Arwel told her.

"You will not be able to do it. I'm very strong."

"So am I," Arwel smiled. "But I experienced first-hand how strong you are, so I might need your help."

The satisfied expression on her face indicated that Arwel had said the right thing. Having empathic abilities sure helped boost one's emotional intelligence.

"This is only going to work if we are equally matched," Aliya said. "Two of you need to pull on that side while I pull on this one."

As Phinas grabbed the ropes on Arwel's side, Orion expected the Guardian to make a macho comment about how he was strong enough, but Arwel only grumbled, "I'm glad Richard had those sleeping potion vials on him, or he would have never been able to overpower Vrog."

The rope on Aliya's side slackened for a split second, and Orion jumped in to catch it, but she renewed her grip. "Vrog is alive?"

"Do you know him?" Arwel grunted as he and Phinas pulled the ropes on their side. "Or do you just know of him?"

Aliya gave the rope a mighty tug, and the boulder moved a few inches. "I was too little for him to notice me, but I know who he is. Was he away during the attack? Or was he left for dead?"

"He was in Singapore." Arwel and Phinas kept the pressure on their side while Aliya pulled on hers, and after the initial drag had been surpassed, the boulder inched off the opening at a steady pace.

"That's big enough." Arwel signaled for her to stop pulling. "We can squeeze through."

Wiping her hands on her pants, she tried to hide her heavy breathing. "Well, now that you can get your friends out, you don't need me anymore. See you later." She turned to leave.

"Stop," Orion commanded. "You are not going anywhere."

"Why not? You said that you and your people mean me no harm and that you only want to get your friends out."

"We need to talk," Arwel said. "Besides, I'm not going to make the same mistake twice and leave this rock unguarded. You and Orion are coming with me. Phinas, you stay here and guard the opening."

"I need a new hammer," Phinas said. "And you need a ladder. Where did you stash the other one?" he asked Aliyah.

"It's in my canoe on the other side of the ruins."

She was lying. Orion was sure of that.

"Tell us the truth, Aliya." He pushed compulsion into his tone. "Where is the rope ladder that we used to go down into the cavern?"

"I am telling the truth." She huffed out a breath. "I thought that I could use it in the lake cavern instead of climbing the wall every time. But there are more ladders around here. I can find you a proper one made of aluminum."

Arwel seemed as doubtful as Orion. "Phinas, check the tent for another ladder and a new hammer."

"Yes, sir."

"Why don't you have a small boat to cross the subterranean pool instead of swimming through it?" Orion asked. "You seem to take what you need without a problem, so why not another boat?"

"I tried. The staircase is too narrow to carry a boat down, so my only option was to build one. I was planning to do that one day, but I never got around to it. There were always more important things to do."

"Like what?" Arwel asked.

"Hunting for food, guarding against intruders, building traps. You know, staying alive."

"Who was after you?"

"Everyone."

Arwel rolled his eyes. "How old are you, Aliya?"

"I'm thirty years old."

"That explains it. You are still a teenager in immortal terms, and you think that it's you against the world. Not everyone is bad, and many people are kind and willing to help."

"Not in my experience." Her eyes flashed red, and her fangs elongated. "Not when I look like this, and not when I'm stronger than twenty human males."

Arwel laughed. "My mate is one-quarter Kra-ell, and I think that her fangs and her assertiveness only make her sexier to me."

The red in Aliya's eyes flickered and turned into deep brown. "Is she the other Kra-ell hybrid that you encountered?"

"No, that was Emmett. He left your tribe a long time before you were born. We didn't even know that the Kra-ell existed, so naturally, we didn't know that Jin had Kra-ell in her until we found Emmett. We believe that she was one of the children who were fathered by the hybrids and given up for adoption."

Aliya didn't seem surprised by that, so she must have known about the practice. "Is she here with you?"

"She is, and you are about to meet her in a few minutes. A word of warning, though. She might punch you in the face first and ask questions later."

75

ALENA

*A*lena had been silently praying to the Fates, pleading, imploring, and making promises just to see the three males return unharmed and for all of them to find a way out.

So far, no one was perishing from hunger or thirst or going into stasis to preserve their resources, but Jacki was pregnant, and she didn't have the option to go into stasis.

Alena shook her head. Talk about overreacting.

No one was going into stasis, but they would most likely have to swim through that lake unless Orion and the others found a way out and brought back an inflatable boat.

For Jacki, of course. But if they already had a boat, then no one else needed to swim in the near-freezing water.

Except, what if the men didn't find a way out and had been led by that braid into more tunnels? What if there were more traps that Arwel couldn't detect?

What if they were—

She shouldn't allow herself to think such thoughts. She had to believe that they'd found a way out and were coming back for the rest of them.

"I'm worried." Alena rubbed her hands over her arms. "They've been gone for a long time."

"It only seems like that," Kalugal said. "It has been less than an hour."

She didn't know whether he was really unconcerned or was just putting on an act for Jacki's sake. The two lovebirds had been sitting on the ground with their backs propped against the stone wall, kissing and whispering things in each other's ears as if they were in the comfort of their bedroom and not stuck in a subterranean cave.

"An hour is a long time." Alena pushed to her feet and walked over to the natural pool's edge. "Do you think it's safe to drink this water?"

Kalugal sniffed. "I don't smell anything funky but take only a couple of sips first. If you start convulsing, the rest of us will know not to touch the water."

"Very funny." Jacki slapped his arm. "We should have swum after them. The water is cold, but it's a very short distance to swim through, and I could have made it easily. I hate all this waiting and not knowing what's going on."

Kalugal squeezed her shoulder. "You're pregnant, my love. The cold water might not harm you, but we don't know how it will affect the baby who is still human."

They all had been thinking that, but not wanting to worry Jacki, no one had said anything.

Jacki put her hands protectively over her small belly. "You're right. How can I keep forgetting that I'm responsible for another life now?"

"I'm sure it would have occurred to you as soon as your little toe touched the freezing water." He kissed the top of her head.

"I hear noises." Lokan lifted the hammer over his head. "Everyone, get ready."

While waiting, Lokan had insisted that they collect rocks and keep them within reach. Other than the hammer, the only other weapons they had were the switchblades and throwing knives that Shamash and Welgost carried. Weapons in hand, the two men got in position next to the opening, while the rest of them grabbed a rock in each hand. It wasn't likely that anyone could get past Lokan and the two fighters, but if anyone came from the lake's side, the rocks could be useful.

"It's us," Arwel called from the tunnel. "Don't attack."

A weight lifted off Alena's chest.

They were back, and they'd either found another entrance to the underground labyrinth or had managed to move the boulder.

When Orion stepped out of the opening, his hand gripping the arms of a very tall female, Alena's joy took a nosedive.

Kalugal walked over to the two. "I see that you've caught your prey, oh mighty hunter. And who is your lovely prisoner?"

"My name is Aliya, and he said that I wasn't a prisoner. But I see that he is a liar." She hissed at Orion, who didn't seem impressed by her posturing.

There were advantages to being a compeller.

"You are not a prisoner. You are our guest." Orion winked at Alena.

Only days ago, he'd been told the same thing by Onegus and Kian.

"Yeah, and I'm Shenlong, the rain dragon."

Her English was heavily accented but fluent, and she was clearly of Kra-ell descent. Tall, thin, nearly flat-chested, with eyes that blazed red in the cavern's dim interior and fangs that protruded over her lower red lip.

"Aliya is from Vrog and Emmett's tribe," Arwel said. "But that's all we know for now. I suggest that we vacate these tunnels first and then hear all about Aliya's troubles."

"What happened to you?" Jin looked Arwel over.

His clothing hung in tatters, and he was covered in mostly healed bruises and scrapes—the crusted blood serving as evidence of the beating he'd taken.

"I was attacked by a wild cat."

"Really?" Jin's eyes widened.

"Yeah, of the Kra-ell kind. But don't punch her. She was scared."

"That's not a valid excuse." Jin bared her own fangs and hissed at Aliya.

The Kra-ell female responded as any predator would, crouching and readying to pounce.

"Ladies." Alena walked in between them. "Please. Let's get to know each other first, and if after that you still want to brawl, that can be arranged."

The two backed away from each other, but Alena had a feeling that this wasn't the end of it. The problem was that Jin was outmatched, and she hadn't realized it yet, or she had and was just posturing.

"The good news is that we can get out of here," Arwel said. "Aliya helped us move the boulder with a cleverly constructed pulley system she'd invented. The bad news is that our drivers have ditched us. We will have to walk until we reach a place with reception so we can call for pick-up."

"What about the girl?" Jacki asked.

"I think this is her." Orion turned to Aliya. "When you were much younger, did you get scared by a nasty-looking mask and run down into the tunnels?"

Her eyes widened. "How did you know that?"

Jacki lifted her hand. "From me. Sometimes I get visions, and I got one when I touched that mask. I saw a young girl scream and run into the tunnels. That's how we knew that the boulder was blocking the entrance and where to go from there."

Aliya dropped to her knees in front of Jacki. "You are a seer. You are blessed by the Mother."

"Please, get up." Jacki looked uncomfortable. "It's nothing special."

"I disagree." Kalugal wrapped his arm around his wife's shoulders. "My mate is very special, and she deserves to be worshiped, but we are in a bit of a rush to get out of here, so let's reserve the worshiping for later."

76

ORION

"*H*ello! Is anybody in there?" A familiar voice called from high above the staircase.

"Jianye? Is that you?" Kalugal called back.

"It is I. Is everyone alright? I brought help, and we are coming down."

"No need. We are fine, and we are coming up. Wait for us to come to you. Better yet, go back all the way to the first chamber."

"Are you sure no one needs help? We brought ropes and a stretcher."

"No one is hurt, Jianye. Go back."

"Yes, sir."

Orion could feel Aliya tense like a coil ready to spring.

"Are you afraid of Jianye?" he asked.

"Afraid of him?" She snorted. "He's nothing. But I don't want anyone to see me. I'm too excited to thrall, and I don't want the humans to see me."

He raised a brow. "Excited?"

She let out an irritated groan. "My English is so-so. I don't know the right word."

"Your English is very good, and the word you are probably looking for is agitated."

"Yes, that's the one." She gripped his arm. "You have to hide me."

"I'll take care of that," Phinas said from behind her. "Orion is needed by his mate."

"Is she the one who is pregnant?"

"No, that's me," Jacki said. "Don't worry about Jianye and his men. Just hunch your shoulders to make yourself look smaller and don't look anyone in the eyes."

"That's not going to work," Kalugal said. "Jianye knows who came here with me, and he will notice one extra female, but that's not a problem. I'll keep him busy."

After climbing the endless stairs and once again crawling through the narrow tunnel, they were greeted by Kalugal's partner and his crew.

"Thank God." Jianye put a hand over his heart. "I was afraid that something happened to you and your friends, and that you were trapped in the ruins. I brought the crew to help dig you out."

"Thank you." Kalugal clapped him on the back and then wrapped his arm around the man's shoulders. "How did you know to come look for us?"

"When you didn't return, your limousine drivers started to worry and came to look for you. When they couldn't find even a trace, they panicked and came looking for me." He looked up at the opening. "I had no idea that there were hidden tunnels under the ruins. How did you know to move that boulder?"

"Intuition." Kalugal tapped his temple. "The boulder looked out of place, and I had a hunch that it was blocking an entrance to a secret chamber. My men and I constructed a clever pulley contraption to move that thing, and we went exploring."

As Jianye glanced at Arwel and Phinas's haggard appearance, Kalugal continued. "We encountered some problems on the way. One of the passages was so narrow that my men had to dig through it, and they got a little banged up while doing that." He smiled at the guy. "We could all use a warm shower and a good meal."

Aliya stayed hidden behind Phinas's broad back, and so far, Jianye hadn't noticed her, but once they started climbing up the ladder one by one, there was no way to hide her.

"Who's she?" Jianye asked.

"A wildlife explorer from Beijing," Kalugal said with a straight face. "Her specialty is wild cats—tigers and leopards of all kinds." He leaned closer to whisper in the guy's ear, "Don't mind her. She's a bit strange. Living for months in the wild as she tracks the migration of the wild cats makes her somewhat antisocial."

"Yes, I can see that."

Orion choked on a laugh, and Alena coughed to hide hers.

Kalugal could have easily shrouded Aliya, but he seemed to be having fun making up stories to cover for her instead, or maybe he wanted to show her that it was all a matter of attitude, and that she shouldn't fear being seen in public just because she looked different.

As they reached the limousines, Kalugal let go of his partner to shake hands with the drivers and thank them for their initiative. He then thanked each of Jianye's men and promised them a hefty bonus for coming out on the weekend to save him.

While he'd been at it, Orion and Phinas escorted Aliya to one of the limousines, and a few moments later, their group was on its way back to the hotel.

"Where are you taking me?" Aliya asked.

"To our hotel," Orion said. "When was the last time you slept in a proper bed?"

Her eyes blazed red. "I'm not sharing any of your beds."

He lifted his hands in the universal sign for peace. "Trust me, none of us are on the menu even if you were interested, so you can relax."

That seemed to be the wrong thing to say.

"Why? Am I not pretty enough for you?"

Leaning over, Alena patted her arm. "You're beautiful, but there are only three single guys in our group, and they are all gentlemen. You don't have to worry about unwanted advances."

Aliya tilted her head. "What does that mean? Unwanted advances?"

"It means that unless you show interest in them, they are not going to bother you."

77

ALIYA

*A*lena was nice, more like a human than a Kra-ell, but then these long-lived people who called themselves immortals were very different from the Kra-ell.

Other than Arwel's mate, the females were kind of docile, not subservient like many of the human females outside of the Mosuo culture, but not aggressive at all. Still, the males seemed just as devoted to them as the Kra-ell males had been to the Kra-ell females, but it looked like they did that out of love rather than duty or honor, and that was nice.

One of the things that had bothered Aliya the most while living in the Kra-ell compound was the lack of love between the purebloods and even between the hybrids and their pureblooded fathers. The only ones who'd been capable of love had been the human mothers and their children, either human or hybrid.

Her best friend growing up was a human girl.

Chyou had been her only friend ever. Aliya often wondered about what had happened to her. She was probably married, and since the government no longer put restrictions on how many kids a couple could have, Chyou could have several.

"Would you like to talk to Vrog?" Alena asked. "Now that we have reception, I can call him, and you can have a video call with him."

"What's that?"

Alena regarded her as if she was some wild woman who didn't know anything. "Do you know what a cell phone is?"

"Of course." Aliya shifted in her seat. "I never had one, but I've seen people use them, especially the tourists."

"I wonder," Arwel said. "How did you get from the Beijing area to here?"

"We walked, we used the train, the bus, and then we walked some more."

"We?" Orion asked. "I thought that you were alone."

Should she feel flattered? Did he think her so formidable that she could have traveled across the country by herself as a child?

She gave him an incredulous look. "I was eight years old. I traveled with my mother."

"What happened to her?" Alena asked.

"She died." Aliya looked down at her mud-covered shoes. "She got sick and died and left me alone."

"I'm so sorry." Alena leaned forward and put her hand on her knee. "It must have been awful."

"It was."

It could have been much worse if they had been anywhere else.

Aliya had been thanking the Mother daily for whispering in her ear to seek the Mosuo territory.

She'd thought that she would find friendly Kra-ell there, but all she'd found were the Mosuo, who'd adopted many of the Kra-ell good customs and none of the cruelty. The matriarch who had taken them in was a tough, unforgiving female who'd run her multigenerational household with an iron fist, but she'd also been kind to accept a single mother and her strange child in exchange for labor.

In a way, nothing had changed for Aliya's mother after they'd escaped the slaughter. She'd been a slave in the Kra-ell compound, and she'd continued slaving away in the Mosuo village until she died.

"You must tell us all about it when we get to the hotel," the leader of their group said. "After you shower and eat, of course." He smiled. "You look like you could use a good meal. What are your nutritional needs?"

She didn't know what that word meant, but she could guess the meaning. "Are you asking what I like to eat?"

"Yes. The two hybrid Kra-ell we know have different preferences or rather needs. Emmett needs fresh blood to supplement his diet, but Vrog doesn't, and they both prefer their meat barely cooked."

"To eat meat when fresh blood is available is an offense to the Mother. Why kill the animal when drinking a little of its blood can fill the hunger?"

"Blood is not on the menu in most restaurants," the leader said.

Aliya had heard someone call him by his name, but she'd forgotten what it was and didn't want to ask. Someone would say it soon enough.

"I don't eat in restaurants," she said. "I hunt for my food."

He looked as if he was losing patience with her. "Let me put it simply. What can you eat that is not blood? Can you eat meat, rice, bread, noodles, vegetables, fruits, etc.?"

"I can eat all of that, but rice and noodles upset my stomach."

"She is probably gluten intolerant," Alena said. "What about milk? Can you have milk and cheese?"

Aliya nodded. "I like cheese." Her mouth watered as she thought of the ru-shan cheese she'd once tasted but never got a chance to eat again. The delicacy was made from cow's milk, and it was toasted, browned, and slathered in rose petal jam. It was made for the tourists who could pay for it, and not for stray dogs like her. She could have use her mental powers to coerce one of the vendors to give it to her, but Aliya never stole things she could survive without, and she could definitely survive without the delicious cheese.

The question was whether she could survive these people.

What did they want from her?

They'd said that they wanted to ask her some questions, but so far, they hadn't asked much. She could lull them into believing that she was cooperating and pretend that she was grateful to them for offering her a meal and a shower.

If they bought her act, Orion wouldn't use his powers on her.

She'd noticed that he was reluctant to use them and had to be coached by the one named Arwel.

Arwel couldn't compel her but knew how to use compulsion better than Orion, probably because he had experience compelling humans. It was the same as the pure-blooded Kra-ell who could hypnotically coerce humans as well as hybrids, and the hybrids who could only do that to humans. Maybe Orion was a pureblood of his kind, and Arwel was a hybrid. It was hard to tell with these immortals. They didn't have distinguishing features like the Kra-ell and looked like humans. Did the males even have fangs?

The only fangs she'd seen so far belonged to Jin, Arwel's mate, and she was one-quarter Kra-ell.

They claimed to have only met two other hybrid Kra-ells beside her. Vrog, whose name she recognized, and Emmett, who she'd never heard of. What if they'd lied about it, though? What if their plan was to sell her to those other Kra-ell who'd attacked her tribe?

It seemed unlikely, especially with the female named Alena being so kind to her, but she didn't know these immortals, and they could be master deceivers.

Her best course of action was to flee as soon as she could.

There was no going back to her subterranean haven.

It had been compromised not only by the immortals but also by the humans. On Monday it would be crawling with the archeological crew digging there for artifacts.

She needed a new home, and the idea from before was still valid. If those human limo drivers were staying overnight in the hotel, and if she managed to get away from her captors, she could hypnotically coerce one of them to drive her somewhere far away.

Hopefully, the immortals had lots of money lying around because she needed some to start a new life somewhere else. She would have never stolen from innocents, but these people owed her for taking away the only home she had.

78

ALENA

"*A*liya, you come with Jacki and me," Kalugal said when they arrived at the hotel. "We have the presidential suite, which has two bathrooms. You can shower in there."

Alena detected the slight compulsion in his tone, which explained why the girl did as he'd commanded, and followed him and Jacki into the lobby.

Once everyone had gathered inside, Kalugal said, "Dinner tonight at our suite. I'll call the concierge and have them set it up. Does five o'clock work for everyone?"

They all needed to shower and change, but they were hungry as well, and Alena doubted they could wait nearly two hours until dinner.

But then that's what room service was for.

"Aliya needs new clothes." Jin walked up to Kalugal. "Jacki's won't fit her, so I guess they would have to be mine."

"That would be greatly appreciated, thank you." Kalugal put a hand on her arm. "Naturally, I'll reimburse you for the expense."

"I'm not a beggar," Aliya grumbled. "I don't want anything from her."

"Well, tough." Jin got in her face. "You're dirty, and you stink, and your clothes are rags. A normal person would have said thank you."

Aliya didn't back down. "Who said I was normal?" And to prove it, her eyes flashed red, and her fangs elongated.

Just as before, Alena got between them, only this time she had to push on both of their middles to get them to step back.

"I thought that you didn't want to attract attention to yourself," she said quietly to Aliya. "If the dirt and the rags don't have everyone looking at you, the red eyes and fangs will surely do."

"*Feihua*," Aliya cursed under her breath as she hunched her shoulders and dipped her head.

Jin snickered. "Crap indeed. I'll see you later."

414

Aliya was taller and slimmer than Jin, but even if baggy, Jin's clothes would be a vast improvement on the rags she was wearing.

As someone with thralling ability, the girl could've gotten herself new clothes with very little effort, and Alena wondered why she hadn't. Perhaps she would ask her over dinner.

She hadn't seen Jacki and Kalugal's suite, but it had to be big to accommodate twelve people for a sit-down dinner.

"I'm looking forward to a long shower." Orion wrapped his arm around her waist as they took the stairs instead of the elevator to the second floor. "Care to share?"

"Sounds lovely, but I'm hungry. Perhaps we can order room service and have them leave the cart outside the door. When we get out of the shower, the meal will be waiting for us."

"An excellent idea." He leaned and kissed her cheek. "I'm so glad that Kalugal is also a compeller and that he took Aliya off my hands. I was afraid that they would foist her on us."

"You were very kind to her." Alena waited for Orion to fish the card key out of his pocket and open the door. "In fact, I was impressed." She walked inside.

"It was nothing." He closed the door behind them and then briefly kissed her lips before heading to the bathroom while unbuttoning his shirt on the way.

Alena stared transfixed, waiting for the shirt to drop so she could admire his muscular back, but he entered the bathroom before dropping the shirt, depriving her of the treat.

Oh well, she would soon have her hands all over his magnificent body in the shower, and there was a lot they could do with the nearly two hours until dinner. Perhaps she should let him get washed up first, though. He'd been covered in dirt even before catching Aliya, and her capture had left him in an even worse state.

Alena wondered why he hadn't used compulsion to prevent the girl from hurting Arwel and Phinas. Had he been too aggravated to summon his ability?

Orion didn't possess Kalugal's finesse, and he didn't enjoy using compulsion, but compelling Aliya to behave had been unavoidable.

He'd been so patient with her, treating her like a skittish kitten, keeping his voice and his eyes soft. Although given Arwel and Phinas's state after trying to subdue her, Aliya was more of a tigress than a kitten.

If the Fates ever blessed Orion with a child, he would make a wonderful father. Blessed the two of them, because Alena was not giving him up.

The trip and the trying events of the day had solidified her conviction that he was the one for her. If he felt the same, she would implore the Fates to give her one more child with Orion, preferably a boy because she wanted to see Orion do all the things that fathers did with their sons.

Alena had raised her thirteen children with the help of her mother and the Odus, but it was not the same as raising a child with a partner. It would be a new and wonderful experience, one she fiercely yearned for.

"Are you calling room service, or should I?" Orion called out from the bathroom.

"I'll call them. Anything special you want me to order for you?"

"Whatever you're ordering for yourself is fine for me."

Orion was so easy to be with. He didn't make a big deal out of anything, didn't complain, didn't grumble, and was always attentive and patient. She couldn't have asked for a better mate.

There was just one more thing Alena needed to do to make her decision official. She needed to tell Orion that she loved him.

79

ALIYA

*A*liya's hair had never smelled so good. She'd spent over an hour in the bathroom, first in the shower and then in the bathtub. Washing in hot water was a luxury she hadn't enjoyed in years, and she'd made good use of all those little shampoos and conditioners. She'd even slathered her face and body with the lotion. All those containers were empty now, but just in case she hadn't been supposed to use them, she filled them with water and put them back where she'd found them.

A towel wrapped around her head and another one around her body, she stared at her reflection in the mirror and grimaced. She was clean, really clean, for the first time in years. She'd washed in the river or in the subterranean lake every other day or so, but she was lucky if she had a crude bar of soap, and she hadn't had one in months. To get a new bar, she would have to row her canoe all the way to the village, compel every person she encountered to forget her, and then she had to steal what she needed because she didn't have any money.

Aliya hated stealing, especially from people who didn't have much to start with.

She had one change of clothes back in the ruins' subterranean system, which were not in a much better shape than what she'd taken off, but at least they were clean, or as clean as she could get them by washing them in cold water and no soap.

What she'd had on this morning had gotten dirty and sweaty and even more tattered than they had been before, and she really didn't want to put them on. But unless she wanted to come out dressed in a towel, she would have to put on the clothes that Arwel's mate had brought over.

During Aliya's hour-long cleansing, Jacki had knocked on the door and put the items on the vanity. The problem was that they didn't include new underwear or shoes, and Aliya had no intentions of putting her old ones on.

She would go without.

For now, she could walk barefoot and put her shoes on later when it was time for her to escape.

Shifting her eyes to the bathroom window, Aliya felt guilty and stupid for not using it to escape right now. It was small and high up, but she was slim enough to fit through and strong enough to hoist herself up to it.

Except, it had felt so good to shower and bathe, and her stomach was growling with hunger. The prospect of a full belly was holding her back more securely than any chains they could have put on her.

The problem was that they didn't need to use physical chains. The leader of the immortals was just as powerful as Orion, and he'd told her not to leave the hotel without his permission. Aliya hadn't tried to defy his command yet, but she was pretty sure that her body would refuse to reach for the small window if her intention was to escape.

A knock on the door startled her, and as she turned around, Jacki opened the door. "Are you almost done? The meal will be served shortly."

"I'll be out in a moment." She waited for the door to close before dropping the towel.

When she was done putting on the borrowed clothes, she took off the towel that was wrapped around her head and let her long black hair tumble down her back. She was so used to combing it with her fingers that she'd started on it before realizing that there was a brand-new comb on the vanity top that she could use.

It had been such a long time since she'd enjoyed such luxuries, and she could easily get used to having them again, but at what cost?

ORION

"*H*ello, beautiful." Orion pulled Alena into his arms. "Do you want me to shampoo your hair?"

He loved her hair. It was thick and wavy and had every shade of blond in it. When the sun hit it, it shone with platinum and gold highlights, and when it was dark, it took on a copper hue.

Before joining him in the shower, she'd released it from the braid, and the long, lush strands parted over her generous breasts, framing the pink erect nipples in copper and gold.

"Have you ever done it before?" she asked.

"I shampoo mine every day."

She smiled. "You know what I mean." Tilting her head back, she let the spray soak her hair.

"No, I never have." When he'd been married, bathing hadn't happened every day. There had been no running water and filling a tub with water that had been heated over a stove had taken a long time, a task he'd gladly performed for his wife twice a week. But Miriam had never invited him to share the bath with her. Back then, it hadn't even occurred to either of them that it was an option.

Why hadn't it, though?

They'd been deeply in love and passionate about each other, so it hadn't been about avoiding intimacy. Or maybe it was?

As she'd gotten older, Miriam had started hiding her nudity from him. She'd stopped undressing in front of him, and their lovemaking had been done in the dark.

"Why are you frowning?" Alena asked.

She probably wondered about his deflated erection, but she voiced her concern in a more polite way.

He shook his head. "It's nothing. Just old memories that have no place here with us."

She cupped his cheek. "You can tell me anything, Orion. Anytime." She smiled. "I

419

have lived for a very long time, and I know that life is not a walk in a rose garden, nor do I expect it to be. I love you just as much when you are sad as when you are happy."

For a long moment, too long, Orion found himself speechless.

Had Alena just told him that she loved him, or had it been just a figure of speech? The same way people said they loved oranges as much as they loved apples? Or they loved the color blue as much as they loved the color red?

"Nothing to say, mate of mine?"

And now she called him her mate as well?

What was going on?

Had they walked through a time warp, and this was weeks in the future?

Alena chuckled. "I've never seen you so dumbfounded before. Is it so difficult to accept that you are my mate?" Wrapping her arms around his neck, she pulled him down and kissed him lightly. "I'll make it easy for you and walk you through it step by step. First, you will tell me that I am your mate, and then you'll say that you love me and that you want to spend the rest of your eternal life with me. You are free to change the order of these statements, but they all have to be there."

"I'm your mate." His throat turning suddenly dry, he swallowed to bring some moisture to his vocal cords. "And you are mine. I've been in love with you from the moment I heard you sing."

It was the truth, and surprisingly, he didn't feel guilty for vocalizing what he'd felt for days. Miriam would have approved of Alena, and she would have been happy for him. And if not, he would just have to beg her spirit's forgiveness.

Throwing her head back, Alena laughed. "I don't know if I should take that as a compliment or an insult. I've been told that I have a good voice, but it's not that good. Besides, I hoped that you were more impressed with my winning personality and my knockout body than with my amateur rendition of 'Let it Go.'"

Her teasing melted away the tension that had crept into his shoulder muscles. Cupping her cheeks, he smiled. "I'm impressed with everything about you, from your kindness to your wisdom, from your selflessness to your assertiveness, and from the beauty of your little toes to the top of your gorgeous hair and everything in between. But I knew all of that before I ever met you. I heard it all in your song. There was power and beauty in it, emotion and determination, a yearning that called to me, was meant for me alone. I knew that the woman whom voice belonged to would be extraordinary, but you've exceeded all of my expectations."

DARK HUNTER'S BOON

1

ALENA

*A*lena, eldest daughter of the goddess Annani, mother of thirteen, grandmother of seventeen, great-grandmother of twenty-three, and a great many times over grandmother of nearly every member of Annani's clan, sat in front of the vanity and gazed at her lover's reflection in the mirror.

It had been one of those days that would forever remain etched in her memory, and it wasn't over yet.

In the span of twelve hours, their team had been trapped under the ruins of an ancient outpost, had found a hybrid Kra-ell female who'd been hiding there for years, and after they'd returned to the hotel, Alena had finally admitted to Orion that she'd fallen in love with him and proclaimed him her mate.

Her heart was full to bursting with happiness and gratitude to the Fates for the wonderful male they'd chosen for her. They had given her a boon—a gorgeous, kind, smart male who loved her as much as she loved him.

Orion had fallen in love with her voice first, but the rest had soon followed. Somehow, hearing her pouring her suppressed emotions into that song had given him a glimpse into her soul before ever meeting her, and he'd liked what he'd seen.

As he caught her looking at him, Orion grinned and flexed his muscles. Alena smiled back and picked up the brush. She could never get enough of ogling her mate's impeccable physique, but she was supposed to get ready for dinner.

They'd made love in the shower, then on the bed, and then again in the shower, so she should be beyond satisfied and content. But as the saying went, her appetite had just gotten sharpened by the first tasty bites, and she hungered for more.

Right now, the male she loved was giving her an eyeful as he got dressed for dinner at Kalugal and Jacki's. It was a shame to cover all that gorgeous tan skin and those beautiful muscles in clothing, but she had to admit that he looked quite dashing in the white button-down dress shirt and the navy-blue suit.

"Do you think I should go with the blazer or without?" Orion asked.

"We are not leaving the hotel, so you can go without, but you look so good all dressed up."

"Not nearly as good as you, gorgeous." He leaned down and kissed the top of her head. "I don't want to mess up your lipstick."

"Feel free to mess it up anytime you want." She puckered her lips.

With a groan, he lifted her off the stool and kissed the living daylights out of her. When he let go, Alena burst out laughing. "Go wash your face. You're covered in red lipstick."

Smiling like a fiend, he turned her around to face the mirror. "I have a feeling that we are going to be late for dinner."

Her makeup was a mess.

With a sigh, Alena sat back down and pulled a tissue out of the box. "I'll just take it off."

She hardly ever bothered with makeup, but tonight was special, and not just because she and Orion were officially in love.

Alena had a feeling that the dinner at Kalugal and Jacki's presidential suite would be one of those events that would affect the future of the clan.

The Kra-ell female they'd captured and brought with them to the hotel was about to tell her story. Probably not willingly, but with Kalugal's compulsion, she wouldn't be able to refuse.

Aliya was like a trapped wild animal, and the only thing preventing her from running away the first chance she got was Kalugal's command to stay put. Hopefully, though, after showering and getting fed, she wouldn't be in such a great hurry to leave.

Aliya wasn't a prisoner, but they needed to keep her from running off just yet for her own good.

The poor woman didn't know who to trust, and she feared everyone. If she didn't allow herself time to get to know them and ran off, Aliya would spend the rest of her life alone and wouldn't get to meet the other survivors of Jade's tribe.

Before allowing her access to Emmett and Vrog, though, they needed to find out how she'd gotten from her tribe's compound near Beijing all the way to the Mosuo village on the shores of Lugo Lake. Her escape from the slaughter of her people and her journey to the remote lake in the Tibetan mountains was no doubt a fascinating tale, but what Alena was even more curious about was why Aliya had shunned society, living hidden in the tunnel system under the ruins of an ancient trading post.

The woman looked half-starved, half-wild, and she was wary of people, whether they were human or other.

A powerful female like her shouldn't have been running scared like that. Physically, Aliya was as strong as or stronger than two well-trained immortal warriors, giving Arwel and Phinas a run for their money. If not for Orion knocking her out with a rock, she might have overpowered them both and run off.

As a hybrid Kra-ell, Aliya could also thrall, and combined with her physical strength, she could have used her gifts to live like a queen. Instead, she'd chosen to live like a pauper.

Why?

Was it grief?

After Aliya's human mother had died, the girl had probably fallen into despair. Depression and anger often contributed to self-destructive behaviors, and in some cases, even suicide. For immortals, ending their own life required such extreme measures that it was nearly impossible, and thankfully, none of Annani's clan had ever gone that far, but over the years there had been some members who'd recklessly endangered their lives in the hopes of ending their emotional misery.

In Aliya's case, her emotional pain might have manifested in withdrawal from society and self-inflicted austerity.

Every motherly instinct she had was telling Alena to take the girl under her protective wing. But Aliya was a grown woman, and it was her choice whether to accept Alena's help or refuse it.

2

ORION

*W*hen all the smeared lipstick was gone, Alena pivoted on the vanity stool to face Orion. "I feel bad about leaving Ovidu and Oridu in their hotel room once again."

"They don't need to eat, do they?"

Alena grimaced. "They eat garbage."

"Really?"

"Did you see *Back to the Future II?*"

"Are you referencing Mr. Fusion? The Home Energy Reactor?"

She nodded. "When I saw that movie, I thought about the Odus. You don't need a garbage disposal with one of them around."

"That would be a very expensive garbage disposal." Orion looped his tie and tied the knot. "I'm surprised that Kian hasn't had one of them reverse-engineered. Imagine a cyborg butler in every house." He chuckled. "The brand name should be Mr. Turbo Clean—the recycling superstar."

He thought it was a very clever name, but Alena didn't seem impressed.

She sighed. "We know how that would end. We should heed the warning of history and not repeat the same mistakes our ancestors made. The Odus were created to be servants, but they were easily converted into killing machines. It got so bad that they were decommissioned and the technology to make them was banned."

"People will always find ways to use things as weapons, but that doesn't mean that new technologies shouldn't be developed just because they have the potential to destroy as well as to build. Computer chips are used in missiles as well as in medical devices." He smiled. "I wish I was more technologically savvy so I could give you better examples, but my point is that with proper safeguards, the amazing technology that created the Odus could revolutionize the way people live and work."

Alena pulled out a calf-long sweater from the closet and shrugged it on. "I get what you're saying. What's interesting is that Syssi's vision linked the Kra-ell with the Odus. Back then, we didn't know that the Kra-ell were real, and we thought that

Syssi's vision was influenced by the virtual reality story she'd created for the Perfect Match studios. As it turns out, it was the other way around. Her precognition created the imagery for what she believed was her own creation."

"That's interesting." Orion pushed the door open. "How were the Kra-ell connected to the Odus?"

As Alena stepped out onto the hallway, Ovidu opened the door and dipped his head. "Good evening, mistress. Should I escort you and Master Orion?"

It was unnecessary, but that was what Kian wanted. "We are just going to the third floor. You can escort us there and return to your room."

"Yes, mistress."

She turned back to Orion. "In her vision, Syssi saw a dark alien world, with skies that had a reddish hue and very strong winds. The vision happened in a spaceport, where Odus were being loaded into shuttles by handlers who she described as looking like the Kra-ell. They were tall, slim, and dark-haired, and the only female among all the male handlers was the one running the show. The most interesting detail about her was that she had fangs."

"Did the females in Syssi's imagined world also have them?" Orion looped his arm around Alena's waist as they took the stairs to the third floor.

"They did. Except for the location, everything about her Krall adventure was eerily similar to the Kra-ell."

He would have loved to see the created world, but he wasn't sure about getting hooked up to a virtual reality contraption. Perhaps there was a way to see it as a movie? Then again, going on an adventure with Alena that wasn't actually dangerous could be fun. After their earlier excitement in the tunnels, he wanted to play it safe, and there was nothing safer than enjoying an interesting experience from the comfort of an easy chair.

"Where did Syssi place the Krall?"

"Greenland. The story was that they landed there a thousand years ago, and their spaceship got trapped under the ice. One day, a massive earthquake shattered the ice, the Krall woke up from their stasis, and then took over the entire Arctic Circle."

"Sounds like a great story." Orion cast her a sidelong glance. "You've piqued my curiosity. Would you like to go on a Krall adventure with me?"

She laughed. "There are so many wonderful scenarios we can pick from, why go to freezing Greenland and encounter nasty, bloodthirsty Krall?"

"That's a valid point. Were the Krall bloodthirsty in Syssi's vision as well?"

"She only said that everyone's eyes were glowing, which led her to believe that it wasn't just nighttime over there, but that it was a dark world. It might have been just her impression, though, because the atmosphere in the vision was so somber. The Kra-ell were sending the Odus out to space, and Syssi believed that they were getting rid of them."

Orion stopped in front of the presidential suite's double doors. "So let me get it straight. In Syssi's vision, the Kra-ell were in charge of decommissioning the Odus?"

"Or sending them to war. The problem with Syssi's visions is that they show her just snippets, and she doesn't know if what she sees is in the past or the future, or where it's happening or why. That leaves a lot of room for interpretation, or misinterpretation. For all we know, the Kra-ell might have been saving the Odus and sending them somewhere safe, or they might have hidden them on some distant moon to be used in future warfare, or it could have been none of the above. If the vision was true, though, which I believe it was, then it clearly connects the Kra-ell to the gods. We know that the Odus were created on the gods' home planet, and if the Kra-ell were handling them, they either shared that planet with the gods or were close neighbors."

As Orion knocked on the door, his head was swimming with the implications. The clan already suspected that the gods and the Kra-ell had a shared ancestry and that they came from the same corner of the universe, but the vision of them being involved with the Odus opened up a whole new can of worms.

Shamash, Kalugal's personal assistant, opened the door. "Good evening. Please, come in."

Ovidu bowed. "Should you require my services, please call for me."

"Thank you." Alena dismissed him.

Kalugal and Jacki's suite was about five times the size of Orion and Alena's hotel room. It had a living room, a dining room, a kitchenette, a bathroom, and a separate bedroom suite.

The dining room was probably designed to host board meetings because the table could comfortably seat the eleven people in their party and Aliya with room to spare. If needed, they could easily squeeze in four additional guests.

Everyone was already there, and two waiters were waiting by their carts to start serving the meal.

Alena glanced at her watch. "I didn't realize that we were late. My apologies."

"You're just in time," Jacki said. "Aliya insisted on saving the seat next to her for you."

When Orion shifted his eyes in the direction Jacki waved her hand, he was taken aback. The female looked like a different person.

With her skin and hair washed clean, her beauty shone through, but her attitude hadn't improved. She looked agitated, and he had a good idea why.

Even from where he was standing, which was at least twenty feet away from her, he could hear her stomach grumbling.

Aliya was hungry and waiting impatiently for the meal to start.

Hadn't Kalugal fed her?

If she'd been placed in Orion's care, that would have been the first thing he would have done. Perhaps the Odus could be moved to another room so they could invite Aliya to stay with him and Alena. The two of them would take much better care of her than Kalugal and Jacki seemed to be doing. Kian wouldn't be happy about that, though. The Odus were there to protect Alena and therefore needed to stay close to her.

"We'd better sit down quickly." He took Alena's elbow and led her to their seats. "Everyone is hungry." He cast a quick smile at Aliya, but she didn't return it.

3

ALENA

*A*lena's heart went out to the young woman devouring food as if she'd gone hungry for days, which she probably had. Even Jin's animosity toward Aliya subsided as she watched her pile yet another serving on her plate and then eat it as fast as was possible in polite company.

Aliya was trying to measure her pace, but she couldn't hide the slight tremor of her hands as she reached for the platters. Casting quick looks around, she checked if anyone else wanted to finish what was left over, and when she was satisfied that there were no other takers, she scooped every last morsel onto her plate.

"I don't know what happened to the portion sizes," Kalugal complained loudly. "They are entirely inadequate." He grabbed the phone and called to order more food to be delivered.

Alena could have kissed him for it. The portions were just as generous as they had been the night before, but with all of them pretending to be full so Aliya could eat her fill, Kalugal had wisely decided to order more.

It had been incredibly sweet of him to do so in a way that allowed her to save face.

Once all the platters were empty, including the additional dishes Kalugal had ordered, the waiters cleared the table and served tea, coffee, and dessert.

Aliya looked catatonic from food overdose, but she still had to make good on her promise to tell them her story.

"Would you like some tea?" Kalugal asked her. "It will help wash the food down so you can tell us what we've been waiting patiently to hear."

"Thank you." She straightened in her chair. "I would love some tea."

He lifted the teapot and actually got to his feet to pour tea into her cup instead of passing it to Alena. "Are you ready to tell us your story?"

Aliya hesitated. "I don't know who you are and if I can trust you, but I know that you can force me to talk like you forced me to help you and to come here. I'm at your sorrow."

"The correct phrase is at my mercy." Kalugal pulled out his phone. "Would talking to Vrog assuage your fears?"

She shrugged. "He could be a traitor. Maybe it was him who betrayed us to our enemies and brought the killers to slaughter our people."

With a sigh, Kalugal put the phone back in his pocket. "I would much prefer it if you told us your story without being forced. But you are a very suspicious young lady, and you leave me no choice. Tell me everything that you remember about the attack, Aliya. Tell me how you managed to escape when all the other Kra-ell and hybrids were either killed or taken. I also want you to tell us what has happened to you since then and why you've been living alone in the ruins."

Alena could see the defiance in Aliya's eyes, and for a long moment, the young woman kept her lips tightly pressed together, trying to fight the compulsion. It was a valiant effort and proof of a strong will, but Kalugal was a powerful compeller, and Aliya wasn't immune.

She stood no chance against him.

"I was eight years old," she spat and lifted her hands to press her palms to her temples. "I still looked human. That's how I managed to escape."

"Go on," Kalugal prompted.

Letting out a groan that sounded like a growl, Aliya surrendered to the compulsion. "When the bad Kra-ell attacked, they let the humans go. They hypnotically coerced them to forget where they lived and put lies in their heads."

"We call it thralling," Kalugal said. "To thrall means to enslave through enchantment. We can do more to humans than just hypnotically coerce them to forget things. We can also plant fake memories in their minds."

"I know that." Aliya glared at him. "That can also be called hypnotic coercion, but thralling is shorter, so I'll use that."

"Thank you." Kalugal gave her a reassuring smile. "So, what kind of lies did they plant in the humans' heads?"

"My mother believed that she'd been in a work camp for all those years, and she didn't remember who my father was because the bad people told the humans to forget about the Kra-ell. But I was a hybrid, and their thralling didn't work on me. I knew who I was, and I remembered everything, including what I learned from Jade and the other pureblooded females." She looked down at the dessert on her plate but didn't touch it. "I was so scared, and I kept asking my mother what happened to my father, but she didn't know who I was talking about. My father was a pureblooded Kra-ell, but he wasn't as bad as the others. When no one was looking, he was kind to my mother and me. He brought us little gifts from time to time, and he gave me money for my birthdays."

Alena wondered if Aliya's father was also Vrog's. She hadn't had a chance to talk to Vrog when they'd been boarding the planes, but she'd heard that he'd spoken with affection about his pureblooded father. There hadn't been many pureblooded Kra-ell in the compound, and most had been described as either cruel or indifferent to humans and hybrids alike. What were the chances that there had been two kind males in that small group?

Was it possible that most of them had been decent males, but given their societal rules they had to keep up the pretense?

Alena knew all about social expectations and how they affected one's behavior.

Not that it was a bad thing, at least not as a rule. Usually, people behaved better when they knew others were watching. In small, close-knit communities, spousal and child abuse were rare, and so were theft and vandalism. People wanted to be judged positively by others.

"Did your mother have family here?" Jacki asked. "Is that why she brought you to the lake?"

Aliya shook her head. "I knew about the Mosuo people, and I told my mother that we would be safe here. It was far away from where we lived before, and the people here respected women. We were alone, and I'd heard stories about human men mistreating females, so I was scared for my mother and a little for myself too. My mother was too terrified to think, but she didn't remember why she was so scared, so she listened to me. We had very little money. The humans in the compound didn't get paid. But I had never spent the money my father gave me for my birthdays because I never left the compound, so it was all still there, and my mother used it to buy train tickets for us. Back then, there wasn't even a paved road leading to the lake, and the train could get us only part of the way. We walked a lot, and we asked kind farmers to give us rides, and finally, we arrived at the Mosuo village. One of the matriarchs took pity on us and let us join her household in exchange for my mother's work. My mother was a hard worker, and she could sew clothes, a skill that was badly needed at the time. The tourism to the lake was growing, and the villagers were looking for more ways to make money off the tourists. They made traditional outfits for sale, but they sewed them by hand. My mother knew how to operate a sewing machine."

"How did you know about the Mosuo?" Orion asked.

"From Jade." Aliya smiled. "I was a rare female hybrid, so unlike the boys who were treated just slightly better than the human children, Jade was nice to me. She liked to keep me around when I was done with my schoolwork and my chores. I was a quiet little girl, and sometimes she forgot that I was there when she talked with the other females, or maybe she thought that I couldn't understand Kra-ell well enough to follow what they were talking about. But I was always good with languages, and if she had bothered to actually talk to me, she would have known that I spoke fluent Kra-ell. One day, she was talking with Kagra about how they were betrayed, and their ship was broken on purpose."

"You mean sabotaged," Orion offered.

"Yes, thank you. Sometimes I don't know the correct words in English."

"Your English is excellent," Jin said. "How did you learn to speak it so well?"

Aliya shrugged. "I have a good ear, and I learned from shows on television, songs on the radio, and from the tourists."

"Television?" Jacki arched a brow. "Did the lake area have reception back then?"

Aliya shook her head. "We had television in the Kra-ell compound. I didn't need as much sleep as the humans, so I snuck out at night and went to the common room to watch TV."

"I didn't know they had English-speaking films on Chinese television," Carol said.

"It was mostly American movies on video cassettes. I think Jade brought them with her from her trips to the US."

That was a piece of information they hadn't heard yet. "Did Jade and the other purebloods leave the compound often?" Alena asked.

"Jade traveled a lot, and she usually took one or two males with her."

"That's interesting," Kalugal said. "But let's get back to what you heard Jade say about the ship's sabotage."

4

ALIYA

*A*liya lifted the teacup and took a small sip to moisten her dry throat. It was difficult to talk about the past, but it was also liberating.

She'd had no one to tell her story to, not even her mother while she had still been alive. Sometimes, she wasn't sure that any of it had really happened and that it hadn't been a dream, or rather a nightmare.

She'd wished it hadn't been true and that she was just a little odd-looking human girl, but she had the fangs and red glowing eyes to prove that she wasn't human and that what had happened in the compound had been real. She belonged to an alien race of people whose customs and beliefs had influenced the Mosuo people, and who'd slaughtered each other for no good reason.

Why had those other Kra-ell attacked her tribe? They couldn't have retaliated for some wrongdoing committed by Jade or the other tribe members because no one had even known that they existed. The attack had been unprovoked, and to this day, Aliya still wondered why.

Then again, the purebloods must have known about the others because they must have arrived on the same ship that had been sabotaged, but perhaps they hadn't known who had survived. Maybe they'd evacuated the ships in small vessels that were like the escape pods she'd seen in science fiction movies, and those vessels had landed in different parts of the world.

Perhaps it had been a territorial thing?

Now that she was older and understood a little more about how the world worked, she knew all about eliminating competition for resources. Even in the wild, one kind of predator killed another's cubs to ensure their own cubs' survival.

Except, even that couldn't explain the attack. Earth was a big place, so big that the two Kra-ell groups had been oblivious to each other's existence until something or someone had betrayed Aliya's tribe to those other murderous Kra-ell.

"Whenever you're ready," Kalugal said gently.

"It was a long time ago, and I don't remember all the details." She looked at him.

"Sometimes I think that I imagined it all, but the proof is right here." She pointed to her fangs. "And if that's real, so is the rest of it."

He nodded, his eyes soft and full of understanding. "You were just a little girl, and you suffered a horrible trauma. It's okay if you confuse some details. Just tell us what you remember, and we will try to piece it together to make sense of it."

That would be helpful.

Perhaps these people could finally fill in the missing pieces for her.

"I heard Jade say something about a scouting crew who were supposed to arrive first and prepare things for her. She told Kagra that she suspected the scouts had sabotaged their ship, so their landing was delayed by thousands of years. I thought that I must have misunderstood because the Kra-ell couldn't live that long. But I knew the Kra-ell word for thousands, and that was what she said. Then I thought that maybe the ship was like a huge village and that the Kra-ell who boarded the ship were not the ones who landed on Earth, but their grandchildren or even great-grandchildren did."

"They could have traveled in stasis," Arwel said. "We don't know anything about their interstellar travel technology, but if it obeys the same laws of physics we are familiar with, then the only way to traverse the enormous distances of space is in stasis, which is a sort of very long hibernation."

That made sense. If the Kra-ell had the technology to travel through space, they probably also had the technology to put themselves to sleep for thousands of years.

"What must have happened was that the scouting team woke up first," Kalugal said. "Their pods were probably programmed to open ahead of the others, and when they did, they decided to give themselves a longer head start on the others and reprogrammed their fellow travelers' pods to stay closed for much longer."

"You are jumping to conclusions," Arwel said. "It might have been a malfunction. If the scouting team had nefarious intentions, they would have killed the others instead of reprogramming their pods."

"Killing with no provocation is an affront to the Mother," Aliya said. "But it didn't stop the killers who attacked my tribe, so maybe they were heretics."

"Or they might have perceived something as a provocation," Kalugal said. "You don't know what Jade did on these frequent trips abroad."

"True, but she never mentioned any other Kra-ell except for that scouting team, and she said that the joke was on them because Earth females were not compatible. They couldn't produce long-lived children for them, so they died out long before Jade and her people woke up."

Jade's exact words had been that the children born to Kra-ell fathers and human mothers were inferior and defective, that they were a diluted breed who couldn't have long-lived children of their own, but she didn't want to repeat those offensive remarks that had made her feel like a failure all those years ago.

When Arwel looked at her with his piercing blue eyes, there was so much compassion in them that she suspected he knew what she'd said only in her head. Was he a mind reader?

"Did Jade think that the scouting team influenced the Mosuo social structure?" he asked.

Relieved at the change of subject, Aliya had no problem answering that. "Jade knew about the Mosuo, visited their villages, and even brought back souvenirs, or what I thought were souvenirs. I think she found some artifacts that caught her interest. She said it was obvious that the scouting crew had lived in the area and influenced the Mosuo society."

"I wonder whether the Kra-ell were put in stasis with venom or with technology." Lokan turned to Kalugal. "If it was done with venom, they would have been skeletal when they landed. But if they were on life support in some sort of pods, they would have probably awakened just fine. Did our father tell you anything about how the gods first arrived on Earth? Or maybe our mother mentioned something?"

Gods? Had she heard him right? Could gods have more than one meaning in English?

Kalugal shook his head. "Frankly, I don't remember either of them mentioning that, but I always assumed that the gods were asleep during the long journey to Earth, so maybe one of them said something to me when I was very young, and it sank into my subconscious. But it's also possible that I was influenced by science fiction movies."

"Does god mean like God Almighty, or does it have another meaning in English?" Aliya asked.

Alena smiled. "Our ancestors weren't deities. They were a divergent species of humanoids, probably from the same place as yours, but they were so advanced compared to humans and had such power over them that humans believed they were gods. Naturally, our ancestors reinforced those beliefs and created a whole mythology around a kernel of truth, aggrandizing everything they did, including their sexual shenanigans. Other mythologies copied from the first one, and that's how most of the world came to believe that they were gods. There is much more to the story, but let's save it for later, or you will never get to finish yours. What happened after you and your mother arrived at the Mosuo village?"

Aliya would have loved to hear more about the ancestors of these immortals, but if she insisted, Kalugal would just force her to go back to her story, and she hated how that felt. She'd rather keep talking and avoid it.

"The people were kind to us, and for a while, things were good. But then I matured, and my fangs started showing when I got excited or agitated, and I became so tall that I was the tallest person in the village. Most of the time, I managed to hide the fangs, never smiling and keeping my head down. But I couldn't hide my height, and people made fun of me, calling me a freak. And then my mother died when I was fifteen, and things got really bad."

"In what way?" Kalugal asked.

"The humans started to fear me. When I got angry, which happened a lot, my eyes turned red, and my fangs elongated. Some people noticed, and I heard them whispering behind my back that I must be possessed by a demon. I didn't want to wait and see what they planned to do about it. And since I knew that I couldn't thrall the entire village to forget me, I didn't feel safe to stay. I gathered my things, left in the middle of the night in a borrowed canoe, and rowed all the way to the ruins. I knew that I could survive there on my own. By then, I'd already been hunting for several years, and I was familiar with the area."

5

ORION

"How long have you been living in those ruins?" Orion asked.

"Since I was sixteen. About fourteen years."

Orion should have added up the years and realized that Aliya must be in her thirties. Her compound had been sacked over twenty-two years ago, and she hadn't been a baby when it happened. But she seemed so young and vulnerable that her answer had taken him by surprise. Aliya might be a thirty-year-old female, but to Orion, she seemed like a young woman who had suffered loneliness for far too long and needed people who would take her in and give her a home.

Casting a quick glance at Alena, he saw the same sentiment reflected in her eyes. Could they become Aliya's foster family?

He and Alena were old enough to be not only Aliya's parents, but her many times great-grandparents. Alena had told him that she would love to have a hundred children if she could, and he knew her heart was big enough to love them all, but would her motherly instincts extend to a grown woman?

Aliya might be chronologically and biologically all grown up, but emotionally she was still a scared little girl, and although she was smart and learned fast, her education level was most likely elementary.

"You remind me of Wonder," Alena said.

Jin snorted. "They are both tall and freakishly strong, but we know that Wonder is not Kra-ell."

Alena waved a hand. "Of course she's not, and that was not what I meant. They are both strong, and they were both isolated, although not in the same way. Wonder was frozen in stasis for thousands of years, and when she woke up, it was to a new world. She needed to learn everything about it and get her education up to modern standards." She turned to Aliya. "What was the last grade you attended in school?"

"Ninth grade," she said proudly. "I'm not ignorant."

"I know that you're not, and given how good your English is just from watching movies and talking to tourists, you are a fast learner. But the world has changed a lot in the last fourteen years, no doubt more so in the West than here. What I'm saying is that if you want to re-enter society, you have a lot of catching up to do."

Aliya's cheeks darkened with embarrassment. "I know about modern things, I just don't have them because I couldn't buy them."

"I bet," Carol said. "What would you like to have?"

"I would like to have a cell phone and learn how to use it. I don't have anyone to call, but I've seen people playing games and watching movies on their phones. I even saw a woman reading a book on it."

"The wonders of technology," Alena said. "We do love it."

Kalugal shifted in his chair, his frown indicating his impatience. "If you are done discussing the wonders of cell phones, I would like to know whether there is anything in that tunnel system that indicates a Kra-ell presence. Did you find any writing, artifacts, anything that didn't look human in origin?"

Aliya pursed her lips. "I've seen weird writing in one place. It was faded, and only a few lines remained, but it looked like letters, not just scratches."

"Can you read Kra-ell?" Carol asked.

Aliya shook her head. "I was supposed to start learning after my thirteenth birthday. Until then, we only learned what our mothers could teach us. The Kra-ell didn't even acknowledge the hybrid children until they reached puberty and started showing fangs. But hybrid females were so rare that I got special treatment. I was allowed to hang around the pureblooded females, and that's how I learned the spoken language. But I've never gotten to see what written Kra-ell looks like."

Orion realized that having been allowed to hang around Jade was a source of pride for Aliya. She'd mentioned it several times, and each time she had, her shoulders had gotten a little squarer.

"Tomorrow, I want you to show me those markings," Kalugal said. "It might be worthwhile to start excavation in the underground."

When Aliya frowned, Jacki leaned forward. "What's the matter? You don't want us digging around in there?"

"It's my home." Aliya glared at her. "Or it was until you came and took it away from me. Now I have nowhere to go and no place to live."

"You can come back home with us," Alena said. "You've been alone for an awfully long time. You must have been so terribly lonely, and I suspect that you went hungry on occasion, and that you were cold and probably bored. I can't imagine living in such isolation. I'm surprised that you didn't lose your mind."

Aliya snorted. "Maybe I did."

6

ALIYA

*A*lena had nailed it.

There had been many times Aliya felt like she was going insane. Often, she talked to herself or sang just to hear a voice, any voice. She hated the quiet of the tunnels, and when the archeological crew had arrived, she'd been equal parts worried about having her home discovered and glad for something to alleviate her loneliness, even though she'd never interacted with them.

They'd been oblivious to her presence even when she'd been so close that she could smell their breath.

Aliya had no television to entertain her, no books to read. Her only source of entertainment was an old transistor radio that didn't work in the ruins, not topside nor underground, and it needed batteries, which she had to steal when the old ones died out. So basically, she had nothing to keep her busy other than hunting for food.

It was difficult to subsist just on blood, and since she didn't want to kill the animals that she drank from, she only took a few sips from each, let them go, and hunted for the next. That alone filled most of her days.

When the loneliness became too much, she ventured into the village during the evening hours when it was getting dark, but the streets were still full of tourists. With the way she looked, going unnoticed was nearly impossible. Usually, she tied a scarf around the lower part of her face, hunched her shoulders, and tried to stick to the shadows, and yet many times she'd been forced to hypnotically coerce people to forget that they'd seen her. It wasn't a problem when she needed to do it to one or two people at a time, but more than that was difficult. It drained her of energy, sometimes so severely that she'd lacked the strength to get back to her tunnels and had to either spend a few hours resting or find a source of blood to replenish her energy. But since hunting also required strength, she usually found a shadowy resting spot under a tree or behind some bushes.

"Where is your home?" she asked Alena.

"In California. Do you know where that is?"

Aliya shrugged. "Somewhere in America."

"Correct. It's on the West Coast of the United States. We have a secret village where only immortals live. You will not have to hide from people there, you'll have friends, and you will no longer be alone."

That sounded too good to be true, which meant that there was a catch. Did they need her for breeding? Or maybe they wanted to experiment on her?

Jade had warned Aliya and the other hybrids that if the humans discovered them, they would be locked in a lab and cut up like rats. Jade had put the fear of the Mother in them, and she hadn't been wrong. Aliya had learned in school about the atrocities the Japanese committed against the Chinese people during the big war. If humans could be so horrible to each other, Aliya could only imagine what they would do to an alien freak like her.

"Why are you inviting me to your secret village? What's in it for you?"

Looking offended, Alena leaned away. "I'm not inviting you because I have anything to gain by it. I'm doing it for you out of kindness." She let out a breath as if to calm herself, and a moment later her eyes softened. "You and your mother were taken in by the Mosuo, so you've experienced kindness from strangers before. You shouldn't be so suspicious when someone wants to help you."

"They needed my mother's skill with the sewing machine. She worked very hard to earn our stay."

"The phrase is to earn your keep," Kalugal corrected. "Alena has a kind soul, and that's why she's inviting you to come home with her, but I'm not sure she should, or even if she has the authority to extend such an invitation to you. You need to prove yourself valuable first." He crossed his arms over his chest. "Alena's brother is in charge of the village, and although he's a fair male, he's not as kind-hearted as his sister. He might refuse you entry to his community."

Aliya shifted her eyes to Alena. "Is that true?"

"I'm afraid so. I can put in a good word on your behalf, but Kian would want proof that you can be trusted and that you are willing to contribute to the community. Since you were not born into the clan, you will have to earn your keep."

It seemed like they needed workers, which made sense. If they were a secret community of immortals, and they didn't have humans to serve them, they would be very glad for a servant girl that was strong and could work long hours.

Hard work had never scared Aliya, but she didn't want to be treated like a slave. She didn't mind cleaning their houses and tending to their gardens, but she wanted to get paid for her work and to be treated with respect.

"How much would I get paid?"

Alena chuckled. "Before we negotiate your pay, we need to discuss what kind of work you'd be doing for the clan."

"I can do many things. I can clean, I can tend to crops and animals, and I can carry heavy things. I can cook a little, but that would be a waste of my abilities. My biggest assets are my strength and endurance. I could probably clean twenty houses in one day."

7

ALENA

*O*nce again, Kalugal had impressed Alena. His move to use reverse psychology on Aliya had been brilliant. By making her acceptance conditional on her actions, he was taking away the invitation and making her work for it.

Aliya was suspicious of their motives, and she couldn't accept that they were offering her a place in the village out of kindness. She also didn't like getting something for nothing or feeling obligated to anyone. Kalugal had put the offer in terms she could understand and accept without feeling like she was being trapped or given charity.

That was why Alena had played along and hadn't corrected him even though what he'd told Aliya hadn't been entirely true.

Theoretically, Kian could refuse, and Alena would have to respect his decision, but she knew he wouldn't. Under his gruff exterior, Kian was just as soft-hearted as she was, especially when it came to a lonely female with no people to call her own.

Heck, if he'd invited Emmett and Vrog to live in the village, there was no chance he would turn Aliya away.

"Twenty houses, eh?" Kalugal sounded amused. "I have a pretty big house. I think it should count as five." He turned to Jacki. "What do you think?"

"I think that Aliya's unique attributes would be wasted on menial labor and should be better utilized. There is nothing wrong with a cleaning job, of course, and if that's what she wants to do, she would have plenty of clients in the village who would be willing to pay handsomely for her services, but I think Guardians are paid even better."

Were Jacki and Kalugal playing good cop, bad cop? Or did Jacki seriously think that Kian would allow Aliya to join the Guardian force?

Alena doubted that. Eleanor, who'd already proven that she was capable and loyal, and who had a niece and a nephew in the village, still hadn't been officially accepted into the training program. Aliya would most likely have to prove herself over an even longer period of time. She was Kra-ell, and she had no one in the village she cared for and was protective of. She would also have to go through several tests before she could start training.

Kalugal's eyes were full of amusement as he took it from there. "As I said before, Aliya needs to prove herself deserving of a spot in the village, and then further prove herself to be considered for the Guardian force."

"What are Guardians?" Aliya asked. "Are they defenders of the village?"

"That's part of the job," Arwel said. "We also wage war against human trafficking."

Aliya looked confused. "Why would you wage war against transportation? Isn't it necessary for shipping goods and transporting people to where they need to go?"

Alena wondered whether it was just the language barrier or was Aliya ignorant of what was going on in the world around her.

Probably both.

In some ways she was like a child, innocent, vulnerable. And yet in others, she was remarkably strong. Aliya had been through hell, losing her place in the world twice, and somehow, she had not only survived but had clung to her principles and hadn't used her abilities to harm people or animals.

That was quite admirable, and Alena was sure Kian would recognize the diamond in the rough that Aliya was.

"Trafficking is a misleading term," Jin said. "It means capturing humans, mainly women, and forcing them into sex slavery."

Aliya gaped at her. "That's terrible. Why is it called trafficking?"

"They use the term because the bad guys capture young women and girls and transport them from one place to another illegally." Jin leaned forward. "But that's like calling murder a misuse of weaponry or some other stupid term that makes a horrific crime sound more palatable to delicate ears."

Aliya pursed her lips. "Is this an American thing? Or do they call it trafficking all over the world?"

"I don't know." Jin leaned back and crossed her arms over her chest. "It doesn't matter what they call it—the flesh market, sex slavery, ruining of lives—it needs to be stopped. I was considering joining the force myself, but my mate, who is a Head Guardian, wouldn't hear of it." She turned a baleful look at Arwel.

He shrugged. "If you really wanted to, you could have filled out an application like everyone else, and I wouldn't have stopped you. You decided that you prefer to run a business with your sister, so don't make me into the bad guy here."

"You're not bad. You're just stubborn and chauvinistic."

"Children." Carol lifted her hand. "This is not about you. This is about Aliya, and I think she'd make a great Guardian." She smiled at the girl. "I trained for a while, but then I met Lokan and my priorities changed. Also, I didn't have the patience to train for years on end. But you most likely wouldn't have to. With your strength and speed, you could probably graduate in months instead of decades."

"It's not just about physical ability," Arwel said. "There is a lot involved in being a professional Guardian—weapons training, strategizing, fighting techniques, negotiation tactics, and so on."

As Arwel listed the things Guardians were supposed to know, Aliya's excited expression turned into a frown. "I don't know if I want to be a Guardian. You said that you wage war against traffickers, but how is that war waged? Do you use machine guns and grenades? Because I don't know how to use them, and I don't think I want to learn that."

Leaning over, Alena patted Aliya's hand. "The Guardians learn how to use those weapons, but that's not how they fight trafficking. They find the places where the victims are held, rescue them, and leave the scum that exploited them to the human police. The clan has a rehabilitation center for the victims, where they get medical and psychological help. They can also learn a trade, so when they are ready, they can re-enter society and live independently."

"That sounds like a very honorable occupation." Aliya regarded Arwel with respect in her eyes. "Mother bless you for what you are doing for these poor women and girls. I would love to help, but with the way I look, I might scare them." She shifted her eyes to Alena. "When people see a woman like you, they think you're an angel. When they see me, they think I'm a demon."

8

ALIYA

"*T*hat's nonsense," Alena said. "You are very pretty, and no one will think that you are a demon."

Aliya arched a brow. "Did you really look at me? What else could they think?"

"I have fangs too," Jin said. "I cover them up with attitude."

"Your fangs are tiny in comparison to mine, but fangs are not my only problem." Aliya let her eyes flash red. "When I'm calm, I can control my eyes and my fangs, but when I'm excited, I can't."

"That's what sunglasses are for," Carol said. "And the rest can be done with the right clothes. Vlad, who is also one-quarter Kra-ell like Jin, is very tall and very thin, has one eye that's green and the other blue, and his fangs used to elongate with the slightest provocation. He adopted a Goth style, and everyone assumed that he was wearing contact lenses to change his eye color and prosthetic fangs. You could do the same thing."

"Goth? What's that?"

"I'll show you." Jin pulled out her phone, typed something on the screen, and then handed it to Aliya.

The girl in the picture had her brows and nose pierced, her eyes lined with heavy black makeup, and her fingernails painted black with purple splotches. Her hair was also black, but the tips were painted blood red. She wore black clothes with rips and buckles all over and boots that added at least six centimeters to her height.

But underneath it all, the girl was just a human in a costume. If Aliya did all that, she would look even weirder than she looked now.

"I don't think that can help me." She handed Jin her phone back.

"I'm tired." Jacki yawned. "It's been a long day for all of us. Can we continue this talk tomorrow?"

"Of course, my love." Kalugal put his arm around his mate's shoulders and kissed the top of her head.

"Where am I going to sleep?" Aliya asked.

With all the excitement, she'd forgotten that her plan had been to escape once her belly was full. She was supposed to pretend that she was excited by their offer, not actually consider it.

"Right here on the couch," Kalugal said. "I want you where I can keep an eye on you."

Aliya crossed her arms over her chest and glared at him. "So I'm a prisoner after all?"

"No, you are a guest, and I'm keeping you here for your own good. We are offering you a better life, a chance to reach your full potential, but you are skittish, mistrustful, and impulsive, and you might decide to run before we can convince you that you can trust us."

He sounded so sincere, but she couldn't trust him. He was too charming, too smooth, and men like him were players and manipulators. Even she knew that.

"Do I have to sleep here? Can't I get my own room?"

Jin snorted. "For someone who's lived in a cave for fourteen years, a couch in the living room of the presidential suite should seem like a luxury to be delighted about. Demanding your own room is kind of obnoxious and could only mean that you're plotting something, and that something is probably an escape."

The woman had a point. "I'm not demanding anything. But you keep telling me that I'm a guest, not a prisoner, so shouldn't I get a room of my own?"

"You can sleep in mine," Phinas offered. "There are two beds, and I only need one."

The mated males seemed safe, but Phinas didn't have a mate. "I'm not spending the night with a bachelor."

"Why not?" Jin asked. "As a half Kra-ell who grew up watching the pureblooded females command a harem of males, you shouldn't be concerned with human propriety rules. Besides, Phinas is quite a catch. He's handsome and he's Kalugal's right-hand man. But if you don't want him, you have nothing to fear because he's not going to try anything, and even if he did, you could overpower him with ease. You are so damn strong that you have nothing to worry about. No male can overpower you unless he holds a knife to your throat, a gun to your temple, or slips drugs into your drink."

"That's not true. Kalugal and Orion can force me to do whatever they want. They are both mated, so I'm not worried that they would take sexual advantage of me, but they could command me to have sex with Phinas or one of the other bachelors."

"Why would they do that?" Alena asked.

Aliya shrugged. "As a favor to the unmated males or for their own amusement."

"They would never do that," Alena said. "Orion and Kalugal are good people and honorable males."

The truth was that Aliya didn't fear any of them would want sex from her, but she needed an excuse to be left alone so she could escape. "You saying that they are honorable doesn't mean that it's true."

"You are so full of it," Jin said. "You grew up in a Kra-ell compound and then among the Mosuo. You shouldn't have any of the human hang-ups about sex."

"I don't." Yes, she did.

Despite being half Kra-ell, and despite growing up in the Mosuo village, Aliya was still a virgin at thirty.

When her flowering time had come, none of the boys indicated that they were interested in her inviting them to her flowering room. She'd been too tall, too skinny, too flat-chested, and too weird.

But those had all been excuses. The truth was that all the boys feared her, and for a good reason.

"Perhaps you'd be more comfortable sleeping with the Odus," Alena suggested.

Aliya looked around the table. By now, she knew everyone's name, but perhaps Odu was a surname?

"Do you mean Carol and Lokan or Jin and Arwel?"

9

ALENA

*A*fter a moment of confusion, Alena chuckled. "Odu is not anyone's last name or nickname. You didn't meet the Odus yet. They are my butlers." When Aliya tilted her head, Alena added, "They are my servants."

Aliya seemed even more baffled. Looking at Kalugal and Jacki and then back at Alena, she shook her head. "I thought that he was the rich one, and he only has an assistant. Are you a princess or something?"

How to answer that?

Her companions would expect her to say that she was, but although her mother was a queen in every conceivable way, Alena never thought of herself as royalty.

Annani had been born to the gods' leading couple and had been groomed to one day take over rulership. The gods had been destroyed, her throne along with them, but she was still a powerful goddess, the head of their clan, and the ultimate drama queen.

Perhaps her mother's supercharged grandness was why Alena had always underplayed her importance and insisted that she shouldn't be treated any differently than any other clan member. Sari and Kian led their respective arms of the clan, so they deserved some deference, but they never referred to themselves as prince or princess either. Only Amanda, who took after their mother in the drama department, was the one nicknamed princess.

"Although my mother, who is the head of our clan, acts like a queen, she doesn't refer to herself as one." As a goddess, Annani probably considered being called a queen a step down in status. "Therefore, neither my siblings nor I are treated as royalty either. One of the Odus has always been my servant and protector, and for this trip, my mother loaned me one of hers, so I will be doubly protected."

Aliya regarded her with suspicion in her dark eyes. "So they are not your servants. They are your bodyguards."

"In a way, they are, but that's not their primary function. Their job is to take care of me the way a servant would."

Aliya's suspicious expression only deepened. "But if their job is also to protect you, why weren't they with you in the ruins? And where are they now?"

"They are in their room."

Explaining to Aliya why the Odus had been left behind required a backstory that Alena preferred not to get into at the moment.

"I was wondering about that as well," Jacki said. "Kian made such a big deal about wanting you protected, and yet you leave your Odus in the hotel room. Why didn't you bring them along on our boat trip or to the excavation site?"

It seemed like the backstory would have to be told after all.

Alena sighed. "Since Okidu's accident, I'm hesitant about getting them anywhere near water. I don't want them to accidentally reboot before we know the consequences of Okidu and Onidu's new protocol's emergence."

"I get it," Jacki said. "But it defies the purpose of them being here. The Odus are supposed to protect you, but since we are near a lake, there is water everywhere, and they are no good to you in their hotel room."

Alena nodded. "I should have thought it through before bringing them along." She smiled at Arwel. "Kian wanted me to take Guardians instead, and I insisted that the Odus would suffice. I'm glad that he sent you anyway. There is no substitute for having a Head Guardian as my protector."

Arwel's upper lip curled in a grimace. "I didn't do such a great job of it, and if we'd had the Odus with us in the ruins, I would have been much less worried when we found ourselves trapped. From now on, I would prefer if they tagged along. There is no reason to fear that they will accidentally drown."

Kalugal cleared his throat. "I disagree. I was told that the Odus are very heavy. If even one of them joined us on the lake, the canoe's center of gravity might have been disturbed, and if the Odu made the wrong move, he could've tipped the boat over." He wrapped his arm around Jacki's shoulders. "I would have been really upset if my wife got dunked in the lake's cold water."

"Yeah," Jacki confirmed. "I would have been pissed as hell. I might be immortal, and getting submerged in cold water won't kill me, but Junior is still human and fragile." She gave Alena an amused look. "Unlike you, the cold bothers me very much."

Pretending to be upset, Alena huffed and crossed her arms over her chest. "It appears that none of you will let me live down that silly performance."

"Silly?" Orion lifted a brow. "That performance made me fall in love with you. It was the most important performance of our lives."

"Oh," Carol sighed. "That's so romantic. Jacki told me about your rendition of "Let It Go," and she said it was one of the best ones she'd ever heard. I would love to hear you sing it."

"Not tonight."

"Why not?"

"Because the entire hotel will hear me, and we are not supposed to draw attention to ourselves. Remind me when we visit the ruins again, and I'll sing it for you in the tunnels. On one condition, though. You will sing with me."

Carol extended her hand to Alena. "You've got yourself a deal. We can sing a duet. You'll be the snow queen, and I'll be the little sister."

That sounded like fun, but then Alena remembered all the taunting she'd heard over the years and reconsidered. "On second thought, that might not be a good idea.

The walls might topple and bury us alive. I was told that my singing could have outdone the horns of Jericho."

As her friends and family laughed, Alena noticed that Aliya remained somber, or maybe just pensive.

"What's wrong, Aliya?"

"I'm confused," the girl said. "If these Odus are so big and fat that it's dangerous to let them sit in the canoe, then they can't be very good bodyguards."

Alena had hoped that talking about her singing would lighten Aliya's mood, but it seemed that the girl's mind was stuck on the previous subject of conversation.

"The Odus are neither big nor fat," Arwel said. "In fact, they look like average middle-aged men. The reason that they are so heavy is that they are part people and part machine, and the parts that are machine are very heavy."

"Were they injured in a war?" Aliya asked. "Did they get low-quality replacement arms or legs?" She cast Alena an accusing look. "The replacements are not supposed to be heavy, and you are rich enough to get your servants the best."

Alena had a feeling that no roundabout explanation would satisfy Aliya. She already knew about the clan, so telling her the truth about the Odus was probably okay.

"They weren't injured," Alena said. "The Odus were never human or immortal. They were not born. They were built, and they are very sophisticated machines." She hated calling the Odus that, but she doubted Aliya would know what a cyborg was. Besides, that wasn't a good description of the Odus either.

Even prior to Okidu and Onidu's reboot, Alena had always thought of them as a different kind of people, an emergent species that couldn't reproduce biologically but that could potentially manufacture their offspring. Was that why Okidu had given Kian the blueprints to their design?

It was a scary idea. Okidu didn't seem capable of being the mastermind behind a future cyborg revolution, but whoever had programmed him might be.

Perhaps the family needed to meet again and discuss Okidu's gift some more. So far, William hadn't managed to decipher the instructions, but he was in the process of assembling a team of bioinformaticians to help him with the genetic code part. If the family decided that it was too risky, they should shut down that project before the clan committed large resources to it.

"Machines?" Aliya tilted her head again. "What do you mean?"

"They look and act human," Alena continued, "but they have a computer for a brain and a mechanical pump for a heart. They also don't need to sleep, so even though I got them a hotel room, they don't use the beds, and you can sleep on one. They are not going to bother you because they are neither male nor female. They don't have sexual organs, they are not aggressive, and they are programmed to be polite, accommodating, and helpful."

Aliya didn't look nearly as flabbergasted on hearing about the technological wonder of the Odus as Alena had expected.

"You don't seem surprised."

Carol snorted. "The poor girl's reached the overload stage. That's all. She's become numb."

"No," Aliya shook her head. "It's just that I must have heard about robot servants before." She rubbed her temple. "I'm not sure, though. Maybe I just saw a movie about cyborgs."

Alena chuckled. "I didn't use the word cyborg to describe the Odus because I didn't think you'd know what that meant. Jade must have brought back a sci-fi movie from one of her trips."

Kalugal leaned over the table, his eyes more curious than Alena had seen them throughout the evening. "Did Jade or any of the other purebloods mention the Odus?"

"I don't remember. It's just that the idea of servants who don't need sleep and are stronger and better than human servants in every way doesn't sound new to me."

10

ALIYA

"*I* wouldn't say that they are better than humans," Alena said. "The Odus have a very limited capacity for decision making." She hesitated for a moment. "We don't really understand their technology, but we suspect that they were deliberately limited by their creators. Still, I doubt that even at their full capacity, they could match human creativity, ingenuity, and problem-solving capabilities."

What Aliya understood from Alena's description was that the Odus were simple creatures that would be easy to fool. Escaping them shouldn't be as difficult as escaping these descendants of gods who called themselves immortals. Except, for that to work, she shouldn't appear too eager to sleep in the cyborgs' room, or the sly Kalugal would guess her intentions.

She would use his own tactics against him.

The male thought that she'd bought his bait and switch maneuver, making her think that Alena's invitation was conditional on her brother's approval and on Aliya's willingness to work.

At first, she hadn't realized that Kalugal had been playing her, and perhaps she wouldn't have caught on to it if Alena was a better actress. But the woman had been so obvious that it had been funny to watch.

The truth was that Alena's bad acting made Aliya like her even more. The woman wasn't fake or smooth like Kalugal, which made her more trustworthy, but Aliya wasn't stupid enough to think that she could trust Alena implicitly.

"Can you take me to meet them?" she asked. "From your description, they sound harmless, but since they are your bodyguards, they can't be that simple. Besides, even though you said that they are neither male nor female, you refer to them as male. I would like to judge for myself if I'll be comfortable sleeping in their room."

Aliya wasn't a great actress either, and learning from Alena's mistakes, she'd chosen to stick as close to the truth as she could. Since she'd meant every word, no one could detect a lie she hadn't voiced.

Nevertheless, Kalugal regarded her with that annoying smirk of his. "Before you get any ideas in your head, you should know that they are incredibly strong, much stronger than even you. If Alena tells them to keep you from leaving the room, they will stop you. And since they don't need to sleep, they will watch you constantly. Even if you manage to overcome my compulsion not to leave the hotel without my permission, escaping the Odus would be even less likely than escaping any of us."

Crap, was she that transparent?

"Who said I was planning to escape?"

He chuckled. "It's written all over your face. You wouldn't make a good spy, Aliya."

She grimaced. "With the way I look, being a spy would be the worst career choice for me."

"So true." Carol pushed away from the table and rose to her feet. "I'll accompany you to the Odus and tell you all about being a spy on the way." She fluffed her pretty blond curls as she waited for Aliya to follow. "No one ever suspects the little curvy blond. The more harmless you look, the better spy you make." She threaded her arm through Aliya's. "And you, my dear, look the opposite of harmless."

"I know. I look scary to humans."

As Alena got up, Orion started to rise, but she put a hand on his shoulder. "You should stay. I'm just going downstairs with Aliya and Carol to the Odus' room and then back up here. I'm supposed to call one of the Odus to escort me, but that would ruin the element of surprise. Welgost can do that."

"It would be my pleasure." The warrior got up.

Orion looked disappointed, and Aliya wondered why. Was it because he wanted to be with his mate every minute of the day?

The males of this long-lived species were overly attached to their females. At first, it seemed pleasant, and Aliya had wondered what it would be like to have a single male so devoted to her, but after watching them some more, she'd decided that it was too much. She wouldn't like so much constant attention.

It would feel suffocating.

"I'm curious to see their reaction to you, and yours to them," Carol said as they walked out of Kalugal's suite.

"Why?"

"You look very Kra-ell. I wonder if they will recognize you as one."

"Did they recognize the other hybrids living in your village?"

"I don't know." Carol glanced at Alena. "Do you?"

"No one mentioned it, so I assume that they didn't react any differently to Emmett and Vrog than to other newcomers."

"Okay, then." Carol tightened her hold on Aliya's arm. "Let me tell you about my pre-matehood days." As they took the stairs down to the hotel's second floor, Carol amused Alena and Aliya with an anecdote from her past as an escort to a powerful man. The few minutes it took to get to the Odus' room weren't long enough to get into more details, and Aliya was dying to learn more about Carol's adventures. Carol was a gifted storyteller, and listening to her was better than watching television. Aliya hadn't had the pleasure of doing that in years.

When Alena knocked on the door, it opened almost instantly, and a short, stockily built male smiled and bowed. "Mistress Alena, what a pleasure it is to be graced by your presence. How can Oridu and I be of service?"

"I have a new friend I would like you to meet." She entered the room and motioned for Aliya and Carol to follow. "This is Aliya, and she belongs to the same people as Emmett and Vrog. She is half-human and half-Kra-ell."

The Odu looked so human that Aliya suspected Alena and the others had been messing with her, but when she got closer and sniffed him, she knew they had told her the truth.

Under the normal smell of flesh, she could scent much more metal than should be in any living thing's body. It wasn't any of the metals she was familiar with either. She hadn't smelled anything like that before.

"Hello, Mistress Aliya," the Odu smiled a fake-looking smile and bowed. "I am Ovidu."

His twin, whose name was Oridu, did the same. "Is there anything we can do to serve you?"

"I just wanted to meet you, but thank you for offering." Aliya scrambled for something to say to get herself out of having to spend the night with the cyborgs.

They were creepy, and she would rather spend the night on Kalugal and Jacki's couch than alone with them.

"Well?" Alena arched a brow. "Now that you've met the Odus, are you comfortable sleeping in their room?"

"Are you sure that they don't need the beds?" Aliya looked around the small hotel room. There was one chair but no couch. "I don't want to make one of them spend the night sitting on a chair."

"I do not mind, mistress," Ovidu said. "Oridu and I will watch television all night long. We want to learn the local customs."

Perhaps she could use that as an excuse. "I wouldn't want to spoil their plans. I also want to watch some television, but probably not the same programs as the Odus. Do you think Kalugal and Jacki would mind if I watched in their living room? I'll keep the volume down."

Thankfully, Alena got the hint. "You can ask, and if they don't want to be bothered by the noise, I can give you a pair of headphones."

11

ARWEL

*A*s the door closed behind Aliya, Kalugal turned to Arwel. "What does your empathy tell you about her?"

"Aliya is very guarded, and she's projecting even fewer emotions than most immortals, and I don't know whether it's because of her Kra-ell upbringing, her life experiences, or her natural disposition."

Orion chuckled. "You don't need to be an empath to know that she's looking for ways to escape. She's like a trapped animal, only much smarter and more cunning."

"She needs new clothing," Jin said. "If we take her shopping, she might warm to us."

Kalugal waved a dismissive hand. "She'll just use the opportunity to split."

"You'll compel her to stay with us." Jin crossed her arms over her chest. "In fact, I think she will feel more relaxed if only the girls go with her. I don't know any woman who doesn't enjoy clothes shopping with her girlfriends. Even a half Kra-ell hard-ass like Aliya wants to look nice."

Kalugal shook his head. "The nearest town with department stores that carry the kind of clothing you want to get her is about two hours' drive away, and I doubt you'll find anything for a female that's over six feet tall even there."

"I'm sure we will find something. At the very least, she needs underwear and shoes. She walked out of here barefoot, if you didn't notice. I don't have any new underwear to give her, and wearing someone else's panties even after they've been laundered is gross, so I didn't give her any, and I bet she's gone commando."

Phinas groaned. "I could have done without that image."

Jacki's eyes widened. "Do you find her attractive?"

"Why wouldn't I? She's pretty, and I like her personality. She's a smart and proud female."

"Aliya looks very alien," Jacki said. "I really can't understand how the pureblooded Kra-ell managed to pass for humans. I'm glad that immortals look for the most part human, and I can't imagine being attracted to someone so alien-looking."

"Doesn't bother me," Phinas said. "I find Aliya rather interesting."

"What about her super-strength and her aggressiveness?" Jin asked. "Isn't that a turn-off for a macho guy like you?"

He gave her an amused look. "Who said that I'm macho? Maybe I enjoy aggressive women?"

"You don't," Jin said with surprising conviction. "You're just messing with us."

"How do you know that?" Phinas asked.

"I just do." Jin uncrossed her arms. "Aliya is not for you."

Arwel wasn't sure about that at all. Despite being a former Doomer, Phinas was a fine male, and he sure as hell was attracted to Aliya. Furthermore, Arwel had noticed her stealing covert looks at the guy. She wasn't indifferent to him either.

"I'll send Shamash to get Aliya new clothes." Kalugal took Jacki's hand. "Can you make a list of what she needs?"

"She needs everything." Jacki sighed. "And Jin is right. We should take her shopping instead. It will build trust and friendship between us."

"Not everyone is like you, my love." He lifted her hand and kissed the back of it. "Aliya will see right through it. Besides, she's intensely proud and doesn't like handouts. She needs to earn her new clothing, and she can do that by guiding us through the tunnels."

Arwel nodded. "Kalugal is right. Aliya would hate to get a new wardrobe as charity. She will be much happier if she has to work for it."

"I can offer her money as compensation for taking over her home." Kalugal ran a hand over his goatee. "Frankly, I feel a little guilty about that, and paying her is the least I can do."

"You're such a sweetheart." Jacki kissed his cheek. "But I don't know what you're expecting to find there. Unless Aliya was lying, the only thing she's ever found in there was illegible scribbles on the wall that might or might not be Kra-ell symbols. And given that she's had fourteen years to explore, that's probably all you're going to find."

"Perhaps." Kalugal lifted her hand and kissed it again. "But maybe my talented wife could put her hand on the writing and get a vision about its origins."

Jacki eyed him from under lowered lashes. "I thought that you didn't want me to have visions while I was pregnant."

"I changed my mind. After you got the vision of Aliya as a young girl, you were more than fine. You were excited, and there was a spark in your eyes. I realized that your visions don't harm you and might actually benefit you."

"Thank the merciful Fates." She gave him a relieved smile. "I didn't want to worry you before, but now that your approach has changed and you've become more reasonable, I can tell you that my visions don't ask for my permission or yours to appear. I was lucky not to get any before today, but that doesn't mean that my luck will hold throughout my pregnancy."

"I know that, which was why I didn't want to take you to Egypt. I was afraid that everything you touched there would bring up visions. I didn't expect to find many artifacts at this site because it has been excavated several times before, so I assumed there was less of a chance of you touching something that would evoke a vision. Besides, you don't speak Chinese."

"I don't speak Arabic either."

As Kalugal scrambled to say something to explain what had probably been a gut feeling, Arwel came to his rescue. "We should call Vrog and tell him about Aliya. He will be happy to hear that one of the hybrid females managed to escape."

Jin snorted. "I wouldn't be surprised if Vrog convinces Mey and Yamanu to leave the echoes alone and take him to her. Aliya is an even rarer find than a Dormant."

12

VROG

"We should call Arwel." Yamanu put his coffee cup down. "We need to tell him about the echoes of the Kra-ell purebloods that Mey saw."

Vrog reached for the carafe and refilled the Guardian's cup. "We should. They called us with what they'd found, we should offer them the same courtesy."

"They had a picture of what looked like the Kra-ell goddess," Mey said. "We have nothing. I didn't learn anything from those echoes except what the pureblooded females looked like. I couldn't understand anything they said. Vrog and I have made some progress with my Kra-ell, so maybe the next time I listen to that echo, I'll understand what they were fighting about, but I doubt I will figure it all out in one go. I would probably have to listen to them many times, try to memorize what they say, and repeat it to Vrog to translate."

"Nevertheless, we need to call Arwel," Yamanu said. "Let's do it right now."

As the Guardian pulled out his phone, Vrog's began ringing, and as he picked it up and glanced at the caller ID, he had to smile. "Speak of the devil." He answered and activated the speaker function. "Hello, Arwel. I know that you're an empath, but I didn't know that you are powerful enough to feel us talking about calling you from so many miles away."

"Do you have news for us?" Arwel asked.

"We've debated whether the echoes Mey saw and heard were newsworthy. She doesn't think so, but I agree with Yamanu that they are. I'll let her tell you about it."

Shaking her head, Mey let out a breath. "I saw two Kra-ell pureblooded females fighting, but they were talking too fast for me to understand what they were fighting about. They looked very alien and were incredibly strong and vicious. Pretty, in a weird way though, like porcelain dolls that had been stretched out. They were both well over six feet tall and very thin."

"That description matches what we found here," Arwel said. "Aliya had trouble blending in because she looked too alien."

Vrog's heart started pounding against his ribcage. None of the Kra-ell females he remembered had been called Aliya. Had the other group found a hybrid among the Mosuo? A live female, or a story of one?

"Who's Aliya?" he asked.

"I'm surprised that you don't recognize her name. She's a hybrid female who escaped the compound as a child. She still looked human when the attack happened, and the invading Kra-ell let her go with her human mother."

Vrog's throat dried out in an instant. "Does she know what happened there?"

"She knows more than you do, but she was just eight at the time, so I don't know how reliable her memories are. The one thing I'm sure of, though, is that your people were massacred by a different Kra-ell tribe. Aliya refers to them as the bad Kra-ell."

Given the girl's age at the time of the attack, he should have known her at least by name. Perhaps Aliya was her Chinese name, and she had another one in the Kra-ell language?

"Can you ask her what her Kra-ell name is?"

"She's not here at the moment. Alena and Carol took her to meet the Odus."

"Why?"

"She's skittish as hell, stubborn, suspicious, and strong of body and mind. We are afraid that she'll manage to overcome Kalugal's compulsion to stay and run away. For her own good, we need to keep her with us."

His gut clenching with worry, Vrog asked, "Did you have to hurt her while apprehending her?"

Arwel chuckled. "We did our best not to harm her, but she didn't extend us the same courtesy. If not for Orion, she might have overpowered both Phinas and me, two well-trained and experienced warriors. Aliya is incredibly strong."

Pride swelled in Vrog's chest. "Did Orion compel her to stop fighting?"

"He knocked her out with a rock."

"Why would he do that?" Vrog asked.

"In the heat of the pursuit, he forgot that he was a compeller."

How could anyone forget their ability? Once they got to Lugu Lake, Vrog would have a talk with Orion and give him a piece of his mind.

"Is she okay?" Mey asked.

"She's fine. The moment she woke up, she started fighting again, but this time around, Orion remembered that he's a compeller and used his ability to subdue her."

"How did you find her?" Mey asked. "Did she live with the Mosuo?"

"She did, but she had to leave once her Kra-ell features became too dominant."

As Arwel told them the rest of the story of how Aliya had trapped them in the tunnels underneath the ruins, and what it had taken to catch her, Vrog found himself infatuated with the female even before he'd laid eyes on her.

Aliya was everything a Kra-ell female should be and then some. Smart, resourceful, cunning, strong, and she even followed the Mother's code of conduct, which was most admirable. As a hybrid who'd lived among humans for most of her life, that was unexpected.

"Does she remember me?" he asked when Arwel was done.

"She remembered your name."

"Does she want to see me?"

"I'm sure she does, but when we offered to call you as proof that we didn't mean her harm, she refused. As I said, she's very suspicious of everyone, and she thinks that you might have betrayed the tribe to those bad Kra-ell."

The baseless accusation felt like a kick to Vrog's gut. "Why would she think that?"

"Because you were away, and you survived," Arwel said.

13

VROG

"I need to see her." Vrog turned to Morris. "Can you fly us out to Lugu Lake tomorrow?"

"What about the echoes?" May asked. "I'm not done with them."

"There is no rush," Arwel said. "Aliya is not going anywhere anytime soon. Kalugal wants her to take us down to the tunnels and show us what she found there, which isn't much, but maybe she just didn't know where to look."

Vrog didn't want to wait for Mey to hear the echoes again. They weren't going anywhere, and she could come back to them at any time. The same wasn't true of Aliya.

"What did she find?" Yamanu asked.

"Some markings that might be in the Kra-ell language. She can speak it, but she doesn't read or write it or even know what it looks like."

Vrog perked up. "Then you need me there. I can read and write it."

"I know what it looks like," Jin said. "And we can take pictures and send them to you, but not right away. Our phones don't work in the ruins. There is some weird interference in the soil that blocks transmission. Kalugal was told that it's caused by copper deposits, but he plans on bringing in a geologist to check."

Vrog couldn't care less about the copper in the soil, the interference, or even traces of Kra-ell habitation. All he cared about was the hybrid female who was probably scared and needed someone to reassure her and take care of her.

If she would let him, he was the perfect choice for the job of her guide and protector. He could invite her to live in the staff quarters at the school, and he could supplement her education himself. He wouldn't expect anything in return either. He would be thrilled just to have her around.

The question was what the clan wanted to do, or rather Kian, who called the shots even though it wasn't his place.

They had no right to Aliya. No one had. She should be offered the choice to either join them, or come live with him at the school, or live on her own.

Hopefully, Kian would take the moral high ground and give her those choices instead of forcing her to live in the village. If he didn't, there was little Vrog could do other than argue on her behalf.

"After you are done exploring the tunnels, what are you planning to do with Aliya?" he asked.

"We want to take her with us to the village," Kalugal's wife said. "The poor girl lived alone in those tunnels for fourteen years. You should've seen her when we found her. She looked like a homeless wild woman. After she'd showered and put on the clothes Jin lent her, Aliya looked like a different person."

"I think she should come live with me in the school. I can tutor her, so she at least has a high-school education."

"Don't take this the wrong way, Vrog," Kalugal said. "But Aliya is not like the Kra-ell females you knew. She's a prude, and she doesn't want to be left alone with bachelors, and that's when she knows none of us can overpower her. With you, she will feel defenseless. Besides, she needs people to hang out with, and she can't do it in your school. She would either have to hide in her room or thrall everyone she meets. She looks too alien."

"I'm sure there is a solution for that. Jade used to travel all over the world, using commercial airlines."

"Jade was a powerful thraller," Kalugal said. "She could probably effect a continuous thrall that worked like my shroud. Aliya is not nearly as powerful, and her solution is to hide and go out only at night when she absolutely has to. That's no way to live."

Vrog realized that Kalugal and the rest of his team had already decided Aliya's future, and he would have to fight for her right to choose after all.

"First of all, the decision should be Aliya's. Her case is no different than mine, and Kian offered me the choice to either join the clan or not."

"Her case is not the same," Arwel said. "You have a son in the village that you want to protect, while she doesn't have ties to anyone. Therefore, letting her come and go as she pleases is not an option. Secondly, you can pass for a human with ease, while she would need to resort to extreme measures to hide her otherness. For Aliya, the village is the safest and the best place."

With Arwel and Kalugal voicing the same conviction, Kian would no doubt accept their opinion and force the decision on Aliya. She had no one to advocate for her except for Vrog.

"What is she going to do in your village? Work in the café? Are they even hiring?"

"They always need more help," Jin said. "But we have a better idea for her. With her incredible strength and her smarts, she could fly through the Guardian training program. Guardians are very well paid, and they are well respected, which seems to matter a lot to Aliya."

"Of course it does. She's a proud Kra-ell female."

"You could join her in the village," Jacki suggested. "I know that the school means a lot to you, but you can take a sabbatical, and visit from time to time to make sure that everything runs smoothly."

Obviously, Jacki had guessed why he was fighting them over the decision to take Aliya to the village. It wasn't all about her right to choose her future, it was also about her possible future with him.

14

ALENA

"Do that again." Aliya clapped her hands with a child's glee.

"Certainly, mistress." Oridu dipped his head, or rather her head.

Aliya was fascinated by the Odus' ability to morph their features from male to female and back, and right now, Oridu was a female.

Thankfully, Ovidu and Oridu hadn't become sentient yet, or they would have been put off by Aliya's demands to perform.

"This is amazing." Aliya giggled. "They would make the perfect spies or thieves. They can go in looking like guys, go out looking like women, and then change again. I wish I could do that." Her happy expression turned serious again. "I heard that many people in the West have surgeries to change their faces." She turned to Carol. "Do you think that would help me?"

Carol shook her head. "You could have your fangs surgically removed and regular teeth implanted instead, but you need them to feed. So unless you're willing to eat an animal's flesh instead of drinking its blood, or if you don't mind drinking it from a cup, you shouldn't get rid of your fangs. You could wear contact lenses, though. Do your eyes glow when they turn red?"

Aliya nodded.

"Then contact lenses aren't going to help, but sunglasses should do the job. And if anyone asks why you're wearing them when it's dark, you can say that you have some rare eye disorder that makes them sensitive to even the dimmest of lights."

Alena didn't think that would do the trick. Aliya could hide the fangs, and she could hide her eyes, but she was going to attract attention because of her height, and once people took a second look, they would notice the other subtle differences that marked her as not human.

"We should get back." Alena rose to her feet. "Are you sure that you prefer to sleep on Jacki and Kalugal's couch? Here you can have a comfortable bed."

"I'm sure." Aliya stood up and walked up to Oridu. "Thank you for showing me your changing features." She patted his shoulder as if he were human.

Smiling, he inclined his head. "You are most welcome, mistress."

"Thank you too." She offered her hand to Ovidu.

"It was my pleasure, mistress." He shook her hand.

"Well, goodnight." Aliya opened the door and walked out to the hallway.

When they reached the stairs, she let out a breath. "At first, I thought that the Odus were creepy, but I like them now. They seem eager to please."

"They are amusing," Welgost said from behind them.

"You need to remember that those are not real emotions," Alena said. "They are programmed to act that way. But I have to admit that I also sometimes forget that they are not real. In fact, I'm very attached to Ovidu. He has been my nanny, my bodyguard, and my butler since the day I was born. I can't imagine life without him."

Aliya sighed. "I wish I had an Odu. Life wouldn't be so lonely if I had a robot who could talk back to me. I wouldn't have even minded that he was a machine and that his emotions were fake."

Wrapping her arm around Aliya's slim waist, Carol leaned her head against the girl's bicep. "Come to the village, Aliya. You'll never be lonely again. You might even find a nice immortal male to love who will love you back."

Aliya stopped mid stairs. "What about Vrog and Emmett? Do they have immortal mates?"

"Vrog doesn't," Alena said. "And from what I hear, he's a decent male. His son, the one who dresses like a Goth, is one of the nicest people I know, and he didn't inherit all that goodness just from his mother. Stella is a good person, but she gets moody, and when she does, she's not very pleasant."

Aliya stopped again. "How come Vrog is not mated to the mother of his son? I thought that your kind had exclusive relationships with just one person."

"We do, but Stella and Vrog are not each other's fated mates. Vlad was the result of a hookup, and Stella found her match twenty-one years after her son was born."

"So she's mated," Aliya said.

Carol chuckled. "Yes, Vrog is up for grabs. Are you interested?"

A blush colored the girl's hollow cheeks. "I don't know. I look like a Kra-ell female, and I'm as strong as one, but I don't want to live like they do."

"And how's that?" Alena asked.

"Similar to how the Mosuo live, but without the love. The Mosuo are human and they are capable of feeling love. So even though they practice what they call walking marriages, and the men don't move in with their lovers, most stay loyal to one partner throughout their lives, and they love their mates. I don't think Jade and the other pureblooded females were capable of love, not for the males in their harem and maybe not even for their children."

Alena shook her head. "I'm sure that the Kra-ell love their children. It's just that their culture reveres strength, and to show affection is considered a weakness. The Kra-ell can't be too different from humans and from the gods or they wouldn't be able to produce offspring with one another. Loving our children is hardwired into our genes. It takes a long time for a human or humanoid child to become independent, and without the feelings of love, the parents wouldn't commit the energy and resources needed to raise their children."

"It's necessary for the propagation of the species," Carol added. "Love is the greatest motivator and the strongest chain. We live for those we love."

"So who do I live for?" Aliya asked.

Carol smiled. "For those you are going to love in the future."

Alena thought of Aliya's restraint, of her preferring to go hungry and cold rather than using her powers to take what she needed from others. "Even though you had to leave, you still loved the people you grew up with. If you didn't, you wouldn't have hesitated to enslave them to your will."

Aliya shook her head. "I don't love them. I just follow the Mother's way."

Alena nodded. "Maybe love is too strong of a word. But you care about them. If they were attacked or if some natural disaster struck and you could've helped, I know that you would have done so even if it wasn't the Mother's way. You care for these people."

"They were kind to my mother and me when we had no one else to turn to. It would be dishonorable of me not to repay them in their time of need, but that doesn't mean that I care about them."

15

ORION

*O*rion listened to his companions' discussion over Aliya's future but decided to stay out of it.

On the one hand, he agreed with Vrog that Aliya shouldn't be forced to do anything she didn't want to. But he also agreed with Kalugal that she didn't have enough information to make an informed decision.

Obviously, she would be better off in the village, but did they have the right to force it on her even if it was for her own good?

Not too long ago, he'd been in a similar situation. If the clan hadn't captured him and held him until he learned more about them, he would have bolted as well. The difference was that he'd had Geraldine and Cassandra to vouch for the clan, and their experience and successful assimilation had helped shape his opinion and attitude toward these immortals.

There was one more difference, though.

He was the descendant of gods, same as them, while Aliya was the descendant of the Kra-ell. Did it matter that they weren't exactly the same?

It shouldn't.

The fact that the Kra-ell were long-lived and not immortal wasn't as important as both species needing to hide their existence from humans. However, there was a hitch in his idyllic vision of peaceful coexistence. Hybrid Kra-ell males could have immortal children with clan females, but hybrid Kra-ell females could not have long-lived children with clan males.

Could two hybrid Kra-ell have a long-lived child?

"How long are you going to stay at the lake?" Vrog asked.

"The plan was to stay two weeks, but I don't think we will have enough to do for that long. We might shorten the trip to a total of one week." When Lokan shook his head, Kalugal continued, "My brother seems to want to stay longer, so we might do so as well." He turned to Jacki. "What say you, my love?"

"I'm not ready to go home yet."

"You heard the boss. We are not going back yet."

"Good." Vrog sounded relieved. "That means that Mey can spend a few more days listening to echoes, and once she's done, we will join you there. I really think that you need me there to convince Aliya she has nothing to fear from you or anyone in the village."

Orion nodded. "I agree with Vrog. If I hadn't had Geraldine and Cassandra to vouch for the clan, it would have been much more difficult for me to trust what Kian and Onegus were telling me."

"You still need to check with Kian," Jacki told Kalugal. "What if he doesn't want her there?"

Kalugal smirked. "I know my cousin. He's a big softie, and there is no way he would turn away a stray like her."

As the door opened and Alena walked in with Aliya and Carol, they all fell silent. Except for Vrog. "Hello? Where did everybody go?"

"We are still here," Jin said. "Say hello to Vrog, Aliya."

The girl swallowed. "Hello."

"*Ni hao*, Aliya. I'm so glad that you survived the attack and weren't taken, and I'm going to join you at the lake in a few days. I would have come right away, but there are some things we need to finish over here before we can leave."

"Who are we?" Aliya seemed to get over her initial shock of hearing that Vrog was on the line.

Orion wondered why they hadn't done a video call. Vrog and Aliya were no doubt curious about each other.

"Mey, who is Jin's sister, has a special talent that she utilizes here in the school, and she's the reason I can't leave immediately. Her mate Yamanu and two Guardians are here to keep her safe, and we also have the pilot who flew us over."

"What's her talent? And why are you in a school?"

"I'll tell you later," Arwel said. "If you want to continue your conversation with Vrog in private, you can take my phone to the bedroom."

She shook her head. "We can talk when he gets here."

Orion had a feeling that she didn't want to talk to Vrog just yet. Maybe she needed time to prepare.

"Before we hang up, I just want to ask you one question, if I may."

Aliya frowned at the phone. "What's your question?"

"What is your Kra-ell name?"

"Kajey."

"That's what I thought. I remembered that the compound had two hybrid girls that matched your age more or less, but neither was named Aliya."

"I prefer Aliya. That's the name my mother gave me."

"Of course. I will not mention your Kra-ell name again."

She shrugged. "You can mention it all you want, just don't call me Kajey because I probably won't respond."

"Your English is very good. Where did you learn to speak it?"

Aliya shifted her weight to her other leg and eyed the half-eaten platter of desserts. "Can we talk about it when you get here?"

"Of course. Goodnight, Aliya."

"Goodnight, Vrog."

When Arwel terminated the call, Aliya let out a breath. "Vrog and I are both hybrid Kra-ell, but that doesn't mean that we have to be friends." She walked over to the table and sat on Jacki's other side. "I don't know him."

Kalugal pushed the platter toward her. "You don't know him yet, but you will in a few days. He's a good guy, and I have a feeling that you're going to like him. But if you don't, that's not a big deal. I'm sure we can find you another male to entertain yourself with."

"I don't need you to find anyone for me. I can do that myself."

"Naturally." He gave her a smile. "I meant we as in the entire clan. You can choose any of the unattached males."

Phinas, who hadn't said a word during the entire talk with Vrog, straightened in his chair and grinned at Aliya, but she pretended not to notice.

"How did it go with the Odus?" Jin asked.

"I had so much fun." Aliya's smile was genuine. "They showed me how they morph their faces and their bodies from male to female and back."

"So are you going to spend the night with them?" Jacki asked hesitantly.

"No. I decided to accept the offer to sleep on your couch. I want to watch television, but I don't want to disturb your sleep. Alena said that if the noise bothers you, she can lend me a pair of headphones."

"I'll give you a pair." Jacki turned to her mate. "What about our plans for tomorrow? Can we go shopping?"

He let out a dramatic sigh. "How can I refuse you anything? We are all going to Lijiang tomorrow." He smiled at Aliya. "My wife and the other ladies are adamant about taking you shopping. I know that you are proud and that you like to work for the things you have, so I'm going to offer you a deal."

She narrowed her eyes at him. "What kind of a deal?"

"I will consider whatever you buy tomorrow as compensation for your lost home. I feel responsible, and I want to make it up to you, so go wild and buy an entire store if you want. After that, I'll pay you for guiding us through the tunnels and helping us find clues about the ancient Kra-ell that might have used the outpost and the tunnel system underneath it. You can spend that money any way you like."

"What if I want to spend it on a train ticket to Beijing? Are you going to let me?"

Kalugal shook his head. "If after you visit the village, you decide that you don't want to live there, I will buy you a plane ticket to wherever you want to go. But before I do that, I will have to compel you to forget ever meeting us."

She cast a sidelong glance at Alena. "Can I trust his promise?"

Alena nodded. "You have my word that what Kalugal offered you will be done."

16

ONEGUS

$\mathcal{O}$negus stood on the path in front of their house and watched Cassandra walk down the steps of their front porch, looking splendid in a loose yellow silk blouse, tailored black slacks, and a pair of low-heeled black pumps.

The gold necklace he'd gotten her for this month's anniversary was draped around her long neck, and the bracelets he'd gotten her for the previous one dangled around her slender wrist. He was already planning next month's gift, another gold chain that was slightly longer and had more delicate links. The two necklaces would look great together.

"What are you smiling about?" She threaded her arm through his.

"I love seeing you wearing the jewelry I get you."

She lifted her other arm and jingled the five delicate gold bracelets. "You have impeccable taste."

"Obviously." He leaned to kiss the corner of her mouth. "I mated you."

"That's right." She grinned.

He loved that Cassandra wasn't modest and knew her own worth. Heck, he loved everything about her.

"I hope Vivian didn't prepare dinner," Cassandra said as they neared Magnus and Vivian's home. "I'll feel really awkward if she did. We didn't bring anything."

"I'm sure Magnus would have told me if she did. They know the reason for our visit is not social."

When Onegus had told Magnus that they might need Parker to use his talent for a private matter, he'd had no problem with that, but he'd said that Vivian had to approve, and that's why they were heading to their house. Vivian wanted to know why they needed Parker and what would be required of him.

As they walked up to the door and Onegus knocked, Parker opened the way. "Hi."

"Hello." Cassandra offered him her hand. "I hear great things about you, young man."

"Thank you." He shook it. "So, what's the mission?"

Onegus chuckled. "Patience, Parker. We need to discuss it with your mother first."

"Can I be there? Because Magnus didn't know whether I should stick around or not."

That was a good question.

Explaining to Vivian why Darlene should leave Leo was a somewhat touchy subject, but nothing a boy Parker's age would be surprised by. Kids these days knew a lot more than they had even a few decades ago, and they were not naive.

"It's up to your mother."

"Don't keep them at the door, Parker." Vivian walked over and smiled apologetically. "Please, come in. I have tea and coffee ready, and Ella baked muffins."

"Is she here?" Cassandra asked.

"She just dropped them off. On Sundays, Ella helps Julian in the halfway house. She organizes social activities for the girls." Vivian motioned for them to take a seat on the couch. "Usually, Yamanu is there on Sundays as well, but he's in China with Mey, and the girls are going to be upset about missing out on their karaoke night again. It's just not the same without him."

Cassandra arched a brow. "I didn't know Yamanu could sing."

"He sings beautifully," Magnus said.

"Can I pour you some coffee?" Vivian lifted the carafe.

"Thank you." Cassandra held up her cup. "I assume that you know why we are here."

Onegus stifled a chuckle. If he were there alone, he would have probably kept the chitchat going for another half an hour or so before getting to the reason for the visit, but his mate didn't like to beat around the bush.

"Onegus said that you need Parker to compel your sister. I need to know more about your plans and what exactly Parker's job will be before I allow him to go on his first mission." Vivian cast her son a smile. "He's so excited, and I hope I won't have to say no."

"I see no reason why you would." Cassandra put the cup down. "We told Darlene about her potential to become immortal, but she couldn't make up her mind on the spot and asked for more time. Naturally, we couldn't let her walk away with the knowledge, and we had to thrall her to forget everything we told her about immortals and gods, etc. The problem is that she can't give it more thought if she doesn't remember anything. So before thralling her, we explained why we needed to do that, and that the next time we would bring a compeller along, so when we release her memories, she would have time to decide what she wanted to do but wouldn't be able to reveal our secrets. Darlene agreed, but since all the adult compellers are currently absent, we need Parker."

"What's the rush?" Vivian asked. "The adult compellers are on other missions at the moment, but they are coming back soon, and if you need it done even sooner for some reason, why not ask one of them to compel your sister through a video call? If Parker can do that, I'm sure the more experienced compellers can do it remotely as well."

Cassandra nodded. "I can explain. My sister is forty-nine years old, which would make her the oldest Dormant to attempt transition. I want her to do it while Annani is in the village and can give her a blessing. The problem is that Darlene needs to leave her worthless husband and then find a nice immortal male to induce her.

Those things take time, and I'm afraid that the Clan Mother will leave before those objectives are achieved."

"I understand." Vivian lifted a plate of muffins and offered it to Onegus and Cassandra. "But what about asking one of the adults to do it over the phone?"

"Timing," Onegus said. "This is a private matter, and I can't demand Kalugal or Lokan get up in the middle of the night to compel Cassandra's sister. Eleanor is extremely busy trying to achieve several objectives in West Virginia, and I don't want to bother her with it either. Besides, I think it's a good opportunity for Parker to flex his compulsion muscles on a mission that is not critical." He smiled at the kid. "This mission is very important to my family, and I wouldn't have asked for your help if I didn't think you were up to it."

"I can do that easily, I think." Parker grimaced. "Other than Lisa, I don't have anyone to practice on, so I don't have many opportunities to test my skills."

"Will Parker need to be there when you talk to Darlene?" Vivian asked. "Or can it be done over a video call?"

"I want to be there," Parker said. "I want to test my ability on Cassandra's sister before they release her memories. If I can't compel her for some reason, they would have to thrall her to forget again, and that's not good for her." He rubbed his hands over his knees. "I also want to see and feel how she reacts. How am I going to get better if I don't get to practice on people? And since I'm not allowed to compel anyone without their permission, and I can only compel humans, my only test subject is Lisa, and by now, I can't tell if I'm really compelling her or if it's a placebo effect."

Poor Lisa.

Perhaps they needed to relax the rules a little so Parker could practice. Onegus needed to come up with a non-harmful and consensual way for the kid to practice on humans. Perhaps Amanda could take Parker to her lab and have him test his ability on student volunteers? She could say that he was a natural hypnotist.

Except, Amanda was on maternity leave because she was nearing her due date and could barely move.

Vivian let out a breath. "Okay. I agree, but it has to be after school hours or on the weekend, and I want all of you to be mindful of Parker's age when you discuss with Darlene whatever you need to discuss with her."

"Of course." Cassandra gave her a thankful smile. "We are going to treat Parker to a nice lunch or dinner, and we are going to pay him for his services."

Magnus shook his head. "No need to pay him. He wants to do it."

Parker cast his father an incredulous look. "So what? If they offer to pay me, I won't say no. You enjoy being a Guardian. Does that mean you should work for free?"

Magnus chuckled. "You've got a point. How much are you going to charge for your compulsion services?"

Parker's bravado was replaced with awkward indecision. "Whatever they are offering."

"Would a hundred bucks do?" Onegus pulled out his wallet.

Parker's eyes sparkled. "Yes, sir."

17

LISA

*H*er phone clutched in her hand and her foot tapping on the carpet, Lisa sat on the living room couch and waited to hear from Parker whether his mother had agreed to let him go on his first mission as a compeller. She was so excited for him. He'd been practicing on her for months, but both of them had started to doubt that it still worked.

She was so used to his little tests that she automatically did what he commanded whether he imbued his voice with compulsion or not.

Parker needed other test subjects, people who didn't know what he was doing. It didn't need to be anything major, and it could be supervised by Magnus to ensure that Parker wasn't abusing his ability, but unless they let him practice, how was he going to get good at it?

In the kitchen, her mother was whistling to the tune of the music playing on her earphones and swaying her hips to the beat. It was good to see her so happy, probably happier than Lisa had ever seen her, and she wanted to be happy for her, but instead she was consumed by worry, guilt, and dread.

Perhaps she shouldn't have encouraged her mother to attempt transition?

Lisa had practically arranged for Ronja and Merlin to have the house all to themselves so they would finally take the next step and stop torturing themselves, pretending to be just friends.

Given her mother's satisfied smile as of late, things were going well with Merlin, and it wasn't only about inducing Ronja's transition. They were bonding, and it was great, provided that the transition went well, and her mother survived it.

Annani was in the village, which was why Lisa had given her mother and Merlin the final push to go for it. As long as the goddess was nearby, Ronja's odds of successful transition were much better, and Annani was only going to stay until Amanda delivered her baby, or perhaps a week or two after.

But what if her mother didn't make it even with the goddess's help?

Lisa would never forgive herself.

"Dinner is almost ready." Ronja walked into the living room, her headphones draped around her neck like a necklace. "Do you want to invite Parker to join us?"

"I'm waiting for a call from him." Lisa put her phone on the couch beside her. "Onegus and Cassandra went over to his house to discuss him using his compulsion ability on Cassandra's sister. Vivian is not too happy about it, but Parker really wants to do it. He's had no one to practice on except for me, and by now, I can't tell if his compulsion is really working on me or if it's a placebo effect."

"He can practice on me." Her mother smiled. "I offered, and I'm still human."

The vise on Lisa's heart tightened. "Not for long." Her chin wobbled.

"Oh, sweetie." Her mother sat down beside her and wrapped an arm around her shoulders. "Don't worry. Everything is going to be okay, and we are going to spend eternity together."

The tears she'd been holding back overflowed their container and started spilling from the corners of her eyes. "I can't help it, and I feel so guilty for pushing you to do it."

"You didn't push me, sweetie." Ronja tightened her arm around her and kissed her temple. "And Merlin didn't push me either. It was entirely my decision, and I don't regret it. Fear shouldn't stop us from going after what we want."

Chuckling, Lisa wiped her eyes with her fingers. "Does that mean I can go bungee jumping with Parker?"

"Not going to happen, my dear. Not even after you turn immortal. Even immortals can't survive getting their bodies smashed to pieces."

Lisa laughed. "Just checking. What about parachuting? With an instructor?"

"I might allow it after I check the instructor's credentials. I'm not encouraging you to be fearless. A healthy dose of fear will keep you from taking reckless risks, like bungee jumping. But if you are really passionate about it and want to try it, make sure you find the best in the field to instruct you and help you do it safely."

"Is that why you chose a doctor as your inducer?" Lisa teased.

Her mother smiled indulgently. "I chose Merlin because he's everything I ever wanted in a life partner. He's brilliant, kind, funny, and he needs me."

He did. Without Ronja, Merlin was hopelessly disorganized, which affected more than just the state of his house. His research could move on much faster if he didn't keep misplacing notes or forgetting to buy ingredients or starting a new experiment and forgetting about the five already in progress.

"And he's also a hunk." Lisa winked.

"That too." Ronja frowned and looked down at her lap. "Your phone is vibrating under my bottom." She pulled it out and handed it to Lisa.

"It's Parker." She read the message. "He's coming over with Scarlet. Is it okay if he comes in with her?"

Her mother loved dogs, but Scarlet shed hair all over.

"Sure." She rose to her feet. "You're in charge of vacuuming after her."

"I'm always in charge of vacuuming." Lisa pushed to her feet and walked to open the door. "How did it go?"

Grinning, Parker walked up the stairs to the front porch. "I got my first paid mission."

"Congratulations. But why would they pay you for it?" Lisa thwarted Scarlet's attempts to lick her face and motioned for him to bring the dog inside. "None of the other compellers get paid for their services."

Parker shrugged. "They offered, and I never say no to money."

"Are you excited?"

He nodded. "I'm also a little scared. What if it doesn't work? I've only had you to practice on."

Her mother walked over to Parker and pulled him in for a hug. "Congratulations on your first official compulsion job."

"Thank you."

"You can practice on me anytime you want," she offered.

"Thank you for that too. I'm going to take you up on your offer. Can I practice on you today? Cassandra said that she would try to arrange a lunch meeting with Darlene next weekend. But if Darlene's husband leaves on one of his business trips, she might schedule the meeting for a weekday, and it might even be tomorrow."

18

ALENA

*I*t had been a long day, and Alena was tired, but the evening dragged on. Kalugal kept ordering more desserts for Aliya, who seemed to have a bottomless pit for a stomach. Carol was on a roll, telling them anecdotes from her new life in China and her old one in the village when she'd still worked in the café and collected all the gossip. Phinas kept flirting with Aliya, who could no longer pretend that she didn't notice but had no idea how to respond.

Alena was starting to think that the girl had never experienced male attention before, which suggested that she was still a virgin. For a hybrid Kra-ell female, that was probably a source of embarrassment.

As soon as there was a lull in the conversation, Alena asked, "When are we leaving for our shopping trip tomorrow morning?"

"Not too early," Jacki said. "I'm so tired that I could sleep for twelve hours straight."

"The city is nearly two hours away," Jin reminded her. "We can't start our day too late, or we will not have enough time for all the shopping we need to do. I suggest that we meet for breakfast in the hotel lobby at eight and be on our way by nine."

"I'll order breakfast to the suite," Kalugal said. "Aliya will be more comfortable here."

Jacki waved a hand in dismissal. "You can shroud her."

"What's shrouding?" Aliya asked.

"I can make the humans see whatever I want them to see, or I can just make them not notice you."

Aliya's eyes widened. "Can you teach me to do that?"

"I don't think it's something that can be taught. I was born with the ability."

"If she can thrall, she can shroud," Jin said. "She won't be able to do it as well as you do, but if she can shroud herself even partially, it would be a game-changer for her."

"Can you thrall?" Alena asked Jin.

"I'm practicing, but I'm not very good. It's like learning a new language as an adult compared to learning it as a child. It's much more difficult, takes longer, and is never as good."

Alena didn't want to point out that most immortals never lost that ability and could learn new languages with a child's ease. Jin already felt different enough with her fangs and venom glands. She didn't need another reminder that she wasn't like other immortals.

"I'm curious to see the selection in Chinese clothing stores," Alena said to change the subject. "I wonder if they export all the good stuff they make or leave some for their own market."

"The Chinese fashionistas love European labels," Carol said. "They appreciate quality and are willing to pay for it. Things have been changing over the last decade or so, though, and there are several domestic luxury brands that have become nearly as coveted as the European ones and are in high demand." She regarded Aliya with a critical eye. "I think that for you we should look for American brands. Typically, they design clothing for taller women than the Europeans and the Chinese brands do. On average, the Chinese ladies are more like me than like you and Jin."

"What about midrange market?" Jin asked. "Can we find the local equivalent of Zara or H&M? I think Aliya would love their designs. They are trendy and inexpensive. Both Mey and I found stuff in those stores that fit us."

"You can search online. Can you read Chinese?"

"Nope. I can speak a little bit, and I understand simple language if spoken slowly. What about you? Did you manage to learn it during the time you were here?"

Carol hadn't been in China all that long, but like most immortals, she learned languages fast.

"I understand almost everything, and I can speak it pretty well, but learning to read and write is going slower."

Alena wondered if Carol was being truthful or if she was exaggerating her difficulties to help Jin save face.

Stifling a yawn, Carol patted Lokan's arm. "If we want to start bright and early tomorrow morning, we'd better go to sleep soon. I need a good rest after today's adventures." She pushed to her feet.

"I'm tired as well," Alena admitted.

It had been such an incredibly long day that the trip into the tunnels seemed like something that had happened days ago, not just a few hours.

Their immortal bodies could tolerate a lot of stress, physical and emotional, but even they needed time to recuperate.

Orion got up and offered Alena a hand. "Big thanks to Jacki and Kalugal for hosting us, and I wish you all goodnight."

"I should get a pair of pajamas for Aliya." Jin pushed to her feet.

"Thank you for your generosity." Aliya bowed her head. "Since Kalugal said I can buy whatever I want tomorrow as compensation for losing my home, I will purchase replacements for all the items you gave me."

Jin chuckled. "Kalugal already promised to reimburse me, so it's all good, Aliya. Don't worry about it. We are going to have oodles of fun tomorrow and spend obscene amounts of Kalugal's money."

As Aliya cast Kalugal a worried glance, he smiled at her. "Don't worry. My wife and I are financially blessed, and we can afford whatever you and Jin spend, and I mean whatever. Don't feel shy about spending a fortune. The caveat is that you will have to do it all tomorrow. The deal is good for only one day."

"There is really no limit? What if I spend a million yuan?"

"No problem. In fact, I dare you to spend a million yuan in one day without donating any portion of it or buying things for the Mosuo village. Everything you get has to be just for you."

"That's impossible," Aliya murmured.

Jacki snorted. "It's easier than you think. Just go into the first jewelry store you see and buy yourself a diamond necklace. You can use up the budget in one swoop."

"That's not fair." Kalugal pretended to be angry at his wife. "She was supposed to figure it out on her own."

Aliya shook her head. "I'm not going to buy diamonds or anything stupid like that. I'm going to buy an apartment. You took away my home, so it's only fair that you buy me a new one."

"Oh, boy." Kalugal sighed dramatically. "You're way smarter than I gave you credit for."

19

ORION

"Are you tired?" Orion asked Alena as they left Jacki and Kalugal's suite. Alena was supposed to have one of the Odus escort them back, but she hadn't called them, and he hadn't reminded her. If there was any danger lurking in the corridors of the luxury hotel, he was more than capable of protecting Alena. He could freeze anyone with a verbal command.

"I am a little tired. Why? What do you have in mind?"

"I wondered if you were up for a walk, but apparently, you're not."

She leaned her head on his shoulder. "A walk along the lakeshore in the moonlight sounds lovely."

"Are you sure? We can go on a walk tomorrow."

"I'm sure. I just need to grab my coat from our room. This sweater is not enough for how cold it is outside."

"I'll get the puffer jacket you got me as well." He kissed the top of her head. "Did I thank you already for making sure I don't freeze out here?"

She'd gotten him everything he needed for the trip and had even packed his suitcase. So far, every item he'd tried fit perfectly and was of the highest quality.

"Yes, you did. It's a shame that jacket is ruined, though. It was such a nice one."

"It's not ruined. I'm sure I can have the tears mended."

She canted her head. "Don't be silly. No one mends clothes these days. We live in the disposable era. Disposable dishes, disposable clothing, and even disposable lovers."

"Ain't that the truth." He opened the door to their hotel room. "As immortals, we had no choice but to engage in fleeting encounters, but it never felt right. We are meant to be monogamous, to cleave to one person for the rest of our lives."

"I don't know about that." Alena reached into the closet for her coat. "According to my mother, the gods were very promiscuous, and having multiple partners was the norm rather than the exception."

He shrugged on his torn jacket. "Really? From what I've seen so far, everyone who's mated is devoted to his or her partner. Did I miss something?"

"You didn't." Alena followed him out the door. "We have the Fates and the addiction to thank for that. True-love mates can't stray."

Addiction? He must have misunderstood, but as he was about to ask what Alena had meant, the door to the Odus' room opened and Ovidu stepped out.

"Should I escort you and Master Orion, mistress?"

She cast Orion an apologetic glance. "Kian would have a meltdown if I don't take one of them along."

"I don't mind. As long as he keeps his distance, he can trail behind us."

When Alena repeated the instructions, Ovidu bowed. "I shall do as Mistress pleases."

When they were outside, Orion asked, "What did you mean by addiction?"

"Didn't I tell you about that?"

"I would have remembered if you did. What is it about?"

"When an immortal couple is exclusive, the female becomes addicted to the male's venom, and her scent changes in a way that keeps him addicted to her and repulses other immortal males. The same was true for the gods, which was why they mixed it up on purpose. Those who weren't true-love mates didn't want to be tied to their partners, and the way to avoid it was to have many different ones."

He chuckled. "So the mythology got that right as well."

"It did."

"Are we addicted to each other?" He pushed the lobby door open.

"I don't know. Would it bother you if we were?"

"No." Orion wrapped his arm around Alena's shoulders. "There are worse fates than being addicted to the woman I love."

"Same here. I feel so incredibly blessed to have found you, and I don't mind one bit being addicted to you."

"Do you want to have a child with me?" he blurted out.

She lifted a pair of wistful eyes to him. "More than anything, but it's up to the Fates."

"What about the fertility doctor? Can he help us conceive?"

"We can try, that's for sure. But isn't it too early to be talking about children? How long have we known each other?"

"Nine days, eternity, who cares? I know you, and you know me, and we both know that we want to spend the rest of our immortal lives together. I don't know if it happens so quickly for other immortal couples, and I don't really care. I know that we were always meant to be together."

Alena's smile was radiant as she stopped and turned to face him. "I love you." She wound her arms around his neck. "It never gets old to say that."

"You are my world." He kissed her softly. "Any more doubts?"

"None. I was just making sure that you didn't have any." Her expression turned serious. "I've never been in love before, but you have. Are you over the guilt of allowing yourself to love again?"

"I am. Miriam never wanted me to stay alone, and she would have liked you."

"There might be a way to find out." Alena started walking again.

"Find out what?"

"Whether Miriam approves."

Orion's steps faltered. "How?"

"You've met Nathalie, Syssi's brother's wife. Her talent is talking to ghosts. If Miriam wants to send you a message, she could use Nathalie as a conduit."

Orion's throat dried out in an instant. "You mean like a séance?"

He was embarrassed to admit it, but he'd sought psychics' help to communicate with Miriam's spirit. After she'd died, he'd been desperate to get proof that her spirit lived on, that it wasn't the end, and that she was okay in whatever realm the spirits lived in.

But none of them could tell him the things only Miriam would know, and he'd given up hope. Deep down, he still believed that the end of physical life wasn't the real end, but without proof, he couldn't be sure.

"Nathalie doesn't do séances, and she doesn't summon spirits. In fact, she does her best to shield her mind against them. Only the most tenacious of ghosts get past her blockades, but if Miriam cared about you as much as you cared about her, she would want to communicate a message to you and tell you to live your life."

20

ALENA

*O*rion looked pained. "Are you sure Nathalie actually speaks to spirits?"

"She does, and she's proven it conclusively." Alena sighed. "I know how you feel. On the one hand, it's such a tremendous relief to know that your loved ones are not forever lost, and that there is more to existence than this physical realm. But on the other hand, you start to wonder why those you lost and miss didn't find a way to tell you that they were okay, that they've gone on in another form. When my brother Lilen was killed, both my mother and I were devastated. Kian was as well, but he kept it bottled inside. I prayed for a sign, a dream, anything that his spirit was still with us in some form, but he didn't come. Not for me, and not for my mother."

"How do you reconcile it? Why do some get visited by their loved ones? Are they more sensitive? More open?"

After Nathalie had given Amanda the message from Mark, Alena had spent many hours trying to understand that, hating herself for being angry at Lilen for not giving her a sign. Eventually, she'd resigned herself to accept that Lilen had moved on quickly because he hadn't left behind any major issues that needed to be resolved.

"It's not easy to gain access to a channel, which is how Nathalie describes what she is. The spirit that took residence in her mind for many years told her that she's like a beacon to those who need to communicate with the living. They were clamoring for access to her, driving her nuts until that one spirit took control and blocked the others. Later, when she learned to do it herself, he moved on. But Nathalie is not our only proof. David, Sari's mate, saw his own previous incarnation during his transition, and his deceased twin brother visited him. What he learned during that visit he couldn't have learned in any other way, and that is another proof of the soul's continuation."

As Orion's natural curiosity took over, his pinched expression relaxed a little. "What did David learn?"

The more she told him, the more at ease he became. "So if Miriam is reincarnated, she is not able to communicate with me. She can only do that between rein-carnations."

"David thinks that the soul might remember its prior lives in dreams, so perhaps it can also find a way to communicate with loved ones while dreaming during those other lives, but we have no proof of that."

"I hope Miriam is happy." The corners of Orion's lips lifted in a small smile. "And I hope that she has many children during her subsequent reincarnations. Now that I know it was probably my fault that she never conceived, I feel so guilty. She loved children."

Alena's heart ached for him, and it ached for Miriam too.

"I had children but no mate to love, and Miriam had a mate but no children." Alena threaded her arm through Orion's and leaned her head on his shoulder. "According to David, reincarnations often happen within the same family, which is a little creepy in my opinion. Imagine if we had a daughter who is Miriam's reincarna-tion. If you knew that for sure, how would it make you feel?"

"Weird," he admitted. "Less so if we have a son. I assume that souls are genderless. Am I right?"

"David and his brother kept reincarnating as males because of what they needed to improve, which were their overly masculine traits. They were too aggressive, too competitive, and not empathetic enough to others. David seems to have fixed all those character flaws, but since he turned immortal, he's done with the cycles."

For a long moment, they walked in silence, with Orion once again frowning. "Isn't aggression a hormonal thing? I'm not a scientist, but I keep reading that nature is as important as nurture, if not more so. If David and his brother were aggressive males, they might have suffered from excessive testosterone, and behavior modifica-tion might not have been possible."

Alena was glad of the change of subject. Talking about Miriam had been upset-ting to Orion, and she shouldn't have started it. It was his prerogative to talk about his first love, and when he did, Alena would listen, but she wouldn't bring it up again.

"Testosterone is not inherently bad, and neither are aggression and competitive-ness if they are harnessed and used for good. Regrettably, humanoid societies cannot survive if all of their members are gentle poets. Testosterone made the men of David's family strong fighters and defenders of their clan. The undesirable side effect was that it also made them jerks and shortened their lifespans. They needed to learn to harness it and not let it ruin their lives or the lives of those they loved. Another good example is immortal males, who are even more aggressive by nature than humans. The males of our clan who choose a career as Guardians use their aggres-siveness to protect and fight for those who have no one else to fight for them. The Doomers, who are genetically the same, use their abilities to conquer and subdue. Or used to. Now they operate drug and prostitution rings while their leader raises the next generation of smart warriors."

Orion shook his head. "How incredible is it that both his sons joined your clan? I guess Lokan and Kalugal are proof that neither nature nor nurture can stand in the way of strong will and a sharp mind. They seem like good men."

Lokan hadn't officially crossed over yet, but he was mated to Carol, which made him a clan member nonetheless.

"Both Lokan and Kalugal have their own agendas, and I don't know if they are purely good." She smiled. "They have a mix of genes, some good, and some not so much. It might be argued that they inherited some of Areana's goodness, and that her genes softened their father's. Navuh is an incredibly powerful and smart immortal, and his sons inherited that from him. His line also suffers from insanity, and that might be in their genes as well."

Orion snorted. "So we are back to nature trumping nurture and free will?"

Alena cast him an amused sidelong glance. "I have lived for over two thousand years, and I've had a lot of time to observe and learn, and the only answer I have is that it's different for each individual. For some, nature is the strongest factor shaping their characters, for others, it is nurture, and for a select few, it's their powerful will."

ALIYA

*A*liya lay on the couch in the hotel suite's living room with the television on, the lights off, and a set of earphones hugging her ears. She luxuriated in the softness of the pajamas Jin had brought for her, the pillows and blankets the hotel's housekeeping had sent up, and the tray of sweets Kalugal had ordered for her.

Perhaps being their prisoner wasn't so bad.

She was clean, her belly was full, and she was more comfortable than she'd ever been. Was freedom worth giving up all of that?

Hell, no.

If the Kra-ell religion included the concept of a devil, she would have sold her soul to him to keep living like that.

But the Mother didn't need a devil to counterbalance her. She wasn't a benevolent entity who needed a bad guy to do her dirty work. Like nature itself, the Mother was both creator and destroyer, gracious and terrible, nurturing and punishing. The Kra-ell who displeased her suffered the consequences in this life and in future reincarnations.

Aliya wished she knew more about the Mother's teachings. In difficult times, talking to the goddess and asking her for help had been comforting, but she was well aware that her knowledge was lacking.

What Aliya had learned about the Kra-ell religion was what she'd overheard Jade preach. As the leader of their community, Jade was the Mother's physical representation and was to be revered and honored almost to the same degree as the goddess.

Now that Aliya was older and had more experience, she suspected that not everything Jade had said was true.

When Jade told the males that those who pleased the Mother greatly were rewarded in the next life with a female of their own, one that they wouldn't have to share with others, it might have been a lie to make them obedient. The harder they worked, the more they sacrificed, the more merit points they earned for the next life.

Jade had told them that they should be grateful for the opportunity to serve her, and that the harsh treatment they'd been getting was for their own good. After all, she was doing them a favor, so they could earn the ultimate reward in the next life.

Had it all been a lie?

Did those who were grateful for the Mother's bounty, those who served her with courage and honor, truly earn a reward?

Aliya had followed what she knew of the Mother's teachings to the best of her abilities. Was her capture by these people a reward?

Was Vrog?

Except, the rewards were supposed to be reaped in the next life, not this one.

What would the Mother want her to do?

Stay, or run?

Aliya probably couldn't run even if she wanted to. Kalugal had reinforced his compulsion before retiring for the night. He commanded her not to leave the suite, specifically telling her not to open the front door or the doors leading to the balcony either.

She could still use the small window in the bathroom and jump down the three stories. The jump wouldn't kill her, but she might break a leg or an arm, and that would take much longer to heal than a flesh wound.

Should she try the suite's front door anyway? Maybe compulsion faded over time? Many hours had passed since Kalugal had commanded her to stay away from the doors. Perhaps she could will herself to refuse?

Taking the earphones off, Aliya listened to the sounds coming from Jacki and Kalugal's bedroom.

They were still awake. She heard them whisper but couldn't understand what they were saying. Whatever it was must have been funny because Jacki giggled, and then Kalugal whispered something, and Jacki moaned.

Grimacing, Aliya put the headphones back on.

After living in a Mosuo household, she was no stranger to the sounds of sex, but it was different hearing Jacki and Kalugal's sounds of passion.

They loved each other, and Aliya was jealous.

She wanted that for herself, and she hated being a thirty-year-old virgin. It was embarrassing even for a human, and tenfold more embarrassing for a Kra-ell.

Even though Vrog was a potential candidate for helping her get rid of her virginity, she would be too embarrassed to admit to him that she'd never had sex. He would think that there was something wrong with her, and he would be correct.

Perhaps she was better off choosing one of the immortals. Phinas was a decent fighter, good-looking, and he kept flirting with her. So far, she'd ignored his light-hearted teasing, mainly because she didn't know how to respond, but maybe tomorrow during their shopping spree, she would indicate her interest.

These immortals didn't live by Kra-ell rules, so she didn't need to be the one to issue an invitation. If she appeared interested, and the male was interested too, he would initiate. She wouldn't have to embarrass herself by having her invitation declined.

Ugh. It was better to stay celibate than deal with all that stupid relationship crap. The Kra-ell were smart to take that out of their culture and make it the males' duty to serve the females. It was an affront to the Goddess to refuse an invitation, and a great offense to the female for which she was entitled to demand retribution.

Not that it had ever happened in Jade's compound. All the males had been eager to please.

If Aliya were still living with her tribe, she would have lost her damn virginity the moment her female urges had started to emerge at fifteen.

Not daring to take the headphones off again, she threw the blanket aside, lowered her feet to the floor, and tiptoed to the front door. That was as far as she made it. She couldn't even reach for the handle. Her arm just refused to move.

More relieved than disappointed, Aliya tiptoed back to the couch and lay down.

22

KIAN

*A*s the phone ringing interrupted Kian's Sunday ritual of late breakfast and newspaper scan, he was tempted to let it go to voicemail, but naturally he didn't.

Everyone knew not to bother him on Sundays unless it was either an emergency or important news that couldn't wait. His bet was on one of the teams from China. It was after midnight over there, so it was probably Arwel reporting at the end of the day.

With a sigh, Kian lifted the device off its charging station, checked the caller ID, and accepted the call. "Hello, Arwel. Is everyone alive?"

"Funny you should ask. We ran into a bit of trouble earlier today. Everyone is okay, and no one got hurt, well other than Phinas and me, but we are fine now."

As Arwel continued his report, Kian was glad that he'd started with the preamble about everyone being safe. After hearing that Alena had been trapped underground, Kian's temper had flared, his venom glands had swelled, and his fangs had punched out.

"Why the hell did she leave the Odus behind? They could have gotten you out right away."

Tomorrow, he would have words with his sister. The Odus were there to protect her, not to stay behind in the hotel.

"True, but Alena didn't want them anywhere near the water, and with three compellers and three warriors at her side, even I couldn't argue with that logic. Besides, if the Odus got us out, we might have never discovered the female." As Arwel continued telling him about the hybrid Kra-ell who'd been hiding in the tunnels under the ruins for the past fourteen years, Kian's anger subsided.

That was a major breakthrough in the investigation, much better than he'd ever hoped for.

"That's one hell of a discovery. You were supposed to find clues about the Kra-ell.

485

Instead, you catch a female who survived the attack. Does she remember what happened?"

"Aliya was only eight years old, and she lived with her mother in the human quarters. She didn't see much, but she confirmed what Vrog had deduced and what Mey had seen and heard in the echoes. The compound was attacked, an unknown Kra-ell male thralled the humans to forget that they ever lived among aliens and told them to leave. Aliya was presumed human, and that's how she got away."

"How could they have thralled away years of memories? That's impossible."

"That occurred to me as well, but their thralling is different than ours. It's a combination of thralling and compulsion, and evidently, it's very effective on humans."

"It would seem so." Kian tucked the newspaper under his arm, took his coffee mug, and headed out to his backyard. "Where is the hybrid now?"

"She's sleeping on Kalugal's couch in his suite. He wanted to keep an eye on her."

"If he compelled her not to run, he could have gotten her a room of her own. I'm sure that his decision to make her sleep on his couch wasn't influenced by monetary concerns. He can afford to rent out the entire hotel."

"Aliya is strong-willed. I assumed that he was afraid of her being able to throw off his compulsion."

Kian chuckled. "I'm amazed at how strong she is. I knew that Vrog, Emmett, and even Vlad were very strong, but she's a female, and she fought off two well-trained warriors."

"Don't forget that we were trying not to hurt her, but I have to admit that I was surprised by her strength. She moved that boulder on her own, a rock that seven immortal males had barely managed to budge. She used a cleverly constructed pulley system, but still. She'd also built effective traps with the most basic materials she found. The girl is smart, resourceful, strong, and fast. She would make an excellent Guardian."

Kian put the newspaper down on the side table and sat on his favorite lounger. "Aren't you getting carried away?"

"I'm thinking long-term. Aliya has nowhere to go, and we can't just leave her here. Those tunnels were her home, and now they are compromised. We need to bring her back with us to the village, and after she proves herself in one way or another, we might allow her to join the training program. You allowed Eleanor to join, and she's much less trustworthy than Aliya, or at least that's my impression. I've never been too fond of Eleanor, but she grew on me."

"We know nothing about the girl. We knew a lot about Eleanor, and she has family in the village that even an opportunistic woman like her wants to protect. Aliya has no one."

"What we knew about Eleanor was nothing good. Aliya lives by a strict, self-imposed code of honor. She could've thralled the villagers to provide her with everything she needed, but she refused to resort to stealing and went hungry and cold instead. Can you imagine Eleanor doing that?"

Kian chuckled. "Eleanor wouldn't have hesitated to steal and coerce to get everything she needed, and she wouldn't have felt an ounce of remorse for taking from those who barely had enough to feed their families."

"Precisely. I think that bringing Aliya to the village is the right thing to do, but I need your consent."

"Does she want to come?"

"She doesn't know what she wants. Right now, she's scared of us and doesn't trust us, but hopefully that will change in the next few days."

"Would you vouch for her?"

"I would, and I'm saying that after knowing her only a few hours. The girl impressed me."

Arwel wasn't easily impressed, and he was an empath. If he felt so strongly about Aliya, Kian had no reason to doubt his judgment.

"You have my consent to bring her, but you'll be in charge of keeping an eye on her."

"I have no problem with that."

23

MEY

"*H*ere we go again," Mey said as Vrog punched in the code and opened the door to the storage building. "Wish me luck." She tucked the yoga mat he'd brought for her under her arm. "And thank you again for the mat. It was very thoughtful of you."

"You're welcome, and good luck." Vrog gave her a tight smile. "I hope today you get your answers, so we can be done here."

"I hope so too." She waved goodbye to Yamanu, crossed the threshold, and closed the door behind her.

Ever since hearing the news about the female hybrid the other team had found at the ruins, Vrog had been in a bad mood. Usually the guy was polite and soft-spoken, but today he'd seemed irritated, which was completely understandable.

In his shoes, she would have been eager to leave as well. For all intents and purposes, Vrog and Aliya were each other's only option. If Mey were a lone immortal with no others of her kind and suddenly one more was found, she would also be impatient to meet that person.

After spreading the yoga mat on the floor, she sat down and crossed her legs in the lotus position, but even though her eyes were closed and her breathing was even, the calm state that opened her mind to the echoes eluded her.

Thoughts of Vrog and Aliya and their possible future in the village stirred up excitement in her, and that wasn't conducive to the feeling of calm Mey needed to enter the meditative state. Instead of trying to banish them, she let her mind wander.

Late last night, Jin had sent her a picture that she'd snapped of Aliya when the girl hadn't been looking. She looked nearly as alien as the pureblooded females in the echoes and was just as beautiful. From what Jin had told her, she was also as aggressive.

Jin thought that Aliya could take the fast track to becoming a Guardian, but was that what Aliya wanted to do with her life?

Were her goals and aspiration aligned with the clan? Probably not.

Maybe she wanted to marry Vrog and have a bunch of babies with him? Nah, Mey was projecting her own wishes onto a female who probably was as alien by nature as she was in appearance. Hopefully, she wasn't a cruel bitch like the pureblooded Kra-ell females who'd gotten rid of babies fathered by hybrid males and human females, or dormant females in the case of her and Jin's mother.

Was their birth mother still alive? Should they try to find her?

Mey wished Eva would resume her detective activities so she could hire her to search for their mother. Once they were back in the village, she planned on talking to her about it. Perhaps Sharon could do that? Since Ethan's birth, Sharon had taken Eva's place as the lead investigator of their firm, and she had probably gained enough experience by now to do the job with remote guidance from her boss.

Once the random thoughts had run their course, Mey's mind finally quieted enough to allow the echoes in. This time around, she was ready for the two long ghostly forms as they entered the building and closed the door behind them.

Focusing on their expressions, she noted that their dark eyes were already emitting a faint red glow, their fangs were slightly elongated, and their high foreheads were creased.

It was obvious that they'd come to the storage room to have a private fight. When they started arguing, Mey understood every third or fifth word, but it was enough to make some sense of what they were arguing about.

"You — — — go. The tribe is— —big— —. I —-ready—-."

Mey filled in the blanks, and the gist of it was, "You need to let me—or us— go. The tribe is too big. I am ready and able—or ripe."

The other one bared her fangs and hissed several words of which Mey understood only a handful, but combined with the tone, it went something like, "You are not the one making the decisions here. I'll decide when you are ready."

The shorter female bared her fangs as well, and her rapid response was nearly unintelligible, but Mey guessed it went something like, "It's your sacred obligation to help me form my own tribe. That's what the Mother commands. You are not letting me do that because you are a greedy pakta."

Mey made a note to ask Vrog what pakta meant, but she had no doubt that it was a very offensive Kra-ell word because that was when the taller female, who was most likely Jade, backhanded the other one and sent her flying into the storage shelving.

The rest of what was hissed and shouted during the vicious fighting was probably more Kra-ell cuss words, but this time Mey endured it to the end.

Exhausted and bloodied, the females sat on the floor and leaned their backs against the wall.

Jade's expression lost some of its harshness as she wrapped her arm around the other female's shoulders and mussed her hair with her other hand. When she spoke, her tone was softer, and her words were measured, allowing Mey to understand most of it and translate it in her head.

"This is not our home," Jade said. "You are too young and vulnerable to split up and lead your own tribe among the humans. We are alone in this world, and there is strength in numbers. We need to stay together."

"What about the other Kra-ell?"

"We don't know if any survived, and if they did, they might not be our friends."

"The tribe is too big. The males are not happy to be shared between all of us.

Maybe we can split up but stay together. Let each female choose her males instead of us sharing them all."

Jade shook her head. "We can't. We need to make as many children as we can, and you know just as well as I do that a larger pool of males increases the chances of pregnancy."

"It feels wrong."

"I know. But we have no choice."

24

ALENA

$\mathcal{T}$he ride to Lijiang took nearly three hours instead of two. They had to stop several times and let Aliya out of the limousine to walk about for a few minutes until her nausea subsided.

Her excuse was that she hadn't traveled by car in sixteen years, and it didn't agree with her stomach, but Alena had a feeling that it had more to do with anxiety about going to the city than the ride in the limo. She'd been fine the first hour of the drive but had grown progressively more nervous as they neared Lijiang.

"Don't worry. Kalugal is going to shroud you, and everyone looking at you will see an average-looking Chinese woman."

"Can he shroud my height?"

Kalugal turned around to look at her. "I can make you invisible if that's what you want, but that might make trying on clothing difficult."

"Just make me shorter and more normal looking. I don't care about anything else."

Alena patted her thigh. "There is a lot to do in Lijiang other than shopping. We can visit the Dayan Old Town. It's one of the four best-preserved ancient cities in China, and it's listed as a UNESCO world heritage site."

"What is UNESCO?" Aliya asked.

"It's the United Nations Educational, Scientific, and Cultural Organization," Alena said. "The Great Wall of China is also one of its heritage sites, so Lijiang is in good company. It has bars, restaurants, cafés, and shops where tourists can experience the Naxi culture. The old city also has 354 bridges spanning over waterwheel-driven canals that are full of goldfish, and it even has a palace."

"How are we going to see all that and go shopping in one day?" Jin asked. "We will need to come back here some other day. It sounds too good to miss out on."

"I have to admit that I didn't expect China to be so beautiful," Alena said. "When I pulled information about Lijiang, I was surprised that I had never heard about it before."

"We can even see a festival." Jin lifted her head from the screen. "This Wednesday is the San Duo festival. The Naxi are gathering to celebrate San Duo, a warrior who is the incarnation of the Jade Dragon Snow Mountain. According to legend, he's the protector of the Naxi people. They sing and dance and ask for his blessing. Should be fun to watch." She tapped Kalugal's shoulder. "Can we go?"

"You and Arwel can go, and if Alena and Orion want to join you, that's fine with me, but I'm more interested in the Mosuo than the Naxi, and I want to keep looking for clues in the ruins."

"I'm sure Aliya wants to attend the festival as well."

Aliya didn't look sure at all. "I can't go. Not without Kalugal shrouding me."

"I can shroud you as well," Alena offered. "But I really don't see the need. After you get new clothing and a pair of sunglasses, you should be fine."

"I don't want to waste today on sightseeing. I have a million-yuan budget to spend, and that will take all day."

So that was the problem.

Alena chuckled. "You shouldn't take Kalugal too literally. He said that you can spend up to a million. He didn't say that you have to."

"I know. But since I have all that money to spend, I want to buy a place to live."

Kalugal turned to look at her again. "Need I remind you that you are coming with us to the US?"

She pinned him with a hard look. "I remember everything you said to me. You told me that if I'm not happy in the immortals' village, you will buy me a plane ticket to anywhere I want to go. If I buy an apartment now, I will have a place to live when I come back here."

"Didn't you want to move to Beijing?" Jin asked.

"I changed my mind." Aliya cast a quick glance at Jin's phone. "Does it say there how many people live in Lijiang?"

"Let me check on *Wikipedia*." Jin scrolled through the page. "About a million and three hundred thousand." She lifted her head and smiled at Aliya. "That's considered a small city in China."

"It's big enough for me to hide in," Aliya said. "But it's not so big that I can't get out of the city and hunt in the wild."

"Speaking of hunting," Arwel said. "I need to stop by the jet and load up on more weapons. When we go into the tunnels again, I want to have explosives, flares, and walkie-talkies. I'm not getting caught with my pants down again."

"Walkie-talkies will be useless there," Kalugal said. "Whatever is causing the interference will also interfere with radio waves. But the flares are a good idea."

"I have a better one," Jin said. "I can tether one of you and stay outside while the rest of you go in. I will be your walkie-talkie."

Aliya looked confused. "What are you talking about?"

Jin opened her mouth to explain, but Arwel interrupted. "Unless Alena agrees to stay out of the tunnels as well, I will have to follow her, and I'm not leaving you alone topside, unprotected. We go or stay together."

If looks could kill, Arwel would be dead, or at least painfully wounded.

"You are so full of it, Arwel," Jin bristled. "You are loading up on weapons and explosives, and yet you would send the rest of the team unprotected if Alena decides to stay with me?"

He glared back at her. "My job here is to protect Alena. I can give the flares and explosives to Phinas and Welgost. I'm sure they know how to use them."

Kalugal cleared his throat. "You forgot one important thing, Arwel. We came here on my jet, and I don't have explosives on board. All I have are flares, handguns, and more knives."

Arwel looked embarrassed. "I didn't forget. I assumed that you carried the same standard equipment as we do, but what you have will do."

Alena had a feeling that Kalugal had nailed it, and that Arwel had forgotten that they hadn't arrived on a clan jet.

"So, what will it be?" Jin turned to Alena. "Do you want to stay with me so the team can communicate with the outside world? We can stay in the hotel and get massages, manicures, and pedicures." She looked at Jacki. "You can join us too."

Jacki shook her head. "I need to be in the tunnels in case they discover something that will trigger a vision. We can do all that on Thursday, and then Aliya can join us." She smiled at the girl. "We can have a girls-only fun day."

Alena chuckled. "We wanted this to be a girls' day out, but the guys wouldn't hear of it. I doubt they would let us out of their sights even to go to the spa."

Not only that, but she also had to take the Odus along because Kian had called and had given her an earful about leaving them behind. He'd eventually conceded that taking them to the ruins wasn't an option because they couldn't cross the rickety rope bridge without falling into the water, and they couldn't fit through some of the narrower tunnels. She'd just omitted to mention that the water was only waist deep and they could walk through. Kian was being ridiculous. With three powerful compellers and three fighters to keep her safe, the Odus weren't necessary, and she planned to leave them in the limousine when their group went shopping and sightseeing.

"I can arrange for the masseuses and manicurists to come to our suite." Kalugal said. "You can commandeer the bedroom."

"No way," Jin said. "If you're so concerned with our safety, you can join us at the spa."

Aliya had remained silent throughout their discussion, but as soon as there was a lull, she repeated her question from before. "What does it mean to tether someone? And why can only Jin do that?"

"That's my special talent," Jin said. "If I touch someone with the intention of tethering them, I can attach a string of my consciousness to theirs and see what they see and hear what they hear until I sever the tether. I used to keep tabs on my sister that way."

Aliya looked horrified. "Is that why you loaned me your clothes? Did you attach a tether to them?"

Jin laughed. "That's not how it works, and I have no reason to attach a tether to you because you don't have anyone to talk to but us. What would I listen to?"

25

VROG

*V*rog unfolded a cardboard box and then changed his mind and tossed it aside.

The ledgers were too valuable to be transported in cardboard boxes. He needed containers that were sturdy and watertight. Perhaps he could load his entire safe onto the plane?

It was heavy as hell, but since they were traveling by private jet, that shouldn't be a problem. He needed to ask Morris, though. The pilot was out with Yamanu and the two Guardians, sitting outside of the storage building where Mey was listening to echoes and playing the stone game with them. The four were bored out of their mind and would probably be much happier in Lugu Lake.

That place was a tourist attraction, and there was a lot to see besides the archeological site and the tunnels running under it.

They could get busy sightseeing, while he got busy wooing Aliya.

Just thinking about her made him hard, and that was without the benefit of seeing what she looked like.

It didn't matter.

He would have liked Aliya to be pretty, but that wasn't the attribute he thought of as most important.

Would she be as cruel as the other Kra-ell females? Or did her human half make her mellower the same way his human half made him?

His dream female would be fierce but not cruel, assertive but not dominant, and most importantly, capable of falling in love with him.

What were the chances of Aliya checking off all those boxes?

Probably slim, and he shouldn't build her up in his mind and then get disappointed by the reality of her.

The problem was that he couldn't help it.

The only love Vrog had ever felt was for his human mother and for his son. How would it feel to love his own female?

Incredible.

If they could have a long-lived child together, all of his wishes would come true. But if they didn't, that was okay. He already had an immortal son, but for her, he would like to have another.

"Get a hold of yourself, Vrog," he murmured as he pushed the ledgers back into the safe and locked the door.

Pushing to his feet, he straightened his collar and adjusted his tie. On his way out, he stopped in Doctor Wang's office. "I'm going out of town in a day or two, so if there are any matters you need to discuss with me, please come to my office later today."

The principal's eyes widened. "Are Mr. and Mrs. Williams done with their investigation already?"

"I believe so."

"Did they make up their minds about buying the school?"

Vrog shrugged. "If they did, they haven't informed me of their decision." He gave the principal a smile before turning on his heel and heading down the stairs.

He'd decided to return to the United States even before they'd found Aliya, and now that they were planning to take her with them to live in the village, he was most likely going to stay much longer than he'd initially planned.

That reminded him of the virtual adventure he was supposed to go on upon his return. Should he still do that now that he had his sights on Aliya?

The female who he'd matched with was waiting for him, and declining to participate after he'd already agreed was akin to a breach of contract and dishonorable.

He would go on the adventure if Aliya showed no interest in him, which was very probable. When he still lived with the other Kra-ell, none of the females had found him attractive enough to invite him to their beds. He wasn't as strong as the pureblooded males, and his mixed genes couldn't produce a pureblooded child, which made him useless to Jade and the other females.

As he walked out of the administrative building, he was surprised to see Mey and her entourage heading his way.

"Did you learn anything new today?" he asked.

"I did." She glanced around the campus. "Perhaps we should discuss what I learned in your quarters."

Classes were in session, so there was no one on the center lawn or anywhere within earshot, but Mey was right to be cautious. "Certainly. I can offer you coffee or tea and we can discuss your plans for acquiring the school."

In case anyone was covertly listening to their exchange, that was what they expected to hear.

"The spirits seem to be resting peacefully," Mey said. "There are still several areas of the school which I haven't covered yet, but I can complete my spiritual investigation in a day or two."

"Can you do that any faster?" He started walking toward the staff quarters. "We have that urgent matter to attend to, and I would like to expedite things if possible."

"I know that you would, but I'd rather be done with my investigation in one shot, so I don't have to come back here again."

"Are you having such an awful time in the school? You shouldn't consider purchasing it if you do."

Yamanu clapped his back. "We are having a great time, but we miss our friends and family, and I miss my own custom-built bed." He winked at Vrog. "A guy my size is not comfortable on a standard bed."

"You forgot to mention Junior," Vrog whispered.

That had been their initial cover story, and they'd stuck to it. Mey and Yamanu had a son who they wanted to teach about his mother's heritage.

"I miss my son," Mey said loudly. "Perhaps sending him to school abroad wasn't such a great idea."

"We can buy a house nearby," Yamanu said. "So we can visit him every day."

Mey chuckled. "He would hate that. Besides, unless we can convince all of our friends and relatives to move to China with us, I don't think I could stand being away from them for so long."

"We will fly back and forth." Yamanu wrapped his arm around his wife's shoulders.

Vrog wasn't sure whether the two were indeed married or if it was part of their cover story. They were mated, though, and given what Vrog had learned from Vlad and Wendy, being mated was more binding than being married.

Supposedly, the immortals' mated bond was stronger than any official document proclaiming a couple husband and wife.

The Kra-ell had neither. No official ceremony, no bond, and no love.

But perhaps things could be different between him and Aliya. They could start a new tradition. Would the Clan Mother agree to marry them?

Damn, he was letting himself get carried away again.

Aliya might not want him, or he might not want her. The fact that they were each other's only hybrid Kra-ell option didn't mean that they would end up together.

26

ALIYA

I have no reason to attach a tether to you because you don't have anyone to talk to but us.

That sentence kept replaying in Aliya's mind on a never-ending loop. It succinctly described her pathetic existence, and it made her stupid plans of returning to China seem even more pathetic.

These people were offering her a lifeline, and unless they were really evil and were planning on selling her to the bad Kra-ell for breeding, she was willing to do whatever they asked of her in return.

"Have you ever seen an airport?" Kalugal asked as the limousine was let through a gate into the private section of the airport.

"I've seen airplanes flying through the sky, but I've never seen one up close."

Kalugal smirked. "You are in for a treat. The first plane you're going to see is my luxurious private jet."

Was that a trap?

Were they luring her into the airplane and planning on flying away with her?

If they didn't have three males who could compel her to follow their orders, that would have been a viable suspicion, but with those powers, they didn't need to trick her into doing anything. They could just tell her what to do and she would have to obey.

"Kalugal likes everything on a grand scale." Carol threaded her arm through Aliya's. "I'm dying to see his jet."

"Haven't you seen it already?"

The petite blond shook her head, her pretty curls bouncing around her beautiful face. "Lokan and I flew separately. This is kind of a family reunion." She sighed. "I haven't seen Jacki and Kalugal in months. I hope to make it back home in time for their baby's arrival. I'm going to be an aunt for the first time."

"That's nice." Aliya said what she thought was expected of her.

Carol looked proud and excited as if she was giving birth to the baby, not Jacki.

497

Thinking of how the pureblooded females had regarded each other's pregnancies, Aliya couldn't remember whether they'd been happy when another female conceived. They had been very competitive, and since conceiving was the ultimate prize, it didn't make sense for them to be happy about a pregnancy that wasn't theirs.

As Carol led her up the stairs into the airplane, Aliya didn't know what to expect, but she sure hadn't expected the inside of it to look like a fancy living room.

"Come." Carol tugged her by the hand toward one of the armchairs. "Sit down."

"Why?"

"The seats recline and turn into beds. I want to show you."

"Okay." Hesitantly, Aliya lowered herself into the seat. "What do I do now?"

"Do you see the metal plate with a picture of a chair on it and arrows? Press the arrow in the direction you want that part of the seat to go. If you want just the back or just the leg part, press the corresponding arrows. If you want to turn the seat into a bed, press the symbol that looks like one."

That was simple enough even for her to understand. Aliya pressed the bed symbol and the entire seat started slowly moving until it was fully reclined. "This is great for short people." She sat up and looked for the button to return the seat to its position.

"You are absolutely right," Kalugal said. "I need to order custom seats that fit Guardian-sized people."

"Is there a special size a Guardian needs to be?"

Chuckling, Carol shook her head. "I was training to become a Guardian, and I'm tiny. But the truth is that other than me, all the other Guardians are on the taller side."

Come to think of it, everyone in their group aside from Carol and Jacki was rather tall, and Jacki wasn't short by human standards. She was average.

"Tell me more about the other immortals in your village. Are they all as tall and good-looking as these?"

"We are the descendants of gods, so obviously everyone is good-looking, but heights vary. The Clan Mother herself is so tiny that she's even shorter than me, but she's the most powerful being on the planet." Carol cast a sidelong glance at Orion, who was sitting with Alena across from them and engaging in covert amorous activities.

The jealous beast inside Aliya started to awaken, but Carol distracted her, whispering into her ear, "We recently discovered that another god had survived, Orion's father, but we don't know how powerful he is. Most likely, he's not as powerful as Annani. She's a force of nature even compared to other gods."

"What happened to them? I mean to the other gods?"

Carol patted her arm. "I'll tell you on the way to the city."

"I'm done." Arwel emerged from the front of the jet with a bulging duffel bag slung over his shoulder. "As soon as Shamash and Phinas are done loading up as well, we can go."

27

VROG

*W*hen the coffee had finished brewing, Vrog poured it into the new mugs he'd had brought to his apartment and handed them out to his guests. During the several days since the team's arrival at his school, he'd equipped his apartment with additional chairs, a small fridge, mugs, teacups, spoons, napkins, and a modest supply of snacks.

Vrog had never hosted people before, but he was discovering that he enjoyed it. He'd also enjoyed his stay with Vlad and Wendy. The breakfasts and dinners they'd shared, hanging out with Wendy in the café during the day, meeting up with Margaret, Bowen, Stella, and even Richard.

It was nice to have friends and family who knew who and what he was, people who he didn't need to pretend to be human with, people to talk to about things outside of school business.

"Good coffee." Yamanu put his mug down. "Where did you get it? It's much better than what you served us the first day."

"I ordered it online." Vrog sat on one of the straight-back chairs. "I'm getting better at entertaining guests."

"You're a gracious and generous host," Mey said. "So, do you want to hear what I learned today?"

"I can't wait."

Hopefully it was good enough to end her investigation, so they could get out of there.

"Jade and the other female were fighting because the other one wanted to leave with part of the tribe and start one of her own." Mey added sugar to her coffee and stirred it in. "By the way. What does pakta mean?"

"I'm not sure what the literal meaning is, but it's considered a great offense to call a female pakta. It's the equivalent of calling a woman bitch in English. I assume that pakta is a female animal from the Kra-ell home that is not held in high regard."

Mey pursed her lips. "I have no idea why humans chose male and female dogs as derogatory terms. I happen to love dogs. If I had to choose, I would have chosen rats or spiders as insults." She made a face. "You are such a greedy tarantula," she gave it a try.

"Nah, that doesn't pack a punch," Yamanu said.

"You're such a greedy rat," Mey tried again.

Yamanu nodded. "That's much better. A greedy snake sounds good as well."

Mey smiled. "Anyway, pakta was what the other female called Jade, and that's how the brawling started. This time, though, I managed to stay in the zone to the end of the echo, and I saw their reconciliation. They acted like bros reconciling after letting off some steam in a fist fight. Jade told the other one that she didn't want her to leave because it wasn't safe. They were alone among humans, and there was strength in numbers."

"The other one was probably Kagra," Vrog supplied. "If the tribe ever split, she would have led the offshoot. So that's nothing new. But I didn't know that they had been fighting over that. They'd always shown a unified front as if there were no discord between them."

"Toward the end of the echo, it became clear that they cared about each other, or perhaps that Jade cared about Kagra. I'm not sure Kagra cared about Jade, though." Mey took a sip of her coffee before putting the mug down. "When Kagra asked Jade about the other Kra-ell, Jade said that she didn't know whether anyone else survived, but if they had, they might not be friendly."

Jay got up to refill his mug. "Did either of them mention the supposed betrayal of the scouting crew that Aliya remembered Jade talking about with Kagra?"

"No, and that's why I want to go back again tomorrow and wait for another echo to play. We might learn more about that."

Vrog groaned. "You might have to listen to endless hours of echoes and still not stumble upon anything relating to the scouting crew. The only echoes you have access to are those that were imbued with strong emotions. What are the chances of Jade or any of the others getting emotionally upset while talking about that particular subject?"

"If I were betrayed by my own people, I would be upset," Yamanu said. "Even decades later, I would get angry every time the subject was brought up."

"Me too," Mey said. "Besides, that was not what we were looking for in the first place. Stumbling upon that fight was just a bonus. What we are really after are echoes left by the attackers or the attacked that will shed light on who they were, how they found your tribe, and why they killed all the males."

"The last one is not hard to guess," Alfie said. "They were after the females. In the old days, when one human tribe conquered another, they slaughtered the males and took the females. It's a tale as old as time."

As everyone nodded in agreement, Vrog's stomach twisted. To them, it was a sad event they'd heard about. To him, it was an open wound that refused to heal. It had been his family that had been murdered.

As his fangs started to elongate, he bent his head and took several sips from the coffee until the sensation passed.

"On another subject." He turned to Morris. "Can we load two medium-sized safes onto the plane? They are about four hundred pounds each."

"No problem," the pilot said. "What do you have in them, gold?"

"To me, it is. I originally thought to put the ledgers Kian asked me for in cardboard boxes, but I realized that they are too valuable to risk transporting in such unsafe packaging. It would be best to take them with the safes I keep them in."

"We can do that," Morris said.

"Good. That's one problem solved." Vrog turned to Mey. "The other one is how long are you planning on staying here? I'd rather leave as soon as I can. I'm eager to get to Aliya. She's all alone and she must be scared. Having me there will make her feel safer." Or so he hoped.

"I can take you," Morris said. "The others can stay here."

"That's a hard no." Yamanu crossed his massive arms over his chest. "We leave together."

"The Kra-ell quarters were burned to the ground." Vrog looked Mey in the eyes. "The echoes of what happened have no walls to cling to. The structures that remained standing will only provide anecdotal information at best."

Mey lifted a finger. "Give me one more day. If I find nothing relevant to our quest tomorrow, we will leave Wednesday morning."

That was progress.

Vrog nodded. "Agreed."

28

ALENA

"*H*ow do I find a home for sale?" Aliya asked as they entered the department store.

Alena wished Kalugal hadn't used a light shroud that affected only humans so she could see what he'd made Aliya look like. He'd said that he made her appear more ordinary but not completely different.

She still attracted attention, probably because she was so tall, but since those were just passing looks that weren't accompanied by murmurs or snickers, Aliya didn't seem to mind, and some of the tension had left her shoulders.

Then again, she was hunching them, so that might have been the reason she looked less tense.

"I'll ask around," Carol offered. "You need to concentrate on buying a new wardrobe."

"Follow me," Jin said. "As a fashion entrepreneur, I know how to spot quality."

Alena didn't plan on getting anything, but she trailed behind them to offer moral support in case Aliya needed it, and since Jin had taken it upon herself to be her fashion adviser, she probably would.

Arwel's mate had the tact of a bull in a china shop. Her comment about Aliya having no one to talk to outside of their group had sent the girl into a melancholy tailspin, and if not for Carol and her talent for storytelling, that bad mood would have ruined Aliya's enjoyment of the day.

"You look bored," Orion said quietly in her ear. "I have an idea of how to alleviate that boredom."

Smiling, Alena leaned against his side. "What do you have in mind?"

He reached to the nearest clothing rack and pulled out a dress. "I want you to try it on."

She laughed. "It's not my size."

"It doesn't matter," he whispered. "You are only going to pretend to try it on while you shroud me and I go in with you."

She rolled her eyes. "This is a department store. There is no privacy in the changing rooms. They are designed like stalls in a public bathroom with the bottoms and tops open."

He looked crushed. "There goes my fantasy."

Carol sauntered up to them. "I don't know what to do about Aliya and the damn apartment she wants to buy. I asked one of the cashiers, and she told me about a nice new neighborhood that's currently under construction. She and her fiancé put down a deposit, and she said that if we want to get an apartment there, we should hurry because they are selling out fast. I was hoping that the cheapest one would be completely out of Aliya's range so she would drop the idea, but the price for a studio or a one-bedroom is within the range of what Kalugal promised her."

A million yuan was only about a hundred and sixty thousand dollars, but it was probably enough to buy a small studio apartment in Lijiang.

"She can buy it and later sell it," Orion said. "Kalugal made her a promise, and if he breaks it, she won't believe anything else we tell her."

"He's right." Kalugal walked up to them. "A million yuan is a reasonable amount as recompense and not a significant amount for me. If it makes her trust us more, I'll help her get it. After she's done shopping, we will drive over to that development and let her choose an apartment."

"You are okay, cousin." Alena pulled him into a quick hug. "Underneath all the bluster beats a good heart."

Wrapping his arm around Jacki, he grinned. "My mate is my heart, and she makes me a better man. Before I met her, I would have just compelled the girl to forget about my slip-up of an offer."

"No, you wouldn't," Jacki protested. "You are an honorable male, and you keep your promises. I have nothing to do with that."

"Thank you." He kissed the top of her head. "I value your high opinion of me."

"Jin is waving us over," Alena said and started walking.

"I want you to see Aliya's new look."

A moment later, Aliya walked out of the changing room in a pair of tight jeans, a white hoodie, white sneakers, and a pair of big sunglasses perched on her nose.

"What do you think?" Jin asked.

"Beautiful," Phinas said, and given his tone, he meant it.

"Great." Jin motioned for Aliya to turn in a circle. "So that's the look we are going for. An international college student."

"Why international?" Aliya asked.

Alena glanced at Kalugal, who nodded. "I'm shrouding what we say as well."

"Because of your height and the fact that your features are not really Chinese. If people think you are a foreigner, they will shrug off your oddities."

"Maybe I should start speaking only English from now on."

"That's not a bad idea," Lokan said. "That will reinforce the perception."

"My accent is terrible."

Alena smiled. "It's gotten a lot better over the past twenty-four hours. You are an exceptionally fast learner."

The girl was like a sponge. Alena had a feeling that given access to quality education, Aliya could excel in any field of knowledge.

Becoming a Guardian was not her only option.

29

ANNANI

"*Mistress* Ronja." Ogidu bowed. "Please come in."
"Thank you." Ronja's smile was full of secrets as she walked into Annani's living room. "Good afternoon, Clan Mother."

"Good afternoon." Annani rose to her feet and embraced her friend. "Every time I see you, you look better than the time before. Is it the physical activity, or is it the love?"

"A little bit of both." Ronja's cheeks pinked, but she kept smiling. "Or a lot."

"Oh dear." Annani laughed as she took Ronja's hand. "I want to hear all about it." She led her to the couch.

"There isn't much to tell." Her blush deepened. "Well, that's not true. I finally did what you encouraged me to do, and I'm floating on a cloud." She chuckled. "And not just because of the wonderful effects of the venom. I'm in love." Ronja sighed. "Merlin is the perfect man for me. He's brilliant, kind, funny, and he's hopeless without me. I couldn't have asked for a better match."

Annani was of the same opinion. The Fates knew what they were doing with these two, and the fact that they were so in love gave her hope for Ronja's successful transition. The Fates had no reason to punish either of the two lovebirds by allowing Ronja to perish. Still, nothing was guaranteed, and assuming that everything was destined for a good ending was overly optimistic and simplistic. Annani's gut, which she usually trusted, was undecided in Ronja's case. It vacillated between being excited about her successful transition and dreading the opposite.

"Congratulations." She patted her friend's hand. "Are you just enjoying yourself, or are you already working on your induction?"

Ronja's smile faltered. "We are not using protection. I figured that it was time to take the plunge and go for it. I have to believe that the Fates arranged for me to be with Merlin because he's so perfect for me and we are great together, so they also have to make sure that I survive the transition."

For some reason, Ronja's hopeful words caused Annani's gut to swing into the dread position of the pendulum's range.

She was excited and hopeful, but she could not help being anxious as well. Ronja was the oldest Dormant to ever attempt transition, and she was taking a big risk because Annani encouraged her to do so, which meant that Annani was responsible for her fate and the fate of her young daughter.

Lisa was only fifteen, and she had recently lost her father. Losing her mother as well would destroy her.

"How is Lisa taking it?"

"She's happy for Merlin and me, but she's also scared."

"Does it bother her that you did not mourn her father for a full year?"

Ronja took in a deep breath. "Lisa encouraged me not to wait, but I'm sure that on some level, it upsets her. She loved Frank. We both did." A tear slid down her cheek. "I still love him, you know. You don't stop loving a person when they are gone. I didn't know it was possible to be in love with a new partner and still love the one you lost." She pushed a strand of hair behind her ear. "That's not true. I knew that it was possible. I loved Frank when I married him, but I also still loved Michael. I don't think I ever stopped loving him even though he'd hurt me."

Annani smiled sadly. "The heart has a boundless capacity for love. It is like the universe that keeps expanding like a balloon."

Ronja crossed her legs. "I remember Michael explaining to David and Jonah that the universe is like dough with raisins. When placed in an oven, the dough begins to expand, and the distance between the raisins embedded in it grows proportionally in all three directions."

"I have to agree that I like the dough analogy better, especially since the universe is supposedly flat." She sighed. "Scientists constantly develop new theories, and it is hard to keep up. I will have to brush up on some reading when I return to the sanctuary. While I am here or in Scotland, I prefer to spend time with my large and beautiful family."

"Can I ask you a question?"

"Of course."

"Why do you live in the sanctuary? Kian and Amanda are here in the village, and Alena might soon join them. Sari is in Scotland. If I were you, I would choose the village as my home."

"I like having my own place," Annani admitted. "And I believe that my children prefer it that way as well. I had the sanctuary built exactly the way I wanted it, and it is a paradise under a dome of ice. It is like a fairyland." She waved her hand, signaling Ogidu to serve the tea and the canapés she had asked him to prepare. "You should come to visit me, with Merlin and Lisa, of course."

"I would love to." Ronja sighed. "If I survive the transition, I will reward myself with a trip to your sanctuary."

"It is not an if but a when. When you transition, I will send one of my Odus with the jet to pick you up. I hope that you will stay for a while."

Perhaps that was the solution to Alena's absence. Annani could invite people to visit her in the sanctuary. She could have a rotation of guests so there was always someone with her, and she would never get bored.

Or maybe she could convince Orion to move in with Alena and stay in the sanctuary. The problem was that Kian might not approve for security reasons.

Then again, if they were trusting Orion with Alena, then they should trust him with knowledge of the sanctuary and its general location. Alaska was vast, and they had made finding the sanctuary as impossible as the technology of the time allowed. Things were changing, though, and either they would need to fortify the sanctuary's defenses and detection countermeasures, or she might be forced to abandon her beautiful fairyland sooner than later.

3 0

ALIYA

*A*fter paying for the lotions and hairbrushes they'd gotten in the cosmetics section of the department store, Jin handed Aliya the shopping bag.

"Do you get periods?" she asked.

Aliya looked over her shoulder to where the rest of their group was scattered, smelling perfumes and checking out makeup. Well, the ladies were. The guys either trailed along or stopped in the men's fragrance section.

Fortunately, they weren't close enough to hear Jin's embarrassing question.

"Why? Don't you?" Aliya asked much more quietly.

"Not since I turned immortal," she said just as quietly. "We only ovulate on demand. And I'm asking so I know whether we need to get you feminine products."

Jin was refreshingly blunt, but she took some getting used to.

"I get periods only twice a year, and the last one was two months ago."

"That's not so bad. When I was still human, getting periods every month was a major drag. I took the contraceptive shot just to get rid of them."

"You are so lucky that your people can activate the dormant genes. If not for your dormant mother, you would have been born human."

On the way to the city, Carol, Alena, Jacki, and Jin had taken turns telling Aliya about immortals, about how they were different from the Kra-ell, about their ability to activate Dormants, and about how Jin and Mey's mother must have been one, which was why they'd been born with the godly genes.

Aliya still didn't understand half of what they'd told her, but it appeared that the female descendants of the gods could transfer their immortality to their children no matter how diluted their blood was.

It was most unfortunate that the same wasn't true for the Kra-ell.

A hybrid and a human could only produce human children, which was why Jade had forbidden the hybrid males to have them.

Mey and Jin's father must have defied Jade and had a secret affair with a human outside of the compound. The girls wouldn't have been given up for adoption at the same time if they'd been born inside its walls. Jade would have given each one away as soon as she'd been born.

They'd been the lucky ones, though. They'd been adopted by a nice couple who loved them very much.

"So, what's next?" Jin asked. "The jewelry store?"

"I think I have everything I need."

"You need a suitcase to put everything in." Jin tugged on her hand. "Come on. The others are getting tired of following us around."

"Let's go." Aliya gave her a smile.

After their initial rough start, Jin had turned out to be a good friend. She wasn't as soft and polite as Alena, or as good a storyteller as Carol, but her temperament suited Aliya's better. Perhaps the blood they shared made them more alike.

It might be nice to have a friend who was at least a little bit Kra-ell.

"Thank you for everything you're doing for me," she murmured under her breath. "And I'm sorry about hurting your mate."

Jin chuckled. "I've already forgotten about it, and so did Arwel. Besides, don't thank me, thank Kalugal. I've been very happily spending his money."

Jin had paid for everything with Kalugal's credit card, and Aliya had lost count of how much she'd spent. It must have been at least three thousand yuan. It might not be much for Kalugal, but it was a fortune for Aliya.

She'd bought so many things, of which the ten pairs of panties were the items she was most happy about.

Perhaps she could excuse herself and go to the bathroom to put one pair on. The leggings Jin had loaned her were comfortable and looked good on her, but they didn't leave much to the imagination, and Aliya felt as if she were walking around half-naked.

To their credit, the eyes of the males in her group never traveled below her collar bone, but other men had been staring at her crotch and her ass, and she'd been too embarrassed to ask Kalugal to extend his shroud to cover those parts of her as well.

In addition to the panties, she now also owned five bras, which in her opinion was a waste of money. Her breasts were so small that they didn't need support, but Jin had insisted that she needed them for modesty to cover her nipples when they got cold and stuck out like a pair of very small knobs.

Aliya had also bought ten T-shirts, but only because a pack of ten cost as much as three if she'd gotten them separately. Jin had been against it, saying that the pack of ten was cheap because the department store wanted to get rid of T-shirts no one wanted, but Aliya didn't care that the designs weren't great. Having ten T-shirts felt like such a luxury. Besides, she planned on using the uglier ones as undershirts instead of the bras. The other items filling her shopping bags were five long-sleeved shirts, three pairs of jeans, two pairs of leggings, two sweaters, four hoodies, two pajama sets, a coat, a scarf, a pair of gloves, and three pairs of shoes—four if she also counted the slippers.

She also had two pairs of sunglasses, a bottle of perfume, and some other toiletries that Jin had insisted every woman needed.

"How much money did I spend so far?"

"You have plenty left over. Don't worry about it."

"Can Kalugal pay for the apartment with that plastic card?"

"Most people can't, but he can. He's very rich."

"What does he do?"

"To get rich?"

Aliya nodded.

"He's an investor. He buys stock and sells it, he also finds promising new start-ups and buys them, and God knows what else. I'm sure that there are some shady deals and other skeletons in his proverbial closet."

Aliya didn't know what stock was, or what kind of deals were done in a closet that had skeletons hidden in it.

"I didn't understand that."

"It's not important." Jin sauntered over to Arwel. "Is it time for lunch? I'm famished."

He lifted his hand and looked at his watch. "It's almost time for dinner. Are you done?"

"Aliya thinks that she has everything she needs, but I need to go over everything we've gotten before we leave the shopping district. Where are Carol and Jacki and the others?"

"Over there." Arwel pointed with his chin. "Let's get them and find a place to get something to eat."

31

ALENA

*A*s they neared the development seller's office, Alena lowered the limousine's window. "This is going to be a very nice neighborhood once it's finished." The buildings, which ranged from six to eight stories tall, were separated by large areas that would most likely become lawns and playgrounds. Those that were completed had large windows, generous balconies, and architectural elements that made them look similar but not the same. A neighborhood like that wouldn't have looked out of place in California or Nevada.

Aliya peeked out the window and frowned. "It's too nice. I don't think I have enough money to buy an apartment here."

"Yes, you do," Carol said. "The clerk at the store told me that you can probably get a one-bedroom apartment for under a million yuan. She and her fiancé just put a deposit on a two-bedroom apartment that was selling for one point two million."

"How much is that in dollars?" Jacki said.

"One hundred eighty-four thousand." Kalugal didn't need a calculator to come up with the figure. "In Beijing, you would pay ten times as much for a nice new apartment. We are fortunate that Lijiang is one of the most affordable cities in China despite being such a popular tourist destination."

As soon as their two limousines parked in front of the sales office, an agent rushed out with a puzzled expression on her face. "Can I help you?"

"Yes, you can," Kalugal said in Chinese and walked over to her. "Do you speak English?" He offered her his hand. "I speak Chinese, but some of my friends don't."

"I speak English." She smiled nervously. "I apologize, but there must have been some misunderstanding. This is the Lo-cur site. The Luckar luxury development is on the west riverbank. I would be happy to give your driver the correct directions."

Kalugal gave her one of his charming smiles. "There is no confusion. I'm looking for a modest apartment for my niece." He motioned for Aliya to come forward. "The young lady fell in love with Lijiang and wants to settle down here."

The realtor's eyes shone with excitement. "Then you are in the right place." She offered him her hand. "I'm Wei."

"A pleasure to meet you, Wei."

"This neighborhood is perfect for young couples who want to start a family. Would you like to see what's available?" She looked over the rest of their group. "Is anyone else interested in purchasing an apartment? It's a great investment opportunity. Lijiang is growing fast, and the demand is rising. In a few years, these apartments are going to be worth much more than they are today."

"Interesting," Kalugal said. "Let's see what's available first and take it from there."

"Do you have anything that's under a million yuan?" Aliya asked.

"I sure do. We have a studio that is offered at eight hundred and fifty, and a one-bedroom that is only one hundred thousand more. Which one would you like to see?"

"Can I see both?" Aliya looked at Kalugal. "If that's okay with you, Uncle."

"Of course it is. I want you to be happy, my dear."

Alena stifled a chuckle. Kalugal loved performing, and he relished every opportunity to do so.

"Is everyone in your group coming to see the apartments?" Wei asked.

"If it's not too much bother." Kalugal fell in step with her. "We were in the city for some shopping, and we heard about this development from a lady who worked in the department store. She was so enthusiastic about the apartment she and her fiancé put a down payment on that we decided to follow her recommendation and visit the place right away. She said that it's selling out quickly."

"It is," Wei confirmed. "It's a beautiful development, and it's affordable." She sauntered closer to him. "As I said, it's a great investment opportunity, and many people are buying apartments because they expect the prices to go up."

"Why is that?" Kalugal asked. "Are new industries coming to Lijiang?"

"Airbnb," she said conspiratorially. "Lijiang is becoming more and more popular with tourists, both domestic and international, and the local authorities have eased up on regulation regarding short-term rentals."

"Interesting." Kalugal smoothed his hand over his goatee. "My niece is not going to be here full time, so she might make some extra money by renting her place out to tourists when she's away."

"Definitely." Wei called the elevator. "I'm afraid not everyone in your party will fit in. Some will have to wait for the elevator to come down. The studio is on the eighth floor, number 823, and the one-bedroom apartment is number 827."

"No problem." Kalugal motioned for Jacki, Shamash, Welgost, and Phinas to join him and Aliya. "We will go first."

As the elevator door closed behind them, Alena let out the chuckle she'd been holding in. "Kalugal should have been an actor. He's happiest when he's performing."

"I noticed," Lokan said. "He amuses himself by pretending to be different people."

When the elevator returned a few minutes later, the three remaining couples and Ovidu got in.

Oridu remained standing by the elevator to guard it.

On the eighth floor, they followed the sound of Kalugal's voice into the apartment.

"It's small," Jin murmured. "But it's big enough for one person."

"Let's see the other one," Kalugal said. "And if you have a two-bedroom apartment available, we would like to see it as well."

"It's over my budget," Aliya said.

"I know, dear. But two-bedroom apartments rent out better on Airbnb."

"What's Airbnb?" Aliya whispered.

"It's a way for people to rent out their homes to tourists for short durations," Orion said. "I used to stay in hotels during my travels, but now I prefer the convenience of having a kitchen, more room, and more privacy, so I use Airbnb whenever I can."

Kalugal grimaced. "I prefer hotels where I know that the bedding is properly laundered. Besides, I like having concierge and room service available."

Smiling, Orion leaned against the doorjamb. "I guess my preferences are more plebeian than yours."

Aliya looked confused. "I don't know what you are talking about. Can someone explain to me how you find these people who rent out their apartments?"

Kalugal patted her arm. "I'll explain everything on the way back to the hotel. We don't want to keep Wei waiting." He turned to the realtor. "When will these apartments be ready for move-in?"

"In about three months."

"Excellent." He smiled at Aliya. "That works perfectly for us."

32

ALIYA

*A*liya lay on the couch in Jacki and Kalugal's suite and looked at her purchases of the day. They were neatly stacked on the coffee table with the price tags still attached to them and grouped according to their function. She was supposed to put them in her new suitcase, but she wasn't ready to do that yet.

She'd never had so many clothes or shoes, and even though Jin had laughed, saying that those were just the bare necessities, to Aliya it was an abundance.

But that was nothing compared to owning a brand new two-bedroom apartment in a new development.

It wasn't the one she'd seen earlier today. That had been a model apartment that the realtor used for showing prospective clients the various layouts.

Hers was still in the process of being built, and it would be ready only in three months, which would give her enough time to decide whether she wanted to stay in the immortals' village or go back to China and live alone in Lijiang.

Had it really happened? Had Kalugal purchased for her a home that cost over a million yuan?

She still couldn't believe his generosity. It was true that his excavations of the ruins and the tunnels had caused her to lose the only home she'd had, but it hadn't belonged to her, and he didn't have to compensate her for it. She was well aware that he'd used it as an excuse to get her things, and that the million yuan hadn't been seriously offered.

He'd made a mistake, and she'd used it to get something she shouldn't have, and yet he'd stood by his offer and paid for the apartment.

Kalugal was either an extremely honorable male or he had a hidden agenda for her. But what could it be? She had nothing to offer him or the clan, not even her womb. Her offspring wouldn't be long-lived, let alone immortal. The Kra-ell were in some ways similar to the immortals, but they didn't carry the godly genes of immortality. The only reason Jin and her sister were immortal was that their mother was a dormant carrier who had transferred the gene of immortality to her daughters.

Despite what Alena had said about finding her a nice immortal male, none of them would be interested in her for anything other than casual sex because she couldn't give them immortal children.

The only one who might find her desirable was Vrog.

It seemed that he was her only option whether she liked him or not, and that was no option at all.

Her memory of him was so vague that she didn't remember whether he was handsome. What she remembered best about him was a conversation she'd overheard Jade having with Kagra.

Kagra had questioned Jade's decision to let him run the tribe's business in Singapore, and Jade had replied that he was smart and loyal to a fault and that she trusted him completely.

To her, smarts and loyalty were the two most important qualities, followed closely by tenacity and generosity. If Vrog had all four, Aliya would give him a chance even if he wasn't handsome.

She should have asked for a picture of him.

As the door to Jacki and Kalugal's bedroom opened, Aliya pushed up on the pillows. "Can't sleep?" she asked Kalugal.

"I'm just getting Jacki a glass of water." He opened the refrigerator and pulled out a large bottle of water. "Do you want some as well?"

She shook her head. "I know that I've already thanked you, but I feel like I need to thank you again. I'm shocked by your generosity."

"Stunned, astonished, or flabbergasted would be better words." He walked over to the couch and motioned for her to scoot and make room for him. "Frankly, I'm a little shocked myself. I don't know why I feel so protective of you. I think that at some point, I started to believe the lie I told and thought of you as my niece." He smiled. "I wanted my niece to get the best deal possible, and the two-bedroom was a better deal than the one-bedroom or the studio."

"I don't feel right about accepting it from you," she admitted. "I was sure that at the last moment you were going to back out. I never believed that you would go through with it. Now I don't know what to do. The right thing would be to give it back, but I can't bring myself to do that. I never owned something so valuable."

He nodded. "I understand your dilemma. If I were in your shoes, I would probably feel the same. The thing is that I'm a hundred percent sure that you will choose to stay in the village, and that this apartment is going to end up being rented out. If it makes you feel better, you can donate the proceeds from the rental to the charity I help fund."

"Is that the one the clan runs for the victims of trafficking?"

He nodded. "That's where the largest chunk of my charitable donations goes, but Jacki also sends money to different causes that involve children."

"I will consider it. If I get a job in the village and don't need the money from the rent, I'll donate it."

Kalugal grinned with satisfaction. "You are an honorable female, Aliya." He offered her his hand. "And I accept your deal."

"And you are an honorable male." She shook what he offered. "I will never forget what you have done for me, and I will find a way to repay you. Jin said that if I become a Guardian, I'll make a lot of money. I would be able to pay you back for the apartment. But it's not just about the money. I owe you a debt of gratitude."

33

ORION

*O*rion put his hands on Alena's waist and drew her to him. "I love you." He took her lips in a kiss that was meant to be soft and loving but quickly turned hungry and demanding.

By now, he knew her well enough not to worry about his inner predator scaring her or turning her off. Despite her mellow demeanor and good manners, Alena was a predator herself, and she loved it when things got a little rough. With her, he could finally let loose the beast inside of him and let it have its fill without worrying that he might hurt her.

They were very much alike in that respect.

They both had polished to perfection the civilized side they showed the world and reserved their immortal wild side for where it belonged—the privacy of their bedroom.

Just as he was about to pick her up and carry her to bed, his phone pinged with an incoming message, but he ignored it in favor of more important things.

Pushing on his chest, Alena planted her feet firmly on the floor. "Aren't you going to check who it is from?"

"Nope." He tried to lift her again.

"What if it's from Geraldine or Cassandra, and they need you urgently?"

"They would have called."

"Just check it. The bed is still going to be there in the next thirty seconds."

Stubborn woman.

"I'll check it on one condition." He pointed at the bed. "You wait for me in there. Naked."

"That's two conditions."

"And your point is?"

A smirk lifting one corner of her mouth, Alena purred, "Pull out your phone, and I will fulfill both and more."

She was planning something naughty, and he was all for it.

As he pulled the device from his pocket, Alena turned around, crossed her arms in front of her, and whipped her sweater over her head.

The bra was next, and when she turned her head to look at him over her shoulder, she caught him staring at her with the phone suspended midair.

"Check the message, Orion."

"Fine." Reluctantly, he did. "It's from Cassandra. She asks if I'm awake and if I can call her."

"Call her."

"I'm sure it's nothing urgent."

"Just call her." Alena reached for the robe that she'd left draped over the bed's footboard. "I'll grab a quick shower in the meantime."

That was a change of plans that he could live with. He'd grown fond of their water play. "Don't rush. I'll join you there when I'm done."

Taking the phone to the chaise lounge, he dialed Cassandra's number. "What's up?"

"Is it a bad time? We can talk tomorrow."

Now she tells me. "It's okay. I'm sure you didn't call to ask me how the weather was over here. What's going on?"

"How *is* the weather?"

His niece had never been good at polite chitchat.

"It's nice during the days and cold during the nights. What do you need, Cassandra?"

"You were the one who arranged the cushy antique gallery job for Leo, right?"

"That's correct."

"So you must know the owner."

"I do."

"Can you ask him to send Leo on a long acquisition trip starting as soon as possible?"

He didn't need to ask why. "Aren't you waiting for me to return to compel Darlene's silence?"

"We are going to use another compeller, and it would be beneficial if Leo wasn't around for at least a few days after we release her memories, so she has some time to think things through in peace. The guy is a controlling jerk, and she can't think straight when she's busy keeping him happy."

Geraldine had given him a summary of their last meeting with Darlene and the not-so-shocking revelation about Roni's real father. Orion had suspected that as well, but because Roni and Leo looked a lot alike, he'd dismissed those suspicions.

"Who's the other compeller? Is Eleanor back?"

"We are taking Parker. Onegus cleared it with the boy's parents, and we are going to run a test before we release her memories to make sure that he can compel her. It's a good test for him as well."

"If his parents agree, then who am I to object. I can call the gallery owner and ask him to send Leo to Pennsylvania. I was supposed to go, but I canceled my plans so I could go with Alena, but Leo can take my place in the estate auction. It's a large estate, but the auction will take only one week. I'll have to come up with several other destinations for him, so he'll be gone an entire month. That should give Darlene enough time to make up her mind."

"That would be awesome, but are you sure? The guy is not too bright. He might overpay for worthless things."

"Don't worry about it. Either Marcelo or I will direct him."

"You're on the other side of the planet. It's going to be nighttime where you are."

He chuckled. "I'll manage. Anything else I can do for you?"

"Yeah, let me know when Leo leaves."

"I will. How is everyone doing?"

"We are good. Geraldine and I are anxious about Darlene. I really want her to leave that jerk and join us in the village. She deserves a second chance, and since she's suffered a lot, the Fates should compensate her with a truelove mate. I'm just trying to figure out who that might be. I think I need to start being more social and invite people over so Darlene can meet eligible bachelors, but I suck at being a hostess. What do I know about entertaining people?"

He laughed. "Not much, but you are Cassandra Beaumont, and you can do anything you set your mind to. I have faith in you."

"Absolutely. I just need to cut back on the hours I work to make time for that."

"You've been saying that a lot. Have you done anything to make it happen?"

"I'm making progress. I've gotten a little better at delegating responsibilities to my team. I'm also doing better with reining in my frustration when others can't do what I want them to do in the time I want them to do it."

"I'm proud of you."

"Yeah, yeah. Say hi to Alena for me."

"I will."

When Cassandra ended the call, Orion wrote an email to Marcelo, checked it once for typos, and sent it.

It was ten at night at Lugu Lake, which meant that it was six in the morning on the West Coast, and Marcelo would probably see the email when he opened the gallery later today, and by then, Orion would have to come up with more destinations for Leo. But there was plenty of time until then, and right now, he had a sexy lady waiting for him to join her in the bathroom.

Planning Leo's month-long acquisition trip could wait.

34

ALENA

*A*lena rested her head on the tub's lip and closed her eyes. It had been a long day, and a warm tub was just what the doctor ordered, as humans liked to say.

That reminded her of Merlin, which reminded her of Ronja, and she wondered how things were going with that. When she'd spoken with Annani last night, there had been no news on that front, but then things might have moved along without her mother knowing about it.

Ronja and Merlin were spending a lot of time together, and they were attracted to each other. They couldn't keep it platonic for long.

Fates willing, Ronja would transition successfully.

Alena offered up a prayer to Ronja's health and long life. Lisa needed her mother, and so did David, even though he was a grown man.

Heck, Alena was over two thousand years old, and she still needed her mother. It was hard enough to imagine living apart from her even if they could see each other every day, harder yet to imagine living in the village while Annani returned to the sanctuary, and inconceivable to never see her mother again.

Suddenly cold, Alena lowered herself into the warm water. Feeling an overwhelming need to hear her mother's voice, she regretted leaving her phone in the bedroom.

It was early morning in California, but her mother was an early riser, and she should be awake already.

Pushing up, she leaned over the tub's lip and listened to the sounds coming from the bedroom. It seemed that Orion was done with the phone call, and all Alena could hear were rustling sounds. Was he taking off his clothes?

If he walked naked into the bathroom, she might forget all about calling her mother.

"Could you please bring me my phone?" she called out.

"In a moment."

"No rush. Take your time." She slid into the water and floated in the large bathtub.

Did the Chinese have a preference for tubs over showers? The tub was easily big enough to accommodate two people, even tall ones like her and Orion, while the shower seemed to have been installed as an afterthought.

"Here is your phone." Orion sat on the edge of the tub, his eyes traveling hungrily over her body. "Who do you want to call this late at night or this early in the morning California time?"

Thankfully, he was still partially dressed.

"My mother. I have a sudden urge to hear her voice."

"Only her voice? You're not going to video chat with her?"

"Why do you ask?"

"Because I want to get into the tub with you, but not if you are video chatting with your mother."

"Annani wouldn't mind, but don't worry, we hardly ever use the video feature. We are old-fashioned, or just old."

"Do you feel old?" His eyes roamed over her breasts, her belly, her legs. "Because you sure don't look old to me."

She wanted to say that she didn't, but the truth was that sometimes she did. Two thousand years was a very long time.

"I don't feel old now." She smiled. "After all, I'm about to call my mother."

He leaned down and kissed her on the lips. "There is something about mothers that always makes you feel like a kid."

"Ha, maybe that's why I stayed by her side for so long. She makes me feel young."

It was true, but for a different reason. Annani was young at heart, adventurous, impulsive, passionate, and being around her was uplifting.

With a sigh, Orion let his eyes roam over her nude body once more. "I'd better not be with you in there while you talk to your mother. I won't be able to keep my hands to myself, and you'll get distracted. I'll take a shower while you call her."

For a moment, Alena considered making a game out of it and challenging Orion, but she knew she would lose. Besides, making out while talking to her mother would be disrespectful.

As he went into the shower, she called her mother.

"Alena, my dear. Is everything alright?"

"Everything is great. We took Aliya shopping today, and Kalugal bought her an apartment in Lijiang."

"Why did he do that if she is coming with you to the village?"

Alena chuckled. "Kalugal didn't mean to get her an apartment, but he painted himself into a corner he couldn't get out of. He told Aliya that she could spend as much money as she wanted, provided that she did it in one day."

Annani laughed. "And the smart girl took advantage of his open-ended offer and got herself an apartment."

"Precisely. Kalugal didn't want Aliya to feel as if she was being given charity, so he said that she should consider it compensation for the home she lost because of us."

"What home? You told me that she lived in the tunnels under the archeological site."

"That was what he meant. She can no longer live there because we discovered her hiding place, and Kalugal's partner is going to excavate the place. Anyway, Aliya challenged Kalugal, asking if she could spend a million yuan, and he said yes, not expecting her to want to buy a home. But he'd given her his word, so he couldn't take it back. To Kalugal, it's not a lot of money, but to Aliya, that's a life-changing amount."

"Did it at least make her less suspicious of us?"

Alena laughed. "I think it made her even more suspicious. Wouldn't you be wary of a stranger buying you a home?"

As Orion stepped out of the shower with his wet hair dripping over his muscular chest, Alena got distracted for a moment.

He stopped by the bath and mouthed, "I'll wait for you in bed."

"I would if he was single," Annani said. "But Aliya knows that Kalugal is mated."

Blocking the microphone with her thumb, Alena whispered, "Don't fall asleep."

"I couldn't even if I wanted to." He let the towel drop, giving her an eyeful of his proud erection.

Her mouth watered. "Don't start without me."

"I can't promise that." He wrapped his palm around his shaft.

"Alena? Are you there?"

Tearing her eyes away from the mouthwatering sight, Alena moved her thumb off the microphone. "Aliya doesn't know what a mated bond is. I don't know how much she knows of the outside world, but you and I know that plenty of married humans keep mistresses on the side, and if they are rich, they buy or rent a place for them."

"I forgot that the Kra-ell do not have truelove mates. They live in a sort of commune, and the females share the men between them. Those are not loving relationships that can result in a bond."

"If they are similar to us, they might be capable of bonding. I think that in their case, their cultural constraints overpowered their physiology. Emmett seems to be in love with Eleanor, and his Kra-ell half is more dominant than his human half. But speaking of bonding, how are Ronja and Merlin doing? Any news on that front?"

"Oh, yes. She and Merlin began the process, and I have my fingers crossed for her."

"It's about time." Alena let out a breath. "Although I would be lying if I said that I wasn't concerned. At least with you there, her chances of pulling through are pretty good."

"I hope that will be enough."

"Other than that, all we can do is pray, and I have already beseeched the Fates on Ronja's behalf."

"I pray every day for her," Annani said. "Thank you for calling me, Alena. It gave me great pleasure to hear your voice."

"Same here, Mother."

"Good night, daughter of mine. Give Orion my regards."

"I will." Alena smiled as she ended the call.

She was going to give Orion much more than that.

35

ORION

*O*rion stroked himself leisurely as he waited for Alena to finish with her phone call. His intention was to keep the embers warm but not let the fire ignite until she joined him, but with the sight of her wet pink nipples imprinted on his mind, it was difficult to pace himself.

When she came out of the bathroom with a towel wrapped around her lush body and licked her lips, he gripped himself tighter. "Come here," he hissed from between his elongated fangs.

"Oh, I am." She sauntered over, dropping the towel on the way.

He sucked in a breath. "You are so incredibly beautiful."

A soft smile brightening her gorgeous face, she straddled his legs and leaned down, and when she parted her lips and took him into her mouth, he jerked up.

"Alena," he whispered her name as if it was a prayer.

Taking him deeper, she looked at him from under her blond lashes, her eyes full of feminine satisfaction at the pleasure and awe that must have been written all over his face. She didn't replace his hand on his shaft with her own, and as he gently pumped into her, he put his other hand on the back of her head, threading his fingers into her thick hair.

It took only a few moments of gliding in and out of the wet warmth of her mouth for him to near the point from which there would be no return, and for a brief moment, he considered letting her finish what she'd started.

After all, the night was still young, and this wouldn't be the end of their lovemaking. He knew it would be heavenly, and he wanted it, but it would also be a wasted opportunity to plant his seed in her womb.

Orion's chance of having a child with Alena might be so slim that it didn't justify the sacrifice, but as the saying went—hope springs eternal.

"I'm not going to last long like that." He forced himself to withdraw from the heavenly heat of her mouth, pulled her up his chest, and kissed her hard before rolling her onto her back and rising above her.

Her eyes glowing, she lifted her head. "Kiss me."

As he took her mouth, his tongue going where his erection had been, he had a moment of regret for stopping her, but he was a man on a mission, however hopeless that mission was.

When he swept his hand down to her breast, she groaned into his mouth, and when he teased her nipple, a throaty moan left her lips. Letting go of her mouth, he moved down to lick at the hard peak and then at its twin. As he kept kissing and licking, his hand traveled down her body, and when he cupped her center, he found her more than ready for him.

Slipping a finger inside her, and then another, he pumped them in and out to prepare her for a much bigger girth. Greedily, she arched up to take more of his fingers inside her, and that combined with the wet heat of her sheath was an invitation he couldn't refuse. In a quick move, he shifted up, rolled her over to her stomach, and entered her from behind.

The connection was electrifying, and as he started moving, she turned her head and looked at him. "Kiss me."

He did, but when the urge to go faster and harder made it impossible to keep their mouths fused, he had to let go.

Gripping Alena's hips, Orion surged in and pulled out. With his thrusts becoming faster and harder, he felt his climax nearing and pulled out. As pleasurable as it was to pound into her from behind, her soft bottom cushioning every thrust, he wanted to be face to face with her when they both climaxed. Rolling her over, he entered her from the front.

In moments, they were both climbing toward the edge again, and as Alena cried out her climax, her nails scoring his back and her head turned to the side, offering him her neck, Orion let himself tumble off the cliff.

With a hiss, he sank his fangs into that welcoming expanse and erupted into her at the same time.

His orgasm seemed to last forever, and when he was finally spent, he shuddered.

Surprisingly, Alena didn't black out, and as her arms closed around him in a gentle embrace, he felt loved, he felt cherished, he was home.

3 6

ARWEL

*a*s the limousine bumped up and down and side to side on the unpaved path, Arwel was thankful for the stability of modern explosives. He'd found a building-supply store in Lijiang that carried them, and he didn't even have to thrall anyone to sell them to him.

Evidently, the use of explosives was common, and their sale was not restricted.

Still, with all that shaking, he was sure Aliya would become nauseous, and they would have to stop for her to have a breather and calm her stomach like they'd had to do during yesterday's trip, but the girl seemed to adapt quickly, not only to rides in a fast-moving vehicle, but also to her new circumstances.

She looked good in a pair of trendy jeans and a hoodie. The hoodie concealed her thinness and her too narrow waist. If not for the shape of her eyes and her unusual height, she could have passed for a college student. With sunglasses on, only the height remained, and that wasn't such a big deal. Unless she suffered from a case of trigger-happy fangs like Vlad had before mating Wendy, she didn't need to worry about scaring people or being pegged as an alien.

Aliya had quite the temper, though, and that was a problem, especially since her aggression was quick to follow. Perhaps she could wear a face mask to mitigate the fangs issue, but even dark sunglasses couldn't conceal the red glow from her eyes.

Ignoring the shaking and rattling, Aliya looked out the window and didn't take part in the conversation going on around her.

Arwel wondered what was going through her head.

The little emotion she emitted since he'd first encountered her had soon changed from fear and anger to resentment and suspicion, then had morphed into surprise and gratitude, and finally had settled on a general state of pensive wariness.

Was she upset about going back to the tunnels that used to be her home?

Was she debating what to reveal and what to keep concealed?

Or maybe she was debating whether she should try to run away or go with them to the village. Although at this point, that was water under the bridge.

Before making the wire transfer to pay for her apartment, Kalugal had gotten her to commit to giving the village a three-month try. If in ninety days she was unhappy, he'd promised to put her on a plane back to Lijiang.

Aliya wasn't the type to go back on her promise, so running didn't seem likely.

Shifting his gaze to his mate, Arwel wondered about her unusual silence. Jin had an opinion on most things and wasn't shy about expressing it. Was she still thinking about serving as their communication conduit to the world outside the tunnel?

When they were minutes away from the riverbank, he turned to her. "So, what's your final decision? Do you want to tether someone and stay topside while we go in, or did you scrap that idea?"

"What do you think? Should I?"

Arwel arched a brow. Usually, Jin didn't ask anyone's opinion, including his. "It depends on your objectives. If you want to stay out of the tunnel and avoid encounters with creepy-crawlies, and if Alena chooses to do the same, then you can tether Lokan or Kalugal and stay behind. Naturally, I'll stay with you. But if you are curious and want to go in, I think that there is no need for you to give up on it. The excavation workers know that we are going in, and if we don't come out at the end of the day, they will know to come to look for us. We are also better prepared this time."

Yesterday, they had all gotten appropriate clothing and footwear in Lijiang, made from materials that wouldn't snag and tear on any sharp edge. They each had a brand-new hardhat with a flashlight attached, a backpack with two durable water bottles, snacks, and more flashlights. Those who were trained in combat also carried an assortment of weapons, including explosives to blast through places that were blocked. He'd also gotten a rope and a harpoon. In short, Arwel was ready for almost anything.

"I want to go in," Jin said after a few moments. "And so does Alena."

"I'm glad." Jacki turned to look at them. "It would have been boring without you. What are we going to find there? Some more illegible scribbles on the walls?"

As all eyes turned to Aliya, she shrugged. "That's all I found during the fourteen years I lived in these tunnels and explored every centimeter of them. So, I don't think there's more to find. But Kalugal insisted that there must be."

"I know there is." Kalugal patted his stomach. "My archeological sixth sense tells me that I'm right, and we are also meeting a geologist who is going to check the soil." He rubbed his hands. "I'm excited about today. I know we will make new discoveries."

"By the way," Jin said. "Did anyone hear from Herb?"

Kalugal turned in his seat. "He went back to the States."

"When?"

"Yesterday. He sent me a text message and said that I should feel free to call him with whatever questions I have about ancient Eastern languages. He suggested that we meet again."

"Are you going to take him up on his offer?" Jacki asked.

"Of course. I enjoyed talking to him, and since I'm moving some of my archeological interests to the east, I might need him."

"What about the other digs you have going on?" Arwel asked.

"They go on," Kalugal said. "I'm not done looking for clues about our ancestors. I just added the Kra-ell ancestors to the mix." He smirked. "I like to keep things interesting."

37

ORION

"*Where* are we meeting the geologist?" Orion asked when they walked through the ancient outpost's gate.

"In the tent," Kalugal said. "Jianye made some improvements while we were shopping yesterday. He said that he'd made the tent comfortable for the ladies. I wonder what he did."

They found out when their group got inside. The tables with the artifacts had been pushed to one side of the tent, and the area that was cleared now served as a place to sit and eat. A long table was covered with a paper tablecloth, and several folding chairs were arranged on both of its sides.

Right now, only one person was sitting at the table, and he rose to his feet.

"Professor Kal Gunter?" His eyes darted to Orion, dismissed him as the possible professor, and moved to Lokan, who apparently fit the image better.

"Mr. Bingwen Zhao." Kalugal stepped forward and offered the geologist his hand. "Or is it Doctor Zhao?"

Looking embarrassed, the young man pointed to a strange device that he'd left on the table. "I'm still working on my doctorate." He lifted the device. "But this has been stealing too much of my time. My brother and I have been working on this since we graduated from MIT."

"How exciting. Did you graduate at the same time?"

"Yes, we are twins."

Orion stifled a chuckle. Kalugal had told them on the way about the twin brothers and their promising start-up, and yet he'd pretended not to know that. Was it a negotiating strategy?

Did he want to appear uninterested so he could get a better deal out of the brothers?

They'd invented a portable device that analyzed soil quickly and accurately. Kalugal had said something about an electron beam microscope or an electron probe, but as usual, anything scientific flew right over Orion's head.

The business part of it, however, he had no problem understanding. Kalugal wanted to invest in the twins' start-up, and he planned to fund the commercial development of their device in exchange for a majority shareholding in their company, the way he did with all his start-up investments. The guy liked to be in control.

"What's MIT?" Aliya asked quietly.

"It's a very prestigious university," Lokan said. "The Massachusetts Institute of Technology produced many important scientists and innovators and is currently ranked first in the world."

Aliya regarded the young man with renewed appreciation. "He must be very smart."

"I'm sure he is," Orion said.

"So, Mr. Zhao." Kalugal motioned for the guy to follow him. "Have you done any initial tests before we arrived?"

"Yes." The guy frowned. "The readings I get indicate the presence of a mineral that my device can't identify, but then we haven't programmed all the possible compounds yet, just the ones that are commonly found. I will have to input its special pattern of iron and carbon into the database and see what comes up. I can't do that from here because of the interference."

"That's interesting." Kalugal smoothed his hand over his goatee. "Is it possible that this peculiar mineral is responsible for the interference we are experiencing here?"

The scientist nodded. "It produces a powerful electromagnetic interference."

Kalugal inclined his head. "What are your thoughts on that, Mr. Zhao?"

The guy opened his mouth, then closed it, fighting Kalugal's compulsion with his mighty brain, but even a brilliant scientist like him couldn't resist a powerful compeller like Kalugal. "I think that the islet the trading post was carved from was created by an extraterrestrial meteorite."

Kalugal looked doubtful. "Meteorites come from above and usually create a crater, not a new islet. New land is usually created by volcanic eruptions."

"A really big meteorite or asteroid strike can cause deep deformations that can lead to volcanic eruptions, but this is not the case here. The crater is too small. Frankly, I don't know what happened here, and I would like to investigate it further."

"Was there a reason you hesitated telling us about it?"

The guy's face reddened. "The competition in the scientific world is brutal. A discovery like that could mean a lot for my career."

"I see." Kalugal smiled apologetically. "But I can't allow you to do that. In fact, I want you to sell me your device and forget what you found here."

Fighting the compulsion, the guy swallowed. "I can't sell this. My brother and I invested years in developing it."

"And you will continue to do that with my help. I just want to test this device on a little side project. Show me how to operate it, and tomorrow, we will teleconference to negotiate the details of my investment in your company." He smiled at the guy. "I assure you that I have no interest in reverse engineering it and manufacturing it myself. That's not how I operate. I identify a potential, provide the funds, and let others do the work."

Kalugal must have used compulsion again because the guy handed him the device and spent a good hour explaining how to use it.

In the meantime, Jianye entertained them by explaining what the various artifacts were and how old he estimated them to be.

When the geologist left, Kalugal handed the device to Shamash. "Is everyone ready to do some investigating?"

"I am." Jin huffed. "But if all we are looking for are more dusty housewares from hundreds of years ago, I'm going to be very disappointed."

"What did you expect to find?" Jianye asked, his defensive tone indicating that he was offended by her comment.

"Something written," she said. "Something that can tell us about the people who lived here. Or weapons. Swords, arrows, knives. How did these people defend themselves?"

"I hope to find that too," Jianye said. "But we can also learn a lot about the people who lived here from the things they used."

"Of course." Jin gave him a perfunctory smile as she slung her supply backpack over her shoulder. "Wish us luck."

38

ALIYA

"*T*ouchy," Jin muttered under her breath as they exited the tent.

"Jianye is passionate about what he does," Alena said. "You offended his profession."

Jin nodded. "Sometimes I speak before I think, and then I regret what comes out of my mouth."

"They repositioned the tent," Aliya said. "There is more room between it and the entrance to the tunnels."

The hole in the ground had been roped off, and triangular red flags had been hung from the ropes to warn people against a sudden drop. The boulder was more or less where they'd left it.

"Should I tell Jianye that I like what he has done with the place?" Jin asked as she peered down the hole.

Aliya glanced down to see what had gotten Jin excited.

A good quality ladder was attached to one side of the opening, the kind that had rails on both sides and looked more like stairs than a simple ladder. Below, the chamber was illuminated with strong floodlights that were connected with thick extension cords to the noisy generator that had been bothering her since the excavation project had begun.

Well, it was not going to bother her for much longer. After today, she would probably never return to these tunnels again, and she would definitely not miss them.

If the immortals' village didn't work out, she would make a life for herself in Lijiang. It was a beautiful city, and so was the new neighborhood where her apartment was located.

She would have to find a job, but first she needed to learn to control her temper.

As Jin had shown her, it didn't take much to explain away her other oddities. The sunglasses covering her strangely shaped eyes could be explained by a rare eye disorder that made them overly sensitive to light, and her height wasn't as big of a deal in a large city as it had been in the Mosuo village. After she'd gotten her new clothes and put them on, Kalugal had stopped shrouding her to prove that she didn't need to hide.

People had turned their heads to look at her, and she heard one kid say that she must be a basketball player, but that was the extent of it.

She could get a job as a cleaner. It probably didn't pay much, but she was used to living on practically nothing, so she could do with very little. The important thing was that she would have a roof over her head that wasn't made of stone, and that she would no longer freeze at night or go hungry.

"Aliya, you're next," Carol said.

Without giving it much thought, Aliya jumped down. She didn't need a ladder to go down seven meters.

"You shouldn't have done that," Jin said quietly. "Jianye saw you jump."

"So what? I've seen human kids do that. It's not such a big deal."

"Maybe not, but you need to be mindful when you're around humans. The less you stand out, the better. Don't draw any additional attention to yourself."

"Is that what you do?"

Jin snorted. "I try. Luckily for me, I don't need to leave the village often, so I can act as I please most of the time."

That village was starting to sound really good, and Aliya promised herself to give life there a fair chance.

Once everyone had made it down to the big chamber, Kalugal motioned for them to gather around him. "You are all probably wondering what I'm going to do with the device Shamash is holding, and why I went to such lengths to acquire it."

Lokan took the device from Shamash and examined it. "You think that the Kra-ell had something to do with that strange mineral, and you hope that this device is going to lead us to them."

"Close. I don't think we are going to find any live Kra-ell, but we might find traces of their vessel." Kalugal lifted Jacki's backpack off and handed it to Phinas. "For an alien mineral to be in such big concentration here, the scouting crew Jade talked about must have landed here. If that happened around two thousand years ago, any metals would have disintegrated by now and penetrated the soil, which would explain the high concentration of it and the electromagnetic interference. If we find where its concentration is the strongest, we might find the exact spot where they hid their pod."

"But if everything disintegrated, what do you expect to find?" Jin asked.

"If any part of the pod was made from glass, we can find shards of that. Glass never disintegrates. Everything else does."

"What if that alien mineral is like glass?" Aliya asked and immediately regretted it.

Her education had stopped at eighth grade. What did she know about minerals and metals and other science stuff?

"Good point," Orion said.

"Indeed." Kalugal nodded. "The other reason I bought the device is that I need to erase all that Mr. Bingwen Zhao found out and recorded in it. We don't want anyone other than us finding out about the Kra-ell or even suspecting that any aliens have ever landed on Earth."

39

MEY

*M*ey's legs were starting to cramp.

She'd been sitting in the lotus position for hours, listening to so many echoes that the stories had all become a big blur in her mind and her concentration was wavering. Letting go for a few moments to rest, she allowed her thoughts to wander.

Those echoes might have been irrelevant to her investigation, but they had been very relevant to those who'd lived them, and they made Mey melancholy.

Or maybe it was just exhaustion weighing her down.

She'd pushed herself hard, keeping her focus for longer than ever before, but nothing important had come up.

Mey hated thinking of the life stories she'd witnessed as unimportant. She was in a unique position to witness people's life dramas, big and small, and she wished she could record them in some way, immortalize the people who had lived them.

Mey supposed that was why Toven wrote about his lovers in his journals. It was the only way he could immortalize those mortal women who'd left a positive impression on him.

Human life was so depressingly fleeting.

Which reminded her that she should visit her parents, and she should do that soon. They weren't getting any younger, and both of their daughters were living abroad.

Talk about guilt.

They had adopted two girls, hoping to one day enjoy grandchildren who would come to visit, and who would spend the holidays with them. They hadn't banked on those girls turning immortal and becoming practically infertile.

She and Yamanu had been faithfully following Merlin's protocol, drinking the vile potions every morning, keeping positive attitudes, avoiding stress…

Yeah, right. Chasing Kra-ell phantoms shouldn't have been stressful, but the circumstances in which they'd disappeared were anxiety-inducing.

With a sigh, she opened her eyes, unfolded her legs, and pushed up to her feet. She was too tired to continue, and there was too much on her mind. She wouldn't be able to reach the meditative state again unless she rested properly and put something in her belly. But the best way to chase away the blues was to make love to her mate.

Heck, just being around Yamanu was a mood booster. He had such an upbeat personality that it was impossible to stay down with him being so up. No wonder the girls in the halfway house loved him and his karaoke nights, which he'd missed out on lately because of the two missions.

It was time to go home.

When she opened the door, Yamanu gave her a pitying smile. "No luck, eh?"

"I think Vrog is right. I've been sitting there for hours, and I've only seen that one echo of Jade and Kagra's fight. All the other ones were created by humans."

"He'll be glad to hear that. The guy is itching to get to that hybrid female, and I can't blame him. If I were him, the moment I heard about her, I would have been on the first flight leaving for Lugu Lake."

"I want to try the laundry again when they close for the day. That's the only place I didn't spend much time in yet. Maybe I'll get lucky."

Yamanu arched a brow and leaned closer to whisper in her ear, "How about I take you to our room so you can rest, and we can both explore how lucky we are to have each other?"

"You read my mind."

Vrog intercepted them on their way to the staff quarters. "Given your exhausted expression, I assume that you had no luck today."

Mey nodded. "This evening, I want to try the laundry again, and if there is nothing there, we can leave tomorrow morning."

A grin spread over his face. "That's music to my ears. I've already made all the necessary preparations, but I was afraid you'd find something new, and we would need to stay longer."

Shaking his head, Yamanu put a hand on Vrog's shoulder. "Aren't you forgetting why we are here? We seek answers about your people. You hear about one hybrid girl and suddenly all the others are unimportant?"

Yamanu was teasing Vrog, but the guy took him seriously.

"The others are just as important to me as Aliya, but at some point, we need to accept that nothing further will be discovered and that it is futile to continue."

Given Yamanu's grin, he wasn't done teasing Vrog. "So says the man who's waited for his mistress to return for twenty-two years."

Vrog let out a breath. "When I started the school, my intention was to preserve and grow the funds the tribe had left behind and wait for those who might have survived to return. But in time, the school itself became my life. I think I stopped waiting a long time ago."

40

VROG

*V*rog wondered if what he'd just said was a lie.

Had he really stopped waiting? Or perhaps his old hopes had been replaced by new ones of a better future that included a relationship with his son and possibly a mate of his own?

Before finding out about Vlad, the hope of finding survivors of his tribe was what had kept Vrog going, which was why he'd clung to it despite the improbability of it ever happening. Now that he had something else to live for, it was tempting to let go of his quest.

But that would be wrong. Perhaps it was irrational, but he believed that as long as he kept waiting and hoping, his tribe wasn't really gone. The moment he gave up, it would be forever lost.

Given Yamanu's doubtful expression, he hadn't fooled the guy. "Whatever makes you happy, my man." The Guardian circled his arm around his mate's waist. "We are going to take a little nap. See you at dinner."

"Have a good rest." Vrog inclined his head. "Is it okay if Morris and I drive to the airport and load the safes onto the jet?"

"Sure. Take Jay with you. You have valuable stuff in those safes."

"Thank you."

Vrog doubted that a Guardian's protection was necessary, but he'd learned that nonchalance was just another facet of arrogance and it never hurt to take extra precautions.

Even though he was at least twice as strong as Jay, the Guardian probably carried a concealed firearm, which would always trump muscle.

"How large are the safes?" Morris fell in step with Vrog.

"A square meter at the base and about a meter and a half tall. There are two of them."

"Do you have a truck to transport them?" Morris asked.

"I can borrow the gardener's truck."

Jay shook his head. "A van would be better. Two safes on a truck would attract too much attention. People will think you have valuables inside."

"We can cover them with a tarp," Morris said. "And tie a rope around them so it doesn't fly off."

"That was what I planned to do." Vrog opened the door to the administrative building. "Can either of you shroud?"

"We can't shroud a moving vehicle." Morris followed him up the stairs.

Vrog chuckled. "I mean now. I don't want my staff to see me carry safes out into the truck. First of all, because no one is supposed to be that strong, and also because they would wonder why I'm taking them out. I'd prefer not to have to explain." He opened the door to his office.

"Won't they realize that they are gone?" Jay eyed the two safes. "Everyone who walks into your office will see that."

"If anyone asks, I can tell them that I transferred them to my personal quarters. No one goes in there."

"Not even the cleaner?"

"I can thrall her."

Jay shrugged. "I can shroud you and the safe, but I can only make you invisible. I'm not good at creating illusions. Morris will have to keep people out of the way. How far is it to the truck?"

Vrog grimaced. "A good five-minute walk. I have a dolly downstairs, so I don't have to carry it all the way."

Morris scratched his head. "You know what would be much less complicated? Getting those documents into these boxes." He pointed at the stack of flattened cardboard resting on top of the safes.

"I'm afraid those are not secure enough. They will not protect the documents from water or fire damage. The only reason they survived the fire that destroyed the compound was that Jade had the foresight to keep them in safes."

Morris looked at him as if he was dimwitted. "You can get stronger boxes that are watertight and fireproof. Theft is not an issue, so those are the only things you should be concerned with."

That was true, but he didn't have time to order those kinds of boxes and have them delivered before leaving for Lugu Lake.

"I checked the delivery time, and it will take three days for them to arrive. If we plan to come back here after the lake, I can leave the documents here."

Morris and Jay exchanged glances.

Jay shrugged. "I'm not the boss, so I can't tell you whether we will or not. Can we get those boxes in Beijing? I can drive over and pick them up for you."

"I checked. The boxes I want need to be shipped from the factory. What they have in the stores is not good enough."

"They probably are," Morris said. "You are not transporting fragile works of art. If you're willing to compromise, getting those lower-quality boxes would solve a lot of your problems."

Letting out a breath, Vrog leaned back in his chair and weighed the pros and cons.

Morris didn't have an emotional attachment to the files, and he was thinking logically. Vrog, on the other hand, was too anxious about moving those files out of his office to think straight.

It was the only tie he had to the past, the only clue that could potentially lead the clan to whoever had survived that attack or to the perpetrators, and that made those files invaluable.

His anxiety wasn't so much about losing the ledgers as it was about them being a dead end. As long as he hadn't used them to investigate the fate of his tribe and hit a brick wall, his hope, however dim, still lived. Once that last avenue was exhausted, and nothing was found, it would die. But perhaps that would be better.

He would finally have closure.

41

ARWEL

"*A*re you sure that you know how to operate this device?" Lokan leaned over Kalugal's shoulder.

"I'll figure it out."

The geologist had taken nearly an hour to explain to Kalugal how the thing worked, and even though Arwel had heard the entire conversation, he wasn't able to help because most of it had been too complicated for a layperson to understand.

The question was whether Kalugal had understood or just pretended that he had. The guy had a huge ego, and admitting that he couldn't master everything on his first go was inconceivable to him.

"I need a flat surface to put it on." Kalugal lifted his head and looked at the rectangular block of stone in the center of the big chamber. "That will do."

He walked over, put the device down, and pulled out his phone.

"There is no reception here," Jacki reminded him.

"I know. I took a few notes while Zhao explained."

Jin let out a breath. "That's going to take a while." She walked over to the stone altar and hopped on.

"You shouldn't sit up there," Jacki said. "If my hunch is right, this used to be an altar."

"So what?" Jin opened her backpack and pulled out a candy bar.

"So it might have been used for making sacrifices. That's why I don't want to touch it."

Jin took a bite out of the candy bar, wrapped up what was left, and returned it to her backpack. "In that case, you should definitely touch it. Maybe you'll get a vision of what they did in here."

"Yeah." Jacki grimaced. "That's what I'm trying to avoid. Funerals creep me out."

"I'll hold your hand," Jin offered. "We might gain some insight into this mystery." She shifted her gaze to Aliya. "Any thoughts on that?"

"I don't think this altar was built by the Kra-ell. Our tribe's altar was much smaller, and it wasn't in the middle of a large chamber."

"What did it look like?" Jin asked.

"Like an oven." Aliya made a domed shape with her arms. "And it was this tall." She indicated the height from the ground. "People had to kneel in front of it and lower their heads."

"Did you ever pray there?" Jacki asked.

"It wasn't used for praying, and I wasn't old enough to participate in any of the ceremonies." She looked at the rectangular slab of stone again. "This was probably built by the people who lived in the outpost."

"Oh, what the heck." Jacki let out a sigh. "You are right. I should give it a try." She put a hand on the altar, and when nothing happened, she added the other one. "No vision." She smiled up at Jin. "Scoot. I want to sit down."

Kalugal paused his tinkering with the device. "Don't jump. I'll lift you."

Jacki rolled her eyes. "I thought that you weren't listening."

"I always listen to you, my love." He put his hands on her waist, lifted her, and set her down on the platform.

"So you were okay with me touching this thing and getting a vision but you were not okay with me hopping up on a three-foot-tall altar?"

"Visions are not dangerous to you or our baby. Jumping up and down is." He turned back to his notes.

Leaning back on her forearms, Jacki looked up. "This was definitely used as a funeral pyre. There are scorch marks on the ceiling."

Jin joined her in the reclined position. "You are right. When we were here before, it was too dark to see, but with the light Jianye put down here, it's very clear."

Following their gazes, Arwel looked at the pattern on the ceiling and had to agree with Jacki's assessment. The darkened area on the otherwise yellow and light gray stone corresponded with a contained fire, and not one that consumed the entire chamber.

Except, if the altar had been used for animal sacrifices, the pattern would be similar to that of a funeral pyre.

He was about to make a comment when Jacki's eyes rolled back in her head and she slumped into Jin, who wrapped an arm around her in time to prevent her from sliding off the slab and hurting herself.

"Jacki?" Kalugal turned to his mate. "What's wrong, love? Are you having a vision?"

She didn't respond for the longest time, but since they could all hear her breathing, they just waited along with Kalugal for her to open her eyes.

4 2

ALENA

P *oor Jacki.*

She'd been so afraid of touching the altar, and if not for Jin's goading, she would have been spared having an unwanted vision.

Alena thanked the Fates for not making her clairvoyant. She was so much better suited for the gift of fertility and couldn't imagine losing control like that, with the vision taking over her mind whether she wanted to see it or not.

It must be so scary and disorienting for Jacki to lose her connection with the real world, getting thrust into the past or the future with no prior warning.

Alena would have preferred carrying and delivering a new baby every year of her adult life than going through a terrifying experience like that even once.

Two thousand babies would have been a bit much even for her, though. She would settle for just one more with Orion—a little boy with black hair and blue eyes and his father's gentle nature.

Their child would be perfect.

As Kalugal took Jacki from Jin and sat on the ground with her cradled in his lap, they all waited in anxious silence.

When Jacki groaned a few minutes later, they all released relieved breaths.

She opened her eyes and smiled at her mate. "That was so worth it. Wait until you hear what I saw."

"I'm just glad that you're okay. You've been out for several minutes." He took in a long breath. "You've never been out for so long before, and I got worried. The Fates got an earful from me."

Jacki put her hands on her belly. "I stayed inside the vision because I wanted to see more. I hope that you didn't cuss at the Fates in your head. We need to stay in their good graces, and we don't want them to become vindictive."

"I don't cuss, love. I threaten and then offer bribes."

Lokan chuckled. "Excellent negotiation tactic, brother."

Alena didn't know whether Lokan's comment was sarcastic or heartfelt, but Kalugal took it as the latter.

"Thank you. It takes one great negotiator to recognize another."

Jacki shook her head. "Now that you're done stroking each other's egos, do you want to hear what I saw?"

"Yes, my love." Kalugal kissed her temple. "Please tell us."

"So I was right, and this altar was originally used to hold funeral pyres." She paused for dramatic effect, glancing at her companions, who had formed a large circle around her and Kalugal. "That's how the Kra-ell dealt with their dead." She paused again, waiting to see their reaction to her revelation. "I saw a Kra-ell funeral service."

Alena didn't know what to think of that. Was the additional puzzle piece confirming the Kra-ell scouting team story a good thing?

"Was the dead person male or female?" Orion asked.

"Male."

"Did you see signs of injury on him?" Arwel asked.

She shook her head. "The male looked old, so I assume his death had been of natural causes, and some of the attendants looked old as well."

"How many people attended the funeral?" Carol asked.

"I counted twelve, not including the deceased, and there were no females. They all wore long robes, but the hoods were down, so it was easy to see that they weren't human. They stood around the altar and chanted prayers." She chuckled. "They reminded me of the Klingons. Not in the way they looked, but in the way their language and their chanting sounded. It was somber and very male. It was pretty obvious that those males were warriors. If they were the members of the scouting team who arrived thousands of years before the others, then it seems like their team was made up entirely of males. But from what I've heard about the Kra-ell society, that doesn't make sense. There should have been at least one female in charge of them."

"The females might have not attended the funeral," Aliya said. "As far as I know, none of the Kra-ell died during my eight years on the compound, so I'm only speculating. But I know that in the Mosuo society, the men are in charge of burials."

"The women still attend, though," Jin said. "It would be disrespectful to the dead if they didn't."

Aliya shrugged. "Maybe their females were older and died before the male Jacki saw on the pyre."

"Or maybe the simplest explanation is the correct one," Arwel said. "The scouting team was most likely comprised of males only. Kra-ell females would have been deemed too precious to put at risk. The males were supposed to prepare a safe environment for them once they landed."

Kalugal shook his head. "There had to be a female, and probably more than one, for those Kra-ell to influence the lifestyle of the Mosuo people. I don't see how that could have been the case if the team was exclusively male."

ALIYA

*A*liya should have felt something for those ancient Kra-ell—pity for how lonely they must have been, regret over their extinction, or anger about their suspected betrayal of their fellow travelers—but she felt nothing aside from mild curiosity.

She had as much in common with that scouting team as with these descendants of the gods. Their ancestors might have shared the same corner of the universe, and Kalugal had told her that the gods and the Kra-ell might have a common ancestor, but they were very different, and they didn't face the same challenges. They could have long-lived offspring, while she most likely couldn't.

It was better not to have children at all than to outlive them. Perhaps Jade hadn't been cruel when she'd forbade the hybrid males from fathering children with humans. She'd been merciful.

"You know what has just occurred to me?" Jin hopped back on the slab, leaned her elbows on her knees, and rested her chin on her hands. "Mey and I might be related to these Kra-ell and not someone from Jade's tribe."

Arwel shook his head. "Jade said that they arrived thousands of years ahead of the rest. If their lifespan is indeed about a thousand years, then the original team is long gone, and if they fathered hybrid children, those are gone as well. The children of the hybrids were born human, so that was the end of the line for them." He shifted his gaze to Aliya. "Did you ever hear Jade talk about the actual lifespans of the pure-bloods and the hybrids?"

As all eyes turned to her, she shook her head. "All I knew was that they were long-lived compared to humans. How do you know it's supposed to be a thousand years?"

"That was what Emmett told us."

"He must know then," Aliya said. "But an average lifespan doesn't mean that everyone lives to be exactly one thousand. The average lifespan for humans is eighty-something years, but some die much younger while others live to be much older. So if some of those Kra-ell lived for twelve hundred years and others for eight hundred, the average was one thousand. Jade said that the scouting team landed two thousand years before the others, so if one or two of them lived longer than one thousand, and his son lived that long as well, he could have fathered Jin and her sister."

"I still say that there must have been a female leading them," Kalugal said. "And if there was, then she could have produced more purebloods. It's very likely that they didn't die out after all."

Aliya shook her head. "Jade assumed that they had. Which means that they didn't have a pureblooded female with them."

"Or maybe she was past her childbearing years," Carol said. "They are not immortal, so a six-hundred-year-old Kra-ell female would be the equivalent of a sixty-year-old human woman and would no longer be fertile."

Kalugal nodded. "That makes a lot of sense."

Carol smiled and fluffed her curls. "I only look dumb."

"You don't look dumb, love." Lokan wrapped his arm around her waist. "You are one of the smartest, most cunning people I know, and anyone who underestimates you is a fool."

"Thank you." She lifted on her tiptoes and kissed the underside of his jaw.

"There is still another possibility," Lokan said. "What if one of those original purebloods hooked up with a Dormant? She transmitted her immortal genes to her daughters, and they to their daughters, and so on, and maybe those genes were altered by the unique Kra-ell genes, and that's how Jin and Mey came to be." He turned to Jin. "You and your sister might have been born to a descendant of that original Dormant who had hooked up with a Kra-ell pureblood or hybrid."

Her arms folded over her chest, Jin frowned. "That's possible. Our Kra-ell features didn't manifest until after our transition. So you might be right about the Kra-ell special genes hitching a ride on the immortal ones." She inhaled and then sighed. "I thought that Mey and I had all the answers as to why and how we turned out the way we did after our transition. We thought that we'd been fathered by a hybrid from Jade's tribe. But now there is that." She waved her hand over the chamber. "I wonder how many other hidden Kra-ell descendants are out there."

Hope bloomed in Aliya's chest. What if there were more people like her? Could she make it her mission to locate them?

Where would she even start?

The Mosuo were the best candidates, but if in order to preserve the Kra-ell genes, the mother needed to be a Dormant, then she doubted that there were any hidden Kra-ell gene carriers among them.

Hopping up onto the stone slab, Arwel sat next to Jin and wrapped his arm around her back. "I wonder if there is special affinity between Kra-ell and Dormants like there is between immortals and Dormants. It seems odd that out of the entire human population, a hybrid Kra-ell male found a dormant female, and another one found an immortal female. It's like two needles in a haystack somehow attracting each other."

"Like magnets," Jin said.

Shifting in Kalugal's arms, Jacki turned to her mate. "Did you figure out how to work that device? Or did I distract you?"

"I figured out what I was doing wrong. I need to keep feeding it new samples and clean the lenses between tests."

"Then let's go." She pushed to her feet and offered him a hand up. "We need to find where that mineral is present in the highest concentration. Now that I know they were here for sure, I want to find material proof of them."

"Are you sure you're up to it?" He pretended to let Jacki pull him to her, but Aliya knew that he hadn't let her bear any of his weight. "Don't you need to rest a little longer?"

"I'm fine." Jacki dusted her pants off. "And if I get tired, I'll ask you to carry me."

"Deal." He grinned as if she'd just offered him a great prize.

These immortals were strange, and their relationships were even stranger. The couples behaved as if they were attached at the hip.

It was nice, but Aliya couldn't imagine having to endure that twenty-four hours a day, every day. She needed her freedom, she needed to roam and hunt, and she needed to do it alone without an overprotective mate hovering over her.

44

ORION

*K*alugal blew out a frustrated breath. "I wish this thing worked like a metal detector."

Their progress had been excruciatingly slow, and Kalugal wasn't the only one who was frustrated. They all were.

Orion felt especially bad for Jacki, who needed more frequent stops to empty her bladder, which required Kalugal to escort her to one of the side tunnels for privacy.

Aliya had reassured them that the tunnels were free of booby-traps, but Arwel insisted on double-checking, especially whenever stairs were involved. That alone slowed them down to a crawl.

Then there was the device Kalugal had bought from the geologist, which required stops at every fork to take a sample of the soil, put it into the device, and wait for it to analyze it.

"Can't we continue tomorrow?" Jacki leaned against her mate's side. "And by we, I mean you and your men. When you find something, you can come to get us."

"We are getting close." Kalugal's eyes remained glued to the readout on the device's screen. "The concentration of the mineral has been increasing the further down we go."

"We are reaching the end of the tunnel system," Aliya said. "There are only two more forks, and they are not very long. I say we finish this today and be done with it."

Orion was impressed. The girl's use of English was improving at an exponential rate. Even her accent was slowly becoming less noticeable.

He was a quick learner of languages, but she was even faster.

She also knew these tunnels inside and out and had led them to every scratch and mark she'd discovered over the years that could possibly indicate a Kra-ell presence.

Kalugal and Lokan had taken many pictures of everything she'd shown them, and the only thing still keeping them in the tunnels was the strange unknown mineral and Jacki's vision of the Kra-ell funeral ceremony.

They'd either lived in these tunnels or had used them for something, and Kalugal was determined to find more clues.

"How long are those two forks?" Jin asked.

"Together with all the small offshoots that terminate in dead ends there is about a kilometer left. I don't know how long it is in miles."

"It's a little over half a mile," Lokan said.

"Let's go." Kalugal handed the device to Phinas. "I'll check the mineral concentration in both, and we will call it a day."

The next corridor, which was how Orion had started to refer to the tunnels, had many branches on both sides, but as Aliya had told them, they were short and terminated in dead ends.

"I think these used to be the Kra-ell living quarters," Jin said. "What if each of these short tunnels led to a private room, but they were walled off for some reason? Maybe they didn't burn all of the bodies, and this is their crypt?"

"Creepy." Jacki shivered.

Orion was surprised to see Arwel nod. "The same thought occurred to me." He turned to Kalugal. "I would like to check one of these to see if there is a hidden opening. Do you want to finish your mineral detecting before we attempt it? Or do we take a break and try that first?"

"We can split up," Kalugal said. "I'll continue with Jacki, Phinas, and Welgost, while the rest of you can check out Jin's idea." He lifted a finger in warning. "Be careful, and don't even think about using explosives. This whole thing could come crashing down on us."

"I want to come with you," Lokan said. "Carol and I are fascinated by the device and the mystery mineral."

"Yeah," Carol said. "I don't get how it can disrupt our phone signals but lets us take pictures and play music. When I put my earphones in, I expect to hear some background noise, or static, or not anything at all, but the music plays perfectly."

Orion had been wondering the same.

"I'm afraid that my scientific knowledge isn't that extensive," Kalugal said. "I will have to ask the geologists when I speak with them tomorrow."

"What about me?" Aliya asked. "Who do I go with?"

"Stay with them." Kalugal winked at her. "They might need your strength to help them dig through." He turned to Welgost. "Since Lokan is coming with us, you should stay with Alena. I promised her brother to keep her safe."

"No problem, boss. I'll stay to protect Alena." Welgost cast a sidelong glance at Aliya.

Was the guy interested in her?

Phinas hadn't flirted with Aliya during their trip to Lijiang, and Orion had wondered whether she'd said something to discourage him, or he'd lost interest.

"Why can't I stay with them too?" Jacki asked.

"Because you are my mate." Kalugal took her hand. "I want you by my side."

"Ugh." She rolled her eyes. "You are such a mother hen. You want me where you can see me."

"I want you with me so I can protect you, and I don't have to worry about you." He led her down the main tunnel with Phinas trailing behind them.

Arwel unstrapped the hammer from his belt. "It's going to get dusty in there, so I suggest you stay out here."

"I can help you dig." Aliya followed Arwel.

"So can I," Orion said and then looked at Alena. "On second thought, I should stay out here with you."

"Don't be silly." Alena gave him a little shove. "You'll be only a few feet away." She threaded her arm through Jin's. "We are going to watch you be all manly, taking turns swinging that big hammer."

"Yeah." Jin waggled her brows. "Give us a good show."

45

ALENA

"Come sit with me." Jin lowered herself to the ground and opened her backpack. "Do you want to share a candy bar?"

"No, thank you." Alena stood at the entrance to the offshoot and watched Arwel, Orion, and Aliya pat the stone walls and knock on them.

Welgost and Shamash were more than happy to stay out in the main artery with them.

"This sounded hollow." Arwel motioned for the other two to step back.

When they moved nearly to where Alena was standing, Arwel swung the hammer at the wall. At first only a few chips flew off, but as he kept going, larger chunks got loose, which encouraged him to keep on swinging.

Alena moved aside so as not to block Jin's line of sight to her mate, for which she'd gotten a smile and a nod.

After several minutes of that, Arwel paused, and Orion took over.

Standing with her arms crossed over her chest, Alena drank in the sight of him working, his arm and leg muscles bulging under his clothing, the determination on his handsome face, the fluidity of his movements. He worked as though demolition had been his primary occupation and he was an expert in it, when she knew for a fact that he hadn't done any menial labor in years.

"I don't think there is an opening there." Candy bar in hand, Jin pushed to her feet and joined Alena. "But if they keep hammering at it, they might create one."

"My turn," Aliya called out.

Orion hesitated for a moment, but then handed her the hammer and stepped back. "Go for it."

Alena was stupidly proud of him for overcoming his chivalrous instincts and not playing the macho game with Aliya.

"This should be interesting." Jin shoved the rest of the candy bar into her mouth.

As Aliya swung at the wall, the impact was so powerful that Alena feared the hammer would break. It was a large tool that was designed precisely for what they were doing, but it wasn't designed to be wielded by powerful immortal males and an even more powerful hybrid Kra-ell female.

"Go, Aliya!" Jin cheered the girl on. "Show them what you can do!"

As big chunks of stone started flying off, Arwel and Orion retreated further out, but after about two minutes of swinging, Aliya lowered the hammer and handed it back to Arwel. "I need to balance power with endurance. When I use all of my strength, my endurance suffers."

There was a small hole where Aliya had been hammering at the stone wall, and she crouched to peer at it.

"Do you see anything?" Jin asked.

"Yeah, I think that there is a cavern on the other side." She pulled out a flashlight from a loop on her belt. "It's not big, and as far as I can see, it's empty."

"That's a relief," Jin murmured. "I was afraid we were going to find a skeleton."

Shamash, who until now hadn't said much, chuckled. "After a thousand years, even a skeleton would turn to dust."

"That's not true," Alena said. "They've found ancient graves with the skeletons intact and even some hairs. They even found skeletons of dinosaurs, and they lived on Earth long before the gods got here."

"I think the dinosaurs were a genetic joke," Jin said. "Maybe the ones who created the gods played around with different species, created the giant dinosaurs, but then realized that they needed too much food to survive, so they annihilated them."

Alena had never been schooled outside of what her mother had taught her, but she'd read a lot, and she remembered that there were all kinds of dinosaurs, big and small, but with the racket Arwel was producing, having a conversation meant yelling, and she decided to keep her comment for later.

After several more minutes of swinging the hammer, Arwel finally stopped. "I think Aliya can squeeze through and let us know what's in there."

She was no doubt the slimmest among them.

Looking down at her new clothes that were already covered in dust, Aliya frowned. "I'll get dirty."

"That's okay." Jin walked over and patted her arm. "We will all need to have our clothes laundered. But if you are squeamish about going in there, I can try to squeeze in."

Aliya looked at her down her nose. "You won't fit. I'll do it."

"If you insist." Jin waved a hand.

As Aliya carefully wiggled her long, thin body through the narrow opening, Orion dusted off his pants and walked over to Alena.

"I haven't done any manual labor in centuries. It was fun."

Leaning closer, she whispered in his ear, "You looked very sexy swinging that hammer."

"Oh yeah?" He nuzzled her ear. "How sexy?"

"I'll show you later tonight."

46

ALIYA

*A*s the light on Aliya's hardhat illuminated the small chamber, she regretted not finding it fourteen years ago when she'd escaped into these tunnels. At some point in time, it had served as someone's bedroom, and the stone platform that must have been the bed was long enough for a tall Kra-ell male.

Naturally, that was no proof that the cavern had been used by a Kra-ell, but the precision with which it was cut out from the stone indicated tools and technology that wouldn't have been available back then. She knocked on it to make sure that it was indeed a slab of stone and not clay, that could have been poured into a mold to create such a precise and smooth rectangular shape.

Could those ancient Kra-ell melt stone? Because that was what it looked like.

"Aliya?" Arwel peeked through the opening. "Are you alright in there?"

"I'm fine, but I think you should see this, or you won't believe me." She described the stone platform and carved-out ledge that could have been used as a table or a desk.

"Take a picture of it with my phone." He handed her the device.

Somehow in all the excitement of buying a home, she'd forgotten to buy herself a phone, but Kalugal had promised to get her one at the immortals' village.

"Do you see the red button on the bottom? You press it when you want to take a picture."

It took her a moment or two to figure out how to operate the camera, and after snapping several pictures, she handed Arwel his phone back. "Before I squeeze myself out of here, look at the pictures."

The others must have huddled around Arwel as he flipped through the photos because suddenly there was more light on the other side of the stone wall.

"You can come out," Arwel said.

When she squeezed through the opening, he handed her a water bottle. "Drink. I haven't seen you taking one sip yet."

She was touched that he'd noticed and that he cared.

"Thank you. I forgot that I had a bottle."

"We should get Kalugal and his contraption here," Alena said. "What if that stone furniture is made of the mineral he's tracking?" She pushed a strand of hair behind her ear. "Maybe these Kra-ell had a 3D printer and used that mineral to build things from."

"Fascinating idea," Jin agreed. "What if they used that instead of metals to build their equipment? Stone doesn't disintegrate as fast, and we might find more traces of them."

As a sudden boom rocked the tunnel, they all braced their hands on the stone walls.

"What the hell was that?" Jin asked.

"I don't know." Arwel grabbed the hammer. "It came from the direction Kalugal and the others were headed. They might be in trouble."

As he started running, they all followed, their boots thundering on the ground. It didn't take Aliya long to overtake Arwel and sprint into the tunnel the boom had come from, but it was difficult to pinpoint sounds in the underground because of the echoes, and she couldn't be sure that it hadn't come from the other one. "Arwel!" she yelled over her shoulder. "Take the other tunnel!"

When she reached the end of it, she knew right away that it wasn't in the same place as it had been before, and not just because of the dust still settling after the ceiling had collapsed ahead.

"Are you okay?" she yelled.

When there was no response, panic seized her. These people were immortal, so they couldn't be dead, but what about the pregnant woman?

What if Jacki lost the baby?

Frantic, Aliya started pulling away stones.

"Over here!" she yelled. "They are trapped!"

How could that have happened? She'd been through these tunnels hundreds of times, and nothing had ever collapsed or even crumbled, except for where she'd dug to hide a trap, but it wasn't in this area.

What if they blamed her for what had happened to their family? Kalugal and Lokan were Alena's cousins. Would she hate her and seek revenge?

Would she lose her new friends?

The prospect distressed her much more than she'd expected, and as her vision blurred with tears, she averted her eyes when the others joined her.

"Kalugal!" Welgost yelled, his voice booming through the tunnel and echoing off the walls.

"Maybe it collapsed long after they passed it," Jin said. "Maybe they can't hear us."

Aliya wished that were true, but there were only a few meters on the other side of the blockage, if at all. The ceiling could've collapsed over the entire remainder of the tunnel, burying the five immortals under tons of rocks.

47

KALUGAL

*A*s consciousness returned, Kalugal first checked on Jacki, who was stirring under him, and then on his brother who was right beside him, sprawled over Carol, who was also stirring to consciousness.

"Are you hurt, love?" Kalugal's ears were still ringing from the boom that had preceded the ceiling's collapse, and when he tried to move to make room for Jacki, he discovered why they weren't crushed under a pile of stones.

He only had scant inches of maneuvering, and his hardhat was gone, but the light from his glowing eyes was enough to see what was above him. A big chunk of stone was wedged at an angle between the walls of the narrow tunnel, saving them from getting flattened.

"I'm okay," Jacki murmured. "The baby is okay too. I think. What happened?"

"The tunnel's ceiling collapsed," Lokan said.

"Phinas?" Kalugal called out. "Are you okay?"

His answer was a faint groan, but he was alive.

"How badly are you hurt?"

When there was no answer, Kalugal lifted his head as much as he could and peered around. "Lokan, can you see him?"

"I can't. He's not with us under this boulder. I think he's buried under the debris."

"Hang on, Phinas," Kalugal called out. "The others will get us out." He dipped his head and sniffed Jacki to make sure that she wasn't bleeding.

When he couldn't detect the scent of blood, relief washed over him.

They'd been incredibly fortunate, and he still couldn't understand how and why the ceiling had collapsed. Aliya had told them that she'd been through these tunnels hundreds of times and that there were no traps or booby-traps anywhere in this area. The only traps in the entire maze had been the ones she'd built herself in the tunnels leading to the underground lake. That was where she'd made her home, and that was the area she'd protected.

Did it have anything to do with the alien mineral? The reading he'd gotten in this tunnel was the strongest so far, indicating that there was a large deposit of it nearby, but him taking soil samples shouldn't have triggered anything. He'd barely scraped the equivalent of a thumbnail worth of stone for the test.

The device he'd gotten from the geologist was probably smashed together with Phinas, but whereas Phinas's body would self-repair, the same wasn't true of the device.

Not that he cared.

Kalugal wanted his wife, his brother, his sister-in-law, and his second-in-command to be out of there and back in the hotel.

Hopefully, the others were okay and could dig them out.

"Do you hear that?" Lokan asked.

Kalugal's ears were still ringing from the boom, but he heard faint scraping.

"I hope those are not rats," Jacki said.

"What I hope is that the others are not buried under collapsed ceilings like we are," Carol said. "And that they will get us out of here soon."

With the ringing in his ears getting fainter, Kalugal thought that he heard someone call his name, and even though he might have imagined it, he called back, "We are here! Phinas is hurt! The rest of us are fine!"

"Hang on. We are getting you out."

That had sounded like Arwel, but it was hard to tell. Hopefully, the guy was wise enough not to use the explosives he'd brought along.

"Don't use explosives!" Kalugal shouted.

When there was no answer, Jacki shifted under him. "I hope he heard you."

"Do you think that Aliya had something to do with this?" Jacki asked. "Maybe she knew that there was a trap here?"

"I don't think so. I would have sensed guilt in her. I talked with her last night, and we reached an understanding. She said that she was willing to give the village a try, and she sounded sincere. I would have smelled guilt if she was planning something like this. We could have been killed."

"She's not like us," Lokan said. "Perhaps pretending to be friendly while plotting murder is considered honorable in the Kra-ell culture."

Kalugal was familiar with cultures like that among humans, so there was something to what Lokan had said. And yet, his gut told him that Aliya had been genuine when she'd thanked him last night and told him that she owed him a debt of gratitude. He was sure she had nothing to do with the tunnel's collapse.

48

ALENA

*W*hen Alena heard Kalugal's answer, the vise squeezing her heart lost its grip, and as her heart expanded, profound relief overcame the confines of her ribcage.

Immortals were very hard to kill, so she'd known that her family would survive, but she'd feared for Jacki's baby. She'd worried about the amount of damage their bodies had sustained and the pain they must be in, and she'd agonized thinking about how long it would take them to recover and how much they would suffer.

Immortals could even regrow limbs, but it took a very long time and was painful as hell.

She'd been praying for them, and hearing that four out of the five were okay was incredibly good news.

She prayed for poor Phinas and his speedy recovery. First, though, they had to get him out, and their progress was excruciatingly slow. The men and Aliya worked tirelessly to clear a small area near the top, but they had to be careful not to further destabilize the tunnel.

The problem was that the blockage went deep, and even though they'd chipped away at the mountain of rock, they'd barely made a dent in it.

Alena, Jin, and Shamash were in charge of moving the stones further away, and the rest were taking turns pulling them out.

Kian had been right. She shouldn't have left the Odus behind. If they were with her, they would have greatly expedited the rescue.

"We should get the Odus here." She helped Jin lift a large boulder and carry it further back into one of the smaller offshoots. "I know it will take time to get them here, but we might not be able to do this without them."

"You're right. But since they obey only you or Arwel, you need to go get them."

Arwel wouldn't be happy about that, but he would have to deal.

"Do you even know how to get back to the surface?" he asked when she told him her plan.

"I do."

"It will take you three hours to get back here. We might get them out by then."

"There is only one road leading up here. I'll ask one of Jianye's men to take me, so you will have the limousines at your disposal. If you are already on your way to the hotel, our paths will cross, and I'll ask the guy to turn back."

Surprisingly, Arwel nodded. "Take Orion with you. I don't want you going unprotected."

"You need him here." She cast Orion an apologetic look. "I'll be okay. I'm not exactly helpless, you know. I can thrall and shroud with the best of you."

"Kian will have my head, but you are right. Go."

"Be careful." Orion stopped to give her a quick kiss.

"I always am."

As she sprinted toward the large chamber, Alena thought of what to tell Jianye. If she told him that Kalugal and the others were trapped under an avalanche of rocks, Jianye would rush down with his men to help, and that would only impede their progress. Even with tools, the humans couldn't do what the immortals and Aliya were doing.

She should come up with a plausible story for why she needed an emergency run to the hotel. She could thrall him, but then she would have to thrall the driver as well. A good excuse would be the easiest way to handle the situation.

Someone needed medication, something that was very important but didn't require a doctor or a rush evacuation to a hospital.

"Carol forgot her insulin at the hotel," she told Jianye. "I need to get it to her as soon as possible. Can one of your men drive me?"

"Of course. But wouldn't it be better if Carol went back to the hotel? She would get her medication faster."

Damn, he was right.

"She can't administer it by herself. I need to do that, and there is still enough time for me to get it and come back. Kalugal also wants me to bring along the two men he left behind. Please hurry. I don't have time to explain." She added a little thrall just to speed things up.

"Right away." He turned to one of his men and spoke in rapid Chinese. "Hu will take you. "

"Thank you."

49

ORION

*A*s it turned out, Alena had been right, and they were still working on getting to Kalugal and the others when she returned with the Odus, who for some reason were dripping wet.

"What happened to them?" Orion asked. "Why are they wet?"

"They are too heavy to cross over the rope bridge. I had them wade through."

It didn't seem to bother the cyborgs, and they went to work right away, allowing the rest of them to take a breather.

"How are they doing in there?" Alena asked.

"They are uncomfortable, and Jacki is desperate to pee, but the good news is that Phinas is responsive, which means that he's doing better. He's communicating with them."

Orion took the bottle of water she handed him and leaned against the wall to guiltily gulp it down. Kalugal and the others were trapped under a big chunk of stone that was the size of an ancient foundation stone. The thing was wedged diagonally between the tunnel walls, which created a small cavity near the ground where the two couples were trapped. They'd been working for the past two and a half hours to clear the stones piled on top of the boulder, but they still had a long way to go, and in the meantime, they couldn't even get water to those trapped on the other side.

"The Odus are incredible," Aliya watched with awe. "We need to help them move the rocks out of the way."

"Back to work." Orion handed the bottle back to Alena and pushed away from the wall.

For the next hour or so, they all worked in tandem, and surprisingly, the first one they were able to get out was Phinas.

The Odus performed an incredible feat of acrobatics to pull him out. After moving stones out of the way, Ovidu lowered Oridu by the ankles into the hole they'd created so he could reach Phinas and take him into his arms. When Oridu had Phinas, Ovidu pulled them both out by Oridu's ankles.

The maneuver was their own initiative, which made Orion wonder whether they were sentient already. What were the chances that someone had programmed them to know what to do in a situation like that?

None.

Phinas groaned in pain, and as they laid him down on the blanket that Alena had had the foresight to bring with her, she got to work on him. "Is anything broken?" she asked.

It was a rhetorical question since Phinas's legs were twisted in odd angles.

"My legs." He lifted his head to drink from the bottle she held to his lips. "I need a doctor to set them before the bones fuse the wrong way."

"We will get you to a doctor as soon as the others are out."

He nodded. "The bones are probably already fused. The doctor will have to re-break them."

Jin crouched next to him. "Can you hang on, or should we evacuate you before we get the others out?"

"I can hang on. Go help them."

"Master Arwel." Ovidu walked up to the Guardian. "Oridu and I will try to lift the boulder, but someone needs to pull Master Kalugal, Mistress Jacki, Master Lokan, and Mistress Carol out while we are holding it." The Odu looked at Aliya. "It should be Mistress Aliya. She is slim and strong."

"Tell me what to do," Aliya said.

How did the Odu know that Aliya was strong? Had someone told him?

Instead of addressing Aliya, Ovidu explained his plan to Arwel. "We will lift the stone, Mistress Aliya will get under it and pull Mistress Jacki out. She will hand her to you or one of the other masters. Then she will pull Master Kalugal out and hand him to Master Welgost. After that, she will get Master Lokan and Mistress Carol."

Orion leaned to whisper in Alena's ear, "I might not know anything about cyborgs, but that seems like an intelligent plan to me. Your Odus might be sentient already."

50

KALUGAL

*A*s the hotel staff finished setting up the table in Kalugal and Jacki's suite, Kalugal lifted his glass. "I want to thank everyone for your valiant efforts today. I'm grateful to all of you and especially to Aliya, who I've been told kept on pulling out stones even when her hands were bleeding and the skin on her fingers and palms was practically shredded." He glanced at her bandaged hands and cringed. "Unlike us, her healing takes longer."

"I'll be okay by tomorrow," Aliya said. "The numbing salve the doctor gave me helped a lot with the pain."

"I'm glad, and I'm forever in your debt."

She shook her head. "It was nothing. I would have done that for a stranger. I owe you much more than you owe me."

"Let's call it even," Kalugal offered.

"Not acceptable."

He knew better than to press the issue. Aliya was prideful, and he was risking hurting that pride.

The poor girl had feared that they would blame her for the tunnel's collapse, and he wanted to reassure her that no one thought it had been her fault.

Well, Jacki had voiced her suspicion when they'd been trapped, and so had Lokan, but Kalugal had explained that Aliya couldn't have rigged the place without risking her life as well. Besides, even though she was smart and resourceful, she didn't have the know-how or the tools to engineer it.

But even if she had, she wouldn't have done it after he'd bought her a home. She was an honorable female.

With her bandaged hands, eating would have been a challenge if not for Shamash, who had found fresh blood for her, which she was now sipping through a straw.

"I'm also grateful to Ovidu and Oridu." Kalugal inclined his head in their direction. "Without your help, it would have taken much longer to get us out."

T. LUCAS

"Mistress Alena commanded us to help in any way we could," Ovidu said. "It was our duty and our pleasure to obey her wishes, master."

"Nevertheless, I'm grateful." Kalugal turned to his second. "I'm sorry that you got hurt, but I'm glad that two broken legs were the extent of your injuries, and I wish you a speedy recovery."

Phinas lifted his glass. "I'm glad that this is over and that Jacki and the baby are okay. When I was lying trapped in there, the pain was secondary to my worry."

"Thank you." Jacki's chin wobbled. "We were so incredibly lucky. It's just now starting to sink in."

Kalugal gave her hand a gentle squeeze. "We are all shaken. I suggest that we spend a few days resting and enjoying the hotel's amenities and leave either Sunday night or Monday morning. By then, everyone's scrapes and bruises will be healed, and Phinas will be able to walk."

"I will walk by tomorrow," Phinas said.

"Until you do, you need someone to take care of you," Jacki said. "I suggest we bring a cot into our suite so we can keep an eye on you during the night."

As much as Kalugal valued Phinas, Welgost or Shamash could do that. Aliya was already sleeping on the couch in their living room, and he didn't want Phinas there as well.

"I'll help you," Aliya offered. "You will need someone to carry you to the bathroom, and I'm strong."

Phinas looked horrified. "I appreciate the offer, but I could never impose on a lady like that."

She gave him a baleful look. "I'm stronger than you. There is no loss of face in letting someone take care of you."

"I know, and as I said, I appreciate your offer, but I'd rather one of my men helped me. Besides, your hands are injured, and you need help yourself."

She lifted her bandaged hands. "It's just skin. My hands are still strong, and I can still carry you."

"I have a better idea," Alena interjected. "Oridu can move into Phinas's room and assist him with everything he needs."

"Thank you." Phinas gave her a grateful smile. "That would be the perfect solution. Oridu doesn't need to sleep, and he'll always be available to help me."

It was impossible to compete with that, and Aliya accepted defeat.

"I still can't understand why the tunnel collapsed," she said. "I've been there many times during the years, and it never showed any signs of weakness. Are you sure that no one felt the earth move? It could have been a small earthquake."

"I checked." Kalugal reached for the dan dan noodles, signaling that it was time to eat. "No seismic activity has been detected in the past few days, including today." He put some on Jacki's plate and then on his own before passing the platter to Alena. "I've been thinking what could have caused it, and I have a theory. I think that the place was rigged, but only when the weight of those standing in that tunnel exceeded a certain limit. That's why Aliya could walk in there safely."

"That kind of makes sense," Jacki said. "Those who rigged it knew to walk in there only one person at a time. It was meant to stop invaders. But the question is, what were they protecting? There must have been something important on the other side or deeper down."

"Correct." Kalugal smiled at his smart mate. "I was following the mineral's concentration readouts on the device. It was weaker in the other offshoot and stronger in the one that collapsed."

"So what now?" Lokan said. "We can't continue the investigation because we don't have the device, and the passage is blocked. But even if we get a new device and clear that passage, there might be more rigs along the way. We can't risk it."

"I agree." Kalugal put his chopsticks down. "I need to talk with the Zhao twins and see if they can combine their invention with a burrowing robot and a robotic arm that would take samples and check them on the spot."

"That would take years to develop," Lokan said.

"I'm not in a hurry." Kalugal reached for another platter. "I'd rather wait than risk lives. I've already told Jianye to keep his people out of the tunnels and proceed with caution with the rest of the outpost."

"Poor Jianye." Jin chuckled. "Since you've erased his and his men's memory of the entire incident, he has no idea why you are being so cautious and probably thinks that you're nuts."

Kalugal shrugged. "He can think whatever he wants. As long as he needs my funding to continue, he will do as I say and keep his crew safe."

51

GERALDINE

"It has been so long since I drove a car." Geraldine clutched the steering wheel with sweaty palms.

Shai cast her an indulgent smile. "We are in a deserted church parking lot. It's the perfect place to practice. Take your foot off the brake pedal and put it gently on the gas."

Taking a deep breath, Geraldine lifted her foot and moved it the few inches to the right. Hovering it over the gas pedal for a couple of seconds, she finally gathered the courage to lower it and apply the slightest pressure. When nothing happened, she pressed a little harder, and the car lurched forward. Immediately taking her foot off the gas pedal, she slammed it on the brake.

"Try it again," Shai said in a calm tone. "But this time, don't take your foot all the way off. You need to find what the right amount of pressure is."

Sweat beading on her forehead, she clutched the steering wheel so hard it groaned under the pressure.

Great, so now her super-strength decided to show up. When she'd needed it to move furniture or heavy planters, it had been nowhere to be found.

The last time she'd driven a car had been years ago, and that car had been very different than Shai's shiny new vehicle with all of its modern amenities and special clan modifications. It felt as if she'd never sat in the driver's seat before.

Gritting her teeth, she moved her foot to the gas pedal, and when the car lurched forward, she eased it just a bit, and the car moved slowly forward.

"You're doing great," Shai encouraged. "Keep the slow pace."

She chuckled. "I have no intentions of going any faster."

The speedometer hovered between ten and fifteen miles per hour, and it was the perfect speed for her first time behind the wheel of a modern car.

After she'd circled the sprawling parking lot several times, her grip finally loosened. "I'm getting the hang of it."

"Yes, you are. Keep going until you feel confident enough to increase the speed a little."

"Okay." She let out a breath. "Maybe it's for the best that the shipping of my car got delayed. By the time it gets here, I will be comfortable enough to actually take it out on the road."

"In three weeks, you will be driving all over Malibu."

She doubted that. "How come the shipping was delayed?"

"The shipping industry can't keep up with the demand. I'm glad that it's delayed only by two weeks." He chuckled. "Kian should have seen it coming and invested in trucking, storage facilities, and other shipping enterprises. Everything is in short supply—containers, chassis to put the containers on, trucks, truck drivers, warehouse operators, warehouse space, and everything else that goes into transporting goods."

"Is it because people buy more and more things online?"

"That's one of the reasons. The other is that manufacturers prefer not to store inventory. They call it just-in-time manufacturing. It's less costly and more efficient for them to manufacture and ship it right away. Another problem is the workforce. Members of the current generation don't want to be warehouse operators and truck drivers."

"Why? I thought that those jobs paid well."

"They do, but they can't drive a truck if they smoke pot, even if they do it on the weekend when they are not driving because it comes up in the testing days after. It was a bad decision, and I hope they will relax the rules a little. It's like Prohibition era all over again."

"Is marijuana use so widespread?"

Shai shrugged. "I was surprised to read that as well. Since the testing started, thousands of truck drivers have lost their jobs, and there aren't enough takers to replace them." He leaned back in his seat. "When self-driving trucks get approved, that will no longer be an issue. Warehouse automation is also on the rise, but in the meantime, we need to be patient and not expect our goods to be delivered as fast as they used to be."

With Shai distracting her with his explanations about the shipping industry, Geraldine hadn't noticed that she'd increased the speed and was comfortably circling the parking lot at twenty miles per hour.

"Your tactic worked." She cast him a quick sidelong smile. "I wasn't paying attention and went faster."

He smiled back. "Are you ready to take it out on the road? This time of day, there are hardly any cars on it."

"Heck, why not? We are immortal, right?"

He laughed. "Stop worrying. You are not going to wreck the car. We have dinner with Darlene at your old house tomorrow, so you can't get into an accident. It will ruin our plans."

He was teasing, of course, and it was working. She was even starting to enjoy herself. As Cassandra liked to say, it was all in the attitude. If she believed that she was a good driver, she would be, and the opposite was true as well.

Geraldine stopped at the parking lot exit and watched the road for a few moments before easing onto it. "By the way, I don't have to get there early tomorrow, so you don't have to cut your workday short. Cassandra has arranged for everything.

A cleaning crew will be there this afternoon, and she ordered tomorrow's dinner from a catering service that brings everything and even sets up the table."

Shai shook his head. "Your daughter is a force of nature. She even found a way to get rid of Leo for the entire month. It was a brilliant move to call Orion and have him arrange with the gallery owner for Leo to go on an acquisition expedition."

Geraldine's heart swelled with pride. "Cassy is very resourceful. When she wants something, she finds a way to make it happen."

Shai sighed. "I hope Parker is not going to fail, for his sake more than for Darlene's. If his compulsion doesn't work, we can wait for Orion's return to compel her silence, but it would crush Parker's ego. From what I've observed, compellers tend to be arrogant people, and I think that confidence has a lot to do with their ability. I don't want Parker to lose his mojo."

5 2

ELEANOR

*E*leanor sat across from Colonel Crowley and a higher-up who'd only offered his last name, which was Wolfe—a name that fitted him so well that she'd doubted he'd been born with it.

"The job is yours, Dr. Takala." Wolfe regarded her with his beady eyes. "You came to us at a pivotal time. Dr. Roberts' untimely death left the program without a leader, and we are fortunate to have you step in. You are not only qualified, but you're also familiar with the program, know each of the program's members, and have been involved in their recruitment as well as some of their training."

"Thank you." Eleanor stifled the urge to ask him how much the job paid.

It was irrelevant, she was not in it for the money, but it still mattered to her. She deserved to be paid at least as much as Roberts. Being offered the same salary would vindicate her for having been kicked out of the program and offered a pittance of severance pay.

Then again, perhaps she should be grateful to the old bastard for kicking her out. If he hadn't done that, she wouldn't have infiltrated Kalugal's stronghold, hooked up with Greggory, and turned immortal.

"How soon can you be available?" Crowley asked.

"I can start tomorrow."

Wolfe grinned like a hyena. "Excellent." He extended his hand to her. "Welcome aboard, Dr. Eleanor Takala."

She liked the prefix and wished it were deserved. Perhaps one day, she would take a break from everything and get a doctorate in whatever. Philosophy or ancient languages, or something else that was totally useless but fun to learn.

She shook his hand. "Before I start, there is an issue I need to discuss with you."

"Right." Wolfe pulled his hand away. "You're probably wondering about the pay. I don't know how much Roberts was paid, but I'll have my secretary check and prepare a formal job offer with the same compensation package."

Triumphant drums sounded in Eleanor's head, but she affected a bored expression. "With all due respect, Roberts might have founded the program with Simmons, but I can do better than both of them. I was the one who brought in all the talent. After I was forced to leave, they failed to recruit anyone new."

"I'm well aware of that," Wolfe acknowledged. "I'm willing to renegotiate in six months."

"That's an acceptable offer, but my pay wasn't what I wanted to discuss with you. In my informed opinion, the program is not doing well because you keep the members underground. That's a big mistake."

Wolfe leaned back and crossed his arms over his broad chest. "And why is that?"

"My theory is that paranormal talents operate on some sort of frequency that science hasn't discovered yet. Those who are sensitive enough to pick up on it, harness it and use it need to be surrounded by nature, and in my experience, as close as possible to the ocean. If you go over the files of our strongest talents, you'll see that most of them lived near a beach or at least spent their summers there. I bet that everyone's talent would manifest stronger when in close proximity to the ocean."

"That's an interesting hypothesis, and I'm willing to send a request to find a new location for the program. Perhaps the naval base has space."

That was where the Echelon spyware was located, and it would have been a perfect location for her to move the program to, but her agenda was to move them to Safe Haven.

Perhaps she could do both.

"That would be a wonderful temporary solution because I don't want them to spend even one more day in that underground crypt. It's killing their talents. But the base is far from perfect. These people need quiet, they need serenity, and they need to feel connected to nature."

Wolfe narrowed his eyes at her. "It seems to me that you have a specific place in mind."

"I do. Have you ever heard about a spiritual retreat called Safe Haven?"

"I can't say that I have."

"It's located on the Oregon Coast, right on the beach, and there is nothing for miles in every direction. There is no better place for honing paranormal talents. We can get our own corner of the property that will be completely separate from the rest of the retreat, and I can get it at a bargain price. On top of that, I suspect that I'll be able to recruit more talent from the spiritual retreat's attendees. Paranormals are drawn to the mystical. They search for answers."

"That's a brilliant idea, Eleanor." Wolfe uncrossed his arms and leaned forward. "And the timing is perfect since we need the space the paranormal research is taking for a different project. Moving it to Oregon is a terrific solution, provided that we can safeguard the research. It is, after all, top secret."

That was twice that Wolfe had said research instead of program.

Eleanor's hackles rose. Had it been a slip of the tongue?

No one was supposed to know about the founders' plan to breed super babies, and even they hadn't called it research. Their term for it was the leap, or some other nonsense like that.

"What kind of research are you referring to?" she asked. "I was under the impression that the paranormal division was about spying on America's enemies, not conducting research."

Wolfe smiled his creepy smile again. "For a smart and ambitious woman, you are surprisingly naive, Dr. Takala."

"I only know what I was told."

"You didn't have the security clearance before, but now that you are heading the program, you need to know what it is really about. The so-called missions they were supposedly training for were just a cover for the real reason the talents were recruited."

The puzzle pieces were starting to fall into place, and the emerging picture was scary as hell. "You were after what made them different."

"Precisely. We want to know what makes these people sensitive, as you coined it, to that mysterious frequency. We hired a new doctor to replace Roberts, and he will continue the research, but he already informed me that he needs fresh talents."

"And that's why you hired me. I was the best at luring paranormals into the program."

"You are a hundred percent correct."

53

KIAN

"William is here. We will talk tomorrow." Kian ended the call with Arwel and motioned for William to take a seat at the conference table.

"Is anyone joining us?" William asked.

"No. Do you prefer my desk?"

"Here is fine." William pushed his glasses up his nose. "Any news from China?"

"Plenty. Both teams are returning Monday."

William frowned. "That's early. What happened?"

"A lot. But the most important discovery was a hybrid female that escaped the massacre of Jade's tribe. She was a young girl at the time, and the attacking Kra-ell thought she was human and let her go with the other humans. She lived among the Mosuo until she grew up and started looking too alien. Since then, the poor woman has been living alone in a tunnel system under an ancient outpost. The team is bringing her to the village."

William's frown deepened. "Vrog and Emmett could easily pass for humans. In what way does the hybrid female look alien?"

"Arwel said that she has a temper and can't control her fangs and glowing eyes well, which in the Kra-ell's case turn red. He also said that the shape of her eyes is very alien-looking."

"That could be solved with sunglasses."

"Precisely. Anyway, Vrog is flying over to see her tomorrow. We might be hosting a Kra-ell couple in the village."

"I have a match waiting for him, and he knows that. Is he going to cancel?"

"I don't know. But given that a hybrid Kra-ell female was found, he might. Just don't tell the lady yet. Who knows, maybe there will be no chemistry between Vrog and Aliya, and he will want to participate in the virtual adventure with the clan female."

Kian assumed that William knew who the clan female was, but he wasn't going to ask. The whole point of Perfect Match was anonymity.

"Is Aliya the reason they are cutting their trip short?"

"She's not. They had an accident earlier in the day." Kian relayed what Arwel had told him. "Kalugal forbade any excavation in the tunnels, and his plan is to end the archeological dig of the outpost soon as well. He suspects that more tunnels are rigged."

William nodded. "The question is by whom, the ancient Kra-ell who died out, or someone else who hid something in those tunnels."

"Arwel mentioned some device that Kalugal wants to develop to search those tunnels remotely, but I don't have details. You'll have to ask him when he returns."

"You seem happy that they are cutting their trips short."

"I am." Kian chuckled. "I like all my ducklings under my wings, and especially Alena. I know she's well protected, and I also know that when she travels with our mother, she's in more danger than she's in now, but I can't help the uneasy feeling I've had throughout their trip. Perhaps it was a premonition."

William arched a brow. "Alena wasn't hurt, so if you had a premonition, it was about your cousins and their mates."

"True. I'm just so relieved that they are coming home." He raked his fingers through his hair. "I'm turning soft. It must be old age, or maybe it's fatherhood."

"I think it's fatherhood. Until not too long ago, we didn't all live together, and you were fine with that. Many of our programmers lived in the Bay Area, and Arwel and Bhathian were stationed there."

It seemed so long ago that Kian could barely remember those days.

"I wasn't fine. I always wanted everyone to live in the same place where I could protect them. That was why I built the keep. But until Mark's murder, I had no reason to order everyone to move into the building." Kian's good mood took a nosedive. "I wish we didn't have to lose him to prove to our people that they were not safe, and that hiding in plain sight was not enough."

"True that." William took his glasses off and used his shirt to clean them. "I like living and working in the village, but I also liked it in the keep, so I'm not a good example. But I think most of our people love living here."

"It's easy to get used to good things. And this is not only good but getting better. The new section of the village is almost ready, and Callie informed me that she's going to run the restaurant. We are going to have gourmet fare in the village."

William's eyes started glowing. "Now, you got me excited. When is it going to open?"

"I assume she'll need a couple of months to get everything she needs, hire staff, and train them. She plans on offering Atzil a position, but I doubt Kalugal would let him go." Kian leaned back and crossed his arms over his chest. "We've gotten distracted. You came here to talk about your progress with finding Toven, not the future of fine dining in the village."

William sighed. "That was a much more pleasant topic, at least for me. I'm afraid that facial recognition is not the way to find Toven. I did as you suggested, and I ran a looser search for men who look like Orion but are not an exact match. I've gotten thousands of results. Roni and I went over them, but none looked close enough to Orion to be Toven. So I ran Orion's picture and asked for an exact match. I didn't even find Orion, let alone Toven. Orion must be using a foreign driver's license or passport as his identification, and Toven is probably doing the same thing."

"Let's check." Kian glanced at his watch. "It's early in the morning over there. I'll text Orion. If he's awake, he'll answer now, and if not, he'll answer later."

The answer came back right away. "Orion uses mostly his Swiss passport as his identification."

"Is he a Swiss citizen, or is it a counterfeit?"

"He's probably a citizen." Kian typed the question.

His phone rang a moment later.

"Thanks for calling, Orion."

"I'm a Swiss citizen, and I have several other passports as well that I use from time to time. Why the questions?"

Kian told him about William's results. "The facial recognition seems to be a dead end. The only thing left is trying to find Toven through his publishers."

"There might be one more thing we can do," Orion said. "I asked Mey if she's willing to come with me to Paris and listen to the echoes in the residence Toven was renting when I met him. It's a long shot, but beggars can't be choosers."

"Did you ever go back there?"

Orion chuckled. "Many times. It was always rented out, and in recent years, it's been offered on Airbnb, so I will have no problem getting access to it. In fact, we can stay there while Mey listens to the echoes."

5 4

EMMETT

*E*leanor entered the hotel suite, kicked her heels off, flung her purse on the table, and plopped down on the couch. "Houston, we have a problem."

Emmett sat next to her and took her hand. "They didn't hire you?"

"Oh, they hired me. They even offered me the same pay as Roberts was getting, which felt really good. And they even agreed to move the program to Safe Haven when the facilities there are ready. In the meantime, they suggested moving the program to the naval base."

"That's where Echelon is located," Peter said. "That's perfect."

"I know. I couldn't have asked for a better outcome of this meeting, but none of that is the problem. Turns out that the paranormal spying division was a cover-up for what they were really doing, which was conducting research on the talents. They want to know what makes them different. What if they discover their godly genes? The government has access to gene sequencing equipment that the clan does not, and their chances of discovering what makes some people have paranormal talents are much better than Bridget's."

"We need to stop the program," Peter said.

"It's not that simple." Eleanor sighed. "Is there any alcohol left in the mini-fridge? Because I really need some."

"Housekeeping replenished the supply this morning." Peter walked over to the fridge and pulled out three little bottles. "What's your pleasure?"

"Can you mix a screwdriver for me?"

"Coming up." He pulled out a bottle of orange juice.

As he mixed the drink, Eleanor continued. "I spent the entire drive back here thinking about what to do. If we get the talents out, they will find new ones and keep testing. We can't allow that to happen."

"How are we going to stop them?" Emmett asked.

"We will feed them fake information." Eleanor took the drink Peter handed her. "We get the program moved to Safe Haven, and we take control of that doctor. We need him to give us the results of all the research Simmons and Roberts did, and if there is anything that even hints that these people have alien genes, we will need to hack into the database and change those results."

"What if the doctor is immune?" Peter asked.

"Then we get him replaced. As the new director, I can fire him for whatever reason like Roberts did to me."

She let out a breath. "Kian doesn't know how lucky he is that he has me on this mission. No one else could have solved this mess."

"We need to call him." Peter sat on her other side.

"I wanted to call him on the way here, but I decided to run my plan through you first and see what you think."

"I think your plan is solid, but the big question is whether Roni can hack into highly secure military data, which I assume is how they classified this research."

"If he can't, I'll make the doctor corrupt the data somehow." She took a long sip from the drink. "I've read somewhere about a clever cyber sabotage of a system that was offline. Top, top security. They infected the scientist's laptop with a virus that stayed dormant until the guy went to work and hooked it into the system. The virus traveled from the laptop into the offline servers and went to work. It didn't do anything noticeable, but it corrupted the data slowly over time, until one day, the whole thing crashed."

"How did they get the virus onto the scientist's laptop?" Emmett asked. "Did he use it online?"

"I don't remember. I should look up that story again."

"Or just call Roni and ask him," Peter said. "I'm sure he knows about every major hack ever perpetrated."

"I don't know about that." Eleanor waved a dismissive hand. "I bet the best hacks never made it to the news."

"The hacker community is not that big," Peter said. "They know when someone manages something big, and they usually know who that is."

Eleanor shrugged. "Perhaps you are right. What I need to figure out now is how to get the two of you into the base."

"We can be new talents," Peter suggested. "Roni has already created fake identities for us."

She eyed him as if he'd lost his mind. "Are you nuts? I'm not letting that doctor anywhere near you with a needle."

"He's not going to do anything to us because Emmett and I will thrall the crap out of him."

Eleanor slumped against the couch cushions. "I need to check whether he's susceptible to compulsion. If he is, then he's most likely susceptible to thralling as well, and then we can proceed with your idea."

55

KIAN

*W*illiam was getting ready to leave when Kian's phone rang again. Expecting it to be Orion, he didn't even look at the display. "Did you think of something else that can lead us to Toven?"

"Was I supposed to?" Eleanor asked.

Kian chuckled. "My apologies. I didn't check the caller ID, and I assumed you were the person I spoke with before. How are things going in West Virginia?"

"I got the job. I'm now officially the paranormal program's new director, and I start tomorrow."

"Excellent work, Eleanor. Congratulations."

"Thank you, but that's not why I'm calling. During my job interview, I've learned new and alarming information."

That didn't sound good. "I'm listening."

"Turns out the program is not a renewal of the government's previous paranormal investigation that was all about spying on the Russians using paranormal talents. That was just the cover story. What they are really after is researching paranormals and learning what makes them different. Now that my security clearance has been upgraded, I was finally told the truth, but I beat myself up for not realizing that before. I pride myself on being cynical and questioning everyone's motives, but I didn't question why Roberts was constantly taking blood samples from the trainees. I assumed that it had to do with the drugs they were giving them to enhance their performance, or the super babies they hoped to breed, but that didn't justify the frequency of those tests. It had research and experimenting written all over it."

"Don't feel bad. I should have realized that as well, and I'm as cynical as they get." Kian let out a breath. "They had four confirmed Dormants to run their tests on, and they have equipment we don't. We need to find out what they know."

"My thoughts exactly. I plan to compel the new doctor they assigned to the program and get him to give me all the relevant information. If there is anything in there that flags abnormalities, I'll have him erase those test results and plant fake ones. I will probably need Roni's help to give the doctor instructions on how to tamper with the data. And if that's too complicated, he can create a computer virus that I'll have the doctor introduce into the system. It's not going to be a big loss if all of their research results are corrupted."

"That's arguable. If we can get access to it, we might learn something, but that's a secondary consideration to ensuring that they don't find out anomalies in the talents' genetic make-up. In any case, I'll tell Roni to provide you with all the assistance you need."

"Thank you. I also pitched them the Safe Haven idea, and they seemed all for it. The big boss, Wolfe, even offered to move the program to the naval base until Safe Haven had the facilities ready for them. The question is whether I should keep pushing it or tell them that the owner changed his mind about leasing it to the government."

"Why would you do that?"

"Because we don't want them breathing down our necks."

"We need to be in control of that research, which means that your stint as its director is going to be a long-term thing. I assume that you don't want to stay in West Virginia for years to come."

"You assume correctly. Safe Haven it is. When do you think you will have it ready? To get final approval on that, I need to at least show them the architectural plans, timeline to completion, and asking price."

"I've already asked Gavin to work on ideas for the place, but he hasn't shown me anything yet. I'll talk to him, and once the plans are finalized, I'll get the Safe Haven project going on a fast track, so it will be ready as soon as possible for the program."

"I need an approximate timeline to completion and asking price as soon as possible. If we want this to happen, I need to strike while the iron is still hot."

"I'll get it to you as soon as I can. In the meantime, you can keep using compulsion to make them cooperate."

She chuckled. "The funny thing is that I barely had to use it, and I didn't even have to work hard to convince them that the underground is detrimental to the talents. They took at face value my bullshit explanation about paranormals' need to be close to nature and especially to the ocean to feed and enhance their abilities. Wolfe jumped on the idea. He said that they needed the space in the shelter for some other project."

"I'm curious about what they are doing in that underground city of theirs, but my curiosity will have to wait. Right now, your first priority is finding out what they know and eliminating it if needed. Your second priority is finding someone in the Echelon system so we can gain access to it, and your third is moving the paranormals to Safe Haven. Naturally, if the opportunity presents itself and you need to do things out of order, then by all means, but keep me informed."

"Will do, boss."

56

ALENA

*A*s Alena entered Kalugal's suite, her eyes immediately darted to Phinas, who looked much better, and then to Aliya, whose bandages were off.

"Good morning." Smiling, she waved her greetings while Orion pulled out a chair for her next to the breakfast table. "How is everyone feeling?"

Aliya lifted her hands and turned them around to show Alena. "I'm mostly healed."

Faint scars still marred her palms and fingers, but they would probably be gone in a day or two.

She was dressed in one of her new outfits, her hair was loose down her back and shone like a black velvet curtain, and her cheeks had a healthy pink hue to them.

Plentiful food, good rest, and new clothes had transformed her into quite a beauty despite her oddly shaped eyes. In fact, Alena was growing accustomed to them, and they no longer jumped out at her as they had in the beginning. Maybe it was because Aliya looked less gaunt, so those alien eyes didn't look as disproportionately large in her small face.

"How about you, Phinas?" Orion asked. "Was Oridu a good nursemaid?"

"He was invaluable," Phinas said. "But I won't be needing his services tonight. Later today, I'm going to remove the braces."

"The doctor told you not to put weight on them for six to eight weeks," Aliya said.

"That advice doesn't apply to immortals." Phinas stuffed another steamed bun into his mouth. "Kalugal thralled the good doctor to remember that I had sprained both legs, not broken them."

Alena shuddered. Watching the doctor re-break Phinas's legs had been painful. The doctor couldn't understand how the bones that had been broken in several places were already fused back, just not properly, and Kalugal had to compel the doctor to re-break them. Phinas had tried to be macho and refuse anesthetics, but Kalugal had ended that nonsense quickly, ordering him to stop being an idiot.

Thankfully, Phinas's knees had somehow avoided being crushed. The delicate and intricate joints would have taken much longer to heal. Alena wasn't sure why, but the big leg bones healed very fast in comparison.

"I spoke with Yamanu earlier this morning," Arwel said. "They will be here shortly after lunch." He looked at the table. "Can we squeeze five more people in here? Or should we go back to dining in the hotel's restaurant?"

"I like us dining up here in privacy, and there is plenty of room once we extend the table." Kalugal reached for the teapot and poured himself and Jacki more tea. "There are two extension leaves stored underneath, and I'll ask housekeeping to bring more chairs."

"Are they going to stay long?" Aliya asked.

"They are going home with us on Monday," Kalugal said. "It's good that this is not the height of the tourist season, so I was able to get rooms for them in the hotel."

Aliya fiddled with the napkin, wrapping it around her hand and unwrapping it. "Are Vrog's eyes like mine? I don't remember him well."

"They are not," Alena said. "They look human."

"Lucky guy," Aliya murmured. "No wonder Jade chose him to run the tribe's businesses in Singapore."

"Do you know what those businesses involved?"

She shook her head. "I was just a kid. No one told me."

"I have an excellent idea," Jin said. "Since all of our fingernails look like shit, I suggest we book appointments at the hotel spa and get manicures and pedicures." She cast Arwel a bemused glance. "And that includes you and the rest of the guys."

"I could go for a massage." Kalugal rotated his shoulders one at a time. "For some reason, our self-healing abilities don't include softening stiff muscles. Any idea why?"

"Call Bridget and ask," Jacki said. "I'm all for a massage at the spa and a visit to the hair salon. Since I turned immortal, my hair grows so fast that I need to trim it every week if I want to maintain my hairstyle."

Alena cast a sidelong glance at Aliya. "Would you like to join us?"

"I would, but I shouldn't. Kalugal can't shroud me in there."

"You don't need shrouding," Jin said. "I'll give them so much attitude that they won't even look at you. They will be too busy trying to avoid me."

Aliya chuckled, which startled Alena. She hadn't heard the girl laugh even once. She smiled a little, but even that had looked sad.

Hopefully, Vrog would be able to cheer her up.

Under the table, Alena reached for Orion's hand and gave it a little squeeze. She had always been quick to smile and laugh, but since Orion had entered her life, she'd been doing both much more often.

He made her happy.

Leaning over, he kissed her temple. "I love you," he whispered in her ear.

"How long will those things in the spa take?" Aliya asked.

"A couple of hours," Jin said. "Maybe three. Why, are you in a hurry to go somewhere?"

"I don't want to be in the spa when Vrog gets here. I want to be ready to greet him."

"Don't worry." Jin waved a hand in dismissal. "We will be done long before that."

5 7

ALIYA

*A*liya had never dreamt of being a princess, but she felt like one now. Her nails and toenails had received a professional manicure and had been painted with clear gloss, her hair had gotten a trim, and her skin had never felt as soft or looked as glowing.

There had been a few tense moments when the beautician had commented about Aliya's unusually hard nails, but Jin had done as she'd promised, going on the offensive and telling the woman to just do her job and stop complaining.

"You look good." Jin put her arm around her shoulders and looked at both of their reflections in the mirror. "I can't wait to see Vrog's reaction when he sees you for the first time." She smirked. "I sent Mey a picture of you, but we decided not to show it to him."

That was news to her. "When did you take my picture?"

"When you first got here and still looked like something that the cat dragged in."

Aliya winced. "Are you sure your sister didn't show it to him?"

"Positive. Don't get me wrong, you were pretty in that picture despite your haggard state, but we decided that not knowing what you looked like would help build up Vrog's anticipation."

Aliya shrugged. "I hope he's not disappointed, but if he is, that's his problem." She'd done her best to look appealing, and if Vrog didn't like what he saw, Phinas was a viable and attractive alternative.

He had backed off during their trip to Lijiang, and she'd thought that he'd lost interest. Admittedly, she'd felt disappointed. But something had changed after his injury. Perhaps he'd had time to think while trapped, and he'd thought about her.

It was a nice feeling to be desired.

The immortal wasn't shy about showing his renewed interest, flirting with her the same way she'd seen the Mosuo boys flirt with the girls but never with her.

Aliya had been just a girl back then, and after she'd fled the village, she'd lived like a hermit vagabond. Thinking about being feminine or desirable had been the furthest thing from her mind.

Still, her body had matured, and she'd become a woman at some point. She just hadn't realized it until now.

Then again, desirability meant different things to different people.

Humans appreciated sweet, soft-spoken women with pretty faces and feminine curves. The Kra-ell valued strength and aggression, and the more of it, the better and more desirable.

She was a hybrid, though, and so was Vrog, and their preferences might be somewhere in the middle.

What did she value in a mate? Was it strength? Intelligence? A sense of humor?

Those were the kind of thoughts she'd never wasted time on before and not just because she'd had no viable options. The pureblooded females hadn't had to choose, and the Mosuo girls could take as long as they wanted to sample lovers until they decided to settle on one. But if she lived in the immortals' village, she would have to follow their customs, whatever they were.

They were monogamous, but perhaps on their way to monogamy, they played around like humans did and tried out many lovers?

Now that she might have to choose a partner, she should know her own preferences.

Out of the group of immortal males, Aliya debated who would have caught her attention if all of them were available. Orion was by far the most handsome, and he was kind and cultured. He was also a powerful compeller, but other than that, he wasn't aggressive at all.

He wouldn't have been her first choice.

Arwel had the most beautiful eyes, and he exuded authority and leadership, but in a calm and collected way. He wouldn't have been her first choice either, but she would have considered him.

Kalugal had everything she wanted in a male, handsome, smart, cunning, innately aggressive, and outwardly cultured, but he was taken, and he was also out of her league. He would have never gone for an uneducated, unfashionable, flat-chested female. Given his wife's ample bosom, he preferred a handful.

The same went for Lokan.

He was gorgeous, and there was a lot of pent-up aggression in him, but he kept it under tight lock and key, and showed the world only his cultured side. That was admirable, and if he wasn't taken, she would have considered him as well.

Shamash was a nice guy, but she didn't find him attractive, so that left Phinas and Welgost. Both were strong warriors, both were handsome, but Phinas was smarter, and he was a leader while Welgost was a follower.

As she and Jin walked into Kalugal's suite, Aliya returned Phinas' smile and nodded, but other than that, she had no idea how to respond to his flirting. She had zero experience.

"Help yourself to some tea and dessert." Jacki motioned at the table.

"Thank you." Aliya sat across from Phinas and gave him another small smile.

"Did you enjoy your massage?"

"I did, but I would have preferred a stronger set of hands on me."

Was it more flirting, and was he hinting that he would have liked her hands on him?

"They are here," Jin announced. "Mey texted me that they are unloading the car and heading to the lobby." She pushed to her feet and pocketed her phone. "I'm going down to greet them. Anyone want to come with me?"

"I'll come." Arwel got up.

Aliya wanted to come as well, but she didn't want to look too anxious to meet Vrog. The Kra-ell females always acted uninterested, letting the males bend over backward to impress them so they would issue them an invitation.

Vrog would expect no less.

Besides, she didn't want Phinas to think that she wasn't interested in him.

"I'll wait here," she said as she pushed to her feet and headed toward the balcony doors.

Phinas might join her there, but she hoped he wouldn't. She needed to calm her nerves.

Except, Kalugal's compulsion made it impossible for her to even put her hand on the door handle. She turned to him. "Am I allowed outside?"

"You are free to come and go as you please," Kalugal surprised her. "You gave me your word that you'd give the immortal village a three-month chance, and I know that you're an honorable woman and would never break your promise."

He had no idea how much his words meant to her.

Her honor was like a shield that Aliya carried around her. It made her feel like a person of worth.

"Thank you." She inclined her head to hide the sudden moisture coating her eyes.

"Do you need company out there?" Alena asked softly.

"Thank you, but I need to be alone for a little bit." Her words had been meant more for Phinas's ears than Alena's, but she didn't want anyone to follow her.

"I understand." Alena gave her a reassuring smile.

As Aliya opened the French doors, stepped outside, and closed them behind her, her lungs expanded to allow a large inhale. She felt free for the first time since they'd captured her, and not just because Kalugal had released her from his compulsion.

It was nice to have people to talk to, people who cared whether she lived or died, but it was also oppressive. Aliya was used to being alone and was comfortable with her solitude. She found the constant company of others fatiguing.

How was that going to work in the immortals' village?

Did they have a hotel? Or would Kalugal and Jackie invite her to stay in their house?

He was a rich man, so his home was probably big and beautiful like the houses she'd seen on television. Would she have a room of her own? Would they let her clean their house to earn her keep?

Later, she would ask him, but for now, she should enjoy the few minutes of solitude before she had to face Vrog and put on an act worthy of a pureblooded Kra-ell female.

58

VROG

"*R*eady to meet your dream girl?" Yamanu wrapped his arm around Vrog's shoulders.

Only Jin and Arwel had come down to greet them.

Why hadn't Aliya?

Wasn't she excited to see him?

Perhaps her injuries were more severe than Arwel had reported, and she was too hurt to walk?

To their right, Mey and Jin were hugging and chatting up a storm as if they hadn't seen each other in weeks.

Ignoring the Guardian's taunting, Vrog turned to Arwel. "Is Aliya okay? You said that she was injured in the rescue."

"Her hands are much better already. She even had a manicure earlier."

That was a relief. But if she'd been well enough to visit the salon, why hadn't she come down to greet him?

Keeping his expression neutral, Vrog slung his travel bag over his shoulder. "I'm glad to hear that she recovered so quickly."

"Her injuries were superficial, just cuts and scrapes that would have taken one of ours minutes to heal. Hers took much longer to mend, and the scars haven't faded yet." Arwel took one of the suitcases Yamanu had pulled out from the trunk of the rented car. "I don't remember your healing after Richard turned your face into hamburger meat. Did it take more than twenty-four hours to heal?"

"Most of it was healed in just a couple of days, but it took longer for the bruises and cuts to fade." Vrog fell in step with Arwel as the Guardians started walking toward the hotel lobby. "Why do you ask?"

Arwel didn't stop by the front desk and continued to the staircase. "I wonder if that has to do with your shorter lifespans."

Vrog wasn't concerned with that. He was still a young man even in Kra-ell terms, and he didn't need to worry about his life expectancy just yet.

"It makes sense." Vrog followed him up the stairs. "Do the others know where to go?"

Arwel turned to look over his shoulder. "What's taking them so long?" He waited until Yamanu entered the lobby. "Where are Mey and Jin?"

"They are coming." Yamanu headed their way. "Jin wanted to show Mey something."

Behind him, Alfie and Jay walked in with the rest of their luggage.

The ledgers had remained on the jet under the pilot's care. Morris had assured him that he had nothing to worry about and that he wouldn't let anything happen to them, but Vrog still worried.

The cases they had gotten on the way to the airport were durable, but they were not fireproof, only fire resistant, and Vrog regretted listening to Jay and Morris and taking the files out of the safes.

"Where are we going?" he asked as Arwel continued climbing the stairs.

"To Kalugal's suite. That's where everyone is right now." Arwel cast him an amused smile. "I know that you're anxious to meet Aliya."

There was no point denying it. The empathic Guardian could no doubt sense his excitement. "I am. Is she excited to see me?"

"She's trying to play it cool, but I can tell that she's anxious as well."

Anxious was not the same as excited or happy, but Vrog was confident that he could quickly change that. He would show Aliya that he was nothing like the cruel pureblooded males and the other hybrids she might remember from the compound. They had been savages, while he was a well-educated, cultured male.

Then again, he knew nothing about her except that she'd lived like a recluse for the past fourteen years. She might prefer a more rugged type of male.

On the third floor, they were intercepted by Jin and Mey, who must have used the elevator. As Jin opened the door, Vrog craned his neck trying to get his first peek at Aliya, but she wasn't in his line of sight.

Was she hiding from him?

"Welcome," Kalugal said as they entered. "I ordered lunch, and it's going to be delivered shortly. I hope you're all hungry."

"We are," Yamanu said. "Nice place you got here."

Vrog scanned the suite for Aliya, finally finding her standing on the balcony with her back to the room as if she was not at all interested in meeting him.

Her height and coloring were Kra-ell, but since she was wearing a baggy sweatshirt, he couldn't see her waist, which in the case of pureblooded females was extremely narrow.

Having a tiny waist had been a source of pride for Jade and the others, but in his opinion, it had made them look even more alien and wasn't all that attractive.

Nevertheless, it was obvious that the woman leaning over the railing was Aliya. His heart sank.

If this was his welcome, he shouldn't expect an invitation from that female anytime soon, or ever.

He'd been prepared for rejection, reminding himself that Aliya wasn't his only option. A match had been found for him, a clan female whose profile and wishes matched his, and he was to join her on a virtual adventure as soon as he returned to the village.

Still, Aliya's dismissive attitude hurt.

Sensing his eyes on her, or maybe just hearing the commotion of the two teams greeting one another, she finally pushed away from the railing and turned around.

As their eyes met through the glass, Vrog felt like he'd been hit by lightning. He couldn't decide whether that was good or bad, but it was powerful, and he suspected that Aliya felt the same.

Her enormous eyes widened and blazed green, which was a dead giveaway of the emotional turmoil she felt. And as she walked over to the glass door and reached for the handle, he looked at her hand and saw the slight tremor she was trying to hide.

Her reaction relieved some of his anxiety, and as she opened the door and stepped inside, he smiled and walked toward her.

"Hello, Aliya." He offered her his hand. "My heart is overflowing with gratitude to the Mother for taking you under her wing and saving your life."

Even though handshaking was not a Kra-ell custom, she placed her hand in his. "I'm also grateful to the Mother for sparing your life. I heard that you were away when we were attacked."

Her palm was calloused, and he held it gently, mindful of the injuries she'd sustained working to save Kalugal and the others. They probably no longer hurt, but he didn't want to take a chance that they did.

"I was in Singapore. When my emails and phone calls went unanswered, I got worried and came back home. I found the compound deserted, and most of it burned to the ground." He swallowed. "I rebuilt it, hoping Jade would return, and in the meantime, I opened an international school on the premises. I knew Jade would appreciate the tribe's money being used for a profitable endeavor."

Aliya nodded. "Alena and Arwel told me about your school."

"Hello, pretty lady." Yamanu snuck up on them, a testament to how absorbed they had been in one another. "I'm Yamanu, Jin's sister's mate." He offered Aliya his hand.

She looked down, and she and Vrog realized at the same time that they were still holding on.

When Vrog let go of her hand, Aliya seemed confused for a moment, but then she shook her head and placed it in Yamanu's enormous paw. "It is nice to meet you, Yamanu. Jin told me a lot about Mey and you."

"I hope only good things." He winked.

59

ALIYA

*V*rog was very handsome, more so than Aliya had remembered, but he also looked more human than she'd expected. Was that a good thing or bad? She wasn't sure. He looked like a teacher, not a warrior, and he talked like one too. His English was perfect, including his accent, and he was very eloquent, polite, and cultured.

The aggression was there, she could sense it just under the surface, and it excited her. The question was how tightly Vrog had it leashed, and whether he was capable of unleashing it.

Did she want him to?

Aliya had no clue. The farthest she'd gotten with her girly fantasies was passionate kisses, which she hadn't experienced but had seen others exchange. As for the rest, she wasn't sure which side of her was more dominant. Would she have to become a snarling beast to get aroused like the pureblooded females had? Or would she enjoy softer touches like the human Mosuo?

The problem was that Vrog most likely assumed that she'd taken plenty of males into her bed and was experienced. Revealing that she was a clueless thirty-year-old virgin would be so incredibly embarrassing.

What if she seduced Phinas first and got it out of the way?

A Kra-ell would expect her not to limit herself to one lover, but if Vrog had adopted human attitudes toward sex, he might not like that.

Kalugal clapped his hands to get everyone's attention. "Lunch is served."

As everyone took their seats, Aliya found herself sitting across from Vrog, which was more awkward than if she was seated next to him. Now, every time she lifted her head, she had to look at him.

"I see that you can eat a variety of foods like I do," Vrog said. "That's very advantageous. Emmett, the other hybrid male who found his way to the clan, can only drink blood and eat nearly raw meat."

I. T. LUCAS

"He shouldn't eat an animal's flesh if he can subsist on its blood. That's wasteful and an affront to the Mother."

Vrog smiled indulgently. "Not everyone interprets the Mother's teachings so literally. There are many interpretations of what the nine commands mean. Some say that you shouldn't eat the meat of animals in the wild, but animals that are raised for that purpose are okay. It's also permitted to eat the flesh when there is not enough blood to sustain you. The Mother does not require you to forfeit your life to obey her commands. Your life always comes first. Others interpret the Mother's wishes still differently. Since she doesn't discriminate between her creatures and allows predators to hunt and kill their prey, it could be argued that since we are predators as well, we should be allowed to hunt and kill our food."

Aliya felt her cheeks heat up. "I didn't know that there were so many interpretations of the Mother's will. I was just eight when I was forced to leave the compound, and my knowledge of the Kra-ell ways was limited. I tried to follow them to the best of my ability."

"That's admirable, and your strict interpretation is the traditional one. I think the others were later adaptations, except for the one that puts your own life ahead. To save yourself, you are allowed to break each of the nine commands."

She let out a breath. "So I can still follow it the way I understand it."

"Of course. We are all free to worship in our own way. There is no right or wrong."

She shook her head. "I don't agree. I still think that killing animals for food is wrong unless it's to avoid starvation."

He waved his hand over the table. "But you don't mind that the people around you are enjoying animal flesh. You don't preach to them that it's wrong. Therefore, you accept their right to choose their way."

"They are not followers of the Mother. They are free to do as they please."

"My brother is vegan," Alena said. "You and he share the same opinion. But since he doesn't need blood to survive, he doesn't drink it either."

Aliya allowed herself to smile. "That is a surprise. I imagined him as a fearsome warrior."

Kalugal chuckled. "One has nothing to do with the other. Kian is fearsome alright, but he's also a sanctimonious prick who has to prove that he's morally superior."

Aliya had no idea what 'sanctimonious prick' meant, but she understood that acting morally superior was not a good thing. Was that Kalugal's way of hinting that she was being rude and also a sanctimonious prick?

Alena chuckled. "That's funny coming from you. Kian just chooses not to eat meat if he doesn't have to. You like to show off in other ways."

"That I do." Kalugal smiled. "I like your brother, and I respect him, but I could do with a little less of his holier-than-thou shtick."

Despite his comment about Kian's moral superiority annoying him, Kalugal had sounded impressed by him, and he wasn't a male who was easily impressed. That meant that the leader of the clan was a formidable man, and she hoped that her drinking of blood didn't offend him.

What if he considered it morally wrong?

"You invited me to live in the village, but you have not secured your leader's permission. What if he doesn't allow me in?"

580

"Don't worry about it." Kalugal waved a dismissive hand. "Kian already approved your visit. Your continued stay is conditional, though. You will have to prove yourself."

"What if he finds me unsuitable in some way and turns me away? Are you going to send me back here even if I don't complete my three-month trial period?"

"Of course. And you still get to keep the apartment I bought you, so in either case, you won't be homeless again." He leaned forward. "But don't worry. Unless you go nuts and start snarling and biting people, Kian is not going to turn you away."

6 0

VROG

*V*rog wasn't sure that he'd heard correctly. "I must have misunderstood." He looked at Kalugal. "Did you buy Aliya an apartment?"

"You understood correctly. I did buy her an apartment in Lijiang, so if she's unhappy in the village, she has a home to go back to." Kalugal smiled at Aliya. "I couldn't think of her ever living in caves or tunnels again. Not that I think she would want to come back after experiencing the village, but if that makes her feel less trapped, then it was worth the money I spent on it."

The territorial rage flaring up in Vrog's chest like a bonfire startled him. As a Kra-ell male, he shouldn't feel possessiveness, but apparently his human side had taken over.

The anger was suffocating in its intensity.

It should have been him buying Aliya a place to live, taking care of her, and making sure she had everything she needed. It was his duty, his obligation, not Kalugal's.

The guy was rich, and the money he'd spent on the apartment was peanuts to him, but Vrog could have certainly afforded it as well. He might have not been able to get Aliya even a rundown studio in Beijing, but he sure as hell could have gotten her an apartment in Lijiang.

Kalugal was lucky that Vrog knew for a fact that he couldn't have been interested in Aliya sexually and therefore hadn't gotten her the apartment to buy her affections. The guy was not only mated but also bonded to Jacki, and Vrog knew what that meant to immortals.

If not for that bond, Kalugal would be a dead immortal, and the irony of that statement was not lost on Vrog.

The Kra-ell females might have shared several males, and the males accepted that as a necessary way of life, but that was not the case for him and Aliya. There were no other Kra-ell, pureblooded or hybrid, for them to form a tribe with, and Kalugal was the exclusive property of Jacki.

"You forgot to tell Vrog that I tricked you into it." Aliya cast Kalugal an apologetic look. "And also about the agreement we reached."

Kalugal waved a dismissive hand. "Feel free to fill in the details."

Vrog was very interested in those details.

Aliya exhaled a long breath as if bracing for the explanation. "Kalugal offered to compensate me for the loss of my hiding place. He told me that I could spend as much money as I wanted during our shopping trip to Lijiang. I challenged him, asking what if I ended up spending a million yuan, and he said I could, but only if I spent it all during that one day. I said that there was no way to spend so much money in a few hours, and Jin said that it could be easily done if I bought expensive jewelry. I said that I would never spend money on such a frivolous thing, and then it occurred to me that I could buy an apartment with such an amount. I expected Kalugal to take it back because he didn't mean it, but he stood by his promise and even bought me an apartment that cost more than the one million yuan he'd promised me."

The whole speech was delivered in under a minute, and at the end of it, Aliya sucked in a breath. "I thought that he would back out and say it was just a joke, but I was wrong. Kalugal is an honorable man."

Vrog didn't know how to feel about that. Should he thank Kalugal for his generosity?

Yes, that was the polite thing to do, even though he hated the guy for taking away what should have been his.

"You are very generous. Thank you for taking care of Aliya."

"It was my pleasure." Kalugal refilled Jacki's plate from one of the communal platters. "But it's all going to come back to me anyway. If Aliya decides to stay in the village, which I'm convinced she will, we will rent out her apartment, and the proceeds will go to one of the charities Jacki and I support."

"Only if I find a job," Aliya corrected him. "If I don't, I will rely on that money for my support."

"You'll make plenty as a Guardian," Jin said. "Even during training."

Vrog arched a brow. "You think Aliya wants to be a Guardian?"

"Why not?" Aliya asked. "I would love to help fight those terrible slavers who trick and abduct young women and then sell them as sex slaves. I cannot think of a more honorable thing to do than saving these victims."

It seemed that Aliya's future had been all mapped out for her without his input. Obviously, it was her prerogative, but Vrog doubted Kalugal and the others had presented her with all the other possible options she might consider.

"You don't have to work for money, Aliya."

She tilted her head. "I don't?"

"I founded the school with the tribe's money, and I've been growing it over the years and saving it for Jade's return. But since it doesn't seem that she and the other females will ever get free from their abductors, this money belongs to you as much as it belongs to me."

Aliya gaped at him, and so did everyone else around the table.

Vrog hadn't planned to say that. He hadn't even thought it through before blurting it out, but he didn't regret making the offer. Aliya was entitled to that money as much as he was. In fact, so was Emmett, but since he'd fled the tribe and

Jade's rule, that was arguable. It wasn't in Aliya's case. She was a survivor, same as he was, and it was her birthright.

Besides, his generous offer to share with Aliya everything he'd worked for outshone Kalugal's generosity.

"I don't know what to say," Aliya murmured.

Vrog wanted to reach for her hand, but she was across the table from him, so all he could do was look at her with fondness and promise in his eyes. "We can work out the details later, but I just wanted you to know that you have options. Living in the immortals' village and becoming a Guardian is just one of them."

He was so glad that he'd made the offer.

The village was beautiful, and life there was good. Kalugal was right that after spending three months there, Aliya would not want to leave. The offer to share the school with her gave Vrog a fighting chance of convincing her to leave the comfort of the village and join him.

61

KIAN

"Come in, Gavin." Kian motioned for the architect to put his plans down on the conference table. "Show me what you have."

Gavin spread the plans out on the table, using the two bottles of water Kian had put there to weigh the thing down so it wouldn't curl back up.

"As per your instructions, I kept it simple so the structure could be manufactured using the 3D printer. As for the finishes inside, I leave that up to Ingrid."

"No problem."

"Grading will be a challenge." Gavin pointed to the area designated for the paranormal division of Safe Haven. "The terrain is rocky, and it will be a bitch to create a buildable pad, which is why I separated the facilities into several smaller structures instead of building one that was large enough to house everything we need. As always, a challenge incites creativity, and creativity offers solutions that turn out to be more interesting and more beautiful than what would have otherwise been done if the conditions were perfect." He smiled proudly.

"I like it." Kian was impressed with what Gavin had achieved in such a short time. What he was showing him was much more than conceptual drawings.

"The small structures are all on different levels, which provides visual interest and landscaping opportunities. Each classroom has its own small building, and the residential quarters are individual bungalows instead of one large lodge. They are small, about eight hundred to one thousand square feet each, but with the abundance of windows and the open space around them, they will feel more spacious. This is the administrative building, which as you can see is about the size of one of these bungalows, and that's the gym, which is slightly larger. The dining hall and kitchen are about fifteen hundred square feet, and there is plenty of space for outdoor dining when weather conditions permit. The bungalow at the top of the hill will serve future potential Dormants and their mates."

"That's less of a concern now that we have Kalugal and Eleanor to compel their silence, but I love having the option." Kian flipped to the next sheet. "Basically, you have kept it to simple rectangles, letting the landscaping and interior design provide the individualized aesthetics and interest."

"Precisely. I will also vary the stucco colors, the shutter shapes and colors, and the roof materials, so it will look like a village that was built over time and not all in one shot."

"Unlike ours."

Gavin shrugged. "You wanted uniformity of design, and you got it. But I introduced enough variety in the different layouts and façades. I knew that you wanted to build the Safe Haven project even faster than what we did here, so I didn't want to complicate it and kept it as simple as possible. All the windows and doors are the same standard sizes, and so are the bathrooms and kitchens. Makes ordering materials and installation a breeze."

"Great work, Gavin. When will the final plans be ready?"

"If there are no changes, I can finish everything in two days."

"Just one thing. How difficult would it be to connect the structures with an underground tunnel system? Winters there are brutal."

"It will be costly, and it will complicate the project."

"Can you give me a time and cost estimate?"

"Sure. I'll need a day or two to do that."

"Try to do it in one. How about the utilities? Is there enough juice left over for the new section?"

"Barely, but since it's not going to house many people, it should suffice. If not, we will have to implement some of what we did in the village, meaning water desalinating equipment and a small nuclear generator."

"I hope there will be no need for that. As it is, I'm spending more than I initially wanted on this project. The lodge renovation has started, and Leon tells me that it's going well, and we are also remodeling the community quarters one room at a time. I expect these people to maintain the paranormal section as well, and I can't leave them living in squalor. I know that they are all into self-sacrifice as a form of enlightenment, but I'm not. Once I'm done with the place, every room and bungalow should be comfortable enough for me to stay in or invite my friends to." He chuckled. "The only one who might find it lacking is Kalugal, but he's welcome to contribute to the project if he wants to visit and lodge in luxury."

"I couldn't agree more." Gavin rolled the plans back and secured them with a rubber band. "Are we using our regular tactics in regard to securing permits, or are we just going to build what we want and plant fake permits later?"

"The second one. No city inspector is going to come all the way out there to check if work is being done. And if one does, we can deal with them. I want this place up and running in a month."

Gavin chuckled. "Of course, you do."

62

VROG

*A*fter lunch was over and several members of both groups had left while others chatted and made plans for the rest of the day, Vrog seized the opportunity to take the vacated seat next to Aliya.

"Would you like to go for a walk with me?" he asked.

She glanced at Kalugal. "I don't know if I'm allowed."

Even though he disapproved of Kalugal having a say in what she was allowed or disallowed to do, Vrog forced his expression to remain amiable. The demigod might be a big deal in the village, but it wasn't his place to rule over Aliya.

Instead, he offered, "We can ask him."

Aliya cast another quick glance at Kalugal, but he was busy talking with Yamanu and didn't notice. "I don't think he would mind," she said. "But why do you want to be alone with me?"

She was blunt, and Vrog liked that even though he wasn't. "Other than Emmett we might be the only survivors of Jade's tribe. We have a lot to talk about."

"I hope the females are alive," she murmured. "But maybe they aren't. The Mother only knows what those evil Kra-ell are doing to them."

Vrog cast a quick glance around. "The same kinds of thoughts torment me as well. I think it will help us both to talk about it."

"Okay. I'll just get my coat." Aliya rose to her feet.

She walked over to the couch, crouched, and pulled out a suitcase that had been tucked under it. Inside were neatly folded clothes. She lifted out a dark gray puffer coat, closed the suitcase, and tucked it back under the couch.

"Where are you going?" Jacki asked her when she shrugged the coat on.

"On a walk with Vrog." Aliya cast Kalugal a questioning look.

"Have fun." He waved her off and turned back to talk with Yamanu.

When they were out the door, Aliya let out a breath. "Until this morning, I couldn't even touch the door handle. Kalugal used compulsion to keep me from running away."

"How come he released you now? Was it because of your heroic efforts to save him the day before?"

"Maybe. He said that he trusted me not to run because I gave him my word that I would give the village a chance."

"Was he right?"

She narrowed her eyes at him. "Of course he was. I would never break a promise."

"Would you have run if not for the promise you gave Kalugal?"

"When they first caught me, I wanted to run. I didn't know who these people were. I thought that the bad Kra-ell found out about me and came to take me too."

Vrog wanted to ask her about the attack, but he decided against it. The subject was no doubt painful to her, and he wanted this walk to be about them getting to know each other. Some reminiscing about the good times in the compound could be enjoyable, and if she indicated an interest in him, maybe he could start with some flirting.

So far, he wasn't sure what she felt toward him. She was polite, but she wasn't friendly, and what irritated him even more was that she was much more comfortable with the immortals than she was with him.

"When you found out that they weren't Kra-ell, did you still want to run?" He opened the lobby door and held it for her.

Aliya nodded. "I didn't trust them. I didn't know what they wanted from me, and I suspected them of cooperating with those evil Kra-ell." She zipped up the jacket and pulled a pair of gloves out of her pocket. "They lured me with the simplest things. Food to fill my belly, a shower to finally get properly clean, and a soft couch to sleep on. Kalugal compelled me not to run, but I don't think I would have even without his compulsion. Then they took me shopping, and for the first time in forever, I had new things that weren't torn or dirty. And then Kalugal bought me a brand new two-bedroom apartment, and I could no longer suspect them of wishing to do me harm. I had to accept that they were good people and that they were sent by the Mother to find me and give me a home." She turned to him and smiled. "I want to believe that it was a reward for observing her rules and for acting with honor."

His heart broke for the hardships she'd endured. "The village is not your only alternative, Aliya. You could come to the school and live in the staff quarters. I can help you catch up on your education, you can go to a university and study something that interests you, and you don't need to worry about earning an income because half of the school belongs to you. You are entitled to half of the net income."

She shook her head. "It's very generous of you to offer, but I'm not entitled to your school. You built it, and you made it profitable. I'm glad that you found something that you are passionate about, but I need to find what that thing is for me, and I don't think I can get passionate about a school."

"And you think that becoming a Guardian is your true calling? You haven't explored all the possibilities. Being a Guardian is just one option among many."

"It appeals to me. I want to help these poor victims who were sold into sex slavery in any way I can, and if I can get paid for doing that, it's even better." She pushed her hands into the coat pockets. "I can't help you run the school, and even if I could, that's not what I want to do with my life. Besides, I would need to keep hiding and pretending that I'm human, while in the village, I can be myself."

"I understand." Vrog mimicked her and pushed his hands into his pockets as well. "I have a son in the village, and I love spending time with him and his fiancée. But I also love my school." He gave her a sad smile. "It's difficult to be torn between two loves that are on opposite sides of the world."

Aliya stopped walking. "Carol and Alena told me that you have a son who is very nice and dresses like a Goth. I was curious about how you met his mother."

Vrog hadn't meant to reveal having a son so soon, but now he was glad that he had. Evidently, Aliya already knew about Vlad, and if he kept it from her, she would have wondered about his reasons.

All he'd hoped for was to get her to like him before telling her about his son, but from her perspective, that could have been perceived as cowardly or dishonest.

"A long time ago, I had a short fling with a lady who I thought was human. When I discovered that she was immortal, I had already planted my seed in her womb. She refused to abort it, for which I'm eternally grateful to her. She vowed to keep the identity of the father a secret, and we parted ways. I never expected to meet her again or to get to know my son, but the Mother had other plans." He put his hand on her shoulder. "I would like you to meet Vlad and Wendy. I think you will find their company very pleasant."

63

ALIYA

"I like all the immortals I've met so far, and since your son is half immortal half Kra-ell, I'm sure that I'm going to like him as well. You are incredibly lucky to have a long-lived son. You must have pleased the Mother greatly to earn such a boon."

Aliya was keenly aware of Vrog's hand on her shoulder. Was she supposed to allow it? Was it a test?

Observing the pureblooded females back in the compound, she had never seen any display of affection between them and the males. The males were respectful, the females domineering, and most of the time, everyone treated each other with respect. Occasionally, though, tempers flared, or something was construed as an offense or disobedience, and then all hell broke loose. She'd made herself scarce at those times, running back to the human quarters as fast as her legs could carry her.

His hand on her shoulder didn't feel bad, though, so she decided to pretend that she hadn't noticed it and ignore it.

"I don't know what I did to deserve Vlad." He took his hand off her shoulder and resumed walking. "I was very young at the time, and I hadn't accomplished much yet."

Aliya missed the contact. She hadn't had anyone touch her with affection in so long that she hadn't even realized how starved she was for it. Fourteen years had passed since her mother's death, and she had been the only person who'd ever loved her. The only one she'd loved.

"I hope to never have children." Her throat constricting, she looked straight ahead. "I don't want to outlive them."

Her mother's death had devastated her. She couldn't fathom losing a child.

Vrog cleared his throat. "I don't want to appear presumptuous, and I know that we've just met, and it's too early to talk about things like that, but if you find me pleasing and invite me to share your bed, we might produce a long-lived child together. The adult hybrid females of our tribe never invited the hybrid males to their beds because they preferred the purebloods to father their children, but I think there is a good chance that two hybrids can produce a long-lived child."

As Aliya's cheeks caught fire, she kept her eyes on the path ahead, avoiding looking at Vrog. "If you mate a clan female, you can have an immortal child for sure. You already have one. Why take the risk with me?"

"Because we are of the same people. Naturally, you can choose any of the clan males if you like, but they can't give you a long-lived child. The immortal genes only pass through the females of the clan."

"I know that. They explained it to me. Right now, I'm not looking for a mate. I need to find my place in the world first."

That was such a lie.

Circumstances had inhibited her feminine urges for many years, but now that her belly was full, she wasn't cold, and she wasn't afraid of what the next day would bring, they were awakening.

"Of course." Vrog bowed his head. "Forgive me for bringing it up."

Great. Now he thought that he had no chance with her, when nothing could be further from the truth.

Vrog wasn't like the pureblooded males or even the hybrids, but that wasn't a bad thing. He was capable of love, and he was growing on her. She liked his calm manner, his eloquence, his quiet confidence. He was more human than Kra-ell, but surprisingly she found it very attractive. He didn't stir her innate aggression, and that was a good thing too. She didn't want to be cruel like the pureblooded females. She didn't want to fight him and hurt him until he managed to subdue her to prove his worth.

More than anything, Aliya wanted to be loved.

Finally daring to look at him, she asked, "When we leave on Monday, are you going back to your school?"

"I'm not. I'm coming with you." He regarded her hesitantly to gauge her response. "My visit in the village was cut short, and I didn't have enough time with my son. Kian wanted me to take Mey to the school so she could listen to the echoes and possibly find out more about what happened in the compound, but he said that I'm welcome to visit any time. I promised Vlad and his fiancée that I would return."

A weight rolled off Aliya's chest. "I'm glad. Maybe we can spend more time together there. You could introduce me to your son and future daughter-in-law."

If the son was like the father, and his fiancée was as nice as the immortals she'd met so far, she would enjoy their company. Maybe they could even become friends.

"I would like that very much." Grinning, Vrog didn't try to hide how happy her wish to meet his son made him.

His human side was definitely more dominant than the Kra-ell.

"Can you tell me how the clan found you?"

"They didn't tell you?"

She shook her head. "Just bits and pieces here and there. I had a feeling that they didn't want to tell me. Did you do something bad?"

He chuckled. "You could say that. I attacked Stella, Vlad's mother."

"Why?"

"I thought she had something to do with the attack on our people."

"Why would you think that?"

"Because it happened shortly after I met her."

64

ALENA

"What are you smiling about?" Orion asked as they entered their hotel room.

Alena walked into the bathroom and sat on the edge of the tub. "Aliya and Vrog. I think there is a spark there. They went on a very long walk, and when they returned, they both seemed much less tense." She chuckled. "Kalugal probably started to worry."

"No, he didn't." Orion leaned against the vanity and crossed his arms over his chest. "He meant it when he said that he trusted her. I trust her too. She is not the type to go back on her word."

Alena turned the faucet on and checked the water until it reached the right temperature. "You like her."

He nodded. "She's strange, and it takes time to peel off her layers, but under the rough exterior beats a good heart."

"It's a miracle that she hasn't gone insane after living in isolation for fourteen years. Humans, immortals, Kra-ell, and even the gods need a community of people to interact with. We are not meant to be alone."

"She ventured into the Mosuo village from time to time, so she wasn't completely isolated. Besides, one can be surrounded by people and still be alone."

She'd forgotten that until very recently, Orion had lived among humans, and his only contact was a half-sister and niece, who he couldn't allow to remember him.

That must have been so damn lonely, and the talk about Aliya's isolation had reminded him of it.

Alena knew exactly how to cheer him up. Pulling her sweater over her head, she tossed it at him. "That's enough talk about Aliya."

"Agreed." His eyes glowing, Orion sauntered over and kneeled at her feet. "Let me help you undress."

Smiling, she lifted her foot for him to remove her shoe.

He gently gripped her ankle and took off the ballet flat. "Pretty color." He looked at her pink toes.

"It matches the polish on my nails." She wiggled her fingers. "My nails weren't as badly chipped as Jin's or ruined like Aliya's, but they needed some tender care." She sighed. "I wasn't as helpful as they were."

"But you saved the day." He gripped her left ankle and took the shoe off. "If you didn't come up with the idea to bring the Odus, Jacki would have for sure peed her pants because it would have taken us much longer to get them out. Actually, I don't think we could have done it without the Odus."

Alena shuddered. "If I never see another tunnel again, it will be too soon."

He chuckled. "You have to see one every time you enter the village."

She pouted. "I don't see it because the windows of the cars turn opaque, but thanks for reminding me. Now I will have a mini panic attack every time I have to go through it."

"I'm sorry." He lifted her foot and started kissing her toes one at a time. "I promise that in a few moments, you'll forget all about it."

As he kissed her instep, she stifled a giggle. "That tickles."

Smiling evilly, he did the same to her other arch. When she laughed, he kissed it again, and then lifted her with one hand while tugging her pants down with the other.

When all she had left on her body was a bra, he pushed up on his knees and pressed a soft kiss to one swell and then the other before reaching behind her and unhooking it.

She held her breath as he blew on each nipple and then kissed them lightly. Licking and nibbling, he tormented her with pleasure until she was writhing on the edge of the tub. Pulling back a little, he regarded her glistening tips with satisfaction.

"Let's get you into the tub." He lifted her and slowly deposited her in the water.

"Come join me." She scooted to the side. "There is enough room."

He shook his head. "If I get in, we will cause a flood. I have a better plan." He reached for a washcloth and squirted liquid soap on it. "I'll be your devoted servant tonight. I'll bathe you, towel you dry, carry you to bed, and give you a massage."

Alena wasn't sure she could survive all that before throwing him on the bed and having her way with him, but she was willing to play along, especially since it involved Orion's hands all over her body.

He would probably snap before she did.

"I like your plan." She sprawled in the bathtub. Resting her head and arms on the lip of the tub, she closed her eyes and surrendered to his ministrations.

65

ORION

Orion took great pleasure in bathing Alena, his palm following the trail he made with the washcloth over her smooth skin, caressing gently, intimately.

He wished she'd let him wash her hair, but she didn't want to ruin the hairdo she'd gotten earlier in the spa. It was a shame. He loved massaging her scalp, working the shampoo into the long, luxurious strands of her hair. But even more than that, he loved washing her breasts, her belly, her thighs, her feminine center.

"You're teasing me," she murmured. "You keep doing that, and I'll pull you into the tub and mount you."

He chuckled. "Is that supposed to be a threat?"

"It's a heads up in case you want to undress first and save your clothes from getting shredded."

She sounded deliciously vicious, and he teased her for a little longer just to hear her threatening him again. He had no intentions of taking her in the bathtub. He had a plan, and he was sticking to it.

"Last warning, Orion." She cut him a mock glare.

With a laugh, he reached for the large towel he'd brought over and fluffed it out. "Come on, princess. Time for stage two of tonight's session."

He helped her out of the tub, wrapped her in the towel, and carried her to the bed.

After patting her dry, he tossed the towel aside and laid her on her belly. "Magnificent." He dipped his head to kiss the round swells of her bottom.

She arched up, and he kissed lower, but he didn't linger. Tearing himself away from the intoxicating scent of her arousal, he reached for the lotion and applied generous amounts to his palms.

"You're such a terrible tease, Orion."

"Patience, my love." When he put his hands on her calves, she groaned. "That feels good."

"I've only just started." He began a slow progression, kneading and stroking up her thighs, and then he was cupping her generous bottom. He lingered there, kneading her lush mounds for much longer than necessary, but then this wasn't about relaxation, it was about slow, torturous seduction.

As he moved up to her back, he kissed her spine, and as she wiggled and writhed over the bedding, he nipped her ear. "Patience is not your strong suit, is it?"

"Patience is overrated." She turned around and pulled him over her. "And you are overdressed."

Orion chuckled. "If only people knew what a tigress sweet Alena really is." He took her lips in a soft kiss. "But I'm glad that I'm the only one you show this side of you to."

Her glowing eyes softened. "I love you, and I know that you love me in all of my facets, the sweet and the spicy. I'm free to explore the other sides of me that have been stifled in favor of the one everyone expects to see."

His heart swelled with love and gratitude for the incredible gift she was giving him and would keep on giving for eternity. They were bonded, there was no doubt in either of their minds that their bond had solidified and was unbreakable.

Alena's lips twitched with a smile. "If you're going to keep staring at me instead of getting rid of your clothes, I'm going to do it for you."

"You're full of threats today." He dipped his head and took her nipple between his lips.

Licking it, he smoothed his hand down her belly to her center and slid a finger into her. When she moaned and writhed on it, he added another one. She moaned again, her hands closing around fistfuls of his hair and tugging his head to her other nipple.

He wanted his tongue to go where his fingers were, not to replace them but to add to the delicious torment, but she was holding on tight, not letting go of his hair.

Impatient minx wanted to get straight down to business, but he would have none of that.

Perhaps he needed to issue a threat of his own.

"Let go of my hair, Alena. Until I make you come with my mouth, I'm not getting rid of my clothes."

When she let go right away and spread her thighs for him, Orion laughed. "Now I know how to get you to cooperate." He slid down her body and positioned himself right where he wanted to be.

"Took you long enough to realize that." She lifted her head and gazed at him, amusement and desire dancing in her eyes. "I'll do anything to get you naked."

"Anything?" He treated her to a long lick.

"Anything." She let her head drop back on the mattress.

66

ALENA

*W*ould it always be like this? The insatiable need to be joined? Their bodies hungry for each other, their minds never wandering too far off the other?

In one way or another, Orion was always on Alena's mind. Everything she did, she considered how it would impact him, would he approve, not because he was demanding or hard to please, but because she loved him and wanted to be the best version of herself for him.

When his mouth replaced his fingers, and he slid his hands under her bottom to lift her, like he was raising a platter so he could feast, her core clenched in anticipation.

He delved deeper, taunting and teasing, giving her just enough stimulation to bring her close to the edge but not to topple over.

Panting, she clutched at the bedsheets next to her, her hips churning on the mattress as much as his grip allowed. She braced for a prolonged torment, but then he let go of one side, plunged two fingers into her, and closed his lips around the bundle of nerves at the top of her cleft.

The climax tore through her like a tornado, and he helped her ride it out—his fingers plunging in and out of her, his tongue lapping at her juices, hungry groans leaving his throat.

When she collapsed, exhausted from the powerful orgasm, he pressed one last gentle kiss to her folds before leaving her for a split second to get naked.

"Finally." Alena cracked her eyes open just as Orion prowled on top of her.

Her male was magnificent. His lean body was made of powerful muscles and smooth, olive-toned skin, his long hair fell forward, framing his gorgeous face, his blue and violet eyes were aglow, and his fangs were fully extended.

She wrapped her arms around his torso and arched up to rub herself against his hard shaft, coating it with the copious juices from her climax.

Baring his fangs, Orion growled and with one powerful surge, joined them.

Alena cried out at the sheer perfection of it. Her inner nerve endings were still overstimulated from the powerful orgasm he'd given her, and as he withdrew and plunged in, she climaxed again.

The look of satisfaction on his face was precious.

"You're mine, Alena, and I can't believe how fortunate I am to have you give your-self to me."

"And you are mine, Orion. And I also thank the Fates every day for the gift of you."

It was a sweet moment, and she was going to remember it forever, but she needed him to move.

As if reading her mind, Orion started with shallow, gentle thrusts that lasted for about thirty seconds, and then he gripped her hips and gave her what she needed.

They were making a racket, and the Odus in the next room over could hear every screech of the bed's legs on the floor, every bang of the headboard on the wall, and every moan and groan leaving her and Orion's throats, but Alena didn't care.

Heck, she didn't care if every immortal in the hotel heard them.

When they both hovered over the edge and Orion hissed, she turned her head, elongating her neck for him, and when the bite came, she didn't try to hold on to reality and let herself soar on the clouds of euphoria.

Orion would keep her safe, and when she floated down to earth, he would be there to catch her.

67

DARLENE

*A*s Darlene entered the hair salon, Judy, her stylist, waved her over to her station. "What a nice surprise to see you here today." She unfurled a big nylon cape and motioned for Darlene to take a seat. "I wasn't expecting you for another two weeks. Do you have an event or a special occasion that you need to look pretty for?" She draped it over Darlene's front and closed it at the back of her neck.

"Yes." Sort of. "I'm invited to dinner with my cousins tonight, but that's just an excuse. I feel like I need a change. Maybe a new hair color? Or perhaps a more youthful style?"

Standing behind her, Judy fluffed up her hair, brought it all forward, and then combed it to the side. "Let me bring you a few style journals to flip through."

"Okay."

Darlene had hoped that Judy would know what to do, magically transforming her into a beautiful young woman with the help of her styling shears.

Right. Only a surgeon's knife could perform such a magical feat. She'd been spending too many hours on that plastic surgery website, looking at before and after images, and wondering whether she would ever have the courage to go for a facelift or a nose job.

Heck, a boob job and a tummy tuck could probably improve her looks more than anything she could do to her face.

Except, she was too much of a coward to do any of that, and Leo would never let her spend the money anyway.

She'd been feeling odd lately, like something was missing from her life.

She also felt resentful toward Leo and had a hard time hiding it.

Well, she always felt that, but lately it was more than usual. She was short-tempered, argumentative, and after one too many snapping comments, Leo packed up his things and left, telling her to calm the fuck down and call him when she was back to normal.

Supposedly, Leo's boss was sending him on a month-long acquisition trip for the gallery, but Darlene doubted that. It was a cover story for what he was really up to, which was most likely shagging a young mistress.

She had no proof that he was cheating on her, but with the way things were between them lately, it was a safe bet that he was.

"So here is what I think." Judy handed her a journal already open on a page. "This hair color." She pointed to the auburn-streaked shoulder-length hairstyle. "With this cut." She thrust another journal into Darlene's hands.

The style was much shorter than what she had now, but it looked young and pretty and was precisely the look she was going for. Not that there was any chance she would look like the model, but she hoped it would be an improvement.

"I like it." She handed back the two journals to Judy.

"Don't you want to flip through them? Maybe you'll find something that you like more? I want it to be your choice."

For some reason, Judy's words brought about a sense of déjà vu. Something about red and blue pills and having to choose one.

She must have dreamt something, and her brain had stored pieces of the dream but not the entire story, so she had no reference to figure out what it meant.

Looking up at the stylist, she smiled. "You've been coloring and cutting my hair for years. I trust you."

She'd been going to the same hair salon for over twenty years, and not because Judy was such a great stylist. Darlene clung to the familiar and hated changes, even simple ones like going to a new hairdresser.

"Thanks." Judy took the magazines and put them back on the waiting area's table. "You will look great. I'm going to mix the color and be right back."

As Darlene waited for Judy's return, she looked in the mirror at the other hair-dressers and their clients. She knew most of them, not by name, but she knew their faces. Most were like her, loyal clients who'd been coming here for years, and yet she'd never engaged any of them in conversation, never asked what their names were, and never took part in the chatting that went on around her.

Was it any wonder that she was lonely?

Her social skills sucked, and that was why she was so dependent on Leo. She had no network of friends, and her family lived far away, so she had only him.

But that was no longer true.

She had a newly discovered family, her cousins Geraldine and Cassandra, and their boyfriends. They seemed just as starved for a connection as she was, or they wouldn't have proactively sought her company.

She should initiate get-togethers and get Cassandra to invite Roni and his girl-friend as well. Darlene still didn't have her son's phone number and couldn't call him even if she had it.

Roni lived in hiding, avoiding capture by the agents that still watched their house. She'd thought that they were long gone, but according to Onegus, her and Leo's cell phones were monitored, and so was the landline to their house.

Perhaps today, she would suggest their next lunch or dinner meeting, or maybe a shopping spree. With Leo gone, she was a free woman and could do as she pleased. It would be so nice to go shopping without him checking where she was every ten minutes and frowning over every little thing she bought for herself.

Looking in the mirror, she eyed the beautician's station and wondered whether the woman could squeeze her in without an appointment. Her eyebrows could use a professional touchup, and she might even go for the eyelashes and brow tinting she'd been wanting to get for so long and was afraid to.

68

RONJA

*A*s Lisa left the kitchen to set up the table in the dining room, Ronja marked the calendar she'd taped to the fridge and sighed. It had been six days since she and Merlin had started working on her transition, and nothing was happening yet.

Well, working wasn't the right term for what they'd been doing. It wasn't a hardship to make love to Merlin twice and sometimes three times a day. Fortunately, or maybe unfortunately, he could only bite her once every twenty-four hours, and he usually did that at night, so she could float on the pleasure cloud for as long as she pleased.

Six days wasn't a long time. Merlin had told her that it had taken some of the Dormants two or even three weeks to transition, and they had been much younger than her. She shouldn't start worrying even if she didn't transition in a month. As a confirmed Dormant, there was no question about her having the immortal genes, but her age was an issue, and the transition might not start because her body couldn't take it.

Ironically, she had never felt better than she felt now, not even as a young woman. The venom was Merlin's best miracle potion. It invigorated her, smoothed out her skin, brought luster into her eyes, and had reversed the clock on her sex drive, so she was as obsessed with sex now as she'd been in her youth.

Thankfully, Merlin's work didn't suffer terribly because of their stolen moments of passion. Well, hours was more accurate. They'd just worked longer days, or rather Merlin did. Ronja had to go home to cook dinner for Lisa and spend time with her.

The first morning after Merlin had stayed the night, things had been a little awkward at breakfast, but Lisa had said that she preferred him sleeping over to Ronja spending the night over at his place. Lisa didn't want to be alone in the house, and even though Merlin's place was only two houses down, Ronja agreed with her daughter.

The result was that Merlin's place had turned fully into a lab and a makeshift fertility clinic, and her place was where they chilled in the evenings and spent their nights.

The three of them were becoming a family, and life was good, but her impending transition loomed over them like a dark cloud.

"The table is set." Lisa walked into the kitchen. "You should call Merlin and remind him that it's dinner time." She chuckled. "That man needs to be reminded to put his shoes on before leaving the house. He's such an absentminded professor."

"That's because he's brilliant." Ronja smiled. "Smart people have so many thoughts circulating in their heads that they don't pay attention to the most basic things."

"Was David and Jonah's father like that?" Lisa pulled out a stool and sat at the counter. "Michael was supposedly brilliant too."

Lisa had been a little girl when Ronja's ex-husband had died. She didn't remember him.

"He was, but in a different way than Merlin. Michael knew a lot, and he was a world-renowned cardiac specialist, but he wasn't an inventor, and his mind wasn't scattered. He had an excellent memory, and he paid attention to detail."

Excruciatingly so.

If anything was out of place, he would notice and make a comment. Ronja remembered how it had stressed her out. Keeping the house in order with twin boys running around was a losing battle, but she and the housekeeper they'd had at the time had done their best. Every night after the boys' bath, they'd stuck them in front of the television in the den, so they could put everything in order before Michael walked through the door.

He never raised his voice or his hand to her or the boys, but his disparaging looks had been nearly as bad. He had a way of making her feel worthless no matter how hard she tried to prove the opposite.

"I don't remember him," Lisa admitted. "But I remember feeling sorry for David and Jonah because he was so demanding and never happy with their achievements. My father praised me for the smallest things." She sighed. "He was a great dad."

"Oh, sweetie." Ronja walked over to Lisa and pulled her into a crushing hug. "This must be so difficult for you."

Lisa nodded. "I miss him, and I wish he were here with us, but I'm not blind. You are happier with Merlin."

It was true, but Ronja couldn't acknowledge it. "I was happy with Frank too, and I miss him. Our love might have been less fiery, but it was warm and fuzzy, and safe. I was contented."

Lisa looked doubtful, but she was smart enough to let it go. "Call Merlin, Mom."

69

CASSANDRA

"They will be here in less than ten minutes." Cassandra put her phone down. For security reasons, they'd sent an Uber to pick Darlene up at her home and drive her to one of the clan's office buildings.

Cassandra had told her that it was where Onegus worked.

He'd picked Darlene up from there and explained that Roni was joining them, which was why she had to leave her phone behind in a locker. It was also the reason he'd given her for running William's handheld bug detecting device over her.

It was a convenient excuse, and it was also partially true.

Roni was there, and his safety was paramount, but even if he wasn't, Cassandra didn't want her house to get compromised. The last thing she needed was for the agents to start monitoring her place.

It wouldn't have mattered if she'd rented the house out like she'd planned to, but she was dragging her feet about it.

That house meant a lot to her and Geraldine, and having strangers live in it just rubbed her the wrong way. It was silly, and it proved that she wasn't as pragmatic as she wanted everyone to believe she was.

"I'm nervous," Parker admitted. "How am I supposed to test whether my compulsion works on her? What if she's the type who goes along with everything she's told to do?"

"That's only true for the man I thought was my father," Roni said. "Darlene always does what he tells her to do. She's not a pushover with anyone else."

"Maybe she feels guilty?" Geraldine suggested. "It might be her way of atoning for lying to him for all these years."

Roni grimaced. "Thanks. So now it's my fault that my mother is punishing herself by staying married to a miserable jerk."

"It's not your fault that you were born as a result of a fling," Sylvia said. "Your mother's decisions and their consequences are on her, not you."

"People." Cassandra clapped her hands. "Let's concentrate on coming up with a good test for Parker. We don't have much time."

"I know how to test her," Roni said. "When I was a little kid, my mother used to sing me this one song that I loved, but only when we were alone. She thinks that her voice is terrible, and if I bring it up and ask her to sing it for me in company, she will refuse. If Parker asks her and she starts singing, we will have our answer."

"That's good." Cassandra moved the vase a fraction of an inch to the right, centering it on the dining table. "Anything else? We need one more as a backup plan."

"I could ask her to tell me the most embarrassing moment of her life," Parker said. "We can pretend to play a game of truth or dare."

"That would have been an excellent idea if we were teenagers." Cassandra patted the boy's back. "Grownups don't play truth or dare."

"It's a backup plan," Shai said. "If the singing one is not conclusive, we can use Parker's idea."

When Onegus's car pulled up in front of the house, Cassandra opened the door and stepped out to greet her sister.

The woman who exited the vehicle looked transformed.

"Oh my, Darlene. You look amazing." She pulled her in for a quick hug. "I love the new hair. And I love your outfit."

"Thank you." Darlene smoothed her hand over her shiny, sleek hair. "My hairdresser suggested the Brazilian blowout. I'm so glad I listened to her."

Cassandra took a step back and regarded her with the critical eye of a fashion executive. "You also dyed your eyelashes and your brows. Well done, Darlene." She threaded her arm through her sister's. "You are on the right path."

"Right path to where?"

Cassandra smiled. "Growth, independence, a new life."

Darlene chuckled. "It's just a new hairdo and professionally applied makeup. I didn't win the lottery."

"Oh, I think you did. You just don't know it yet."

DARLENE

*C*assandra was a strange woman.

Darlene didn't know why she had formed that opinion about her cousin, but it had been there even before the comment about her winning the lottery but not knowing that she had.

When they walked inside, Geraldine rushed over to her and hugged her as if they hadn't seen each other in weeks. "You look so beautiful, my Darlene. This new hairdo is perfect for you."

"Thanks." Darlene kissed her cousin's cheek and looked over to where Roni was sitting with his girlfriend.

"Aren't you going to give your mother a kiss?"

He got to his feet, walked over to her, and gave her a peck on the cheek. "What's the occasion?" He waved a hand over her new hairdo. "Is it your and Leo's anniversary?"

She tilted her head. "Our anniversary is in March. Did you forget?" And since when had he started calling Leo by his given name?

"I have a bad memory for dates." Roni led her to the dining table, where a gangly teenage boy was sitting. "This is Parker. Parker, this is my mother, Darlene."

"Nice to meet you," the boy said.

"It's nice to meet you too, Parker. Are you Onegus's or Shai's nephew?"

"Parker is the son of a good friend of mine," Onegus said.

He didn't explain why the boy was there, but she assumed his parents were vacationing somewhere, and Onegus was hosting Parker while they were gone.

As everyone sat at the table, Cassandra lifted her wine glass. "To family, and many more family dinners."

"I'll drink to that." Geraldine lifted hers and clinked it with Cassandra's.

When the salute was done, and everyone had clinked everyone else's glasses, Cassandra and Geraldine removed the lids from the chafing dishes. "*Bon appétit*, everyone."

"Wow, Cassandra, you cooked up a feast." Darlene salivated over the selection. She filled her plate with thin beef slices and steamed asparagus, but she skipped the mashed potatoes even though they smelled divine. Today was the start of her new self, and along with the new hairdo, she would also start watching what she ate and include exercise in her daily routine.

"I didn't cook a thing." Cassandra put a big scoop of the yummy mashed potatoes on her plate. "I ordered catering." She gave Darlene a sly smile. "I love having the family over for dinner, but I don't have time to cook."

"Then it's a wonderful solution." Darlene admired her cousin for her resourcefulness.

If only she could be a little like Cassandra, assertive, determined, a go-getter who went for what she wanted and didn't stop until she got it. But first, she needed to figure out what she wanted.

That wasn't it.

Darlene actually knew precisely what she wanted, but there was no way she could ever get it, so what she needed to figure out was what would be a satisfying substitute for having everything she wanted in life.

Family, friends, something fulfilling to do, and no financial worries. She didn't need to be rich, but it would be nice not to worry about paying her bills.

"Do you remember the song you used to sing for me?" Roni asked out of the blue.

"'You Are My Sunshine.'"

"Yes, that's the one. I wanted to sing it for Sylvia, but I couldn't remember the words or the melody. Could you sing it for me?"

There was no way she was going to sing in public. Leo said that she sounded like a deaf goat. "I could recite the words for you."

"I want you to sing it."

She shook her head. "Maybe when we are alone. I'm too embarrassed to sing in company."

"I want to hear you sing," Parker said. "Sing for me."

Shocked at the boy's audacity, Darlene wanted to tell him to mind his manners, but instead, she found herself quietly singing the song.

"Louder," the boy commanded. "Sing louder."

Her eyes bugging out, she raised her voice even though it was the last thing she wanted to do.

"You can stop now." Parker smiled like a fiend.

"What the hell was that?" she croaked. "What kind of a trick did you use to make me sing? Was it hypnosis?"

"Close. It was compulsion." The kid turned to Onegus. "I've done my part. Now it's your turn."

71

GERALDINE

*G*eraldine's heart started pounding as frantically as it had the first time they'd told Darlene that she was her mother.

This was round two, and it might not go as well as round one had, which hadn't been great either. Darlene had listened to her explanation, so that was good, but she hadn't forgiven her, and she hadn't warmed to her. She had treated her much better when she thought that they were cousins.

As Onegus switched places with Cassandra and sat next to Darlene, Geraldine had to force herself to take a breath.

"Look at me, Darlene," Onegus said. "I'm going to release the memories I suppressed before, and as they flood back in, it might feel a little overwhelming, and you might get a headache, but the sensation shouldn't last long. I only erased the memories of what we told you during our last meeting."

She narrowed her eyes at him. "What are you talking about? I remember everything that happened during our lunch last week."

He smiled at her. "You remember what I planted in your head to fill up the gap created by what I suppressed."

"How can you do that?"

He smiled. "Instead of explaining everything once again, I'll release your memories, and if you have more questions after that, I'll try to answer as best I can. Ready?"

Looking doubtful and suspicious, she nodded nonetheless. The doubting expression turned to awed, then pained, and then she clutched at her head and whimpered. "You weren't kidding. Not about the pain and not about all the rest."

Her eyes closing again, Darlene slumped in her chair. "Give me a moment. It's all a jumbled mess in my head."

"Take all the time you need," Cassandra said.

As the seconds ticked by, and Darlene's expression vacillated between confused and angry, the change marked by the depth of her frowns, Geraldine couldn't fill her lungs with enough air.

When Darlene finally opened her eyes, she shifted them to Geraldine, and the anger in them didn't bode well. "How could you?"

Geraldine swallowed the lump in her throat. "I explained. I had a very bad accident, and I lost my memory. I didn't know that I had another daughter. I only found out recently."

"I understand about the memory loss, but you pretended to be my cousin." She turned to Cassandra. "You also lied to me." She then shifted her eyes to her son. "You should have told me. You knew all along who they were, and you didn't say anything."

"Would you have believed me if I told you that Geraldine was your mother? You would have thought that we were all on drugs. In order for Cassandra and Geraldine to come forward, we had to tell you about the gods and immortals, but since we believed that you were too old to transition, we decided to spare you the pain of knowing you missed your chance."

"So why are you telling me now? What has changed?"

"Before, we didn't know that we were direct descendants of a god," Cassandra said. "We found out about Orion through Rudolf, and when we caught Orion, he told us that his and Geraldine's father was a freaking god. With a god's blood flowing in your veins, you have a much better chance to transition successfully, even at your age, than Dormants who are younger. That's why we came forward, and that's why we offered you a chance of immortality now and not before."

Slumping in her chair, Darlene closed her eyes for a long moment. "I need a drink. Something stronger than wine, please."

"Coming up." Cassandra rose to her feet and walked to the kitchen. She returned with a bottle of brandy. "Will this do?"

"It's perfect." Darlene lifted her empty wine glass for Cassy to fill.

After taking a long sip, she turned to look at Parker. "You are the compeller they were talking about?"

He nodded. "The other compellers are scattered on missions all over the world, so that left me. You are my first mission." He took in a long breath. "What I did before was just a test to see if I could compel you. Now I need to compel you for real. You will keep everything you learned about gods and immortals a secret and never mention it to anyone unless they are immortals or gods as well." He stopped and looked at Onegus. "Is that good?"

Onegus shook his head. "You need to clarify that she can only talk about immortals with clan members."

"Right." He turned to Darlene. "You can only talk about immortals and gods and everything else they will tell you with clan members."

"How would I know who is a clan member and who isn't?"

"It's simple," Onegus said. "You can only talk to those you know for sure are clan members."

"Is everyone here a clan member?"

"Yes."

"Then go ahead." Darlene waved a hand at Parker. "Compel me."

"I just did."

"That's all? That's all it takes?"

He nodded. "It's in the voice. But don't ask me how it works because I don't know."

"What about the adult compellers? Do they know how they do what they do?"
He shook his head. "The ability is hereditary. We are born with it."
"I see. Well, thank you for coming here and doing this for me. I appreciate it."
Parker grinned. "No need to thank me. Onegus paid me a hundred bucks to do it."

72

DARLENE

"Good for you," Darlene gave the kid a smile before shifting her eyes to Roni.

The look of hope in her son's eyes gave her pause.

He wanted her to say yes to leaving the human world behind and joining him in immortality, and she wanted that as well, but she still couldn't believe that what they were telling her was true.

Then again, all these people, including her son, couldn't be crazy or part of a conspiracy to separate her from Leo.

She also had personal proof of the paranormal power Onegus wielded. He'd made her memories disappear and reappear by just looking into her eyes.

Onegus could potentially be a powerful hypnotist, but the kid was too young to have mastered the technique, and she'd never heard of the ability to hypnotize being hereditary.

Parker looked perfectly normal and acted like any other teenager. It had been easy to see that he'd been nervous before conducting his compulsion test on her, unsure of himself, but now he seemed relieved, and his confidence was through the roof.

The truth was that she had enough proof to believe everything Roni, Cassandra, and the others had told her, but she was hiding behind her disbelief and using it as an excuse to avoid having to make a life-altering decision.

What if she didn't have to, though? What if she could give living among the immortals a month-long trial while Leo was away?

They were all looking at her expectantly, Roni and Geraldine in particular, but so were the others, even Parker, who wasn't related to her, didn't know her, and had no stake in her decision.

"I know that you are all waiting to hear my decision, and I have to admit that I'm more inclined to say yes today than I was the other time, but I'm really bad with making big decisions on my own and without having enough time to mull them over. Is it possible for me to come live among you during the month Leo is gone and make my decision then?"

Onegus shook his head. "Thralling away a month's worth of memories is difficult and might cause damage to your brain."

"You don't need to thrall me now that Parker compelled me to keep quiet about you."

"That's true." Geraldine turned a pair of pleading eyes at Onegus. "Darlene is my daughter, and she's Roni's mother. She will never betray us. I'm sure special accommodations can be made for her."

Onegus still looked skeptical. "If you decide not to go for it and return to Leo, I can't allow you to have memories of our village. Leo has proved that he can't be trusted, and compulsion is not a hundred percent airtight. You might blurt something out, he might become suspicious, and I can't allow it."

They'd accused Leo of betraying Roni, but she still had a hard time believing it. Then again, she might be using her disbelief again to avoid making a decision.

Leo was a jerk, and she needed to leave him for a thousand and one little reasons even if he hadn't betrayed Roni. All those small insults, put-downs, and let-downs had a cumulative effect, and the resentment she felt toward him had become too much to contain.

She was such a damn coward, though. She had chosen to stay with him not because she loved him but because she was afraid of the alternative and because she had no energy and no confidence to take the necessary action.

If only they would allow her to stay in the village for a little while so the decision would become easier to make.

"What's the maximum length of time I can stay before you have to erase my memories?"

"The standard is two weeks," Onegus said. "I doubt that would be long enough for you. Usually, we only allow it for Dormants who are already in a relationship with a clan male and are working on their induction. In most cases, it takes up to two weeks for the transition to start, and if it doesn't, it means that the person does not have the godly genes."

"It took much longer for Richard," Shai said. "Mey also exceeded the two-week mark, and Kian allowed an extension."

"True, but their circumstances were different." Onegus crossed his arms over his chest. "Both Mey and Richard were willing to stay in the village indefinitely. Mey because she was in love with Yamanu, and Richard because he didn't want to live anywhere else. Darlene still hasn't decided what she wants to do with the rest of her life, and two weeks are not long enough to meet someone, fall in love, go through the induction, and transition."

"She is a confirmed Dormant," Shai said. "She doesn't need to do any of those things right away. All she needs to do is decide whether she wants to stay."

Onegus nodded. "I'm aware of that. But what I was trying to say is that she would have a much easier time with deciding to stay if she found love with a clan male and transitioned."

Darlene struggled to come up with a counterargument, but perhaps there were other options. "What if I come for two weeks, and at the end of them decide whether I want to stay forever or go back to Leo? Or what if I'm willing to take the risk of sustaining brain damage at the end of a month if I go back?" She chuckled. "If I give up immortality for Leo, I should get my head examined anyway. I don't know why I cling to that failed marriage. He's probably shagging someone on the side, and she's warming his bed on this so-called business trip."

"The business trip is for real," Cassandra said. "I arranged for Leo to be sent away for a month so you would be able to make up your mind without him hovering over you. You need time to think."

Darlene nodded. "I do."

With a groan, Roni pushed to his feet and started pacing. "Stop being such a pushover, Mother. What are you clinging to? Dancing around Leo's moods? Jumping when he says jump and asking how high? Don't tell me that you love him."

She swallowed. "I've been married to Leo for over two decades. I don't know how to live without him."

73

RONI

*F*rustrated, Roni glared at his mother, who shrank back under his gaze.
Was he any better than damn Leo if he was making her feel smaller?
She needed encouragement, not derision.

The problem was that out of everyone in the room, he was the worst at providing support and guidance. Cassandra wasn't much better than him, Geraldine was crumbling under a ton of guilt, and the others didn't want to influence Darlene's decision.

It was up to him.

Letting out a breath, he pulled out a chair and brought it over next to his mother. "I know that it's a difficult decision to make without seeing the village with your own eyes and meeting the people. It was easy for me because I fell in love with Sylvia and would have followed her to the ends of the world, but also because I was basically a prisoner, and anything was better than the isolation I lived in. You don't have a lover in the village, and you're not a prisoner, but you have me, Sylvia, Geraldine, Cassandra, Onegus, Shai, Orion, and plenty of other nice people you can be friends with. None of us can fully compensate for the lack of a life partner, but you will not be alone. You can come live with Sylvia and me, or perhaps with Geraldine and Shai. Geraldine doesn't need to leave for work and can keep you company. Come stay for the weekend, and if after that you decide that you need more time, Onegus will thrall your memories of the place away but leave the rest intact so you can go home and give it some more thought."

He turned to Onegus. "Can you do that? Can you leave some of my mother's memories of us and erase the rest?"

Onegus nodded. "It will take time to sift through them, but two days' worth of memories is not that much. I can do that."

Roni turned back to his mother. "What do you think?"

"I love you," she whispered, tears misting her eyes. "When did you become so grown up and so insightful?"

He chuckled. "I'm still working on it."

"You're doing really well, and I like your plan."

There was a collective sigh of relief, and then Cassandra took over. "So, how are we going to do it?" She turned to Onegus. "I can pick Darlene up in the office building on Friday and take her to the village."

Darlene's eyes widened. "Oh heck, you will want me to leave my phone there again. What if Leo calls me?"

They all exchanged looks and then shifted their eyes to Onegus.

"I can give you a clan phone, and you can forward your calls to it, but they will have to be monitored by the village's security. You can't tell him where you are or with whom."

"What should I tell him?"

"Tell him that your cousins took you for a weekend in a mountain cabin," Cassandra suggested. "He won't be able to verify that."

Roni rubbed his chin. "If you want, I can find out if Leo took a woman on his business trip. If he did, it should make your decision much easier."

Darlene swallowed. "I prefer not to know, but that's a coward's response. I can't be a coward if I want to transition into immortality."

"Damn right." Cassandra clapped her on the back. "It's time to grow some balls, Darlene, and you couldn't have asked for a better instructor than me to show you how."

When everyone laughed, Roni let out a breath. For the first time ever, his mother was choosing him over Leo, or even better, she was choosing herself over them both.

"I'm proud of you, Mom." He leaned to kiss her cheek. "That took guts."

"Not really." She caught his hand and gave it a squeeze. "I keep telling myself that it's only one weekend, and that Leo is probably not cheating on me. Even if I decide to leave him, I don't want to look back on my time with him and berate myself for not seeing him for who he really was. I know it's difficult for you to understand because none of you have spent so many years with your partners. Imagine waking up one morning and discovering that it was all a lie, and that you wasted your life with the wrong person."

Cassandra's eyes softened as she regarded her sister. "When you're an immortal, these decades with Leo will seem like a blink of an eye. Your life is just beginning."

"Or ending." Darlene smiled sadly. "I might not make it. I might die instead of turning immortal."

"That's why I was pushing you so hard," Cassandra said. "I can't tell you too much because that's really sensitive information, but I can tell you that there is no better time for you to transition than now. We have a narrow window of opportunity that I don't want you to miss."

Cassandra was adamant that Annani's blessing was absolutely necessary for his mother's successful transition, and even though Roni was a skeptic, he also wanted Darlene to get all the help she could get, and Annani's blessing had proven helpful. The goddess planned to stay in the village until Amanda's baby was born and probably for a few more weeks after that, which gave his mother plenty of time to find an immortal male she liked and who liked her back.

Perhaps William could arrange a virtual Perfect Match for her? That would speed up the process of finding her a mate. It would also allow her to experience adventures she would have never had the guts to try in real life.

Roni was getting excited. That was the best idea he'd had so far.

During the three hours she would be hooked up to the virtual fantasy machine, Darlene could experience weeks of adventures with a compatible male. It could be just the thing she needed to cure her of her indecision and give her confidence in herself.

ALIYA

liya hadn't slept much, but this time it wasn't because of the television. She'd tried to watch, but her thoughts had kept wandering to Vrog and their walk last evening. They'd talked for hours, first on the walk and later in Kalugal's suite.

Vrog had left only when Kalugal had practically thrown him out because it had been time for everyone to go to sleep.

They'd talked about Vrog's journey from being a novice businessman working for Jade to becoming the head of an international, well-regarded high school. He'd told her about the misunderstanding with Stella, and how he'd been captured by an untrained newly turned immortal who'd outsmarted him.

Vrog's humility was one of the things she liked best about him. He didn't boast, didn't try to make himself look more important than he was, and had no problem admitting his shortcomings.

It wasn't a typical Kra-ell attitude.

Humility hadn't been valued in the compound, and it was a very human quality, although not all humans were the same in that regard.

The heroes and heroines of the American television shows and films she'd watched weren't humble. Well, most of them weren't. Did that reflect on the American culture?

The British were self-deprecating and courteous, but humility seemed to be valued more by the Eastern cultures. That was what she was familiar with, so perhaps that was why it appealed to her.

"A penny for your thoughts?" Jacki sat next to her on the couch.

Aliya frowned. "Is that a saying? Because a penny is not a lot of money, right?"

Jacki laughed. "It is a saying. You have been sitting here all morning, staring at the blank television screen, and you seem to have a lot on your mind. I wondered if you needed to talk."

Aliya shrugged. "I was thinking about the cultural differences between people. Easterners are humbler than Westerners."

"Are they really? The fact that people act a certain way doesn't mean that they truly are that way on the inside. If it's considered rude to boast and polite to show humility, then people would attempt to appear humble even if they are not. In my opinion, people are the same everywhere, and that includes immortals and even the Kra-ell. We all want to be appreciated, loved, and accepted, and no one wants to be ignored, put down, or marginalized. We all want a family, traditional or otherwise, we all want to have our basic needs met, and we want to feel safe."

As Aliya nodded, her stomach growled, and Jacki chuckled. "We all want to be well fed too." She pushed to her feet. "Breakfast should have been delivered already. I'll call the concierge to check what's happening with it. The others will start coming and we don't want a bunch of hungry immortals in one place." She winked. "They are much easier to deal with when their bellies are full."

When a knock sounded at the door, Jacki was still on the phone, and she motioned for Aliya to open it.

Pushing her feet into her new cozy slippers, Aliya walked over to the door and opened it.

"Good morning." Phinas grinned at her.

His braces were off, and he wasn't even using crutches. The immortals' healing ability was truly exceptional.

"Are you all healed up so soon?" She opened the door all the way.

"I wouldn't go dancing just yet, but by tomorrow, I will be good to go." He walked up to the dining table and pulled out a chair for her. "We can drive to Lijiang and find a club."

"I've never been to a club before." Aliya sat down. "What do people do there?"

He sat next to her, his body turned in a way that their knees were almost touching. "They dance, they drink, they talk with their friends." He leaned closer to her, and his eyes started to glow. "They also kiss and make out in dark corners, enclaves, and nooks."

Was he flirting with her?

Aliya had no experience in those things, but it sure looked like he was. But she might be wrong, and this sort of behavior could be commonplace between immortals.

"That sounds like fun. We should all go."

Phinas smiled, but it wasn't a friendly smile. It was predatory, and it stirred something in her. "The offer was for you, not everyone."

"I doubt Kalugal would let me go. He likes to keep an eye on me."

"I'm his right-hand man. He will have no problem with it, but your boyfriend might."

"I don't have a boyfriend."

Phinas's grin was broad enough to split his face in half. "In that case, you should have no problem going to a club with me tomorrow."

"Leave her alone, Phinas." Kalugal walked into the room.

"Why? She's single, I'm single, and we have nothing better to do."

Kalugal turned his gaze to her. "Do you want to go out with Phinas, Aliya? Don't feel obligated to say yes. If you're not interested, just say so."

Was she interested?

Yeah, she kind of was. But she was also interested in Vrog. As a Kra-ell female, she could enjoy both and not feel an ounce of guilt about it, so why did she feel bad about being attracted to Phinas while contemplating a future with Vrog?

They were both fine males, and from having no choices, she now had one too many and didn't know what to do.

"I need to think about it," she said just as another knock sounded at the door and saved her from having to say more.

VROG

*V*rog felt the tension as soon as Jacki opened the door and let him in. Not from her, but from Aliya and Kalugal's second-in-command.

What was going on?

"Good morning." He plastered a smile on his face. "Am I early? Or is everyone else late?"

"You're on time, and everyone else is late," Jacki said. "Including room service. I just got off the phone with the concierge, and he promised me that breakfast was on its way and should be served in the next ten minutes." She motioned for him to take a seat at the table. "Can I offer you coffee in the meantime?"

"I don't want to impose." Vrog inclined his head.

"You're not imposing." Jacki walked over to the suite's kitchenette. "I'll bring the carafe and the mugs to the table, and everyone can serve themselves."

"In that case, I would love some. Thank you."

As Vrog pulled out a chair on Aliya's other side, Phinas's body language didn't escape his notice. The guy was sitting sideways on his chair, facing Aliya, and their knees were almost touching.

"I see that you no longer need to use braces." Vrog pinned the guy with a hard look. "But given your sitting angle, I assume that you didn't regain full range of motion yet."

Phinas wasn't dumb, and he got the message. "Thank you for your concern, but my range of motion is just fine." He moved his legs to where they were supposed to be, beneath the table.

Aliya shifted as well, aligning her body straight with the table and making sure that she was smack in the middle of the two of them.

Aggression swelling inside him, Vrog regretted not being able to challenge Phinas to a fight. He would win, there was no doubt about it, but he was not in the Kra-ell compound, and these days that was not how males competed for a female's attention in the human or the immortal world.

He'd never done that before, but he knew how other males did. Money and status were the aces in their deck of cards, while humor and sarcasm were the jokers. The wild card could trump the ace if wielded correctly. Charm was king, intelligence and eloquence were queen and prince, and brute force was reserved for the plebs.

What card should he open with?

Phinas was a salaried employee, but he had no idea how much Kalugal paid him or if Phinas had been smart managing his money. He was also older and had had more time to amass his fortune. Still, the guy was a fighter, not a businessman, and Vrog probably had more money. As for status, being the head of an international school was much more prestigious than commanding a bunch of former hoodlums.

The question was how to present these advantages without sounding too obvious or boastful.

Perhaps he should start with humor?

"Here you go." Jacki put down the coffee carafe and four mugs on the table. "I'm so glad that this hotel caters to foreigners. I need my coffee in the morning."

Vrog seized the opportunity to flash his prince card. "It is true that China is traditionally a tea-drinking nation, so much so that tea became an integral part of Buddhist practice, and it is said that Zen and tea have the same flavor. But coffee is rapidly gaining popularity. In fact, Shanghai has the most coffee shops in the world and even has a coffee festival. Starbucks has opened over five thousand stores in two hundred cities in China, and they are planning to expand into at least a hundred more."

"How many do they have in the US?" Jacki asked.

"Over fifteen thousand."

"Let me see." Kalugal smoothed his hand over his short beard. "That's one store for every twenty-two thousand people in the US, compared to two hundred and eighty-thousand people per store in China. I say Starbucks still has a long way to go here."

Vrog stilted a smile.

Kalugal was a sophisticated player, but fortunately, he wasn't competing for Aliya's attention. Phinas, on the other hand, had nothing to contribute to the conversation.

Perhaps he should continue to dazzle Aliya and the others with his vast knowledge and intelligence.

"Whiskey is also a rapidly growing segment of the Chinese high-end liqueur market. Urban consumers who consider themselves trendy and sophisticated perceive whiskey as an international drink. And as with all things that carry that designation, the demand for it is growing."

"What about cigars?" Kalugal asked.

"Oh, the cigar market is booming. China is officially the biggest market for Cuban cigars, and that's despite the government's restrictions on tobacco use. There is a huge demand for all luxury products, and cigars are an outward sign of success."

"I should call Kian," Kalugal said. "Perhaps hearing about the whiskey and cigars will tempt him to visit China."

Vrog cast a sidelong glance at Aliya to see whether she was impressed but was disappointed to see her gazing out the window with a vacant look in her eyes.

She hadn't been paying attention, and the only one he'd managed to impress was Kalugal. Was Phinas impressed?

Even if Aliya had found the subjects of their conversation boring, Vrog still considered intimidating Kalugal's second-in-command with his superior intelligence and knowledge a worthwhile endeavor.

76

ALENA

*A*lena gathered her hair in a loose bun on top of her head and examined her reflection in the vanity mirror. Her cheeks were rosy, her eyes were shining bright, and her lips were curved in a smile that just refused to abate.

She was so stupidly happy that it scared her.

To say that she was in love was an understatement. Her heart was so bloated with emotion that it was close to bursting, and she was so consumed with Orion that she could scarcely think of anything else.

Everything about him pleased her, his gentle demeanor, his innate curiosity, his intelligence, his love for art and his appreciation for beauty in all forms, and it didn't hurt that he had the body of a god and the stamina to match.

They'd made love seven times last night, or rather last night and this morning. They had gone to sleep only a few hours ago, and they were terribly late for breakfast at Kalugal and Jacki's suite, but Alena couldn't bring herself to care.

"What's the smile about?" Orion leaned over her and kissed her neck.

"I'm happy." She leaned into his touch.

Crouching next to her, he put his hands on her thighs. "I've never been happier in my life. Does that scare you as much as it scares me?"

Alena nodded. "It's overwhelming."

"Is it the bond?"

"Part of it is, but not all. We are just good together."

"Yes, we are." He pushed up and took her lips. "But if we keep this up, we will miss breakfast and end up in bed again, and I'll be neglecting my duty to you."

"Which is?"

"For starters, making sure that you are fed." He pushed to his feet and offered her a hand up. "The others are waiting for us, and they won't start until we get there."

She let him pull her up. "We can't have that. Hungry immortals are antsy."

"Not to mention a hybrid Kra-ell who went hungry for so long that she can't get full no matter how much she eats." He handed her the long sweater coat she'd left draped over the arm of the lounger.

An arm that had seen a lot of action recently.

Right. She needed to shift gears and get her head out of the sex, or they would end up missing breakfast and ordering room service, which wasn't such a bad idea.

"Let's go." She shrugged the coat on and walked toward the door before her hormones had a chance to take over.

Ovidu and Oridu trailing behind them, Alena and Orion held hands as they climbed the stairs to the third floor and walked down the corridor to the presidential suite.

When the door to the suite opened, and a procession of servers with carts rolled out, they moved aside to let them pass.

"I guess we are not late after all." Orion held the door open for her.

"Good morning, everyone." Alena walked in. "I'm glad that we are not late. I was afraid that you were all waiting for us."

"Good morning." Vrog pushed away from the table and approached her with a big grin on his face. "Congratulations." He offered her his hand.

Was he being sarcastic? Was he congratulating her on making it to breakfast?

"Thank you." She shook his hand. "What are you congratulating me for?"

His gaze shifted to Orion, then back to her, and again to Orion. "Forgive me. I forgot that immortal males don't have the ability to sense when they create a life like the Kra-ell do."

There was a gasp, and then all conversations stopped, the silence in the room becoming deafening.

Alena's heart hammered against her ribcage.

Vrog had said that she and Orion had created a life, but that was impossible. How could Vrog possibly know that? But what if it was true?

Pulling her hand out of Vrog's, she put it over her belly. "What are you talking about?"

"Kra-ell males can sense a pregnancy at the moment of conception. You created this life last night. It wasn't there the day before."

Someone inhaled sharply, and someone else started clapping but was quickly silenced.

It felt as if the entire room was holding its collective breath, waiting for her to say something.

Her heart did a somersault, and then happy butterflies took flight in her stomach.

Could it really be true?

Alena had felt that last night was special, but she'd never expected to get pregnant so soon. She'd prayed to the Fates to give her and Orion a child, but even in her most rosy fantasies, that didn't happen for many years to come.

"Are you sure?" Orion croaked.

"I'm positive," Vrog said. "I've never been wrong about a pregnancy yet."

77

ORION

*T*oo stunned to react, Orion gaped at Alena's belly. She had her hand on it, already protective of the life growing inside of her.

He wanted to wrap his arm around her and not let go for the next nine months.

Damn, he didn't even know if immortal pregnancies took the same time as human gestation. Were they shorter or longer? More or less dangerous to the mother?

"Are there any risks?" he managed to ask through his constricted throat.

Seemingly stunned and as speechless as he was, Alena shook her head.

"Immortal bodies are very resilient." Kalugal pushed to his feet and walked over to them. "Congratulations, cousin." He pulled Alena into his arms and kissed her on both cheeks. "I know it's a human custom, but I would be delighted if you chose me to be your child's godfather."

"And I his godmother." Jacki got up and walked over to Orion. "Congratulations, Daddy." She hugged him and kissed his cheeks.

The same continued with the others, and the last one to congratulate them was Aliya. "May the Mother keep you and your child safe and healthy." She made a fist and punched her own chest. "Congratulations."

When everyone had returned to their seats, and he and Alena were the only two still standing, Orion took Alena's hands and kissed them one at a time. "Thank you. You've made me the happiest man on earth." Ignoring the oohing and aahing, Orion pretended that they were alone in the room, took Alena into his arms, and kissed her gently on the lips. "I'm grateful beyond words, to you and to the Fates that brought us together and granted us this unexpected boon. I don't know what I did to deserve it, but I promise to spend my eternal life proving that I do."

"Oh, Orion." Alena wound her arms around his neck. "You are more than deserving of this boon. You loved, and you lost your love, but you healed and loved again."

Behind them, someone cleared his throat.

"As touching and lovely as this is, we are all hungry," Lokan said. "Let's celebrate this joyful occasion with a feast."

Smiling, Alena let go of Orion's neck. "I need to be mindful of what I eat now. Once again, I'm feeding a baby." She chuckled. "Wait until I tell my kids that they are about to get another sibling. They will be overjoyed." Her eyes widened. "I need to call my mother."

He put a hand on her arm. "Food first, phone calls later."

"Yes, sir." She beamed at him happily.

"Here." Jacki passed her a platter of steamed buns. "Load up."

"Have some breakfast biscuits." Carol pushed another platter toward Alena.

She laughed. "Right now, our baby is just a fertilized egg. I don't need to eat for two."

As Alena ate and chatted happily with the other ladies about the joys and woes of pregnancies, about raising children, and the joys and woes of that, Orion sipped on his coffee, unable to take a bite. He was elated and terrified at the same time.

He'd been given so much in such a short period of time, and it was wonderful to have and terrifying to lose.

"So, what's next?" Jin asked. "Are you going to hole up in the sanctuary for the duration of your pregnancy?"

"No way." Alena wiped her mouth with a napkin. "We are going to Paris."

Orion arched a brow. "We are? When was that decided?"

"Right now. We need to find your father." She turned to Mey. "Are you up for a trip to Europe and more investigating of echoes?"

Mey glanced at Yamanu. "I am if you are."

"I want to come," Jin said. "I've never been to Paris."

She turned to Arwel. "Can we?"

"I don't see why not. Kian wants to find Toven, and Paris holds the only clue we have so far. Or so we hope. Toven might not have left any echoes in that townhouse."

"I don't think we can come." Carol pouted. "Can we?"

Lokan leaned back in his chair and crossed his arms over his chest. "Paris is still the capital of fashion. I can justify a trip there provided that there is a fashion show going on."

"There is always some show going on in Paris," Jin said. "When do we want to go?"

"I can't leave until Amanda has her baby," Alena said. "She is due in three weeks, and I promised her to be there for her. I can't go right after either. I need to stay for at least a week or two."

"That actually works better for us," Lokan said. "We need to put in some work between vacations."

From the corner of his eye, Orion caught a glimpse of Aliya, who seemed distressed.

Lifting his hand, he halted the discussion. "What's the matter, Aliya?"

"If all of you are leaving to go on a trip to France, what is going to happen to me? Are you just going to leave me in the village?"

"Oh, sweetie." Alena reached for her hand. "By the time we leave, you will have plenty of new friends. And if you still don't feel at home in the village, we can postpone the trip. Amanda would be very happy if I stay longer."

"I'll keep you company," Vrog said. "I'll stay until they all come back."

"I'll be there as well," Phinas said. "I'm not joining Kalugal this time." He cast a quick glance at his boss. "You don't need me there, right?"

"There are no Kra-ell lurking in Paris, and I doubt Toven is a threat." Kalugal took Jacki's hand and brought it to his lips. "Unlike this trip, Paris is going to be decadently luxurious. No dusty archeological sites, no tunnels, and no nasty surprises."

ALENA

"Come sit with me." Alena looked up at Orion and patted the spot next to her on the couch. "I want us to tell my mother together."

"Hold on." Orion sat down and took her hand. "Before you call her, I want to discuss a couple of things."

"Okay." Alena put the phone down.

"I want to get to know all of your children. You said that most of them live in Scotland. Correct?"

"Yes. All except one."

"Then let's include Scotland in our European trip. It can be before or after Paris."

Alena smiled. "Did I already tell you today how much I love you?"

"Many times. So, is it a yes?"

"It's an enthusiastic yes. I would love for you to get to know my children. Forgive me for not thinking about it first. I should have."

Leaning closer, he kissed her forehead. "You are forgiven. The second thing I want to discuss involves the ring that I didn't have time to purchase yet. I want us to get married before the baby is born. I know that marriage ceremonies are not part of your tradition, and that making it official is not important to you, but I grew up in the human world, and it's important to me."

Alena's lips were going to be permanently stuck in an upturned curve because this man was making her so happy. "Annani would love to officiate at our wedding. Do you want a small ceremony or a big one?"

"If possible, I want the entire clan to attend."

"A big one, then. That would make my mother even happier."

He took both her hands in his. "I want to know what would make Alena happy."

"Being with you makes me happy. Everything else is optional."

COMING UP NEXT
Dark God Trilogy

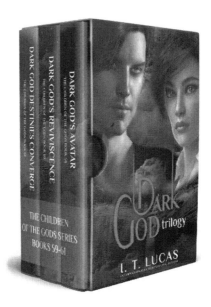

Dear reader,

Thank you for reading the *Children of the Gods*.

As an independent author, I rely on your support to spread the word. So if you enjoyed the story, please share your experience with others, and if it isn't too much trouble, I would greatly appreciate a brief review on Amazon.

Click **HERE** to leave a review

Love & happy reading,

Isabell

To find out what's included in your free membership, click HERE or flip to the last page.

If you're already a subscriber, you'll receive a download link for my next book's preview chapters in the new release announcement email. If you are not getting my emails, your provider is sending them to your junk folder, and you are missing out on **important updates, side characters' portraits, additional content, and other goodies.** To fix that, add isabell@itlucas.com to your email contacts or your email VIP list.

DARK GOD EXCERPT

Toven put his wine glass on the side table, propped his slippered feet up on the worn brown leather ottoman, and clicked the television on.

"Are you depressed?" asked the actor playing a sympathetic doctor. "Does your life feel like a long road to nowhere?" He looked directly at Toven. "Neurotap offers hope to those who no longer believe it exists. In clinical trials, seven out of ten—"

Annoyed, Toven clicked over to another channel.

That damn commercial had been popping up on different cable and broadcast stations for days. If he were human, he might have been tempted to give Neurotap a try, but no medication could alleviate a god's ennui, and neither could therapy sessions with the best psychoanalysts.

Philosophizing about the meaning of life with the greatest human thinkers was pointless as well.

He should know.

Toven had conversed with the most renowned philosophers humanity had produced.

Socrates, who had believed that the secret to happiness was found in enjoying less, Confucius, who had advocated meditating upon good thoughts as a way to make the world a better place, and Seneca, who had preached that people should be happy with their lot and not strive for more. Lao Tzu advocated living in the moment, Nietzsche valued power above all, and Kierkegaard explained that life was not a problem to be solved but a reality to be experienced.

Ironically, most of those thinkers had been influenced in one way or another by Toven's own writings, and yet they had arrived at very different conclusions about the human condition and how to best endure it.

Toven agreed with some and disagreed with others, but he'd given up on solving that age-old problem centuries ago. Humans were doomed to their misery, and even a powerful god like him could not help them.

He'd tried, failed, tried again and again, but at some point, he had to resign himself to the fact that humans were bloodthirsty, power-hungry savages. Not all of them, but enough to make everyone else's life miserable.

Out of all the philosophers, Kierkegaard had been the wisest. Trying to solve humanity's problems was futile, and living in the moment and just experiencing life was all that was to be had, even for a god.

A god.

What a joke that was. He should've abandoned thinking of himself as a god eons ago. He was no deity, he was not deathless, he was just the scion of a superior race of people, who had long ago been worshipped by primitive humans.

But the gods were no more, destroyed by his own brother in what had turned out to be a suicide mission, and Toven was all that was left of that superior race of beings.

A rare burst of anger rising in his chest, Toven wished that Mortdh had survived the bombing so he could've killed the murderous bastard himself. His insane, power-hungry brother had dropped a bomb on the gods' assembly to escape his punishment for murdering a god, but the idiot had miscalculated the weapon's destructive range and had been swept away in its deadly wind.

His anger subsiding just as quickly as it had risen, Toven let out a sigh. Killing Mortdh would have been intensely satisfying, but he knew that he would not have prevailed against his older brother. Mortdh had always been more powerful, but since the bastard was dead, Toven could allow himself the fantasy.

Except, Toven was well aware of how absurd even fantasizing about it was.

He was a scholar, not a killer, which was probably the reason for his lack of effectiveness. The pen might be mightier than the sword, but the sword was still necessary to implement and enforce the pen's creations.

Toven had never wielded a tool of death.

Hell, he couldn't even bring himself to end his own miserable life.

Humans didn't realize it, but they had the better deal.

Their short lifespans were like rollercoaster rides, the slate wiped clean with each new rotation. Once they grew bored and disillusioned with life, which was inevitable, they didn't have to suffer long. Their lives ended shortly thereafter, and they were given a fresh start in a brand-new body and no memory of their previous incarnation.

Not all humans believed in the cycle, and even he couldn't be absolutely certain that reincarnation existed. But after witnessing too many cases of humans who'd remembered past lives and could prove that those memories were real, Toven had become a believer, and he envied humans for it.

A god who had lived for over seven thousand years and was tired and bored had limited options to end it all, and Toven was too much of a coward to jump out off a plane or pay someone to behead him.

Instead, he tried to amuse himself the best he could, passing the never-ending time by traveling from one metropolis to another and penning romance novels about love he couldn't feel.

He used to enjoy his human lovers, but even that had become boring. Nowadays, he rarely sought out female company, preferring his solitude and the realities he created in his head to pleasures of the flesh that no longer excited him.

It took someone very special to stir even the slightest emotion in him.

As a loud car commercial began playing, pulling him out of his head, Toven groaned.

Why did he even bother watching television? It wasn't as if he was really interested in what was happening in the human world. The players and costumes kept changing, as did technology, but history kept its cyclical ebb and flow, and humans seemed to learn nothing from their ancestors' mistakes.

Was it morbid fascination that prompted him to follow global affairs? Or was it hope that humanity would one day break out of the cycle and reach the enlightenment he'd tried to steer them toward and failed?

Hope springs eternal.

Apparently not only humans fell victim to hope's allure. Toven had thought that his had died a long time ago, but perhaps a kernel of it still lived in a corner of his dark heart. Perhaps that little spark was what kept him from hiring a killer to behead him and end his misery.

As the car commercial finally ended and the news program tune started playing, Toven put the remote down and lifted his wine glass.

"In today's news, a Bayview resident is accused of…"

Toven switched to another channel. He wasn't interested in local drama.

It was time to move to his next destination.

The San Francisco home he was renting was lovely, but he didn't like staying in one place for too long, and he was looking forward to the change in environment his next stop would bring. The old-world charm of the Victorian house on Webster Street had inspired a historical romance, while the ultra-modern seventy-second-floor Park Avenue apartment in Manhattan would hopefully inspire a contemporary novel.

As a loud commercial for a cleaning product started, he clicked over to the next channel and yet another commercial, but the stunning visuals snagged his attention and he lingered to watch more.

Toven assumed that what was being promoted was a computer game, but as a pretty young lady walked in front of the screen and presented a service that was not about playing a game on the computer but rather playing inside of it, Toven's interest was piqued.

It was a fascinating idea.

"Are you a busy professional with no time to search for your soulmate?" she asked in a sexy, slightly raspy voice. "Are you tired of surfing endless profiles on dating apps and going out on disappointing dates?" Several snapshots of humorously overdone disastrous first dates flashed across the screen. "If so, then Perfect Match Virtual Studios has the answer for you. For more details, go to www.PerfectMatch-VirtualFantasy.com. Your dream partner is only a few keyboard clicks away."

Intrigued, Toven pushed to his feet and walked over to the desk to retrieve his laptop.

Back in the armchair, he typed the URL into the search box and started reading the online brochure explaining the service. Could it be for real? Surely it was impossible to turn into someone else for the duration of the virtual adventure. A computer couldn't take over a person's mind and let them live out a fantasy. The brochure claimed that in the span of three hours, weeks of virtual adventure could be enjoyed. They promoted their service not only as the safest and most scientific way to find a soulmate, but also as the best vacation solution for busy people.

If genuine and not paid for, the numerous testimonials confirmed the service's claims, singing its praises. People were finding their perfect matches, and if the wedding photos of happy customers weren't fake, the number of featured couples was impressive.

Others were going on adventures with their spouses, rekindling their passion by either choosing beautiful avatars to represent them or going in as themselves.

It wasn't cheap, but the one thing Toven had no lack of was money. The savages he'd tried to civilize had paid him tribute in gold, and while it was the only tangible good he'd gotten from wasting centuries trying to improve their lives, there was lots of it.

There were many adventures in a variety of environments to choose from, and the service promised a perfect match with a real person who was interested in the same sort of adventure.

Toven wasn't hoping for a soulmate, and he'd been on enough real-life adventures not to crave fake ones, but what appealed to him the most was the promise of stepping out of his own mind and becoming someone else for a spell.

Mia turned the cream-colored envelope around, looking for a hint of what was inside, but other than the hand-scribbled *Happy 27th Birthday* there was nothing, not even a Hallmark logo or that of one of the other greetings card brands.

Patting the envelope didn't help either. It didn't feel like a gift card, which was what her friends had gotten her for her 26th birthday, or cash, which was what her grandmother always put inside the cards she'd gotten for her at Walgreens.

Margo and Frankie were smiling like a couple of fiends, so it was probably a gag gift.

"What is it?" She narrowed her eyes at her besties.

"Open it," Margo said.

Frankie waved the waiter over. "Another round of margaritas, please." She winked at Mia. "You're going to need it."

Mia rolled her eyes. "Did you get me a subscription to Boys Down Under?"

The three of them were obsessed with the Instagram sensation. They'd been tempted to subscribe to the private channel nearly every time the guys posted new pictures of themselves in provocative poses. Those who paid for premium access got to see more than just a sliver of muscular chests peeking from unbuttoned shirts, but Mia wasn't sure that she was ready to see more, especially if the guys exposed anything other than their abs and pectorals. She wasn't into pornography.

Frankie looked at Margo. "Damn, why didn't we think of that? That could have been so much cheaper."

"Indeed," Margo pretended to agree. "Next year, that's what we are getting you."

Laughing, Mia opened the envelope, and as she pulled out the card and saw the logo embossed in its center, her eyes widened. "You got me a Perfect Match adventure? Are you nuts? These cost a fortune!"

"It was on sale," Frankie said. "They opened a new studio a few blocks down from my office building. There was a big sign on the front window that they were offering fifty percent off to the first one hundred customers. I was sure that it was no longer available and that all one hundred were sold out." She waved a hand. "You know how everyone and their grandma is talking about it."

Mia laughed. "You're right. My grandma talks about it nonstop. She says that she's not interested in the hookups, and she just wants to try the Russian spy virtual adventure, but I think that she's full of it. She wants a hookup with 007. I know that she's been fantasizing about it ever since the Perfect Match commercials started."

"What does your grandpa have to say about it?" Frankie asked.

"You know him, he just smiles half-indulgently, half-suffering and goes back to his newspaper or his television show." Mia looked at the card. "But even at half off it is still a very expensive gift."

Frankie waved a dismissive hand. "Margo and I split the cost. You can pay us back by telling us all about it after you're done. And if you find your perfect match, I'm going in there and buying a token at full price for myself even if I have to sell my vintage record collection to pay for it."

"It's just an advertising gimmick." Margo lifted her margarita and licked the salt from the rim before taking a sip. "To be able to find people their perfect matches, the Perfect Match Virtual Studios people would need to have hundreds of thousands of profiles in their database, which they can't have because their service is so costly that only the wealthy can afford it. But if I had the money, I would love to experience a virtual hookup, or two or three, in some exotic location just for the fun of it."

"You know what the best part is?" Frankie leaned forward. "Time moves differently in the virtual world. In the span of three hours, you can have a two-week romantic vacation with enough sex to last you for a year."

Mia forced a smile. "Awesome."

What Frankie had really meant to say was that in Mia's case it would have to compensate for the four preceding years, and unless she could afford another trip to cyber world, probably even more going forward.

Besides, there was no guarantee that she would enjoy it. The service was hyped up by a big advertising campaign and celebrity endorsements, but that didn't mean it was all that. It only meant that there was a lot of money behind the national chain of virtual adventure studios. Or was it international by now?

"Hey, maybe we should follow their website so we'll know where and when they open their next branch." Margo pushed her half empty margarita aside. "Maybe we can get more tokens at half off."

Mia lifted her purse from the back of the chair and put the envelope inside. "If my children's books gain some traction, I will buy you each a token for your next birthday."

Margo's lips twisted in a grimace. "Your illustrations are brilliant, but the stories suck. You need to find a different writer or write them yourself."

"I can't. That's the deal I have with my publisher. I'm just the illustrator."

Her agent had told her that they'd loved her illustrations but hadn't liked her stories, and the condition for a publishing deal had been that they provide the writer. The guy was okay, better than she was at coming up with compelling stories, but the books lacked something. They just weren't exciting, not to the kids, and not to the parents reading them to their children.

The publisher had said that her stories weren't happy enough, but they weren't supposed to be. Not everything in life was happy. In fact, most of it was not, and pretending otherwise was dishonest. Children should not grow up in a bubble, unprepared for life's challenges. Thinking that life was fair and that everyone got their happy ending was just setting them up for disappointment.

Margo lifted her margarita, took a sip, and as she put it down her expression was somber. "Just be careful with the type of adventure you choose, Mia. Don't go for the Russian spy one. Go for something sweet and romantic."

"You don't have to remind me. I know."

Too much excitement might kill her.

Literally.

Four years ago, it almost had.

Kian closed the last of the files Shai had put on his desk and handed the stack back to him.

His assistant rose to his feet. "I'm going down to the café. Do you want me to get you something?"

"Only coffee, please. I'm having lunch with Syssi at home later." Kian swiveled his chair around and looked out the window at the village square below.

At this time of day, the café was teaming with people.

My people.

"I built this village for our clan, a safe place for the immortal descendants of Annani to live in and thrive as a community. I didn't expect to welcome the descendants of other gods, and I sure as hell didn't expect to invite three members of a different breed of long-lived people, who we had no idea coexisted with us and humans on this planet."

"The Fates have been busy lately," Shai said.

"Indeed, they have been, and they are not done yet."

Not too long ago, they'd discovered that Annani's half-sister had survived as well. In a bizarre turn of events, Areana had ended up being mated to Navuh, the clan's archenemy who was bent on the clan's annihilation. Areana had lived in seclusion for thousands of years, locked away in Navuh's harem and unaware that Annani was alive and that her mate sought her sister's demise.

But even more bizarre than Areana being mated to Navuh was that both their sons had joined forces with the clan.

And now they were searching for Toven, another god who'd been presumed dead.

The Fates had worked behind the scenes, weaving their plans and orchestrating the seemingly random encounters that had first led Toven's granddaughter and then his daughter and son to the clan.

Their invisible fingertips were all over it.

If not for the two immortal children Toven had fathered with human mothers finding their way to the clan, they would have never learned about Toven's survival.

Shai walked over to the window and peered at the busy café below. "When we built the village, we believed that the only other immortals on the planet in addition to us were the Doomers."

Kian chuckled. "I wonder if Navuh knows that we call his order DOOM and his followers Doomers. We couldn't have come up with a more fitting name for our enemies if we tried."

Shai shrugged. "That's their acronym in English. The Brotherhood of the Devout Order of Mortdh. It doesn't work out as well in the old language."

Kian turned to look at his assistant. "Do you speak the old language?"

Shai shook his head. "I never had the chance to learn it. Maybe I could ask Edna to teach me the basics, and then I could continue on my own."

With the guy's eidetic memory, he would have an easier time than most learning the complicated language, but Shai had enough on his plate.

"When you hire an assistant, maybe you'll have time for a side project like that. Right now, you don't."

"No one wants to be the assistant's assistant. I can't find anyone for the job." Shai pushed his hands into his pockets and leaned back on his heels. "Maybe when we find more of Toven's children, one of them will turn out to be a capable administrator."

Kian chuckled. "If they are all like Orion and Geraldine, which given Toven's preference for artistic females they probably are, none will make good administrators."

It was ironic, or maybe fated, that Geraldine and Shai were truelove mates. The woman with memory issues had mated a man with an eidetic memory.

"You never know." Shai smiled. "Cassandra is artistic, but she's also good with numbers."

"True, but since she's Toven's granddaughter, she's further down the line and might have inherited a good head for numbers from her father. First, though, we need to find Toven himself. He's too smart to leave tracks for us to follow, and even if we somehow get lucky and find him, he might not want anything to do with us. If the god is so cold and indifferent that he turned away his own son, there is no reason to believe that he'll want to join forces with us."

"We will do what we can, and the rest is up to the Fates." Shai pulled his hands out of his pockets, turned toward the desk, and tucked the files under his arm. "I'll put these away and go get you your coffee. Your mood will improve after an infusion of caffeine."

"Thanks. Get me a pastry as well, please. It will tide me over until lunch."

"You've got it, boss."

When Shai left, Kian sighed, turned his chair around, and rolled it closer to the desk.

Perhaps when they found Toven and he met Annani, she would have a positive impact on him. She was the only one who had any hope of influencing the god to at least cooperate with the clan, and maybe to stay in touch with his children.

While Annani had despised Mortdh, she'd been very fond of his younger brother.

If Ahn had promised his daughter to Toven instead of Mortdh, the world would have been a different place today. Annani wouldn't have pursued Khiann in a desperate move to avoid marriage to the hateful god, and Mortdh wouldn't have murdered Khiann in retaliation for the humiliation. The gods' assembly wouldn't have sentenced Mortdh to entombment for the murder, and he wouldn't have bombed the assembly to avoid punishment, destroying the gods and altering the course of history. But engaging in a game of what-ifs was futile.

The past couldn't be changed.

Kian could only look to the future, and he hoped that Annani's upbeat personality and positive attitude would rub off on Toven. Perhaps her light could banish the darkness the god had allowed to smother his spirit. And if the Fates really wanted to do some good, Annani and Toven would be each other's second chance.

They could never be truelove mates, but they could at least have friendly companionship with benefits, which would solve the problem of replacing Alena as their mother's companion.

Kian shook his head. Once again, he was letting himself travel down the road of what-ifs, but unless those what-ifs had to do with clan security, he had no business engaging in them.

That brought to mind the next subject keeping him awake at night—the damn Kra-ell.

Discovering that two more gods had survived the bombing was a mere curiosity compared to discovering a different breed of long-lived people who, like immortals, had been living undetected among humans.

The Kra-ell were a potential threat to his clan.

The three hybrid Kra-ell they'd found so far were not much of a threat, but those who'd massacred the rest of their tribe were. If those other Kra-ell had no qualms about killing their own males so they could steal their females, they would not hesitate to do the same to his people, if and when they discovered the clan's existence. In fact, immortal females would be even more valuable to them than their own.

The Kra-ell were long-lived but not immortal, and mating with immortal females would be a new lease on life for their species. A daughter born to a hybrid Kra-ell male and an immortal female would transfer the immortality gene to her children. The Kra-ell did not have enough females, and breeding with humans was pointless for them because their longevity genes seemed to be recessive. The product of a union between a Kra-ell and a human produced a hybrid with longer life span than that of the human partner, but the children of the hybrids with humans did not inherit the Kra-ell longevity, which meant that the Kra-ell were doomed to eventually die out.

If he could avoid them detecting the clan for the next thousand years or so, the danger would be over, but Kian hadn't been as careful as he should have been.

He'd already taken a big risk by allowing two survivors of Jade's tribe into the village, and now he was admitting a third.

The rare hybrid Kra-ell female had lived in hiding, terrified of being found by the Kra-ell who'd massacred the males of her tribe. She had no one and nowhere to go, and he couldn't in good conscience turn her away, especially since Arwel had vouched for her.

The Guardian might be an empath, but that didn't make him soft-hearted. Arwel didn't vouch for Aliya out of pity but out of respect.

Perhaps the three hybrid Kra-ell arrivals were part of the Fates' grand design?

If that was the case, it was too early in the game for him to see what that design might be.

Kian just hoped that he wasn't letting a Trojan horse into the sanctuary he'd worked so hard to create for his people.

Books 59-61: Dark God's Trilogy

THE CHILDREN OF THE GODS SERIES

THE CHILDREN OF THE GODS ORIGINS

1: GODDESS'S CHOICE

When gods and immortals still ruled the ancient world, one young goddess risked everything for love.

2: GODDESS'S HOPE

Hungry for power and infatuated with the beautiful Areana, Navuh plots his father's demise. After all, by getting rid of the insane god he would be doing the world a favor. Except, when gods and immortals conspire against each other, humanity pays the price.

But things are not what they seem, and prophecies should not to be trusted...

THE CHILDREN OF THE GODS

1: DARK STRANGER THE DREAM

Syssi's paranormal foresight lands her a job at Dr. Amanda Dokani's neuroscience lab, but it fails to predict the thrilling yet terrifying turn her life will take. Syssi has no clue that her boss is an immortal who'll drag her into a secret, millennia-old battle over humanity's future. Nor does she realize that the professor's imposing brother is the mysterious stranger who's been starring in her dreams.

Since the dawn of human civilization, two warring factions of immortals—the descendants of the gods of old—have been secretly shaping its destiny. Leading the clandestine battle from his luxurious Los Angeles high-rise, Kian is surrounded by his clan, yet alone. Descending from a single goddess, clan members are forbidden to each other. And as the only other immortals are their hated enemies, Kian and his kin have been long resigned to a lonely existence of fleeting trysts with human partners. That is, until his sister makes a game-changing discovery—a mortal seeress who she believes is a dormant carrier of their genes. Ever the realist, Kian is skeptical and refuses Amanda's plea to attempt Syssi's activation. But when his enemies learn of the Dormant's existence, he's forced to rush her to the safety of his keep. Inexorably drawn to Syssi, Kian wrestles with his conscience as he is tempted to explore her budding interest in the darker shades of sensuality.

2: DARK STRANGER REVEALED

While sheltered in the clan's stronghold, Syssi is unaware that Kian and Amanda are not human, and neither are the supposedly religious fanatics that are after her. She feels a powerful connection to Kian, and as he introduces her to a world of pleasure she never dared imagine, his dominant sexuality is a revelation. Considering that she's completely out of her element, Syssi feels comfortable and safe letting go with him. That is, until she begins to suspect that all is not as it seems. Piecing the puzzle together, she draws a scary, yet wrong conclusion...

3: DARK STRANGER IMMORTAL

When Kian confesses his true nature, Syssi is not as much shocked by the revelation as she is wounded by what she perceives as his callous plans for her.

If she doesn't turn, he'll be forced to erase her memories and let her go. His family's safety demands secrecy – no one in the mortal world is allowed to know that immortals exist.

Resigned to the cruel reality that even if she stays on to never again leave the keep, she'll get old while Kian won't, Syssi is determined to enjoy what little time she has with him, one day at a time.

Can Kian let go of the mortal woman he loves? Will Syssi turn? And if she does, will she survive the dangerous transition?

4: Dark Enemy Taken

Dalhu can't believe his luck when he stumbles upon the beautiful immortal professor. Presented with a once in a lifetime opportunity to grab an immortal female for himself, he kidnaps her and runs. If he ever gets caught, either by her people or his, his life is forfeit. But for a chance of a loving mate and a family of his own, Dalhu is prepared to do everything in his power to win Amanda's heart, and that includes leaving the Doom brotherhood and his old life behind.

Amanda soon discovers that there is more to the handsome Doomer than his dark past and a hulking, sexy body. But succumbing to her enemy's seduction, or worse, developing feelings for a ruthless killer is out of the question. No man is worth life on the run, not even the one and only immortal male she could claim as her own...

Her clan and her research must come first...

5: Dark Enemy Captive

When the rescue team returns with Amanda and the chained Dalhu to the keep, Amanda is not as thrilled to be back as she thought she'd be. Between Kian's contempt for her and Dalhu's imprisonment, Amanda's budding relationship with Dalhu seems doomed. Things start to look up when Annani offers her help, and together with Syssi they resolve to find a way for Amanda to be with Dalhu. But will she still want him when she realizes that he is responsible for her nephew's murder? Could she? Will she take the easy way out and choose Andrew instead?

6: Dark Enemy Redeemed

Amanda suspects that something fishy is going on onboard the Anna. But when her investigation of the peculiar all-female Russian crew fails to uncover anything other than more speculation, she decides it's time to stop playing detective and face her real problem—a man she shouldn't want but can't live without.

6.5: My Dark Amazon

When Michael and Kri fight off a gang of humans, Michael gets stabbed. The injury to his immortal body recovers fast, but the one to his ego takes longer, putting a strain on his relationship with Kri.

7: Dark Warrior Mine

When Andrew is forced to retire from active duty, he believes that all he has to look forward to is a boring desk job. His glory days in special ops are over. But as it turns out, his thrill ride has just begun. Andrew discovers not only that immortals exist and have been manipulating global affairs since antiquity, but that he and his sister are rare possessors of the immortal genes.

Problem is, Andrew might be too old to attempt the activation process. His sister, who is fourteen years his junior, barely made it through the transition, so the odds of him coming out of it alive, let alone immortal, are slim.

But fate may force his hand.

Helping a friend find his long-lost daughter, Andrew finds a woman who's worth taking the risk for. Nathalie might be a Dormant, but the only way to find out for sure requires fangs and venom.

8: Dark Warrior's Promise

Andrew and Nathalie's love flourishes, but the secrets they keep from each other taint their relationship with doubts and suspicions. In the meantime, Sebastian and his men are getting bolder, and the storm that's brewing will shift the balance of power in the millennia-old conflict between Annani's clan and its enemies.

9: Dark Warrior's Destiny

The new ghost in Nathalie's head remembers who he was in life, providing Andrew and her with indisputable proof that he is real and not a figment of her imagination.

Convinced that she is a Dormant, Andrew decides to go forward with his transition immediately after the rescue mission at the Doomers' HQ.

Fearing for his life, Nathalie pleads with him to reconsider. She'd rather spend the rest of her mortal days with Andrew than risk what they have for the fickle promise of immortality.

While the clan gets ready for battle, Carol gets help from an unlikely ally. Sebastian's second-in-command can no longer ignore the torment she suffers at the hands of his commander and offers to help her, but only if she agrees to his terms.

10: Dark Warrior's Legacy

Andrew's acclimation to his post-transition body isn't easy. His senses are sharper, he's bigger, stronger, and hungrier. Nathalie fears that the changes in the man she loves are more than physical. Measuring up to this new version of him is going to be a challenge.

Carol and Robert are disillusioned with each other. They are not destined mates, and love is not on the horizon. When Robert's three months are up, he might be left with nothing to show for his sacrifice.

Lana contacts Anandur with disturbing news; the yacht and its human cargo are in Mexico. Kian must find a way to apprehend Alex and rescue the women on board without causing an international incident.

11: Dark Guardian Found

What would you do if you stopped aging?

Eva runs. The ex-DEA agent doesn't know what caused her strange mutation, only that if discovered, she'll be dissected like a lab rat. What Eva doesn't know, though, is that she's a descendant of the gods, and that she is not alone. The man who rocked her world in one life-changing encounter over thirty years ago is an immortal as well.

To keep his people's existence secret, Bhathian was forced to turn his back on the only woman who ever captured his heart, but he's never forgotten and never stopped looking for her.

12: Dark Guardian Craved

Cautious after a lifetime of disappointments, Eva is mistrustful of Bhathian's professed feelings of love. She accepts him as a lover and a confidant but not as a life partner.

Jackson suspects that Tessa is his true love mate, but unless she overcomes her fears, he might never find out.

Carol gets an offer she can't refuse—a chance to prove that there is more to her than meets the eye. Robert believes she's about to commit a deadly mistake, but when he tries to dissuade her, she tells him to leave.

13: Dark Guardian's Mate

Prepare for the heart-warming culmination of Eva and Bhathian's story!

14: Dark Angel's Obsession

The cold and stoic warrior is an enigma even to those closest to him. His secrets are about to unravel...

15: Dark Angel's Seduction

Brundar is fighting a losing battle. Calypso is slowly chipping away his icy armor from the outside, while his need for her is melting it from the inside.

He can't allow it to happen. Calypso is a human with none of the Dormant indicators. There is no way he can keep her for more than a few weeks.

16: Dark Angel's Surrender

Get ready for the heart pounding conclusion to Brundar and Calypso's story.

Callie still couldn't wrap her head around it, nor could she summon even a smidgen of sorrow or regret. After all, she had some memories with him that weren't horrible. She should've felt something. But there was nothing, not even shock. Not even horror at what had transpired over the last couple of hours.

Maybe it was a typical response for survivors--feeling euphoric for the simple reason that they were alive. Especially when that survival was nothing short of miraculous.

Brundar's cold hand closed around hers, reminding her that they weren't out of the woods yet. Her injuries were superficial, and the most she had to worry about was some scarring. But, despite his and Anandur's reassurances, Brundar might never walk again.

If he ended up crippled because of her, she would never forgive herself for getting him involved in her crap.

"Are you okay, sweetling? Are you in pain?" Brundar asked.

Her injuries were nothing compared to his, and yet he was concerned about her. God, she loved this man. The thing was, if she told him that, he would run off, or crawl away as was the case.

Hey, maybe this was the perfect opportunity to spring it on him.

17: Dark Operative: A Shadow of Death

As a brilliant strategist and the only human entrusted with the secret of immortals' existence, Turner is both an asset and a liability to the clan. His request to attempt transition into immortality as an alternative to cancer treatments cannot be denied without risking the clan's exposure. On the other hand, approving it means risking his premature death. In both scenarios, the clan will lose a valuable ally.

When the decision is left to the clan's physician, Turner makes plans to manipulate her by taking advantage of her interest in him.

Will Bridget fall for the cold, calculated operative? Or will Turner fall into his own trap?

18: Dark Operative: A Glimmer of Hope

As Turner and Bridget's relationship deepens, living together seems like the right move, but to make it work both need to make concessions.

Bridget is realistic and keeps her expectations low. Turner could never be the truelove mate she yearns for, but he is as good as she's going to get. Other than his emotional limitations, he's perfect in every way.

Turner's hard shell is starting to show cracks. He wants immortality, he wants to be part of the clan, and he wants Bridget, but he doesn't want to cause her pain.

His options are either abandon his quest for immortality and give Bridget his few remaining decades, or abandon Bridget by going for the transition and most likely dying. His rational mind dictates that he chooses the former, but his gut pulls him toward the latter. Which one is he going to trust?

19: DARK OPERATIVE: THE DAWN OF LOVE

Get ready for the exciting finale of Bridget and Turner's story!

20: DARK SURVIVOR AWAKENED

This was a strange new world she had awakened to.

Her memory loss must have been catastrophic because almost nothing was familiar. The language was foreign to her, with only a few words bearing some similarity to the language she thought in. Still, a full moon cycle had passed since her awakening, and little by little she was gaining basic understanding of it--only a few words and phrases, but she was learning more each day.

A week or so ago, a little girl on the street had tugged on her mother's sleeve and pointed at her. "Look, Mama, Wonder Woman!"

The mother smiled apologetically, saying something in the language these people spoke, then scurried away with the child looking behind her shoulder and grinning.

When it happened again with another child on the same day, it was settled.

Wonder Woman must have been the name of someone important in this strange world she had awoken to, and since both times it had been said with a smile it must have been a good one.

Wonder had a nice ring to it.

She just wished she knew what it meant.

21: DARK SURVIVOR ECHOES OF LOVE

Wonder's journey continues in *Dark Survivor Echoes of Love*.

22: DARK SURVIVOR REUNITED

The exciting finale of Wonder and Anandur's story.

23: DARK WIDOW'S SECRET

Vivian and her daughter share a powerful telepathic connection, so when Ella can't be reached by conventional or psychic means, her mother fears the worst.

Help arrives from an unexpected source when Vivian gets a call from the young doctor she met at a psychic convention. Turns out Julian belongs to a private organization specializing in retrieving missing girls.

As Julian's clan mobilizes its considerable resources to rescue the daughter, Magnus is charged with keeping the gorgeous young mother safe.

Worry for Ella and the secrets Vivian and Magnus keep from each other should be enough to prevent the sparks of attraction from kindling a blaze of desire. Except, these pesky sparks have a mind of their own.

24: Dark Widow's Curse

A simple rescue operation turns into mission impossible when the Russian mafia gets involved. Bad things are supposed to come in threes, but in Vivian's case, it seems like there is no limit to bad luck. Her family and everyone who gets close to her is affected by her curse.

Will Magnus and his people prove her wrong?

25: Dark Widow's Blessing

The thrilling finale of the Dark Widow trilogy!

26: Dark Dream's Temptation

Julian has known Ella is the one for him from the moment he saw her picture, but when he finally frees her from captivity, she seems indifferent to him. Could he have been mistaken?

Ella's rescue should've ended that chapter in her life, but it seems like the road back to normalcy has just begun and it's full of obstacles. Between the pitying looks she gets and her mother's attempts to get her into therapy, Ella feels like she's typecast as a victim, when nothing could be further from the truth. She's a tough survivor, and she's going to prove it.

Strangely, the only one who seems to understand is Logan, who keeps popping up in her dreams. But then, he's a figment of her imagination—or is he?

27: Dark Dream's Unraveling

While trying to figure out a way around Logan's silencing compulsion, Ella concocts an ambitious plan. What if instead of trying to keep him out of her dreams, she could pretend to like him and lure him into a trap?

Catching Navuh's son would be a major boon for the clan, as well as for Ella. She will have her revenge, turning the tables on another scumbag out to get her.

28: Dark Dream's Trap

The trap is set, but who is the hunter and who is the prey? Find out in this heart-pounding conclusion to the *Dark Dream* trilogy.

29: Dark Prince's Enigma

As the son of the most dangerous male on the planet, Lokan lives by three rules:

Don't trust a soul.

Don't show emotions.

And don't get attached.

Will one extraordinary woman make him break all three?

30: Dark Prince's Dilemma

Will Kian decide that the benefits of trusting Lokan outweigh the risks?

Will Lokan betray his father and brothers for the greater good of his people?

Are Carol and Lokan true-love mates, or is one of them playing the other?

So many questions, the path ahead is anything but clear.

31: Dark Prince's Agenda

While Turner and Kian work out the details of Areana's rescue plan, Carol and Lokan's tumultuous relationship hits another snag. Is it a sign of things to come?

32 : Dark Queen's Quest

A former beauty queen, a retired undercover agent, and a successful model, Mey is not the typical damsel in distress. But when her sister drops off the radar and then someone starts following her around, she panics.

Following a vague clue that Kalugal might be in New York, Kian sends a team headed by Yamanu to search for him.

As Mey and Yamanu's paths cross, he offers her his help and protection, but will that be all?

33: Dark Queen's Knight

As the only member of his clan with a godlike power over human minds, Yamanu has been shielding his people for centuries, but that power comes at a steep price. When Mey enters his life, he's faced with the most difficult choice.

The safety of his clan or a future with his fated mate.

34: Dark Queen's Army

As Mey anxiously waits for her transition to begin and for Yamanu to test whether his godlike powers are gone, the clan sets out to solve two mysteries:

Where is Jin, and is she there voluntarily?

Where is Kalugal, and what is he up to?

35: Dark Spy Conscripted

Jin possesses a unique paranormal ability. Just by touching someone, she can insert a mental hook into their psyche and tie a string of her consciousness to it, creating a tether. That doesn't make her a spy, though, not unless her talent is discovered by those seeking to exploit it.

36: Dark Spy's Mission

Jin's first spying mission is supposed to be easy. Walk into the club, touch Kalugal to tether her consciousness to him, and walk out.

Except, they should have known better.

37: Dark Spy's Resolution

The best-laid plans often go awry...

38: Dark Overlord New Horizon

Jacki has two talents that set her apart from the rest of the human race.

She has unpredictable glimpses of other people's futures, and she is immune to mind manipulation.

Unfortunately, both talents are pretty useless for finding a job other than the one she had in the government's paranormal division.

It seemed like a sweet deal, until she found out that the director planned on producing super babies by compelling the recruits into pairing up. When an opportunity to escape the program presented itself, she took it, only to find out that humans are not at the top of the food chain.

Immortals are real, and at the very top of the hierarchy is Kalugal, the most powerful, arrogant, and sexiest male she has ever met.

With one look, he sets her blood on fire, but Jacki is not a fool. A man like him will never think of her as anything more than a tasty snack, while she will never settle for anything less than his heart.

39: Dark Overlord's Wife

Jacki is still clinging to her all-or-nothing policy, but Kalugal is chipping away at her resistance. Perhaps it's time to ease up on her convictions. A little less than all is still much better than nothing, and a couple of decades with a demigod is probably worth more than a lifetime with a mere mortal.

40: Dark Overlord's Clan

As Jacki and Kalugal prepare to celebrate their union, Kian takes every precaution to safeguard his people. Except, Kalugal and his men are not his only potential adversaries, and compulsion is not the only power he should fear.

41: Dark Choices The Quandary

When Rufsur and Edna meet, the attraction is as unexpected as it is undeniable. Except, she's the clan's judge and councilwoman, and he's Kalugal's second-in-command. Will loyalty and duty to their people keep them apart?

42: Dark Choices Paradigm Shift

Edna and Rufsur are miserable without each other, and their two-week separation seems like an eternity. Long-distance relationships are difficult, but for immortal couples they are impossible. Unless one of them is willing to leave everything behind for the other, things are just going to get worse. Except, the cost of compromise is far greater than giving up their comfortable lives and hard-earned positions. The future of their people is on the line.

43: Dark Choices The Accord

The winds of change blowing over the village demand hard choices. For better or worse, Kian's decisions will alter the trajectory of the clan's future, and he is not ready to take the plunge. But as Edna and Rufsur's plight gains widespread support, his resistance slowly begins to erode.

44: Dark Secrets Resurgence

On a sabbatical from his Stanford teaching position, Professor David Levinson finally has time to write the sci-fi novel he's been thinking about for years.

The phenomena of past life memories and near-death experiences are too controversial to include in his formal psychiatric research, while fiction is the perfect outlet for his esoteric ideas.

Hoping that a change of pace will provide the inspiration he needs, David accepts a friend's invitation to an old Scottish castle.

45: Dark Secrets Unveiled

When Professor David Levinson accepts a friend's invitation to an old Scottish castle, what he finds there is more fantastical than his most outlandish theories. The castle is home to a clan of immortals, their leader is a stunning demigoddess, and even more shockingly, it might be precisely where he belongs.

Except, the clan founder is hiding a secret that might cast a dark shadow on David's relationship with her daughter.

Nevertheless, when offered a chance at immortality, he agrees to undergo the dangerous induction process.

Will David survive his transition into immortality? And if he does, will his relationship with Sari survive the unveiling of her mother's secret?

46: Dark Secrets Absolved

Absolution.

David had given and received it.

The few short hours since he'd emerged from the coma had felt incredible. He'd finally been free of the guilt and pain, and for the first time since Jonah's death, he had felt truly happy and optimistic about the future.

He'd survived the transition into immortality, had been accepted into the clan, and was about to marry the best woman on the face of the planet, his true love mate, his salvation, his everything.

What could have possibly gone wrong?

Just about everything.

47: Dark haven Illusion

Welcome to Safe Haven, where not everything is what it seems.

On a quest to process personal pain, Anastasia joins the Safe Haven Spiritual Retreat.

Through meditation, self-reflection, and hard work, she hopes to make peace with the voices in her head.

This is where she belongs.

Except, membership comes with a hefty price, doubts are sacrilege, and leaving is not as easy as walking out the front gate.

Is living in utopia worth the sacrifice?

Anastasia believes so until the arrival of a new acolyte changes everything.

Apparently, the gods of old were not a myth, their immortal descendants share the planet with humans, and she might be a carrier of their genes.

48: Dark Haven Unmasked

As Anastasia leaves Safe Haven for a week-long romantic vacation with Leon, she hopes to explore her newly discovered passionate side, their budding relationship, and perhaps also solve the mystery of the voices in her head. What she discovers exceeds her wildest expectations.

In the meantime, Eleanor and Peter hope to solve another mystery. Who is Emmett Haderech, and what is he up to?

49: Dark Haven Found

Anastasia is growing suspicious, and Leon is running out of excuses.

Risking death for a chance at immortality should've been her choice to make. Will she ever forgive him for taking it away from her?

50: Dark Power Untamed

Attending a charity gala as the clan's figurehead, Onegus is ready for the pesky socialites he'll have a hard time keeping away. Instead, he encounters an intriguing beauty who won't give him the time of day.

Bad things happen when Cassandra gets all worked up, and given her fiery temper, the destructive power is difficult to tame. When she meets a gorgeous, cocky billionaire at a charity event, things just might start blowing up again.

51: Dark Power Unleashed

Cassandra's power is unpredictable, uncontrollable, and destructive. If she doesn't learn to harness it, people might get hurt.

Onegus's self-control is legendary. Even his fangs and venom glands obey his commands.

They say that opposites attract, and perhaps it's true, but are they any good for each other?

52: Dark Power Convergence

The threads of fate converge, mysteries unfold, and the clan's future is forever altered in the least expected way.

53: Dark Memories Submerged

Geraldine's memories are spotty at best, and many of them are pure fiction. While her family attempts to solve the puzzle with far too many pieces missing, she's forced to confront a past life that she can't remember, a present that's more fantastic than her wildest made-up stories, and a future that might be better than her most heartfelt fantasies. But as more clues are uncovered, the picture starting to emerge is beyond anything she or her family could have ever imagined.

54: Dark Memories Emerge

The more clues emerge about Geraldine's past, the more questions arise.

Did she really have a twin sister who drowned?

Who is the mysterious benefactor in her hazy recollections?

Did he have anything to do with her becoming immortal?

Thankfully, she doesn't have to find the answers alone.

Cassandra and Onegus are there for her, and so is Shai, the immortal who sets her body on fire.

As they work together to solve the mystery, the four of them stumble upon a millennia-old secret that could tip the balance of power between the clan and its enemies.

55: Dark Memories Restored

As the past collides with the present, a new future emerges.

56: Dark Hunter's Query

For most of his five centuries of existence, Orion has walked the earth alone, searching for answers.

Why is he immortal?

Where did his powers come from?

Is he the only one of his kind?

When fate puts Orion face to face with the god who sired him, he learns the secret behind his immortality and that he might not be the only one.

As the goddess's eldest daughter and a mother of thirteen, Alena deserves the title of Clan Mother just as much as Annani, but she's not interested in honorifics. Being her mother's companion and keeping the mischievous goddess out of trouble is a rewarding, full-time job. Lately, though, Alena's love for her mother and the clan's gratitude is not enough.

She craves adventure, excitement, and perhaps a true-love mate of her own.

When Alena and Orion meet, sparks fly, but they both resist the pull. Alena could never bring herself to trust the powerful compeller, and Orion could never allow himself to fall in love again.

57: Dark Hunter's Prey

When Alena and Orion join Kalugal and Jacki on a romantic vacation to the enchanting Lake Lugo in China, they anticipate a couple of visits to Kalugal's archeological dig, some sightseeing, and a lot of lovemaking.

Their excursion takes an unexpected turn when Jacki's vision sends them on a perilous hunt for the elusive Kra-ell.

As things progress from bad to worse, Alena beseeches the Fates to keep everyone in their group alive. She can't fathom losing any of them, but most of all, Orion.

For over two thousand years, she walked the earth alone, but after mere days with him at her side, she can't imagine life without him.

58: Dark Hunter's Boon

As Orion and Alena's relationship blooms and solidifies, the two investigative teams combine their recent discoveries to piece together more of the Kra-ell mystery.

Attacking the puzzle from another angle, Eleanor works on gaining access to Echelon's powerful AI spy network.

Together, they are getting dangerously close to finding the elusive Kra-ell.

59: Dark God's Avatar

Unaware of the time bomb ticking inside her, Mia had lived the perfect life until it all came to a screeching halt, but despite the difficulties she faces, she doggedly pursues her dreams.

Once known as the god of knowledge and wisdom, Toven has grown cold and indifferent. Disillusioned with humanity, he travels the world and pens novels about the love he can no longer feel.

Seeking to escape his ever-present ennui, Toven gives a cutting-edge virtual experience a try. When his avatar meets Mia's, their sizzling virtual romance unexpectedly turns into something deeper and more meaningful.

Will it endure in the real world?

60: Dark God's Reviviscence

Toven might have failed in his attempts to improve humanity's condition, but he isn't going to fail to improve Mia's life, making it the best it can be despite her fragile health, and he can do that not as a god, but as a man who possesses the means, the smarts, and the determination to do it.

No effort is enough to repay Mia for reviving his deadened heart and making him excited for the next day, but the flip side of his reviviscence is the fear of losing its catalyst.

Given Mia's condition, Toven doesn't dare to over excite her. His venom is a powerful aphrodisiac, euphoric, and an all-around health booster, but it's also extremely potent. It might kill her instead of making her better.

61: Dark God Destinies Converge

Destinies converge, and secrets are revealed in part three of Mia and Toven's story.

62: Dark Whispers From The Past

A brilliant scientist and programmer, William lives for his work, but when he recruits a young bioinformatician to help him decipher the gods' genetic blueprints, he find himself smitten with more than just her brain.

A Ph.d at nineteen, Kaia is considered a prodigy and expects a bright future in academia. But when William invites her to join his secret research team, she accepts for reasons that have nothing to do with her career objectives. Wiliam's promise to look into her best friend's disappearance is an offer she just can't refuse.

63: Dark Whispers From Afar

William knows that his budding relationship with the nineteen-year-old Kaia will be frowned upon, but he's unprepared for her family's vehement opposition.

Family means everything to Kaia, so when she finds herself in the impossible position of having to choose between them and William, she resorts to unconventional means to resolve the conflict.

64: Dark Whispers From Beyond

The sacrifices Kaia and her family have to make for a chance of gaining immortality might tear them apart, and success is not guaranteed.

Is the dubious promise of eternal life worth the risk of losing everything?

65: Dark Gambit The Pawn

Temporarily assigned to supervise a team of bioinformaticians, Marcel expects to spend a couple of weeks in the peaceful retreat of Safe Haven, enjoying Oregon Coast's cool weather and rugged beauty.

Things quickly turn chaotic when the retreat's director receives an email with an encoded message about a potential new threat to the clan.

While those in charge of security debate what to do next, Safe Haven's first ever paranormal retreat is about to begin, and one of the attendees is a mysterious woman who makes Marcel's heart beat faster whenever she's near.

Is the beautiful mortal his one truelove?

Or is she the harbinger of more bad news?

TRY THE SERIES ON

AUDIBLE

2 FREE audiobooks with your new Audible subscription!

THE PERFECT MATCH SERIES

PERFECT MATCH 1: VAMPIRE'S CONSORT

When Gabriel's company is ready to start beta testing, he invites his old crush to inspect its medical safety protocol.

Curious about the revolutionary technology of the *Perfect Match Virtual Fantasy-Fulfillment studios*, Brenna agrees.

Neither expects to end up partnering for its first fully immersive test run.

PERFECT MATCH 2: KING'S CHOSEN

When Lisa's nutty friends get her a gift certificate to *Perfect Match Virtual Fantasy Studios*, she has no intentions of using it. But since the only way to get a refund is if no partner can be found for her, she makes sure to request a fantasy so girly and over the top that no sane guy will pick it up.

Except, someone does.

Warning: This fantasy contains a hot, domineering crown prince, sweet insta-love, steamy love scenes painted with light shades of gray, a wedding, and a HEA in both the virtual and real worlds.

Intended for mature audience.

PERFECT MATCH 3: CAPTAIN'S CONQUEST

Working as a Starbucks barista, Alicia fends off flirting all day long, but none of the guys are as charming and sexy as Gregg. His frequent visits are the highlight of her day, but since he's never asked her out, she assumes he's taken. Besides, between a day job and a budding music career, she has no time to start a new relationship.

That is until Gregg makes her an offer she can't refuse—a gift certificate to the virtual fantasy fulfillment service everyone is talking about. As a huge Star Trek fan, Alicia has a perfect match in mind—the captain of the Starship Enterprise.

Made in the USA
Las Vegas, NV
15 January 2023